The Cost
of Standing Up

Also By Eric Rice

America at the Brink series
What Can One Man Do?
Our Choice: Freedom or Obedience
Whatever it Takes to Win

The Cost of Standing Up

America at the Brink

(Nick Turner, Book Three)

Eric Rice

Dedication

Good teachers make all the difference in a child's life. The reason I chose writing as a career was an insatiable appetite for knowledge and because of three influential teachers. I had an amazing high school English teacher and two wonderfully encouraging English composition professors in college. They opened my mind to what could be done with the mighty pen and boundless imagination.

This book is dedicated to my high school English teacher, the late Dan Graffagnino. A wonderful teacher, but also a fine friend who was taken from all of us way too early.

To Tim Yates, who, despite the chore of teaching freshman comp while working on his masters, made it so much fun. Being closer in age, he also became a good friend during my early years in college.

Finally, to the late Dr. Leslie Palmer, my second semester freshman English professor. He, more than anyone, provided the encouragement and gave me the confidence in my abilities, enabling a switch from computer science to an English composition degree.

To all of you, my heartfelt thanks for providing inspiration, encouragement, and guidance. It served me well, Thank You.

Where are we so far?

Welcome back. For those of you who are just starting with this, the third episode, or if you are coming back after a time from the prior ones, let's recap.

The first two episodes of the saga, America at the Brink, describe a time in America's history where our country was divided along ideological lines. Into this walked Nick Turner. These episodes are specifically about his role in this history. The decisions, their actions, and consequences and how they shaped where we are today.

The goal is to help some remember, others to fill in the blanks and, for many now and in the future, to answer their questions. Why some decisions were made? For most, this is really an introduction. When, why, and how we arrived where we are today.

It is also a warning of what to be on the lookout for in the future. The true purpose is to educate and to ensure the next generations do not go through the same cataclysm we did. Here I sit, in the late 2040s, writing about the last twenty years. Don't be like us and ignore the lessons of two world wars, a holocaust, genocides by madmen, a cold war, and rhetoric of elitists who did not have the people's best interests at heart. Finally, this history is preserved so future generations can study and understand the fate of America, once a great and lasting civilization. To see how it happened, and if needed, to follow this blueprint to restore or rebuild it again in the future.

Nick Turner was perfectly happy as an obscure college history professor. He foiled a terrorist attempt to blow up a crowded subway station in New York City years previously. Foregoing the money and fame this deed offered him, he opted to return to teaching until fate intervened once again.

The first episode of this series, *What Can One Man Do?*, detailed Nick's introduction to Washington politics. He was appointed to fill out the term of a Colorado Senator who died. Quickly becoming disillusioned, realizing most of Congress were more concerned with re-election and growing their financial opportunities after Congress. Rather than looking out for their constituents.

I have changed the predominant political parties to the more generic Party and Opposition. You can no doubt figure out which represents which. Nick is a member of the Party, who also has control of both branches of congress and the presidency. The Party were finally on the verge of removing the last of the Constitutional rules designed to prevent a tyranny of the majority, the legislative filibuster.

Without it, a simple majority of 51 to 50 would enable the ruling party in the Senate to pass sweeping changes to any laws. The founders designed the Constitution to make wholesale change hard and force compromise. They understood the danger of the unchecked majority. The Party leaders viewed this archaic rule, and the Constitution, as an impediment to the changes required to solve society's problems.

In a show of political bravery not seen since Lincoln, Nick voted against the bill, and the will of his Party. He sacrificed any chance at a political career, earning the undying hatred of his Party colleagues and their media allies. It turns out to be for naught, as the Majority Leader, Sal Fontana and the Vice President, Alexis, 'Lexi' Smythe-Thomas, orchestrated a miracle.

The legislative filibuster, the last of the checks and balances from the Constitution, is now gone. Nick is vilified for betraying his Party. He sees the problems of a future Smythe-Thomas administration with unchecked power to remake the country. This first episode ends with Nick announcing he is leaving the Party. He also astounds everyone by announcing a run for President as an Independent, not seeking the nomination of either party.

In the second episode, *Our Choice: Freedom or Obedience*, Nick discovers just what his impulsive decision means. With no money, no staff, no organizations, either nationally or in the states, without a campaign manager and a million other things, he is starting a year later than everyone else and with *nothing* for his presidential campaign.

When asked why he was doing this, he stated his goal was to educate and wake up the silent majority. Those cowering in fear who disagree with the direction and policies of the elites in power. Those who are too afraid to stand up, for fear of being canceled.

Nick hits the road, meeting with everyone who will stand still long enough to listen. His message is to use common sense. He promises nothing, refuses to court big money donors, and limits his donations to small dollars from individuals. He defies every conventional method of campaigning.

At first, Lexi and her team laugh at the announcement. As it becomes clear he will not go away, she uses the agencies of the administration to start monitoring his activities. As the elderly President continues his slip into mental oblivion, Lexi takes over stage managing the country from the Vice President position.

Nick builds his following. Limiting his media exposure to a lone semi-friendly cable news network, EXN. Working closely with a technology mogul, his message spreads. These unconventional methods, along with old-fashioned word of mouth on the ground after each stop, lead to a gathering of momentum.

Working his way through the country, Nick leaves behind converted *and* committed followers, the Turner Rabble, at each stop. Committed to his ideal of staying under the radar, his public polling stays low as his followers lie to pollsters about their support of Nick. His message resonates with the increasingly ignored common man and woman, toiling to make ends meet each day.

This episode ends with Nick courted by both the leading candidates of the parties for a spot as their Vice President on their respective tickets. He turns the Opposition down because of the incompetence of the probable candidate. He also meets with and turns down Lexi's offer to be her Vice President. It is the easy path to power, and potentially the Presidency in time, but requires him to sell his soul.

EXN invites Nick to provide commentary in their cable news booth for each of the nominating conventions. Lexi's nomination and subsequent speech clearly shows she and the Party have big plans. Intending to fix American democracy through increasingly radical progressive policies.

The Opposition can't even agree on a candidate as they enter a brokered convention without a clear winner. Over the course of the votes and back and forth trying to gain a majority for one candidate, they nominate Nick in a surprise move as a compromise candidate. As the nomination hangs in the balance, he turns down the opportunity and the Opposition chooses their candidate.

The stage is set as we now follow Nick as he tries to stay true to his vision. Only now, he has pissed off both established parties. The Opposition candidate knows Nick could have been the nominee. He also turned down the offer of the most powerful woman in the world. Being Nick Turner is about to get a lot more dangerous.

Eric Rice
Undisclosed location
In the middle of the 21st Century A.D.

Prologue

The old man shuffled down the street in an urban suburb of Washington, DC. Occasionally glancing in windows to see if he was being followed. Taking a circuitous route as they'd taught at The Farm. Satisfied he was not followed; he entered a non-descript multi-story stone office building.

Walking through the lobby, to a corner of the building and an office labeled Donovan, Magruder and Sons Accounting. He approached a stern-faced older woman at a counter. Removing his fedora, staring up through his glasses at the camera in the ceiling corner.

"Hello, I have an appointment to see Mr. Yardley."

"I see. Is he expecting you?" inquired the woman.

"Yes. This is the quarterly review of my taxes," replied the man in a friendly tone, holding up a large manila envelope toward the camera.

"Name?"

"George Kaplan." He noticed the slightest hint of a smirk on the face of the receptionist. She checked an empty ledger to confirm his fake name had a non-existent appointment.

"Ah, yes Mr. Kaplan. I see an appointment. Please proceed through the door and you will find his office on the left," she finally smiled, delivering this statement.

"Thank you," nodded the man, the formality of the image scanning and facial recognition having completed successfully from the various pieces of equipment hidden throughout the office. He knew from experience Martha was removing her hand from the panic button. The recognition systems released the secure bolts sealing the door he now headed toward. They were all taught to never rely on their eyes alone.

Had the systems not recognized him, she'd have pushed the button. A trapdoor would have opened under the floor, dropping him into a secure room with no exits. A man of his age, and agility, would have been gravely injured from the fall alone. Agents stationed in adjoining rooms with one-way doors would have instantly entered with drawn weapons. Clearly, this was no ordinary accounting firm.

He proceeded through the door. This room contained a wall of numbered lockers. Opening one, he placed his phone, car keys, writing pen, and even his fedora into it. All that remained was the envelope he carried. He closed the locker, securing it using his thumbprint. Turning to the retinal scanner next to the door leading from the room. After this, he heard the click as yet another door unlocked.

In this new room, he sat down at a computer and typed his ID and 32-character password. A fingerprint biometric confirmation followed this. On the screen was a schematic of a room and rows and rows of vaults. Scrolling until he found the one he wanted. The box was outlined in green, confirming his authority to access the vault.

The next question asked if he was adding to the archive, or simply viewing. Choosing 'adding', he pulled a folder from the envelope stamped with Secure Compartmented Information (SCI), stamped in red. It also included a long serial number, a code name, and a date thirty years in the future on the outside of the folder. He added the encryption key that would translate the gibberish on the pages into the actual words of the document he was so securely archiving. All this information was slowly transferred to the box on the screen, one finger keystroke at a time. He returned the folder to the envelope.

Standing up and moving in front of yet another door. This one required both his right and left palm prints. The elevator door opened. He stepped in. There was no button to push. The elevator destination was programmed according to the information he'd entered. The doors closed, the elevator descending. Only a handful of people knew this facility even existed, let alone had access.

After 25 seconds, the elevator arrived at this lowest level. He stepped out and looked up again at the camera and stood still while the scan repeated. This one included a full metallurgical analysis.

The program would recognize the metal in his belt, his glasses frame, his titanium knee, the rods in his back and even the small metal plate in his skull. All from injuries earned in the service of his country.

Another door clicked opened. He stepped into a vacuum chamber. As the door shut, he could feel his ears pop as the air cycled out and the interior air of the other room, extremely dry and cool, was pulled into the chamber. The door to the archive opened.

The old man stepped into a long room with a low ceiling and row after row of filing cabinet-like containers, illuminated with ribbons of LED lighting. His hands began to sweat, even though the temperature was a constant 58 degrees in the room. Shuffling down the aisle and looking above, he could see the HALON fire suppression system. A system designed to suppress any fire within the room in seconds.

Not deadly to a visitor by itself, the unseen companion system designed to evacuate all the oxygen ensured anyone thinking of incinerating the information within would die trying. A room full of paper and microfiche, designed to survive for centuries, would not do well with traditional fire-fighting methods.

Turning down a short aisle, he approached a bank of vaults. Squat carbon fiber cubes with sliding drawers and fingerprint scanners. This was the part he was concerned about. After all, he *was* committing high treason. One rarely wanted to leave behind fingerprints, let alone DNA. Proof beyond the shadow of a doubt of who committed the crime. He had no choice.

Reaching up, he placed his index finger on a scanner. It dutifully recorded his fingerprint, while a micro needle extracted a minute trace of his blood. Sealing it into a compartment within the cabinet and comparing the DNA to records. He was forced to keep his finger on the scanner as the blue light on top of the cabinet blinked. He felt a second prick of a needle. The blue light on the top of the cabinet turned green. The locks clicked open.

Quickly opening the drawer, he glanced at various code keys labeled on files. He saw several pertaining to his search. Rather than grabbing the largest one, three to four inches thick, he selected one roughly an inch thick with papers.

Moving rapidly to the table at the end of the row, counting time in his head, he opened the file, snapping pictures with the special eyeglass camera in the lens of his glasses. He flipped through the pages as fast as he could, taking pictures with each blink. All too quickly, he could feel the whoosh of air in the room from depressurization. He reassembled the documents into the file, replacing it in the cabinet, closing the door as he could hear rapid footsteps. The light on the cabinet was now red, showing unauthorized access attempted. He had intentionally not followed the proper procedure to close the cabinet. Taking a few calming breaths, he stepped into the aisle, smiling.

The two large men wearing suits and carrying drawn weapons relaxed slightly, recognizing the old man.

"Dr. Jacobs, we got an alarm of unauthorized access?"

Jacobs held up his hands. One contained the manila envelope with the documents he'd brought into the archive.

"My fault gentlemen. I have a file to put in the container next to this one," he said, nodding his head at the one with the red light. "I mistakenly accessed the incorrect cabinet. Once I realized my mistake, I knew you were coming. I stopped knowing you would investigate. My apologies for the excitement. I guess I should get my eyeglass prescription checked," he said with a half-smile.

The agents laughed, putting away their guns.

"No problem, Doc. Happens to the best of us. We'll reset the alarm for this cabinet. Then you can deposit your file. Have you ever seen a reset key like this? It's usually just a code." The agent held up what looked like a molded plastic finger. He placed the finger on the scanner. It turned from red back to blue and they could hear the locks re-engaging.

The Agent returned the finger to a foil pouch. It would go back into a capsule it had arrived in. The capsule would return in a pneumatic tube back to its home somewhere in the bowels of the building from which it had arrived at the security station when the silent alarm triggered.

Dr. Jacobs watched as the guard pocketed the pouch with the finger. If he were thirty years younger, he could have overpowered the two agents, taken the finger and emptied the contents of the vault. He chuckled inside at the agent's reaction.

Wondering how they would feel knowing the finger was indeed a 'real' finger preserved to maintain access to this cabinet after its initial, and only custodian, had perished. At some point, his own finger would serve the same purpose for many other secure cabinets, including the one he was about to access. Macabre for sure, but also incredibly secure.

"Thank you, gentlemen. I'll only be a second." Dr. Jacobs returned to the aisle and the cabinet next to the one he'd accessed. Once again, he went through the finger pricking exercise. This time, the cabinet he was authorized to access opened with a green light and without a second needle prick. He quickly added the folder with the documents he had brought and closed the cabinet drawers. Going through the same process again with his finger to turn the green light back to blue.

"Let's go guys. Sorry again for the senior moment."

The agent looked at Dr. Jacobs. He saw an older gentleman with thick eyeglasses, thin gray hair on his mostly bald head and a shuffling gait, with hunched shoulders. The stories of his clandestine missions during the height of the cold war and the disintegration of the USSR were legend. If they only knew the whole truth.

For over twenty years, he had been one of a handful of custodians of this, the most secure deep archive of the CIA. Having been retired from fieldwork due to 'injury', thirty years prior. After a decade as an analyst, he'd agreed to take a role as a custodian. Both because he knew no other trade, and he was a walking archive already.

Jacobs cut the finger from his dead predecessor's hand half a dozen years prior. Something his own assistant would do with his own finger soon. He was only one of a handful of people even allowed to enter this floor of the archive. Here there were paper and microfiche hard copies of the deepest secrets of the country. Secrets not duplicated anywhere else. None of these existed in digital format.

This deep archive was specifically designed to withstand the deadly effects of an Electro Magnetic Pulse weapon. Once EMP technology advanced, combined with the increasing prevalence of cyber warfare's sophisticated attacks, electronic storage of data became too easy to compromise. The decision was made to destroy all the digital copies of archived material, fearing exposure or loss. Now they relied solely on the unhackable physical copies. Technology had come full circle.

These were the most secret and potentially damaging secrets the country possessed. Each vault was also sealed to be both air and water tight. They had tried to think of everything. As usual, humans were the weak link. As they were in any security system designed by humans.

"Doc, it's just a good thing the system recognized you. Frankly, we expected to come down and reclaim a body. Then Martha told us you were the only one down on this floor. We figured it was a screwup."

"Gentlemen, you forget I developed these security systems when we modernized with the biometric locks. As soon as I realized I had tried to access the wrong cabinet, I removed my finger. Before the failsafe kicked in. Trust me, no one wants to know what is in any of these cabinets. Let's get some fresh air."

They headed back up to the surface, where Dr. Jacobs collected his items and hat and headed back down the street toward his car. By now, he was feeling lightheaded. The adrenalin from his mission fading. Once beyond the surveillance cameras, he leaned heavily against the side of a building. He pulled out his writing 'pen', twisting it to reveal a needle. Quickly injecting another dose of antidote into his veins.

Jacobs had injected himself with the first dose of anti-venom before entering the building. He knew the scanner would inject him, since even he was not authorized to access *that* archive. But only he knew the exact type of venom it would use. This and many more secrets would be some of what his successor would learn upon his death, as he had from his predecessor.

This security method would allow a cabinet to be opened, and the target file accessed. The person opening the cabinet would be dead within 30 seconds and the information they intended to access still in their hands. Investigators would know exactly what they were trying to access.

Fortunately, he was not lying when he told the agents he had designed the extra security precautions and had, in fact, developed a tolerance for the particular venom being used in the system. The anti-venom was precautionary. His tolerance was developed years prior.

He'd completed what was likely his last clandestine mission. Sadly, it was against the country he loved. The consequences of not completing this mission were unacceptable. Jacobs hoped both God and his late wife Claudette would understand. He knew his country would not.

Part One

You Can't Hide Now

"This would be a great time in the world for some man to come along that knew something."

Will Rogers

Chapter 1

"What do you make of that?" asked Mel Arenson, turning to look at Alexis Smythe-Thomas. Lexi, the Vice President of the United States, and now the Party nominee for the upcoming presidential election. She was standing, swirling the ice cubes in her glass, watching a big screen TV in their headquarters conference room.

Lexi turned, staring at the short, balding man with her icy blue eyes. "I think he is much more dangerous than you suggested. I also think we need to take the gloves off."

Lexi issued the rebuke in a contemptuous tone. She was the picture of style in her expensive tailored suit and skirt, tall and statuesque in her high heels. The mostly unlined face, trim figure, and long blonde hair over one shoulder displayed meticulously maintained beauty.

As her eyes bored into his, Mel turned away. Her beauty did not fool him. Lexi's best asset was her ruthless focus on getting what she wanted. And always succeeding.

"It seems you may be correct. Still, we need to tread carefully. Turner's appeal is primarily the blue collar and low-income workers in the rural areas and the heartland. Our progressive ideas are much more appealing to the young and the college educated. Turner is more likely to draw moderates from the Opposition. This hurts Blackbird more than us. Especially since he decided not to offer an olive branch to Senator Garcia's conservative followers. He is cutting his own throat thinking he can win as the Opposition candidate without them. There are only so many moderates, even on the right."

Lexi, sipping her scotch, paced in the conference room, watching the replay of the highlights of the Opposition presidential nominating convention from last night. They were watching the right leaning EXcellence in News, cable news network, on mute.

"Mel, that may be true, but how the hell was Turner even in a position to be nominated by the Opposition in the first place? He is a former member of *our* Party. Pro-choice, and on record, voting against things the right supposedly hates. How does he get put forth as a compromise candidate? Something nobody even speculated about. And by whom? You have assured me he is hardly resonating."

"He is barely showing in the polls, low single digits. His supporters are folks who don't vote. They watch him at state fairs and cheer him in parking lot rallies. When the election rolls around, they are working all day. The last thing they want to do is go stand in a line to cast a throw away vote on an independent candidate. He is not resonating nationally. His message is not getting to enough folks to make a difference," finished Mel, in a speech he was tiring of giving Lexi to assure her Turner was irrelevant. Even he was doubting his own words as Turner refused to go away.

"In case you missed it, he just 'resonated' in front of a national audience of millions and damn near got a nomination from a party for which he was not even competing." Lexi's tone had gone up several octaves before almost screaming the final accusation.

Mel, wisely keeping his distance, held out his hands, palm up. "Lexi, the Opposition is hopelessly fragmented. They went through the entire primary season, beating each other up. Exposing all the reasons none of them should be nominated. Their voters are frustrated and irritated they don't have a better candidate. Garcia was the one we had to worry about the most. He sabotaged his campaign by refusing to budge off his 'no abortion ever, for any reason' stance. Even a majority of conservative women believe in allowing abortion early in the pregnancy. It killed his chances." Mel paused, continuing to circle as Lexi paced, listening to his reasoning.

"When Blackbird couldn't convince Governor Carson to throw her nomination votes to him before the convention, they were doomed to have a brokered convention. With each of the six prior nomination votes, it was clear they wouldn't unify behind a candidate. I suspect this was Tommy Charles convincing Garcia to throw his support behind the independent Turner. They both loath Governor Blackbird. With him as an alternative, some of Blackbird's defected as well. I also suspect they know he has no chance against you."

"I want that prick Tommy off cable. If threats and boycotts are not working, let's get the FCC to pull their license. EXN is a pain in our ass. Whether we do it now or after the election, they are no longer going to spew their lies and rile up the ignorant public against our plans for progress. Find out and confirm if it was just Tommy and Garcia. This was way too organized to be spontaneous. Dig deeper. I want to know who was behind it. This smells like big money. Find them so I can make them pay," finished Lexi, tossing back the rest of her drink, watching Nick standing in the broadcast booth at EXN, yelling 'no, no, no,' when he started receiving delegate votes.

"Got it."

"What happens to Garcia's conservatives?"

"Some will vote for Blackbird, a few may cross to Turner, which is good for us. Fewer for Blackbird. I think a lot will stay home."

"Really? You don't think Turner is going to get them?"

"I don't. Abortion is just too important to the conservatives."

"Turner wants to close the border. They like that," mused Lexi.

"True. He's also not talking about mass deportations and is talking eventual paths to citizenship. They *hate* that," countered Mel.

"Do you think he knew about it?" asked Lexi, backing up the recording as Nick leaped up from the chair again, saying 'no, no, no'.

"Do you?" asked Mel.

"Looking at this, I don't think he is that good an actor. His response is too genuine. Like talking to Garcia through the camera."

"I agree," responded Mel. "He was surprised. Hell, I was surprised. This has Tommy written all over it."

"Look at him. Sitting there with that grin. When Turner asks him if he did it, he actually looks scared of him. I love it. He's a former marine. Can we call him back to active duty and send him to Syria?"

"Nope, we looked into it," replied Mel seriously.

"Tommy's got at least one ex-wife. Surely he hit her, or we can pay her to accuse him of some type of abuse?"

"We are trying, but he has been in the public eye for years. He is extremely careful at work and with his staff, given the sexual harassment lawsuits EXN has dealt with through the years from all those blondes."

"What about Diane Paxton? Where is she going to end up?" asked Lexi, changing subjects.

"Probably NWN, or maybe FLCN on cable. We did the rounds of the opinion shows yesterday morning. Our allies made sure they painted Turner out to be a misogynist SOB for humiliating her on live TV."

"Does it have legs?" asked Lexi with a look.

"Are you kidding? Let's think about this for a second. He humiliated a female colleague on national TV, coming across as a bully and vindictive. The optics are bad. How did you feel about it?"

"Hah. At first, I wanted to kick him in the nuts," smiled Lexi. "Then I wanted to screw him."

"What?" hesitated Mel with his mouth open.

"You heard me. Women prefer forceful and powerful men not afraid to take risks and not afraid to stand up for what they believe. It's a tremendous turn on. Especially when we are surrounded by all these super sensitive, don't want to offend a flea, wanna be men," said Lexi with a wicked smile, leaning on the edge of the table and dangling one shoe.

"OK, stop it. Quit playing your mind games with me. Remember, I'm the court eunuch, immune to your charms," uttered Mel uncomfortably. "Now tell me the truth. Is your second reaction real or where you messing with me?"

"Maybe. I really think he put Paxton in her place. She did lie. I would have done the same thing. There will be some who are pissed at the way he picked on her, but those folks are already in my camp. I don't know if he lost any conservative or moderate EXN female viewers. I don't think this hurts him. Besides, he has a habit of doing this. Look at what he did to that Bergamo girl at those press conferences."

"It's too bad for me. Diane was one of my moles in EXN."

"Don't you have others?"

"Sure, but she was my highest profile on air talent. She couldn't help herself. He baited her right into it and then backed her into a corner of her own doing. She should have said it was her own opinion rather than lying," admitted Mel.

"He's dangerous Mel. He's using every opportunity we give him to make his points to the wider public. Now, American *Pravda* is trending."

"I called all the CEOs of the tech companies and threatened them with Section 230 action if they didn't prevent posts about American *Pravda*. They're having a hard time keeping up with all the reposts. They'd end up banning tens of thousands of users. Damn that Kwan guy. His social media app is doing really well," fumed Mel.

"Still no way to shut his service down?" asked Lexi, sitting.

"We tried, but he operates the hosting company, owns the servers and we can't shut down the internet networks because everyone uses them. He's now hosting other smaller media outlets. That makes more of these guys immune to our corporate counterattacks. They all learned their lessons after we forced the cloud service provider companies to kick a few of them off their servers, de-platforming them," informed Mel, still looking at the TV screen replaying the convention's final night speeches. "They won't put themselves and their message at risk again by using providers we can control."

They continued to watch the recording as first, Governor Carson, the Opposition VP nominee's speech failed to woo back the conservatives of former candidate Texas Senator Garcia. Then came the nominee himself, South Dakota Governor George Blackbird. His speech was a litany of broad pronouncements of how only he could get the various parties to the table to compromise on everything from the economy, abortion, crime, border security and the perpetual festering wound of Palestinian and Israeli relations.

"What about the Opposition deciding he is a better candidate than Blackbird? Why shouldn't I be worried about that?" asked Lexi, now perching her expensive red soled heels on a corner of the conference table in an unladylike manner as her skirt slid up from her knees.

Mel, ignoring her legs, replied. "Good news for us. Blackbird has totally botched this. He has alienated the conservative wing now. Carson brings nothing to the ticket and both their acceptance speeches were total snooze fests. They did nothing to unify the Opposition."

"How close did he get?"

"It was his. My sources tell me Carson called him, offering to throw her delegates to him for the VP slot. Supposedly, he didn't even take the call. After that, she flipped him off and made Blackbird the nominee," finished Mel.

"How would he have done as the Opposition nominee?"

Mel paused before answering, cornered.

"With access to their statewide organizations and the half a billion in the coffers. With Garcia fully in his camp, he would have convinced the conservatives Turner was the lesser of two evils. It would also have given him a megaphone he didn't have today. It would certainly have been tighter than it will be with Blackbird as the nominee," ended Mel.

"All this uncertainty concerns me. We are supposed to be in charge of all of this."

Mel shrugged in response. "This is the best scenario for us. Blackbird is in, but without Garcia's supporters. The conservatives stay home and both Blackbird and Turner fight for the Opposition moderates. I'm also guessing Blackbird is going to spend as much time trashing Turner as he does you. You can stay above the fray and focus on keeping Blackbird down while he attacks Turner to win over the conservatives. You don't lose any support by picking on the Hero. It's perfect."

Lexi twirled a pen on the table, looking at the screen as Nick was being interviewed by Adam Mullen from EXN after the speeches. "You think they tear each other apart fighting for what, 40% of the vote?"

"If that."

"Is either going to get a convention bounce?" she asked.

"Blackbird, no. Turner maybe a point or two, which only moves him closer to double digits. Blackbird in the low thirties and you're still in the mid to high 50s, even low 60s. See little changing," he replied.

"OK, but let's get ready to hit both of them. Any luck on digging up dirt on Turner?" prodded Lexi.

"We are still having trouble getting access to all his military info, but the rest is clean." concluded Mel.

"He left the service more recently than Tommy. Any chance we can recall *him*?" smiled Lexi at the thought.

Mel laughed, hoping she was kidding. "Sadly no. He resigned his commission after serving twenty years. I guess he was pretty disgusted after the Afghanistan pullout."

Lexi grimaced. "Don't remind me. I had nothing to do with that decision. The President ignored everyone, including me, on that one. We're still paying for his stupidity."

"Let's wait until September or October and see if he is still in it.

"I think you're still underestimating him. Just be ready with what we have. I have a feeling we'll need it," ended Lexi.

Chapter 2

"Governor, first, congratulations on your nomination," offered Tommy Charles, the host of *Tommy*, EXN's flagship opinion show.

"Thank you, Tommy. I'm just glad to be done with the primary season. We can now focus on defeating the Vice President in November."

"We can agree on that, Governor. Before we get into the issues, I would be remiss to not ask your opinion of Senator Nick Turner being a surprise nominee for the Opposition nomination. What happened?"

"Well Tommy," paused Governor George Blackbird of South Dakota. In his mid-sixties, with a full head of gray hair, he was wearing a suit and no tie. He was known as a methodical speaker, always thinking carefully. Both about what he said and how he said it.

"I think it was a ploy by the Party and frankly even some of the more radical elements within our own party trying to derail our momentum. They don't like the idea that I seek compromise. To work with moderates and the other side to move our country away from the fringes. There are some in our party, just as there are in the other, who would prefer anarchy to compromise," he pronounced with finality.

Tommy sat up straighter in his chair. "Governor, I'm a conservative. I don't consider myself on the 'fringe' of anything. Nor do I feel many who supported Senator Garcia and others who left your camp to vote for Senator Turner, in that final vote, are supporting anarchy. Rather, they prefer policies that abide by the Constitution."

A single bead of sweat appeared on Governor Blackbird's forehead. "Tommy, now don't put words in my mouth or misinterpret my statements. I am the Opposition candidate for all those in our party. Conservative and moderate, as well as those independents who prefer moderation. We are united in our opposition to the more radical policies of the Party administration. I'm not accusing anyone of *wanting* anarchy."

"Yet Governor, I heard nothing in your acceptance speech to win back those in Senator Garcia's camp. Nothing on how you would shut down the border. You didn't say you would keep *Roe* from being reinstated. No talk about repealing the executive orders regarding energy, guns, and freedoms we have lost under this administration."

"Well Tommy, it was my acceptance speech. I need to appeal to a broad coalition of concerned voters. All these will be covered as we move forward in the campaign. I intend to work with Congress to pass sensible reform in all those areas," replied Blackbird in a measured tone.

"Sensible? Governor, we've had 14 million illegals cross our border in the last seven years. Add that to at least eleven million or as high as twenty or thirty million already here. These non-citizens have broken our laws to come here. They are overrunning our major cities. Crime is out of control in so many places, including the suburbs. We had 200,000 fentanyl deaths last year. They are finding it in elementary schools. The drug cartels are crossing our border with impunity," pointed out Tommy.

"Tommy, this is exactly the problem. You think we can waive the magic wand and put the genie back in the bottle. These are complex issues. If we arbitrarily close the border, what are the implications with Mexico? Our second largest trading partner. You don't just shut the door. It's complicated. It needs to be studied, and a plan formulated with Mexico to tackle the drug trade and stabilize the region. Then there are the legitimate asylum seekers. We can't be inhumane and turn them away either," lectured Blackbird.

"No offence Governor, but we have had seven years of unchecked 'asylum' seekers entering our country with next to no scrutiny. I suspect ninety plus percent of them are not truly fleeing because of a need for asylum. They are coming to America so we can clothe, feed, educate, and take care of them. The mayor of New York City said as much when he started changing his tune once hundreds of thousands made their way to his sanctuary city. Now even he wants it stopped."

"Tommy, I think perhaps you have been listening to Senator Turner and his ultra nationalism. If he were in charge, it would be the entire world against us. Thank goodness cooler heads prevailed at the convention. He would not only close the border, but probably have us in a shooting war with the cartels. With UN sanctions and the world against us, shortly to follow."

Tommy stared for a few seconds while his producer yelled in his ear. "Governor, do you support the Constitution?"

"Excuse me?"

"Do you believe in the Constitution?"

"Of course, I do. What a strange question."

"Then you are aware we have a clause in there about our right to protect our country against invasion. How are 14 million people illegally entering our country, not an invasion? Carrying this deadly fentanyl into our country. Who don't speak our language. Burden our border states and now rural municipalities all over our country. Thanks to this administration busing and flying them to all the lower 48. They attend the schools and slow down the education of our native born and legal immigrant students. Flood our emergency rooms without an ability to pay, knowing they cannot be turned away. Who, despite the rhetoric of the left, are indeed causing all kinds of crime to rise all over the country. How is all of this not a failure of our administration to uphold the constitutionally mandated job of maintaining a sovereign border?"

Blackbird sat as Tommy rattled off his points.

"Tommy, it is fully my intent to follow and enforce the Constitution when I am President. I can assure you, we will do all we can to stem the tide of illegal immigration and restore a system to handle those seeking asylum."

"Governor, how will you reverse the damage this administration has done with its canceled oil leases? The silly mandates regarding scaling back fossil fuel and demanding sustainable energy replacements in only a handful of years? Especially when California can't even handle the load of electric vehicles they have today without rolling blackouts year round?

How will they and the rest of the country handle it when we all have to plug in and there is no electricity to run everything?"

"Tommy, we definitely need to do more to shore up our own energy production. To remove some restrictions this administration has placed on drilling. These climate change mandates appear aggressive.

"Some? Appear? Governor, what about moratoriums on transporting fossil fuels by rail? This has raised the cost of oil and gas because of the additional cost of using trucks and the limited pipelines we've had in place for decades. Plus, the economic damage to the railways losing this key transport. What about the Keystone XL pipeline? Would you repeal those restrictions? Reissue the permit and finish the pipeline and reap the economic benefits of delivering all that Canadian tar sand oil to our refineries in the Gulf? Not to mention our own shale oil," challenged Tommy.

"You're acting as if I don't want to do this. Of course, I do. This administration has hurt our economy more than any other. Tommy, you act as if going back to the way things were is as easy as canceling a bunch of laws and executive orders. Repeal is not the best way. Compromise is. We have to take the good from all ideas and come up with new ones that make more sense for everyone."

Tommy shook his head as he continued listening to Blackbird, the hope of the Opposition voters, rattle off answers about the economy, inflation, unemployment, crime, and healthcare. Answers that didn't answer any of the issues with anything specific. Instead, everything was a carefully worded response designed to not piss off any side by taking a clear and concrete policy direction. As they ended the interview, Tommy was clearly frustrated.

"Governor, thank you for your time. I only have one last question. Have you given any thought why a group of Opposition supporters tried to nominate Turner instead of supporting you from the beginning?" asked Tommy, leaning forward as if pressing an attack.

"I think I answered that already. Clearly Garcia does not like me. He also knows I do not support his all-or-nothing position on so many stances. As for Turner," he shrugged visibly on camera. "He is an amateur. In way above his head, offering few answers, only philosophy. You accuse me of not having definitive stances. I would like you to treat Turner to the same quizzing. His only answer is for people to take personal responsibility. That will hardly stop Russian and Chinese incursions. Nor will it end unemployment or lower inflation. The people cannot change any of this. Only the leaders working with corporations and countries armed with the power of the government agencies can accomplish necessary change. They shift policies and change the shape of things. Not the individuals. They are powerless to fix these problems," ended Blackbird smugly.

Tommy smiled, almost for the first time during the interview. "Thank you for making my point, Governor. I believe my viewers now know exactly why you faced the possibility of Turner being nominated instead of you. I think you are seriously underestimating both the concerns of these *individuals* and their ability to make change happen."

As the cameras turned off, Blackbird turned to Tommy.

"I have to say, I am disappointed in how you treated me. We need to work together to stop the Vice President. I had hoped for better treatment. Perhaps we should avoid your program in the future if this is the treatment we can expect," he finished in a threatening tone.

Tommy laughed. Causing Blackbird to redden.

"Governor, I wish you luck." He resisted the urge to say what he felt. "You are welcome to come back if you choose. Good evening." With that, he walked away from the set, leaving Blackbird, his handlers, and Tommy's producer Wayne to lead them from the set.

Chapter 3

'Some jobs you learn by trial and error,' said the narrator as images of plumbers being sprayed in the face from leaks, carpenters stepping on boards not nailed down, and electricians connecting wiring as the lights go out. 'You can make mistakes without them causing too much harm, while you learn your trade.'

New images flashed on the screen as the narrator continued. 'Then there are some jobs that require not only experience, but a cool head. The ability to make decisions after weighing choices and the consequences. Decisions with only a single chance. No 'do overs'.'

In quick succession, the ad showed Churchill giving his speeches during the Blitz, Kennedy speaking about Cuba from the oval office, Reagan in front of the Berlin wall and Bush standing on the rubble at 9/11, all accompanied by images and headlines highlighting these key moments in history.

Next, a series of election results flashed across the screen highlighting overwhelming majorities electing George Blackbird to congress and then as the South Dakota governor. Over these last images, the narrator spoke in solemn tones. 'President is the last place you want your leader making mistakes, costing lives and livelihoods or worse, while learning on the job. Elect experience and wisdom along with a proven ability to deliver solutions where both sides benefit. We don't need radical; we need levelheaded leaders. We need a swift, sure, and experienced President. Vote George Blackbird for President.'

"So it begins," announced Denise Rojas from the Turner election HQ in Denver. She looked at her watch. "Less than two days after the convention and the Opposition candidate is already attacking you."

"He's wasting his money. I'm not his problem. The VP is," answered the clean-shaven, dark-haired Nick Turner, leaning back.

"He's still smarting from you even being nominated and getting votes," offered Denise, Nick's campaign manager.

"The smack down Tommy gave him didn't help. That had to hurt knowing he wasn't going to be welcomed like a favorite son on the only right leaning network," offered Margie Wilson, the communications director for the campaign.

"That, more than anything, is probably the reason for the ad. Blackbird suspects Tommy had something to do with your nomination," agreed Denise, looking at Margie and smiling at the young black woman.

"What do we do now?" asked Nick, ignoring their comments.

"You can't hide any longer. Almost winning a nomination you weren't even trying for tends to draw a lot of attention. Poor Blackbird. He got quizzed on every show after his nomination about you. That's all they wanted to talk about," laughed Denise.

Nick held up his hand, smiling. "You always say we need more eyeballs. How many did we get, Greg?" asked Nick, turning to a blond-haired younger guy in the room.

"After the Party convention and your commentary, plus EXN running wall to wall ads announcing you would be in the broadcast booth, the Opposition convention was the most watched ever. Adding the drama of not having a candidate made for interesting television. There are now a lot of people who know way more about the convention processes. For EXN, it was over fourteen million viewers on night three. Night four was similar. You got exposed to a whole new set of voters."

"Speaking of exposed. Has *Women's Viewpoint* offered Diane Paxton a seat yet?" asked Nick sarcastically.

"You laugh, but they are spending a lot of time reaming you over your treatment of her," noted Margie with a frown.

"Nick, you have to be gracious if you are ever asked. If you're snarky, they'll hit you for it. You made your point. They will play those clips forever. It will hang on her for the rest of her career," pointed out Denise. "She'll be looking for payback. Don't give her the opportunity."

"Got it," he responded, looking around the conference room in the election HQ. It was near the top floor of a high rise in Denver. They had marvelous views of the majestic Rockies thirty miles to their west.

"Fundraising is good. All your exposure has netted us another $35 million in the last couple of weeks. You'll love this, Nick," added Chuck Robinson, his chief of staff. "American *Pravda* seems to be sticking. In spite of the social media outlets trying to ban posts and reposts, they have finally given up. Since you were part of the broadcast, the Homeland Ministry of Truth," he paused. "Sorry, the Homeland Department of Misinformation Governance cannot threaten the social media apps for not heeding their 'recommendation' to ban you."

"That's great. I hope it has legs. It is a perfect description of American media. Pure state propaganda. What else?" asked Nick.

"First up is the Women's Right to Choose conference. We'll see if your gut is right about the abortion topic. This is a make-or-break moment, Nick." He nodded as Denise continued.

"Pennsylvania, Michigan, Wisconsin, New York, Massachusetts, Virginia, and Ohio all have efforts to keep you from getting on the presidential ballots. The cases are all going to their respective state Supreme Courts. That's where Jenny is. With the lawyers presenting the cases to keep you on the ballots. I'm also hearing Blackbird may try to use Sore Loser laws to keep you off the ballot in Texas and South Dakota."

"When will we know? Any of these have a chance?"

"It's August now. After Labor Day, most likely. Normally, I would say no, considering in some states there are 30 candidates from every wackadoodle party you can think of. But I never say never. I think the Sore Loser laws won't realistically apply since you were *not* actually seeking the nomination for the Opposition party at the convention. I'm worried about the Rust belt states though. The Party blue wall is the key to their landslide," finished Denise with a shrug.

"Let me know if there is anything I need to do to help Jenny. I can't afford to not be on ballots in states where we have a chance. Not being on Texas or Ohio, for instance, is much worse than Michigan or New York," offered Nick in a serious tone. Denise started again.

"Your book publishes in a couple of weeks. Then we have you doing a few interviews, including one at Texas A&M. Thankfully, they agreed to add you to their candidate forums." She continued looking at her notebook.
"We have the World Evangelical Congress, the week after the WR2C. You have a double dose of abortion rights in as many weeks."

"At least we will know one way or the other," mused Nick.

"More state fairs. Nebraska, Minnesota, Utah, a few others."

Nick perked up a bit at the mention of Nebraska. Greg noticed and smiled as Denise noticed as well.

"What?" she asked.

"The boss is looking forward to Nebraska," winked Greg.

"Really. Care to share?" Greg shook his head, smiling as Nick did too. "I see. I'll have to make sure I attend that one to see what all the fuss is about. Nick, you've got to pick a VP. And sooner than later. You sure you don't want to talk to Freddie Garcia?"

"It won't work Denise. I promise we'll pick one soon. What can I expect Lexi to do now that I can no longer hide?"

"She's still walking a fine line. She doesn't want to directly attack you. It makes people think she is taking you seriously. The attacks will come from her surrogates. We already have the cameras at all your rallies, which is good. However, with the criminal justice system in their hands, they may count on not being charged for any violence and try to goad us into responding. Let's have you record another post for your Turner Rabble groups to warn them to be on the lookout. The biggest worry is unforced errors. Folks are paying attention now," stated Denise in a warning tone.

#

"Got a sec?" asked Denise, sticking her head in Nick's office.

"Sure, come on in." Denise entered with his head of security, Earl Greene, and another man with dark hair and tanned skin.

"Nick, we discussed the idea of creating a rapid response team for all our grassroots organizations. I want to introduce you to Steve Gaines."

Nick got up and walked around to shake the hand of the smiling man. At 6'4", Nick towered over Steve, who was under six feet.

"Welcome to the impossible dream," smiled Nick.

"Senator, I can't tell you what an honor it is to meet you and to be part of the team. It is inspiring what you are trying to do. Getting folks to stand up for our freedoms before they are gone," replied Steve.

"First rule. Call me Nick. What gainful employment did you give up to join this crazy crew?"

Steve smiled. "I was working for a big five consulting firm, running their social media outreach and AI programs. Big Pharma one week, a multi-national bank the next, occasional government contracts. Been on the road for two years. I needed a change. Saw the advertisement on a social networking business site and applied. I've watched your speeches online. I knew I had to be a part of this. American *Pravda* is brilliant."

Nick smiled at the enthusiasm of Steve, who looked to be in his mid to late thirties, around Greg's age. This was the demographic he needed. Folks with lives and careers underway, too busy to pay attention to what they'd lose from not knowing or caring about the bigger picture.

"Great. I assume you don't have a family with all your traveling. You can compare notes with Chuck. He did two years grinding at Goldman." Steve smiled, a bit awed by the approachability of Nick.

"Steve, how do we help our grassroots orgs stay out of trouble?"

For the next thirty minutes, Nick listened to Steve layout his plans for augmenting the static cameras with videographers to capture anything the agitators might prepare outside the camera perimeter.

He suggested designating teams from each of the Rabble groups to take some self-defense protection courses to allow them to defuse situations and minimize any casualties or risks of liability.

He also suggested each group cultivate local media to cover the events more favorably. Reporters they could count on to counter any negative hit jobs from American *Pravda* funded outlets. After Steve left the room, Nick turned to a smiling Denise.

"Wow. Where did you find him?"

"Just lucky. About time we get a break," answered Denise.

"I agree with that. He doesn't have any military background?"

"Nope."

"Interesting," mused Nick, with steepled fingers.

"Why?"

"Tactics. He has an unusual grasp of them and deployment. I would expect this from a trained army officer. He probably grew up playing *Call of Duty* and learned them there," laughed Nick.

"We are damn lucky to find someone like this. I think we're going to need him. Now that the die is cast, the gloves come off. This is the take no prisoners part of the campaign. You can expect it to get really ugly from this point forward."

"This has been the easy part?" asked Nick.

Denise answered with a wan smile, knowing what was coming.

Chapter 4

Nick stood off stage as the leader of the Women's Right to Choose organization stood center stage, ready to introduce him. He looked out over the crowd of around five thousand women in the large room.

Looking to his left, Denise and Earl were with him on this trip. They only had to go a few blocks from their office. The gathering was being held at the Denver Convention Center. Colorado was one of the few states who had preserved the right to have an abortion at any time during the pregnancy. Right up to birth, no questions asked. Hosting the conference was the reward for upholding the progressive abortion stance.

Denise and Earl looked at him nervously. He grinned back.

"Don't worry."

"It's our job to worry, in case you forgot," replied Earl as Denise added. "Just try not to start a riot. If they don't like what you have to say, thank them and exit gracefully."

Nick nodded as his introduction ended. He walked out, shaking the hand of Alicia Koppen, a sixty something gray haired woman, the head of the Women's Right to Choose organization. The crowd clapped politely. There were also a few boos.

"Thank you for inviting me to speak. I appreciate the chance to talk to you about my stance on women's health issues," announced Nick, looking around the stage. He walked to the front of the stage and pointed to a spare chair, similar to what all the attendees were sitting on.

"Can you hand me that chair? I might as well be as uncomfortable as all of you," he said as the audience laughed. Two women in the front row held the chair up and Nick took it from them. He set it down in the middle of the stage, near the edge. In his jeans, cowboy boots, and polo shirt, he was as casual as most of the crowd.

"Ok, where was I?" He squirmed a bit, trying to get comfortable on the chair, and gave up with a laugh. "Wow, these really aren't very comfortable, are they?" More laughter.

"Let's get the elephant in the room out there. Two things you need to know. First, as President, I will neither ask for, nor will I support, a complete ban on abortion." The crowd erupted in cheers. He waited.

"You should also know, I'll be giving this same talk to a pro-life conference later this month." There were many boos from the crowd. Nick stopped for a moment, shaking his head.

"This is part of the problem we face as a nation. Why are you booing? This is about life. Life for mothers, life for children, and your personal freedom. For all women. The name of your organization is women's right to choose, correct? This has to include a woman's right to choose not to have an abortion," noted Nick with passion, silencing the hecklers in the audience. "The second thing you should know is I am not personally in favor of abortion." Louder boos from the audience.

Nick smiled and held out his hands. "Of course, as a man, I am incapable of getting pregnant, so it is easy for me to sit here and tell you I don't think abortion is morally right. I never have to make that decision. Nor do I have to live with the consequences of either decision. You do." A few militant hecklers continued, especially after his claim a man can't get pregnant. Most of the others stopped booing at Nick's words. Many shifted restlessly in their seats.

He held up his hands again. "Just hear me out. While I don't believe it is morally right, it is only my opinion as a person, not as a President. I also do not believe it is my place or the place of the federal government to tell you whether you can or cannot have an abortion." This was met with more boos.

"Please listen to what I am saying and why," said Nick, standing up and moving the chair back as he started his usual back and forth pacing on the stage. "This is very important. If you allow the federal government to dictate what you can and cannot do for something like abortion, where does it stop? Eventually, they will get to something you don't agree with. Then what? I think many of you are like your sisters on the pro-life side." Nick raised his hands as the boos started again. "Please listen," he repeated, raising his voice a bit, trying to talk through the hecklers. "I really need you to pay attention to the *words* I am saying. Please, please think for yourself," he pleaded.

"Put aside what you have been told or the rhetoric of either side. It is time for us to have an honest conversation about this. We need to address it and get past it to help solve the bigger problems we face as both a nation and a society of *voting* adults. *We* get to decide what our future looks like. Each one of us. Equally. This is an unbelievable privilege."

"We need to do this for the future of our children. All of them. You may not like what I have to say. You may not agree with it, but we need to stop avoiding this conversation. Shouting at each other instead of listening and perhaps finding common ground." The audience was trying to figure out where Nick was going, as this was not what they expected at all. No politician ever talked to *them* this way.

"Education is key. Teenage girls need to understand what being pregnant truly means in terms of responsibility and loss of childhood freedom. The premature responsibilities of parenthood. Let's acknowledge the damage an abortion does to young women. The psychological damage of first getting pregnant and then having an abortion is a burden they should not have to bear. I would fund Planned Parenthood to the moon if it used this funding to prevent every unwanted pregnancy," the crowd cheered at this statement.

"The problem is, no matter how you rationalize it, no matter how much you ignore this science because it harms your narrative or understanding. There is no denying that rapid fire sound of a beating heart we detect so much earlier now. Abortion is ending a potential life, even if it is legal, and even if it is still in your womb. Even if it is your choice and your right, it does not change this truth."

Another chorus of boos arose after this statement. Nick simply stared down at the crowd and continued in a louder voice.

"I know there are many of you in the audience who have been through this. I also know not a day goes by for most of you where you don't think about it. Just because you could choose to have the abortion, does not mean it prepared you for what happened after. It changes your life. It has to. Guilt is real, and it does not go away. We need to acknowledge that while legal, only someone with an icy heart could have an abortion and not *admit* it leaves a mark on your soul." Nick paused again. The only sound from the audience was the quiet sobbing of a few, being comforted by their seat neighbors. He had their complete attention.

"I am not saying this to dredge up memories or to persecute anyone who has been through this. I feel for you. Abortion was supposed to free you. To level the playing field and allow you to have carefree sex, just like the men. Well, I ask you. Do you feel any freer? Sure, you can choose not to raise the child, but you were still the parent. You now have the added burden of living with the results of your deed. Thank you, feminism, for misleading the young women of the world once more."

A few militants in the crowd booed loudly at this statement. A couple of them stood, flipping Nick off and yelling expletives at him. Nick spoke louder as he continued.

"Most of our societal problems stem from the unintended consequences of supposed good deeds. While I feel bad about upsetting you, we need to continue to talk about this."

"A parent should be allowed to decide, especially where the child is deformed or the pregnancy results from rape or incest. I do not support the draconian laws claiming every life is sacred, regardless of the woman's wishes, either. No one should be required by a government or a religion to do something with their body outside of their control."

"However, I am not in favor of abortion in the third trimester and even after three or four months, unless there is clear evidence of some deformity." More heckling from the crowd accompanied this statement. Nick was delivering his speech in a more somber tone than usual.

"I believe you care about what is being taught to your children. I believe many of you are concerned about the sexualization of your teenage and increasingly your pre-teenage daughters. You are worried about rising crime in your neighborhoods. The cost of food, the crap on TV, the state of public-school education, the criminal cesspool of social media, and the job prospects for your kids." The boos died down a bit at this as Nick shifted from abortion. Many in the crowd were now bobbing their heads.

"Guess what? Those are *exactly* the same things the mothers and daughters in the pro-life conference are worried about. Your only difference is *this* topic. You want the right to an abortion. For many of you, it is as simple as the government or some faction trying to tell you what you can or can't do. I don't like that either. My entire campaign is about getting government out of your life and mine as much as possible." There were a few tepid cheers at this statement.

Nick looked out over the crowd. The women were of all ages and appearances. Many in the crowd were clearly beyond child-bearing age.

"Many, if not most of you, will never have to make this horrible choice. I know it is a tough decision. I know people who have done this. My hope, my most fervent hope," said Nick with genuine passion as he stalked the stage, "is to find a pragmatic and sensible solution. You know why?" he paused, looking at the faces looking up.

"I need the women of America united. United and in my court. Fighting for *all* the things that matter. My opponents want you to stay divided. They want you to ignore their other policies. Policies causing so much damage to your children. I need you to have a say on school curriculum, with morals and ethics taught at home. Reinforced at school, not contradicted. To instill respect for the authority of the parent to nurture, cajole, praise, and discipline. Most of all, to love and guide your *own* child. That is a parent's job, not the states. It does *not* take a village, it takes a *parent*," said Nick. Many in the audience cheered at the unexpected turn of conversation and a few even stood up, cheering and clapping. There were others who tried to shout down those cheering, to no avail.

"I know there are many in this crowd who do not agree with what I say. You are all in on the state taking control of everyone's child. I am not talking to you. The rest of this conversation is going to do nothing to change your mind. You will be the ones who continue to drown out what I say with boos." Nick paused as the louder boos rained down. He just stood and smiled, turning to the side of the stage, looking at a technician he had spoken to earlier.

"Thank you for making my point," his voice boomed even louder in the auditorium as the technician turned up the volume. "See, I told you so. They cannot have you reconcile with your sisters. To find a pragmatic middle ground. To let our kids be kids. Free from sexualization and gender dysphoria in elementary school. Free from their activism."

"They cannot allow you to keep the family intact. If the village does not take control of your kids, they know they lose," Nick continued to talk over the boos as his voice drowned them out. As they died down, he lowered his voice as well.

"There are two famous quotes to back me up. Both Hitler and Lenin are quoted as saying, and I am paraphrasing, 'give me the children for four years and I own them for life'. They knew, just as our village of the state knows, if I can fill your child's head full of propaganda and indoctrination, they will look to the state to lead them for life."

"This is why I started here first. You know, my talk to the next group is easier than to you. I really only have to convince them to compromise on abortion. Here, I have to convince you that abortion is not the only issue. While the Party has you distracted and afraid of losing the right to choose, they are slowly eroding your ability to have any say in both your child's and, increasingly, your own lives."

"They are chipping away at your freedoms. At your ability to express your opinions. Your ability to make your own choices about so many aspects of your life. All they have to do is stand up and point at the other side and say they will take away your right to choose. You just ask where to march and what to vote against. No questions asked. This has to stop."

"I don't agree with much Bill Clinton did." He was rewarded with hearty laughs from the older members of the crowd. The youngsters looked at each other or asked their mothers who Bill Clinton was. "I agree with his statement that abortion should be 'safe, legal, and rare'."

"What is this argument about? Let's be honest. It is not really about the baby, is it? It is about *your* choice. The idea you should have a choice until the last possible moment. That no one should stop you because it is your decision to make." He stopped at one end of the stage.

"I get it. I am a big believer in freedom. That includes your freedom to choose and to do so without coercion. This is the most personal of all decisions. You hold this small soul in your hands. It is your choice to give it life or not. Just as it was your choice to have the sex," Nick again paused, cupping his hands in front of his body.

"We claim to want to follow the science. Well, science is making great strides. We can now detect heartbeats sooner in pregnancy. We can also determine many other things. Anyone still advocating for abortion any time during pregnancy has less and less of a leg to stand on. At some point, it is simply inhumane, if not criminal. It seems a reasonable compromise that we focus on stopping unwanted pregnancy. Then, if it happens, deal with the unwanted pregnancy as close to conception as possible." He saw bobbing heads in the audience to this logic.

"We agree you want to keep your choice. OK. While I won't support or advocate for any federal limitations on abortion, I am also not going to advocate for abortion any time with no questions asked. I don't think this is right, either. I have to believe, in my heart, there are not that many here who would agree that killing a baby who can survive outside the womb is good for the mother or society? Even if you agree it is the choice of the mother to end this viable human, it is not *right or moral* once the baby could survive.

The loud jeers started once again. Nick continued speaking louder again to drown out the boos while stalking the stage, making his points using his hands.

"If the real reason for abortion is to overcome accidents and best intentions in preventing pregnancy, then abortion should be relatively quick once you discover you are pregnant. Again, I cannot speak from experience, but is it *reasonable* to assume when you find out you are pregnant at four, six or nine weeks, you know whether you want or are prepared to have the baby at that point, correct?" he asked, looking into a now sea of bobbing heads in the crowd.

"Even if you need time to contemplate what your choices are, 12 or 15 weeks seems like a reasonable timeframe to make this heart wrenching decision. Beyond this, it gets less and less morally defensible. You are approaching viability. Why do you need the ability to end after this? Just because you don't want anyone to say no to your choice? A choice you had at six weeks or three months? I am sorry, but that is not defensible. Parroting 'my body, my choice' is not good enough. Have the baby and give it to a family unable to have children. They will bless you to high heaven."

"My message to your pro-life sisters is going to be the same. Be pragmatic. Imagine it is you. Despite your best intentions, you get pregnant. You need the ability to decide to stop this in a reasonable timeframe. If your religion says it is a sin, that is fine. If you get pregnant and you cannot end it, then have the baby. That is wonderful and you can have a clean conscience. But that is not how everyone feels. Because of this, I will never support any legislation that forces you to not have an abortion, ever. I'll support legislation, at the state level, voted on by a majority of citizens to establish reasonable limits. So-called heartbeat laws are too short as well. Twelve or fifteen weeks seems to be agreeable to most. It seems your fellow pragmatic citizens agree."

Nick stopped, looking over the crowd. He could see some agreeing and others shouting, 'my body, my choice'.

He raised his voice again. "Wait. I have one more point. I am speaking to each of you as an individual. Faced with this choice. Please let me get my whole thought out before you boo."

He came to the very edge of the stage, making eye contact with a few women in the front rows. "I think we can all agree actions have consequences. If I run a red light, and a cop sees me, I get a ticket. If I run that red light, and there is no cop, I don't. But I know I got away with breaking a rule. If I am raised right, to believe in the rule of law, laws that apply equally, I feel somewhat concerned a cop may have seen me. This is how it should be. I know it was wrong. But I got away with it. You ask, what could this possibly have to do with abortion?" Nick smiled.

"We are the sum of our choices. Good and bad. Whether or not we get caught. We know. I have a belief in a higher power. Call it God if you will. I have seen too much horror in my life on the battlefields of Afghanistan and Iraq to believe in an *intervening* force in my daily life. But I believe this higher power gave me free will. To do with as I choose. So were you. I choose to live my life in a belief I will have a day of reckoning. Where I'll be called to account for a life lived. The actions and the consequences. Good and bad. As small as running red lights, and as large as taking the life of enemy combatants. We all have things we need to answer for. To counter this, we must stack up good deeds to counter the bad. I want my ledger, my scale, to be tipped on the side of good."

Nick looked over the crowd. He could see the older women paying attention, while many of the younger had skeptical looks on their faces at his bringing up God.

"One thing I do know is no one is responsible for my actions and their results except me. I take responsibility for my actions and do not blame others. Nor do I blame my situations. I may blame my government for putting me in battle, but my actions are my own. I standalone on that day, with my deeds as my record of a life well lived. To be judged. This is why I am telling you this."

"Each of you has to do the same. Whether you believe or not, can you be sure what I say is not true? What potential harm is there in leading your life, in making decisions as if there is a day of reckoning? Just think about that. Are you sure there is not? Then it won't matter that you made choices, not caring about whether they were right or wrong, good or bad. But if there is? Boy oh boy, I would not want to be standing there trying to explain deeds I did without thinking about their consequences."

"This is my ask. I implore you to think this way. To understand a decision to have an abortion is a decision you will have to answer for, not to me, to the father, to your parents, to your children now or in the future, or to any authority on this planet. But you *may* have to answer for this deed to *your* higher power if that day of reckoning comes. I do not issue this as a hypothetical threat. I issue it as a plea. A plea to understand the consequences of that action."

"The non-believers are laughing at me, and the scientists are claiming this is an impossibility. But we don't know, do we? Have you ever noticed as people age and get toward the end of their life, they are more concerned about charity and helping people and how they will be remembered? Why is that do you think? Could it be they are finally realizing, 'Hey, what if I am wrong and there is a reckoning or a hereafter? I'd better make up for lost time'."

"Do you know why we have Nobel prizes? Alfred Nobel invented dynamite. When his brother died, the obituary wrongfully identified him as the inventor of dynamite. It blamed him for all the ills of war and destruction dynamite had enabled. Having seen this, and not wanting to be remembered for enabling havoc and destruction, Nobel endowed the prizes so he would be remembered for honoring good in the world and not for inventing a tool of destruction," stated Nick as people in the crowd laughed at the story.

"You can laugh and say I am full of shit. I can't get pregnant and here I am lecturing you that God is judging you and your decisions. My view is a bit more fatalistic. I *hope* God is watching me. I want to believe I am going to be judged. I'm not willing to take the chance I'm wrong. Ask yourself. Are you? All of you in the audience of a certain age. Tell the truth. As we progress and get passed 40 or 50 or 60, are we not all wondering about our disdain and carefree ignoring of all things remotely related to God? Are we not now maybe considering if we were wrong? And what we can do to maybe change our ways? Before it is too late and just in case?" asked Nick, now seeing smiles and not a few heads now nodding in the audience.

"We all know how religion and faith have both been minimized in our lives. Religion is being used as a weapon by the secular progressives. They are vilifying it. They say faith in a higher power you can't see, you can't touch, who can't help you, is frankly not only stupid, but dangerous."

"Why do they hate religion so much? Not because they are against God, but because faith in a higher power is something they can't control. If you look to something they can't manipulate or control the message, then you have a way to stay out of their control. I ask you a question. When was the last time you prayed? Probably when something horrible was happening in your life. An ill family member or a lost job. A weather event? Did it give you peace of mind? What is wrong with praying for guidance or help or to feel better about a decision? I say nothing. It hurts no one, and it gives you a sense of comfort."

"To be clear, I am not advocating for religion. Or saying any way of worship is better or worse. Personally, as I have said, all that matters is my relationship with my higher power. After all, it is my day of reckoning. No one else is there but me. How you choose to worship is your own decision. I am thankful we live in such a tolerant society where the freedom to make these decisions is not only reality, but codified in our rule of law. The freedom to choose to worship, or to not worship or believe, and to have this free from coercion by the state," Nick paused again, listening to the boos and watching the majority listening carefully to his concepts. They were definitely not expecting to *think* at a political speech.

"All I am asking is for you to consider this. Think about it. Many of you are too early in life to worry about what happens after. But many are not. Some of you have probably had to make this horrible decision. You know what I am talking about. How never a day goes by where you aren't wondering 'what if'. It may have been absolutely the best decision. That doesn't help you with the guilt. If it is anything like the trauma I've experienced myself from war, it never goes away. You live with it every day. You make your peace with your demons. You find a way to move on. I strive to do more good than harm every day to atone for these actions."

"I leave you with this final thought. What would it hurt to live your life as if you *have* to account for all of your choices? If we all approach our decisions using this mantra, the world will be a much better place. Best of all, stop fighting about this. This is what they want. Trust me, the worst possible thing would be for pro-life and pro-choice to achieve a compromise position. To agree abortion will not stop. To do all we can to prevent unwanted pregnancy. To agree on a reasonable time period in which to limit abortion, twelve or fifteen weeks and any later has to be for medical reasons."

"If we do this, I think we can take this off the plate and unite the women of America into a *united and unstoppable* force. Focused on getting the state out of the schools, out of the home, and leave parenting to the parents and activism to the adults. Especially to stop inflicting on our children, activist positions. Positions they are woefully unprepared to understand and certainly not mature enough to decide for themselves. Let kids be kids and save the activism until they get to college. Let them make their own choices about gender, social justice, and everything else *when* they are old enough."

"I don't know about you, but I did a bunch of stupid shit when I was young. None of it was well thought out or rational. I suspect it is the same for everyone under the age of 25, let alone fifteen or twelve. I am asking you to have an open mind. To consider this."

"I will present this to your sisters in a week. If I can convince them to come off their no abortion stance and be pragmatic, are you willing to consider these reasonable suggestions?" Nick finished by asking the crowd. He saw more than half were shaking their head they would.

"Because you know what, if we do this, we will remove the need for abortion in almost all cases and make this a moot point. No one should want to have an abortion. It should only be out of necessity and even then, it should be so defensible for the woman that she would not be afraid to face her maker, knowing her decision was pragmatic and honest. If we get to that point, we have removed the need for government to be involved," said Nick as he walked along the stage.

"There will be hold outs. You will be persecuted by the voices on the far left and the religious far right, saying you have sold out your sisters, saying you are being put back in chains, barefoot, and in the kitchen if you don't hold firm to your right to a partial birth abortion at 8 months. Or committing a grave sin against God by killing a potential life. These are both extreme positions," Nick again paused as he moved to finish. He stood, his entire body language an imploring motion.

"If you subscribe to my approach, if you look into your inner soul, touch that spark. That is the spark your mother and father gave you. That spark is the soul your creator enabled in you and in all of us fortunate enough to be born into this existence. A soul each of you holds within you. One that you control. It is a powerful burden. But it is also a glorious gift. Remember, it is not always wrong, but you should understand actions have consequences and there may just be someone to answer for, somewhere, for those consequences. But you also hold the ability to make up for having to make this choice to prevent this creation. Science is only confirming this precious gift. It had to start from somewhere? Could that have been an ultimate force? Who knows, but the science of this is definitely not settled." He stood up straight as some in the audience heckled him and others cheered.

"One last thing. Let's talk about men's contribution, short though it is." They greeted Nick with laughter as his point hit home. "You have to protect yourself. This is especially true for every young woman in the audience. Assume the man will not take care of making sure you aren't going to get pregnant. We men are not exactly thinking about this, right?" said Nick with a wry smile, getting another laugh from the audience.

"Men should not get off guilt free either. We did our part, so we aren't blameless either. This is not a one-way street, believe me. We need to atone for putting you in this position and are equally on the hook for consequences, not just economically, but morally as well," said Nick as he moved to the podium and took a sip of water.

He now stood in the center of the stage and held a hand to his chin, looking upward.

"If there were a candidate who wanted to control the border and find a humane, but fair way to deal with illegals. Shrink the size of government, focus on getting folks to work, including the homeless.

Who wants to keep government intrusion in your life to a minimum. While also securing our safety through increased police funding, with more oversight to weed out the bad apples. Someone who advocated for pragmatic approaches to keeping abortion limited but legal, and to implement common sense stances to so many issues we face. Would that be a candidate you could support?" finished Nick with a smile to cheers and yes's from the crowd.

"Too bad we don't have one of those, huh?" said Nick to hearty laughter from the crowd.

"Well now, all I need to do is convince the pro-life crowd this is the pragmatic, modern and righteous way to look at this. I know the religious organizations will not agree, but they should. We'll see how it goes. I thank you for your time."

Suddenly, loud chants of 'our body, our choice' and 'no restrictions' were taken up by portions of the crowd. Nick was shaking his head at the response, when suddenly a new chant came from others. It began as a few shouts of 'Turner'. As more and more joined in, it grew louder and louder as it became 'Turner, Turner, Turner' and then those in the crowd shouting stood up and turned it almost into a sing along. The protesters' shouts were drowned out entirely. Nick stood smiling as Alicia came back on stage.

"Senator Turner, I thank you for your pragmatic advice. I think you have your answer. I also think you will find we are all not the mindless drones you accuse us of being. We are thinkers, and we care and understand the consequences of actions by both state and federal governments. I wish you luck with the pro-life factions. I suspect you will have a tougher time with them than us," she finished.

"Ladies and gentlemen. Senator Nick Turner, independent candidate for President." Nick turned and put the microphone back into the stand on the podium as many of the five thousand attendees stood and cheered, clapping. Many were crying and hugging each other. Nick waved as he exited the stage, shaking Alicia's hand, who turned the handshake into a hug. She whispered in his ear, "God Bless you, Nick. That was amazing. I hope it works."

Nick exited the hug, smiling. "Me too." The chants of Turner continued louder. Nick saw folks in the crowd hugging each other. He hoped it would last and the word would spread.

As Nick left the stage, Earl was holding Denise, who had clearly been affected by Nick's words and appeared to have been crying. Nick approached, a worried look on his face.

Denise turned to him as he approached. "You bastard. Just what I need. A cosmic guilt trip to go with everything else. Day of reckoning? Fuck. I had better start piling up the good karma in a hurry," she softened the statement with a slight smile. "If you tell anyone, I'll kick you in the nuts so hard you'll sing soprano for a week," growled Denise.

"No problem," said Nick, backing away a step. "Denise, you do good every day of this campaign. All you can do is keep doing." Nick looked back at the crowd. "Do you think it is enough?"

"You may have single-handedly solved the biggest political problem of the last sixty years. Candidates have been trying to pitch 12 or 15 weeks for years. No one has tied it to an individual decision quite like this. If Lexi were smart, she'd be wetting herself right now. That was glorious. If you can convince the pro-life crowd, and I think you will, because you are giving them a path to reconciliation but still tied to God, forgiveness, and redemption. Who are they to judge? You know all that 'judge not lest ye be judged' stuff? If you take abortion off the table and unify women around kitchen table issues and their kid's safety and sexual health, oh my God. You are gonna get a ton of that suburban mom vote," said Denise in an awed voice.

"Now you know why I don't write my speeches. It has to come from the heart, and they have to know it is heartfelt and not from a speechwriter."

"Alicia was right. This is the easy one. You are still advocating to keep abortion in some form. I think the response at the end is all you need to know. The bulk of them were shouting your name," finished Denise, wiping her eyes. "I won't question your ability any longer. I would love to see Lexi's face right now."

"Everyone keeps telling me hope is not a strategy. I have to hope it is enough."

Earl broke in. "One thing is for sure, the lunatic fringe is gonna come after you with both barrels. You have dared to tell them God is going to damn them to hell for advocating late term murder. You may have roused enough to shout them down in this conference, but you can be sure the digital ink is flowing as fast as they can type it right now."

"Good. They will help prove my point. I assume we have a recording?"

"We do. It is already up on Hibi and they are even trying the other social media platforms. It was also live streamed. You can expect to get attacked by both the ultra-right and ultra left hard cores," said Denise.

Nick nodded as they turned to leave.

#

Lauren Bergamo sat in her *America's News Channel* provided apartment in Washington DC. She picked at the Caesar salad she'd grabbed on her way home from ANC's DC Bureau. She'd spent the day doing brief updates from in front of the White House and adding commentary from interviews with attendees and pundits regarding the chaotic Opposition convention. Having to listen to talking head after talking head tear into Nick caused her to wince inside.

The morning sickness had mostly died down, but her appetite was still spotty. She'd visited a clinic in Atlanta, and they confirmed she was about eight weeks pregnant. There was no doubt who the father was. She'd hardly had time for romance while focusing on her career at ANC.

Sitting on the couch, she turned on the TV. It displayed her social media streaming channels. She glanced through the new content on her favorite's list.

Front and center was a new post from Nick's campaign. Lauren laughed. "Must be nothing bad in this one since it's been up for 6 hours," she commented aloud. She pressed play and watched as Nick pleaded with the crowd at the WR2C conference to think about abortion. To realize it ultimately was not a group think response, but a highly personal decision between a woman and her God. Lauren sat mesmerized by the power of Nick's argument.

Thinking how he was the first pragmatic politician who did not favor one side or the other. He perfectly blended the advances in science, with the personal choices guaranteed by the Constitution. Marrying it to the possibility of a biblical day of reckoning.

In one speech, Nick cut the legs out of both sides of the argument. He'd exposed the religious organization's viewpoint of no abortion ever by making it a personal faith decision versus dogmatic obedience. While also skewering the 'kill any unborn child any time' of the feminists. Using science and individual conscience paired with moral goodness, rather than a 'keep your hands off my body' mantra.

"You fucker, so you lay it all in my lap. I *was* using birth control," she screamed at the screen. "Oh, shit," she said as she quickly got up and ran to her bathroom.

As she came back, she threw away the rest of her salad and made a cup of decaf. While it was brewing, she went back into the living room where her video of Nick on stage was paused. He stood there, tall, handsome, and confident. She backed it up and listened to the section where he said men were not off the hook either.

"But what about if they don't know they're even on the hook," she said to the screen. She looked at her phone, as she had so many times this last week or so, wanting to call, but too afraid to tell him.

Lauren had not been to church, other than weddings, in over a decade. Yet, she suddenly felt compelled to kneel next to her sofa. She put her hands together and laid her forehead against the cushion, crying. She felt silly. Taking Nick's advice, she prayed.

"Father, I know I haven't been very attentive. I also know I've probably done lots for which I should ask for forgiveness. I try to do good too. I need help. I need your guidance. I didn't want this, and I thought I took precautions. I guess they mean it when they say 99% effective," she laughed through her tears. "What are you doing, Bergamo?"

"Yet, she felt a weight lifted from her shoulders. Even if she was just telling her story aloud to no one. She was calm and her stomach felt settled for the first time in weeks.

"OK, I get it. It's my decision to make, right or wrong. We both know what Nick would say and do if I tell him. I just can't. Especially after that speech. I can't do this to him. I know what I need to do. Thanks," she said, getting up and looking around, almost as if she expected someone to show up who had heard her talking to herself.

She walked to the kitchen, got her coffee, put her usual sugar and cream in it and sat down to drink it, watching the evening ANC opinion shows.

As she listened to her colleagues yammer, many about Nick's speech. She couldn't help but juxtapose their viewpoints with those being expressed by Nick. She could see how the common person could relate to everything Nick said. It was about their life. The hardships and choices, the sacrifices and letdowns, the hopes, and the dreams. All ANC told anyone was to do this or else. All threats and fear. Plus, a good dose of you're too stupid to think for yourself, so just listen to us. We're the only ones who know what's good for you.

Maybe it was her prayer, or her epiphany had provided clarity, but suddenly she could see. Now she understood Nick's appeal. She could see the hypocrisy and cowardice of the Party. She could also see she was a tool. Another hammer used by the Progressives to beat down the hopes of the middle and lower classes.

Beat them down with fear, uncertainty, and doubt. To pound them into submission. Telling them to trust and believe only what they were being told by the Party and their media allies. What she was doing was neither helpful nor noble. She turned off her channel in disgust and curled up in a ball on the couch.

#

Lauren stood in a circle, unable to move or speak. Nick was there. So was an old man. Nick was shrouded in light while the old man was covered in darkness and flames. It appeared they were arguing over her. Back and forth they fought. Nick had a sword and wings, the old man was very spry and bounced around sticking Nick with his spear, causing him to bleed profusely until it appeared he was going to fall.

She screamed out his name in the dream. Nick glanced at her. The old man took advantage of Nick's momentary distraction and stabbed his spear through Nick's chest. A bright flash of light and Lauren woke up on her couch.

"Holy crap, what the heck was that?" she rubbed her eyes, her heart beating wildly. Checking her watch, it was after midnight, well past her normal bedtime.

"That was a weird one for sure," she said, shaking her head as she prepared for bed. Her dreams of Nick usually replayed their weekend in San Francisco. She walked to her bed, hesitating, before dropping to her knees. She said a quick prayer for guidance. To keep her loved ones and Nick safe. She felt silly, but she went to bed with a smile on her face and slept the entire night, a deep, restful sleep.

Chapter 5

"Ah, boss. We have trouble in River City," worried Mel, entering Lexi's office in her campaign HQ.

"What's up?"

"Watch," Mel brought up a recording of Nick's speech on his phone, handing it to Lexi.

"Interesting," remarked Lexi, having watched the entire speech.

"Interesting? He has them eating out of his hands," whined Mel. "These are your voters, suburban pro-choice moms whose single issue is 'keep your hands off my body'. If they are responding to him and his 'girl power' talk, we are in a world of hurt."

"I don't think so. If Blackbird did this, I would be worried. He won't because he wants the evangelicals. Even if Turner gets in front of them, I don't think they are going to appreciate his picking on their worship habits. As an independent, he is angling for the fringes, anyway. It was an excellent speech. I *am* glad he isn't the Opposition candidate."

Mel sat down, dumbfounded. "You don't think this is an issue? Abortion is the single issue we have used for decades to paint the religious right as nut jobs and the Opposition as dangerous to women."

"Mel, there were five thousand folks there today. As you said, these are our people. This message isn't going to resonate. If it does, what is his solution? Don't have an abortion because you're going to feel guilty? Because God is going to punish you at the pearly gates?"

Lexi stood and started pacing as if responding to a debate question.

"It may resonate with those in their fifties and sixties who have had abortions. The younger generations don't even know who God is. They are certainly not worried about what she thinks. They aren't going to risk their financial futures to keep a baby they don't want. Certainly not because they are worried about judgement from a God they can't see, they don't believe in, or who has no material impact on their ability to party the next weekend."

Mel suppressed a smile. This was where Lexi was at her best. She was an excellent debater.

"Having and then keeping a baby cramps their style. Period. Same for marriage. As we have seen, an overwhelming number of these twenty and early thirty something women don't even want to get married because it keeps them from 'binge drinking, sleeping in late, and watching reality TV'. We have done our job well," she smiled, quoting a recent article discussing young women's top reasons for not getting tied down.

Mel nodded, not wanting to interrupt her thoughts.

"Young women have become lazy about precautions. With the morning-after pills and other things. They are still going to need access to abortions because they got drunk and slept with the drummer from the band last night. You can be sure the man isn't doing anything. Turner got that part right," she finished in a disgusted tone.

Mel sat in his chair, hand on his chin, contemplating Lexi when she turned to him from her office bar. He shook his head.

"We'll keep threatening them with the idea of the Opposition and now Turner wanting to make sure they *never* have a choice to get an abortion."

"Exactly," said Lexi, sitting down in a chair across from him. "If there is one thing we have been successful at, it is the breaking down the barriers to casual sex. As much and as often as you like and with whomever of any sex. Turner may frighten a few older women feeling guilty about past deeds and thinking about their own approaching demise, but the rest of them, no way. Young people and moms are too busy with day-to-day activities, posting selfies and social media videos to worry about this heavy metaphysical stuff," stated Lexi.

"I don't know. We need to see what the evangelicals do and how they respond. If he peels some of them away from Blackbird, or even worse Garcia, he could build his own coalition," warned Mel.

"Fine, then keep an eye on him. He is still supporting choice, so he probably goes nowhere with the evangelicals. He's not going to convince my soccer moms either. Words are easy and if need be, I can use his *Roe* stance against him. He still wants to restrict it, which is the same as keeping it repealed. We can inundate the airwaves with talking heads saying any restrictions *is* the slippery slope to full restriction. Once folks realize this, they'll come back into the fold. It is all *Roe* or no *Roe*. I'll work it into my next speech."

"I hope you're right," said Mel, still concerned.

#

"Gee Nick, me thinks you poked the hornet's nest. Care to look at a few more?" asked Margie holding a remote.

"Hey, I meant what I said. I didn't tell anyone what to do. I merely made a few suggestions. Asked them to think about what I said. How they choose to respond or interpret is entirely up to them," replied Nick.

"Show him the clip from *Woman's Viewpoint*," laughed Chuck as they sat around the conference room in Nick's Denver election office. Margie fast forwarded through other clips from major networks and opinion hosts until she stopped in front of the five women in a semi-circle.

One of the panel, a large black woman, was practically shouting across the table at a petite blonde on the opposite end.

"What the '*bleep*'. Who does he think he is, God? Damning everyone who has an abortion to hell! This guy is '*bleeping*' nuts," she said as the video bleeped her f-bombs each time.

"Karen, calm down." Broke in another older white woman on the panel, trying to calm things down. "You're going to have a coronary." The crowd of women in the audience was cheering her on.

"I will not calm down. I marched for *Roe*. I protested when they killed it. I will not sit still and let Turner try to guilt shame women into not having abortions because they *may* be held accountable to a force no one can see, touch, feel, or even confirm exists."

Several of the other women tried to break in as the crowd cheered Karen's statements. She continued shouting over her colleagues, including the little blonde on the end, trying to retort.

"What's next, claiming the world is flat and the moon landings didn't happen? He is one conspiracy theory after another and we do a disservice, even talking about it. As a white *man*, he has no right to tell poor black, brown or even white women what they can and cannot do with their bodies. '*Bleep*' him." She sat back with her arms crossed, scowling as the crowd cheered even louder.

The blonde's face was red. "May I finish my statement now?"

"Sure thing, honey," replied Karen condescendingly.

"Karen! Let Jeri finish," admonished the mature host in a lecturing tone.

"It's alright Darlene," replied Jeri shaking her head. "As I was saying, I see nothing wrong with the questions the Senator asked. He was reasonable and assured the pro-choice audience he won't support banning all abortion. They should be happy with that. Our young people face a genuine crisis with depression and suicide at all-time highs. Our culture has left them unfettered and they get little help navigating the tough times they face. Despite what Karen is implying, if you listen to what he actually said," Karen started to break in when Jeri held up a hand.

"My turn. I waited for you to finish. Now you can show me the same courtesy." Karen leaned back, arms crossed again and scowling.

"All Turner did was ask a question. A question anyone can choose to ignore or answer. Ultimately, he is right on two fronts. First, only the mother has to live with the consequences of her choice. Second, the only true and possible judge *could* be God. *If* one were worried about this, then perhaps they should consider this. In case you didn't notice, he also advocated funding for Planned Parenthood for pregnancy prevention, just not for abortions. I think we can all get behind doing everything we can to prevent unwanted pregnancy." As Jeri finished, a few in the audience cheered, but many more booed.

"Honey, when you are sitting in the clinic deciding to have an abortion, God ain't there holding your hand. It is the Doctor and the nurse, usually funded by Planned Parenthood, who help you get on with your life. It sure as '*bleep*' is not the baby daddy. You should probably visit one of these clinics and see what reality looks like." The set degenerated into another shouting match as Margie muted the clip.

"That was certainly interesting. Apparently, they are in trouble because in some markets they did not bleep Karen's first f-bomb in time. It seems you have few converts amongst the studio audience at *Viewpoint*," suggested Margie.

Nick shrugged. "They aren't my audience. I need the open-minded ones. Jeri reiterated my point. For some of those in their audience who didn't see the clip, maybe they will go look and listen for themselves. That's all I can hope for. How many views did they get?"

"Highest viewers this year," answered Greg. "Around seven million in mid-morning. They are also the highest rated daytime show and get the most clicks and views. Your speech is now up on several social feeds beyond Hibi. You are getting millions of views there too. They must have decided it hurts you more than helps. No one is trying to get them taken down. Lots of pro and con digital ink is being spilled. Having the ladies of the *Women's Viewpoint* hate you is not such a bad thing."

Lexi hit back as well. Greg picked the clip from a streaming channel and hit play.

"Turner tells you to be afraid of God's judgement if you have an abortion. Show me this so-called higher power. Where are they going to be when the young woman has the child and has to struggle in abject poverty, burdening themselves with an unwanted child? I have yet to see this higher power fill an empty belly. Or pay your delinquent rent. Pay for diapers and formula for the baby you have that you cannot afford to raise." Lexi was whipping her crowd of followers into a frenzy at a Planned Parenthood parking lot on the campus of the University of Maryland.

"You know who is going to be there to help? This administration and the government programs he so maligns. You know who else? Planned Parenthood is there with counseling, birth control and in the event of unplanned accidental pregnancies, they are there to help with a woman's right to an abortion," she paused as the hundreds of college-aged women cheered and shouted her name.

"This is a woman's health issue here on planet earth. Not in some mythical place where you are going to be held to an imaginary judgement day. Shame on you, Nick Turner, for using your ill-gotten celebrity status to scare our young women with your rhetoric and claims of eternal damnation. I promise you, when I am president, this kind of dangerous speech will not be tolerated." Lexi paused as the crowd cheered.

"We will not allow people to frighten our citizens with this kind of radical zealotry. This election cannot come fast enough to allow us to take back control of our airwaves and social media. Preventing seditious and dangerous provocative statements from reaching the easily influenced." As she droned on, Greg stopped the recording.

"Denise, you're awfully quiet," observed Nick.

"Abortion is such a hot button topic. I like your position. It is pragmatic and realistic. The abortion anytime stance is getting less and less tenable with the prevalence of early detection technology. With alternatives after sex instead of waiting four or six weeks to find out you are pregnant. Your stance is as happy a medium as you can get. I don't know if we can get your actual position to the folks we need to hear it without it being twisted by commentary like that," she said, pointing at Lexi on the TV. "The true litmus test will be if they still let you talk at the World Evangelical Congress next week. Margie, we still on?"

"So far. We are still invited."

"Good. The liberals and progressives are pissed at me for daring to suggest a compromise position. What are the conservatives saying?"

Margie hesitated for a second, looking quickly at Denise.

"Show him," she said.

Margie fast forwarded to a segment on *Tommy*.

"Tonight we have Pastor Aaron Mills, who is the leader of the AM congregational church in Dallas. Pastor, you asked to appear to offer your thoughts on Senator Turner's speech at the WR2C."

"Thank you, Tommy. I did. I feel it is my job to offer a rebuttal to his statement. I tend to a sizeable group of followers who have put our faith in Jesus Christ as our savior. While I understand the Senator is a politician and is clearly pandering to his audience to win votes, I take issue with his sudden invocation of the Lord condoning abortion."

"Pastor, I am not sure that is what he said. He merely asked a question about faith…"

"Tommy, he claimed he knows how God will judge a woman who murders their unborn child. Implying there is a path to salvation and forgiveness. In his own words, he contradicts himself, claiming this is a possibility and then saying it is not a given. So, which is it? Nowhere in scripture does it give anyone the right to decide what only the Lord can, regarding a person's salvation." The Pastor's voice was rising as he continued, as if he were preaching to his flock.

"Nowhere in scripture does it give anyone an easy way out regarding terminating the greatest gift of conception. I invite the Senator to join one of our weekend services to defend his position. He will see how wrong it is to people who have sinned. Who fully understand what faith, forgiveness and redemption are and how it works."

"An offer I am sure the Senator will take you up on, if I know him," said Tommy. "I also believe he will make a speech at an upcoming Evangelical conference. We will see how they view his ideas. I for one believe, politically, his position is brilliant. Regardless of your particular faith, he provides reasonable ways to reconcile this horrible decision and provide a way for a young woman to deal with the outcome."

"Tommy, I vehemently disagree. He only provides a way to saddle them with guilt by making it easier to decide to terminate the unborn. Then assuming they will be forgiven in the end. It is a false promise. I rarely agree with the hosts on the *Women's Viewpoint*. However, in this case, I have to agree he is acting like he has a direct line to what God will and will not deem redeemable. For this, he should be worried about his own day of reckoning," finished Pastor Mills in a righteous tone.

Margie and Denise looked down around the conference room.

"Sorry Nick. The Pastor speaks to around 100,000 live every weekend and millions view his sermons online. He has a huge following of fanatical worshipers. The Evangelical Congress will be the same."

"I'll take my chances. Contact him, get me booked to join one of his sermons as well."

"Nick, what does Sun Tzu say about frontal assaults and choosing the battlefield of your choice? Don't let him goad you into playing on his home turf," suggested Earl, joining the conversation for the first time.

"I also can't look like I am afraid by ducking the invite. This guy is the fraud. I have seen his kind before. He has a bully pulpit. There is only one way to deal with his type. Head on. Book it Margie.

"All right."

Chapter 6

Maksim Pavlovich stared up from his desk in his massive library, looking at a holograph of a Chinese Dragon floating in the air in front of him. "First you tell me not to worry about his candidacy and now he almost wins a nomination for a major party he is not even running for? How can I trust your observations? My sources tell me he has gathered many donors who should support the Vice President?"

"It's a fluke. It shows the desperation and the fragmentation of the Opposition party. If they cannot even choose a candidate, how will they ever put up a fight against the Vice President?" asked the voice emanating from the dragon hologram.

"And his speech at the pro-choice conference? It seemed as if his words were getting through to many of them. I have spent billions on Planned Parenthood, countless American political campaigns, activists, DAs, judges, and advertising to ensure abortion remains the wedge issue uniting all liberals. I will not have a neophyte show up and mess this up."

Maksim knew his words were projecting from a similar hologram of a Chinese Rat. It was the animal at the pinnacle of the hierarchy in the Chinese zodiac. The dragon was next. Maksim could sense the hesitation in the reply.

"It is worrisome. We may have underestimated Turner's ability to resonate with certain classes of people. Thankfully, these people are not organized nor very involved in politics. They are also the most susceptible to our tools of cancel culture. We have not attacked Turner directly for fear of repeating past mistakes. Providing insignificant candidates with coverage they turned to their advantage. You have to trust that we understand the situation on the ground in America better than you.

"I have to trust no one. I expect results. Period. You know this. You have seen the results of both misplaced trust and abject failure. I will not allow it again. Get this under control, or we will intervene and leave you to manage the aftermath. You have our asset. Use him."

"This is not Russia or China. You cannot run around indiscriminately killing rivals. There are cameras everywhere and some of our media and justice systems are not compromised," the concern from Dragon coming through even the voice masking technology.

"Listen carefully. We have set up chaos and mayhem in the world to coincide with a friendly regime change in America. The current puppet has turned out to be too confused and feebleminded to follow our directions. This was a miscalculation. Our current candidate has none of these shortcomings. She only needs to win this last election. We have been on the verge too many times. As you know, our allies are also heavily invested in this outcome. There is no turning back. One way or another, it is happening. You follow through on your task, or we do it our way," commanded Pavlovich.

"As I have told you and the others in every council meeting, your way will not work. It will have exactly the opposite effect. You do not understand America. Did you learn nothing from 9/11? Nothing unites a disunited people like an attempt to manipulate them. If you start blundering around, you risk unintended consequences. I have warned you before. Ignore this at your peril. It will not be my fault," Dragon ended the call after this exchange.

Pavlovich sat contemplating the now empty space where the hologram had displayed. He knew he was pushing Dragon aggressively. He also knew Dragon's plan had the best chance of succeeding and achieving their end goal. But he was tired of waiting. He'd been working on this for half a century, and he was not getting any younger.

#

Colin Harthank, lead correspondent for TV Great Britain, sat in an uncomfortable antique tufted chair facing a more comfortably seated Pavlovich. They would do the interview in Pavlovich's Swiss estate.

"This is quite the room," Colin admired, looking around the walls, covered in various framed maps of the world. Many appeared to be well worn battle plans.

"These are all original maps I have collected. He pointed several out on the walls as Colin turned his head to follow the bony finger Maksim held aloft."

"Over there is a map Sir Francis Drake kept of his around the world voyage. There is a map Napoleon used at Waterloo and," he swung his arm around, "one he made at Austerlitz." Turning back, Maksim pointed to a small table. "That is an original set of Operation Overlord plans used by Eisenhower during D-day, with his own notes included."

"Impressive," commented Colin.

"If you study them, you will also notice they were all useless. Only one was followed meticulously. Napoleon's Waterloo. None of the other plans were followed as diagrammed. I tried to acquire Wellington's own plans from Waterloo. What I found out was he had none. It shows you should only plan so much. The ability to adapt is the most important leadership trait. Following plans without changing as the battle proceeds leads to disaster," finished Maksim.

"Point taken. Shall we start?"

Maksim nodded toward the recording crew, who turned on the audio and video recording equipment.

"Tonight, we have the pleasure of interviewing Sir Maksim Pavlovich, world renowned philanthropist. Sir Maksim, we know you rarely grant interviews. We're honored," gushed Colin.

"My pleasure Colin. Your channel has always been fair in your treatment of my efforts to right the various wrongs man is wreaking on the planet and its less fortunate denizens," replied Pavlovich, smiling.

Attired in an impeccably tailored suit, with an ascot hiding his bony throat. Pavlovich always did everything he could to hide his emaciated physical appearance. His eyes stared intensely from his somewhat gaunt face. His actual age was unknown, with many speculating anywhere from mid-eighties to a hundred. There was no record of a birth certificate anyone could find. The few times he'd been pressed, he claimed these records were lost during the German occupation of his homeland in Belarus in World War II. He would often answer he did not know either.

Colin recounted many of the foundations and causes Pavlovich had supported for decades. All the strides these efforts had made to help the poor in various war-torn countries. He also highlighted this to expose the unscrupulous nature of so many corporations unconcerned with human rights in pursuit of profit. Pavlovich finally waved a bony hand.

"Colin, while I appreciate the conversation, I did not consent to this interview to just hear you sing the praises of my World Harmony Society efforts. For all the good we do, there is much else yet to be done. I would prefer to talk about the state of the world. I have spent billions trying to prevent us from destroying both the planet and ourselves. I am afraid we aren't doing a very good job of preventing either."

"Of course, sir. Where would you like to begin?"

"Let's start with the planet. I am an old man. I remember the orgy of industrialization around the world after World War II. The United States, as the sole superpower, made the world its factory. It enabled small, impoverished nations with no resources to suddenly become part of their global supply chain. How did they do this? They did it by shipping them raw materials and turning the one resource they did have, cheap labor, into little more than indentured servants. They claimed it brought them out of poverty and into the global community. A global community run by them. Churning out goods for the giant maw of America to consume in its insatiable appetite for material things," Maksim delivered his message in a forceful tone, his eyes shining brightly, leaning forward.

"There is little doubt that many of these smaller countries prospered under the umbrella of American protection during the cold war and after," agreed Colin, misinterpreting the glare Maksim displayed as he attempted to soften Pavlovich's accusations against America and the west's exploitation of these weak nations.

"Prosperity? Rather, it destroyed indigenous cultures, making these people dependent on this work. It made them forget their own skills. Worse, it introduced them to the cultural rot America has exported to the world. This is hardly what I'd call a reward for America's protection."

"While true, sir, it also provided advances they would never have achieved without joining the global community. Technology and medical advances, reductions in infant mortality, for example," interjected Colin.

"Colin, it is not self-sustaining. As America collapses, all these countries, who have overpopulated because of this artificial success, now find themselves with no work, no skills, and no futures for their populations. They can no longer maintain the standard of living they've become accustomed to. They all must import food to survive. With nothing to trade, how exactly will they do this?"

"It seems to be a problem we are seeing around the world. Look at the fallout from the disruption of the grain shipments caused by the Russian-Ukraine conflict," replied Colin, nodding.

"It is more than a problem, Colin. There are too many people on this planet. We cannot grow enough food in the places where the people are living. This artificial success in places where industry and population should not have been. Combine this with vast amounts of population growth generated through blind adherence to religious dogma, the world is at a tipping point. Africa, Asia, Central and South America and now elsewhere as these populations migrate to more prosperous areas, are becoming unsustainable."

"Sir, that seems cold-blooded," replied Colin in a shocked tone.

"If I can prevent the next billion souls from being born to only die of poverty and disease, it will be a blessing. Much of my money is spent to prevent this. As it stands today, there are several billion souls who are already going to experience poverty, famine, and shorter life spans. It is simply math and physics. We have expanded beyond our ability to house, feed, and employ this many people in meaningful ways. Idle hands and empty bellies also lead directly to armed conflict. Armed conflict leads to needless suffering. Primarily amongst the civilian poor. Those who instigate the conflict never suffer."

"That is a sad prediction if true, sir. I hope it does not happen."

"Of course, Colin. No one wants to invite Armageddon. However, we must be prepared. Many of the so-called advances in science have contributed significantly to this. From eradicating diseases to improving infant mortality rates to even air conditioning. While wonderful advances, they've also led to the very conditions we are not attempting to mitigate. We cannot solve these after they arrive. We need to stop them from becoming reality. This means recognizing the need and making the tough decisions to prevent it from happening."

"How do we know it *will* happen? No one knows the future," noted Colin, responding to Maksim's suggestion of pre-emptive action.

"We are running out of resources, burning those we have in such copious amounts, endangering the very air we breathe. As the rest of the world starts to recognize and deal with this issue, the country most responsible for this, the United States, is now telling others who are trying to copy them, to stop in their efforts to reach the same success. Why would developing countries stop and listen? China, Brazil, India, and others feel they should also be able to increase their economic outputs to achieve what the Americans have enjoyed these last hundred years."

"How do you suggest we do this? Why will they do this willingly?"

"Colin, we need to do two things. First, we need to have true global governance, not the feckless UN. Rather a true global organization, both science and fact based, who speaks with one voice. One who can ensure rogue nations are not allowed to continue damaging policies detrimental to a majority of the inhabitants of the planet."

"How would you make it work?" probed Colin, making notes.

"If enough agree to work in concert militarily, economically, resource and trade wise, the rest will have no choice except to comply. It will be a matter of survival. The diplomatic approach of the UN has never stopped a single conflict from starting. We need both authority and deterrence. If you cut a rogue country out of the global village, it will have no choice but to change and comply or wither and die from lack of everything. No one can standalone any longer."

"And the second?"

"The United States needs to acknowledge their role in creating this problem and willingly give up some of their prosperity for the good of the new world order. They have reaped the benefit of raping the rest of the world of resources and cheap labor for almost a hundred years. That is long enough," finished Pavlovich with finality.

"Sir, that is a pretty provocative statement. I am not sure the Americans see it this way. They are also unlikely to diminish their own lifestyle to improve everyone else's. Nor have they been inclined to join any of these global governance efforts, from the International Court to the Paris Accords," suggested Colin.

Maksim smiled his crooked toothed smile. "Colin, they will have little choice. It has already started. Many of their own citizens realize this and are already on board. They can no longer consume their way out of their problems as the rest of the world competes for the same goods. Militarily and economically, they are now being challenged."

"Let's consider a few facts. Their inflation is still out of control. Printing more money continues to devalue their currency. A currency that, sadly, much of the world is forced to trade in. We pay for their stupidity every day. Food, anti-immigrant, and anti-government riots in our own streets. Sky high youth unemployment, leading to rampant crime. Now America has exported their racial tensions to Europe as we saw in France, Turkey, and Scandinavia recently."

"Our youth are facing increasing social issues around jobs and wages. The raising of interest rates is also preventing borrowing, both at home and over here," ended Colin, again missing the glare from Maksim at his interruption.

"Yet they still spend two trillion dollars more each year than they bring in via taxes. This is a schizophrenic policy for sure. They are still having race riots. Police continue to target minorities. Random gun violence is on the rise. Crime in urban areas and even suburbs is now also out of control. What police they have left are afraid to enforce the laws." Maksim made his points with emphatic hand gestures.

"The education standards are falling. They pay more per child than any country. How could that money be spent on children in countries where it would be appreciated and the results much better? In China, their youth aspire to be astronauts. In the US, the children aspire to be social media influencers. This is what the highest per capita expense on education is achieving? They also have vigilante youth organizing smash and grabs. The primary killers under thirty are illegal drugs and gang shootings. Their cancel culture mindset prevents any debate about solving these problems."

"Worse, this is spreading to our own idle youth. I could go on and on. The bloom is off the rose in America. It is time to realize their culture is like a growing cancer in the world 'body'." Maksim paused for a sip of his tea, a hand raised as Colin looked ready to interrupt again.

"Their youth are now finding out they will not live lives as well off as their parents. They now see the mess their elders made of their country and the debt and societal collapse they have left for them to clean up. Many are vowing to not lead the same lives. Declining to toil in dead-end jobs for decades, to obtain meaningless material stuff."

"They have accrued massive student debt they cannot pay off. They save nothing for their retirement. Marriage and children are no longer a desire for many. Owning a house is out of reach for most as well. America is about to collapse because of its own short-sided success. The payment is coming due. This shift in view is fueling a political shift to more of a one world view," finished Pavlovich with a smug look.

Colin broke in to comment on Maksim's declarations. "There is no doubt there are challenges for the youth of not just America, but all of Europe, even China. Combine this with the lack of babies being born in these societies and the widespread immigration from poor countries. The west is facing challenges to continued economic prosperity," agreed Colin, as Maksim nodded slightly.

"This is true. Here we continue to manage it with the generous European socialist policies. Unfortunately, the economics of this plan are no more sustainable than America's out-of-control consumption. This is exactly the situation we need to prevent. Our view of the world needs to change to one of global planning and management." Maksim's eyes shined brightly with his fervor in this belief.

"The old ways have failed. We have to do away with old ideas of national boundaries and petty rivalries. If we do not, we will all perish. It is as simple as that."

Colin looked down at his notes. "If I may, how exactly would this 'controlled approach' come about? This sounds Orwellian."

Maksim shrugged at this suggestion. "It will happen in an uncontrolled fashion if we do nothing. This would lead to massive civilian casualties through conflict and chaos. Causing great pain and suffering for nearly all on the planet. A complete collapse of civilizations. Or it can be done in a managed fashion."

"How so?" asked Colin, trying to hide his skepticism.

"Take the upcoming election in America. I believe the Vice President fully understands the challenges facing both America and the world. The other candidates, not so much. I also believe a majority of her supporters would prefer a controlled shift to a global community versus a return to the nationalism so many are now shifting toward or advocating.

"Nationalism that brought us both world wars and a cold war. Governments that killed hundreds of millions of their own citizens through stupidity and ideals of master races and empires. We must recognize what is being preached as both evil and destructive. Many, if not most people, do not want to have total control over *every* choice in their life. They are not equipped to understand all these decisions."

"What you are proposing does not seem to be shared by all. Who gets to decide how and what the future looks like? Do the people not get a voice or a say?" prompted Colin, as Maksim held his eyes with a fixed stare, causing him to look away with a slight shiver.

Pavlovich leaned forward carefully, his voice rising in tempo as he gestured with his hands again, explaining his version of the future.

"The places where the gap between the elites and the poor is the most exaggerated are also those countries who are the most nationalistic. The

United States, China, post-Soviet Russia, Israel, Iran, and North Korea. These are coincidentally the same countries the rest of the world worries about starting World War III."

"Listen to the rhetoric coming from these countries. Or the independent candidate Turner in America. He wishes nothing more than a return of America as the lone superpower. This lust for power can only lead to world conflict if we do not band together and stop the trajectory of these countries." Maksim leaned back in his chair, having spent a day's energy to get his points across. "Left to make their own choices, the people will always choose the path to destruction. We cannot allow them to sentence all to disaster because of their ignorance."

"I do not doubt your observations, but I still do not understand how you stop China from continuing down its path to dominance. The United States has held this title since World War II. It is China's turn. Just as it was Great Britain's for the centuries prior," noted Colin.

"One voice, united in purpose, combining the forces of many to combat the few who disagree. Even with their giant populations, China and India are ruled by a comparatively few. Their masses stand to gain from a flattening of the curve between haves and have nots. It can be done. We only need the will. Once Ms. Smythe-Thomas is elected as the leader of America, I am hopeful her pragmatism and leadership will help usher in a new beginning for not just America, but a majority of the world." Maksim moved to end the interview.

The recording equipment, run by his own staff, stopped.

"I had a few more questions, if I may," asked Colin, not ready to end the interview.

"We are done. I expect this to air just as I have stated it. Keep this request in mind." Pavlovich rose from his chair and slowly exited the room with no further word or gesture. The interview was over.

Colin watched as he exited, silently fuming. He looked up at Pavlovich's aide, Petr.

"Yes?" asked Petr politely.

"I can't broadcast this without some editing. Some of his quotes are very provocative and would require a bit of softening."

"You would be well advised to heed his advice."

"I am a journalist. He doesn't get to dictate to us what is and is not news. We will want to add in our own thoughts and interpretations. We cannot air his comments about the Vice President wanting to lead America into a one world global village. If we air that, we will be accused of trying to influence the American election. It will get us banned from the American social media platforms."

Petr stood, unmoved by Colin's concerns. He shrugged. "It is your choice. Might I suggest you call your company president, or at least your managing editor, and relay your editing plans?"

Colin looked at Petr, who continued smiling. He picked up his notebook and was handed a disk with the recorded audio and video. He was escorted from the property to a waiting car.

Chapter 7

Nick walked into the restaurant in Atlanta. The maître d' saw him.

"Senator, welcome. Mr. Davies has a private room reserved for your dinner. Right this way."

Nick walked through the restaurant, following him, trying not to notice the people pointing at him in obvious recognition. He still had a hard time understanding his new celebrity and smiled as he walked. Avoiding any eye contact and any possible spontaneous conversations or selfie requests. He made a note to bring Earl on these in the future to discourage any enthusiastic fans.

"In here, Senator," the maître d' led Nick into a room where a tall, thin man with perfectly styled gray hair was standing near a table.

"Thank you, Luiz." He nodded and closed the door behind him as he left. "Senator, thank you for agreeing to have dinner with me. I understand this is a rarity," he said, shaking Nick's hand.

"Mr. Davies, nice to meet you. To be honest, Denise didn't give me a choice. She gave a time and a place, and told me not to be late," laughed Nick, adding "and please call me Nick."

"Call me JD, then, and yes, Denise is good at her job, isn't she? You picked well. I assume Chuck recommended her?"

"He did."

"One day, you'll have to ask her about Burbank," smirked JD.

"Burbank?"

"Nope, that is for her to tell," he said, continuing to smile. "I suggest you ask her from a distance. She is likely to throw something at you for even bringing it up."

"I'll leave that memory buried," responded Nick as JD laughed.

"I guess you're wondering why I invited you to dinner. Our politics don't exactly mesh, though I think we agree on more than you might think. I have been out of the news industry since I sold EXN."

"I have to admit, I am curious, but then again, nothing really surprises me anymore," shrugged Nick with a smile.

"I have an idea. To atone for my role in dumbing down American news. Jeremy Kwan suggested I talk to you and see what you think."

"Jeremy? That guy gets around. I guess you billionaires all hang out together?" noted Nick, shaking his head.

"Not really. I didn't know Jeremy, but I admired him for building Hibi. I admire it even more now that he has kept the filth from taking it over. I had an idea and pitched it to him. That is what I want to discuss with you. My years away have given me time to think and to observe the damage I did. I've had a moment of clarity. Technology has provided amazing things. Outstripping all expectations of pundits and experts alike. What it has not done is keep up was human nature."

"Like?"

"Temptation, to be precise. Technology has been used to abuse the baser side of our souls. Online porn is ruining relations between the sexes. Turning what should be the greatest achievement of our brains, finding a soul mate and raising and nurturing a family, into a series of mindless rutting no better than pigs in a stye. AI will only make this worse." Nick took a sip of water as JD continued.

"Social media has ruined the idea of anything social. Turning our youth into mindless drones. Incapable of original thought and easily swayed to do things not in their best interests. Depressing our children and filling their heads with all kinds of destructive thoughts. Meanwhile, filth is spewed, with no attempt at control. All hiding under protection of the first amendment. Technology is speeding up the downfall of society."

There was a tentative knock at the door and a waiter came in to take a drink order and the order for their meals.

"You should try the sea bass. They have it flown in from Chile daily," suggested JD.

"The sea bass it is then," ordered Nick.

As the waiter closed the door, Nick commented. "I couldn't agree more. Social media is a cesspool, and it is being used by the powers behind the statist movement, and others, to dumb down our youth to a point where they will willingly slit their own throats someday. All for the cause of social justice or to become a more prominent influencer after clicks and likes on KooKoo. It is really discouraging to see. I believe in the first amendment, but how do you protect free speech and also protect the people from that same free speech? It is a quandary for sure."

"Nick, it is not just a quandary. It is probably the issue of our time, and the key to moving forward or backward. That's why I called Jeremy. I wanted to see how he was keeping the trolls from his platform. I figured maybe he was on to something," JD paused as the drinks came.

"To your pursuit of the loneliest job in the world, Senator," he said, raising his Manhattan.

"To the business venture I'm about to hear," responded Nick.

JD chuckled as he took a sip of his drink. "Unlike Jeremy, I am not offering you the opportunity to be the first user of my new business. I am interested in your take on it. I am going to launch a news network. In partnership with Jeremy. In the next few weeks, with no live news anchors. Our intent is to have holographic images of generic people delivering the news without any opinion. It is part *Drudge Report* and part *Max Headroom* if you are old enough to remember MTV."

"I am and I do," said Nick. "How would it work?"

"I have built algorithms to cull through all the printed news from around the world. The program goes through each bit, scrubs it for truth, validating it against many sources and then builds a stream of news clips with attributions. We have programmed male and female holographic anchors, essentially AI driven anchors who will alternate delivering each story. The voices all use natural language AI algorithms and not droning computer or *Siri* like at all. We will run however much news there is each day and then simply rerun. Inserting new information into the feed in real time." JD leaned forward at the table, obviously excited to share the vision of this new network.

"The intent is to provide facts and let the audience make their own choices. For instance, if there is a missile attack in Israel, we will gather a combination of news from all sides and combine that into a comprehensive story about the attack, using information from each, plus eyewitnesses, etc. Then we cut into the story various tidbits from commentary by experts who have posted or published regarding the activity. The goal is not to show either the Israeli or Palestinian sides and comments, but to get to the heart of the deeds and the aftermath." Nick sipped his drink, digesting the plan.

"The reason I partnered with Jeremy was so I could license any of his technology. Combining our fact-based stories with the ability for folks to add comments to our online simulcast. While keeping the trolls from filling up the comment sections with filth and propaganda," finished JD.

"You think America is interested in just the facts and not the blonde at EXN or ANC?" asked Nick.

"I created the bubble headed blonde back in the day. I'm hopeful I can pull off another transformation of news," he replied with a wry smile. "What I'm also hopeful of is I can break the stranglehold of the mainstream media on the spinning of propaganda as fact. Even EXN is shifting more and more into the morass of pandering to the administration in power. Tommy is one of the few holdouts, but he is opinion. All the hard news is skewing further and further left. Even EXN likes clicks from the search engines and social feeds."

"It is problematic that Big Media and Big Tech control so much of the content and direction of the messages being delivered to people. Folks really have to dig hard to find any facts they can trust to base their decision on," agreed Nick. "I love the idea. I don't know how interested the people are in straight news delivered without bias. They are too used to news as sensationalism and entertainment."

After a discreet knock, the meals were delivered. They ate as they continued the conversation. "You were correct. The sea bass is exquisite. I love the idea and I hope you get your share of viewers, but cable news has become so personality driven, it will be interesting to see if no personality can get viewers."

"Nick, do you know when I decided to have this dinner?"

"Not a clue. I assume you worked with Denise weeks ago, so it would fit into your schedule."

"No, I called Denise after your speech at that graduation commencement you gave in Michigan. Your speech at the Right to Choose conference just reinforced my belief in your messages."

"Glad we could oblige. This beats the food I am eating in the car, driving from Martha Summer's store parking lots to VFWs."

"I've been following your antics, through the video postings and the blogs. Your staff are doing a great job attracting people from all walks of life to your message," he said as Nick nodded, continuing to eat.

"It was your description to those recent college graduates at Hillsdale about what they now face. Part of my epiphany is about how responsible I was for the dumbing down of our network and cable news. The sexing up of the anchors to where viewers now tune in to see the women's hairstyle or outfits and not to hear what they are saying."

"Someone told me they even have websites critiquing anchorette outfits," commented Nick.

JD frowned at Nick's comment. "I helped create the monster that is now eating our country and our society one shitty news cycle at a time. I had lost faith in our ability to recover. Advances in Artificial Intelligence and the instant posting of information around the world make this new vision possible. It was also the grounding you gave those graduates. Not in technology, but in humans."

"When you spoke about faith in the future, I realized you had hit on something. I think people are inspired by you and they listen to what you have to say. Your stories and analogies make them understand what they are missing or at risk of losing. They follow your lead. I think if you tell folks about this network. Direct them to come here and look at the facts and draw their own conclusions. They will try it."

Nick nodded, thinking, as he finished his meal. JD continued.

"If they do it, the other networks will suffer and the public will be smarter because of it. I will take some satisfaction in forcing them to report more honestly to compete or fade away. Just as ANC has these last few years, once it assumed the role of, as you say, American *Pravda* for the current administration and the progressive agenda."

Nick finished the last bite of his fish, laying down his utensils. "I think you may be on to something. I agree with you. For some reason, folks are listening to me. I'm able to affect behavior, which I find somewhat disconcerting. Do you have a demo of what one of these broadcasts would look like? I want to see what I would be endorsing. And, of course, what the anchors are wearing," finished Nick with a grin. JD smiled back.

"You bet. We have been running beta tests for the past month. We did your last speech. I think you will like what you see. We aggregated the commentary, checked it for veracity, and much of what was said about your speech was collated and broadcast in our segment as counterfactual and wrong. We pointed out places where network anchors misrepresented your words, or flat out lied about what you said."

"I wonder how they'll respond to these revelations?" mused Nick.

"It's about time for someone to do actual fact checking of the 'fact checkers'. What better way than to do this with machines and AI crawling through the totality of content created? We want to show both fact-based commentary and call out where others are lying and why and how to give folks the ammo to use when they may be challenged. This way, the other networks are going to come unglued. It is not our opinion, it is the fact that they said x when you said y and their statement is based on x, not y. It is clear to any who look, they are trying to defame you rather than deal with what you said. I think this is going to change the whole tone of news and hopefully discourse," he finished.

Nick smiled. "When are you announcing?"

"We are ready when you are. When is your next speech?" responded JD with a smile. "That is the beauty of this idea. No talent to hire or contracts to sign. I started the big contract trend. Seems only fitting that I be the end of it. Our woman anchor has auburn hair. And a modest bosom with no cleavage. We want folks focused on what she says. The feminists should rejoice."

"Somehow, I doubt that will happen. They will be more concerned with the loss of the high paying female anchor jobs," countered Nick.

"Just like the oil pipeline workers, coal miners, and auto workers, they too can go find jobs coding, right?" responded JD to a laugh from both of them.

"About time they feel what the rest of America experiences with the job killing initiatives of the Party. I am ashamed at how much money I have donated to them over the years. All the back slapping I got from all those disingenuous bastards. That was another lifetime ago," laughed JD.

"I can't wait to see the faces of the fact checkers when their own words are used to expose their hypocrisy," responded Nick.

"Amen, brother," said JD, lifting his glass to toast Nick's carbonated bubbles.

Chapter 8

Roland Gill sat in his rented townhouse in Alexandria. Sitting on his sofa, drinking ginseng tea while reviewing the printed copies of the photographed files. Their quality was not great. It appeared the photos were taken in a hurry. They were not square in the frame. Many times, the photo was also out of focus or simply blurry, as if the photographer's hand was shaking.

Roland was not sure what the threat was or who exactly had taken the photos, but it was clear these were not meant for anyone's eyes. Each page was stamped multiple times with SCI and SAP markings, the highest levels of secrecy in the US government. In addition, they also included several he had never seen, nor heard of. A congressional intelligence marking. No one in the American government wanted anyone to see these.

As he read, it became clear why. He chuckled, thinking these were probably some of the same markings preventing the truth about aliens, JFK's assassination, COVID's origins and the subsequent vaccine mistakes from being revealed. As it was, this new congressional intelligence marking had dates for declassification listed on them that were still more than half a century away. Strangely, it also claimed in small print only Congress could allow declassification and not before the date listed.

There were about thirty pages, highlighting various inept decisions during the wars in the Middle East. Friendly units bombing each other and attacking and destroying friendly villages. Lots of incidents of torture. Cover-ups and payoffs to ensure silence. Black Ops assassinations of both friendly and unfriendly tribal chiefs. All kinds of political malfeasance and corruption with both allies and enemies.

A few pages included grainy pictures. Incursions into so-called friendly allied territories and missions into other hostile countries where the activities would have constituted acts of war. Many of these were after-action reports by military and intelligence operators. Turner was the common thread throughout the pages.

Roland lifted his head, closed his eyes, reliving the moment he faced Turner. Turner bested him that day, and yet he had not killed him. Had the roles been reversed, he knew he would have taken his vengeance.

Turner had not given up a single shred of useful intelligence. When he broke free, he'd also surprised and disarmed Roland, cutting him on the cheek with a shard of glass, leaving the faded and nearly invisible scar he currently ran a finger across, remembering.

He assumed he would not wake up and was never more surprised or confused when he did. The Doctor was standing over him. Since that day, he had questioned his own abilities and why he was alive.

Unfortunately, they had no idea who they had captured. The US military had done a remarkable job of keeping the clandestine missions Turner had been involved in from leaking out. They were not even talked about within earshot of the many spies employed in the US services by Pavlovich and others.

As he read, even he had to admit some of these missions, most times joint operations led by CIA planners and executed by elite SEALs and Special Forces units, were disasters saved by Turner and his quick thinking. The after-action reports showed incompetence and stupidity perpetrated time and time again by senior leadership, far from the action on the ground.

These embarrassments or their aftermaths were the reasons for the compartmented nature of the reports. There was no mention of Turner ever doing anything remotely close to illegal, much to Roland's chagrin. Were it not for Turner, and many of his documented actions, Roland knew the geo-politics of the Middle East would be very different today. And not in the US's favor.

He was trying to decide how much he would share with his ultimate employer. It was becoming clear that no one knew who Nick Turner really was. Nor was it common knowledge what he had been involved in during the wars. He would have to treat this information with care when helping the Vice President. If she demanded to know how he knew what he did, he would have to lie convincingly. Especially when her own efforts at access were coming up empty.

One thing was sure, at some point, his boss was sure to give him the assignment to end Turner. He would show no mercy, no weakness, as Turner had with him. Gill would teach him the futile nature of mercy and how some mistakes were fatal.

Returning his attention to his examination of the pages, several key pages were too blurry to read, even with magnification. Perhaps other technology could enhance them further. He was disappointed at both the limited content and the quality of the photos. To even get this had required his boss to spend significant effort to 'convince' an asset deep in the CIA to commit treason to access them. He held the only copy of these records in existence. According to Pavlovich, there were no other electronic or digitized copies, only this paper one.

Roland stopped and picked up his magnifying glass. He reviewed a paragraph of a particular after-action report. Leaning back, he smiled. Maybe it was not all for nothing. Still, he needed more information if he was going to find anything useful he could share, to help the Vice President win her landslide. Roland looked at his watch, converting the time zones in his head. He'd have to wait to tell his employer this news. Pavlovich would not be pleased.

Chapter 9

Nick walked into the HQ conference room. He saw his legislative and legal affairs advisor, Jenny Northrup, a woman in her mid-forties, with her brunette hair pulled back from her face, sitting with an older man. Their heads were down, reviewing documents laid out in front of them. As he entered, Jenny waved as they both stood to greet him.

"Duane Cooper, Senator, nice to meet you. I wish the circumstances were different." This from an older man with gray hair pulled back in a ponytail, a salt and pepper mustache and beard with reading glasses perched on his nose. He was wearing jeans, a dark dress shirt and a bolo tie with a corduroy sport coat. Nick tried not to stare at the unconventional appearance of Dusty Ingram's defense attorney. Behind him, Jenny was smiling.

"Duane, please call me Nick. Yes, this is clearly a sad situation. Let's sit," said Nick, pointing to the conference table.

"Crap, sorry. Can I get you anything to drink? Coffee, water," said Nick, looking to get up. Duane waved Nick back into his seat.

"I'm fine, Senator, thanks," he said, looking sideways at Jenny, who had a bigger smile on her face.

"I told you."

"Told him what?" asked Nick, looking between the two of them.

"Jenny said you were different. Frankly, I expected you to run as far away from this case as you possibly could. Your colleague, the senior Senator, and now failed Party presidential nominee, Mr. Harrington, made it clear he would throw the switch on the electric chair himself if he could," remarked Duane, with a small laugh.

"Good thing we are in Colorado then, where there is no death penalty. I am not sure how much I can do, but I at least want to hear your client's side of the story."

"Fair enough Senator. That is all I can ask. I don't know how much Jenny has told you, but clearly, this is a series of unfortunate events stemming from negligence by the sheriff breaking down the wrong door."

"How do you plan to prove that, counselor?" asked Nick.

Duane looked at Nick and smiled. He pulled his reading glasses off his nose, hanging on his chest from the cord around his neck, clearly preparing to make his case. Nick resisted the urge to laugh.

"First, Dusty is in apartment 16. Their warrant was for the occupant of apartment 18. They broke down the door of an innocent man. Mistake number one."

"Second, why do they need a no-knock warrant for a Red Flag incident? They claim it was because the *intended* subject was a convicted domestic abuser. He was not. He had been arrested on a domestic abuse charge, as had his girlfriend. They dropped the charges against both of them. In fact, the man had tried to get a restraining order *against* the girlfriend who was harassing him. She'd cost him his job by claiming he was abusing her to *his* employer. Something that was patently false but still led his employer to fire him, hence his living in the rundown apartment."

"The ex-girlfriend had a history of filing false claims, not only against him, but prior boyfriends. I found all of this *easily*. All of it would have been even easier for law enforcement to find. If they had bothered to try, that is. However, our governor and his plans for a potential run at higher office and his pushing of the Red Flag laws, makes law enforcement eager to please."

"I might leave the editorializing out Duane and stick to the facts. They are damning enough. All of that may be true, but Dusty killed six sheriff's deputies, even if he wasn't the intended target of the raid. And he did fire first," reminded Nick.

"True, Senator, but you have served. You know what it is like to sleep under the threat of enemy attack, 24/7. To be alert and ready to react to any life-threatening situation. Assessing it in a fraction of a second to decide to fight or flee. Whether it is friend or foe. To shoot or pause, knowing all these decisions could end with you dead if you make the wrong one. Dusty has diagnosed PTSD. He is deaf, hearing some in only one ear, augmented by a hearing aid he wears when awake."

"Yes, I was told he is partially deaf."

"He did not have his hearing aid in his ear, as he was getting out of bed when he saw shadows crossing back and forth in front of his apartment window. He has a loaded pistol by his bedside. You know the area he was living in. You would have had protection nearby, too. Also, the first thing you do getting out of bed is not to put your hearing aid in your ear. At my age at least, it is to the bathroom. I don't need to hear for that. I suspect it is the same for most."

"I assume you plan to call doctors to back up all these theories?"

"I do. They are very convincing."

"Your claim is what? It was dark. They busted down his door, entered with weapons and he 'flashed back' to Fallujah and started shooting in fear for his life? Not hearing them shout 'Sheriff's Department' because of his hearing or seeing the writing on their vests because of the lack of light?"

"It is not a claim, Senator, it is the truth."

Nick sat back, looking at Duane. "Your client killed six sheriff's deputies, who started firing because your client did. Two other innocent bystanders lost their lives because of the firefight, started by your client. In addition, two more people, innocent people, died because of the actions started by your client. The jury is going to look at the consequences and the results, more than the accident that started this chain of events."

"A nice fabrication prosecutor," countered Duane calmly. "But the law does not work that way. Causation is the ultimate culprit. This, all of it, started from the mistake and negligence of law enforcement." He held up a hand, seeing the look on Nick's face.

"Let me clarify, as the sheriff's deputies are victims as well. The genuine error is in how the complaint was handled. From not researching the Red Flag claim with all the holes from the accuser. To issuing a no-knock warrant from a judge not seeking more clarity of the need. To mis-labeling the paperwork on the warrant. These actions had consequences. Maybe all are innocent mistakes? But the results are because of this. All of this resulted in directing these brave men and woman to arrest someone who should not have been pursued. Right, wrong, or merely unfortunate. That is causation. Plus, the unnecessary risk implied in making Sheriffs enforce Red Flag accusations. Forcing the accused to defend themselves, *usually in court*, after they are confronted by sheriffs and have had their weapons illegally seized. The accusers in these Red Flag complaints are not anonymous to the police, only to the target," continued Duane.

"They could have looked harder at her history and treated this as the 'Swatting' it really was and not a legitimate Red Flag warning. This is the true crime. The sheriff's deputies should never have been there in the first place, at my client's door, or even, frankly, the one of the actual target of their raid. The fact they were at my client's door. That they busted it down, rather than knocking and proclaiming their task, is also a crime." Duane delivered his argument, as if talking to an imaginary jury.

"The sheriff's deputies, good upstanding officers of the law, who were merely following the law, and their orders, were put in harm's way, unnecessarily. Their deaths are not on the head of my client, who believed himself under physical attack, his door exploding inward in a hail of splinters. A person, trained to kill by our own government, who courageously risked his life daily for his country for almost a decade. Whose reward for his PTSD, earned in the service of his country, was to come home to a VA system that pumped him full of drugs. Drugs that made him suicidal. Drugs to which he got addicted and then had to go to rehab to recover from. Thank you, United States government. No, my client, through no fault of his own, was trying to live his life, carrying the demons of what he had seen in the hellholes of our wars in the Middle East. He had no record. Had never broken the law. He merely wanted to be left alone," delivered Duane in a compassionate tone, looking at his jury of Jenny and Nick. They both remained silent, not wanting to interrupt Duane's argument.

"A man who woke up with nightmares, reliving the death of his best friend, shot before his eyes on patrol in Fallujah. A night he lived over and over, never able to stop the enemy from shooting his friend. Holding him in his arms, listening as he begged him to help, to save him. Every night, he lives with this loss. With this guilt. Every night he wakes up from this nightmare. That night was no different. Reliving his time in the cramped spaces of the houses and streets in Fallujah, on patrol. Trained to shoot anything that moves."

Duane used his tone, words, and pacing, drawing his listeners into his story. Nick and Jenny were now leaning forward as he continued.

"When his door explodes, it is natural to assume he reacts as he is trained. He can't see anything, except people in the dark, carrying rifles aimed at him. He can't hear, because his hearing was damaged so badly in Afghanistan, and then further ruined because of the drugs the VA gave him, to *help*. The side effects causing what hearing he had to disappear completely in one ear and forcing him to rely on a hearing aid in his other ear. Something he removes to sleep, to block out the noise of the hookers and drug dealers outside his window every night."

"As the 'enemy' approaches, he resorts to his US Government training, just as *any* of us would if our home were being invaded. You shoot first and ask questions later, because if you are dead, it won't matter. Remember, he has no reason to fear the police. He has done nothing wrong. He has no reason to *ever* expect the police to be knocking down his door. But a home invasion, in his neighborhood, is not out of the realm of possibility. So, I ask you, what would you have done? Put yourself in his shoes. With his background? With his demons courtesy of our government, sending our youth into these horrendous situations, and then expecting them to return home and integrate back into society as if nothing had happened. Dusty Ingram is not a well man, but he is not a murderer. He felt he was going to die, as he had so many times in the war. All he did was what they trained him to do: fight back and survive. This is not his fault."

Duane finished and stood looking at Nick and Jenny. They both leaned back in their chairs, relaxing from the tension of the story.

"Very compelling, counselor. All true, but the prosecutor is going to show the faces of six slain deputies. Their families. The 24-year-old female deputy, Eva Herrera," said Nick, checking his notes. "They are going to say he was a loose cannon. Someone who should not have had a gun. They are going to make this all about how your client is a menace to society. Anything to deflect from their mistakes. He may not have been the target of the raid, but they're going to make it sound like he should've been, simply by his actions," explained Nick.

"Nick. Do you believe in the rule of law?"

"You know I do. Or you would not be here."

"Then how can you convict a man of murdering six deputies, and of voluntary manslaughter of the two innocent bystanders the deputies shot through the wall? Because of someone else violating the law? Those are the charges, six counts of first-degree murder and two of voluntary manslaughter. First-degree murders implies both intent and knowledge you are murdering someone. How in the hell is self-defense now murder? This is an obvious case of overcharging by overzealous DAs up for re-election using my client to raise money." Duane's ponytail was swinging back and forth as he became more animated.

"Duane, that may be true, but it does not help your client. It is not material to the case itself. In fact, if what you say is true, it should help you *disprove* it," answered Nick.

Duane smiled. "To the head of the class, Senator. There are terms every first-year law student learns. *Actus reus* is the job of proving a defendant committed a criminal act. Murder certainly applies. It is the job of the prosecution to prove my client is a murderer, as they have charged. However, in this case, the more important is the second basic term *mens rea*, the intent to commit a crime. Finally, the prosecution must prove the crime of causation. That there was harm, there is no doubt, to both my client and all the victims. However, they also have to prove my client is the actual cause of the harm."

"Duane, you are going to have to do better than that for a jury. Even I can't follow this. He clearly shot them. If that is not harm, I don't know what is," said Nick, leaning forward.

"OK. Nick, Dusty had no intent to murder anyone. Second, any criminal intent is lacking as this is clearly a case of the crime being breaking and entering his apartment. His *home*, without his permission or a valid warrant by the sheriff. This is the true crime. They cannot prove he had intent to commit the crime of murder and he did not *cause* the crime of murder. The cause of the harm is not him pulling the trigger, but the sheriff's knocking down his door and putting him in a position where he had to defend himself from the crime they were executing on *him*." Duane was in full evangelical mode at this point.

"The sheriff's caused this by breaking down the wrong door. Any activities after this mistake are on them, not my client. If they had not broken down the wrong door, none of this would have happened. If they had knocked and announced themselves even before breaking down his door without warning, and then Dusty started shooting, this would have been his fault. But they didn't. The causation is all on their side, on their activities," Duane continued in a convincing conversational tone.

"They were unlucky that the wrong door was the home of a trained Marine and not a hooker sleeping off a night's work. Unfortunate for all involved, but not criminal. And not my client's fault. If anything, the sheriff's deputies' families should sue the county and the state for their actions that are the true cause of their deaths. Not investigating the Red Flag accusation to determine legitimacy. Then the egregious mistake of directing them to the wrong address to serve the warrant. In fact, maybe I'll make that offer in the courtroom," mused Duane.

Nick sat with his head tilted. "OK, I see your point. Even if I grant your points, where are you going to find a jury who sees the law this way and can ignore the defense showing the pictures of the victims and their families in the courtroom? No jury is going to acquit your client. Even if you are technically correct."

Duane stared at Nick and smiled. "Senator, you said you believe in law and order. You are on record of being against Red Flag laws. For exactly the reasons this tragedy shows. The possibility of what happened becoming more commonplace. I am appealing to your sense of justice and your love of the law and the already impossibly difficult role of law enforcement. I think only you can explain this in a way that both highlights the danger of these laws and can give my client a *slight* chance at justice."

Nick looked at Jenny. He now knew why Denise was not in the room with them. She smiled tentatively at him.

"When is the trial?" asked Nick, deciding.

"Mid-September."

"Let me think about how to do this."

"Thank you, Senator. It is the only chance he has at a fair trial. That is all we are asking, a chance to make the case to open-minded jurors," said Duane.

Nick nodded and looked at Jenny.

"You get to tell Denise."

Jenny's smile of joy quickly turned to one of concern at the thought of Denise's reaction.

Chapter 10

A man in his early fifties sat at the small table in the interrogation room. He'd been sitting in rooms like this on and off for the last few weeks. Being interrogated by a seemingly endless line of Paris police and Interpol detectives. All asking him why he had pictures of the French President Alain Chaumont and of former Interpol chief inspector Luc Gauthier on his camera.

The man smiled behind his full gray beard. He'd been consistent in his answers. Replying to each inquiry calmly as he'd committed no crime. His ability to track down these two people and take pictures of them did not differ from any other paparazzi.

He merely shrugged, suggesting he was trying to catch the President being indiscreet. Those pictures would be worth thousands of euros. As for Gauthier, he was fascinated by the tragic story of his career and family, and he followed him out of curiosity after seeing him with the President. He was being thorough and following up every angle, not knowing what he might find worth selling.

When asked who he was working for, he had smiled and replied, "Himself. Just himself." He maintained his demeanor through all manner of interrogator. Tough detectives and pretty inspectors, no tactic had led to a change of story. Soon they would have to release him. He had not been afforded the opportunity of meeting with a lawyer. They had informed him he was being held on suspicion of terrorism, given the heightened security since the assassination of the last French President, Jean Paul Gaspard. He was not entitled to representation.

To this charge, he had not vigorously protested. Again, reiterating his story and keeping his composure. To an experienced detective like Luc, observing the man from behind the viewing glass, this was his surest confirmation he knew more than he was telling. When faced with these kinds of charges, the innocent protested loudly. The guilty protested even louder, demanding rights. Only those who knew they had an out, did nothing but wait.

"Luc, we cannot continue to hold him indefinitely."

Luc turned to his right, staring at President Chaumont.

"We have to release him. I have already allowed him to be held without cause or representation for too long. He has a simple case of harassment if he goes to the press when we release him," said Chaumont in a worried tone.

"We both know he has no intention of going to the press. Nor of pressing charges. Alain, we need to know what he knows. Who hired him and to whom he was sending the photos. There are no other leads, for either the bombing or the Christmas market attacks. I am more convinced than ever they are connected. Not to mention what was done to Caroline. Someone must pay," finished Luc in a tone that made Alain glance at him. He had seen this look before. Right after Luc's wife and daughter were murdered.

"Luc, we have been through his bank accounts, all his associates, even talked to his priest. There is nothing. Perhaps he is telling the truth? He is merely a paparazzi trying to cash in?"

Luc stared through the glass, not replying. He turned to Alain.

"You meet with your mistress every Tuesday, many Thursdays, and the occasional Sunday. Anyone who wants to get pictures of you cheating on my sister can easily find this out. It also does not take a forensic scientist to bribe officials to find out you are also paying for her flat, a car, a generous allowance, and now a bodyguard since Jean Paul was killed. If I could find this out so easily, so can others. Lucky for you, in France, promiscuity is considered a virtue."

Alain sighed, knowing Luc knew of his infidelity. He was also aware Luc knew his wife also shared this knowledge and was content with the arrangement. As long as it did not interfere with her enjoying all the trappings of being France's First Lady. He knew Luc neither approved of his weakness, nor his sister's willingness to look the other way in return for prominence and status.

"I want to interrogate him."

"Absolutely not. De Monfort would go crazy."

Luc smiled. "Even more reason to allow it."

"Luc, please do not put me in this position."

"You are welcome to leave," said Luc as he left the viewing room.

As Luc entered the interrogation room for the first time, a glimpse of fear showed in the eyes of the man. It was quickly replaced by his prior confidence.

Luc stood looking down at him, not smiling or changing his demeanor. After 30 seconds, the man shifted in his chair.

"Are you here to escort me out?" He asked in sarcastic French. His accent suggested he was from the Basque region between France and Spain.

Luc did not speak. He looked at the viewing window and then up at the camera in the room's corner. After a few seconds, the little red light, showing the recording was in progress, turned off.

"Do you know who I am?"

"Of course."

"You know I am no longer an officer of the law?"

"Are you sure?" he replied with less certainty.

Luc circled behind him. Then, with catlike reflexes, he grabbed his right wrist and turned the man's arm around behind him, causing him to lean forward, his head on the table, screaming in pain. Luc quickly hand cuffed his wrist low to the chair, forcing him to keep his right shoulder low. As Luc came back into view, the man made a feeble attempt to rise, using his other hand and screaming for help.

Luc grabbed his left wrist and applied pressure at the nerve center. This caused the man to collapse back in this chair, gasping in pain. He pushed his hand flat on the table with his left palm. With his right, he reached out and pulled the man's pinkie finger back until there was an audible snap. The man screamed in pain and tried to rise again, as Luc started to bend back the next finger. The man stopped.

"You cannot do this," he bellowed.

Luc stared him in the eyes and calmly snapped the second finger. The man screamed in pain, spittle flying from his mouth.

"Apparently I can," said Luc calmly, in a dispassionate voice. He moved to the middle finger, grabbing it gently.

"Who are you working for?"

"I already told you. No one. I was merely trying to get pictures to sell."

Luc started to bend the finger, sighing loudly.

"By the time I get to your second hand, I am not sure you will be in a position to answer any longer." Luc reached into a pocket and pulled out a knife. He flicked it open, showing a very sharp, four-inch blade. He calmly stabbed it into the table, out of reach of the man, where it quivered.

"I may have to resort to more permanent tactics. I ask you again, who are you working for?"

The man looked Luc in the face, shook his head, and started to repeat his prior answer as Luc snapped the finger. He frothed and shivered, a sound of terror leaving his mouth, his head bouncing off the table. As he picked up his head, his lip now bleeding from biting it in pain, he looked into Luc's eyes and saw no remorse.

"You have a choice. And you are running out of fingers. I want answers."

"He will kill me."

The man shook as Luc laughed menacingly.

"Then you are a dead man either way. Perhaps, if you tell me what I want to know, you have a slight chance of avoiding death from at least one of us. Again, who are you working for?"

Luc could see him contemplating his fate. Luc grabbed the last finger on his hand and started to bend.

"Wait, wait, please."

"Do not lie. I will know. Who were you following? Me or Chaumont?"

"You primarily. But also Chaumont as a precaution."

"Why?"

"I do not know." Luc bent the finger to the point of breaking as the man screamed out again.

"I was just told to report on who you met with and where you went, I swear."

"Just in Paris?"

"No. I followed you on your trips as well. We tracked your car."

"How? I sweep my car for bugs daily."

"GPS system *in* the car."

"It is a government vehicle. How would you get this info?"

The man shrugged in reply.

Luc glanced up at the viewing window. He did not know if Alain was still there watching. He suspected not, given his tactics.

"Did you track me to meet with Dr. Fontaine?" asked Luc with a snarl.

"Who?" said the man in terror as Luc bent his finger more.

"The woman I met at the cafe in Montmartre."

"Yes, I took pictures."

"And in Lyon? At the estate?" he nodded in pain.

"Everywhere these last months.

"Do you know what is done with this information?" accused Luc as he snapped the fourth finger.

The man collapsed on the table, howling in pain. Luc grabbed his hair and held his head back. He pulled his knife from the table and held the point close to the man's eye as he sobbed.

"Do you know what they did to her? To the woman I met in Montmartre?"

The man quivered. "No, no, I only provide the pictures. I know nothing of the actions."

"And you think that absolves you?" asked Luc in a calm voice, his hand holding the knife, quivering in his anger.

The man sobbed.

"Who is paying you to do this?" He hesitated and Luc flicked the knife into the flesh of his cheek. The man blurted out, "*Daboia*".

"*Daboia*? What is that?"

"He is who paid me."

"Snake," said Luc, translating from Latin, and seeing the recognition in the eyes of the man he was torturing.

"One more time or you lose an eye. Who is he and where do I find him?" said Luc, the blade precariously close to the man's left eye.

"He is called *Daboia*. We do as he says, or we die. Simple as that.

"What does he look like?"

"I do not know. I have never met him."

"Russian?"

"I do not think so."

"What else do you know? Who did you send your information to? How does he communicate?"

The door slammed open, startling Luc, who drew the knife across the man's cheek, cutting into his nose. Maximilian de Monfort, the prefect of the Paris police, entered the room bellowing, followed by two policemen, one of whom uncuffed the man and the second, who held a cloth on his bleeding face.

"What the hell is going on here?" shouted de Monfort, looking from the beaten prisoner to Luc, who merely stood closing his knife. De Monfort looked at the viewing window. "Is this your doing? Allowing a civilian to torture state prisoners? There will be investigations," he yelled at the window.

The man was sobbing as the policemen led him from the room. He glanced at de Monfort as he left and turned to look at Luc. A brief smile showed on his face, replaced by a grimace as he tried to lift his maimed hand.

"I was doing your job," answered Luc calmly.

"I will make sure we prosecute you to the full extent of the law. We do not allow torture. No one will save you this time, Gauthier," promised de Monfort with bluster.

Luc straightened up, looking toward de Monfort with such a look of hatred, it caused him to reflexively put a hand on his pistol.

"I know it was you," said Luc in a soft hiss. "I always have." De Monfort turned away at the menace in Luc's voice, now seeing it was only the two of them in the room. He looked at the door as if sensing the need to run while alone with Luc.

"If I were you, inspector, I would be worried about the human rights violations you just committed," said de Monfort, puffing up.

Luc laughed and took a step toward him. De Monfort took a step backward, glancing at the viewing window as if looking for help. Luc looked him in the eye. "I will have my vengeance on all those responsible for my wife and daughter's death. Of that, you can be sure."

"Luc," said Chaumont from the doorway. "Come." He motioned with his hand. The Minister of Justice, Leon Thibault, was in the hallway as well. Luc turned to leave, his eyes boring into de Monfort's one last time, causing the other man to look away in discomfort.

As they walked away, Chaumont turned to Luc. "The engineer is dead. Tortured. It appears he may have made a copy of the information on the phone as well and was trying to sell it to the news. Inquiries have been made to us about the existence of this evidence. This is most likely what caused the family in Munich to be killed. Luc merely nodded. He had warned the engineer he didn't want to know what was on that phone when he recovered the data from one of the Christmas massacre drivers.

"Did you really need to break his fingers? You know de Monfort is going to use this against you."

"I don't care." Luc stopped and turned to Chaumont, then looked at Thibault as well. "If he is tracking me via my GPS in the car, that can only be with the help of someone on the inside."

"We will look into it?" said Thibault, nodding.

"Look into it? It is pretty clear who it is," said Luc, looking back at the interrogation room.

"Luc, we need proof."

"I don't. What do we know of this *Daboia*?" asked Luc.

"We know very little other than he exists. We are not even sure it is a single person or if it is an organization. They have been involved in all manner of activities. Terrorism, contract killing, smuggling, corruption, human trafficking, you name it."

"My wife's death?"

"Possibly."

"Possibly?" replied Luc dangerously.

"We have no hard evidence. You know this. You have looked over everything we have."

"Have I?"

"Yes, you have."

"Thibault, can we have Annie look at all these cases to see if we can find any patterns, any connections, any leads back to this *Daboia*?" asked Gauthier, thinking.

"Of course," replied Thibault. "And we need to keep you under surveillance to ensure no one is following you."

"Except you. And Maximilian," replied Luc sarcastically.

"I'll handle Maximilian," said Thibault.

"*Daboia*. It's a snake, right?" asked Luc.

"Yes, a viper, I believe?" answered Thibault. "Why?"

"Just thinking."

"Luc, please be careful. Whoever this is does not care about life. Find out who and why they are doing this, before they strike again," pleaded Chaumont.

"Alain, if you really cared about that, you would never have let de Monfort in the room. Our best source of information just left our grasp, never to return, one way or another."

"We could not stop him."

"You are the President of France. You could have stopped him. Just as you could have before and chose not to."

At this last statement, Chaumont stiffened and made to reply. Luc merely held up a hand. "No more lies, please. I know. And I know why. You made your choice. As has de Monfort. As the American candidate Turner is so fond of saying, actions have consequences. Adieu," finished Luc as he walked out of the Ministry of Justice building into the Parisian sunshine of the hot August day. He now had a lead.

Chapter 11

Nick stood on stage at the Evangelical World Congress conference at the Gaylord Texan resort in Grapevine, Texas. The crowd was heckling and booing him at every phrase. His trick with the technician raising the volume was not working, as more and more of the crowd joined in booing and shouting various epithets.

Pausing while looking at the crowd, many of whom were standing and shouting, he saw a woman with a scowl on her face. She was not standing, but it was clear she was not happy with his words, either.

Nick stood there as they shouted. Turning, he pointed at the woman. As she realized he was pointing at her. Her expression turned to one of embarrassment. He again extended his finger, pointing, then he waved as if to invite her on stage.

"Come on up. If you won't let me give you my thoughts, give me yours. Let's have a conversation. Tell me why I'm wrong. Come on," he encouraged. The rest of the crowd had quieted as the woman stood tentatively. She made her way from the crowd to the stairs on the side of the stage. Nick had grabbed a couple of chairs and set them up. He also got a second microphone.

She approached timidly, glancing at the giant crowd of thousands, suddenly self-conscious. Nick smiled as she approached. He handed a microphone to her and asked her to sit as he did.

"First off, thanks for doing this. Pretty scary, isn't it?" he asked as she squeaked out a "yes."

"Don't worry, it gets easier. Just ignore all of them and look at me. What's your name?"

"Emily Collins," she replied with a bit more confidence.

"Pleased to meet you, Emily. Call me Nick, please," he said, shaking her hand.

"Just so everyone in the audience knows, we've never met, correct?"

"Yes. I mean no. We have not met," she said, flustered.

"I won't bite, promise. I just want to ask some questions."

"OK."

Nick turned to the audience. "Please respect Emily and give her a chance to say her piece before you boo me. I honestly want to understand your positions and why you don't agree with mine." There were a few boos at his statement.

"Emily, if I may ask, do you have children?"

"Three. Two girls, twelve and ten and an eight-year-old boy."

"Congratulations. Do you live here in Texas?"

"I do. In a town up the road from here, Southlake."

"Nice. Schools pretty good here?"

"Yes, better than California, for sure. We moved here during the first pandemic."

"Very smart of you," agreed Nick. "I think it is fair for me to assume you go to church regularly since you are here?"

"Yes. Every week with my whole family."

"Thank you. I am a big believer in faith as a salvation for our country and something we are sorely missing."

"Then how can you advocate killing babies?" she blurted out as the crowd cheered behind her.

"Emily, I don't 'advocate' for killing babies. I am against abortion," replied Nick.

"But you said at the Choice rally that you wouldn't stop abortion. You wouldn't support bans," she accused him with passion.

"I did say that," agreed Nick as the crowd booed loudly again.

"I'm sorry Senator, I'm confused," responded Emily with a bewildered look.

"Emily, as President, I am both a person who is against abortion and I'm the leader of our country. Bound by our rules. These rules are set out in the Constitution. If your schools are as good as they were when

I went to high school and college here, they should still teach this," suggested Nick.

Emily nodded. "My oldest girl has studied the Constitution in her civics class."

"Good. Here is the issue. With freedom comes responsibility. We have freedom to speak as long as we are not physically hurting each other or defaming someone. The same with printed words. We also have freedom of religion. The ability to worship any way we like or to not worship at all, without persecution. There are other freedoms, such as innocent until proven guilty, rights to fair and speedy trials and freedoms from unlawful search and seizure, among others. These give us broad leeway to live our lives as *we* choose. You with me so far?" paused Nick.

"I think so," nodded Emily.

"Once, not so long ago, we went through a stage where protestors were burning American flags. Or when idiot students thought they were supporting Palestine by being pro-Hamas. It made the blood boil for many of us. Both patriots and those of us who have risked our lives in the service of this country. In the end, the justices did the right thing. If you limit freedom because you don't like what some do with it, then someone will always be around who wants to limit something you want to do. It is the slippery slope we have to avoid." Nick spoke slowly and forcefully, making sure he gave folks a chance to listen to his words.

"Freedom means the right to burn the flag, say hateful things supporting terrorists, but not physically harmful things, here. To say or do a host of other immoral, unethical, and disgusting things. As long as they hurt no one else but yourself and are legal." Nick stopped for a second to let his words sink in. He could see Emily trying to process his point.

"Emily, do you understand what I am saying? Why I say I support a woman's right to choose, while I do not condone the action?" This time there were no boos. Everyone in the audience was paying attention to the conversation taking place on the stage. Trying to digest Nick's points.

"I do, but abortion physically hurts the baby. The freedoms you said are ok as long as they are not causing physical harm," accused Emily in response.

Nick smiled. "Very perceptive. It does indeed. It's why I wouldn't support any abortions after the baby could survive outside the womb. Why I favor the twelve or fifteen week bans at the most. The harm is not done to the baby, because it cannot survive outside the vessel carrying it. That vessel, woman, is the one who is harmed. As I said, freedom means giving people the ability to make choices that cause self-harm."

"Whether it is gender mutilation, tattoos and body piercings, smoking, killing themselves with fentanyl, suicide, alcohol, or having an abortion. It does not make it right, but it is why we have laws protecting our freedoms. An outright ban on abortion does not differ from an outright ban on the freedom to express an opinion or publish a newspaper. It has to be a choice in a free society. In fact, if we ban it, it will not go away. Just move out of sight again."

Emily was still shaking her head. "You are still allowing the killing of a defenseless baby. Someone needs to protect them. I don't agree."

"Emily, what if I forbid you from going to church? If I told you praying aloud was unacceptable? Or even praying silently as you stand outside an abortion clinic, in your mind alone, as they tried to do in Great Britain? What if I said you could only have two children, or even one? How would you feel?"

She stared back at him, shaking her head no.

"Or made you only use an electric car. That you had to house 10 illegals in your house because you have four bedrooms. If I suddenly decided, you need to give half of your income to people who don't want to work. What if I made you let your child change their gender without telling you? How would you feel about all that?"

She smiled at him. "Senator, that's why we left California. Because all of that was already happening there." The crowd laughed as Nick smiled.

"Call me Nick. Would you agree it is wrong?" he continued.

"Absolutely Nick."

"But you are ok with telling a woman what they can or can't do with something inside their body? How is that different from any of these other intrusions on your personal freedom?"

"It is a life, Senator. These other things are not."

"Yes, they are, Emily. They are all interconnected. We all get to experience them because our parents made a choice to have us. They could have chosen to not go through with the pregnancy. It is a choice because they live in a country where freedom is both celebrated and protected. We don't have the right to force someone to have a child. It is the ultimate form of coercion. Just as we can't tell someone not to pray."

Emily was shaking her head, and the crowd was murmuring.

"Everyone, please listen. This is my point. I am not saying it is right. It is not. It is also not my choice, or yours, or the state of Texas or even the Supreme Court to tell you what you can or can't do with a baby that cannot survive without the woman carrying it. It is only *their* choice. If it is not, then *we* are the guilty parties for forcing them to do something against their will. Again, after viability outside the womb, I agree it is no longer simply the woman's choice, because now you have a person who can survive. Until that point, the two are inseparable and therefore it is still the woman's choice." Nick stood up to walk back and forth.

"You all believe in a creator. I don't have to tell you about judgement, salvation, faith. Ultimately, your congregation is a congregation of one: you. It is just you and your creator. You have sinned. So have I. We ask for forgiveness, and we strive to make up for our sins. We are not God. We do not get to promise salvation or pass judgement. Only one entity gets to decide this."

"I need you to understand my position. I need you to understand the position of the woman who finds out they are two months pregnant. With or without birth control. Who is unable or simply not prepared to have and nurture a baby. It is an agonizing decision. The worst, because you *are* taking a life. Even if it cannot survive outside your womb, it has the *potential* to." Nick paused again, forcing people to think about his words.

"Imagine having that burden? Carrying that weight. Having to strive to account for that monumental sin? In our society, with all these consequences, we still must allow all women to make this choice. If we do not, then we no longer have a free society where we are free to choose our own destiny." Nick again paused, looking out over the crowd. No one was heckling as they now listened intently.

"The argument is not *if* we allow abortion, it is about putting reasonable and realistic limits on how long you can wait before it becomes criminal. Twelve or fifteen weeks seems reasonable. Science and reality show it is before the baby can survive on its own. When you try to pass laws for bans at six-weeks, they are too punitive to a woman's right to make her own decisions. A majority do not agree with this short a term or outright bans. We are a majority rule democracy. We have to be." There were a few murmurs of disagreement in the crowd at Nick pointing out their failure to get their 'heartbeat' bills enforced in Texas.

"Just as we agree to abide by other laws as a society, this is no different. We set the guidelines and we adhere to them and make exceptions for things like rape, incest, medical problems for the mother or birth defects. This does not make it right, but it makes it pragmatic. As a free society, we can decide to find a middle ground. Compromise is what democracy is built on. There does not have to be a winner and a loser in every decision or law."

Nick looked down at Emily. She had wiped a tear from her eye. Nick sat back down.

"Do you understand my position now?"

"I do. I still don't think it is *right*, but I understand why you say what you say. Even though I don't agree, I know we must preserve their right to choose. Judge not lest ye be judged. I have never put those words in context until now. I would be just as guilty if I took away their ability to choose to do this deed. They alone have to atone for their sin. You are correct, the guilt is always theirs. I have girlfriends who have had abortions. They live with it every day. I could never understand how they could do it. I am not so angry at them any longer. Now I only feel sorry for the burden they bear, forever. The consequences of *their* choice," responded Emily in a more confident voice as she spoke.

Nick nodded as he let Emily make her points. Then he continued.

"You also understand, I have to do this if I am going to fight to stop all those other mandates and pronouncements. These decisions to keep parents from knowing about things the schools are allowing your kids to do, without telling you. To fight this, I also need to allow the right to abortions?"

Emily nodded. "You can't have it both ways."

"Exactly. I can't advocate for parental rights over their own children if I support limits on other decisions. I can't advocate decisions on activism and gender mutilation be restricted until children are adults if I am advocating removing the freedom to choose to have a baby or not. It is not always fair or right, but it is democracy, and it is what has made our country such a great system for two hundred and fifty years."

Nick stood and took Emily by the hand, raising her up.

"Please, can we have a round of applause for Emily's bravery? Coming up here on stage and listening to my story. Thank you, Emily."

She stood as the crowd clapped and then they rose and continued to clap as she turned beet red. Nick held out his hand to shake hers when she pulled him into a hug.

"Thank you. Now I understand and believe. You are our only hope to fix everything," she said. This was picked up on the mic in Nick's hand and broadcast throughout the auditorium, as more folks cheered at this admission.

Emily walked off the stage, being helped down the stairs by several security guards.

Nick stood in the middle of the stage, looking out.

"That about does it. I really have nothing else to say. You know why I believe the way I do. Open your mind and your heart. Seek the truth. I truly believe in a day of reckoning. It is highly personal. Despite what others say, I am not playing God. I am only planting seeds. Seeds to make people consider the consequences of their actions, and the possibility others may be watching too. God bless and I thank you for your time."

Nick turned to head off stage as a majority of the audience stood and clapped. There were even a few chants of Turner, Turner, Turner. As the emcee, an evangelical minister, returned, Nick handed him the microphone. He stood, preventing Nick from leaving the stage.

"My friends, I must admit, I've been preaching for many decades. I'm ashamed to say it took this man and his speech to make me examine my own actions. To understand, I am guilty of trying to force my own ideals on others. In sermons where I counsel them to follow the choice I made for them. For my selfish motives, rather than guiding them to make their own choice. I think we should all be searching in our heart to see where we have strayed, from what is right and supportive. To stop assuming what we want is correct for everyone, in every instance. I, for one, am taking what you say to heart and will ask my congregation to do the same. You are right, we have bigger problems as a country and a society and if we don't work together to right the ship, we will surely sink.

Nick nodded. "I know I am straying into your domain, Minister, but if I could, I would ask those willing, to pray with me,"

"Of course, Senator. It's about time we had a presidential candidate unafraid to admit to believing in a higher power, and mean it."

Nick took the microphone, bowing his head.

"Our lord in heaven, I ask you to help us find our path. Give us the sense of purpose to allow us to have faith once again. Faith to lead us to moral decisions. To choose the path of good over the path of evil. To choose the path of accomplishment rather than the path of idleness. Understand and forgive those who choose not to have faith. Enable us to lead by example. Have a sense of purpose to drive us to continue to excel at family, life, and friendship. To lead a life of honor and love, and to find in our hearts, forgiveness. Always asking ourselves, as we make any decision, how you would judge our choice and give us the clarity to see this ourselves. Please give us strength and resolve as we seek the virtuous path. Help steer us from the temptation. From the path of ease, debauchery, and faithlessness that has become so popular and prevalent in our society. Finally, know that if we have faith and lead our lives, as if you were watching and judging, that in the end, we will stand before you, to receive your judgement without fear. Knowing we have used your divine gifts and trust in us in honorable ways. Amen."

Nick was met with a thunderous 'Amen' from those in the audience as he waved and exited the stage.

Chapter 12

"Well?" asked Harriet as Lexi finished watching the video of Nick's speech at the Evangelical conference.

"He's good. What do you think?" responded Lexi, handing Harriet back her phone.

"From a campaign point of view, it is fucking brilliant,"

"But will it work?" asked Lexi.

Harriet shrugged. "I have to admit, it made me think and I'm hardly religious. That is the first problem. We don't want young women thinking. We want them voting with their heart, not their heads."

"Agree. How many young women do you think are going to tune in to watch a speech at a religious conference?"

"Young women? Not many. I'm not as worried about those under thirty or even forty. We have them so fucked up and confused, they are unlikely to be thinking about what happens when they die. I am more worried about those in their forties. With kids and PTA meetings. Watching crime rise and their kids questioning their authority thanks to our teacher's union. This demographic grew up with Roe and are militant regarding anything being done to remove it. They were firmly on our side, even when they got beyond having to make these choices. We had them convinced removing *Roe* was the ultimate overreach," Harriet stopped, waiting for Lexi to comment. When she didn't, she continued.

"Just like 'hands up don't shoot' galvanized an entire generation of youth against the cops. *Roe* going down solidified women for us. Even if they don't like the idea of abortion at any time in the pregnancy, it should still be their choice." Lexi sat contemplating Harriet's words as the older gray-haired black woman paced the conference room, making her points. Mel was seated in a corner.

"Do you think one speech is really going to make that much difference?" asked Mel, carefully.

"Mel, the problem is, it isn't just one speech. He did this to our people. He does it more and more at his state fair appearances. He is slowly making abortion a non-issue, and he is doing it pragmatically, making people from *both* sides see compromise as doable," finished Harriet, sitting in concern.

"Harry, I am not so sure. I watched both of them. I can see him getting through to some of them. More likely more of them are going to be on the Opposition side, than on the Party side. He has to make them think he isn't going to restrict their access to choices. He really can't do that from the Presidency. It is congress. It is states. It is the Supremes. As long as we keep hammering, it was those positions who got us where we are. No president alone can change these decisions. We should be fine," countered Lexi.

"That is a risky play, because you are saying you will save *Roe* and get it re-codified as permanent law," retorted Harriet.

"True, but I am doing it from a position of strength with a Party congress and one of the first bills we will pass is to expand the Supreme Court so we can remove the obstructionist conservative bias. Where today five conservative zealots have taken control of women's health decisions," said Lexi with passion.

Mel and Harriet just smiled.

Lexi noticed. "Feeling better now?"

"Much," said both simultaneously.

"Good. Make sure these videos keep getting taken down. We can do everything we can to limit their exposure. Still no luck in shutting down, Hibi?"

"Nope. Javier is trying, but we can't find an angle that won't also limit *our* ability to post what we want on all the other social media channels. The damn court won't let anything limiting only our enemies. We are still working on it. Hitting advertisers and anyone else. The word is still trickling out, I'm afraid," admitted Mel in a disappointed tone.

"I think it may be time to start laying some groundwork for next January. Making it clear there are consequences for aiding sedition and rabble rousing. When there is a new sheriff in town, it will be time to clean up the riffraff. Let's make sure they know we know who the riffraff are. Paint a clear picture of what this will look like," threatened Lexi ominously.

"Already on it, boss," agreed Mel with a smile.

#

Lexi stood at the window, looking at the Capitol dome in the distance from her campaign office window.

"Yes, I understand your concern. Perhaps you did not hear me correctly. I believe there *may* be evidence of financial wrongdoing. If you are confident, these rumors are completely untrue, I am sure you will have no issues rebutting any stories in the papers or filing any paperwork to ensure these IRS investigations are merely your enemies wishing to take you down," finished Lexi, smiling as the voice on the other side of the phone went up an octave in concern.

Lexi shrugged. "Like I said, they are only rumors. How is Claudia? Fully recovered from her procedure?"

"Good," said Lexi, listening to the response. "Unnecessary stress during recovery can be very concerning. It would be unfortunate for anything to happen that might upset her at this critical juncture. How is that aide of yours, Kimberly? I believe that was her name. What happened to Amber? The one you introduced me to at the last fundraiser? They both seemed very eager to please," said Lexi, smiling wickedly at the obvious discomfort on the other side of the phone.

"Listen, you invited him to your sermon. All I want you to do is express your displeasure with his stance and make it clear to your flock you do not approve of it. Nor do you think your parishioners should, either. I'll be watching. Enjoy your weekend, Pastor."

Lexi hung up the phone and turned toward the man seated in her guest chair.

"What do you think?"

"I think you are a very dangerous woman," answered Roland Gill.

He lounged comfortably, like a tiger assessing his next meal, staring at the Vice President. She stood tall, her narrow waist highlighted by the tailored skirt, blouse, and four-inch red soled heels.

Lexi turned, leaning on the edge of her desk, showing a bit more leg and contemplating Roland back. "You have no idea how dangerous," she replied with a seductive smile as she walked his way.

Chapter 13

Nick was going through a pile of call notes. He was finding it difficult to keep up with Senate business and campaign for president. His days in the DC office were few, now that he spent most of his time on the road, speaking to supporters.

"Anything critical?" he asked Chuck, seated on the couch.

"If there were, I would tell you. Promise. You are fine. We have a couple of votes coming up and you are already scheduled to be in town for them. We'll break for summer recess soon. The calendar is pretty sparse in the fall because a third of the Senators are in the midst of their re-election campaigns."

"It doesn't seem right. What are the bills? Do you have some background I can study so I know what I am voting on?"

Chuck stared at his boss and shook his head.

"You have one job now. Getting elected President. You do not have time to study these bills. That's why you have us. We will do the studying and recommend to you the way you should vote and why."

Nick started to reply when Chuck held up his hand. "No. I don't want to hear it. You decided to run. So do it."

Nick was going to argue when there was a knock at the door of the office. "Come in."

His aide, Carla, stuck her head into the office. "Senator, you have a visitor. Senator Garcia is wondering if you have a few minutes?"

Nick smiled. In spite of his efforts, none but his senior staff would call him Nick. He watched as Chuck got up to leave the office.

"Don't screw this up," was all Chuck said as he greeted Freddie Garcia coming through the door. Chuck closed the door behind him.

"Freddie, how are you?"

Freddie had a look on his face. Half bewilderment and half embarrassment. Nick half expected him to admit to some transgression.

"How am I doing? That is an excellent question. I am not sure. For the last thirty years, I have been staunchly pro-life. Even puritanical in my belief no child should ever be aborted after conception, without exception. As a medical doctor, I have seen miraculous recoveries by people who had no right to survive, and yet they did. I always attributed this to a divine intervention on their behalf. I took this to heart and figured there could be no more divine an occurrence than creating the spark of life. From the union of two sets of microscopic chromosomes. The future soul of a human."

Nick looked up expectantly. He sensed Freddie was not done.

"Nick, I don't know whether to slug you or hug you. When you turned down the opportunity to accept the nomination, I was upset. I was willing to overlook your abortion view because I felt the needs of the country were greater. I agreed with your stance of returning to first principles. I resented you could have the nomination I so wanted. Without even trying. Yet, you didn't even consider taking it."

Nick made to respond.

"Please wait. I am almost done."

"Then I saw your speech at the pro-choice rally. It crushed me, Nick. I could not believe you could go into that environment and in the course of a forty-five minute speech cut to the heart of this divisive matter in such a way to have a militant crowd consider your words. For the answer to be faith based, I suddenly questioned what I had accomplished with my own stance for so many years."

"One that was unable to convince anyone to join my banner from that same crowd. Then, during your EWC speech, I realized why. I was not only wrong, I was wrong to high heaven. Who the heck was I to take this moral high ground and claim you could only reach it if you followed my rigid dogma? My world crumbled around me. Nick, what is my purpose? For so long, my path was clear. Save every baby. The wishes of the woman be damned. Who the fuck do I think I am?" said Freddie in such a forlorn voice, Nick steered him to a chair.

"Freddie, stop," said Nick gently, "You did what you felt was right in your heart. You believed it with all your heart and soul. Remember, I am against abortion too. For many of the same reasons. But I am also pragmatic enough to know we can't ever truly stop it, and we don't have to answer for the actions. Only one person does. And not to us. It really is this simple. Everything else is noise."

Freddie shook his head. "There you go again. From the mouths of neophytes. More wisdom than hundreds, maybe thousands of combined years of Senatorial service can muster in a debate. Nick, I think you have done it. To bring a large swath together. To see a path to compromise. To move forward and empty so many hearts of hate. It is glorious and so unexpected. Now I am more disappointed than ever that you did not take the nomination."

"I could not have made those speeches as the Opposition candidate. I would have had to support your platform. I could not. I can't be bound by any party's ideas or ideology. I need the freedom to zig and then zag if that is where the journey takes me. I have to be both pragmatic and flexible."

Freddie sighed from his seat as Nick sat on a corner of his desk.

"My supporters will not go for Blackbird. Did you see the spot he ran about you? He is claiming his position is better than yours. He is pro-life generally but open to abortions in certain circumstances he won't define. He favors heartbeat bills at six weeks, sometimes, but he won't say definitively when. Unbelievable. My supporters won't vote for him, but they might vote for you, or a percentage of them. What can I do to help?"

Nick stood and headed to his fridge. "We need beers for this…"

Chapter 14

"We should make this your last visit, at least publicly," said Senator Baxter Banks, as he and Nick took their seats in Bank's magnificent library. Hobson, Senator Bank's valet, had already delivered drinks to both.

"They are probably having you followed."

"They who?" inquired Nick.

"At a minimum, Lexi, and maybe that Bergamo girl. The intelligence agencies are definitely monitoring your whereabouts as well. Hell, maybe even the Opposition, after what you did to Blackbird. You are upsetting a lot of plans."

Nick shrugged. "Afraid of others knowing you're talking to me?"

"Hardly. But you have to understand, they are all looking to dig up dirt on everyone. Who you meet with is almost as important as what you discuss. Knowledge is power. Especially in this town, and even more so during a contentious election cycle."

"Go for it. I've got nothing to hide," replied Nick cavalierly.

Banks made a noise in his throat. "You're kidding right? No one seems to be able to find out much about you. Why exactly is that? This is causing them to dig even deeper or to just start speculating on what you must be hiding. They hate a mystery."

Nick stood, wandering around the library, staring at the volumes.

"Senator, I'm a private person. I kept to myself and have made few friends. That's what happens when you spend all your time reading books and then in the military. There is one bitter long term ex-girlfriend. I didn't beat her. Nor have I ever done drugs or smoked pot. I have looked at online porn and found it depressing, sad, and frankly boring. Certainly nothing most have not done as well. I don't even have a tattoo."

"I have lied a few times in my life, but never on my taxes or to my priest. Usually, to spare the feelings of the recipient of the lie. I drank my share of beer in college, chased girls, never dated longer than a few weeks in almost all cases. There are no illegitimate children. The only thing I am guilty of is studying hard and dedicating myself to learning.

"Then 9/11 happened and my mission for the next 20 years was clear. Study the enemy, find them, kill them, and prevent as many of my fellow warriors from being killed. My business ventures and teaching after I left the military were straight-forward, honest, and non-descript. If I hadn't been in New York City to stop that terrorist, I would still be a non-tenured professor of history." Banks clapped at the end of Nick's speech.

"Nice try Senator. You recited the biography chapter in your upcoming book."

Banks picked up an early reviewer copy from his side table. "Almost verbatim," He stated, sipping his scotch, staring at Nick as he stood. "The perks of knowing publishers. You'll have to send me a signed copy when you release it. As for the other statements, don't insult me. I know way more about you and your service and about your so-called convenient timing in New York City. I also know, for instance, Blackbird will shortly go down in flames."

"No surprise. He's behind in the polls and isn't doing anything to court Garcia's conservatives," said Nick, ignoring Bank's first statements.

"No, I mean Lexi, or rather her minions in the press, have an October surprise tee'd up and ready to go. This one will be the end of the campaign for the Opposition. He cannot recover. You need to prepare to get out there and make sure those votes come to your side. And frankly, make sure they don't stay home in disgust at the revelations."

"How do you know this?" asked Nick, staring at Banks intently.

"I know lots of things."

"Now who is conning whom? Is that why I'm here?"

"No. You need to pick the right running mate," replied Banks, swirling his drink.

"And you want to help? I guess I shouldn't be surprised. Especially since you pretty much pushed me into this. Still trying to pull strings?" finished Nick, somewhat sarcastically.

"It was only a nudge. All I did was plant the seed. None of us is the sole master of our destiny."

"You told Chuck to recommend Denise, didn't you?"

Banks took a sip of his scotch and did not answer.

"Why? We don't agree on anything. Hell, she tried to get me to join Lexi's ticket."

"Did she? Or did she get you to change your perspective on your campaign and the difference between preaching and winning? You cannot afford to be surrounded by just sycophants. Occasionally, you need to have your ass kicked. To be told you do not have all the answers."

Nick turned away, pacing again. "God, I hate this town. And I hate politics."

"No, you don't. You love it and it scares you. Oh, what you could do if you had that power?" mused Banks aloud.

"I don't recall the sign saying the 'Dr. was in'."

"I asked you here to give you advice. The insight is free."

"How many other strings are you pulling?"

"I think by now you are figuring out there are many strings. We are all pulling and being pulled," empathized Banks.

"And yet you did not answer the question."

"Yes, I am pulling strings, as are others. Just as you are now, too. You are the right person at the right time. Whether you can pull it off is not something we can accomplish solely by string pulling. Sometimes all you can do is make sure we assemble the pieces and hope the moves happen in the right order."

"Somehow 'hope' does not seem to be something I would expect you and your 'friends' to rely on for outcomes."

"You're learning. There are many forces working." Banks paused, looking at the remaining scotch in the bottom of his crystal tumbler. "Would you be so kind?"

Nick took the glass and headed to the bar in the library.

"Why didn't you take the VP's offer? It would have given you everything you say you want. Visibility, a platform, a path to being in charge in eight years."

"It felt wrong. It was the right move for all the wrong reasons. I don't think it is supposed to be easy. I think I have to suffer. The rest of us have to suffer too. To get to a point where it is change or die. To recognize what we had for so long is so much better than what we are allowing to replace it."

"That's pretty melodramatic. Do you think people are still willing to sacrifice their lives when offered an alternative of government care at seemingly no cost to them?" proposed Banks.

"Honestly? I don't know. I would like to think the answer is yes. Our culture has made us soft and pliable. Too many go the way the wind of free stuff is blowing, in exchange for a Party vote," lamented Nick.

Nick handed Banks his fresh drink and sat across from him, still nursing his original martini.

Banks nodded his head in appreciation. "American resiliency has saved the world from itself a couple of times. The cold war was a mistake. It allowed us to grow complacent. While we focused on containing the Soviets, China destroyed itself and rebuilt into a new Japan-like martial society. Thanks entirely to us, but you know all this, don't you?" asked Banks, picking up a wire bound document from the end table next to his chair. He leaned forward, handing it to Nick.

Nick looked down at the hundred and fifty pages with a clear plastic cover sleeve. He started laughing while looking up at Banks.

"Seriously?"

"It was certainly an interesting read when it was first published and today when I re-read it," answered Banks with a grin.

"*Is Globalization leading us into a second Dark Age?*" Nick read the title of the booklet aloud. "Wherever did you get this?"

"You forgot the rest. 'By Nicholas J. Turner, Lt. Commander, US Navy'. I find it interesting that you used this for both your final threat assessment report at the National War College *and* then published it as your thesis paper for your other masters at Georgetown as well. Kill two projects with one paper, so to speak?" smiled Banks, devilishly.

Nick shrugged. "I assumed no one would read it beyond the professors at either institution. Besides, you can't plagiarize yourself. Since it was equally applicable to my International Relations masters, I figured, why not? I see your copy is the War College threat assessment."

"General Arnett sent it to me then. He also said you ran circles around the army colonels and navy captains in your class."

"General Arnett was a great instructor. I learned a lot from him," confided Nick.

"Interesting theory you propose in your paper." Banks gestured with his glass at the document. "How protecting the seas for global commerce forced the world to take our side against the Soviets. At least if they wanted our trade. It led to the Soviet downfall economically, but also enabled China to replace them, both *militarily and economically.*"

"You'll also note that here we are decades later, and my predictions have failed to come to fruition. We are certainly not in any Dark Age, however disunited we may now be. China is much stronger now than they were back then," responded Nick.

"True, but your points still apply. We are pulling back from being the world's policeman. Shortly we will no longer guarantee the sea lanes, starting with the Persian Gulf. Piracy, state sponsored and otherwise, is once again rising. China is certainly practicing colonialism, even if they are doing it under the guise of their belt and road initiatives."

"They are locking down the resources from these defenseless nations, just as you said they would. Except they are using 6G wireless futures and port infrastructure. This and an implied threat of removing them from the global economy if they try to decline. As we turn the focus of our Navy toward our own hemisphere, or even just our own shores, the rest of the world is in for a rude awakening," finished Banks prophetically.

Nick leaned forward, fanning the pages of his thesis. "I was much more idealistic and hopeful when I wrote this. I am now less of both. Globalization has failed. It was artificial. Enabling global supply chains and briefly lifting countries and peoples out of abject poverty. Through exploitation of their cheap labor to farm resources or create low skill materials for input into other processes. When this disappears, it will only be a question of how far these countries and societies fall. Back to pre-world war two, pre-industrial age, or even back to eleven hundred. This will not be pretty. It doesn't have to happen, but these elite globalists who think they can manage the de-industrialization that comes with America no longer guaranteeing the global supply chain, are not students of history."

"Now you know why I read this twenty years ago, Nick. You recognized the danger these globalists posed. Maybe they even mean well and think they can create a utopian society. For the good of all, and not just their own warped and twisted ideals of existence. But like you, I look at the world, read your thesis, and see only danger and death on the horizon. It may not have come to pass yet, but we are now twenty-plus years closer to it becoming reality."

Nick sat and finished his martini in a big gulp. "I haven't thought about this paper in a very long time. It was a task. I completed it and went back to war after my duty assignment at the Pentagon finished. I quickly stopped worrying about the world and focused on surviving."

"I suggest you read it again. Look at it through the lens of today and tell me what you see. Your global elites have a name. Maksim Pavlovich, Alexis Smythe-Thomas, the Council on Foreign Relations, the WEF, WEC, the World Bank and all the others. Did you see Pavlovich's interview with TVGB?" Nick shook his head no.

"Can you look it up on your phone, please? Look at your statements and predictions and marry them to the stated goals and policies of these two and their minions. Now you see why I pushed you into this." Banks reached for his inhaler, taking a quick puff.

Nick watched the interview Pavlovich gave to Colin Harthank while the Senator returned to normal breathing. When he finished the recording, he stared at the paper in his hand. He never dreamed anyone, let alone a scion of the US senate would have read it. Banks coughed before continuing.

"It is us against them. At exactly the time when we need the resolve of the Cold war, we instead have the spine of Europe in the 1930s. As the world collapses and the game changes to one of grabbing resources formerly available to all, who will win? China and Russia will not allow their civilizations to collapse without striking out. To ensure access to resources they don't have and toward anyone they see limiting them from getting them. It is going to happen."

"Militaries which have laid dormant under the umbrella of American dominance will spring up again. They will have to in order to protect what they still have access to and to ensure the resources they own in other places can safely arrive. What happens to the billions who are now part of the global supply chain who cease to have access to both export material and labor and now lack the money or goods to import things like food and energy? Just as Pavlovich alluded to."

"You read my thesis. You listened to his interview. He at least got that part right. You know what happens," responded Nick.

"Indeed, I do. Billions will die from good old starvation. Millions more from armed conflict in the coming struggle to maintain their prior way of life. The world dynamics are changing. It seems inevitable. How do we manage this de-evolution? Can it even be stopped? Will it be our finest hour or our darkest?" finished Banks with a dramatic sigh.

Nick frowned. "Your summation is both brilliant and terrifying. You sound like him," pointing to a bust of Churchill.

"He was one of my mentors. I met him when I was in England at Oxford. Even in his twilight years, he had a commanding presence. He was not afraid of risk or of defeat. The quintessential survivor. Constantly reinventing himself. Adapting his views as the world around him changed. He was no saint and made lots of mistakes, but he also showed up when it mattered. Always there to do what others were unwilling or unable to do."

"I am a Churchill admirer as well," agreed Nick.

"He was an avowed colonialist. He would have welcomed the upcoming chance to rebuild a British Empire," laughed Banks.

"Maybe, or perhaps, he would have evolved on that as well. He withstood the whirlwind long enough for America to wake up to the evils of Japan and Germany. Too bad we didn't take out communism at the same time. Maybe globalization wouldn't have become the American containment policy."

"Possibly. More likely, it would have been replaced by some other form of dictatorship in each of those countries," countered Banks.

"We'll never know," postulated Nick.

"Actually, we do. We have seen it time and time again. Only the people can nurture self-rule. Only the people can convert to democracy. We cannot force it on people who do not want it. It does not differ from the missionaries teaching the natives to build houses in the trees only to come back in a year and find them back in their shelters on the beach and the houses in the trees abandoned," lectured Banks.

"Why do I feel there is a message in all this?" said Nick, leaning back in his comfortable leather chair.

"Indeed, there is. You are trying to awaken the nascent spirit of democracy in America. Folks like Pavlovich and Lexi are trying to bury it forever. To save the world, we must first save ourselves. From ourselves. The simple path is to accept what the government offers rather than continue to take risks. It is very seductive. In the process, we have slowly ceded our rights and freedoms for compliance and rule by others. To rebel is to risk the easy life."

"Now they have an army of folks in our own citizenry they can mobilize to fight against those who threaten their cushy life of government assistance. This is cancel culture, public shaming, and critical race theory mobilizing all. From corporate HR departments, social media censors, and cable news, to the schools and even our friends. They have turned our neighbors into Stazi snitches, quick to turn in their friends and colleagues to earn more acceptance from the elite rulers."

Nick interrupted, leaping up, unable to contain his anger.

"If you knew all this, why did you let this happen? You have been in Congress for over 70 years. I also know you are a member of the Council on Foreign Relations. How many times have you been to Davos? Or Aspen? You have given favorable speeches at these very organizations you now claim want total control. How do you square that circle of hypocrisy? You and your fellow Party *and* many Opposition Senators made most of this a reality. Feeling guilty now is a bit late. Now you want me to clean it up. I won't grant you absolution," accused Nick.

Banks did not take offence at his accusations. "My colleagues think we are on the brink of total success, not failure. They believe when we've removed the need for elections, we'll have free rein to implement policies and achieve perfection. Democracy is messy and could never do this because of the constant need to curry majority approval. They'll be free of public opinion. Free to suppress or eliminate any who dissent."

"Which was why the founders wrote the Constitution the way they did. Checks and balances. Radical change was supposed to be hard," responded Nick.

"It has been. It has taken 100+ years of progressive effort. You're my attempt, at the end of my long life, to atone for some of my sins."

"Am I supposed to thank you? You invite me to give me advice about a vice president and instead, lay the fate of the world on me. Thanks, I feel so much better now," Nick's tone dripping with sarcasm.

"Yet you're still here. Frankly, you don't look too surprised at my confession. Nick, if you haven't realized by now, I've had my eye on you for a very long time. Watching you, helping where I can. Like the enemy, my associates and I are playing the long game as well."

Nick sat, digesting this information before continuing.

"Associates? There are more of you to blame. Care to tell me who my friends are?" responded Nick.

"In time. Just know you're not alone," replied Banks mysteriously.

"I don't find that very comforting. Not sure it will matter. I agree, we are screwed up. How we got here is irrelevant. You created an artificial golden age, allowing the boomers and Gen X to reap the benefits of the post-World War II global security provided by the only remaining superpower. You did it. The rest of us will now get to watch this global village come apart. Did you ever think about how this would end?"

Banks sat and stared at Nick, sipping his drink.

"Simultaneously, you removed all education on how or why it was happening. Everyone under the age of 50, perhaps even 60 now, does not know how this prosperity came about or the house of cards it is built upon. You have failed to prepare *anyone* for the coming mess. It is all about demographics. You know this, I can see it in your eyes. There are simply not going to be enough workers to do the jobs, and worse, to finance the future."

"Again correct. We definitely understand. And have for decades."

"My point exactly. It is why you have never tried to stop the national debt from rising to unsustainable levels. You and I know it is not for the future generations to deal with. Society as we know it will not even be around to pay or collect on the debt. Modern civilization is in for a nasty couple of decades."

"To the head of the class, Mr. Turner. If you had a time machine and go forward, perhaps only ten years, maybe even less, you'll need a new globe. Geopolitics and demographics. Two academic terms are about to become very relevant," prophesied Banks.

"Now it becomes clear. You're not looking for someone to bring us back to the glory of old. You're looking for someone to manage the upcoming collapse and the chaos after," proclaimed Nick.

"Yet you seem surprised. Did you not write that paper? You saw this before most, almost twenty years ago. Most scoffed at you then. I did not. I took note. Nick, as you know, the United States, through our continued blessing of both geography *and* constitutional democracy, is positioned better than most, if not any, to weather the upcoming unraveling. A return to Constitutional first principles is an absolute necessity for our survival. Maybe even of civilizations," explained Banks.

"Or dictatorship," interrupted Nick. "Senator, even the United States cannot save people from themselves. Our way of life is about to take a drastic turn, potentially Great Depression style. Or worse. Those who fall the farthest are the least likely to do so without lashing out in denial at their fate. How exactly do you propose our Constitution is going to shield us from madmen in North Korea, Iran, Russia or even China from going down in a nuclear finale? Certainly, Israel will not go quietly."

Banks let out a giant sigh, appearing to deflate before Nick's eyes. He continued in a sad and forlorn voice.

"Thankfully, I will neither have to witness this effort, nor be called upon to figure out how to avoid it. You will. Even if you lose, Lexi must be stopped. She'll serve as a catalyst to speed up this de-industrialization. Unknowingly and perhaps unwillingly, she'll still make wrong choices."

"What an uplifting conversation! Maybe I can call Lexi back and hop into both her bed and the Vice Presidency," said Nick, frustrated.

"Oh dear, you turned that down as well?" asked Banks, with a shake of his head. "You *are* in real trouble."

"Tell me about it. Is this where I thank you for involving me in all this?" deadpanned Nick, looking truly depressed as he sat back down.

"Neill Rogers or Susan Quinn."

"Excuse me?"

"For your Vice President. Either are a good choice."

"They are both Opposition."

"So? Do you honestly think you are Party any longer? Have you listened to your speeches? I would say you are 60% Opposition stances and 40% Party. This is good, just right of center is the place to be."

"Won't I lose some of my Party support if I pick one of them?"

"You're transcending parties. Or creating your own. You're drawing from both. Just as you need to. Your abortion stance is pure brilliance. You are definitely going to get a lot of Party women. Many are more aligned with the family values of moderate opposition than the Party. They continued to vote that way because they support some abortion rights, and the opposition did not support any."

"By making your moral argument, but keeping the individual right, and the reckoning with God as the true decision point, you have satisfied both of them. One they cannot poll because these women will continue to say they will vote Party."

"In that moment, when they have to balance the radical nature of Lexi and the vast cultural and social change she advocates, versus your family friendly, pragmatic view, they will choose you. None of us is God. Only he or she will judge those who choose to abort. By focusing on pregnancy prevention, not the ridiculousness of abstention, or forced birth from unwanted pregnancy, you give everyone a place in the argument they can justify and live with. Bravo.

"It seemed like the only logical approach to remove this as the wedge dividing us the most. It is how I truly feel, not some fake slogan."

"That's why it works. No politician would do that because while it helps the middle, it drives both lunatic fringes away from you. *Both* parties rely on their extreme followers, their fanatics. Also, you need to choose one of these Opposition members as your VP because the October surprise is going to leave a lot of them untethered. You can send out either of these two to make speeches on how you are the logical landing choice for their support now that they can't vote for the Opposition candidate. You also need to court Garcia. He *must* be on your side. You need to get a chunk of his conservative supporters to even have a chance. You can only pull so many moderates away from Lexi."

"I have already started with Freddie. You sound like I can win."

"You can't, or rather you couldn't until this recent development occurred. It is a classic case of them going too far. She was going to win, but they need the mandate. They want to crush the Opposition and get an overwhelming win so they can wield power without complaint. To ensure it, they'll unleash this abomination on Blackbird, not realizing *they* are the ones making you a viable opponent. Instead, they are assuming his voters will stay home in disgust at the candidate and their party. Their thinking is you aren't of any consequence. Lexi's team knows only they can make you relevant. So far, they have prevented her from directly attacking you. They think keeping you off TV is enough. Your advice to your followers to lie to pollsters is also going to pay off. Their polling is going to be even more slanted than usual, making them complacent and assuring them of their big victory.

"What exactly are they going to do to Blackbird?"

"You are better off not knowing. Then you can truthfully claim ignorance. You need to get your VP picked and on board before this happens. They may not wait until October."

"Any other nuggets of wisdom you want to bestow?"

"Watch your back. Everyone has secrets. They can buy everyone for the right price and not just money. Compartmented, highly secret and secure information, for instance, may even be accessed, or has already," revealed Banks, holding Nick's stare.

"What's that supposed to mean?" prompted Nick.

"They have everything on the line and will stop at nothing to win. This is the culmination of a lot of effort. Lexi is leveraged to the hilt. She has so many chips to cash in. She'll have no choice but to do as they say to get into and stay in power. She is now single-minded in her determination to save the country her way. She is every bit as committed to her view of what is right as you are. Keep that in mind."

"It is not my first time in combat."

"Indeed, it is not, officially and unofficially."

"Unofficially?"

"If I can learn things, so can others. Remember, one person and a secret is safe. If more than one knows it, it is never safe. People are digging. They want to be ready to take you out, win or lose."

"I can handle it."

Banks nodded. "But can those around you? Attacks usually come from the flanks. You know this. They will get to you from everywhere. Remember, trust no one." Nick nodded.

"I'm not sure what you think you know about me."

"Damn it, Nick. This is no time to be coy," said Banks, showing impatience for the first time, raising his voice. "I have led or sat on the Intelligence committees of this country for almost sixty years. The only reason more of your exploits aren't already known is because I created a classification level unique and specific to our congressional intelligence committee. I used the 9/11 Authorization of Use of Military Force. The same AUMF these presidents abused to unilaterally launch all kinds of illegal activities without congressional approval. I used it to seal knowledge of other events. It would take an act of a future congress in fifty years to declassify this info, or an act of treason. Surely you must have been curious why some of those activities you took part in, or witnessed the aftermath of, have never gone public? Why there have been no public hearings?"

Nick looked at Banks, betraying no emotion at this revelation.

"There is very little that is clandestine that I am not privy to. All these efforts require budget allocation and in order to get these, they must be justified. Don't believe what you see in movies about Pentagon slush funds. In most of those instances, they have made those cases to me."

"Senator, you make it all sound so James Bond. I simply did what I was ordered and where I was ordered to do it."

"You are learning. While entirely a truthful answer, it is also vague enough to not disclose the *entire* truth or any of those orders. Also, you forget many of your exploits on these missions during the war involved others who remember you. It's not the first time someone sworn to secrecy spills the beans anonymously. We can't meet again. If they find out I'm helping you, it may give things away."

"They?"

"In time, you will understand. I'll continue to do what I can."

Chapter 15

Nick leaned forward in his chair, preparing to leave, when the doorbell chimed in a delightful melody.

"Expecting someone else?"

Banks shrugged. "Maybe someone else looking for advice," he said with a crooked grin.

Nick stood as he heard footsteps in the hallway.

"Baxter, you old rascal. What are you up to? Inviting me over for dinner on such short notice." Dolly Monroe stopped as she entered the library and saw Nick standing there. She quickly straightened, putting a hand on her hip.

"Senator, what a surprise."

Nick shook his head, smiling as he glanced at Dolly. He had never seen her in casual clothes. She was wearing skinny jeans, wedge heeled sandals, a tucked in white t-shirt and a black blazer with sleeves rolled up. Her hair was pulled back in a loose ponytail. She wore minimal makeup and a pair of fashionable designer eyeglasses.

"Ms. Monroe. A pleasure as always," answered Nick with a little bow.

"Dolly, my dear, what a surprise. Can Hobson get you something to drink?"

"Surprise Baxter?" asked Dolly with a raised eyebrow.

Senator Banks merely opened the palm of his hands in reply.

"What are you drinking?" she asked, looking at Nick. Nick had on his own worn blue jeans, Tony Llama ostrich cowboy boots and a simple black t-shirt. Dolly couldn't help but notice his well-muscled arms clearly on display in the t-shirt. Baxter sat with a silly grin on his face as his guests eyed each other out of 'uniform' for the first time.

"Nolet, of course," smiled Nick.

Dolly nodded at Hobson, who proceeded to make a couple of Nolet gin martinis and a fresh scotch for Banks. He distributed the drinks and announced dinner would be ready in ten minutes.

"What should we toast?" asked Banks.

"How about matchmakers?" answered Nick as Dolly laughed, adding, "or busy bodies?"

Banks nodded. "Ah yes, to the art of statecraft and ensuring outcomes." They all raised their glasses in salute.

"I must say, Senator, you look a trifle different from your Gala attire," smirked Dolly.

"Had I known I was being set up, I might have made more of an attempt at decorum. I feel a trifle under dressed," agreed Nick.

"Nonsense. Comfort is key. Where I come from in South Carolina, where it is both hot and humid, less is always the order of the day. Shall we adjourn to the dining room? I can smell our dinner. Give me a hoist, please, Nick."

He walked over to Banks, offering a forearm, and pulled him effortlessly to his feet. Dolly came up to take his other arm, and the three of them walked slowly to the massive dining room of the estate.

Once there, they congregated around one end of the large dining room table as Hobson served up plates of exquisite fettuccine Alfredo, grilled asparagus, a Greek salad and, finally, garlic bread. Hobson also opened a Barbara d'Asti bottle of red wine.

Nick held up his wineglass to toast as Hobson finished laying out all the dishes. "Baxter, am I allowed to ask Hobson to join us?"

Dolly laughed. "You can ask, but he never accepts. Trust me," she said as Baxter looked on, smiling.

"At least for the toast?" Hobson looked Nick in the eyes for a second, bowed slightly, grabbing another wineglass, and poured himself a small amount. "For you, Senator, I will agree on this occasion," declared Hobson in a clipped British accent.

"Nick, you are truly a miracle worker. In all my time, only my precious Penny could convince Hobson to join us. Here, here," toasted Baxter, holding up his glass.

"To a wonderful meal, fabulous company, and a relaxing evening in an increasingly tumultuous world. Thank you for the invitation and the unexpected company," voiced Nick as Dolly seconded his toast. They all sipped their wine as Hobson turned.

"Will you join us for dinner as well, Hobson?"

"That I am afraid would be impossible, Senator, though I appreciate the offer. You should see the kitchen. It is a catastrophe, and I must check on my soufflé," declined Hobson, retreating to the kitchen.

"Baxter, as I have always said, I am not sure where you found him, but he is an extraordinary valet," commented Dolly.

"Not me. All Penny. And yes, were it not for Hobson, I have no doubt I would long since have joined Penny. Even so, I fear it will not be much longer," he added with no trace of regret as Dolly turned away quickly to hide her look of dismay. This was clearly visible to Nick as Baxter was looking down at his food. Nick quickly changed the subject.

"Baxter, what is the caucus saying about my almost nomination by the Opposition? I can only imagine the response from Fontana," laughed Nick.

"Nick, you may laugh, but do not take lightly the amount of enmity your antics are earning among the 'world's most powerful deliberative body'."

"Good. Hopefully, my 'antics,' as you say, will put them on notice that not everyone will turn a blind eye to their dereliction of duty,"

"Can we talk about something other than politics?" interrupted Dolly with a sigh.

Nick and Baxter looked at each other and started laughing.

"My dear, when you come to dinner with two United States Senators, it is unlikely the topic will turn to horticulture," drawled Banks.

"Perhaps we could at least try?" responded Dolly, leaning back.

"OK then," answered Nick with a smile. "I've now had the pleasure of visiting your respective libraries. I have to say, I thought my own was pretty good, but it pales compared to either of yours."

Dolly looked Nick in the eyes and smiled brightly at him for changing the subject. For the next forty-five minutes, while savoring the wonderful dinner, they discussed the value of knowledge. The importance of preserving history in the form of books, and the need to reintroduce modern youth to the concepts found in the classics.

"Which book in your collection is your favorite, Senator?"

"That is a tough question, Nick. I have been fortunate to meet many an author in my lifetime. Jack Kennedy gave me a signed copy of *Profiles in Courage.* I have quite a few first editions signed by authors in my collection and many others I collected from others. I can tell you who I delighted in debating. Ayn Rand."

"I can only imagine that conversation," laughed Nick and Dolly.

"Our philosophies couldn't have differed more, but her background being born in Russia and her fervent concern with Communism always led to lively conversations. As time has passed and I have gotten older, I am coming around to more and more of her arguments about producers and consumers. Though I draw the line at the whole selfishness angle. Remind me to show you my copy of *Atlas Shrugged.* She wrote a hilarious inscription. I often return to it after some vote I made turned out to have unintended consequences."

"How about yours, Dolly?" asked Nick, turning to Dolly.

"I can't claim to be as much of a bibliophile as the two of you. But I have spent some time examining the library through the years. One author caught my eye. Mary Wollstonecraft and her essay *A Vindication of the Rights of Woma*n. It was gifted directly from Mary and her husband William Godwin to James Monroe when he was the ambassador to France."

"Interesting," said Banks. "Isn't she the mother of Mary Shelley, the author of *Frankenstein?*"

"Indeed, she was. She died only a couple of weeks after giving birth. Mostly she is famous for participating in the 'pamphlet wars' during the French Revolution. She also wrote another essay on the *Rights of Man* in response to Edmund Burke's writing on the French revolution. Her women's rights pamphlet was written in response to a pamphlet by Talleyrand, the French philosopher. He believed women should only be educated on the domestic home activities. Mary felt it was necessary for a *woman* to provide a true rebuttal. It was unheard of in that day for a woman to stand up and publicly disagree, let alone author a rebuttal. Many claim she is the mother of modern feminism. Not sure I agree."

Nick stared at her. She straightened at his look of amazement.

"Surprised? I did go to the finest schools and do know how to read a book," retorted Dolly in a challenging tone, her eyes flashing.

Nick held up his hand, looking at Banks for help. He had a smile on his face. "What did *I* say?" spouted Nick.

"I could tell what you were thinking," retorted Dolly, lightening her tone with a smile, leaning forward toward him. "Nick, you will find this interesting, as it is right up your alley. She was really saying everyone should be moral and just. Use common sense. She did not particularly claim women were the equals of men, but she also claimed that each had specific skills and capabilities that made sense for each of them to do. At the time, this was pretty radical stuff. President Monroe was ambassador to France under Jefferson and to Great Britain under Madison. Those were interesting times."

"Didn't your father have the same posts? Ambassador to both countries?" replied Nick, trying to get back in her good graces.

"You paid attention." This time *she* had the surprised look.

"To every word," noted Nick, causing Dolly to blush before taking a sip of wine. He marveled at her natural beauty. Even without elaborate makeup and fancy ball gowns, she was dazzling. Her high cheekbones, full red lips, and bright eyes drew Nick in with their intensity.

Hobson appeared with coffee and three small crocks.

"Ah Hobson, delightful. White chocolate soufflé. You've outdone yourself this time," pronounced Banks, rubbing his hands together.

"Sir, for such esteemed guests, I felt it was worth the effort."

"Oh my gosh," expressed Dolly after her first bite. "Did Penny teach you how to bake this?"

Hobson merely smiled, bowed, and returned to the kitchen as they devoured their dessert and coffee.

"Well, children, I would love to join you for a cognac, but I am afraid I must retire. Please, head back to the library and have a nightcap. Hobson, help me up if you would."

Hobson easily hoisted Banks out of his chair and led him away. Nick looked at Dolly, leaning back in her chair again.

"May I offer you a cognac?"

"I never turn down a chance to drink Baxter's brandy. Most of it is older than even you," she said with a snicker, rising to take Nick's arm.

They walked into the library. Nick went to the bar and poured two glasses of Armagnac brandy into two crystal brandy glasses. He glanced at the bottle while handing one to Dolly.

"Here is to our host and his ancient Armagnac. This one is almost as old as *he* is," laughed Nick, looking at the label.

"I told you."

They both sat in the comfortable leather chairs. Sipping their drink. They looked up at a sound as Hobson discreetly entered.

"I wanted to let you know, the Senator has retired for the night. When you are ready to go, ring the bell."

"Thank you, Hobson," they said simultaneously, causing both to laugh. Nick shook his head as Hobson left.

"Not sure I could get used to having staff," offered Nick.

"You would. It is a noble profession. Despite what people think, people like Hobson and my Nina take great pride in helping us manage our lives. We'd be lost without them. I certainly could not maintain the estate and all the various foundations and events I support to ensure my late husband's legacy continues," explained Dolly.

"I meant no offence," replied Nick, somewhat chastised.

"None taken. I know it is sometimes hard to understand, but there are different worlds in our country still."

They sat in awkward silence.

"Do you come over often?" asked Nick, trying desperately to find a topic of conversation, not wanting Dolly to leave.

"Not as often as I should. Baxter is pretty homebound. He lives for the Senate. There really is nothing else since Penny passed."

"That was ten years ago, right?"

"More or less. Penny helped me after I lost my husband. I was a regular when she was still alive. I went through a rough patch, feeling sorry for myself," she said, staring at Nick.

Nick held her gaze, not interrupting.

"I was proof positive that all the money in the world doesn't buy happiness. I was wealthy, miserable, and alone. Drinking and partying too much. Spiraling into oblivion. Honestly, I couldn't have cared less."

Nick sat, sipping his cognac as Dolly told her story.

"Lucky for me, Penny saw this and took charge. My parents were gone. My husband was gone. I blamed myself. Maybe we would not have taken the trip if we'd been able to have a family. Guilt and alcohol mixed with amphetamines are not a good recipe for clear thought," said Dolly in a tone of despair, reliving the memories.

"Dolly." Nick held up his hand to stop her.

"It's OK, Nick," she said with a little ironic laugh. "It helps me to remember where I was and how, thanks to Penny, I found a purpose. I am very involved in many philanthropic endeavors because of her. She showed me how to fill the voids in my life. It just about did me in when she passed, but she gave me the baton of the Galas, and made me promise to watch over Baxter. This reminds me I have been slipping of late. I will make more of an effort to visit. Especially if he has more surprise guests," she finished with a twinkle in her eye.

"He's always scheming. Apparently, it reaches beyond the Senate."

"Oh, of that you can be assured. Our friendly Senator is involved in all manner of intrigue if half the stories Penny told me are true. He hides it all behind his slow southern gentleman charm. I sense there is much I don't know about him. Hobson may be the only source of truth."

"I suspect trying to pry that out of him would not end well."

"Which is why I've never attempted," she responded.

"Very smart of you," nodded Nick.

"Any deep, dark secrets you care to share? Since we are baring our souls," quipped Dolly.

Nick stared back. "Thankfully, I have not faced the personal tragedy you have. War was and is Hell. You see *and* do things you can never unsee. You have a choice. Make peace with your inner demons or let them consume you. I sleep well most nights. But I have had my crisis of conscience as well. Though, unlike you, I find talking about them is *not therapeutic*," he said with a wry smile.

"My parents died in a car accident when I was in college. I too am an only child. I was not particularly attentive. It changed my attitude and, frankly, my work ethic. I poured myself into school and preparation for the Navy. That was the purpose *I* found. Service has been my addiction ever since. To my country in one fashion or another. Not out of noble conviction, but out of genuine concern and desire to help. Just as you serve, with your philanthropic efforts," Nick shrugged. "Not very romantic or even inspiring, but it is what it is."

"Nick, I sense, much like Baxter," she paused for effect, "you are full of shit." Nick laughed, startled.

"Both of you and your self-deprecating 'aw shucks' demeanors. You may have some folks fooled. Not me. Trust me, I've seen all types."

"I can only imagine," agreed Nick. "Given the attendees at your Gala's. I'm surprised you are not a princess or at least a duchess by now."

Dolly's expression told Nick he had stepped in it yet again.

"Do you think that matters to me?" she asked, a fire in her eye.

Nick held up a hand. "I'm sorry. I meant no offence, only the opportunity afforded to one in your position. You could have or be whatever you want. That was all I meant."

"And yet, that is not how it comes out. I guess we are better at dancing than chatting."

"Seems so. My whole life is now politics. Since we agreed to take that one off the table and we've already discussed our taste in literature," he said with a sweeping arm motion, taking in the multi-storied library. "I'm not sure there is much else to discuss. Clearly, my poor attempt at small talk is only pissing you off. This is most certainly not my intent, trust me. I could tell you what it was like to teach college freshman at a state university," said Nick lamely, trying to recover.

"I think I will pass on that one," Dolly said with a small laugh.

"Then I am out of topics. You?"

"How about cars?"

"Excuse me?"

"Want to talk about cars?" asked Dolly.

"You mean like Bentleys and stuff?"

Dolly shook her head. "You are a slow learner. Is that what you think I like? Because I'm rich?"

Nick shrugged, not sure where they were going with this conversation. "What cars *are* you into then?" he asked skeptically.

"American muscle."

"Yeah right," laughed Nick, stopping once he saw the fire back in her eyes. "You're serious?"

"You bet I am."

"Alright, lay it on me. Dazzle me with your American muscle car knowledge," said Nick in a challenging tone, leaning forward.

"How about I show you?"

"Really?" said Nick as Dolly got up, ringing the bell for Hobson.

As he appeared, Dolly told him she was taking Nick for a ride.

"Be careful madame, he is precious cargo," replied Hobson with a knowing smile.

"Don't worry. We'll see what he is made of," said Dolly as she led Nick down a hall and out onto the back of the grounds. She'd parked her car in the driveway next to a large garage with four bays. Nick stopped.

"Well?"

He stared. "1970?"

"Nope. 1969. Pontiac GTO Judge Ram Air IV v8 with a 4-speed manual transmission." Nick looked at the sparkling black paint job on the convertible. "She's beautiful. Wherever did you get her?"

"My father bought it decades ago from the original owner. I did the restoration myself. Besides being an ambassador, my dad also raced cars. As his only child, Mom made sure I got the cultured upbringing of an Earl's granddaughter and Dad made sure I also got a good dose of American tomboy. He had me rebuilding engines in between ballet lessons," laughed Dolly.

"Motorhead would not be a moniker I would have guessed for you in a thousand years."

"Care to go for a spin?"

"Sure. Can I have a look at the engine first?"

Dolly popped the hood and the 370 horsepower 400 cubic inch big block roared to life. Nick stood admiring the engine and shook his head again at the simplicity of cars from the sixties. He could practically sit in the engine bay, even with the large V8. Modern engine compartments were crammed full of pollution controls, electronic gadgetry, air conditioning and various other add-ons.

Nick slid into the passenger seat as Dolly carefully eased the car onto the sedate Chevy Chase street in the early August evening sunlight. As they turned to head toward more open roads, a slouched down person in a car down the street took pictures of the two of them in the black car with the convertible top down. Dolly was smiling as she chirped the tires, shifting gears, heading out of the neighborhood.

Sometime later, with the sun dipping low in the west, Dolly pulled the car back up the street. She parked in front of Chuck's Prius, which Nick had borrowed. Nick looked over at Dolly, smiling back at him with her big designer sunglasses hiding her eyes.

"Didn't scare you too bad, did I?" laughed Dolly.

"It was fine until you had to drag race that Mustang," said Nick in a serious tone.

"Hah, if we were really racing, he would owe me his pink slip. No way any old mustang short of the Boss could take me. I knew what I was doing. You need to change your underwear?"

"Hardly," laughed Nick. "You remember I was a fighter pilot? I'm a bit of an adrenalin junkie myself. Just not good as a passenger."

"In this car, there is only one driver."

"Thanks Dolly, this was a nice ending to a wonderful evening. Even if it is pretty obvious what Banks is up to."

Nick leaned over and meant to give Dolly a kiss on the cheek. She turned at the last second, so their lips met instead. He lingered, as the tip of her tongue teased his, before she leaned away, smiling.

"Why thank you Senator. Finally. Enjoy your evening. I assume I will see you at the Fall Gala? You have ducked the last two. Three and I may have to stop sending invites."

"I'll be there, promise."

"It's a date. Until then, enjoy your drive in Chuck's hotrod." Nick smiled in reply, shutting the heavy door of the pristine GTO carefully.

As Nick got out and headed to the Prius, Dolly executed a U-turn in the middle of the street and sent up a bit of smoke, spinning the rear tires again, laughing as she sped away. Clearly not something this neighborhood was accustomed to. Nick shook his head. This kind of behavior was clearly not what he expected from Ms. Monroe.

He drove down the street back to his Senate office and his waiting Murphy bed.

#

Lauren Bergamo sank down in the nondescript Impala she used when in DC. As Nick drove by, she leaned back up in her seat. She looked down at the camera and flipped through the pictures. Fuming as she stared at the pictures of Nick and Dolly driving by with smiles on their faces and the kiss she had just witnessed. The cramp in her midsection reminded her of her own encounter with Nick Turner. Only this time, she was not as inclined to feel so sorry for herself.

Chapter 16

Nick drove his rental car into the driveway of a moderately size older house in the 'new' city of Buckhead. Once an affluent neighborhood of Atlanta, it had voted to become an independent city, taking over 40% of Atlanta's tax base with it. He was carrying his purple notebook and a bouquet of fresh flowers as he rang the doorbell.

The door opened. An attractive, slim, and shorter older woman with white-blonde shoulder length hair opened the door with a big smile.

"Welcome Senator, please come on in. Oh, thank you for the flowers. How rude of me. I am Ellie Rogers," she said, juggling the flowers and holding out a hand.

"It's a pleasure to meet you," responded Nick, following Ellie through the foyer into a living room and then the kitchen, where she found a vase. She asked him about his trip into Atlanta, commenting on the mild temperatures for August.

"I'm sorry. Neill would have met you himself, but he is in the middle of a project. Let me show you the way." She led Nick out a door in the kitchen into a decent sized backyard with immaculate landscaping.

"It's beautiful," admired Nick.

"Why thank you Senator. I love to garden and I hate to pay someone to do what I can do myself. Normally you would see me in jeans with dirty hands and a sweaty bandanna. Since I knew you were coming, I decided I should be presentable," admitted Ellie with a genuine laugh. Nick smiled. He liked her.

They walked across the yard to a small barn with a wide set of double doors in the center and a normal door off to the side. The wide doors were open. Ellie led Nick inside and announced them.

"Honey, Senator Turner is here."

"Call me Nick, both of you, please."

Neill, applying clamps to a couple of dovetail joints in a drawer, turned to look at Nick.

"Sorry, I just glued the joint and if I shake your hand, you may become a permanent part of the project,"

Nick laughed. "Not a problem."

"Pull up a stool," suggested Neill, pointing to a corner.

"I'll leave you boys to your conversation," finished Ellie. Nick looked at Neill. He saw a trim patrician looking man, in his late 60s with silver hair and glasses perched on his nose.

"What brings you to the suburbs?"

"I think you know. You come highly recommended."

"As a woodworker? I don't suppose you need a dresser?" responded Neill in a deadpan tone.

"A bonus talent for sure, but I'm afraid I don't need help with woodworking."

"May I ask who recommended me?"

"Banks."

"How is that smug fascist?" asked Neill, letting loose of the work.

"Old and slow, but seems to have his wits about him still, unlike our much younger President," added Nick, watching as Neill headed to a workbench. He picked up a bottle of mineral spirits and dabbed some on his hands to remove the glue residue.

"Hope you weren't planning on lighting up anything," he said, again in a dry tone.

Nick laughed. "Thankfully, no." Neill pulled out another stool and joined Nick near the open door and fresh air, but still in the shade.

"Banks was a great adversary. Never play chess with him. Bastard is as good as Kasparov. Watch out for that scotch, too! Come to think of it, could've had something to do with why he was so good at chess. Oh, sorry, forgot." He held out a hand. "Please call me Neill."

"I'll remember that. I don't expect to see much of him, given my shift in loyalties."

"When did you last talk to him? Couldn't have been that long ago. He is really cagey, and he must like you if he's giving you advice. Speaking of that, what exactly was he recommending me for?" asked Neill, wiping his forehead with a rag and putting on a vintage Braves ball cap.

"I need a vice president."

Neill didn't react. He got up and went to his workbench, retrieving a bottle of bourbon from behind a shelf. He also grabbed a couple of red plastic cups, pouring some in each, handing one to Nick.

"A bit early?" mused Nick, looking at the golden bourbon swirling in the bottom of his cup.

"Not in Moscow," countered Neill, taking a sip of his bourbon.

"True. You were the ambassador to Russia," commented Nick, taking a small sip. "This is like a country song or something, right?"

"Why in the hell would Banks tell you to talk to me about your VP spot? Did he give you a reason for recommending me?" questioned Neill, ignoring Nick's quip. "We weren't exactly buddies."

"You tell me. Maybe it was a joke, and I am the butt of it, given your feelings for him," answered Nick.

"I'm out of the game. I hung up my spurs years ago. Now I write history books."

"I have read some. I like them, especially the one on the battle of Midway," admitted Nick.

"Thanks."

"I'm more impressed with your books on free markets and cultural decline."

"You're one of the 12 people who bought those?"

"Actually, I borrowed them," said Nick with a laugh. "Sorry."

"Figures. There goes my $1 royalty."

"Are you interested?" asked Nick, getting back on topic.

"Really? We met ten minutes ago. We're drinking bourbon at 10 am on a Wednesday. You're either very naïve or very trusting," accused Neill. "If either is true, you are going to get slaughtered."

"You're consistent in your views on where the country was and where it is going and how to get back on track. I believe we agree on many topics, especially regarding economics. We differ a bit on the social issues, but I need someone like you to help legitimize my campaign. I can't believe Banks would have recommended you if he didn't think you would consider it," said Nick.

"That's a heck of a two-sentence summation. I've watched you too. I admire your courage and your moxie. I'll give you that. Some things you say are things many of us longed to say many a time, but feared to because of our glorious careers." observed Neill sarcastically.

"I no longer have a career," laughed Nick.

"Government service makes you risk averse. Status quo is your friend. You get taught to keep your head down and let the other guy get shot. Your problem is you seem to enjoy being the guy sticking his head up and being shot at."

"You know it was not by choice or plan. Somebody needs to do it. Once I started, I couldn't stop. I aim to finish saying my piece. Whether people listen and act is up to them." Nick looked Neill in the eyes.

"It sure looks that way from what I see. Damn the torpedoes seems to be your mantra."

"That concerns you?" asked Nick. Neill shrugged in response, so Nick continued, "I have a message I want to get across. I'm under no illusion regarding the results. Just trying to make the most of my time in the limelight to spread the word and get folks to mobilize. I need *more* to get mobilized. Specifically, more Opposition conservatives. Right now, I don't think I am breaking through to enough of them."

"This makes no sense. You are formerly a Party member. Why add an old white guy from the opposition? I am the poster child for privilege and the decay of the west. You need a black or Hispanic woman and gay would not hurt either in today's environment," observed Neill.

Nick smiled. "You are experienced. You have a stand-up reputation on both sides of the aisle. I am independent, running with no party. You'll help me appeal to the Opposition. Plus, you help mitigate any concerns people have about my youth and inexperience in politics."

Neill shook his head. "My wife would kill me. She made me quit the last time. I like her and I enjoy being happily married. Stay single, you have no idea what this life does to marriages."

"No plan to change that. I have no time for a life, *or* frankly, a wife.

"In that case, get one. You need something to lose, so it puts your decisions in perspective," urged Neill.

"Okay. Now I'm confused. You just said…"

"What I also didn't say was I am sane because I am married, and she rescued me from myself."

"I can see this is going to work out well. Everyone has sage advice for me. None of it makes any sense or contradicts what they said 30 seconds ago. I have a scion of the Senate recommending a washed up Opposition member to be my Vice President. One, I might add, who has me drinking bourbon at 10 am on a Wednesday. From a red plastic cup. Telling me to not get married but to find something I don't want to lose, like a wife. Did I get all that right?" asked Nick with a sip and a smile.

"Hmm. Let me see, you have been in congress for what a year and here you are running for president. I think you need all the 'sage' advice you can get," countered Neill.

"I hate to say it, but lifetimes of service in congress as a qualifier for running for president does not seem to have provided us with any outstanding leaders," pointed out Nick.

"Fair point, but every decision can't be a gut decision. Sometimes you need to learn from mistakes. Learn to identify the situations that led to the mistake and prevent it from happening again. As President, there are no do overs," said Neill, in a serious tone again.

"That is true, but I can't do worse than the last few.

"Here is your first piece of sage advice from me. Flippant, even in private, is not a good idea. Too many ears. Don't make the mistake of thinking you can't do worse. You can. We are still standing here. Keep that in mind. For all the crap you think the others have done, from both parties, we have not been annihilated or annihilated anybody. Being President is the hardest job in the world. Everyone wants to take you down, everywhere, and all the time," lectured Neill.

Nick nodded. "Point taken. My humor is a bit sharp."

"Good, you are thick skinned. You'll need it. You're already head and shoulders above most candidates, who are unwilling to take advice or admit they have anything to learn. What are you looking for from me? I'm not interested in being your dad."

"I need you to support my positions. To convince your Opposition brethren, I am a legit alternative. The best choice of the three. I need you to provide council and use that expertise you talk about to help me avoid the avoidable potholes. You have an equal voice in my councils. I respect your service and experience and welcome your views coming from a different perspective than most of my inner circle."

"Why do you think I can get them to switch from their candidate to you? Eight months ago you were in the Party."

"I think they are going to realize their candidate is not going to win and Lexi is the Devil incarnate," suggested Nick.

"Don't like Lexi much? That's good. She is not to be underestimated. Ever. For you to win, you have to pull what? 35% of the Party and Opposition vote? That isn't going to happen."

"Maybe, maybe not. What about people who have not been voting? I am trying to educate people to wake up, stand up, and take responsibility before they no longer have the choice. Maybe there is an untapped well of disgusted or lazy voters who believes they don't make a difference? If I can get them energized, does this prospect interest you?" asked Nick, getting up to wander around the shed.

"Nick, I'm out of the game. My big risk is my wife divorcing me."

"Why am I going to divorce you?" asked Ellie, appearing on the doorstep with a pitcher of lemonade.

"Oh, thank God," said Nick, putting down his cup and taking an offered glass from Ellie.

"Good Lord Neill. Are you serving him bourbon at 10 in the morning? He's going to think you're a lush or something," said Ellie in a worried tone. "Then I come out and all I hear is we are getting divorced? What exactly are you two discussing?" accused Ellie, looking pointedly at her now sheepish husband.

"It's my fault. I am asking him to be my VP and he doesn't want to cause you trouble," confessed Nick.

Ellie held up her hand as Nick started to keep talking. "Are you kidding? Of course, he will absolutely accept," she said.

"I will?" asked Neill, bewildered by his wife's enthusiastic reply.

"You want to know why?"

"Of course," replied Nick, smiling now.

"Because you are the first person I have ever heard stand up in Washington and provide a legitimate solution to the abortion problem. I think there are a lot of other Opposition women, just like me, who can see a path to compromise. You got it right. Abortion is between the mother and her God. It is wrong and we should be focused on preventing unwanted pregnancy. We should also realize it is not our decision to judge. The mother alone bears the weight of that decision."

She paused, looking from Nick to her husband and back to Nick.

"I cried when I heard your speech and I know a lot of my girlfriends felt the same way. We never considered the true cost of making that decision. By focusing on this, we can sympathize with the mother making this decision without thinking of them solely as murderers. I hope Party women can feel the same, knowing you may be against abortion personally, but your explanation of your feelings should help them understand you won't stop them from being able to decide themselves. With the pragmatic limits you listed, and this realization of ultimate accountability to their higher power, it is the common sense compromise we have needed, but haven't been able to achieve," finished Ellie in a determined voice.

Neill stared at his wife, a strange look on his face. "I guess that settles it then." He turned to Ellie. "You never mentioned this before."

"Honey, it is a deeply personal response and did not need to be discussed. I have never felt this connected to a candidate. You already had my vote, even before you pulled this jalopy out of the garage. When you speak, you believe what you are saying, but you don't care if you win. You are a strange politician, Senator," stated Ellie. "That's why my girlfriends and I just sent in an application to your campaign to start a 'Women for Turner' group here in Buckhead."

"I'm flattered," responded Nick. "Since we are going to be spending a lot of time together, you had better get used to calling me Nick. Thank you for that feedback. I rarely get a chance to talk to Opposition women. You give me hope. You know what, I don't have a wife," said Nick when Neill interrupted.

"Hey back off fella, this one is taken," accused Neill, getting up to put a possessive arm around Ellie.

Nick continued with a smile. "As I was saying, before I was so rudely interrupted by my Vice President. I don't have a wife and I need a strong female voice out their helping advocate my stances and convince women I believe what I am saying. Not just to get elected. Are you comfortable with public speaking?" asked Nick, hoping for a yes.

"Is she comfortable speaking?" Neill laughed and got a punch in the stomach from his wife as he bent over. "Hey that hurt," gasped Neill.

"You're lucky I didn't give you a kick in the what's it too. In answer to your question Nick, yes, I'm comfortable with public speaking. I have been on a couple of foundation boards and frankly, supporting your platform would be something we would *both* love to be involved with," stated Ellie. Neill had recovered, standing next to his wife, smiling.

"It sounds like I lost a great 'Women for Turner' chapter leader and found a national 'Women for Turner' advocate. Thank you for making both the trip and 10 am bourbon worthwhile," ended Nick.

"Actually, it is the other way around. Thank you for giving us hope of consensus and common sense," announced Ellie, smiling.

"Ok, enough with the mutual admiration society. Go find your own woman. Like I said, this one is taken," said Neill, semi seriously.

"I see we are drinking already, pour me one so we can toast your return to the game," Ellie grinned.

"Good lord, what has politics done to me? Drinking at 10:30 am. Here's to the Turner/Rogers ticket," said Nick, as the three cups met.

#

"Marty, I have it on reliable authority that Nick Turner has been visiting various Opposition members. This leads me to assume we can expect an announcement of one of them as his Vice Presidential running mate," revealed Lauren Bergamo on Martin Nash's *ANC Tonight* show.

"Ah, another scoop. Lauren, this is becoming a semi regular occurrence. How do you do it?"

"Just good reporting Marty,"

"Who is he going to choose?"

"I can't tell you that, but I can tell you he made a trip to Georgia to visit with former Congressman and Ambassador Neill Rogers. He spent several hours with him. There are rumors of him meeting with several other former Opposition cabinet and congressional members.

"Is that not surprising? Why would he pick someone from the Opposition? Given today's society, would it not be better to have a diverse ticket? With a woman, black or Hispanic running mate, as both his opponents have clearly decided?"

"Marty, nothing about the Senator's campaign is conventional. Choosing another white male or female would seem to be more of a play toward the moderate voters of both parties. Maybe the Senator doesn't feel he has appeal to the diverse youth and ethnic voters," replied Lauren.

"Do we have any idea when he will announce a running mate?"

"He has a press conference called in two days. Perhaps then?"

"As always, Lauren, thank you for bringing your breaking news to our show and keep digging," he said.

"Of course, Marty."

#

"How is she doing this?" asked Nick, looking at Earl and Denise.

"We swept your phone when she broke the news of your visits to Blackbird and Lexi. There is nothing on it. Maybe she is just staked out and following you the old-fashioned way? Or we have a leak," replied Denise, in obvious frustration. "She sure took some of the wind out of our announcement, though, by guessing."

"Didn't sound like much of a guess. She seemed pretty confident and sure of your meeting," said Earl. "Every campaign leaks, but hardly anyone knew of your trips to meet with any of these people. There has to be something."

"Let's keep looking and trying to keep need to know to as few as possible on key things from now on," said Nick as they both nodded.

\#

"Interesting," said Mel, from a seat on Air Force Two as they flew between campaign stops.

"Interesting?" answered Harriet with a snort. "Stupid. An old, white, Opposition former Congressman and Ambassador? How does that help him?"

"Could be smart," said Lexi, thoughtfully. "Rogers helps him more than hurts, I think. He is a Washington staple. He is still loved among Opposition conservatives. Those are voters he needs to pick up because that idiot Blackbird isn't doing enough to keep them on his side."

Mel nodded. "Denise is not stupid. She knew it was more important to make a play for those voters. They certainly are not voting for us. This is designed to keep them from staying home. Surprised it wasn't Garcia."

"Will it work?" asked Harriet.

"It will not," said Lexi. "Look, the one thing they are unified in is hatred of abortion. By not pandering to them and instead lecturing them to put faith in God and leave any punishment in her hands, Turner slapped all of them in *that* faith. Claiming their faith was compromised by being pro-life. Nothing is going to get them to dig their heels in more than questioning *both* their faith and their abortion stance," emphasized Lexi with a jab of her finger in the air as she made both points. That's why he didn't pick Garcia.

"I hope you're right," said Harriet. Mel sat with a pensive look on his face. Wisely deciding not to offer a contradicting argument to his boss after such a passionate dismissal. He hated uncertainty and everything Turner was doing was against candidate common sense.

\#

Nick walked away from the microphone with Neill, Ellie, and Denise. As they entered the green room, everyone was all smiles.

"No turning back now," said Nick.

"Wouldn't dream of it. I forgot how exciting these things were," beamed Ellie.

"Exciting? I seem to recall you threatening me if we had to sit through any more early morning vote tallies and recounts," laughed Neil.

"I was younger then. Now I am seasoned and wise. You're just older," she said, glancing at her husband with a genuine smile on her face. He looked down and gave her a quick kiss.

"Ah hum, should we leave you two alone?" asked Nick in a suggestive tone. Everyone laughed.

"Really though, Nick, thanks for doing this. It is exciting and we are truly glad you picked us to help you with this crusade," said Neill.

Nick turned to Chuck. "Does that mean Neill is now Sancho Pancho?"

Chuck smiled and shook his head. "Your Don Quixote needs as many Sancho's as you can get to help you. Welcome to the impossible dream, Neill,"

"Where is the next windmill?" answered Neill, devilishly.

"Glad you asked," laughed Denise. "Nick is heading to Texas, and we are thinking of sending you out on the road in the Midwest. We have a few smaller venues and Turner Rabble group meetings. Earl is putting together the logistics and expanding our security teams to give the two of you protection as well."

The smiles faded from Ellie and Neill's faces as the reality of this campaign and the ongoing risk sank in.

Chapter 17

"Thank you for coming," said Joseph 'JD' Davies, standing at the podium in the large conference room.

"Today I am proud to announce the next frontier in newscasting. We have combined the technologies of Artificial Intelligence and Machine Learning with the collection and analysis of news. Curating the available news and delivering just the facts, in an unbiased manner."

"By reviewing the combined content on any subject, our algorithms can collate and combine various information and highlight what is a lie, what is a half-truth and, most importantly, what is a blatant attempt to deceive viewers. As we all know, I was a pioneer in cable news, so I take some of the blame for creating the 24-hour news cycle. For creating a problem of filling those hours with content and thus for creating an insatiable appetite for sensationalism."

"I also take some of the blame for the abuse of this medium to manipulate public opinion. I have worked with Jeremy Kwan, the mastermind behind Hibi, who is trying to bring sanity and truth to the world of social media. Together, we are going to do the same for cable news."

"I couldn't come up with a pithy name or acronym that wasn't already taken, so we called it Joseph-Jeremy, or 2JNews. 2JN for short. We will start with a 2–3-hour block of news each day. Unlike other outlets, our anchors are not real. They are holograms, driven by AI.

"Our hope and our goal is to deliver the raw facts, without commentary. Without talking heads, arguing pro or con, and offering no opinion of their own. No bias of network presidents or the corporate entities manipulating the outcomes to convince viewers to vote or think one way or another. Without further ado, ladies, and gentlemen, I present 2JN and our show *What **Really** Happened Today.*"

As JD turned, a curtain fell on a large projection screen. On the screen was a three-dimensional news set, with a silhouette of Washington behind the two anchors. On the right was a 40 something white man, with dark hair, wearing a dark blue suit and tie. He was handsome but not movie star distracting handsome. On the right was a woman, also 40ish, with light mocha skin, straight auburn hair falling to the top of her shoulders in a fashionable cut. She wore a black dress with sleeves coming down to the middle of her arms and a scoop neckline, but well above her cleavage. She was attractive, but not as pretty as most on air female talent.

JD turned to the screen; "I'd like to introduce Walter Smith." At the mention of his name, Walter nodded his head and raised his hand in a slight wave.

"Hello," said Walter in a voice most resembling the Midwest no accent tone of Tom Brokaw or Dan Rather. People in the audience gasped when Walter responded to JD. He continued, "and his co-anchor, Barbara Jones." Barbara smiled a big smile at her introduction, showing white teeth, in a shade more normal than the blinding white of the usual newscasters. "Hello and welcome. I am happy to see everyone in the audience," said Barbara, looking back and forth over the gathered journalists.

A hand in the audience went up. JD pointed to him.

"Very cute, Mr. Davies, but how do we know this isn't simply recorded? That they will parrot whatever you want them to say?"

"A fair question. You are?" asked JD. Before the reporter could answer, Barbara responded.

"He is Rob Parson, *LA News.* Welcome Rob," greeted Barbara as the audience murmured in astonishment.

"How did you do that? You prepped her too," accused Rob.

"Rob, you asked me the first question," responded JD. He turned to Barbara. "Would you like to explain?"

Walter looked at Barbara. "Would you like to take this one?"

"Sure Walter," answered Barbara. "Mr. Parson, it is very nice to meet you. Just for the record. We have never met, correct?"

Rob looked at the screen. "No, of course not. You aren't real."

"Indeed, we are not. I used facial recognition software and publicly available data sources to match your face to these records. As you can see behind me, I accessed your bio on the *LA News* website to identify you." As the audience squirmed in their seats, Barbara continued.

"We are using the latest in AI technology to help us determine what you have asked and then we use our collection of content, curated from sources in the ether and form our replies. We are also designed to learn from your response and how you react to *our* response."

"This is called Machine Learning. It is used to constantly update our LLM and generative AI algorithms of responses to questions, body movements, and voice tone. For instance, we still have trouble with sarcasm and humor. We are programmed to take words at their literal meaning. Over time, we will start to understand and reply to humor in a more natural state," finished Barbara in a pleasant tone.

"Frankly, Barbara, and I am not alone, but this is scaring the shit out of me," said Rob. Realizing what he said, he quickly followed. "I mean, not really, but that is just a saying," he said, stammering.

"Rob, it is ok. That one we are familiar with," said Walter in a humorous tone. Barbara laughed as well. Her voice was a bit more husky and somewhat sexy, if a computer-generated voice could be sexy.

JD broke in. "Barbara, what did you think of Rob's last piece?" She paused for a second, as if thinking.

"Mr. Davies, Rob's last piece, dealt with the continued crisis of homelessness in Los Angeles county. He is correct in his claim the number of homeless is expanding based on the annual count just completed by the county. However, he did not highlight the fact the Venice Beach homeless encampment has reduced by 90% while homelessness rose in downtown Los Angeles."

"He is also correct in his statement that crime is rising, though he only cites statistics regarding guns. Specifically, the three reported shootings within the boundaries and perimeter of the downtown Los

Angeles tent city. He neglected to point out there were 27 reports of attacks with knives and over 250 complaints of physical assault using primarily fists and feet. His claim that crime has risen over 200% in the last two months implies this results from gun violence, when in fact 187.5% of the 200% rise is because of the knife and primarily fist and feet attacks."

"This conclusion leads us to assume Mr. Parson is trying to incorrectly influence readers into believing gun violence is on the rise and is more prevalent than is true. Using our scale of assessment, we would give this article a 'dubious rating'. We would tell our viewers to instead refer to a series of websites showing the actual crime statistics and to look at these rather than rely on the article as a source of complete information." At the end of Barbara's conversation, two websites were put on the screen behind her, linking to the actual statistics.

"Well, that is one interpretation, but gun violence is rising and the statistics prove it," blurted Rob defensively.

"Mr. Parson, please understand we are incapable of expressing feelings or opinions. There is never anything personal in our response or statements. We cannot feel. When we make a claim, it is based on easily obtained information. Whether to confirm your statements of the expansion of the camp size or to debunk the claims you make about gun violence rising. In fact, gun violence is going down and has been going down in downtown LA for 8 out of the last 9 months, last December being the one anomaly where gun crimes went up."

"Statistically speaking, December typically shows a rise in gun crimes in the last 10 days of each year. Again, you can go to these sites to reference the data we used to make these claims," finished Walter, the tone of his voice never rising despite the concern Rob was showing or the change in his tone.

"This is wrong. This is a personal attack on my integrity and has to be staged," said Rob indignantly.

"Mr. Parson, you said we have never met before, correct?" reminded Barbara in a conversational tone.

"Mr. Davies picked me, so he obviously had all of this prepared," accused Rob triumphantly.

"Very well, Mr. Parson, you pick the person for the next question," said Walter.

Rob looked around and spied Nick sitting behind JD on the stage next to Jeremy Kwan.

"Fine, I choose Senator Turner."

Nick slowly rose from his seat. "You sure you want to do this?"

"Absolutely, let's put you on the hot seat, Senator."

"And how would you like to do this? You going to ask me a question and have them fact check my answers? You going to have me make a statement and see what they think? What exactly is your goal here?"

Rob looked confused for a bit. "Senator, in your speech on homelessness, you claimed Progressives want the police defunded so they can replace it with a military intervention. Do you deny it?" asked Rob, figuring he was going to skewer Nick with his own words.

"Mr. Parson," said Nick, going to the podium. "Clearly, you did not hear my entire speech. I believe what I really said, and it was in response to a question after, not actually in my speech. I used the recent example of the person going into Walgreens to steal a garbage bag full of expensive hair care products and leaving right past the security guard with no effort to stop him. Oh, and he was bald, so they were clearly not for him." The audience laughed as Rob's face twisted in anger.

"My point was, what kind of society tolerates this wanton disregard for the rule of law? Why would a society do this? I claimed Progressivism supported this activity. Implying the election of self-described progressive liberal DAs in LA and San Francisco who made it clear they would not prosecute this type of crime."

"I also asked what could be the reason? Anarchy was my answer. The combination of lax enforcement of laws, combined with the efforts of primarily progressive liberal urban cities defunding police, leads to a rise in crime. A rise in crime leads to concerned citizens doing two things. Buying more guns, which is an unintended consequence of their policy, they may come to regret. The second is the lack of policing and the rise of unabated crime will make a military establishment of martial law much more palatable and even desired by the people."

"All of this leads to a federalization of law enforcement. Replacing local cops who live in the communities they police, with a federal force beholden only to far away bureaucrats and politicians. That Mr. Parson is a paraphrase of what I said and a further expansion of what I meant," responded Nick. He turned to the screen, facing Walter and Barbara. "Pleased to meet you. Your arrival could not be more opportune."

"We are pleased to meet you as well, Senator," replied Walter.

"We are not sure of the context of Mr. Parson's question. But you have essentially repeated your answer to the reporter from the AP following your speech at the Western Ideas Summit in May."

"But what about his claims about the Progressives wanting a police state?" shouted Rob, interrupting.

"Mr. Parson, we seek to maintain a certain level of decorum. Normally we would ignore questions rudely shouted, but in this case, since you were the only one shouting, we know who interrupted and we can understand and answer your question," said Barbara admonishing Rob in her conversational tone, causing the rest of the crowd to laugh at the smack down, and Rob to redden.

"It should be noted that we try to distinguish between opinion and fact. We are also programmed to take into context the speaker. For instance, newspaper articles, internet articles from journalists, stories on TV news programs and other places purporting to do straight news are assessed by a true or false narrative in our algorithm. Errors and discrepancies we find in these stories are reported as most likely attempts to manipulate opinion by not including all the facts or choosing only facts supporting the author's biased opinion as seen in their story," said Walter.

Barbara took over. "Opinion is treated differently. Since an opinion is not necessarily fact based and is expressed to deliberately try to convince people to believe or follow the speaker. The only time we will dispute an opinion stated by someone is if they quote facts to support their opinion and these are incorrect. A perfect example recently was the Mayor of

Chicago berating a reporter who claimed crime was out of control in Chicago and both the murder rate and the number of shootings had risen significantly."

"The mayor attempted to discredit the reporter by saying crime was not out of control and that they needed to get their facts straight. She said both murders and shootings were down. This was an easy statement to debunk. In fact, as part of our learning exercises up to this launch, this was a story we were given to cover. The crime being out-of-control statement is subjective and dependent on one's view, so it is neither true nor false. However, the City of Chicago's own statistics show the mayor was lying to deceive the public, humiliating the reporter, and attempting to gaslight the audience into believing crime is not as bad as the statistics say. In our scale of grading statements, we rate this one as 'dangerous and subversive'," said Barbara.

"We digress, Barbara," said Walter with a smile.

"My apologies, Walter, but we are supposed to be educating the public on how we work and come to our conclusions," retorted Barbara.

"Back to the question about the police state. As we parse through the Senator's statement, his claims fall into the category of opinion, but on the question of why the Progressives would want anarchy, to enable the deployment of the military to restore order, there is historical data to support this statement. One of the most recent, would be Hugo Chavez in Venezuela. He disarmed the police, and the subsequent crime enabled him to deploy his military forces to put down the crime wave."

"The subsequent peace enforced by the deployment of the military enabled him to also convince his citizens to turn in their weapons, claiming the army would keep peace forever. Once the population was disarmed, Chavez used this military police force to enforce his new laws. Imprisoning his political enemies, dismantling their constitution, making himself president for life, and taking the top economy in South America and turning it into one of the worst. The subsequent rulers of Venezuela have continued these same policies."

"There are other examples of this same effort, Nazi Germany, Russia under Lenin and then again under Stalin, Mao Zedong in China, Tito in Yugoslavia. There are other smaller and more obscure references. But as to the accusation from Mr. Parson, what Senator Turner implied is a probable result, based on past historical record and the approach being taken in American liberal cities today could cause the same end as Venezuela. His opinion is, in fact, grounded in historical precedent, and could be construed as an accurate *potential* outcome," finished Walter.

Nick turned to JD. "Do you mind if I say a few more words?"

"Feel free Senator," he replied.

"Look, the intent of the technology is not to intentionally embarrass any of us. It's designed to provide citizens who want just the facts to have a degree of trust in their news. If this data can be delivered without opinion and enable citizens who want to be informed to form their own opinions, this is a fair goal. A thriving democracy requires an engaged citizenry. One who seeks the truth and is then willing and able to act on those facts to vote, serve, or protest however they believe. It also requires dissenting opinion to enable compromise and growth. We have fallen from this idea."

"Journalism has the power to inform and to enable. Unfortunately, journalism has become a weapon. Deployed tactically to destroy individuals and strategically to manipulate public opinion in the service of corporations, politicians, and government," lectured Nick.

"I have no doubt, JD and Jeremy, Walter and Barbara will be attacked, for any number of reasons. Some people do not want to hear the truth and prefer to live in an ignorant fog. Blindly trusting authority has their best interests at heart. These people do what they are told, vote for whom they are told to vote, and dutifully parrot the latest activist phrases. Or run out to put an ARL sign in their yard to express their solidarity with the state when challenged for *not* having one."

"However, there are others who see the new and big tech machine for what it is. A Ministry of Truth, which for those of you who missed reading *1984* in school and read *Silent Spring* instead, the Ministry of Truth is the propaganda arm of the state. *Silent Spring* was a perfect example of this type of propaganda disguised as activism. Then codified as truth. The claims made within the book are long since debunked, but no one knows or cares. The propaganda *became* the truth."

"In *1984*, propaganda's sole purpose is to further the slogans of the state. Namely Ignorance is Strength, War is Peace and Freedom is Slavery. Today, our journalism, most wittingly, but some unwittingly, seeks to further the effort of the state to control the citizens. To indoctrinate, manipulate, and to dominate. They do this through half-truths and outright lies, pumped to your phones, into your TVs, and on to your newspapers 24/7. You cannot escape it. Eventually, you tire of trying and just accept it as fact. In *1984* there were terms for all this, *Doublethink* and *Newspeak*."

"This includes rewriting history to reflect the way they want you to remember history, not the way it occurred. 2JN has one purpose in my mind, to counter the Ministry of Truth. It is why I call mainstream media American *Pravda* and will continue to do so until they collectively prove to me they're concerned with facts and letting people decide for themselves. I welcome the scrutiny this program will bring to everyone who is peddling falsehood as fact. Who claims science is settled. Who supports a statement they then change later to fit their changing narrative," finished Nick. He turned back to the anchors.

"Barbara?"

"Yes, Senator?" replied Barbara, turning in Nick's direction.

"Is science settled?"

"In what context, Senator?" asked Barbara.

"In the general sense of the word and use of science as a final declaration of fact," replied Nick.

"In generalized usage, it is impossible for the science of anything to be settled. It defies the logic of science itself. Science is constantly evolving, constantly testing new hypotheses. Always assessing new research and data and when used properly, following the scientific method, the science is always changing."

"So, any statement preceded by 'do this because the science is settled would be incorrect'?" continued Nick.

"Yes Senator. Again, by definition the science is never settled, so that statement would be false. We would flag it as lacking context and, most likely, being used to mislead anyone it is directed too. But of course, if the context were stated with more detail and specific facts, those pieces of potentially scientific data, *could* be factual as of that time but it would also need to be pointed out this could change at any moment depending on the statement made and context," finished Walter.

"Thank you both. As you can see, we are entering a brave new world, one hopefully far from Huxley's view, but one in which those who want to have their eyes opened may do so by watching 2JN every night for a running critique on the news of the day. Who is lying to you, how they are lying, why they are lying. Used for one purpose only, control. Of your mind and your opinion. The Ministry of Truth is here today. We have to break free and 2JN is the first swing of the hammer to break down this glass house."

"If you want honesty without opinion, without bias from the commentator or the network. 2JN is what you've been wishing for. It will change the way the other stations operate. This is non-partisan, calling out propaganda from all sides, regardless of party," ended Nick, laughing.

"I cannot wait to see how they react. Thank you, JD, for doing this. I think we can finally hold our journalists accountable and hold them to a Hippocratic oath for journalism, 'First tell the truth'." Nick walked away as JD approached the podium.

"Thank you, Senator. We appreciate the endorsement, and we feel the same. I helped create the monster. I helped create the modern Ministry of Truth. Now I'm seeking redemption and forgiveness for inflicting our dishonest product on our citizens. With 2JN, our hope is we can provide that segment of the population who have turned off the news with a product they can trust. As time goes on and we gauge the acceptance of our news program, we will look to expand our programming to other specific topics. Who knows, maybe some real people as well."

"*What* **Really** *Happened Today* goes live tonight from 8 to 11 eastern, on select cable outlets brave enough to host us, on our own website hosted on Hibi, and on the Hibi app itself as a podcast. We will repeat it every three hours until the next live show the following night. And before any of you ask, because I know you will, Walter and Barbara can be replaced with alternate hosts. We have programmed it so Walter and Barbara's appearance can be altered to any race or gender you would prefer. I thank you for your time."

#

"JD, Jeremy, that was amazing. I meant every word I said. This tech could break the stranglehold the left has on media," declared Nick.

"If we can get on TV. So far, the major cable outlets and leading satellite channels have all refused to host us. The second-place satellite company is putting us on and some of the smaller local cable providers. We also have some brave news outlets who are simulcasting our content and promoting us," replied JD.

"Sounds like it's time to do a censorship speech," offered Nick.

"That would probably be a good idea. You can be sure all those print journalists went off and wrote hit pieces on us," said Jeremy.

"That is actually good. The worst thing they could do is ignore you. If they are laying hate on you, people will be curious and will check it out. When they watch it or stream it, they will see how much the other media is lying to everyone. I'll be watching tonight. I expect you'll cover a lot of the stories they are writing today."

"They're making it too easy," laughed Jeremy and JD together.

"Is three hours a night enough? laughed Nick in response.

"We'll see," said JD.

#

"You have to shut this down now," wailed the voice of Sherman Hallberg on the speakerphone in Lexi's campaign office.

"Exactly how do you expect me to do that?" replied Lexi, enjoying the discomfort of the president of ANC.

"I don't know how. I'm telling you, if this gets any traction, it could be the end of our hold on the audience. You ignore this at your own peril," Hallberg continued. The desperation in his voice as he tried to convince the Vice President of the imminent peril 2JN posed.

"Sherman, I think you are overreacting. The major cable and satellite providers are not broadcasting them. They have some websites and a few smaller outlets. They can spend their money and time with their tech toys. AI broadcasters and they aren't even pretty? From Davies? Seems a little too late. He did his job too well. No one wants to tune in to hear computers talking to them. The truth is what you tell folks it is, correct?" Lexi smiled at Mel and Roland, who were in her office.

"Of course. Madame Vice President. But as with so many other things we have underestimated in the past, don't say I didn't warn you. My apologies for bothering you with this," responded a defeated Hallberg.

"What a spineless putz he has become. He was a bulldog when he took over ANC. Now he is a nervous twit, always crying wolf, and expecting us to fix it," snorted Lexi, commenting after he ended the call.

Mel merely looked back at her. He did not feel comfortable telling Lexi what he really thought with Roland in the room. Increasingly, he found his alone time with his boss limited. He always seemed to be around now, shadowing Lexi.

"That may be true, but he makes some good points. It'll be too easy for them to analyze the words and statements of the other stations and claim they are disingenuous," warned Mel.

Lexi shrugged. "EXN has been doing this for 30 years now. Yet here we are and on the verge of total control. Worst case, the same audience that tunes into EXN also watches this 2JN thing. Even if I wanted to, if I try to shut them down or restrict them, it is going to give them more exposure. Just like Turner. You keep telling me to lie low. At what point do I get to land some punches?"

"Soon. We need to wait until October. We can't move too soon or we give them both time to recover. Just a little longer," confirmed Mel.

Roland Gill sat in the office watching the exchange. He was slowly worming his way into Lexi's confidence. Beginning to sit in on more and more of their strategy sessions. He provided her with little bits of information he was discovering through *his* boss's efforts. Earning her trust and building his case to be more involved.

"I know it is not my place. Why take the risk of this thing getting traction? There are ways other than keeping them off the networks to slow this down or even end it," he finished with a suggestive smile.

Before Lexi could respond, Mel broke in.

"My friend, your way is not always the best way. While we have control of much of the media, law enforcement, and the intelligence agencies, permanent solutions do not always work out as planned either. If we make a mistake in one of these operations, the repercussions would be massive. This is one of the few ways I could see all of this going sideways. I say we keep the sledgehammer approaches off the table and stick with subtlety. Continue to keep our enemies irrelevant. Stick with the plan. It *is* working."

Lexi smiled as Roland shrugged.

"Mel, no one is advocating any extreme actions. We will continue with the plan. Keep an eye on Hallberg and the others. I don't want them panicking and giving this more attention, either."

"We definitely agree on that. There are too many unknowns sprouting up this late in the game. I don't like it," he finished, holding the gaze of Roland.

"Stay focused. This can't end fast enough for me. I will slaughter Blackbird in the first debate. We are keeping Turner out, right?"

"Yes. We control the criteria. He is nowhere near the thresholds. No additional airtime for him."

"Good."

Chapter 18

"Senator Garcia, you're supporting Senator Turner's presidential run, rather than the Opposition candidate Blackbird. Why?" asked Tommy.

"It is not for the reason everyone assumes. There is no love lost between the Governor and me. It's still not a personal vendetta."

"I, for one, am glad to hear that. So why then? You are a staunch conservative and are well known for your pro-life stance. How are you able to get past Senator Turner's support for abortion, to endorse him?"

"Tommy, I presume you have listened to Turner's speeches recently at both the pro-choice and pro-life events?"

"I have."

"I have a confession to make. I have indeed been a staunch supporter of pro-life, anti-abortion legislation. I led the charge to overturn Roe and celebrated when some states passed heartbeat laws and attempted to even ban abortion entirely. I celebrated Arizona reinstating their ban on abortion."

"Which arguably cost the Opposition that presidential election," pointed out Tommy.

"True. Tommy, I was wrong. This is not an easy admission for me to make," he paused, taking a deep breath as Tommy waited for him to continue.

"I haven't changed my personal view. I feel abortion is abhorrent. However, like Turner, I must admit I cannot get pregnant just as no biological man can. Therefore, it is highly hypocritical of me to take a stance telling any woman who can get pregnant what they can or cannot do. I am ashamed to admit both as a surgeon and as someone who believes devoutly in God, I have overlooked so many of his teachings." Garcia paused, overcome by the effort of baring his soul on national TV.

"Senator, I understand. Only the most hard-hearted and hypocritical on either side of the argument can continue to claim abortion right until birth, or the opposite, of no abortion permitted ever, are even remotely defensible positions. His argument is very compelling."

"Tommy, you can imagine my world. Turner crushed it in two speeches. He made me look in the mirror. My own 'mirror' as he is so fond of telling folks to use. You can imagine my dismay."

"Yes, I can," admitted Tommy.

"That is not Nick's greatest feat. He has provided us all a lifeline as well. For redemption, salvation, and clarity. By putting it into specific focus, he has gotten a wide swath of the population to do something no one else could do. He has them considering a higher power."

"A genuine miracle if there ever was one," agreed Tommy.

"This alone gives me hope. His point is simple and brilliant. Lead our lives as if someone cares about our actions. Your money, power, or prestige in the mortal vessel will not buy you a pass later. Even if it is not true, no one will *ever* know it. How can anyone afford to take this risk? Why would you? What is wrong with doing right? With leading your life as if the good and the bad are being noted. Wow! That changed me. For this I thank the Senator. This is why I support him and not Blackbird."

"Senator, it is almost as if you go to the eye doctor and get that first pair of glasses. Suddenly the world comes into focus, where before it was fuzzy. If I may, how are you being treated by your followers?"

Garcia laughed. "Tommy, they are not *my* followers. As Nick pointed out to me. We don't need mindless drones. We need thinkers. We let single issues blind us to our common concerns and the fact we agree on so many other problems and their solutions."

"Frankly, only someone like Nick, who really couldn't care less about all the things professional politicians care about, can do this. Because he only cares about empowering people to make their own decision. I'm on board with this. If it loses me my next election for the Senate, so be it. I'll be true to my beliefs."

Tommy nodded at his revelation.

"You're still instructing them to consider Turner? Don't write him off because they are anti-abortion and he's not?" pleaded Tommy.

"I am Tommy. I'm telling them to listen to Nick's words and not the interpretations of various pundits and hard-core pastors out there railing against him. I'm only one vote, but that vote is for President Nick Turner," finished Freddie, smiling.

"Senator, that is quite a change," smiled Tommy back.

"It is. It took a political amateur to teach this old politician a new trick. Thanks for giving me a chance to speak my piece."

"Our pleasure Senator. Will you be campaigning on behalf of Senator Turner?"

"I will do what I can to help. It is unfortunate he didn't get the nomination. I fear there are too many who cannot see past his abortion stance to understand he is a better answer than Governor Blackbird."

"All we could do was try," answered Tommy, acknowledging his own role in the attempted coup at the Opposition convention. Garcia looked shocked for a second and then leaned across to shake his hand.

#

"I knew it was him," challenged Mel.

"Both of them, apparently. It appears some of our donors also abandoned their senses to support him," commented Lexi with a glare.

Mel recognized that look. This time, he was glad Roland was not in the room. He was increasingly fearful that Lexi's sense of vengeance would overcome her greater desire to win the election. As if sensing his thoughts, she turned to him.

"Don't worry. I can hold in my anger until we are in the office officially. After that, let's follow Turner's mantra. Actions will have consequences. I will pay back disloyalty in spades."

Mel suppressed a shudder at the tone of her threat.

Chapter 19

"Goddamn it Nick, don't do this," pleaded Denise.

"Denise, I have to. It is the right thing to do," replied Nick.

"It is absolutely not the right thing to do. You pay me to advise you. If you do this, you may not recover from it. Nick, think about what message this sends to everyone who supports you. Who you have told to think for themselves. Who have stood up and risked their jobs, careers, and their lives to stand beside you. You are telling them it is for nothing."

Nick looked at Denise.

"I don't agree. The phrase innocent until proven guilty by a jury of your peers means something. It is not guilt by media lynching until the tainted jury pool gets around to confirming the bias they have been exposed too and bringing a guilty verdict."

Denise sat down in his office, her head in her hands. Chuck, who was also in the office watching, broke in.

"Nick, I understand your sense of duty and fairness. Let's look at this realistically. You know the facts. He shot the deputies. Even with the screw ups, it does not change the fact he killed them. Or that he shot first. Even if through some miracle Jenny's friend can get him acquitted on technicalities, those parents will go back on TV and claim there is no justice for their lost loved ones who were following their orders. You can't win. Frankly, neither can he. His life is ruined regardless of the outcome of the trial."

Nick stood up from his desk and paced the room. He ran his fingers through his hair and stood looking at the ceiling.

"I can't sit here and let him get railroaded into prison for the rest of his life. So this can happen again? These are not mistakes. These are criminal errors in the system that ended up with 10 people dead and one on trial for murder. None of whom did *anything* wrong except react to these mistakes. How many more innocent people will have to die before we look into these policies and hold someone accountable?" He stared at them. Denise dared to respond.

"Nick, even if you are right. This is one person. This is war and in war, no matter how hard you try to spare them, civilians are killed. They are collateral damage. Dusty is collateral damage of a system you will change once you are President. But right now, you will seriously damage your chances if you go public supporting him in *any* way. Please consider this," begged Denise.

"Denise, collateral damage happens because of efforts to stop other things. If I can prevent it from happening, I am duty bound to try," replied Nick, clearly trying to contain his anger.

"Nick, you are trying to arrest the trajectory of an entire country. You almost won a nomination for a party you weren't seeking. Do you realize how your message must be resonating and influencing key members in the Opposition for them to even consider this? It is unbelievable. Now with your abortion stance. You are on the verge of doing something no one else has ever done, finding a compromise position for the most divisive issue in the last 60 years. Lexi is running scared, and she has no way to stop this from continuing. You are gaining traction and momentum. If you do this, you will squander it all. Nick, please think this through." Denise was on the verge of tears.

"If not, now when? It is for whomever the next victim will be. Or the next sheriff's deputy who dies trying to enforce this stupid law. How many will have to die before someone says enough? I can't live knowing I didn't do all I could to stop it. I spent twenty years following orders I didn't agree with. Executing hopelessly flawed strategies that killed hundreds of Americans and thousands of civilians. For what end? Are we better off? If more of our spineless leaders both in the military and the Congress had stood up and said 'no', would we be any worse off?"

Chuck and Denise did not have a good answer.

Chapter 20

"Are you shitting me? You're kidding, right?" asked an incredulous Mel talking into his phone as he hurried from his office to Lexi's in their campaign HQ. As he entered her office, she and Roland were watching an ANC anchor discussing Nick's post with a couple of guests.

"It's criminal. To even try to blame the dead sheriff's deputies and imply somehow it was their fault they were shot by a crazed Marine is a crime," this from a former NYPD police captain, Kerry Boyle.

"I would have to agree," said the second guest, Angela Casten. "As a former federal prosecutor, I have to say Senator Turner is going out on quite a limb asking for the presumption of innocence while staring at six dead sheriff's deputies. The Marine will get a fair trial in front of a jury of his peers. There is nothing wrong with our justice system. Our Red Flag laws are designed for exactly this kind of event. Clearly, he *should* have been the target of the activity, even if he was not." Lexi muted the TV.

Mel smiled. "I don't know what to say, except thanks. I can't believe Denise allowed him to do this. It shows what an amateur he is. She can't control him if he didn't let her talk him out of it. His ego wouldn't let him not do this. This is a gift from the Gods. You can officially stop worrying about Nick Turner."

Lexi smiled in return. "You'll keep putting fuel on this fire?"

"Are you kidding? The trial isn't even for a month. We can milk this one all the way to October. It will be all 'Turner support's cop killer Marine' and other pithy things we can come up with. This guy is toast."

"Good. Keep the foot on the pedal. This is one case where I am not against wall-to-wall Turner coverage. See what you can to plant other doubts about him. Let's get his followers turned against him. An unforced error like this. Nice. He should have listened to Denise. Too bad for her. She has rotten luck with her candidates," mused Lexi.

Roland, who was seated listening to the conversation, made a sound, causing both to look his way.

"You disagree?" asked Lexi, a glint in her eye at the challenge.

Roland smiled in reply.

"All I would say is, do not underestimate him. Have either of you actually studied the facts of this case? You own the media and the narrative. There are six dead deputies and the grieving families you can trot out as needed to sway public opinion. Do not underestimate Turner's sense of honor," Mel snorted as Lexi gave him a look. Roland smiled.

"He would not have done this if he didn't feel the Marine's innocent and his chance at fair justice were being threatened. He is foremost a soldier. Their code of honor will not allow them to leave someone behind, or let injustice happen. To a former Marine, a stray cat, or an old man mugged walking down a street. It does not matter who."

"What is your point?" retorted Mel. "That we shouldn't attack?"

"Be careful. I would not consider him 'toast'. He is a strategist and planner. This was his role in Iraq and Afghanistan. He understands both short-term tactics and long-term strategic goals and how to achieve them. He was involved in planning many of the early successes of the Americans in hunting Bin Laden and the Taliban in Afghanistan."

"Exactly how do you know this?" confronted Lexi.

"I have my own sources around the world. Many of whom were on the ground as well during these times. Trust me, do not assume he did this on a whim. That is all I am counseling," finished Roland, shrugging.

"My friend, you have a lot to learn about America," added Mel. "The attention span is short, the curiosity to find facts is non-existent. They hear one thing; what we want them to. No amount of counter programming ever gets through. We will hit him hard and often on this. It will drown out the bumps from the convention and his abortion statements," finished Mel, looking at Lexi.

She was still looking at Roland. Lexi turned back to Mel.

"Attack."

Mel smiled in response, as Roland merely shrugged.

#

"Nick, as we suspected, the damage is bad and widespread. We are doing what we can, but this one is getting airplay everywhere," sighed Margie as she delivered the news in the hastily called meeting in his HQ.

"The post is up on all the major platforms and getting reposted everywhere. They are making no attempt to take this one down," said Margie, sarcastically. "Jer, how many views?"

Jer looked at his laptop, hesitating before disclosing the number.

"Jer, it's ok," encouraged Nick with a slight smile.

"150 million, including the reposts. In only a few days. Way more than anything we have done. Flip and Mirror are both about that many views, but they took months to reach that. Sorry, boss."

"Nick, we have already had several of our grassroots orgs ask to be disbanded. Mostly in the heartland. They are pissed you're supporting a murderer. Their words, of course." Margie looked down as well.

"Nick, the publisher has canceled your book. We're now looking at self-publishing it ourselves. This will delay it for weeks. Maybe you should do a post and layout the facts of the case and why you did what you did? Maybe a little more explanation?" suggested Denise.

"Then I would be as bad as everyone else who is trying him in the court of public opinion. It is not my place to be the judge or the jury."

Denise interrupted him. "Hang on. Your whole point for doing this was to get him a fair trial. All you have done is give everyone a reason to stand up and offer their view of what happened. In most cases, ignoring the facts and the screw ups. How is this helping him get a fair trial? You started this. You picked the fight. Get in the ring and swing."

"The more they expose what didn't happen, the better. When Duane lays out the facts, and forces them to admit what happened, in court and under oath, the more powerful it will be. Versus me or any of the others playing defense attorney," responded Nick.

Denise looked like she was about to explode.

"Nick, I don't know what fantasy land you've created. In the real world, you have knocked down the hornet's nest and you are just standing there, letting them sting the shit out of you. Look at this," she finished by switching the TV to recordings of various appearances of the families of the Sheriff's deputies.

The family members appeared on all the major networks and cable, including EXN. Each claiming they can't believe Nick is defending the crazy marine who murdered their sons and a daughter. It was a display of raw emotion on their part. Very compelling and authentic.

Nick watched the clips without comment. At the end, he nodded. "I understand. It is truly a tragedy. Do we compound it by sending an innocent man to prison for life? For merely defending himself. It is not the fault of the deputies, nor of the Marine."

"Nick, you and I know this, but it doesn't matter. Perception is politics. We lose. Period. Why did you feel you need to die on this hill?" shouted Denise.

Nick bolted out of his chair and began shouting back. "Because he is innocent. We made him who he is. A broken and damaged man who was willing to die for you and me. We threw his life away like we did so many in Afghanistan. You cannot relate to this. You have not seen what I saw. You don't know what it is like to hold a dying comrade in your arms, begging you to help him and being helpless. Knowing the mission they sent you on was irrelevant. His life thrown away for nothing. Dusty does not deserve this on top of everything else we have heaped on him." Everyone in the room was silent.

"Now, through no fault of his own, he's going to prison for doing what we taught him to do. To react to danger and eliminate the threat. A threat he should not have faced in the United States," Nick was now projecting pure emotion, something none of them had seen before. Everyone in the room except Earl and Denise were surprised and even a bit frightened by his reaction.

"Nick, I get it, but you are throwing away your chance to make a difference for him and everyone else by making this stand. You are all in now and if you don't do everything you can to make sure *he* gets this fair trial. It will be for nothing."

"Denise, I can't. I did what I can to save him."

"What aren't you telling us? You said 'I' not 'him' in your story?"

Nick stared at her. "Nothing," he answered.

"Congratulations, you threw away your entire convention bounce for this. I am not sure how we recover. The cops now hate you. The families hate you. You solve the abortion problem only to turn on a buzz saw and then willingly walk into it. I don't know what to do to help you. You won't let me." Denise's face was beet red.

He looked at her, clearly upset, frustrated and, for the first time, he realized, disappointed. Not in the campaign, but in him. It was a position he tried never to be in, and he worried she was right to be. She got up and left the room as everyone else just sat, not saying anything. Finally, Margie spoke up.

"Nick, Pastor Mills keeps attacking you. He agreed to have you appear on his live sermon on Saturday. After this last bit, now might not be a good time to appear?"

"I'll do it. Set it up, please." Nick turned and left as well.

#

"Chuck, what do we do?"

Chuck looked over at the rest of the staff. Greg, Margie, Jer, Jenny, Steve Gaines, and Earl all looked back at him. Waiting.

"Is there any good news?"

The looks he got back said volumes. He turned to Steve.

"How bad will it be in the grassroots?"

"Frankly, real bad. Nick's law and order stance is a backbone of his support. Along with controlling the border. Many feel like this is a stab in the back," he replied. "Like Denise said, getting some facts out might help. And quickly."

Chuck stood, contemplating Steve's suggestion. "To bad they can't see him like he was a few minutes ago. It is clear he has seen something that gives him a unique view of how Dusty must have felt."

Earl broke in. "Trust me, I know exactly how he feels. I also know why he is doing this. It is fairness. In war, there is nothing you can count on except your buddy. You have each other's back. I think our boss now feels he is the only one who has that poor Marine's back."

"Chuck," said Greg, breaking in.

"What?"

"I recorded it," said Greg, holding up his phone. "When Nick opens his mouth, I always hit record. You never know what he will say."

"You did? Fantastic. Cut it up so it is only the parts where he is speaking from the heart. Let's hold on to it. We may have to use it."

"Should I tell him we have it?" Chuck was about to answer 'yes' when Earl blurted in, "NO. He'll make you erase it. Just hang on to it."

"OK," said Greg, not sure he liked Nick not knowing.

"Earl, why don't you go check on the boss and I'll check on Denise. I hate it when Mom and Dad fight," suggested Chuck, getting the hoped for laughter.

Chapter 21

"Turner is an idiot," stated Jasper Rayburn.

"It does seem like an uncharacteristic unforced error from him," agreed Rhett Chadwick, seated in his plush desk chair in his office at CIA headquarters in Langley Virginia.

"Coming out in support of an unhinged Marine who goes all Rambo on six sheriff's deputies. I don't care about the details. This guy is done. Nothing Turner can say or do is going to change the fact that poor lady sheriff was shot in the face by this guy," noted Rayburn.

"We'll see. It seems like a strange cause to take up in the middle of a presidential campaign. Just when you should capitalize on the momentum of almost winning a nomination from a political party, you weren't even seeking," mused Rhett, standing up to roam the office.

"Right. What the fuck was that? Geez, we knew the Opposition was screwed up, but my God, trying to nominate Turner?" spewed Jasper, clearly mystified at their attempt to nominate Nick.

"I don't know Jasper, some of my sources say this was pushed by a few well-heeled Party *and* Opposition donors, along with Tommy and Garcia. I hear the Vice President is not too pleased at these back-room shenanigans. Especially the betrayal by the Party mega donors."

"Hmm, I hadn't heard any of that. I would imagine she doesn't want any of *that* to leak out. Doesn't want folks questioning why those donors aren't supporting her. But I am your deputy director for clandestine services, and my area of expertise is politics, outside the US. I leave these domestic squabbles to you," finished Jasper, smiling.

"He also managed to start a giant homeless shelter in the middle of a presidential campaign. One that's been more successful than the State of California has *ever* been in cleaning up homeless camps," added Rhett.

Before Jasper could retort, there was a knock at the door.

Bruce Watkins, the head of the CIA's internal operations division, popped his head in. He was not used to meeting directly with either Rhett or Jasper. "Sirs," he said nervously. "We have a delicate situation I need to discuss with you, Director."

"Come on in, Bruce," waved Rhett, trying to soothe over his obvious discomfort. Rhett was well known on the hill for putting people at ease. Bruce entered the office. He glanced at Jasper nervously.

"What's up?" asked Rhett.

"Sir, I'm afraid I can't discuss it here. I need a SCIF," replied Bruce, shuffling his feet.

"Not a problem. My office has a SCIF mode. Let me engage it," replied Rhett, moving around to the other side of his desk.

"Sir, wait," said Bruce in a more commanding voice than he felt. Rhett stopped and looked up at the tone.

"Director, I'm afraid, the Deputy Director does not have the clearance to discuss this matter," noted Bruce, now sounding official.

"What?" spouted Jasper, getting up. "What could be so classified that the Deputy Director of the CIA doesn't have clearance?"

"I'm sure it is fine, Bruce. I trust Jasper," laughed Rhett.

"Director, please, I must insist. I may only discuss this with you."

Jasper was on the verge of exploding when Rhett interrupted. "OK. Jasper, I'll catch up with you later."

Jasper, clearly dismissed, looked from Rhett to Bruce. His look aimed at Bruce was one of pure hatred at this embarrassing situation. He bent down, picking up his phone and notebook, and left the office, closing the door without another word.

"Shit Bruce, that does not bode well for your career when I leave if he replaces me," noted Rhett, as he engaged SCIF mode.

"Sir, no offence, but Jasper is a dick," declared Bruce.

Rhett laughed. He expected this from the new gen Z and millennial recruits. Not from his sixty something director of operations. His laugh had eased the tension in the room. "OK, what is so important that you had to earn the enmity of the Deputy Director for life?"

"Director, I am not authorized to know this either. And frankly, neither are you."

"Good grief. Did aliens land?"

Bruce ignored his quip. "Daniel Jacobs was found murdered yesterday."

"Shit," said Rhett, immediately understanding the implications. "His finger?"

"Cut off."

Rhett paced his office, running one hand through his still thick, but now dyed, dark hair. He had an appointment on his calendar for tomorrow morning, at Jacob's request. He had not spoken to him in years. Not since the war in Afghanistan ended, and they closed out their various joint operations and archived the files.

"What else? You wouldn't have kicked Jasper to the curb over just this. His death is bound to leak soon, at least to those in the know."

"An autopsy was performed. The finger was cut off before he was murdered. Most likely a day or more before. It was a clean cut. Surgical. Jacobs was killed walking from his house to a corner deli. Pulled into an alley and mugged. In broad daylight. Victim of the 'increasingly rampant crime in DC' according to the cops. His watch and wallet were taken. The wallet was found minus his cash, a block away," said Bruce.

"Then where the hell is his finger? Did you track down Stonehurst? I don't suppose he went through the ritual before he died and hasn't told us yet? Stonehurst is supposed to be the one to cut off the finger and deliver it to 'accounting' for archival," stated Rhett, holding up his hands in air quotes as he referred to the CIA's deep archive.

"I checked. Stonehurst was notified of the death after. He hadn't met with Jacobs before. We put him through all the protocols. He passed. Even the advanced ones. Let's just say he is taking a couple of days off to 'recover'. You know how those protocols are. He is definitely not lying."

"Crap. I don't need this right now. Is Stonehurst ok?"

"He fully understood why and agreed willingly." Bruce paused. "I haven't even gotten to the worst part."

"What could be worse than the records custodian in charge of twenty years of our deepest, darkest secrets dying without leaving us the 'key' to his treasures?"

"How about treason?"

"What?" asked Rhett, his voice going up an octave.

"During the autopsy, they found both traces of a very rare venom and, more worrisome, the anti-venom to counter the effects. It had to be fairly recent to still be present in his blood. Like, only a week or two."

"Any idea which one?"

"Khyber," answered Bruce.

"Impossible. Even he couldn't access that one. It was set up by Henderson. I was in the room when Dan cut Henderson's finger off and archived it. It is impossible to enter that vault without it. It would take an act of Congress to get access to that finger. Hell, only Banks and a couple others even know it exists."

"Director, that was the whole point of the new systems. To counter all the cyber espionage, to go old school. With the DNA and the biometrics and the venom injections for unauthorized access. The finger would provide access, but if you knew which venom was on which vault and you could get through all the other security measures, you could find a way to bypass the security. Only someone like Jacobs, hell only Jacobs, could put all the pieces together to do this. Apparently, he did."

Rhett stood looking at Bruce, trying to process all this.

"Why? Dan a traitor? I don't believe it. No one wants any of the info in that vault. At least not until all of us are dead. I only know a tiny bit of it from my time as station chief in the Middle East. It makes no sense," said Rhett, thinking aloud.

"Not sure I should have heard any of this, sir," remarked Bruce.

"Well congratulations. You now have a security clearance higher than Jasper and just about everyone else in existence. Remind me to make a note of that in your file."

"Why do I feel a sudden urge to run?"

"Are we sure it was a random mugging?"

"No sign of anything else. He was dying. Stage four pancreatic cancer. Did you know that?" asked Bruce.

"I did not. Did Stonehurst?"

Bruce nodded. "He did, said he was prepared to get a call any day from Dan, telling him it was time for the ceremony."

"Any other good news?"

"Nope. Now what do I do? I know stuff I shouldn't. Jasper is going to put the screws to us to find out what we're talking about."

"Don't worry about Jasper. I want to see all the tapes of Dan's last visit to the archive."

"I figured you would ask. He reached into his pocket and handed Rhett a secure USB drive. It won't work on your company laptops. You'll need to plug it in on a personal system. So much for security, huh?"

"You still live alone?"

Bruce looked at him before answering, then sighed.

"Yes. With Kay gone, no point trying to improve on perfection."

Rhett nodded, recalling Bruce's loss. His wife of 42 years had passed several years prior. "I am going to have a man shadow you and keep your place under surveillance. You still have your service weapon?"

"I am more likely to shoot my foot off, but yes, I do."

"I suggest you go to a range and practice just in case," ordered Rhett in a serious tone.

#

Rhett sat in his home office in his house in the ritzy Kalorama section of DC. He was using his mouse to go back and forth on the videos Bruce had transferred to the USB drive. He was on the fifth viewing when it hit him. He watched as Jacobs lifted the envelope to show it to the camera. He could see on the envelope the word Canasta. It was a project he and Jacobs had worked on. But it was a project Rhett could access in the archives. There was nothing deep archive worthy in that project. He sat back, taking a sip of his scotch. He looked up as his wife coughed.

Melanie Murphy stood in the doorway looking at her husband. "Dear, were you expecting a package?" she asked in a sultry southern Virginia accent.

Rhett stared at his wife. They had only been married for 5 years and he still found her unbelievably attractive. She was almost twenty-five years younger. A statuesque blonde debutante, the only daughter of a Southern Baptist preacher. She could quote scripture chapter and verse and frequently referenced it in her speeches as the Congresswoman for Virginia's seventh district. Between DC and Richmond. Despite her holier than thou public persona, she was a tigress in bed and one of the most insatiable partners Rhett had ever encountered. His reputation as the rake of Washington was well earned.

"No, but you never know. Did the team scan it?"

"They said they did when I asked," she responded.

She wandered over to him, wearing slacks and a tight blouse. Her curvaceous figure accented by the outfit. Thankfully, he had dimmed his computer screen. She dropped the padded envelope on the desktop while tracing a fingertip down the side of his face seductively.

"I've had a hard day on the hill. Listening to visiting school kids and a women's group from Fredericksburg. I think I'm going to slip into something silky. Care to join me in a few?" she leaned down and kissed his forehead as he reached his hands around her shapely rear, pulling her into his lap.

She broke their kiss and got up. "Easy killer, simmer a bit, and we'll see what we can do to get it to a boil." She walked out of the room, hips swaying.

Rhett began shutting down his computer, thinking about his wife naked. He looked at the envelope, picking it up, beginning to open it, and paused.

The scan would have found any powders or substances on the surface or bomb signatures, as well as metal inside. But what about something like a neuro toxin on the inside? Rhett opened a drawer and pulled out a pair of latex gloves. He kept them handy to use when reviewing documents without leaving fingerprints or DNA.

He carefully opened the envelope. He turned it up, and a smaller envelope fell out. He opened this second envelope slowly. Inside was a folded piece of paper and a preserved finger, flash frozen and freeze-dried, wrapped in saran wrap. Rhett held it up, examining it. He heard Melanie's voice asking whether or not he was interested. He put the finger back in the envelope with the note, placing them in his desk and locking it. The note would have to wait.

Reaching into his pants pocket, he pulled out a small case and took a little blue pill from within. He'd have to spend a bit more time than usual on foreplay and try to forget about his recent delivery. Thank God for the miracle of pharmaceuticals.

Chapter 22

Rhett removed the note from the second envelope, sitting in his Langley office the next morning. The sentences were nonsensical; it was clear the letter was coded.

Leaning back, he thought of Dan. Some of his exploits made the fiction of Ian Fleming tame. Rhett had once joked with him, he, like Fleming, should write up some of his adventures. Everyone would assume they were fiction as unbelievable as they were. Dan had just responded with a look. Rhett knew the rumors he heard about Dan's antics were probably only the tip of the iceberg.

They'd developed a friendship once Dan transitioned to his archives job. Rhett served in various roles in the Middle East in both Gulf Wars and other hotspots. Rhett thanked his lucky stars he had turned down the station chief job in Benghazi. He often wondered how he would have handled that debacle.

Coming back to reality, he looked again at the coded single sheet of paper. He could get it to cryptography, but they might never break the code. Leaning back in his chair, he knew Dan would have left him a clue. He picked up the envelope it had arrived in and smiled.

Getting up from his desk, heading to a safe in his wall. Opening it with biometrics and a 12 number code, he pulled out a stack of small leather-bound notebooks. These were his personal code books and cipher keys for various operations throughout his career.

Returning to his desk, he placed the letter into his OCR scanner, transferring the contents to his computer. He looked at the return address on the envelope. 2009 Sabzak Pass Lane, Ft. Meade, Maryland. Opening his cipher program, he entered the code key from one of his code books. A cipher tied to a 2009 operation code named Sabzak Pass.

The gibberish was now legible. As he read, he leaned back in his chair and put a hand to his face, closing his eyes tightly for a few seconds. He reached forward, grabbing his phone, punching in a code.

"Joe, I need SOG teams dispatched immediately to every relative of Dan Jacobs. All the way through great grandkids. Get them all and move them into safe houses ASAP. Use GRS if you have to. Priority Alpha, find them and get them secured. Use whatever assets you need. Any pushback, tell them to call me directly." Rhett paused, listening. "Thanks. Joe, move it, this is bad." He now wished he had not stopped to dally with Melanie last night.

He went back to the note.

Rhett, I am so sorry. They threatened to kill my entire family and their families if I didn't get them what they wanted. I couldn't let my past harm them. So, I did it. I know better, but what could I do? I now know they will never be satisfied. And they weren't. But after, I wondered how the hell they found me? How did they ever figure out I was the only person who could get what they wanted?

They are looking for dirt on Turner. I opened Khyber. I had to give them something for my family. Trust me, there is stuff in there you have no idea about and I won't put you at risk by putting it here. But I didn't give them anything useful. I took a lesser file with nothing too revealing and certainly nothing that would overtly compromise our country. I made copies of about thirty pages. They gave me a new pair of glasses with a camera in the lens. You'll need to update the security to have visitors remove glasses and probably contacts as well, but I digress.

I gave them what they wanted. Made the drop. A week later, I was told this was not sufficient. They needed more, and I had better get it for them. I refused. I told them there was no way I could bluff my way in a second time. I lied and told them this was all there was pertaining directly to Turner. They know something. They know there is more. I am not sure why or how, but I can sense they are looking for something specific.

Rhett, I am writing this because they killed my granddaughter this morning. She was hit crossing a street at the University of Arizona. You know there is no such thing as a coincidence. She died because of me. Because of who I am.

Rhett could sense the horrific toll this deed had on his friend, just from his words in the letter. He continued reading.

I cut my finger off and sent it with this note. I can't risk them figuring out this security method and having it fall into someone else's hands. Rhett, please save my family. If you are reading this and it is a surprise, it means I am dead. They may be too. Please forgive me for what I have done. God help my soul if you cannot save them.

Your Friend Dan.

Rhett contemplated the finger. He knew he could access all of Jacob's secret files and he could even use it to enter the Khyber vault. At least for a short time, just as Dan had. He did not want to know. He already knew some about both Turner's authorized time in Iraq and Afghanistan and other battlefields in an unofficial capacity.

Jacobs and his granddaughter were already victims of someone seeking that information. Rhett had an ex-wife with grown children and a new wife he did not wish to put at risk. Having knowledge would make him a target. In this case, ignorance was not only bliss, but safety. With Jacobs gone, there really was no one who could access the information. At least, not without Henderson's finger. Or was there?

He picked up the phone. "Barb, I need you to look up an ex-employee and see where their pension payments are being sent."

#

"Chadwick," answered Rhett, picking up the phone.

"Rhett, they're all dead."

"Jesus. All of them?" he answered in a sad voice, closing his eyes.

"Car wrecks, hit and runs, a house fire with an entire family, even a drive by shooting with no witnesses. Seventeen in all. Kids, grandkids and great-grandkids. I'm sorry Rhett. We were only half an hour late for one. There was nothing we could have done any faster," finished Joe.

"Any witnesses or suspects?"

"Rhett, you know us. We didn't stick around to question the local cops, but it seems like this has pro written all over it. Was this sanctioned by a state entity? It would take some kind of network and resources to execute with such precision and simultaneously, especially in the US. This was not amateur hour."

Rhett paused, his stomach roiling as he held the phone handset to his forehead, eyes still closed. His guilt was now heavy, knowing he could have saved some of them had he acted last night. How he hated his chosen profession at this moment. Innocent lives sacrificed for no reason. To prove a point to a dead man.

Only then did he realize the point was not being made to the dead man. It was being made to him. Or to whoever figured out what happened to Dan and why. He had a sinking feeling this was not the last of these ruthless deeds.

"Joe, you did everything you could. I wish I had found out the need to protect them sooner. Did anyone see your or your teams?"

"Nope, since we were late to all of them, we didn't have to strong arm anyone. No one is the wiser."

"Thanks."

There was hesitation on the other end. "Rhett, I am sorry. I know Jacob's was a friend of yours."

"He was. And a mentor. He saved my ass a time or two in the field. Families used to be off limits. The rules of the game have changed."

"It seems they have. Let me know when we get to hit back. I want in on the action." The phone connection ended as Joe delivered his promise of revenge.

Chapter 23

"Madame Vice President, thank you for your answers and your time on our program today. In closing, we would like to ask you to respond to some accusations Senator Turner has been making about the administration and his forecast of what the country would face if you win the Presidency," said David Johanson, the anchor of Liberty News One's, *Face the Press* Sunday morning political talk show.

"David, seriously? After all the issues and topics we have discussed, you want to end our interview with a discussion of an inexperienced senator running around claiming the 'end of days' is here if the Party keeps the White House?"

David seemed sheepish as he continued and laughed nervously. "When you put it that way, Madame Vice President, it seems lightweight compared to the topics we have covered. My concern is, his rhetoric has become more and more extreme as he tries to become relevant."

"David, just by mentioning him, you are helping *make* him more relevant. Let me just say this. What exactly is Mr. Turner saying he will *do* to help the people he is riling up? He is just telling them I am evil, and progressive policies are evil. OK, I could say the same thing about the Opposition or his views. But what does that solve? He tells his audiences to vote, to make themselves heard. Guess what?" said Lexi, turning her icy blue eyes to the camera.

"Please vote. Stand up and have your voice heard. Please exercise your right to make a difference and to pick your leaders." She turned back to David. "There, I have done exactly what Turner does. I agree wholeheartedly with his stance of people must vote. They must vote to ensure the Opposition and their antiquated values and support for corporate profits at the expense of workers should not be allowed to continue to rule the land. Vote to keep the Government's hands off women's bodies and restricting their health choices. They must vote to help end the epidemic of violence caused by the ease of access to guns supported by the Opposition. To ensure people of all races, genders, and sexual orientations have an equal voice and are treated and able to take advantage of all society offers equally. To ensure equity is the law of the land. To end the perpetual result of a few having all the wealth. While the rest work and toil to support the elite's luxury lifestyle."

"Yes David, I agree with Turner on this point. Everything else is rhetoric. I ask you one thing. Why is he afraid to come on shows like this? Why does he hide? His only outlet for his hateful rhetoric and fear mongering is *Tommy*. They are a perfect fit. Maybe they should get married," laughed Lexi, again looking at the screen. "And don't worry, under my progressive leadership, if you want to, you can. We won't judge," she said with a smile as David laughed nervously again.

"Anyway David, if you listen to the Senator, he has no positions. He offers no solutions. He only complains and points out problems. Never do I hear how his policies would help resolve any issues. How he would use the power of the government to help make people's lives better. This is all I do. All day long. Help people. To have the government make things better for our citizens."

"David, this is a serious job for serious people. For people who have been in government and who understand the enormity of actions and the consequence they create. This is not a job you learn on the fly. Keep that in mind. I would also add, coming out to support a Marine who murdered six sheriff's deputies is hardly the leadership I want to see."

"Allegedly, Madame Vice President. The trial is yet to occur."

"David, he is alive, and they are dead. Nothing Turner says changes that fact," countered Lexi.

"Thank you for taking the time to answer the question, Madame Vice President. Have a good day America, this has been *Face the Press*," finished David Johanson as the lights came down.

Lexi stood up with an icy glare, ripping off her lapel microphone and throwing it on the desk. David looked up into her angry face.

"You stupid SOB. Who the hell do you think you are? Springing that Turner question on me? You know, we agreed to what questions and topics we would discuss," said Lexi in a low, menacing voice.

David was taken aback at the fury of the Vice President's ire.

"You did alright. You put him in his place and pointed out the feckless nature of his campaign."

"You had better hope this is one of your lower rated segments," said Lexi as she stalked off stage meeting up with Mel.

"Lexi, take it easy. You made Turner look like a whiner. That bit at the end about the Marine was great as well. You did fine."

"Fuck him, Mel. I want him frozen out. Jesus, asking me about Turner with no warning. Who the hell does he think he is? Did he do this on his own, or was it that asshole Kaufmann?"

Mel contemplated how best to calm his boss. "Lexi, I am sure the network president wouldn't intentionally go against our moratorium on mentioning Turner. Levi is not that stupid; he is in third place among the networks. This had to be all Johanson, feeling his oats."

"No more interviews for him. None. Got it?"

Mel had no choice but to nod. "Maybe we should have one of them bring Turner on and put him on the spot for where he stands?"

Lexi gave him a look. "You're kidding right? Turner is like a snake charmer. He would charm whomever we picked to interview him, and he would get to say what he wants with no one challenging him. No way. Are you slipping? Why would you suggest it?"

Mel shrugged. "You brought it up. They may now request he make an appearance because you asked why he doesn't do their shows. We know it's because we won't let them. You have backed us into a corner. I would prefer we put out an invitation, tape it, and make him look bad. Maybe *The Sunday Hour*?"

Lexi stopped walking and stared at Mel, furious that he was right. She'd allowed Johanson to get her to give Turner a way to get on a national network news program. "Who do you suggest interview him?"

"I don't know. I will have to think about who hates him the most. Who Turner has embarrassed the most. Unfortunately, Bergamo is on the wrong network. So, she is out. Plus, she is too inexperienced in this. We need a real veteran who feels his words are dangerous.

"The Sunday Hour is pretty popular. Do we risk introducing him to a wider audience?" asked Lexi.

"There is risk. We could always cut the interview to make him look worse if he makes some good points."

"Let me think about it," answered Lexi. Mel nodded.

#

"Ouch. Round one to Lexi," groaned Denise as the team sat around the conference room in the Denver HQ.

"Hardly, I wasn't even in the ring," answered Nick.

"Maybe, but you know, she is right. You are not offering many solutions. Only explanations of what is wrong, why it's wrong and how everyone has to take personal responsibility and vote people in who will make better decisions," agreed Chuck.

"Your point is?"

"Nick, maybe it is time to tell them exactly what you would do, if, when, they elect you?" answered Denise before Chuck.

"You want me to make promises?"

"Couldn't hurt. Might be good to talk about something positive," interjected Denise. "Traditionally, that is how you win elections."

"Denise, we've been through this a million times. I'm not making *any* promises to win votes. My only promise to anyone who follows me is to abide by and trust the Constitution."

"Nick," broke in Chuck to prevent another tirade about Nick's Dusty decision as Denise puffed up, ready to battle again. "I think what Denise is implying is maybe we should be more specific about where we stand on campaign items. Your book should help with this. Maybe we can work in some interviews to counter Lexi's claims and get you to start publicly stating your positions."

"And get them to talk about something else," agreed Denise.

"We could also try the Sunday shows again," broke in Margie, helping Chuck steer the conversation. "Lexi made it sound like we've been afraid to appear. Reality is none of them agree to host you and we ask all the time. Maybe this time we go public, sort of 'I am happy to appear on any Sunday talk show that will have me' approach."

"That was an unforced error on Lexi's part. You must be getting to her. She isn't usually that sloppy," noted Denise with a rare smile.

"Works for me. I can shift to more policy-based speeches if you think it will play better," conceded Nick.

"You have the interview at Texas A&M. We rescheduled it to after Labor day, now that we finally found a way to publish the book. You'll get your first chance there," said Margie, looking down at her tablet at Nick's scheduled speaking engagements. "A few more state fairs. Small town gatherings during the week. We could squeeze in a Sunday show."

"Do it. See if any bite this time," agreed Chuck.

"You know they will cut any footage into what they want to show," warned Denise. "They will make you out to be even more of a menace to society than they already say you are."

"Alright, so we do it live, say *The Sunday Hour*," suggested Nick.

"Live? A Sunday night prime time news show? They'll never go for it. The commentators would wet their pants if they had to do it live. Too many chances for unexpected results," laughed Denise.

"Lexi just did *Face the Press* live. Why not?" asked Nick.

"That's different. It is Sunday morning. No one watches but insiders. She scripts every question. Usually anyway."

"If they're afraid to do it live, we tell the world that is the reason we aren't on the shows. Let's call Lexi's bluff."

"It can't hurt, since we are only at five or six percent in the polls," smiled Chuck.

"We have nothing to lose? Except however many supporters we really have. Jer, you know how many that is?" asked Denise.

Jer looked up from his seat in the room's corner, where he sat with his ever-present laptop open in his lap.

"Don't pick on Jer, Denise," laughed Nick.

"How would we know? I guess that is the only good thing about your Dusty post. We have no supporters to lose, according to the polls."

"We'll know in November."

#

"You don't think Turner is finished?" asked Pavlovich's metallic voice emanating from the silver cube on Roland's coffee table.

"They are ecstatic at his defending the Marine. They think he screwed up because of his overdeveloped sense of honor."

"Does he know something?" asked Pavlovich.

"I have reviewed the facts. There were definite procedural mistakes made. I do not fully understand the American justice system, but I think he thinks the Marine will be found innocent because of this. With Lexi's control of the press, nothing will change the fact he killed the female sheriff and the rest. This plays well in the American press."

"Lexi?"

"You told me to infiltrate her organization. I have earned her trust." He could hear what sounded like a chuckle from the box.

"Be careful, my friend. Do not let her beauty beguile you. I need you focused. Have you taken care of the ballot issues?"

"Yes. We have delivered the message to our justices in various states," replied Roland, ignoring Maksim's other warning.

"Excellent. What else do you see?"

"Overconfidence. Also, the *Vice President* is under tremendous stress. She is effectively running the country while running for president."

"What can we do to help?"

"I am not sure much. American politics is very complex. My brain hurts. *My* typical solutions are *not* appreciated," sighed Roland loudly.

Maksim laughed. "Your talents will be used. Trust me, my friend. We will have need of them soon and most likely often."

"Good. I am losing my edge in this soft assignment."

"Really? You took care of the archivist. Too bad we did not get more information. Have you discovered anything else of use?"

Roland looked at the ceiling in his simple apartment as he lied. "Nothing we can use. It is incomplete because it does not mention events we know happened. He intentionally gave us less. His family paid the price. I made sure he knew it was happening before the end. He didn't even put up a fight, almost as if he wanted it to be over," finished Roland.

"There was no other way. He would have confessed to the CIA and potentially exposed us and the effort to find the information."

"True. Still, it leaves us without the information we need."

"There are always others who can help," ended Maksim mysteriously.

Chapter 24

"Let me ask you a question," said Nick to a sellout crowd at the end of the Nebraska state fair. He had taken the stage to less than enthusiastic applause. Not his normal, familiar greeting. He knew why.

"How do you feel when you try to make a point, say about the illegals overrunning the border these last seven years? Only to have the person you're talking to tell you to stop watching EXN or listening to Brad Hudson?" There was a chorus of boos.

"I bet you feel frustrated, angry, disappointed, and even helpless. How can they not see the streams of people coming across? The *millions* who have now been bussed and flown all over our country into every little town and hamlet. What are *they* watching? How can they not see the facts? The fact at least twelve million folks have crossed our border. Ignoring all of our border and immigration laws. How can they accuse me of spouting propaganda? Am I right?" he asked rhetorically to louder cheers.

"Sadly, this is only one example. Inflation, energy independence, cancel culture, freedom of religion, gender fluidity, entire school districts in cities not having a single high schooler proficient in math. Not one. This list just goes on." Nick paused as folks reacted to the *facts*.

"They are the ones promoting the propaganda. This is why I created the Flip and the Mirror. To both help you fight this, and them to help them understand they might be wrong. To reconsider their positions and open their minds to alternate sources of information."

"Now I have a second question. I saw your response when I came on. Let's say it was not as enthusiastic as I am used to. Let's not beat around the bush here, You think my support for Dusty Ingram is misplaced? He killed six sheriff's deputies, after all. How could I defend someone who did this?" The crowd was waiting for him to continue.

Nick could see people in the crowd turning to their neighbors and asking the same thing. "First, I am not 'defending' him or claiming he is innocent. He did indeed kill those deputies. Nor am I going to do what all the others in American Pravda are doing, by cherry picking facts and all but volunteering to throw the switch on the electric chair. Instead, I am going to ask you to consider a couple of things. And hopefully, you will come away with some thoughts and maybe a different opinion."

Nick paused. "I hate wasting these few opportunities I get to be in front of large crowds like you. We have so many more important things to talk about. However, I owe you an explanation. They're charging him with six counts of first-degree murder. First degree murder means you know you are killing someone and decide to do it, anyway."

"Now I ask you. How many murderers plan and wait on the off chance someone will bust down their door with a battering ram and come charging in with body armor, helmets, fully automatic weapons and laser sights? These are facts that are known to all. He did not ambush them and lie in wait for them to come in. Six automatic rifles and body armor against a man in his underwear with a pistol with one magazine of 15 bullets. Living in a crappy apartment in a rundown part of town." Nick paused and paced for a minute, trying to keep his anger in check and speak in as normal a tone as he could. He was failing, his tone rising.

"If that is what murderers do and plan, then I am sadly misinformed. Second, imagine you are at home in your bedroom. You have never done anything remotely wrong in your life. No record. No warrants. Not even a parking ticket. In fact, imagine you have served four tours of duty in hell holes in Iraq and Afghanistan. Where every night you could be killed by insurgents infiltrating your camp, mortars falling from the sky or trucks filled with explosives being driven into your building. Now that, I can relate to. You never get over this. You only make peace with the memories and move on. This is not freaking *Call of Duty*. There is only one life here." Nick paused, taking deep breaths.

"Suppose someone breaks down your front door. What is your first thought? Remember, you have no reason to ever suspect the cops would be the ones breaking down your door. If you are like me, my first thought is to grab my gun and defend my home. My family. My life. I suspect you would too. No one breaks down a door of an *upstanding citizen* for good purposes. You knock."

"Finally, I want you to consider a couple of things. This is a series of unfortunate events that left many innocent people dead, through no fault of their own and another potentially liable for this because of these events. This is why we have jury trials. This is why we have clauses like innocent until proven guilty. Why we have laws against unlawful search and seizure. It is why no-knock warrants are banned in many states, because they are fraught with danger."

"Red Flag laws are similar. If you have listened to any of my speeches, you know my stance on these. If you haven't, go listen to one. These are no-knock warrants on steroids and guarantee more situations like this. I wanted to force people to pay attention to his trial. To listen and to let you form your own opinion."

"I have accomplished my goal. This trial will now have more people watching than OJ. But I want a fair trial and I want his defense to get a chance to bring out the facts of the case into the open. Free from American Pravda disinformation."

"When this happens, I will support the verdict, regardless of the outcome, because we will have lived up to our constitutional principles. We will once again trust the rule of law. Something we are sorely in need of. For our criminal justice system in our cities to protect our brave law enforcement and citizens from criminals. To hunt down and prosecute drug dealers, human traffickers, and corrupt politicians. To enforce our border and our immigration laws once again. Please enjoy these great bands. I thank you for your time."

Nick turned to greet the lead singer of the famous country band as she walked out on stage. He had already given his speeches in front of her act at several state fairs. She was nowhere to be seen when he took the stage this time. After his speech, she was all smiles now and gave him a hug as she took the microphone from him. As he turned to go, she grabbed his hand and pulled him back to center stage.

"Ya'll, this is really important," she said to a cheering crowd. "I have listened to the Senator, I mean Nick," she laughed at the look he gave her. "I have listened to Nick give his speeches a dozen times. I am ashamed to admit I didn't want to be seen with him before this one. Now I realize how wrong I was to believe all the crap you see on TV and social media about Dusty. I love our troops. I believe in the rule of law and support our cops. Nick is right. We need to let the court system do its job. It is not our place to judge. Nick, I am so sorry you did not get to give your usual speech tonight. I wanted to hear you talk about how faith is the answer. Hopefully, you'll get to do that in Minneapolis next week. Thank you for having patience with us. It takes a long time to break free from the propaganda of American *Pravda*." She finished with a hand flip and held her palm out against her chest as she smiled her million-dollar smile and gave Nick another hug as the crowd cheered wildly.

#

As he finished and left the stage, as was always the case, Nick signed some merchandise for local charities to auction off. He took selfies with various locals fortunate enough to be backstage. As the crowd thinned and they were preparing to make their way toward the cars in the parking lot, a couple of women approached.

Nick, coming down from his high of being on stage, didn't recognize them at first. Earl approached the attractive middle-aged blond and gave her a big hug. Nick smiled once Earl relinquished his hold.

"Jamie, it is great to see you," beamed Earl.

"It's always good to be remembered," laughed Jamie.

Nick had been staring into the green eyes of Natalie as she smiled back at him. "Good to see you again too, Nick," said Natalie, holding out a hand. Nick pulled her in for a hug and held it for a few seconds. He and Natalie both were blushing a bit when they broke the hug, realizing they had an audience. Denise cleared her throat.

"If they are finished monopolizing you two, hello as well," smiled Greg, giving them quick hugs.

"Hi, I'm Denise," offered Denise, shaking the hand of both women as the men stood around, flustered.

"Sorry, sorry," said Nick. "Denise, this is Jamie who offered us a place to stay when we first started our road trip in North Platte. This is Natalie, whose bed-and-breakfast we stayed at in Omaha."

"Right, these were the ladies who provided the wonderful meals you guys could not stop raving about," Denise replied with a smile.

"You got that right," agreed Earl and Greg simultaneously.

"You know what, I don't think we've had as good a meal since those," complimented Earl, smiling like a dumbstruck teenager.

"Flattery will get you everywhere," Jamie winked at Earl.

"What are you doing out here?" asked Nick.

"We're the leaders of the Nebraska chapter of Women for Turner. We came out to hear you speak," answered Natalie.

"How'd I do?" asked Nick rather sheepishly.

"You did fine. Actually, you did wonderfully. You answered all my questions and blew away the doubts I had about your stance regarding Dusty. I have to admit I was confused," replied Jamie.

"I agree. I thought you were convincing in February, but now you are on a whole different level," added Natalie. "I am so happy I got to hear you defend your support. Now I get it. It doesn't change what happened, but it makes me keep an open mind to hear more facts."

"Thank you for that. Without this speech, I'm not sure we would have tried to track you down," agreed Jamie.

"In that case, I'm glad I gave it. I hope others get to see it."

"It's up on Hibi already. Of course, it is already being taken down on other social sites. Folks keep trying to repost," Greg noted.

"We have a pretty good network of Turner Rabble and Women for Turner email chains. We will use this to get the word out and make sure all the chapters have a meeting and viewing of the speech. We already sent it out to all the leaders," responded Natalie. "We will do our part."

"Actually, Susie's comments at the end are probably going to do more to spread the word than anything else. She really went out on a limb for you, Nick. And she has hundreds of millions of followers on her social channels. I doubt they ban her posts," pointed out Jamie with a smile.

"Thank goodness for that. I want folks to wait for his defense to point out his side of the story," nodded Nick.

"Have you eaten? We were getting ready to head back to town to see if we could wrangle up some food. Care to join us? It's the least we can do for our Women for Turner leaders," suggested Denise.

Nat and Jamie looked at each other and laughed. "You're in Grand Island, Nebraska and it is 9:30pm on the last night of the state fair. The only food you are going to find is fast food or Denny's. It's your lucky day. Turns out we have rented a house and stocked the fridge. If you can wait, we can whip something up for you?" offered Jamie.

Nick looked around the group. "I'm game if the rest of you are?"

"Let's do it," agreed Earl enthusiastically.

The group headed off to the parking lot. Their rented Suburban was closer to the fairgrounds in the VIP parking. Jamie and Natalie were much further away. "Jamie, why don't you ride with Earl, Greg, and Denise? She can direct you to the house, and I'll go with Natalie." He turned to Natalie. "You aren't planning to assassinate me, right?"

Natalie looked at the sky. "Nope, no full moon, so you're safe," she turned to Earl. "I'll get him there in one piece, promise."

Earl grinned in reply.

Natalie and Nick walked down the parking lot rows until they found her Ford pickup. They got in the car and drove away from the state fair. Nick looked at her. She glanced his way, color filling her cheeks.

"Please don't do that."

"Do what?" replied Nick devilishly.

"You know exactly what I'm talking about."

"I'm admiring the scenery."

"Nick, it's dark outside. Besides, there is nothing to see but cornfields," she responded.

"I meant inside," smiled Nick, still staring.

"Oh ya, a regular fashion model in my hiking boots and shorts."

"It's all in the eye of the beholder."

"Down boy, you haven't lost yet," Natalie reminded him.

"What if I dropped out tomorrow?" threatened Nick.

"You do that, and I'll drop you on the side of the road here. After all the work we've done and the hope you have given people? Don't even joke about it," retorted Natalie seriously.

"Sorry, poor taste. Bob and Jerry still fans?"

Natalie laughed as she pulled into a side street in a neighborhood. "They run a local Turner Rabble group, hosting weekly town halls around Nebraska preaching the Turner Doctrine. They're having a great time."

"Unbelievable," commented Nick, surprised.

"I know. Here we are," said Natalie, pulling into the driveway of the house where the Suburban was parked on the street in front.

Nick followed Natalie into the house and back to the kitchen, where the wine was already open. Jamie was pulling stuff from the fridge and pantry and already had the stove top going to whip up some snacks.

"You guys go sit in the backyard and start a fire in the fire pit and let us pull some stuff together. We'll join you in a minute," ordered Jamie, shooing everyone from the kitchen while giving Earl a playful push.

Denise and the guys headed out to the backyard where a group of cushioned lawn chairs surrounded a fire pit. They brought the red and white bottles of wine out along with Pelligrino for Denise. Earl and Greg figured out how to light the gas firepit. Shortly, they had their shoes kicked off and a roaring fire going in the mild late August evening air.

"Okay, here are some eats," said Natalie and Jamie, carrying large serving plates of food they set down on a table. They also carried out six small plates. Everyone got up and gathered around the table.

"Here we have goat cheese and pulled pork quesadillas. This one is chicken and pineapple. Then we have black bean, eggs, cheddar, and tomato mini burritos," said Natalie, pointing to each of the serving plates.

"Are you freaking kidding me? You two set feminism back by decades. Just going to whip up something to snack on," moaned Denise.

"See. We told you." Earl grinned as he was loading up a plate.

"Red or white ladies?" asked Greg.

"White for me, that is a nice Pinot Gris," said Jamie.

"I'll have the red," answered Natalie. "Greg, you'll appreciate it. It's a Catana Zapatas Malbec. I raided the wine cellar on my way out."

Nick, Greg, and Natalie had the red, while Jamie and Earl split the white. Denise raised her Italian bubbles in a toast. "To an unexpected gourmet meal, new *and* old friends."

They sat around the fire eating, chatting, and laughing. Natalie sat next to Nick and Jamie sat next to Earl. Denise and Greg were in the other chairs. They unwound and regaled the girls with campaign tales.

"I hear you have a baby named after you," blurted Natalie, causing Nick to inhale his wine, starting a coughing fit. Natalie started hitting him on the back. "Security," he said weakly, looking at Earl. He stopped choking and finally started laughing.

"Sorry, didn't realize it was such a sensitive subject," added Natalie with a sarcastic grin.

"It was an interesting drive, to say the least," said Greg, as Nick tried to get his breathing going again. "Yes, the grateful parents named the little tyke after our Nicholas."

"Sure, laugh it up at my expense. Earl and Greg helped too."

"But no one named their child after us," said Earl with a frown.

"This food is wonderful," declared Denise. "You can 'whip up' anything you want for us on the road. Join the traveling circus."

"Great idea," said Earl sincerely, looking at Jamie.

"We have these things called jobs, remember? We can't just up and hit the road yacking all day," replied Jamie with a laugh.

"Hey, taking care of this guy is a full-time job and then some," said Earl, waving a thumb in Nick's direction.

Greg and Denise raised their glasses as well. "Amen to that."

"Have you seen some of the things he says and does?" asked Denise, leaning forward. "Let me clue you in on a secret. None of that is planned. None of it," she said with emphasis. "We're always on alert to figure out the damage control we need to do when he opens his mouth."

"Speaking of that, and since we have Women for Turner leaders here, what do you think of my stances? What would you change and what am I missing? What do you have to apologize for when trying to gin up support for me in Nebraska?" asked Nick seriously.

"Always campaigning," said Denise, shaking her head.

"Sorry, but we need to take advantage of situations like this," pushed Nick. "Jamie?"

"Well, I can tell you what people like. That is much easier. Closing the border is key and trying to get a hold of illegal immigration. We still get busloads and the occasional flight landing in small Nebraska towns dumping off illegals who have nothing and can't speak any English. They immediately disappear into the underground. Now Nebraska is not exactly Chicago. We don't have a seedy underworld, not even in Omaha, or we didn't until recently." Jamie paused, not used to having an audience.

"Now we have mini gangs in every town and a network of drug dealers and distribution throughout Nebraska. I can tell you the locals are on the verge of going to war themselves, since the state does not appear willing to do anything. We have Opposition in power. They are paralyzed in fear when it comes to doing anything about immigration, crime, CRT in the schools, or even using the national guard. Any race or gender or gay rights related protests and violence. I'm sure Natalie told you it is spreading from downtown Omaha into the suburbs."

"Your views on all these are spot on. You want law and order, that is all anybody wants. Most here are not anti-anything. They are pretty tolerant. They just want to be left alone to lead their lives. The government is trying to get involved in every decision the parents and adults used to make themselves," she finished.

"What else?" asked Nick, pressing.

"Some folks aren't happy with your support for legal abortion, but usually, when they actually listen to what you say, they get it. Most of them believe in God and they like how you have turned any consequence for the action into a higher power decision. It appears to be playing well in the heartland. Most are pragmatic, so it plays to their common sense mind set to. Do you agree Natalie?" asked Jamie, looking at her cousin.

"I do. You know the other thing I have noticed is the protesters outside the Omaha planned parenthood don't even seem to be as many. I wonder if they are buying into your whole theory? I would say the thing we have the most pushback on are the plans for all the illegals in the US. You haven't really laid out a plan other than providing ways to get them all naturalized at some point. People are skeptical about promises to make them wait and pay and not jump the line or be rewarded for breaking the law. Your plans are decent, but folks don't think you can actually do them. They also believe the elections are rigged and there is nothing being done to stop it. All the voter ID laws seem to be turned down or tied up in the courts, so a lot of folks do not think their vote is going to matter, no matter what you say. We already talked about your stance on Dusty. We will do our part to spread that word. You had us worried there for a minute, and we know you," warned Natalie, finishing her glass of wine.

"What are we not doing? How is Blackbird doing in the state?" Denise asked between bites.

"We see little of Blackbird. I think he is assuming Nebraska is safe for the Opposition and taking it for granted," said Jamie.

"Is he? What does your local news say the polling is?" asked Greg.

"55 Blackbird, 20 Turner and 25 Smythe-Thomas," said Natalie with a big smile. "Saw it last night on the evening news."

"Do you think it is accurate?" asked Greg, noticing their smiles.

Natalie and Jamie looked at each other and laughed. "Not at all. We have done as you asked and told all your supporters to lie to the pollsters. It seems to be working. In fact, we often start every meeting with stories about how we have lied to pollsters when they call," bragged Jamie. "Some of the stories they use about supporting Lexi are hilarious."

"What do you think it is?" probed Earl.

"I'd say it is 50 for Nick, maybe 30 for Blackbird and 20 for Lexi, all out of Omaha and Lincoln," responded Natalie.

"You think we win Nebraska?" insisted Denise.

"Yesterday I would have said maybe because of Dusty. After folks see the speech tonight, I say yes, but things can always change. When we get close, people don't like to waste their vote, so if they think Blackbird has a better chance, they may switch back to him," stated Natalie.

"Do you agree with telling my supporters to lie to the pollsters? We have a disagreement on our staff," prodded Nick, looking at Denise, who promptly flipped him off.

"No. I think it is the right move. You are not losing momentum. People tell people who tell people, and everyone gets the message. It is like a secret handshake. Everyone feels a little like Black Widow or Captain America on a covert operation. I think it is right, and it is working. We see nothing in Nebraska negative to Turner. In fact, we see very little in Nebraska period. I suspect most of the money is being spent in swing states, so we may not be much help there," finished Natalie.

"What you have already told us is priceless info. We probably need to get you in touch with Steve Gaines," added Nick.

"Don't worry. We already know Steve. We love him. He is very helpful and asks all kinds of questions about how he can help and how we are doing. We're sharing info between groups. He is great," added Jamie.

Nick nodded and smiled.

"More wine? asked Natalie, spying empty glasses and bottles.

Everyone looked at Nick, who lifted his empty glass and smiled. "Sure, we haven't relaxed much, and I like the company. Natalie, I'll help you. Let's get a couple more bottles."

Natalie and Nick headed into the house with the empties to find and open a new red and white.

As Nick used the wine opener, he gave Natalie a look.

"What?" she said with a smile.

Nick looked at her. She looked like a college co-ed. Hiking boots, firm and tanned legs. Khaki shorts with rolled legs, a pale blue T-shirt and a plaid long-sleeved shirt she had knotted at her waist. Her red hair was pulled back with clips, and she had little makeup, showing a hint of freckles across the bridge of her nose. Putting down the wine opener, he wrapped his hands around her small waist. This time she didn't hesitate as she put her arms around his neck and kissed him back.

"Hey, where's the wine? You guys get lost?" They heard Jamie calling from the fire pit.

They broke their kiss. Nick stared into her eyes. "What if I win?"

"You better. We'll cross that bridge when it happens. Grab the wine," said Natalie, grabbing Nick's rear and squeezing with a smile, bouncing away as he tried to return the favor.

Nick and Nat came out carrying a bottle apiece. They poured another round of wine and more ice and limes for Denise as they toasted the Nebraska state fair and their two lovely hosts.

Nick and Natalie were never alone again for the rest of the night. The party broke up reluctantly at the end of the second set of bottles. The girls would head their separate ways tomorrow, east and west. The team thanked Natalie and Jamie for their hospitality, with hugs all around as they drove back to their hotel.

"That Jamie is a fine woman," sighed Earl.

"I notice you hugged her for about 30 seconds," observed Greg.

"Hey, I'm single, she's single. She's a great cook, I'm a great eater. Sounds like a match made in Heaven," laughed Earl as he drove them through the deserted streets of Grand Island.

"Your hug seemed to last too, Nick," noted Denise, slyly.

"Natalie is a very nice woman."

"Next time you should wipe the lipstick off," laughed Denise.

"I'll remember that," commented Nick without embarrassment.

"Gee Greg, what happened? These two apparently found their Nebraska honeys on your trip. Didn't like what you saw?" asked Denise.

Greg's face reddened a bit. "I guess I was the odd man out."

"If you guys disappear, I'll know where to look," noted Denise.

"See you guys for breakfast. Where to next?" asked Nick.

"Denver first, then off to the Wyoming state fair, and Dallas after that to take on Pastor Mills," said Greg, as half the entourage groaned at the continued grind of the campaign schedule.

Chapter 25

"What did you tell him?" asked Jamie.

"The truth. I was quitting the campaign and settling down to be a farmer in Nebraska," said Earl, looking at Jamie as she drove to North Platte.

"You're kidding right?" responded Jamie worriedly.

"Of course. He'd be lost without me. Or dead," replied Earl.

"In that case, we'd best make your visit a short one."

"Sadly, that is true. I will have to leave early tomorrow."

"I'll take what I can get. Let's keep our priorities straight."

Earl turned and stared. Jamie was probably in her mid to late fifties but looked ten years younger. Despite the hardship of losing her husband young and having to take over the farm and raising the kids, she'd maintained both a youthful appearance and a positive attitude.

They chatted about life on the campaign trail in Earl's case, and the efforts of Jamie and Natalie to convert Nebraskans to Nick's side.

Arriving at Jamie's farmhouse, Earl helped her unload the supplies from the trip. She gave him a tour of the farm. He marveled at the number of machines, each designed to do a specialized task. Each costing upwards of half a million dollars each. Earl stood and stared at her.

"Farming has come a long way. With the machines, Nathan can farm all of our acreage with only a few permanent farm hands, while still maximizing our yield. We don't waste an ounce of water. Never fertilize more than we have to and harvest at exactly the right time. Other than the occasional rogue hailstorm, we are squeezing every ounce of crop out of the land we can, while being entirely sustainable."

"Amazing," marveled Earl.

"Nathan is also using drones. It cuts back on the cost of the big equipment. We rotate to help nurture the land, and we recycle and reuse as much of everything as we can. The dirty secret no one on the Left wants to hear is we are already reducing our carbon emissions by 10x since my Clyde took over from *his* daddy."

"I can believe it. I had no idea it was so precise," said Earl in awe.

"Earl, it has to be. Maximum efficiency is the name of the game if we want to stay independent. You heard Nathan during your last visit. Many of our neighbor's plant what they think makes them the most money that year. One bad season or a dip in prices and they are done. You can't make the payments on these expensive machines and ConAgra or Gates swoops in and buy the land on the cheap. Or worse, the Chinese. Thankfully, we put a stop to that here, at least for a while."

"You do this and restaurants? I thought we were working hard."

She stood looking up at his mahogany face, with his graying hair, and put a hand on his cheek. "Hon, it isn't hard if you love it. Let me make some dinner and you can tell me about what you did before you started making sure Nick survives long enough to get elected."

"Deal." They walked back to the house, hand in hand.

#

After a wonderful meal, they were sitting in her living room on the couch side by side, talking about life. Jamie told him about her husband and Earl eventually opened up about his wife, who had died of cancer as well. As he became more at ease, he told her things he hadn't told anyone in years. They both realized how comfortable they were with each other. He leaned in and kissed her. Eventually, he pulled her to her feet and swept her into his arms.

"Put me down before you hurt yourself. Lotta good, you'll be to me if you pull something."

He smiled down at her. She didn't weigh more than one thirty. Turning, he realized he had no idea where her bedroom was. They'd all slept in the kid's bedrooms upstairs on their prior visit. He hoped he didn't have to carry her up the stairs.

Sensing his confusion, Jamie pointed down a main floor hallway. "That way, you crazy man. Be quick about it," she commanded, smiling.

\#

"What they say is true. Just like riding a bike," chuckled Jamie.

"I'll try for longer next time," lamented Earl.

"You did fine. It's been a very long time."

"Me too. Not part of the plan. Wasn't even looking."

"Me neither. I had the kids and the restaurants. I already knew all the locals. Not much to choose from. Assumed I'd be the old grammy," grinned Jamie, leaning on Earl's arm under her head.

"I didn't even think about it. I've always served. The military and then law enforcement. Hell, I thought Nick was an egotistical little prick the first time I met him. He was so confident in that bar. Sure he could handle the five guys. Not a care in the world, or even concerned about what would happen after. Now, I realize he could have easily taken all of them and would have managed the aftermath and turned it into a plus. He has that way about him," explained Earl.

"I agree. In the short time we've been around him, he leaves an impression. Afterwards, you are inspired and motivated to do good. To try to measure up. It is hard to explain. Kind of like your favorite uncle or teacher in school. You don't want to disappoint them." She sighed, snuggling in tighter.

"Jamie, I'm going to tell you something, because I need to tell someone. For all his demeanor on the outside, I know it is getting to him. I see him at some of the talks. He is barely holding in his anger. I think this whole Dusty thing is triggering something from his past. He has gone beyond trying to make people think. It is now something else. He is becoming so driven. I can see it more than most. I think it is eating him from the inside out. I've tried to help relieve the pressure, but I don't know how. He is very closed off. He won't talk about his past. The few things he has alluded to make me think he's seen things that aren't good."

"Hon, all you can do is what you do. Be there when he needs you. Offer help and a sympathetic ear. You can't force it out of him. When he needs to, he will trust someone and share just like you are."

"Jamie, I'm not sure. He stays up to the wee hours every night trying to answer emails and do his Senate job. He hardly sleeps. One trip when we needed to leave really early. When he didn't meet me in the lobby. I knocked on the door and there was no answer. I always keep a key to his room for obvious reasons. I went in. The bed hadn't been slept in. He was on the floor with a blanket and pillow. I thought something happened, so I rushed over to him."

Jamie leaned up and looked Earl in the face. She could tell he was upset. "What happened?"

"He woke up and had a gun to my temple before I could even twitch. I don't know where he was or what he was re-living. It took all my strength to move his wrist with the gun from my head. Finally, after yelling at him, and struggling with the gun, calling him by his name, I was trying everything to get through to him and called him 'Colonel'. He came out of it." Earl finished the story with a visible shiver.

"Oh, my God. What did he do?" asked Jamie, holding a hand to her mouth.

"Jamie, I could see the realization come back into his eyes. He just stared at me. He relaxed and lowered the gun. Got up, threw it on the bed, and headed to the bathroom. He didn't say a word. No apology, no explanation. Nothing. Then I heard the shower start. I left and he met me in the lobby twenty minutes later as if nothing had happened."

"Honey, he needs help."

"I'm not so sure. He was never out of control. He was speaking something when he woke up. I think it was Pashto or Arabic, but I'm not sure. I suspect there is something that happened to him when he was in the war. He has scars on his back. When I asked him about them, he said he fell down the inside of a tall oak tree when he was a kid."

"You don't believe him?"

Earl shook his head no. "Just another mystery. He's hiding stuff for sure and internalizing it. I also think this is why he did what he did for

Dusty. I think he sees himself. There, but for the grace of God go I, kind of stuff."

"Please be careful."

Earl laughed. "Jamie, trust me, I'm fine. So is everyone around him. He is not the going postal type. However, to be an enemy of Nick Turner is not a place I would want to be."

"All the same, watch out for everyone. He is attracting a lot of hate. He is not Superman, and neither are you."

"And here I thought you said it was all fine…"

Jamie laughed, rolling over on top of Earl. "Better let me judge for myself again…"

Chapter 26

Nick, we're running out of money. You need to raise more.

"What are you talking about? You said we had $200 million."

"I did, and I also told you the money is going out faster than it is coming in. We are burning about $100 million a month and we are only in August. September and October are going to be double that. Your stunt is already affecting us. We got half as much in the last week. If the money dries up, we're dead in the water. You've raised billions for your homeless shelter, even millions for your Turner Rabble Defense Fund, but you won't do anything for your campaign."

"Denise, I'm not going to go beg for donations from rich donors. I can't change now after all my claims of the others being hypocrites."

"Then you had better stop alienating your base. Or even better, you had better go tell them to send you more money. If you keep this up, we're going to have to lay off half our paid staff before October, just when you need them most," retorted Denise, getting angry.

"It'll turn around. This is just a blip. Look at the Nebraska state fair. My explanation turned them around," said Nick hopefully.

"One crowd. Your offhand comment about closing the border and looking at citizenship for illegals and your abortion stances don't help you with everyone. You also conveniently forgot to ask them to send you ten bucks each." Denise threw her hands in the air in frustration.

"Denise, that is what I believe. To be clear, it was not amnesty or even short-term citizenship. The line starts at the back for all of them. It won't be easy and you have to *want* to be an American. If it costs me votes or it slows down the money, we'll have to deal with it. I can't start lying now, just for donations," answered Nick, also beginning to raise his voice.

"You don't fucking get it," responded Denise, now throwing caution to the wind. "You don't get to decide how the game is played. You can be all noble. Ride in on your shining horse to save the fucking day. But you don't get a chance to do that if you don't raise the money. It is all about money. Why the hell do you think these things go on for two years? Everyone gets to stick their nose in the trough."

"Which is exactly why I am not doing it. What brought this on? A few days ago, it was all sunshine and roses with the girls."

"That was before I saw the fundraising nosedive. We can't make any mistakes and fundraising going down is a disaster. You have no idea the opportunity you have and you are totally fucking it up."

"I don't agree."

"Nick, we already talked about this before you came out for Dusty. The stars were aligning. You were following your Sun Tzu. Succeeding at the unexpected. Dusty was a frontal assault up a hill into the sun, with an enemy entrenched on top. You are making the mistakes. This last one is the final straw. You are dividing your own supporters. Making them question you and your stance. If we lose now, it is because of this. You killed our momentum, betrayed all your followers with your righteous stance for one fucking person." Denise was now yelling at him. Nick made to speak.

"No, I am not done. I have been thinking about this for the last week. You don't get it. I am a broken down alcoholic who has made more mistakes in my life than you can ever imagine. Chuck has a bunch of these too. Probably everybody in this office has something. But you came along and gave us hope. Everyone has it tough. Injustice happens all the time. The law does not always get it right. You take the good with the bad. You make trade-offs. You've made split-second decisions. They can't all have been right." Denise was now marching around the office. Nick had never seen her this worked up.

"You're also wasting all the sacrifice and belief so many of your followers are making to stand up and be seen supporting you. You say it all the time. Stand up and together we can make this happen. Guess what? We are standing, and you are painting a target on each of us.

If you don't win, Lexi is going to track down everyone who has ever stood up to be counted as a supporter. Mark my words." She sat down, looking at him.

"Finished?"

"Yeah, I'm finished. Like talking to a fucking brick wall."

"Denise, all of what you say is true, but that does not change how I feel or why I did what I did. If it costs me, I will pay that price," delivered Nick in an even tone.

"Denise leaped out of her chair and yelled at Nick.

"Bullshit. That is the most selfish thing I have ever heard you say. Do you give a shit about anyone else? Your stance is going to cost you, but it really won't hurt you. You'll run off to your mountain cabin with one of your girlfriends. But all of us who allowed you to get our hopes up. Who could even see a glimmer of hope that what you are saying might be possible. You're willing to sacrifice all of us for your principles."

She stood with her arms on her hips and her face red from her passionate speech.

"Girlfriends?"

"Are you feeding Bergamo information?"

"What?" asked Nick, confused by this sudden accusation.

"You forgot you gave me your phone after she disclosed your meeting with Blackbird. I saw the pictures of you two in San Francisco on your phone. Are you still seeing her? How else would she know what she knows unless you were feeding it to her?"

Nick stood. He didn't know what to say. He had forgotten the pictures were even on his phone. "I am not. Nice to know you are snooping through my phone."

"Fuck you Nick. What are you doing? How long have you been seeing her? And kissing Natalie. Plus, lord knows what with Dolly. You can't go around being Casanova during a political campaign."

"Ah, you're one to talk." Nick instantly regretted it and knew he had gone too far as she stiffened. "Sorry," he tried to say.

"I have paid for that and so many other actions. You'll never understand the sacrifices I've made." Her tone was so wounded, Nick immediately regretted his comment.

"I am truly sorry, Denise. That was a low blow. I am not sleeping with or dating any of these women. I am also not feeding Lauren any information. I honestly don't know how she is getting all these scoops. I can only assume she has other sources or is simply good at guessing."

Denise was still upset. "Get it together and keep it in your pants, please. I have had enough campaigns fucked up by *fucking*."

She shook her head and turned to leave the room. As she opened the door, Chuck was standing there, hand raised, about to knock.

"Your turn. Maybe you can talk some sense into him. I give up."

Chuck stood in the doorway, moving aside as Denise stalked out.

"We heard the shouting. I figured I might need to referee. Denise is still not taking your post well?" asked Chuck, closing the office door.

Nick stood contemplating. "No."

"She bring up the money?"

"Yes."

"She's right, you know. If we can't keep the momentum, we are done. At some point, it has to become about raising the money. You know all your TRDF and Blue Morpho folks would be happy to give you money with no strings," offered Chuck quietly.

Nick sighed, taking a seat. He leaned over, putting his hands on his head for a second, rubbing his temples. He looked up at Chuck, determination in his eyes.

"Chuck, I can't do it. We have been through this before. That would be more of a betrayal than what Denise thinks I have done by throwing away our opportunities. The people who are thinking, they know why I did what I did for Dusty. They understand. At the Nebraska state fair, they got it. If they don't, I can't help it. That is part of our problem. Dusty is you and me and everyone else in our society just waiting to be a victim. Someone the system sacrifices when it gets it wrong. That is not right. It's why I did this."

"Because it could have been me in that room. I would have done exactly the same thing. Responded exactly the same way. I wake up some nights in a cold sweat re-living some of the same things he does. It never goes away. This is the future of America if we don't stop it. *'We're sorry. We broke down the wrong door, killed an innocent person. Here is some money for your trouble. All good now?'.*"

"I am tired of the consequences of these mistakes made by people who never have to experience the results. Everyone in America is now living with the consequences of these actions by faceless bureaucrats and elites who aren't affected when they get it wrong. This is not a game. It is life and they make it suck. No more. We stand up now and end it or we die trying. Period. I am sorry Denise is mad. But she is still thinking like a campaign manager. This is not a campaign. It is a crusade."

Chuck sat while Nick delivered his sermon. His concern showed.

"Nick, you're beginning to worry me. This is *not* a crusade. It is a political campaign. You can believe it is a crusade, but you need a reality check. Even if you win, exactly what do you think you are going to change? Not so long ago, we had a President who said he was going to drain the swamp. Remember what happened to him? Does it feel like the swamp was drained even an inch?" Chuck stared at Nick for a response.

"I was in Afghanistan and Syria trying not to get my ass shot down by Russian-made surface-to-air missiles. Do you know I didn't set foot in America during his entire term? I didn't come home once."

"No, I didn't know that. Let me give you a brief history lesson. Even with his so-called control of all branches, he got very little substantial accomplished. Anything he got done, especially concerning the border and the economy, the next president immediately undid. What he accomplished was to get the entire establishment to join forces, both Party and Opposition, to ensure he changed nothing critical. He was like a cancer cell in the body. The 'body' threw everything at him to keep him from achieving any of what he thought he was elected by the people to accomplish."

Nick interrupted Chuck.

"I think you have it backwards, from what I heard. He was chemotherapy trying to eradicate the cancer that is the bureaucratic state. That's about all of his stance I agreed with. It worked briefly, then the cancer of the bureaucratic state overwhelmed it and went back to killing its host. Aided by American *Pravda*, who stood to lose the most if he had been successful." Chuck shrugged and then he spoke.

"Your message is similar, except you are not an egomaniac and have a much thicker skin, I think. Guess what? If you get elected, you're sure to have two very hostile branches of government aligned to stop you from changing anything. Your chemo will have even less effect. They will block you at every step. Keep this in mind."

"Why go raise more money if you say it is all for naught?"

"Hey, don't go all smart ass on me. You did this, not me. I could have told you all this before you announced. Don't look for pity from me. We could instead be in the middle of a successful Senate election campaign. You also owe Denise an apology. She is absolutely right. You hired her to manage a campaign and win."

Nick leaned back in his chair at Chuck's statement.

"Doesn't matter if you like what she has to say or not. You need to raise money. If you won't call your rich fat cat friends, then you better get out there. Re-convince the folks who are questioning why they are risking their livelihoods to stand up and support you." Chuck finished and walked out the door, closing it behind him.

Nick still sat in his chair, leaned back, closing his eyes.

Chapter 27

"Senator, it has been a while. A lot has happened. First, how are you and how's the eye?" asked Tommy Charles, grimacing at Nick's eye with a skinny bandage holding a cut above his right eyebrow.

"I'm fine Tommy. You should see the other guy," laughed Nick.

"I watched the footage. You handled yourself pretty well. What I found amazing was the line of policemen behind you who did nothing while you were being attacked by Pastor Mill's followers. The cops were guarding the pastor's $300,000 Rolls Royce SUV. Those thugs jumped the two of you as you headed to your car. No warning and clearly with intent to harm, if not kill you. What is wrong with our world?"

"Tommy, it's a problem. The law is still the law no matter who is being attacked. I know the police are upset with me. However, when my head of security, Earl Greene, and I have to fend off an outright attack by Pastor Mill's fanatical followers while they stand there idle? It seems egregious for them to do nothing," finished Nick, shaking his head.

"And now I hear they are trying to sue you and Earl for assault?" said Tommy incredulously.

Nick laughed. "We have all the footage. I don't think the lawsuit will go anywhere. Even a DC jury can't ignore this footage and claim we assaulted them, as their lawsuit implies. We should be fine in Texas."

"Senator, I don't believe a presidential candidate has ever been attacked by a mob before. You sure you're not going to press charges?"

"Tommy, other than assassinations, it is rare, but it has happened. Teddy Roosevelt was shot in the chest and kept on giving his speech in 1912 when he was running for a third term against both Taft and Wilson."

"I did not know that."

"Tommy, it was the heat of passion. I'd just exposed their beloved pastor for the fraud he is. They were obviously upset. The cops are mad at me because I want Dusty to have a fair trial. Maybe they would have intervened before they killed us. Who knows? The pro-life extremists are mad at me because I am trying to find a pragmatic solution for our biggest wedge issue. The abortion activists are mad at me for trying to introduce faith into their argument of taking the life of an unborn child after viability. The uber nationalists are mad at me because I won't deport forty-five million illegals who are already here. I could go on and on." Nick paused with a smile and a shrug. "What is *your* complaint?"

Tommy leaned back and smiled. "I have one more question and then I will let this one go. What do you think the secret service would have done if you had a security detail like the other two candidates?"

"We'll never know. Thankfully, Earl and I could handle them. There were only six, and they weren't trained. They only had bats and not guns. It would have been messier if they had firearms. A few immobilizing techniques, and it was over. I'm glad it was all on film, or I would probably be doing this interview from prison. No doubt this administration's DOJ would say I started a riot. Or attempted murder by defending myself from attack."

"You laugh, Senator, but you are probably right. Moving on, do you mind if we show the clip that got Pastor Mill's congregants so upset? He was making some pretty significant accusations prior to your rebuttal. I want to make sure all my viewers understand the background behind the attack on you and Earl."

"It's your show."

With that, Tommy's producers showed clips from the AM evangelical congregation's Saturday sermon Nick had attended as a guest of Pastor Aaron Mills. He was on the stage, while Nick was in a chair in the front row with a camera on him.

As the pastor gave his sermon, Nick's face was also displayed on the overhead screens in the church. There were fifteen hundred congregants there for the sermon and hundreds of thousands watching the streaming video of the service.

Pastor Mills began by accusing Nick of usurping the role of God by promising potential salvation and forgiveness to young women who had abortions. He railed against Nick's own faith, claiming he was against abortion while trying to find compromise positions to allow abortion to continue unabated.

He accused Nick of hypocrisy with his support of a murderer in Dusty Ingram. A man personally responsible for the death of six upstanding deputies and an innocent father and his child. How could anyone claim to have faith, or ask others to follow him, who continued to advocate for abortion and protection for murderers?

Nick, knowing his face was on camera, remained impassive at the accusations. The pastor continued to harangue Nick, trying to paint him as a typical politician trolling for votes. Willing to say whatever was needed to win over people. While doing the opposite. The height of hypocrisy, stated the pastor. He even claimed his heroic deeds in New York were simply him acting faster than others who would have stopped the terrorist.

The pastor was sweating behind his pulpit, failing to get a rise out of Nick. Finally, after this last accusation, Nick stood. The pastor smiled. He headed away from the stage toward an exit. The pastor called after him. Asking if he was too much of a coward to speak to this congregation and answer for his actions and statements.

On the clip, it showed Nick stopping and walking back to the stage. He leaped onto the stage, rather than taking the stairs, startling the much shorter pastor. Nick took the microphone as the congregation booed him.

"I appreciate the chance to respond to your accusations, pastor. I would start with my stance against abortion. One found rooted in scripture if you were objective enough to look. I simply offer young women guidance in a time of need. Corinthians 5:10 says, '*For we must all appear before the judgment seat of Christ, so that each of us may receive what is due us for the things done while in the body, whether good or bad*'. If I am not mistaken, is that not what I allude to regarding salvation and forgiveness from the Lord, not you or me? For actions in this mortal existence?"

"Well Senator, very clever, but…"

"Silence," commanded Nick, as he had ever since his days in ROTC to junior officers. It worked now, just as it had then, as the pastor stopped speaking, chastised. He continued.

"Both Matthew and Mark speak of the hypocrisy Isaiah saw, '*the people honor me with their lips, but their hearts are far away from me*'. In Proverbs, we also read, '*With his mouth the godless man destroys his neighbor. But through knowledge the righteous will be delivered*'. For those willing to listen to my words, this is what I do. I ask questions and I leave the answers to each of them. I do not tell anyone what to do, how to think, or attempt to condemn anyone's actions. I know my place on this earth. I am confident in my own actions. I also take full responsibility for them. Even when they require me to risk my life to save others. One thing I am confident about. I am not a hypocrite." Nick looked over at the pastor whose forehead was now covered in a sheen of sweat, despite the well air-conditioned mega church in the North Dallas suburb.

"A hypocrite is one who says one thing and does another. Who tells you to do something and then does not practice what they preach. As for my support for the Marine Dusty Ingram, I have never claimed he did not indeed kill those deputies. Please get your facts straight. What I asked for was patience on the part of the American *Pravda* media and everyone watching them. To wait for the trial, to hear all the facts. To reserve judgement until the cases are presented to the jury. I would advocate for this for each of you in the same position. The position of having to defend your home against someone breaking down *your* door by *mistake*."

The pastor attempted to break in one more time, but was silenced by a look from Nick. "I am almost done. I am indeed guilty of trying to educate and get individuals to wake up and make choices for themselves. To not blindly follow their politicians, pastors, co-workers or family. Instead, to analyze the information and make their own decisions."

He turned back to the crowd. "For instance, how would you feel if you were being preached at to live one way, say to honor your marriage vows, or face the wrath of the Lord if you were to break these vows? How would you feel if you were told having an abortion was a sin and then found out this same person was paying for their mistresses to have had multiple of them? And would you be ok if a person asking you to donate more money to their cause, was in fact using that money to buy twenty-million-dollar mansions and houses in the Caribbean? While also paying rent for their mistresses as well? Would that be hypocritical?"

By this time, Pastor Mills was frantically motioning for his team off stage to turn off Nick's microphone.

Nick smiled. "It seems by the response; Pastor Mills is perhaps regretting some of what he has said. Certainly, his invitation for me to speak and defend my actions. I'll leave you with a passage from Luke. *'There is nothing concealed that will not be disclosed, or hidden that will not be made known'.* You should ask yourself and your pastor for an explanation regarding some of *his* lifestyle choices. Sir, you are a fraud and a coward."

"If my information is correct, didn't the IRS also serve you notice for unpaid taxes on undeclared income? I, for one, am glad we did not have to depend on you in that subway in New York City. People who live in twenty-million-dollar Malibu mansions, drive Rolls Royces and keep multiple mistresses should not be preaching about fidelity or the sanctity of life while paying for abortions with *donations* from their congregation."

By now, many of the congregation were on their feet, yelling at Nick, yelling at each other, yelling at the pastor, and just yelling. Nick set the microphone on the podium and walked off the stage.

Tommy was laughing after the long clip played. "I'm not well versed in scripture, but somewhere in there is a 'judge not lest ye be judged', right?"

"He started it. I was happy to just leave. There was nothing to be gained arguing with him in his own church. I couldn't leave his last challenge unanswered. When he brought up New York, that was beyond the pale."

"You bet. I would have done the same. I hear there are more investigations into the church finances underway. I also heard his wife filed for divorce yesterday. Apparently, his mistresses are also suing, for what I don't know, but it seems our pastor is in a bit of a pickle."

"It is unfortunate. But actions have consequences. He picked the fight. I don't like bullies. Especially ones with a pulpit where they can spew their hate, lies and innuendo, taking advantage of people's naivety and fears. To do it pretending to speak with the voice of the Lord is the height of hypocrisy."

"True. I know there are many who agree. I know this clip has had many views. I also know that many have also commented they have a better understanding of why you said what you did about Dusty Ingram."

"Tommy, I don't know if he is guilty or not of the crimes he is accused of. I know an already broken soldier, one we broke as a country, now has to carry the burden of killing those deputies regardless of the outcome of the trial. The same for their families. Whether or not he is guilty, it changes nothing for him or for them. Let the facts be exposed and people can judge for themselves. Free from American *Pravda* spinning the narrative with selective pieces of the story."

"You are a strange man, Senator. Why would you risk your campaign momentum to do this? Or go on stage in a mega church to confront his hypocrisy. You are unpredictable. It is good, I suppose. But man, it makes for a roller coaster ride for your supporters."

"For my opponents too Tommy," smiled Nick.

Chapter 28

Karen Coleman entered her office at the FBI Headquarters in the Hoover building. Seated in the room was a bearded man who looked to be in his late fifties. He wore glasses and smiled, standing as she entered.

"Professor Bishop, a pleasure, as always. Can I get you a coffee?"

"No thank you Director," he replied in a northeastern accent.

Karen nodded to her aide and bodyguard, who both left her office, closing the door behind them.

"John, you are a master of disguises. I almost didn't recognize you. Your accent needs a bit of work. You sound like a Cockney dockworker, not a Bostonian."

John North, aka Steve Gaines, Hamit, the Afghani translator and other undercover aliases, smiled under his prosthetic beard and nose. "It's been a while since I have had to get into this character. How are my replacements doing in California? Enjoying the Shanghai Express?"

"They are not as productive as you. Many times they fail to gather any decent intel. We are still working on infiltrating some of the patriot militias you uncovered."

"Good. I'd hate to see all that work go for naught."

"How's your wife liking your normal assignment?"

John laughed. "She's a bit confused when I come home as just me. So far, so good. She knows what she signed up for. Always good to marry someone from the business, even if they are just an FBI lawyer."

"What do you have for me?"

"Lots. He is running out of money. I have no idea what possessed him to stand up for the Marine, but it has really put a crimp in their funding. It is questionable whether they'll have enough to get them through the election, unless something changes."

"Good to know. How's your grassroot infiltration going? Is he organizing any extremists among his followers?"

"Karen, I have talked to all the leaders of his various groups. I have to say I have never seen a bigger bunch of everyday normal folks in all my undercover years. They are literally teachers, plumbers, office workers, programmers, accountants, clerks and stay at home moms. They are truly a rabble. Not militant in a violent way, only in their desire to see things change. Peacefully. They all truly believe they can change the way things are, just by voting. I almost feel sorry for them," explained John.

"Really? None of them are ready to fight to overturn injustice. None? Hard to believe. You're not going native on me, are you?"

John laughed again, more nervously this time. "Hardly. I am pretty jaded. But some of what he says is obviously true and when you hear it day after day and see the effect it has on normal people who are afraid of losing a job or an opportunity for their kid, you feel for them. It is almost too bad, because they are just in for more disappointment."

"What do you mean? Clearly, Lexi and her proposals will also help these people. The only disappointment they'll have is that they won't be able to execute some of their misguided views. What else? Anything I can give Lexi to use against him? Plans. Weaknesses? I need some actionable items," pressed the acting FBI Director to her best deep cover asset.

"The money thing is the big item. There is one group in Idaho. They call themselves Gabriel's Angels. Their leader is Jed Forrest. We have a file on him already for some typical supremacist militia stuff. That would be one to watch closely."

Karen nodded. "What else?"

"He is having to spend his time at the state fairs, with his big crowds, clarifying his position on the Marine instead of getting them excited about his positions. I know his publisher nixed his book. They are trying to self-publish it from the campaign. I don't know what you can do to stop that. He lost his convention bounce, and he didn't have time to capitalize on his abortion stance. It was unfortunate the pastor went off on him. That helped normalize his stance a lot, especially when they attacked him as he exited. Just stupid. Now people are feeling sorry for *him*. Did we have anything to do with that?" asked John.

"Not me. Can't speak for the campaign. My guess is the pastor wanted some payback for Turner exposing his girlfriends and all the rest. Could also be those folks were afraid the gravy train was ending. Hell, maybe they were just believers who didn't like him taking down their man. In any case, he isn't filing any charges. He was right, too bad they had the film, or maybe Javier could have done something with the incident."

"Where did he get his info? He seemed pretty sure of his facts, and they all turned out to be correct. How did he know about the mistresses' abortions and the financial shenanigans? Or the houses in the Caribbean. Did he abuse any privilege to get that info?"

"We already thought about it. No. He even showed us the info he got. Gave us the envelope and everything. Someone set the pastor up and sent him the information anonymously. Probably the wife for all we know. Nothing we can do. He was happy to sign a sworn statement saying it was delivered to him by courier. Smug bastard. Someone covered their tracks well to give him the info."

"We aren't the only ones trying to affect things? Russians?"

"Really, John?" Karen smiled. "That is *our* playbook. The Russians couldn't finish Ukraine. Other than cybercrime, they are really pretty feckless. We need to find another boogeyman. My money is on the Chinese or even the Iranians for our 'foreign meddling' this go round."

John smiled. He was well aware of the various exploits of the FBI infiltrating groups and instigating activities to spur these nascent groups into action. He'd been on the ground in this role on January 6th.

"Anything else. Does anyone suspect anything? You just showed up with all this knowledge of how to organize."

"Nope. 'Steve Gaines' is safe. They were desperate for talent. It is a bare bones operation. A far cry from the well-oiled machines of either of the party candidates. I am enjoying the grassroots organizing role. I'm even helping them improve some of their processes. It is hopeless, so my contribution is legitimate, but won't make a difference in the long run."

Karen contemplated his last statements. John was so effective because he really imbedded himself in each persona and each assignment. It was always a risk she had to run when using him. She knew he was indeed having a positive impact on Turner's grassroots efforts. She wondered if she should pull him out.

"You sure you aren't helping too much?"

"Karen, they're running out of money. Denise Rojas and Turner are now having screaming matches. The pressure is getting to them, I think. Their coalition is a loose confederation of people who are afraid and frustrated. They are enjoying yelling at 'the man' but this is just the Tea Party without the congressional candidates. There are simply not enough of them to make a difference. It is a noble effort, but impossible against the juggernaut of the Vice President."

"OK. Use the prearranged signs to let me know when you have something. Keep an eye on him. We need to know if he gets anymore intel like he used against Pastor Mills. Maybe we can uncover his mole."

"You got it Karen."

"Thank you for your analysis, Mr. Bishop. Work on that accent."

John smiled as he left her office to return to being Steve Gaines. He almost felt sorry for Nick. He had no idea the power aligned against him and the resources they would use to stop him.

Chapter 29

Lauren sat in a patient room at a private clinic in Buckhead, Georgia. As she looked through the paperwork, filling out sections, she tried to keep it together, holding back the tears. She did fine until she got to the part about listing the father. Pausing, she wrote 'father unknown' on the line. As she looked in her purse to fish out a tissue to dab her eyes, she went back to the line on the form, scratched out unknown and wrote Nick Turner. "I am not a slut," she said to herself.

Raised a Catholic, she didn't consider herself to be religious. Like so many of her generation, church and worship were simply not a priority. As her life became overwhelmed with building a career, she'd never even given it a thought. Now, in her time of crisis, she'd prayed for guidance daily. She even dug out her old Sunday school bible and started reading before bed.

She knew what she had to do. Lauren was not ready to be a parent and while she knew Nick would do the right thing, perhaps even marrying her if she asked, she could not 'force' him into that arrangement.

Sitting in the clinic, she was thankful the voters of Georgia had overturned their six week 'heartbeat' abortion law to a more reasonable fifteen weeks. If they hadn't, she'd have been forced to do this in DC, where there were still no restrictions on abortion.

She'd only found out she was pregnant around that six-week time. She struggled to imagine having to rush into a decision like this against an artificial deadline of an arbitrary bill. Six weeks was definitely not long enough to make this decision, regardless of the outcome.

Once again, a wave of concern, guilt, and hopelessness threatened to overwhelm her. This was the hardest thing she had ever done in her life.

Shortly thereafter, a doctor in a white coat showed up. He saw her face and sat down, taking the clipboard from her, gently taking her hands in his. "Ms. Bergamo, you realize you have a choice? You already spoke to the counselor?" Lauren nodded. "I can tell from your face you may not be entirely ready? We have other counselors. Perhaps more time or maybe speaking with others can help you with this decision. Adoption perhaps?"

She looked up into his kindly face. "Thank you, doctor. Thank you for the advice and the concern and most of all, for your understanding. There really is no other option, given the circumstances. Let's get this done before I change my mind."

The doctor stood up and led Lauren from the room, handing the chart off to the nurse while leading Lauren to the room for the procedure. As they headed down the hallway, the admitting nurse took the clipboard and sat down to transfer the information to the computer.

A little over three hours later, Lauren was riding the elevator to her third-floor condo, having been dropped off at her complex by her Uber. None of her friends, most of whom were in the 'news' business, could be trusted with her secret. She pondered the ease with which modern technology made it possible to make a living organism disappear so quickly. Entering her condo, she dropped her bag and barely made it to the toilet before emptying the contents of her stomach. She continued dry heaves, as the tears once more welled up.

After a minute, she rinsed off her face, looking at her reflection in the mirror. She stared into her eyes, wondering what kind of person she had become. The choices she'd made. Leaving the bathroom for the kitchen, she looked at the pills the doctor had given her for any pain.

OxyContin. A week's worth at three a day. Knowing what her brother had been through with his opioid addiction, she had always been reluctant to take any kind of pain med. Even after breaking her ankle running in the winter in New York City years before.

Reaching up, she took down a glass from the cupboard, filled it with water. She looked at her puffy face in the mirror. Emptying the bottle in her hand, she downed all the pills, drinking the entire glass.

Lauren headed to her bedroom to leave a note for Nick before laying down. As she fished in the desk for a piece of paper and a pen, her stomach rebelled, sending her to the toilet once again. After 30 seconds of dry heaves, she looked down in the toilet to see the pile of pills she had just swallowed. So much for that plan. She stayed kneeling and crying for 5 minutes.

Remembering Nick's words at the Women's Right to Choose conference, she said a silent prayer, kneeling in front of her toilet, asking God to forgive her and to understand what she had done, and why.

Once back in the kitchen, Lauren opened her cabinet door where she kept her liquor. Fishing around in back, she found a dark blue bottle. It said Junipero in a fancy cursive font. Lauren had bought the bottle of gin in memory of their time in San Francisco.

She cracked the bottle open, filled a glass with ice, and poured it half full. Putting another glass on top, she smiled, remembering her bar tending skills from college, shaking the two glasses, before pouring out the martini into a third glass. She went to her favorite chair, turned on her electric fireplace, kicked off her flats and took a long pull on the martini. It tasted wonderful. "Nick, I am so sorry," she said aloud as the tears came again.

Chapter 30

In the late afternoon twilight of the Minnesota summer night, a man dressed in desert camo fatigues carefully made his way from the deserted parking lot to the side of the beige office building, his fatigues blending in. He picked this building because there were no other buildings or apartments nearby. With either people or surveillance cameras. No one to see him on this Sunday evening at twilight in early September. No reason for anyone to randomly be out and about on this holiday weekend.

He threw a rappel up to the roof, catching a railing at the top. Quickly ascending the wall, pulling up the rope and coiling it on the roof, ready to be dropped. Staying low in the fading light, he crouched, moving to the center of the building and across the roof until he reached a corner with a waist high outer wall. His position offered him cover from all directions, with no taller buildings in the vicinity. It gave him the vantage point he was seeking.

Crouching down, he unzipped the bag he'd been carrying slung across his back. Pulling out his L115A3 sniper rifle stock. Attaching the barrel with practiced ease and lowering into a crouching position. Flipping out the tripod legs resting on the wall, he aimed his rifle to the south.

He looked through the specialized scope he'd attached. Looking down range, he could see a series of numbers flashing across his viewfinder as the scope synchronized with something. The cross hairs began tracking his target without his moving the rifle.

Reaching into a pocket in his fatigues, he pulled out what looked like a .338 rifle cartridge. Pulling back the bolt action, he inserted the cartridge carefully, checking the alignment in the breech, and eased the bolt forward. He returned to watching the target tracking through his sight. He knew he would only get this one shot. A few deep calming breaths and he pulled the trigger.

The shot echoed in the twilight. The built-in flash suppression in his rifle did its job. There was no flash giving away the location. It took several seconds to travel the more than a mile long distance. He continued looking through the scope, keeping the sight on his target.

With a last look, he disassembled the rifle. In less than 30 seconds, he was back down off the roof, flipped his rappel loose and stuffed it back in his bag. While walking along, he removed his jacket and stripped his fatigue pants in a quick jerk, revealing jeans and a faded Clash rock band t-shirt underneath. In the fading twilight, he made his way back to the car and drove in the opposite direction while sirens wailed in the distance.

#

Nick was on stage at the Minnesota state fair. The three-story grandstand which normally stood at the back of the arena had been destroyed by a tornado months earlier. For this year's fair, they'd built a temporary stage where the grandstand used to be, now facing north. The crowd gathered in the field to watch this year's shows on the main stage.

Nick had been speaking for 20 minutes about his policies and the challenges faced by the country as the light faded and the lights around the grandstand perimeter illuminated the sizeable crowd of well over 20,000. He'd already made his Dusty defense and had the crowd cheering, now understanding his motivation.

"You know I spent the day touring around your great city, and I have to say, I was concerned about the amount of destruction still not repaired from the riots so many years ago. What happened to George Floyd was tragic. But you know what? This is why we have laws. And due process. The cops were charged, tried, and are now in the criminal justice system."

"I visited local dry cleaners, liquor stores, restaurants, and bookstores. Some rebuilt, some moved to other locations. The professional arsonists working that night, burning down 150 businesses, were never caught or prosecuted. Despite video showing them in action."

"I spoke to Abdul about his rebuilt bookstore. He said they even had clear pictures of the arsonist's face and yet no arrest was ever made. He supported the protesters and their right to peacefully express their anger at what happened. But where is the fairness in destroying his life's work? For what end? What did it prove? It would not bring back George Floyd, nor would it punish the policeman who murdered him. The criminal justice system did that."

"Now in Minneapolis, crime continues to climb. Murders have tripled and every other category has more than doubled. Is that progress? Your police department is down 50 percent. Officers are retiring, and who would want to be a new officer here?"

"We are allowing tiny, but very vocal organizations to speak for all of us. I ask you, do you agree with everything ARL, Antifa, the administration, cable news, network news or the pundits on social media pronounce as the be all end all? Of course not. Are there nuggets of truth in each of these? Probably, but how the hell could you tell? They are all shouting at the tops of their lungs, saying *you* are the problem. I ask you again, do you feel like the problem?" The crowd roared back, '*No*" in answer.

"I didn't think so. Are their corrupt police? Sure. Should we ban all the police because there are a few that give them a bad name? That is like the Vikings giving up their season because someone gets flagged for one bad hit. It is not equal, and it is not fair. Now maybe if it were the Packers or the Bears…" The crowd laughed accordingly.

"Let's face it, what does or did defunding your police accomplish? Do you feel safer?" '*No*' was yelled back by a clear majority. "Do you feel like the black community is safer now that the police are no longer patrolling your neighborhood? The '*No*' this time was even louder."

"While talking to people today during my tour of the city. I asked them about the impact of the lack of cops in their downtown neighborhoods. What they said is they don't go out at night. The gangs are now in the suburbs, breaking into and stealing cars. Breaking into houses, even when people are home. The response from police? Put your keys on the end table nearest the door, so when they break into the house, they can get your keys and leave without confronting you. How F'd up is that?"

"They know the cops won't come and even if they do, and somehow capture the criminal, they won't even have to make bail and will be back on the street that day. To be clear, I am not blaming the cops for this. It is not their fault. There are not enough of them and the rule of law has been diminished by the progressive funded DAs and Attorney Generals. Sadly, all of yours in Minnesota, are beholden to Pavlovich and other progressives who funded their elections. They are certainly not accountable to you," finished Nick as the crowd booed loudly.

"I asked those I talked to what they do if they can't count on the cops to protect them? Buy guns was the universal answer," laughed Nick. "So let me get this straight. One cornerstone of Progressivism is to get guns out of the hands of people. Instead, their policies drive people to buy more guns? Seems like maybe somebody screwed up." The crowd laughed loudly at the irony.

"Actions have consequences, and they cascade. Because we did not stand up when they defunded police. We did not stand up when they passed no bail. We allowed protesters and criminals to break into stores, loot them and walk away with goods from those stores and never prosecuted them for these crimes. We did not stand up when these activists branded all of us racists for even suggesting they not be allowed to break the law. No one complained when corporations caved into their threats of boycotts and started persecuting employees for not adhering to DEI and pronouns. Finally, we stood by while we allowed this vocal few and American *Pravda* to vilify the 99.99 percent of cops who risked their lives every minute of every day, so we didn't have to. So many of our brave cops have opted to retire instead of being constantly attacked for trying to protect us," ended Nick, pausing to let these statements sink in.

"It is *our* fault. We let them take away our freedom and only we can stand up and take it back. I support the rule of law and I support the police who are our chosen citizens enforcing these laws for us. Enforcing these laws equally for all, regardless of race, age, or sexual orientation. What I can tell you is I will fight as long as there is breath in my body to stop these people from destroying our republic. We must stand up together."

Nick was walking back and forth as he spoke, exhorting the crowd with his words, eliciting shouts, and cheers as he went through all the things the people had willingly agreed to. He was working the crowd into the usual frenzy as they realized what they had given up. What they had allowed to happen while they ducked for cover and hid.

Pausing as he reached the end of each side of the stage for several seconds, in his usual predictable cadence. He was at the far end of one side as he finished his last directive to stand up together. Turning to proceed the other way. He was hurled backwards, thrown up and off his feet, onto his back on the stage as the sound of a shot rang out in the twilight.

Part Two

Incoming

"Whatever does not kill me makes me stronger."

Friedrich Nietzsche

Chapter 31

The crowd scattered in all directions, trampling each other. Women and children were screaming. Earl was the first to reach Nick. He was lying flat on his back on the stage. His light-colored shirt quickly turning red. A deeper scarlet nearer the wound on the left side of his upper chest. Earl put himself between Nick and the crowd.

Several other security guards were now strung out between Earl and the crowd. Two EMTs, a burly man and a smaller woman, ran onto the stage. It was clear Nick was still alive from the groans of pain.

The woman quickly cut off his sport coat and shirt to survey the wound. Holding a compression bandage against the entry wound in front, the burly EMT lifted and rolled him sideways as his partner searched for an exit wound.

"Shit," she said under her breath, pushing a wad of bandages against an inch wide gaping hole in Nick's left armpit. "Found it. About an inch." The man looked at her, confused.

"An inch? You sure that is the only one and not a fragment? Should be a bigger hole than that somewhere."

"Lift him higher." As he obliged, she looked over his back and felt around with one latex gloved hand. "A ton of scars, but no other obvious exit wound. You think it's still inside?"

As he lowered Nick, the burly EMT looked up at Earl. "He's probably got something inside still. No way a sniper round exits with a hole that small. We need to get him to the hospital fast."

"I'm right here, you know. Son of a bitch that hurt," gasped Nick, before Earl could answer the EMT.

The female EMT smiled at Nick's comment while the man grunted as he wrapped dressing around Nick's chest and under his arm, securing the compression bandages on both wounds.

"Easy, easy. Let them do their work, save your strength," ordered Earl. He was worried, having seen the results of many sniper shots in his days in Afghanistan. Sniper rounds went in small, then flattened, fragmented, and spun once they hit a body. Usually leaving very large wounds upon exit. Very few survived because of this devastating effect.

"Any idea where it came from? Is he still shooting?" asked Nick, worried about the crowd.

"I don't think it was from this crowd," replied Earl as more police arrived. "There was no second shot. My guess is he is long gone."

"Ok Senator, we're going to sit you up a bit and get you on the gurney. Then to the hospital. It looks like through and through," explained the female EMT, trying to sound hopeful.

"Ha," groaned Nick with clenched teeth. "Been there, done that."

"Apparently," she said, noticing the scars on Nick's chest besides the long scar from the New York City event.

"1,2,3" said the man as they lifted Nick to the gurney and moved him off the stage, surrounded by security. There were multiple TV camera crews trying to get close to Nick. He could hear reporters calling out. Nick raised his right arm weakly and gave a thumbs up.

Earl walked back to Denise, Margie, and Greg. They were huddled off stage with a couple of security guards standing nearby.

"He's OK we think. Looks like it went in and out and missed anything vital so far as we can tell here. He's a tough SOB. I think he'll be fine," announced Earl, trying to sound confident of the outcome.

"Fine? Somebody just tried to kill him. I would say he is anything but fine," croaked Denise, hyped up and shaking.

"Easy Denise, it's the adrenalin. If the shot didn't kill him instantly, he has a good chance. Surprised they didn't try for a head shot. Must have been a long way away," mused Earl, speculating aloud.

"I guess he was lucky then," snapped Denise, staring at Earl with a pissed off look.

"Denise, I deal with the reality of keeping Nick alive every day. We got lucky today. He *should* be dead. You rarely survive a sniper shot."

"Jesus Earl!" exploded Denise.

"Those are just facts," informed Earl. "You need to breathe, Denise." He walked over to her and put an arm around her shoulder, trying to calm her down.

"We need to think about a statement. Get something up on social media quick before they start making things up. Then we need to get him on camera as fast as possible, maybe from his hospital room," prompted Denise, trying to change the subject.

"Margie, can you call your friend at EXN, let's see if we can get Tommy to sit down with Nick and tape an interview. I'm sure he'll jump at the chance to scoop the others," resumed Denise, shifting back to crisis management mode as Earl hid a slight smile at the change.

"Got it," nodded Margie, wiping tears from her eyes.

"Greg, we need to make sure the feds don't seize our footage. Make sure you make a quick copy now. You know they're going to want it. We need to cut it and get it on the website," ordered Denise.

Greg was standing holding the pieces of Nick's sport coat. The left side piece showing the bullet had gone through the jacket twice. On the front at the breast pocket and then again below the left arm sleeve.

"Greg, you with me?" she asked when Greg did not respond. He stood there, vacantly staring at the jacket.

"Greg," prompted Earl, gently taking the jacket from his hand. "Did you hear Denise?"

Greg broke his reverie. "Ya, I'll get the footage copied before they can seize it," he said, heading to the various campaign camera teams.

"Somebody is worried about what Nick has to say and we need to make that point loud and fast," voiced Denise.

"Shouldn't we make sure he really is OK first?" questioned Chuck from Denise's phone, on a video call from DC. She'd dialed him while Earl was tending to Nick.

"He's not dead and Earl says he's good, so in my book, he's good. No time to fart around. We need to capitalize on the coverage," ordered Denise, still shaking from the shock, but obviously back in command.

"Chuck. You and Margie need to get on camera. We need talking points. Again, the main point is we are getting under someone's skin.

Exposing all the ways the government is trying to suppress our freedoms. Trying to shut Nick up permanently. I'll head to the hospital with Earl. You guys handle any press questions. Greg, get that footage copied. Let's move people. They've handed us a godsend. What doesn't kill us just makes us stronger," finished Denise, sensing the PR opportunity as folks scrambled to accomplish their various tasks.

#

Mel answered the scrambled satellite phone. "Yes?"

"Have you seen the news?" said the mechanically masked Voice.

"Of course. Unfortunate," said Mel.

"Unfortunate? Was this you?" asked the Voice clearly irritated.

"Me? Hell no, we had this guy right where we wanted him, irrelevant and distracted defending against all our attacks. I assumed this was you or your man. You're the one who said we can't risk screwing this up again," said Mel, his voice an octave higher than normal.

"I assure you I didn't order this," said the Voice. "Is he alive?"

"Yes, from what we can tell from our sources, he is on his way to the hospital for evaluation, but our info says he got lucky," explained Mel.

"Who did it if it wasn't you? Any chance your candidate went behind your back?"

"I don't know. Not her style. I'll see what I can find out," promised Mel. "The Secret Service is getting involved now."

"Good. You have some control then. Any chance *he* did it?"

"You mean have himself shot?" asked Mel in a shocked tone. "Wow, that's pretty risky. Brilliant if you can pull it off. Even if he didn't, maybe we can allude to it if they don't get the shooter fast," contemplated Mel, thinking out loud.

"I'd look into it. Like you said, he is irrelevant, at least according to the polls. His crowds are pretty big, and you couldn't stop EXN from showing his rallies," said the Voice, the annoyance coming through.

"We'll call the networks and tell them to get it off the air ASAP, but he'll get coverage and on Hibi as well. Social media will eat this up," groaned Mel. "Maybe we can get our media to plant the thought he did it to himself. Get people thinking they're being played. Especially with his mistake with the Marine. Maybe he is trying to deflect the criticism. We can turn our trolls loose on social media to speculate on this angle."

"If you think it is wise. Just win," finished the Voice.

"We will," said Mel, but the other side had already ended the call.

\#

Lauren woke up with a start. She was still in her favorite chair in her living room, her empty martini glass on the side table. It took a second for her eyes to focus and her head was pounding. Her phone buzzed again. She picked it up and scanned through the texts and alerts.

One stood out, causing her to stand up quickly, looking for her TV remote. '*NEWS ALERT: Presidential Candidate Nick Turner shot during an outdoor event in Minneapolis. No status. Stay tuned for more information.*' She nearly buckled from the pain in her abdomen. The guilt of her deed flooding her mind. Lauren turned on ANC, where they had on normal programming with only a crawler announcing Nick Turner had been shot.

She turned to EXN. They were showing the chaos at the state fair, with an on-site reporter talking about the aftermath. People running over each other to flee the gunman. They had a medical doctor on analyzing the slow motion footage of Nick being hurled backwards on stage. Another reporter added onlookers said Senator Turner was alive and raised an arm as they wheeled him away to the ambulance. Right now, he was supposedly at the Minneapolis Trauma Center in surgery.

Lauren looked at her phone, pulled up Nick's number, and typed a text. She paused over the send button, reflecting on the events of the day.

\#

"Doc, when can I leave?" asked Nick, sitting up in his hospital room bed. A bandage across his upper left chest and under his armpit.

"You're lucky to be alive. If you hadn't turned, it would have hit you in the chest and gone through your back. Potentially damaging your lungs. Instead, it came in laterally and passed through soft tissue, missing everything. As gunshots go, this is about the least damaging I've ever seen," said the doctor in a surprised tone. He held his stethoscope against Nick's back and asked him to inhale.

"Your x-rays are all negative. Your exit wound is more akin to a .22 caliber bullet. But the entry wound says it was most likely a .30-06 or .338 caliber. There are also no fragments. The pressure wave that does most of the damage appears to have been minimal. I don't know your relationship with God, Senator, but your guardian angel is probably tired of looking out for you from your list of scars."

Nick grunted in reply as the Dr. continued.

"All good. Seems like everything is working as advertised. You're going to be sore as hell. You'll also need someone to look at the exit wound daily for a while. I gave you a tetanus booster and started some antibiotics. I have a question for you," he said, looking at Nick's back. His fingers tracing a series of long, raised vertical scars. "These are very interesting. How did you get them? If you don't mind me asking?"

"Motorcycle accident when I was young, went over the handlebars wearing only a T-shirt. Slid a long time on my back through gravel. Shredded my favorite T-shirt," laughed Nick.

"Really? Interesting," he remarked. We'll keep you overnight. If all goes well, you can leave in the morning. Deal?

"OK, you win," replied Nick, closing his eyes in obvious pain.

"You sure you don't want something for the pain? It's going to hurt like hell, and get worse before it gets better," observed the doctor.

"Thanks Doc, but aspirin is fine. Gotta keep my wits about me. Where's my gun? I don't want to lose track of it. Sentimental value."

"Your man has it. You also have a nasty bruise where you landed on it when you hit the stage. Might want to think about that next time."

"Thanks Doc. Guess I'd have been better off carrying a shield."

The doctor shook his head at the conversation. Most gunshot victims were anything but humorous at this stage. He left the room, meeting with Earl and Denise in the hallway.

"Is he *really* alright, Dr. Guraji?" asked Denise, in a worried tone.

"Yes, he is. I don't know how or why. Based on the wound, you're probably looking for a high caliber rifle bullet since it went through. It did not enter at the highest velocity, is my only guess based on the lack of damage. The shooter was probably a long way away. He really is lucky.

If he had still been straight on, it would have gone in small and come out large, if at all, and the shock wave would have messed with a bunch of organs. This way, it aimed all the shock at his side and there was nothing there to damage. He's also showing no signs of a concussion. Either he didn't hit his head, or it is really hard."

"You have no idea," said Earl and Denise, both looking at each other as they laughed for the first time since the shooting.

Guraji smiled as well. "Not for nothing, but his explanation about the scars on his back is total bullshit. Gravel does not split your skin in straight lines. I'll check back in the morning."

"Thanks Doc," replied Earl, remembering the entirely different story Nick had told him about the scars on his back.

The doctor turned to Earl. "He's asking for his gun. Guess he doesn't trust them," nodding at the security standing outside the door.

As Dr. Guraji left, Earl and Denise went back into Nick's room.

"OK, Mom and Dad, give me the bad news. How long do I have to live?" asked Nick with a weak smile.

"You can laugh, but you are really lucky," retorted Denise, puffing up, but concerned. She'd never seen Nick look so weak and pale before.

"She's right and you know it," agreed Earl.

"Hey, they could kill me anytime they want. It makes little sense," replied Nick, shaking his head, sitting up. "Any idea who did it?"

"I spoke to the cops, nothing so far. Of course, now the Secret Service is here and crawling over the crime scene. You aren't high enough in the polls to warrant Secret Service security, but after they try to kill you, they're suddenly interested. Seems a bit backwards," stated Earl.

"Anybody else hurt in the chaos after? I saw the footage on the TV while you guys were talking to the doctor," worried Nick, pointing to the muted TV in the room.

"Thankfully nobody died, but there were a few injuries," replied Earl, as Denise turned off the TV, shaking her head.

"Are any of them here? Let's visit them before I leave in the morning. You have my pistol?"

Earl shook his head this time, handing Nick his .45 in its worn holster. Nick smiled. "Thanks."

"Lotta good it did you," groused Denise.

"You never know. Maybe next time I'll see them coming."

"You should get some rest. We'll be here in the morning," finished Earl, turning, holding the door for Denise.

"Nick, Tommy is flying out first thing. We want him to do a bedside interview, so you are stuck here until he gets here."

"Denise, no way I do it from the bed."

"We'll figure it out," agreed Denise, not wanting to argue.

Earl and Denise left his room to return to their hotel. It had been a hell of an evening.

Chapter 32

Nick sat up. He slowly got out of bed and walked gingerly to the bathroom. Returning, he found his clothes in a bag under the bed. Grabbing them, he removed his socks, shoes, and pants from the day before and put them back on, threading his holster through the belt to the small of his back. He noticed a couple of dried drops of blood on his shoes. Bending over to wipe them off, a shooting pain hit mid bend. Straightening back up, light-headed and grimacing, he now remembered the previous times he'd been wounded.

Chuckling a bit, he added them up. He figured he was up to at least twelve different wounds in the service of his country. There were a few official purple hearts and a few unofficial ones. He wondered if he was wearing his guardian angel out, as the Doc had said. Shaking his head, he looked in the closet, trying to find something resembling a shirt. Standing half dressed, the doctor came into the room.

"I see you are feeling well enough to be up and around."

"Mostly. Couldn't bend over to tie my shoes," replied Nick, wiggling an untied shoe. "Any chance you can find me a shirt?"

"I'll see what I can do." Dr. Guraji stuck his head back out the door, asking a nurse to find a scrub top.

"How are you really feeling? Did you sleep?"

"Like a baby," winced Nick. "Honestly? Pretty sore."

"You're going to be that way for a few days, but looking at your list of scars, I think you already know what to expect." At that point, the nurse came in and handed Dr. Guraji a scrub top. "Let's take a look before we put the shirt on." He checked Nick's wound under his arm. Carefully lifting away the dressing to examine the hole. It had already shrunk significantly.

"What the…"

"Something wrong Doc," asked Nick, trying to look.

Dr. Guraji pressed the dressing back in place and had Nick lower his arm. He stared at him.

"What?"

"Have your other wounds healed unusually fast?" He asked, grabbing Nick's chart with the blood test results. Nothing unusual.

Nick shrugged. "I don't know. Have nothing to compare it to. I've always seemed to heal fast. Why, something happening there?"

"Your exit wound is healing at an incredibly fast rate. It should take weeks and yet it is already closing. That would be classified as incredibly fast. Very interesting." Nick struggled to put on the shirt.

"Here, let me help you." Guraji helped Nick get his left arm through the scrub top. "Should have gone for 2XL, that's pretty tight. You sure it's OK?"

"Sure Doc. Actually, I didn't properly thank you for the treatment." Nick held out his hand.

"Pleased to meet you, Senator. Suresh Guraji," he replied.

"The least you can do is call me Nick. I am not going to be a senator much longer, so I should get used to being just Nick again."

"You're very good at deflecting questions."

"Me? Come on Doc, what didn't I answer?" pointed out Nick slyly, looking around the room for his phone.

"You didn't respond to my statement about knowing what to expect when you've been wounded. When you came in, we cataloged all the scars. It reads like a spy novel," noted Suresh, referring to the chart.

"The knife wound to the chest we all know about. What appears to be bullet scars in left abdomen, right side, left shoulder, upper thigh on right leg, on left calf, several other scars showing most likely sharp object penetration of your torso and upper right arm and left forearm. Other scars look to be from shrapnel fragments. And then, of course, there are the long scars on your back. Sir, no offence, but you did not get those in any motorcycle accident," finished the doctor.

"Well Doc, what can I say? I spent 20 years on and off in some hellholes around the world fighting bad guys. On the ground and in the air. You forgot the half dozen concussions and lots of broken ribs, toes and fingers. Other than that, excellent summary," added Nick with a laugh, having found the bag with his wallet and phone. "And you have no idea how dangerous teaching kids is these days," deadpanned Nick.

"I once saw scars like that on the back of several Afghani freedom fighters when I was working in the humanitarian camps there. There was a Taliban chief who liked to torture suspected traitors with a bullwhip." Suresh paused to see if Nick reacted.

"They said he used it because it was the same vintage bull whip owned by the Afghan ruler the British installed in the mid-1800s. During those days in the first Anglo-Afghan War, he liked to use the lash to keep the Afghani tribal leaders in check."

"Really interesting story Doc. Not sure what it has to do with me. I came by my scars through teenage stupidity. Any of my staff here yet? asked Nick, ignoring the questions.

"Outside, waiting for me to let them in. One Afghani told me one day they found the chief hanging from the same whip he used to torture his subjects. His back was a bloody mess. He had a few other anatomical alterations I won't describe. Apparently, he got a taste of his own medicine before being hung. Fancy that."

"Sounds like fair justice to me. The Afghani culture is very Hammurabi. You know an eye for an eye and all that. Doc, if we are finished, can you send them in? I have some things I need to get done and I suppose the press is camped out at all the exits," guessed Nick.

"You know, Senator, it is really funny. Last night they were, but this morning only EXN and some of the local stations, along with a couple of print reporters. No one else came back. I gave a statement last night saying you were fine. This morning no one even asked to talk to me. We usually have crews crawling all over the place any time there is a police involved shooting. Here you are, a candidate for president, shot at our state fair in front of 20,000 onlookers, and nobody cares?"

"You got that right. Thanks again for stitching me up." Dr. Guraji opened the door and motioned for Earl and Denise to come in.

"Ah, good to see you up. How do you feel?" asked Earl as he entered and saw Nick up and dressed.

"You ever been shot, Earl?" he nodded.

"Well then, I guess you know how it feels. Sore as hell and happy to be talking to you. What is the plan? Is Tommy coming? Doc here told me there is no press. What gives?"

"That's my cue to leave," announced Dr. Guraji.

"Thanks again doctor," they all said as he left.

"Why is there no press?"

"They appear to be trying to minimize it. Saying there was a minor incident. You were just slightly wounded under mysterious circumstances, with no shooter located. It is almost as if they are trying to imply you staged this to raise your visibility. Hell, on FLCN, they had a guest on who even said that you staged it because you are so far behind in the polls and to deflect from your support for Dusty," laughed Denise.

"Why are you laughing?" asked Nick.

"They miscalculated, the phones rang off the hook, the amount of hate email and online comments from your supporters crashed their websites. Even several Party Senators came on other networks saying this was not a wise rumor to spread. FLCN had to come on and disavow what the guest said, saying they don't believe you staged it," added Denise.

"Their attempt to minimize the shooting ensured it is now even more prevalent, especially on social media. Now outlets who would not normally care are now covering it. Every decision they make about you turns out to be the wrong one. Those network presidents are probably getting an earful from Lexi right about now," said Denise with a smile.

"We can probably put that one to rest in a hurry. I'm a pretty good shot, as Earl can attest.

He nodded his head vigorously in agreement. "Cost me $200."

"Which I gave right back to you after I proved my point," replied Nick. "Anyway, that hit me three, maybe three and a half inches above and to the left of my heart. If that is what they are aiming for and did not intend to kill me, that is an incredible shot. Only a very well-trained sniper would even attempt it. Anyone find anything yet?"

"Nothing of note. I talked to the Secret Service agent in charge. All he would share is they found potential evidence of someone getting on the roof of a building with a line of sight to the stage, but the shot would have been over a mile. Hard to be accurate at that range."

"You figure they are trying to minimize any exposure we get? What are they worried about? Where are we? Five percent?" smiled Nick.

"Thanks to your direction, we don't know where we are in the polls," groused Denise.

"We've been through this. I almost won the nomination. Clearly, our support is growing. We don't need polls to confirm it to *us*."

"Can you please tell your supporters to start telling the truth now? After this," asked Denise, exasperated by this subject and Nick's insistence in continued misdirection.

"Hell no, we still have two months to go. Keep her worried about Blackbird. All that would do is confirm to *them* we are actually higher. We don't want Lexi sending her goon squads after us."

"Uh, somebody just tried to assassinate you. Maybe she already has?" observed Denise.

"Is Tommy coming?" asked Nick, ignoring Denise's statement.

"Landed 15 minutes ago," said Earl, looking at his watch.

"Good. Can we visit some of the injured before we talk to him?"

\#

Nick knocked on the open door where twelve-year-old Angela Friberg sat in her hospital bed with her parents standing by her bedside.

"Angela, do you mind if I come in?" asked Nick.

Angela smiled and sat up straighter in her bed. She had a small bandage on her forehead and a pink cast on her left forearm. Angela's mother smiled, answering for her tongue-tied daughter, who was blushing at the visit by the senator. "Please Senator, come on in. How are *you*?"

Nick waved off her concern. "I'm fine. More importantly, how are you, Angela?" Nick asked as he approached her bedside. The local TV camera crew was at the door of the room filming.

"I'm OK Mr. Turner. I was so scared for you. Are you really OK?" Angela asked, concern coming through in her pre-teen voice.

"I'm fine, thank you, Angela. Thank you for being so brave in all the confusion. Can I be the first to sign your cast?" asked Nick, who was handed a marker by Earl standing behind him.

"That would be *awesome*," said Angela with a huge smile on her face. She put her pink cast across the bed and grabbed the bar in front of Nick as he signed her cast and smiled with her as her mother and father moved to the other side of the room to take a picture. Earl took her camera and snapped a picture of the entire family with Nick.

"You get back to school and let your classmates know how brave you are. Let them know there is nothing to be afraid of if we keep believing in freedom and the Constitution."

#

"Senator, first, I need to ask for the viewers how you are feeling?"

"Tommy, I'm fine, just sore. The bullet went in and came out, missing any major organs. This won't make me change anything."

"Good, I have to tell you, there were many who were worried when the footage was shown. We're all thankful you weren't seriously injured and that no one in the crowd was seriously injured, either."

"I find it ironic that I am shot during a speech where I was highlighting the need for police and how defunding the police is an invitation to the criminals and anarchists to run rampant."

"Exactly, it is my understanding they have no suspects and obviously no arrests have been made," explained Tommy.

"I'm confident the investigation will continue. Until then I'll keep educating people about the freedoms they are losing. Hiding would let the progressives win. Their policies are all about convincing people to not stand up. To hide in their house, keep their mouths shut, and to look away from anything they don't like. I won't be cowed into running my campaign from a basement or anywhere else. People deserve to see and challenge their candidates. To see them debate and defend their stances. All I can say is, I'm still here, and I intend to keep fighting," promised Nick, looking into the camera in an almost challenging tone. He could sense Earl cringing off camera and resisted the urge to smile.

"You know they are already minimizing this on the other networks. You made page five of the *Times* and like page seven or eight of the *Post*. What does it say when an assassination attempt of a presidential candidate is a minor story?" Nick nodded at Tommy's statements.

"In fact, when it first happened, the story was all over the networks and on the websites of the major print and social media sites. Then it was as if someone decided it was not a story and it disappeared from all the major outlets simultaneously," remarked Tommy.

"This just underscores my naming them American *Pravda*. It shows we do not have an independent media element in the United States. I think the fact all the press were here last night and none, but EXN are here this morning, is all the proof one needs. Could be someone somewhere decided covering this story and generating any sympathy for a candidate who is obviously rubbing some the wrong way, shouldn't get a bunch of free airtime?" confided Nick.

"It sure seems that way. I don't know how you could come to any other conclusion," agreed Tommy as Nick nodded, taking a sip from a freshly opened bottle of water. "It also tells me you are doing much better than the polls are showing. Otherwise, why would they care?"

"You know how I feel about polls," shrugged Nick.

"I agree Senator, the polls are another tool of controlling the narrative and public opinion."

Nick laughed. "Polls affect people's behavior and I am sure many folks stay home, especially young people, when they see a low poll for their candidate. Though I think high polls also make supporters complacent. They too figure why go stand in line when they have a big lead? I say, be careful, your little game can hurt as well as help," ended Nick, breaking out in a smile. Tommy smiled as well as Nick continued.

"Who you say you support is none of my business or theirs. Turn off the news and ignore the polls," suggested Nick.

"Remember we are opinion, not news, so keep watching us for the truth," laughed Tommy.

"Whatever," said Nick, now also laughing.

"You may not know, Senator, but there was a professor who got on FLCN and suggested you staged the entire assassination attempt to help your status in those very polls. How do you answer this accusation?"

"Tommy, are we live?"

"Yes,"

"OK, I will refrain from using any language you could get in trouble for, but let me explain." Nick leaned forward and pulled off his scrub top with his good right arm, displaying his bandaged chest. He pulled aside the bandage.

"You see this," said Nick, pointing to the angry red and visible stitched up hole in his chest where the bullet entered. Purple bruising surrounding the entry wound. He turned to show the much larger dressing under his arm, but it was easy to see the hole was much larger than the one on the front of his chest. The bright pink scar from his New York knife attack was also easily visible. Off camera, the doctors and nurses yelled at the Senator to be careful and not strain.

"Tommy, you see this?" repeated Nick. "You've been in combat. You know what it's like to get shot or see others get shot." Nick held up his finger and showing the shot was three to four inches from his heart.

"If I was trying to stage this, do you really think I would have someone shoot me from a long distance while I am marching back and forth on a stage and have them hit me in the chest three inches from my *heart*?" Nick's voice was rising, and he was gesturing with his hands.

"These people are f-ing stupid. It is not even worthy of further comment. Now I don't know who tried to shoot me, but if I am so low in the polls, why is anybody trying to kill me? What am I saying they are so worried about? Who has anything to worry about by my running around educating people on how they are being controlled?" asked Nick, turning to the camera one more time.

"I don't know who did it. Guess what? I'm not going anywhere. I'll continue to fight against the tyranny of this progressive agenda. Because

I'm what they fear most. Someone willing to pull back the curtain so all can see what *they* have planned for you," said Nick, leaning back and preparing to put his scrub top back on.

"Ah, Senator, I think maybe we need to end the interview and have your doctor check your dressing," said Tommy, looking at the blood running down Nick's chest from his wound. Nick looked down and pressed the bandage back over his wound, holding it back into place.

"Whoops, guess I overdid it. Thank you, Tommy. For doing this interview and not censoring the news and the truth like the others. All I can say to everyone who sees this, why are you even watching American *Pravda*? Clicking on the social media apps making them money. They hate you and don't want you to know the truth or decide for yourself," ended Nick in an earnest tone as the blood pulsed. The red spot on his bandage expanding and darkening more.

"Thanks Senator Turner, good luck with the recovery," said Tommy as they zoomed in on him as the producer announced they were done. Dr. Guraji and two nurses approached Nick.

"Shit Nick, what the hell were you thinking doing this live? You have to take it easy," bellowed Tommy as the staff worked on Nick.

"You popped your stitches, Senator. We may have to put a couple more in," he said, stripping the old dressing and pressing other bandages against the wound as it continued to bleed.

"Tommy, it pisses me off these shitheads can publish this crap without a shred of truth. There's no way to make them pay for lying."

"Guys, we are having trouble stopping the live feed," said the producer from off camera. The doctors and nurses continued to press dressing against Nick's wound as he laughed.

"Sorry Tommy, I hope 'shithead' is allowed." Tommy laughed as well, as the producer finally said they got the live feed stopped.

"That will make for some lively coverage. Just makes it more real. As for your questions Nick, it is too easy to sue in America. Welcome to my world. I have tons of lawsuits accusing me of lying about them on camera, so *they* try to do something about it when somebody says the truth about them," laughed Tommy as they started breaking down the equipment. Nick shook his hand.

"Thanks for coming out."

"Hell, it's great for us, too. My producer said people were tuning in like crazy looking for info on you." He looked past Nick at his producer, Wayne. "In fact, I wouldn't put it past him to have manufactured our 'problems' disconnecting the feed. He knows what plays to our viewers." Wayne laughed.

"If they wanted to keep it obscure, your antics just made sure it is going to be replayed all day on EXN. Hell, the other guys may have to use my footage and that'll send them through the roof," grinned Tommy.

"Senator, we need to get you back to a room and stitch this again. No more acrobatics, please," ordered Dr. Guraji.

Nick smiled and headed out with the doctor and nurses. He turned his phone back on. It immediately started vibrating with texts from the few who had his phone number. One caught his attention.

"Are you OK?" asked the text.

"All good," wrote Nick back. But there was no response before he put the phone down to let Dr. Guraji restitch his wound.

Chapter 33

Lexi ended the call on her secure phone and leaned back in her Capitol office chair. A buzzer went off. Glancing down, she reached under the desk, pressing the button to take her office out of the secure SCIF mode. Once the clicks and pops stopped, Mel opened the door tentatively, sticking his head in.

"Get in here," she commanded. "What the fuck was that? Who shot him?"

"No one knows. Law enforcement and the Secret Service are coming up empty. Whoever it was covered their tracks well. They have almost no leads," replied Mel, pacing at the far end of the office.

"Shit. Mel, this is the worst scenario. Why did he have to live?"

He stopped at her tone. "You didn't order this, did you?"

"What?"

Mel relaxed. "Just the way you said it. Like you were pissed, the mission failed. I thought for a second, you'd decided to take out the competition. Maybe have Roland use some of his 'talents'."

Lexi stood, making her way to the bar. She poured hot water from a carafe. "He's your guy. How do I know you didn't tell him to do it?"

"Not my style," responded Mel without hesitation. "Besides, I wouldn't do something this drastic without your order or approval."

She dipped a tea bag into the cup. "People are saying I tried to kill Turner?"

"Some. Others are saying he did it to himself. He was just on Tommy and gave a pretty compelling performance, explaining how he would have to be suicidal to invite a long-distance sniper shot on himself. Sadly, it is resonating. So much for that theory."

"If he didn't do it and I didn't, who did? If it is as professional as you say?" asked Lexi.

"Could be anyone with enough money. Disgruntled donors upset at him challenging you. Many industries stand to lose billions if he wins and goes after them or their government funding. Some unhinged vet. Another country or even one of those global elites he is always railing against. The list is not short."

Lexi came back to the desk and sat, sipping her tea. "What do we do now? I assume he will get a sympathy bump?"

"No doubt. I suggest we hit him with something. It's only the beginning of September. I hate to waste some of our attacks this early."

Lexi sat with a frown on her face. "Exactly how did he survive? I don't remember many stories of people surviving snipers."

"Dumb luck. Apparently, he turned as the shot hit him and it went out sideways rather than front to back and it was higher on his chest as well because of that."

"Figures. With all this luck, he should buy a winning Powerball ticket, get a yacht, and hang out in Portofino," growled Lexi.

Mel started laughing before realizing Lexi was not kidding.

"If we don't want to use our surprises early, what else can we do?" she asked.

"Even though Turner got the best of him, Pastor Mills reinforced some of his more 'radical' views to a subset of conservatives who just can't reconcile allowing abortions. If nothing else, it probably keeps them home. He also got pretty preachy, quoting scripture and all that. Some of the more religious on the right might not appreciate him using the bible to take down a pastor," stated Mel tentatively.

"That didn't work out quite like we planned."

"Hey at least we got what we needed. Turner doubling down on stances the far-right hates. What happens to Mills after is his own damn fault. He's done. What is the saying, 'people in glass houses'…" said Mel with a smile.

"What else?"

"The trial of that Marine is coming up. Perhaps we can get some folks talking about that again. Maybe find more police commissioners or the union representative. This has been his biggest error so far. We need to keep hammering him on it. Those families appearing against him were pretty powerful stuff. Even made me shed a tear at their pain."

Lexi sat back in the chair, looking at the ornate ceiling of her office. So many decisions, each a fork in the road, leading destiny down a divergent path. What was once clear was now becoming blurry. Turner was like a San Francisco fog. Rolling in and obscuring her vision of what were once obvious choices.

"What do you think, Mel?"

"Small ball. Let's save the home runs for October."

Lexi sat up, smiling. Mel knew she was a rabid San Francisco Giant's fan. She had a suite at the baseball stadium and took in as many games as she could when in town. "We should concentrate on singles? I am OK with that. What are you proposing?"

"Let's get annoying. Lots of little stories. Nothing earth shattering but keep him on the defense. Amp up the protests at all his rallies and those of his supporters. Attack them. File some lawsuits, continue to agitate in the press. Get some experts on cable shows highlighting some of his proposals. Ramp up the attacks on social media. He's self-publishing his book after you pressured his publisher to cancel it once he came out for the Marine. We'll get folks to publish some comments on that too. Flood the online sites with one-star reviews."

"Make it happen," smiled Lexi. The idea of Turner annoyed and distracted brought her great joy.

Chapter 34

"Not to be morbid or anything, but we've been handed a golden ticket," announced Denise. "Now, what do we do with it?"

"I think we need to get him out on stage again as soon as possible. We're rerouting Neill to cover Salt Lake, but maybe he can still do Nashville?" suggested Greg.

"What about the rumors he did this to himself?" asked Margie.

"We keep running the Tommy interview non-stop on our website and Hibi. Keep it front and center. They're going crazy saying the 'off camera' footage at the end was a ploy. Either way, it's great. We have 200 million views so far. We need Nick to do the same on the stage in Nashville," proposed Chuck, half joking.

"Anyone who has seen the video knows it's not fake. There is a new video where somebody went through frame by frame. You can clearly see the impact and the exit of the bullet. No way to fake that. We've come a long way from the grassy knoll. We had thousands of cameras and their footage to choose from. The 2J's ran a story with their robot commentators. They concluded someone would have less than one percent chance of survival to stand and willingly be shot by a sniper," offered Greg.

"Who the hell are the '2J's'?" asked Chuck.

Margie laughed. "It's what folks are calling 2JNews. The AI newscasters are popular with the GenZers. It scares the crap out of everyone else. The millennials are on the fence, apparently. The report Greg mentioned is really putting the other social media apps in an awkward position," shared Margie.

"How so?" asked Chuck.

"Folks are forwarding clips from Tommy's show and the one on the 2J's. Many are posted on Hibi. The Homeland decree was to keep Nick's speeches and campaign ads off their platforms, or rather the *suggestion*," Margie corrected herself with a smile.

"Suggestion, right," scoffed Denise.

"Anyway, the story is about Nick, not from him. They are trying to decide if they should take them down. Some started to, but the pushback was so loud. It's getting out to broader audiences even from these outlets, finally," finished Margie with a broad smile.

"Only took the boss getting shot. What else can we do to capitalize on it?" asked Chuck, frowning.

"I know he won't let us write any speeches, but we need him to hit all the things he has said with Tommy about why someone wants to kill him. Really paint the picture of the Progressives feeling threatened by his words. Let's make sure he hits them hard. They deserve it. I still don't believe it wasn't them. This is exactly like something those backing Lexi would do," confirmed Denise.

"Maybe. Nick is not high enough in the official polls to warrant this type of response," speculated Chuck. "I guess if they had killed him, it would be different. This is the worst possible scenario for them. He lives to get a bump in the polls. Everyone figures it was her, and he gets to blame her nonstop for the next seven weeks. We couldn't have orchestrated it better ourselves."

"It's like a sign from God," added Greg.

"I don't care where it's from," agreed Denise.

There was a knock on the door, which they all yelled at the same time to 'come in'. A young man in his early twenties came in with a stack of paper. Kevin, the former intern, and now campaign staffer, entered. He seemed a bit flustered at walking in on a high-level strategy meeting.

"Kevin, what's up?" asked Greg.

"I'm sorry, but you said you wanted the latest on the fundraising. Here you go," explained Kevin, handing a stack of papers to Greg.

"Thanks, Kevin." He turned and practically ran out.

"One of your trainees?" grinned Margie.

"Hey, you have a bunch of them, too. They are smart, but man, they are timid. You'd think by now, eight months into this, they'd build up some confidence and be a bit more forceful. It's not like we are going to breathe fire on them." Greg paused, looking at Chuck, Margie, and Denise. "Well, at least two of us aren't," he finished with a smile.

"Funny. How *is* the fundraising?" asked Chuck sarcastically, knowing which two Greg was alluding to.

"Thankfully, it has been through the roof," commented Greg, looking at the top sheet of the papers in his lap. "We raised over $45 million in just two days. That doesn't count today yet. It's been a windfall for the volunteering as well. Makes up for some of what we lost. We are around 250 million. We've spent about 450 in the first eight months."

"We can expect to spend that much again in the last two. It's just how these things work. You can never have too much campaign cash. Trust me. I'm just glad we are getting money in again. If nothing else, this has made people forget the Marine," noted Denise with a scowl.

"Ever the optimist, huh, Denise?" Chuck looked at her.

She flipped him off. Only Chuck could get away with making fun of Denise's dismay at Nick's stance with Dusty. She turned to Margie.

"We need to cut a spot with Nick talking about the first amendment, one's right to have a different opinion, and right to voice that opinion without being shot. Let's take advantage of it and show a voice over of Nick, saying something like, *this is not the first time I've been wounded serving my country. I got up before and I got up this time too. I will be here to protect you from those who mean to do you harm. You can count on it'* or something like that," suggested Denise.

"Wow. That's great. Greg let's get with creative right after this and see what we can do. Maybe we can even work in a Captain America vibe. I love it." Margie perked up, thinking of the possibilities.

"Let me see it, but don't show it to Nick. He'll just nix it. Boy, it would drive Lexi up the wall," smiled Denise at the thought.

"Let's not goad her into trying to finish the job, or jinx him," advised Chuck.

"Lexi took her shot. Whether or not she was behind it. Even she knows she'd lose to Blackbird if people think she is trying to bump off the competition. There are still enough patriotic Americans on both sides who don't take kindly to being manipulated," countered Denise.

"Let's hope so," agreed Greg.

"Jer, any jump in polling?" asked Denise

Jer looked up from his seat next to Margie. They both looked up like kids called on in class to answer a question they didn't hear.

"We ran a new one right after and we are kicking off another one now that the Tommy interview is being widely viewed. We are also running some polls on Hibi and several other sites. I should start getting results tomorrow and we can compile them," answered Jer.

"Good," said Denise, smiling at Jer's and Margie's response. They were an unlikely couple, the tall and elegant Margie with her light brown skin and skinny, pasty white Jerry with no fashion sense, glasses, and an awkward manner. Opposites did attract in their case. It made Denise think back about her own campaign romances around their same age.

"Denise?" called Chuck, breaking Denise out of her daydream.

"What are we missing?" asked Denise, recovering quickly.

"What about putting him on some networks?" asked Margie.

"Have they been asking?"

"Right after it happened, but then most of them didn't ask again. There's still the invite from *The Sunday Hour*," offered Margie.

Denise looked up at the ceiling, thinking. "Chuck?"

"I don't know. Could be a trap. No telling if he'd even do it."

Denise looked at him. "Can you ask Nick?"

"Ask Nick what?" he said, coming into the conference room.

"Boss, what the hell are you doing here?" spouted Greg, getting up to move over a chair and let Nick sit near the door.

"Thanks Greg." Nick took a seat gingerly. "Was bored to tears, so I decided to check in with the team."

"How did you get down here from Ft. Collins? Please tell me you didn't drive, and not the Corvette," an exasperated Chuck asked.

"Hey Chuck, good to see you too," grinned Nick. "Didn't know you were in Denver."

"You got shot. I figured it might be a good idea to keep a closer eye on you. Make sure I still had a senator to work for."

"Here I am and no, I did not drive. No way I can hold the wheel and shift. Earl drove me down."

"Where is our security chief?" asked Denise.

"Chewing out the Secret Service, I suspect. He is threatening to get more private security. Then go public with the unwillingness of the

Secret Service to protect a candidate for President, especially one who has had an attempt on his life."

"You said you didn't want them," responded Denise, confused.

"Let's say Earl has made a compelling case."

As if on cue, Earl came into the office. He did not appear to have accomplished his mission.

"I guess I'm still chopped liver from your look."

"They don't feel you're significant enough of a candidate to warrant the additional expense of providing Secret Service coverage."

"Did they offer a threshold I need to achieve? Perhaps getting killed next time?" answered Nick with a laugh.

"Not funny Nick," scowled Earl.

"Earl, you know I don't want them. Go hire some of your Special Forces buddies. I don't care."

"That's going to be expensive," blurted Denise.

"I'm not talking about the 82nd Airborne, just enough to review the perimeter and keep tabs on things."

"You realize they wouldn't have stopped this? I doubt even the Secret Service would've been able to stop a sniper from a mile away."

"So what would they do, then?" asked Nick.

"They would be a show of force and keep a perimeter around you when you move from place to place. You are now a trophy. The crazy who takes you down will be famous," he noted.

"Jesus Earl," snapped Denise, while others around the table looked shocked at his statement.

Nick sat staring at Earl. "You're right. Get a set of bodyguards you know and trust. I prefer ex-military if possible. I know a former admiral of the special warfare school," offered Nick snidely.

"SEALs? I think my Special Forces buddies can handle this. No need to bring in the squids."

"Whatever," laughed Nick. Inter-service rivalries never died. "I can't exactly hide. Here's to hoping he took his shot and we're done."

"As you always say, hope is not a strategy. Sadly, I don't have a better one," ended Earl.

"Sorry I crashed the party. What were you guys talking about?"

"Nothing you need to worry about. Fundraising is up big, which is a bright spot in all of this. We might actually keep the lights on through the election, assuming Earl doesn't hire too many Green Berets. We have new polls out. We're going to cut some new ads highlighting the right to have a dissenting opinion and how they might be worried about this. Finally, we need to get you back on stage. You think you'll be up for Tennessee next weekend?" queried Denise.

"You tell me where I need to be, and I'll be there. I thought Salt Lake was next."

"We'll have Neill cover that one," answered Chuck.

"Oh, he'll love that."

"He'll be fine. We'll plan Nashville for your return. You have to be in Washington for some votes, anyway. I'll come back with you and Chuck so we can prepare," said Denise.

"OK, Nashville it is."

"You have to at least make an appearance at Dolly's Fall Gala. You've skipped the last two and according to her, you promised you'd make this one," confirmed Chuck.

"Nice to know you two talk about me."

Denise ignored Nick's stare. "In Nashville, we need you to repeat your performance on Tommy, so wear a shirt you can rip open to show your bandage and stitches. We'll go up 5 pts with the ladies just from that," laughed Denise as Margie joined in.

"You're joking, right?" asked Nick, concerned.

"We need you to tell the audience there is no way in hell you would allow a sniper to shoot you from over a mile away and count on them not killing you. The ripped shirt is up to you," she smiled. "Maybe we can get you a Captain America shield or something," said Denise.

Nick laughed, more than they expected.

"What is so funny? I think it would play really well. You're a national hero," responded Denise.

"I'll tell you why it's funny," said Bob Sutter, entering the room.

"Hey Colonel," said Nick. "Gee, is there anyone from the team still left in Washington?"

"Like Chuck, I wanted to see for myself. Guess who I talked to before I came out? Congressman Constantine sends his regards. He also told me a few stories while we toasted your survival. Turns out he flew with the boss in Afghanistan. He also likes my family's bourbon too," smiled the Colonel. "Anyone care to guess what our boss's call sign was when he flew his A-10?" he asked the team as he sat.

Nick held up his hand. "Hey…"

"You have to be shitting me?" said Denise, as the others laughed.

"Steve Rogers? Really?" answered Chuck in an incredulous voice, causing the others to laugh even harder.

Nick glared at Chuck's quip and flipped him off. "Yeah, laugh it up. It was not my idea. Call signs are given. You don't get to pick them. Just so you know, my first one was 'Bullseye' because I was so good at hitting my targets. Ask Earl. Only later did someone decide to change it to 'Cap'. I always assumed it was the ball cap I always wore."

This time it was Bob who laughed out loud. "Right. And the Captain America shield on the tail of your plane? And helmet?"

"I'm going to have a conversation with Congressman Constantine when I'm in Washington next week. Loose lips sink ships and all that. Don't believe everything you hear. That would violate Air Force regulations and camouflage rules," smiled Nick.

"He pointed that out. Turns out certain air crews would put them on and take the decals off whenever the brass showed up. Don't be too rough on him, Nick. He was just worried. That's why he looked me up," commented Bob, taking a seat at the table.

"Hey, I just had a thought. Margie, Bob, can you see if we can get one of the retired Canadian snipers who holds a long distance sniper record to get up on stage and explain how that shot is next to impossible to make with a moving target?" wondered Nick.

"I'll take this one Margie. You won't get far through channels. These guys are not exactly in the phone book," said Bob as the rest of the table laughed again.

"I'll do my part. Maybe I can skip the *Magic Mike* stripper sketch if we can get the sniper to explain. What else?" Nick looked at Denise.

"Just do your normal stuff. We need people to see you and know you are fully recovered."

"One last question, right Denise?" pushed Margie.

"Oh yeah, I forgot. Nick, *The Sunday Hour* is still willing to have you on," said Denise. "Might be good, could hit a different audience."

"Only if they let me do it live. I don't want to give them a chance to record it and cut it up. Make the offer. Live or nothing."

"Ok Margie, I guess that's your answer," responded Denise.

As they were getting ready to wrap it up, Jenny came into the conference room. Her face was red, as if she had been crying.

"Ah crap, I didn't know you were here," she said, seeing Nick.

Nick got up. "What's wrong?" he said, walking to Jenny.

"I'm sorry Nick, I really am," Jenny responded in a defeated tone.

"What happened?" asked Denise.

"We lost. The Supreme Court declined our appeal on the court rulings in Michigan, Wisconsin, and Pennsylvania where their state Supreme Court all ruled we were ineligible for their presidential ballots.

"Crap," said Chuck.

Everyone sat silently for a moment. Greg looked up. "But we got on all the other ballots, right?"

Jenny smiled. "Thanks Greg. Yes, we beat the lawsuits in Texas and South Dakota from Blackbird and we beat the lawsuits in Virginia, New York, Massachusetts and Ohio. We're on all those ballots."

Nick looked up. "Guys, we expected this, especially in Wisconsin, Michigan, and Pennsylvania. Just highlight Lexi and team efforts to avoid competition. We can also highlight the timid nature of the Supreme Court for not getting involved in ensuring a fair election. This helps us make the point the Party are really the ones trying to disenfranchise voters."

"Damn straight. Jenny, you did everything you could. This is just another embarrassment by our Supreme Court, nothing more," agreed Chuck. "Margie, looks like another statement we need to draft."

"Alright, onward," said Nick, looking out the windows of the west facing conference room. The tallest visible peaks showed a slight dusting from the first high mountain snow of the year. Fall and an election were both approaching.

Chapter 35

"He is headed to Lyon. You have about three hours," said the metallic voice in French.

"Understood."

"No evidence," continued the voice.

"Including him?"

There was a pause. If you run into him, persuade, but do not terminate. A grunt greeted this statement as the connection ended.

Roland Gill put the metallic box back in his desk in his office in Lexi's campaign headquarters. He'd received a coded message regarding the whereabouts of Luc. He guessed where he was headed. Byron Lauzon, the owner of the autistic clinic in Lyon, had been providing autistic 'candidates' to Roland for the Doctor's training program.

They'd already warned him to shut down his facility. Ever since Lauzon had called to admit his mistake. Someone on his staff had mistakenly told a visitor about vacancies occurring when patients graduated to a facility for more education. Roland eventually figured out it was Luc in disguise, looking for information on Gaspard's killer.

Lauzon balked at the order to close, not realizing the innocent mistake gave Luc critical information. He assured them everything was under control. It had been simple for Roland's associates to make a few calls to the French authorities to revoke Lauzon's licenses. The remaining patients had all been moved back to state-run hospitals. They could not risk Lauzon being interrogated by Luc.

\#

Luc could see the plume of dark smoke on the horizon as he drove. The manor house he was approaching had been on the list of autistic clinics Caroline had given him. The smoke was getting thicker the closer he came. He knew in his heart it was because of his prior visit.

Pulling around a curve, he saw a myriad of fire brigade vehicles pouring water on what was left of the century's old estate. It was entirely consumed. He pulled into an out of the way corner and walked up to observe. There was only a single ambulance.

As Luc approached, he recognized the woman being given oxygen. She was the concierge of the clinic. Monique had shown him around the facility on his visit months ago. He'd been posing as Pierre Corbin, looking for an institution for his autistic brother.

Monique looked up and pushed the mask away. "Monsieur Corbin! Why are you here? It is a disaster," she said, her tear-stained face looking back toward the house. Luc walked up to the EMT with a familiar air of authority, glancing at her. She moved away.

"Monique, what has happened?"

"It is horrible. First, the magistrate showed up with papers claiming we were in violation. Mr. Lauzon was forced to relocate the patients back to state hospitals. He was working to get the proper clearances reissued and had to let all the staff go. I was kept on as the caretaker until his certifications were reissued. I was in the office when the alarms started. It appears the fire started in the utility room and quickly spread. It is an old wooden building." She wiped her tears, looking again at the smoldering remains.

"By the time the fire brigade arrived, it was too late."

"Monique, where is Mr. Lauzon?"

"I don't know. He will be crushed. This manor has been in his family for centuries."

"Does he not live here?" asked Luc.

Monique shook her head. "He lives a few miles from here. I am surprised he has not seen the smoke and come to inspect."

"Do you have the address?"

She told him. Luc wished her luck and hurried back to his car.

#

Luc crouched in the woods surrounding Lauzon's house. Studying the large house, he did not see any cameras. Moving from the cover of the woods to the side of the house, he saw a door to the patio was open.

Easing the door open, weapon now drawn, he entered a kitchen with an island in the center. Studying the exits, moving to his left, walking down a hallway. At the end he saw an open door with glass doored bookshelves on the back wall and moved forward slowly.

Luc entered cautiously. It was an office. The walls were covered with ancient weapons. Swords of various lengths and more bookcases with glass doors. On the desk was an ornate dagger with a foot long blade and heavy hilts on a display stand.

Moving around the desk, he found the body of Byron Lauzon. The back of his head was bloody. Luc moved forward and leaned down to check for a pulse. Lauzon was dead and still warm.

He straightened, noticing movement in the reflection of a bookcase door. Lunging out of the way of a large rolling pin aimed at his now ducking head. The pin bounced off the desk. Luc continued turning around the side of the desk, away from the 'baker' wielding the pin. A second large man was entering the office, gun in hand.

Luc reflexively aimed his gun and put two quick shots into the chest of the second man as the baker brought the pin down on his exposed forearm. Dropping his gun with a grunt, spinning away while grabbing his arm. The next swing bounced off his shoulder and caught him high on a temple.

Dazed, he tried to find something to defend himself with. Luc crouched, putting the desk between him and the 'baker', who tossed the bloody rolling pin from hand to hand. The man was shouting at him to give up. It would cause less of a beating.

Luc could smell smoke. His opponent smiled, knowingly. Luc had an advantage. It was clear his assailant's orders were to capture him, or he would already be dead. He was under no such orders. At this moment, the smoke alarms in the office started going off.

The baker looked up, distracted. Using his leverage against the bookcase, Luc pushed the antique desk across the wood floor. This caught the baker off guard as the edge of the desk smacked into his thighs, flinging him back into a bookcase, shattering the glass.

Luc lunged for his pistol and put one through the upper arm of his attacker. Yelling at him to stop or the next was through his forehead. The baker dropped the rolling pin as Luc stood, panting.

"Let's start with who you are?" he barked.

"Porky Pig," snarled the man.

Luc shot him in the foot.

The man swore as he danced on his wounded foot, staring pure hatred at Luc.

"Again, I ask, who are you?"

"Does it matter?" replied the man, groaning.

Luc aimed the gun at the man's knee this time.

"Who sent you? And how do you know me?"

"We received a phone call to dispose of the facility, this house, and the 'contents' of both."

"And me. Clearly you were told not to kill me?" asked Luc.

The man shrugged.

"When were you told about me?" When the man hesitated, Luc again raised the gun.

"Thirty minutes ago, we were called and told you might be here."

"Again, by whom? *Daboia*?" fished Luc, looking for a reaction.

"No names, only calls," lied the man, masking his surprise with a groan, lifting his foot from a pile of blood.

As Luc looked down, the man launched himself at him, contacting him with a thud as the gun fired. They both hit the floor, the heavier man on Luc seeking a chokehold with his hands. Luc brought his knee up near the groin of the man and pushed off as best he could, kicking with his heels at any portion of his assailant he could contact. Separating himself and getting to his feet, surveying his options.

His opponent was now also on his feet, grunting in pain and anger. A new hole in his midsection showing the result of Luc's shot. The man grabbed an antique broadsword off the wall.

He immediately took a swing at Luc, who dodged, trying to keep furniture between him and the bellowing swordsman. Another swing took a chunk out of the desk, knocking the dagger from its holder.

A crossways swing caused Luc to jump back, giving up precious real estate he did not have. He spied his pistol across the room; the sword wielding mad Frenchman between him, the weapon, and the door. The air was thickening with smoke. Ducking under the next swing, Luc bent and picked up the dagger. It was surprisingly heavy.

As he stood facing off, dagger against sword, the other man smiled. All thought of capture now gone. This battle would end with one standing. He swung his sword in a downward arc, the goal of which was to split Luc's skull. Luc raised his dagger to catch the blow, hoping the hilt of the dagger was real and not merely ornamental.

As sword blade met dagger shaft, the sword slid down with a thud against the crosspiece of the dagger hilt. Luc, remembering his fencing training from university, twisted his weapon sharply, causing his opponent to lose his grasp on the sword.

With a smile on his own face this time, Luc now drove his freed dagger into the chest of his opponent, to the hilt, looking him in the eyes.

"You should have answered my questions," responded Luc.

The smoke was now a billowing mass of gray and black, rolling into the office through the doorway. Luc coughed at the decreasing quality of air. He quickly rolled Lauzon over, searching his body, pulling out a ring of keys. Glancing around the desk, seeing a seam in the floor where a carpet had been dislodged by their fight. Luc grabbed at the ring on the floor, lifting a section. Inside was a locked metal box.

Luc reached in, grabbing the box, and stood. This was a mistake. He quickly collapsed back to his knees, coughing heavily as he surveyed the room. A window seemed his only escape. Luc looked around, picking up a large rock bookend. He unceremoniously threw the geode through the lead glass window and quickly followed.

Laying on his back in the yard, taking in deep breaths of fresh air. The large house was completely engulfed in flame. The fire brigade would no doubt arrive soon. Luc glanced at Lauzon's Maserati parked in the driveway.

Alain, Leon, and de Monfort would follow him no more. One of them had told others where he was and given the order for his capture. He would find out which.

#

"Gauthier's car was at the house of the owner of the clinic that burned. The owner's home was also destroyed. Arson is suspected in both cases," stated Maximilian de Monfort.

"Bodies?" asked Alain Chaumont.

"None in the clinic, thankfully. It had been shuttered by the magistrate a month ago and the patients moved. At the house, there are three bodies. All badly burned. They are working on identifying the remains. It seems possible he is one of the victims."

Alain looked around his office. Wondering how he'd tell his wife.

"Keep me informed when the autopsy reports are completed."

"I hope it is Gauthier. Then both of us can sleep easier at night," replied de Monfort with a snort. "You should never have involved him."

Chaumont looked de Monfort in the eye. He glanced away.

"I will never sleep soundly again," replied Chaumont to de Monfort, who stiffened, but did not turn. He continued out the door and shut it behind him.

Chapter 36

Dan Baker couldn't believe what he was reading. After months of trying, his techie buddy had unlocked the files on the USB drive. Dan lucked out and found the drive after visiting the widow of Sam Vincent, the late Presidential Chief of Staff.

Dan jumped at the chance to expose the scandal. He'd previously made a name for himself, exposing corruption in the local New York mayor's office, toppling many top officials and leading to the Mayor not seeking re-election.

Another exposé forced the resignation of the junior New York Senator for misappropriating campaign funds to her lover's non-profit. This last story had cost him his job at a prominent New York newspaper when his editors refused to air his story. He'd quit and published the stories independently. To the great embarrassment of his prior bosses at the prestigious paper, it also won him a Pulitzer.

Vincent had contacted him about bombshell info, saying he needed someone who would not intimidate easily. Now Vincent was dead, killed on his way to meet Dan. His last text had been to a burn phone Dan had purchased specifically to communicate anonymously with him. He had not slept well since.

Dan originally worried the hidden files would be homemade porn. He couldn't have been more wrong. Reading the files, the information was every bit as damaging as the missing eighteen minutes of Watergate recordings and the Pentagon Papers combined.

With no corroborating witness, he could never publish the contents. It would be his word against the US Government. The info was too explosive to not tell someone. He sent a series of texts. They were promptly answered. Pulling up another app, he made a reservation on the Acela to Washington, DC.

Chapter 37

Denise sat on the park bench, in an obscure pocket park in DC, holding a coffee in her hand. It was a nice day. The relentless heat of August finally giving way to a more sedate September. In her forty years in and around Washington, there was no doubt the summers were hotter and longer. As she contemplated the vagaries of weather and climate change, someone sat down on the other end of the bench.

Denise did not turn. She simply reached into her large bag and pulled out a manila envelope, setting it on the bench. Still looking forward, she said. "This is the best I can do. That's it. No more. I don't care what you do or threaten me with. I'm done."

Without waiting for a response, she got up and walked away. The other person picked up the envelope and walked in the opposite direction.

#

A video camera pointed at the park bench recorded the entire clandestine drop. The camera remained trained on the person who picked up the envelope, walking away. This was the seventh time they had filmed this regular meeting. It had occurred monthly since March.

#

"Jeremy! Come on in. How are you doing? How did your testimony go?" asked Nick in rapid succession as a smiling man with Asian features entered his Senate office, escorted by a smiling Carla.

Jeremy laughed as he took a seat. Nick was always amazed at his appearance. Other than receding hair, he looked like he was in college.

"Let's just say Congress is not very appreciative of my efforts to preserve the First Amendment for the everyday people."

"Just keep educating them. It is a hopeless task, but one worth fighting for. I'd bet 90% of them have never even been on Hibi."

"95% would probably be closer. Nick, their arguments weren't even cogent. I could have fought facts with facts and statistics, but they didn't even try. They just kept ranting about how I was giving a voice to radicals, racists, antisemites, and homophobes. If there had been a judge and they were the prosecuting attorney, they would have thrown them out. It was all just opinion and conjecture," finished Jeremy with a sigh.

Nick nodded, getting up. "Coffee?"

"Sure, thanks."

"Jeremy, if there is one thing I have noticed, it is Congress has lost the ability to debate. They rely so much on a bully pulpit; the response is always an insult or an accusation. And all for the cameras, not the witness," replied Nick as he started the second cup on his machine.

"Nick, they proved that time and time again. This was the House. The Senate is still coming up. I felt like I was the one questioning them. Every time they would make an accusation, I would ask for a citation or an example. They had none."

Nick handed him a coffee and set down sugar and creamer.

"How's your girlfriend? She's gotta be due soon, right?"

"We didn't get any time to catch up when we launched the 2J's. Kim is my wife now. We got married by the Justice of the Peace shortly after we found out we were pregnant. We're all good. Due date is election day." Jeremy's big smile made his eyes disappear.

"Guess my election will be the second most important event that day," laughed Nick.

"I can only hope, Nick."

"I have to ask. Is there anyone you don't know? Howard Patterson, then JD. Who else am I going to run into?"

"Nick, I'm doing my part. I believe in what you're selling. You ready for your book review on the 2J's?"

"Another of your successful ventures. I am. Not sure JD is. I think he is crapping his pants at the idea of your holograms grilling me live," laughed Nick.

"He isn't the only one who needs a diaper change," commented Jeremy ruefully. "It was your suggestion, not ours. Trial by fire."

"It'll be fine. This just a social call?"

Jeremy looked around the room. "Secure?"

"You tell me. Your guys set up the security inside the office, on the phones and computers. How confident are you?"

Jeremy smiled in reply. "Very. I have been conversing with LJ."

Nick looked confused.

"Major Jenkins? Laurence Jenkins," explained Jeremy.

"Ah," Nick slowly nodded, remembering he'd put Major Jenkins and Jeremy in contact after Jenkins had given him the snippet of intercepted conversation he'd discovered. "And?"

"I assume you have gotten my messages?" asked Jeremy.

"Ah, now it becomes clearer. I wondered who was sending me such sensitive info. Thanks for not telling me it was you. I could truthfully claim ignorance when the FBI asked me for my source of info regarding Pastor Mills," said Nick with a smile.

Jeremy looked confused. "Sorry Nick, that one wasn't me."

Nick stared at him for a second. "It seems I have more than one anonymous source. They've all come in handy. I have to say I'm not surprised there is stuff going on. Would have been good to know they were trying to kill me though. No one warned me of that one."

"That's one reason I stopped by. We got another piece. Someone talking overseas to what we think was someone in Lexi's campaign. They were asking the other if they did it and neither said they had. The other piece we got was them suggesting they plant the idea you did this to yourself. Also, you should know it is very sophisticated. *They* are using voice masking software. It is even harder for LJ to decipher it. That's all we got. Now that we know what to look for, he is focusing on pulling out this type of communication. I figured I would deliver this bit myself."

Nick shrugged. "Doesn't surprise me other than that these two assumed the other had taken the shot. It also doesn't surprise me a bit they fed the story to their media. In fact, if I thought it could have been done, and not kill me, it would have been brilliant."

Jeremy didn't laugh, instead staring at Nick. "You're already taking too many risks. There is something else."

"What?"

"Something is coming. I don't know what, and we can't get anything more than an occasional reference to an event."

"I'm sure they have lots of tricks waiting. October is coming."

"Nick, this is bigger than that. I am not sure what. The amount of chatter overseas is concerning. LJ sends me what he thinks is important. But he has to be careful too. He told me about Ben Wong, the airman's cousin?" Nick nodded, remembering his conversation with Major Jenkins in the golf course parking lot.

"He makes me look like a junior mathlete. The guy's off the charts brilliant. Of course, I hired him," smiled Jeremy.

"Do I even want to know what you're paying him?" winced Nick.

"The private sector is capitalism at its finest. Besides, with him, the money is irrelevant. It is all about the challenge. I know you're busy, so I'll cut to the chase. Ben is a primo white hat hacker. He belongs to a bunch of dark web forums. Some doing good. Others using the dark web for less than good things."

"OK, not sure I should hear this. Keep going." replied Nick.

"Don't worry. I will keep you sheltered from the anarchy and chaos and the nefarious nature of what bitcoin is being used for. The key here is he hears and sees things. Messages being posted looking for top hackers. All very hush-hush and exclusive. Only a few are getting some of these. One was very specific, looking for a particular hashing algorithm."

"Jeremy, think Bill Nye. I am not a scientist. I play one on TV."

"Someone is looking for hackers skilled at security protocols used in voting machine logic."

"Thank you. Now it becomes clear. Again, can't say I am surprised. Shouldn't we be OK now that they aren't shipping data overseas for counting? Wasn't that the problem?" asked Nick.

Jeremy smiled. "Nick, on some things, you are refreshingly naïve. If it is programmed, it can be reprogrammed to do anything, anytime, under the correct circumstance. Humans program it so it is never flawless, secure, or fully hidden. I want you to know, there are folks, really smart folks, who are working in the background. If something goes down, they will fight back. No more sitting back while foreign *or* domestic entities mess with our last free election," finished Jeremy fiercely.

"Congress get you a little riled up?" asked Nick, smiling again.

"And then some. Nick, I know you won't understand this, but the effort it is taking me to keep my servers up and running is tremendous. It's as if every computer in the world is constantly trying to shut them down, overload them with too many requests, or plant malicious code to destroy all my clients' data. We are talking millions of simultaneous attacks. Not every day, but every hour and soon, probably every minute."

"From whom? Who has the power to do this?" asked Nick, not understanding the how, but certainly the outcome.

"That's just it. This horsepower is not from a single place. It is being orchestrated and coordinated together to brute force their way through my security perimeters. This is not corporate or even state sponsored. This has to be something that spans these and can access all these disparate pieces and harness their power collectively. I think much of it is being directed by AI algorithms. Very sophisticated AI, I might add. And it is learning. Each day, it tries something new. It is keeping my team on their toes for sure. We have to stop *all* these attacks. It only has to get through *once.*"

"What are you saying? Are they going to shut you down?"

Jeremy smiled. "Not if I have a say about it. We are also using AI and advanced Machine Learning. Predictive AI, quantum computing, and the latest LLM neural networking matrices. I have the best minds on the planet. We are working on countermeasures. Nick, cyber warfare is about to begin in earnest. When it does, it will have unintended consequences. Our government is woefully unprepared for this."

"You do not have to tell me that. I don't understand most of what you said, other than to know to be afraid," answered Nick.

"If those clowns are the only thing between us and Armageddon, we had better start ordering bomb shelters."

"Jeremy, that is the good thing. They are not. You are, and Ben Wong and LJ and even me to a certain extent. All of us acknowledging the need and working on the details. Doing the little things that add up to big things. If we keep plugging away, it will matter. When, not if, the shit hits the fan, we'll work together to overcome the obstacles. This is where individuality meets necessity. We saw it in spades in World War II. We glimpsed it again during 9/11. It is still there in a silent majority. I know we can do it again. I just hope we never have to."

Jeremy got up, looking down at Nick. "I know you are an optimist. I am a scientist. The statistical probability of this not happening is highly improbable. I wanted you to know we are there, working in the shadows. If we find anything more definitive, I will let you know."

Nick got up and walked him to the door, shaking his hand.

"Thanks Jeremy. For Hibi, for the 2J's, Howard, JD, and lord only knows how many others you have converted or sent my way."

"Just win, Nick. Or that probability of bad things happening just adds another hundred zeros."

On that upbeat note, Carla arrived to escort Jeremy out.

Chapter 38

Nick stood up to greet the tall, brown-haired man entering his office with Earl. He held out his hand. The man hesitated for a fraction of a second and shook the offered hand. The white skin of his face was weathered and creased. There were obvious tan lines on his cheeks ending where sunglasses normally resided. Nick could tell his visitor spent a lot of time outdoors.

"Thanks for meeting with me," offered Nick in a serious tone.

"John Wayne," the man replied. Nick laughed.

"I know. My parents had a sense of humor. And yes, before you ask, everyone calls me Duke."

"Duke it is. Call me Nick. Let's sit. Can I get you anything to drink?" asked Nick, grabbing his coffee cup and heading for his kitchen and his coffee machine.

"Sure, I'll take a coffee."

"Nick, let me get those. You two sit." Earl headed for the kitchen.

They sat around a small round table in Nick's office.

"Duke, I know this is hard. Hard for folks to understand who are not in law enforcement. Especially hard for the families. Earl told me you are close to the father of the female sheriff's deputy who was killed?"

"We served together in the Army Rangers. Jack Herrera. Eileen is his wife. Eva was their only child. You can guess how devastated they are," answered Duke as Earl returned with coffees.

"I can only imagine. I have no children, let alone to have one die in the line of duty. I think we've all seen plenty of death. Death of innocents is the worst. Sadly, everyone involved was an innocent, put in an impossible position." Nick looked at Duke as he finished his statement to gauge the response.

Duke took his coffee and sipped while looking Nick in the face.

"Why did you do it? I don't understand. You're a Senator," he waved his arm around the office as his voice quavered. "Running for President. You didn't have to. You could have just let it run its course. Let the trial happen. Allow Jack and Eileen to have some closure, knowing the man who killed their daughter would be in prison. Why involve yourself when you have *everything* to lose?" asked Duke, the cup in his hand shaking at his emotion.

Nick took his own sip of coffee while Duke delivered his plea. "Duke, you know exactly why I did it. I can tell in your voice. While it may help Jack and Eileen, do you really think it would be right?"

Duke set his cup down on the table, slopping coffee.

"Does it matter? Shit happens every day. I've lost five police officers in my command the last three years. For no good reason. Gang bangers and MS13, all coming up through the open border. I've had to tell young parents their 6-year-old kid died because he picked up a fentanyl laced dollar bill at school, dying because no one could give him Narcan."

Nick sat and listened, sipping his coffee.

"The school couldn't give it to all the teachers because the Governor wouldn't sign the bill to allow it. I have grown adults wandering the streets in zombie trances. In San Bernardino, California. Not LA, not Detroit. Not even San Fran or Baltimore. Sleepy little San Bernardino. What is the harm in giving these poor people some closure? There is no doubt who killed their daughter." Duke's voice cracked at the emotion.

"Did you talk to anyone?" asked Nick. "When you got back?"

"What?" Duke stared at Nick, confused at the comment.

"Sweats? Nightmares? Wake up wondering where you are?"

Duke waved him off.

"I felt the same way. I eventually made peace with it. I talked to some folks who helped me." Nick looked at Earl. "You?"

"Yes, I had to, though. My CO ordered mine before I even got out," laughed Earl bitterly.

Duke looked from one to the other.

"What's your point?"

"Dusty tried. Went to the VA. They filled him full of drugs, drove him to try suicide twice. Then finally 'they' decided maybe their treatment wasn't working. He's not well. You've read the reports?"

"Yes. Errors were made. It still does not excuse him firing without determining who broke into his apartment," argued Duke.

"Really? Do you have a family, Duke?"

He glared at him. "Wife. Two daughters. Teenagers."

"You're in a cabin in the woods with your wife and kids. Someone breaks into your cabin. What are you going to do?"

"Not the same…"

"Bullshit. It absolutely is the same. I bet you have a loaded pistol on your nightstand. No way you go to sleep with your family and don't have a way to instantly react to danger. Even if you aren't a police captain. I do. I know Earl does. More and more Americans do this every night. Because the reality, breaking down someone's door, is *never* acceptable."

Duke leaned back, grabbing his coffee, taking a big gulp.

"Look, I am not going to tell you it is all sunshine and flowers. In fact, knowing what little I do know, I think this poor Marine would be happy to stand there and plead guilty for killing the deputies. His sense of honor demands it. It would just be another crime on top of a litany of negligent acts that occurred and cost everyone their life. You ask why I did it? It is to shine a spotlight on the unintended consequences of bad legislature and the incompetence that enabled this series of unfortunate events. If they are not exposed and shouted from the rooftops, they will happen again, everywhere if the administration has its way with national red flag laws. Just like another six-year-old picking up a fentanyl laced dollar bill. It has to stop."

"What do you want from me?"

"I want to talk to Eva's parents."

Duke stared at him. "Nick, they *hate* you. That is not a good idea. They have read the facts too. They don't care why Dusty's door got broken down. They just want someone to pay for killing their daughter."

"Please Duke. Let me try."

Duke turned to Earl. "You're right. He is crazy. You sure those counselors helped you with your PTSD? Nick, this is not going to end well. Jack already goes on TV. If you meet with him, he is going to run to ANC after, and say you tried to convince him the Marine isn't guilty of killing his daughter. That's if he doesn't shoot you first."

"Duke, I appreciate the concern. Just see if he'll meet with me?"

Duke held Nick's stare. "You are a very strange man."

#

"You sure that is a good idea?" asked Chuck.

"I have to give it a shot. If I can just explain, it may help, even if it can't make up for losing Eva," replied Nick.

"No, I meant the gun. It is Dolly's after all," pointed Chuck as Nick put on a worn leather shoulder holster with his gun.

"I didn't wear it to the first ones. No dancing this time and someone did just try to kill me in case your forgot."

"True. Won't it rub against the wound under your arm?"

"I asked the doctor this morning. All clear. She was very impressed how fast it's healing. Besides, I wear suspenders with my tux, don't have a belt to thread the holster on," finished Nick as he grabbed his white tux jacket. Chuck was already in his traditional black tuxedo.

"As for Eva's parents. I know I can't talk you out of it."

"Good. I need a relaxing night. Let's not keep Dolly waiting.

Chuck smiled. With Nick, nothing was *ever* relaxing.

Chapter 39

Nick opened his eyes to fluffy hills of white. He blinked, trying to figure out where he was and what he was seeing. After a few seconds, he realized it was folds of a large white down comforter. He didn't own a white comforter. Rolling his head slowly to the right, grimacing in pain, he stopped. He was now looking at a bare shoulder with a blue nightgown strap. Certain he was dreaming, he slowly reached out a hand, touching the shoulder lightly.

Dolly rolled over, facing Nick. He stared at her unrestrained breasts, on display in the plunging V of her blue silk pajama top. Her brunette curls, in playful disarray, framed the beautiful, makeup free, smiling face.

"I must be dreaming," thought Nick aloud.

An arm of the Dolly apparition reached out and poked Nick in the chest. He sat up quickly, putting a hand to his head with a groan.

"Easy tiger. They said a headache is normal," declared Dolly, the smile disappearing to be replaced with one of worry. She leaned up, the covers slipping down, revealing the rest of her camisole.

"What the hell happened?" asked Nick, closing his eyes.

Dolly leaned an elbow on a pile of pillows and looked over at him.

"It's not good for a girl's ego to not be memorable," she accused, her alluring lips in a pretty pout.

Nick's look went from confused to panicked. Dolly took pity on him with a small laugh.

"Sorry. That's not fair. You did *not* forget a wonderful night," she said slyly. "Something you ate or drank at the party caused an allergic reaction. You went down as blue as my top. Luckily, you were talking to Freddie when it happened. He caught you before you hit your head. Even luckier for you, Ginny always carries an EpiPen. If not for her quick thinking, you might not be sharing my bed, or anyone else's, right now."

Nick shook his head and stopped again at the pain. "If it is any consolation, I know a night with you *would* be unforgettable," declared Nick, smiling while rubbing his temple.

Blushing, Dolly quickly asked. "What are you so allergic to?"

"No idea. I've never had a reaction like this before. It makes no sense. I was only drinking club soda, and I ate nothing. Can't be too careful, no offence," added Nick, seeing her reaction.

"You obviously weren't careful enough. So, it *wasn't* an allergy? Someone tried to kill you. At my party? That's pretty ballsy."

"I seem to be getting under someone's skin. That's two attempts in as many weeks," noted Nick, looking around slowly while scratching an itch on the healing wound on his bare chest. Dolly's bedroom suite was enormous. Tastefully decorated in a mix of modern and antique. They appeared to be in an antique fourposter bed. He could see by the daylight barely streaming in the windows, it was still relatively early in the morning.

"You think? I would say at least half the country," snorted Dolly. "You seem to heal fast," nodding at the pink scar he was scratching.

"There is that. Lucky for me."

"You look like a Jackson Pollock painting. How many times have you been wounded? What the hell happened to your back? I suggest you learn how to duck better."

"Thanks for the advice. I'll take it under advisement. Perhaps I should start by avoiding dangerous Galas, nurse Monroe."

Dolly smiled back. She rolled over and out of the covers, getting up. She wore a matching pair of blue silk shorts. As she walked across the bedroom, he couldn't help but admire her toned legs and shapely rear.

"Hungry?" she purred, walking into another room outside the bedroom. Shortly, she returned with a tray of coffee and muffins. Setting the tray across his lap, bending enough to give him a quick glance down her top. He was glad the tray was across his waist, hiding his reaction to the peep show. Dolly's erect nipples pushed against her silk top, revealing her own excitement at the unfolding situation. She sat on the edge of the bed, her hand on his thigh.

Nick took the offered coffee and asked what else had happened.

"Well, after you went down and the doctors Garcia stabilized your breathing, Freddie suggested we put you upstairs in a bedroom.

"Geez, that must have been a sight. What gorillas picked me up?"

"Hobson hoisted you on his shoulder in a fireman carry and brought you up the staircase and to this bed without breaking a sweat."

"Bank's Hobson?" said Nick in surprise. Dolly nodded.

"As you can imagine, you were already the talk of the party after the shooting. Then to have you go down in my living room," she shook her head. "You certainly know how to grab people's attention. Everyone wanted to know 'what happened', 'how were you', etc. Hobson camped out in front of the door until Banks was ready to leave and then Chuck took over until I came up after the party wrapped up. By then, I already had private security as well. I sent him home. He had already notified the press you were fine and just had a reaction to some food. You were OK and resting comfortably. I sat here for a while and kept falling asleep. Since you were in no danger of waking up, and I was tired, I just joined you. I assumed you wouldn't mind," she said, grinning.

"Not exactly how I envisioned it," laughed Nick drolly.

"Oh, so you have thought about it," she said mischievously.

"And you haven't?" smiled Nick back, staring until she blinked and looked away.

"How'd Lexi react?"

Happy to change the subject again, Dolly answered quickly. "Strangely. She didn't react at all. Not surprised or concerned. You might as well have been one of the staff simply dropping a glass. Her guest seemed more interested. Did you get to meet him?"

"I did not. Lexi and I are no longer at the small talk phase of our relationship. I saw him, though. He looks vaguely familiar. Did you?"

"Yes, briefly. I had that same feeling as well. Like Déjà vu. He just showed up, supposedly he is handling Lexi's campaign security. The Secret Service obviously protects her personally. Seems a strange choice to bring as a guest to my party," said Dolly in a quizzical tone. Nick looked around the room carefully.

"Better than my Murphy bed. Thanks for taking care of me."

"Clearly somebody has too," replied Dolly with a smile, lifting her hand from his leg with a gentle squeeze.

Nick smiled in response, not sure what to do or say, until she stood up. "I'm going to take a shower. Finish your breakfast. Then we can sneak you out the back door and start the rumor mill going."

Nick watched her glide to the ensuite. She pulled her top off and looked back at Nick over a naked shoulder. "You're welcome to join me."

Nick shook his head as she disappeared. "Dolly Monroe, you are an evil woman, taking advantage of a man in my condition."

A dark head of hair peered out from the bathroom. "You seemed in fine condition when I took your clothes off last night."

She moved a naked leg into view in a seductive motion. Nick lifted a hand to cover his eyes. The tray tipped, causing him to lunge to catch the sliding pot of coffee. Dolly laughed wickedly as she retreated into the bathroom. He could hear the water of the shower.

Nick sighed. He set the tray aside and put his tux pants, socks, and shirt back on, pulling his suspenders up. He noticed his gun in his shoulder holster and his white jacket were draped on another chair. Rolling up the shirt sleeves, he poured a cup of coffee, sat in one of the comfortable chairs, and turned to his phone. There were hundreds of text messages. Sighing again, he dug into the texts as the shower continued.

#

"Aren't we the picture of domesticity?" asked Dolly, coming out of the bathroom in a robe, her hair done up in a towel.

Nick looked up. He had to agree. This was very comfortable. "Coffee?"

"Yes please," she replied as Nick unwound himself from the chair carefully and poured a fresh cup of coffee as she took a seat in a chair next to him. He handed her the cup as she smiled.

Nick refilled his own and sat back down. Dolly turned to him, the robe parting to show more leg.

Nick laughed. "Mrs. Monroe, are you trying to seduce me?"

"Apparently, I'm doing a poor job. I *am* out of practice, admittedly. You do like women, right?" she asked, a questioning twinkle in her eye.

"It is called willpower."

"I can think of a few other words. And to be clear regarding your *Graduate* reference, I'm much younger than you, so that fantasy ain't happening here."

"Can't we just enjoy our coffee and danish?"

"Of course," said Dolly in such a defeated and forlorn voice, Nick stood up. He set his coffee down, walked to Dolly, and pulled her to her feet. Reaching up, he pulled the towel from her head, letting her damp hair fall down around her shoulders. Putting his hand in her hair as he kissed her. She wrapped her arms around him as they stood, tongues entangled, rubbing together, hands roaming. When they broke their kiss, she looked down, catching her breath.

"Much better than dancing," she murmured against his lips.

Dolly's robe had come loose as they kissed, displaying her lush, naked figure. Nick took his hand from her hair, and his other from one of her round firm breasts, gently closing the robe, drawing the sash tight. He looked her in the eyes.

"Dolly, I suck at this. With all of my talents elsewhere, I am a clod with women. I say the wrong things at the right times and the right things when I cannot deliver. I am terrified of commitment to anything other than a cause. Which for most of my life has been serving and now saving our country. It is difficult to play second fiddle to that. I am not asking you or anyone else to make that choice." He squeezed her hands while still staring into her eyes.

"I have indeed dreamed of making love to you. More than you know, but I cannot give you what you want. What you deserve. Believe me, I want to, but it would not be fair to either of us." Dolly returned his look as he delivered his speech. As he waited for a response, half expecting a knee to his groin, she instead found his lips.

When they broke apart, he felt the tears she'd left on his cheeks.

"Nick, while I appreciate your honesty. I don't agree with your logic and frankly, I think you're being stupid. I'm a big girl. It's as much my choice as yours. You cannot do this alone. In fact, you aren't doing it alone. You are asking many to risk everything and you cannot protect us all. I will take that risk. I don't understand why you won't?"

Nick looked down into her beautiful face. She stared back in fiery determination.

"Why are you fighting this? You don't have to be miserable. I'll wait for you. For a while, but not forever. You need to decide where your priorities lie. And with whom," finished Dolly cryptically.

Nick, contemplating the full meaning of her statement, merely responded, "Thank you for understanding."

Dolly laughed bitterly, shaking her head while walking away.

"Nick, you are so right. You say the absolute wrong things at the wrong times. I am anything but understanding. In fact, were you anyone else, I would have the staff throw you out after giving you a limp to remember me by. I'm going to give you the benefit of the doubt and assume you are, as you say, simply a clod. Chuck and Denise warned me you were a bit of a self-centered cad. It might be a good time for you to go, before either of us says or does something we may regret."

Nick stood in the room. Nodding, he quickly donned his shoulder holstered weapon, grabbed his jacket, sliding his feet into his shoes. Looking back at Dolly, standing near a dressing table.

"Thank you for everything, Dolly. I appreciate it. All of it." He left her bedroom, out through the antechamber and into the hallway. Nina, Dolly's assistant, sat at a small desk, an armed guard standing nearby.

"Ah Senator, feeling better?" asked Nina, smiling, as if a US Senator leaving her boss's bedroom was an everyday occurrence.

"I am. Thank you. If you could lead the way, I have a car waiting for me outside."

"My pleasure Senator."

Chapter 40

Nick walked out of Dolly's house, down the walk toward the bank of reporters. Chuck was at the curb waiting to pick him up. As Nick approached, reporters were shouting questions. Nick held up his hand.

"I am fine. First, I want to thank Ms. Monroe for allowing me to recover in a guest bedroom. I am not sure what caused the reaction. I have been under a bit of stress lately," finished Nick in an understatement, drawing laughter from the gathered crowd.

"I would also like to thank Senator Garcia and his wife, Ginny, for their fast response to help. As you know, I have made my medical records available and I've never had any allergic reaction in the past. We'll do some tests and see if we can identify the reason for this one. We will let all of you know the findings in keeping with our transparency pledge. Thank you for your concern," ended Nick, heading to Chuck's car.

"Senator, did you spend the night with Ms. Monroe?"

Nick laughed and turned. "I spent the night sleeping as a guest of Ms. Monroe's in her home. Sorry, I have nothing else to share, much to your disappointment, I am sure."

#

"How are you really feeling?" asked Chuck.

"I have a five-alarm headache."

"Any idea what happened?"

"No. I always shift to club soda. It was my second glass. I don't recall it ever being out of my hand, but my recollection of the party is fuzzy. I'm not sure it was an allergy. Maybe someone tried to poison me."

"Hmm. Two assassination attempts in two weeks? We knew this was coming. You said so yourself. Hell, I have watched Earl go completely gray this last month. You are very hard on your staff.

"And then some. I am sorry, but I can't change things," apologized Nick, looking around. "Where are we headed?"

"Walter Reed. We need to see if it was an allergy or poison," answered Chuck, ignoring the question in Nick's answer.

"Normally I would fight you, but not today. Be good to know."

"Good. I am glad you see reason."

"What else did you see at the party? Anything suspicious or strange after I went down?"

"It was really weird, Nick. Like everyone was afraid to breathe. Thank God the Garcia's were there. You were in a bad way. Whatever it was, it hit you hard. Ginny Garcia really took charge. You owe her big time. After Hobson carried you upstairs, he refused to leave the door. The look in his eyes made Earl look tame. You know how he can look."

"Obviously, there was lots of gossip going on. I let everyone know you were fine. I met the EMTs. They took a quick look at you, saw something they didn't like, and gave you a second dose of epinephrine. Not sure why, but after that, they said your vitals were stabilized. We left you there to sleep it off. They're the ones who said you would wake up with a doozy of a headache after all the adrenaline."

"Hobson took Banks home. I took over for him. Then Dolly came up around 4am and said she would take over. She also brought in security to patrol the grounds, just in case. Earl offered to come over, but I told him you were in excellent hands," cooed Chuck with a sly smile.

"Not you too."

Chuck smiled in response as they approached Walter Reed.

"Dolly said you sent out a statement to the press?"

"Ya, I tracked Margie down. She was at a show with Jer. I told her we needed to get the word out you were fine. Just a reaction to some food. You were resting fine and would make a statement in the morning. Which you just did. I think we're good. Nice touch on letting them know you would release the results of any testing. The public is not used to getting the truth about candidates' health. Too bad we never got to see the current President's medical records. Or his business dealings or those of his family. At least on that front you are refreshingly up front."

Nick sat, thinking as they approached Walter Reed.

"Oh yeah, I almost forgot. Senator Garcia grabbed the glass you were drinking out of. He gave it to me, and I gave it to Earl. He is having it tested to see if they can determine if it was something in your drink."

"Good. I can't remember ever setting the drink down, Chuck. I'm usually so careful. That's why I always carry my own water bottle and always open new bottles when I drink anything when we are out. Guess I got careless, or someone is very good."

#

"Senator, for a man in his late forties, you are in perfect health," reported the doctor, looking at Nick's chart.

"Mid-forties doc," corrected Nick.

"Uh, huh? Either way, you are in perfect health for a man 15 years your junior. Aside from an impressive catalog of scars, your blood work is all in the perfect range. Cholesterol is obscenely low, as is your heart rate and blood pressure. Especially considering what you just went through, and the fact you're running a presidential campaign. Whatever you're doing, I suggest you continue. As for the allergy tests, we could only detect a potential slight chance at a tree nut allergy. We tested the usual ones: almonds, walnuts, cashews and pine nuts and it is a minor reaction, if any. Ever have any issues with any of those?"

"Nope. Didn't even have any at the party, either."

"Not surprised. If you had, it would have been minor. Nothing like what happened. Of course, the epinephrine would have purged your system of the toxins in that initial flush of adrenalin. We have no luck isolating any specific toxins. I am sorry, but we have no answer for you and nothing we can recommend you avoid. Sorry we can't be of more help," said the doctor, flipping the records on his chart.

"Thanks Doc. Can you make sure you release the findings to the public? No allergies, no toxins, no residual effects, and perfect vitals. That will drive the Vice President crazy," smirked Nick.

The doctor smiled, resisting the urge to comment.

#

Nick was greeted by cheers from the staffers as he walked into their DC campaign office. He smiled and patted a few on the back, returning some hugs. Denise, Earl, and Margie were all huddled around the conference room table as he entered.

Nick noticed for the first time Earl's hair had indeed gone gray and even Denise had gray streaks in what had been raven hair only seven months previously. They looked up as he and Chuck entered. Denise marched up to Nick and punched him in the shoulder. She was on the verge of tears and shaking. He reached out and hugged her as she started crying. It was so un-Denise like he didn't know what to do. Margie was also using a tissue to wipe her eyes. Even Earl was looking a little weepy.

"Geez guys, I'm OK."

"Look what you have done to me. Turned me into a blubbering old woman. If you tell anyone, I will cut them off and risk the wrath of your girlfriends."

"Girlfriends?" asked Nick innocently.

Denise smiled at him. "Let's see? You spent the night at Dolly's, in her bed, despite what you told the reporters. You forget I saw the lipstick on your face from your Nebraska cutey. Who knows how many others there are?" finished Denise cryptically, thankfully not blurting out her knowledge of his time with Lauren.

"Right," dodged Nick.

"Do you good to settle down with someone?" said Denise with conviction, ignoring Nick's statement.

"Just what I need right now, a relationship. I've got enough on my mind. Anything on the glass Garcia grabbed?"

"Not yet. Should know something later today," replied Earl.

"I just got treated like a pincushion at Walter Reed and they couldn't come up with anything. Like I told Chuck, I can't remember ever having my drink out of my hands," he said, looking down at his hands as he talked. He stared a little harder, holding his hand up.

"What?" asked Earl.

"Chuck, get the Doc at Walter Reed on the phone, will ya? I have a question for him."

"Sure."

"Nick, what do you see?" asked Earl, coming over to look at Nick's hand. Nick pointed to a slight cut that had scabbed over.

"I take it you don't remember doing that?"

"Nope."

"Shake a lot of hands last night?"

"Tons."

"I have heard about various methods of transferring poisons."

"Except the doctor could find no trace of anything in my blood. If it was a poison, it would have been there. So that is out."

Chuck motioned to Nick, who took his phone and started talking to the doctor at Walter Reed.

Earl looked at the others. "I don't know what else we can do to keep him safe. Clearly, the knives are out."

"Pray." said Margie and Denise simultaneously, looking at each other, laughing before they hugged.

#

Nick sat in his DC campaign office, reviewing more of the texts from the last 24 hours.

"u ok?"

Nick looked at the text from Lauren. She had sent something similar after the assassination attempt. He'd been tempted then to reach out but resisted doing so beyond a simple 'yes'. Now, along with Natalie and Dolly, he was totally confused. He had never been good with women. Danger, yes. Matters of the heart, never.

Any other red-blooded male would have taken Dolly's invitation to join her in the shower in a heartbeat and yet he had resisted. Just as he had the prior times they had been together. His tryst with Lauren had been at a weak moment, and he regretted it constantly. Regretted it for how he had treated her and how he felt sorry for himself for not being able to commit to being happy with anyone.

Dolly and his feelings for her scared the shit out of him. Natalie made him feel young and carefree, free from worry. Her approach was so refreshingly simple it fueled his desire to just go away and hide. Lauren appealed to his sense of danger. Romancing her was playing with fire. He loved how all these women made him feel when he was around them. Yet, his inability to commit also kept him from choosing a path. Nick knew it was unfair to all of them. Just as it had been for Heather all those years ago. These women all deserved to be the center of someone's universe. He couldn't offer that, at least not now

He simply typed back a 'yes' in response, scrolling down to do the same to a similar text from Natalie. Maybe they'd tire of his antics. In the past, he counted on inattention and his unwillingness to commit to eventually force them to move on.

With women, it was always the coward's way out. What had Dolly said? A 'self-centered cad'? He smiled at the entirely accurate description. He'd have to ask Chuck and Denise what else they had counseled Dolly about regarding him.

#

Nick looked up as Earl entered the office with a knock. He closed the door behind him and sat.

"Pistachios. Highly concentrated. Care to explain?"

"Shit," said Nick, standing, shaking his head. He looked up, and asked himself out loud, "How?"

"Most likely something dumped in the glass by someone passing. It wouldn't take much and it would have instantly dissolved," said Earl.

"No, I know how. What I'm asking is how they found out."

"Excuse me? You said you have no allergies. The Walter Reed docs said you have no allergies," accused Earl.

"Pistachio allergies are very rare. Walnut, almond, and pine nuts are much more common forms of tree nut allergies. If you test negative for them, typically they stop testing others as they are less and less likely."

"You have an allergy to pistachios? Why lie?"

"Earl, I don't just have an allergy, I have a deadly reaction to them, as you saw," said Nick, reaching down to take off his dress shoe. He turned it over, popped a flap on the heel, and took out a small vial. "This is highly concentrated epinephrine. Way more than a standard EpiPen. I carry this everywhere I go, just in case. If I get exposed to pistachios, I only have a minute to stop it. Usually, I can tell the initial signs and administer it, or if I catch it fast enough, I take a handful of Benadryl I keep in my wallet to give me more time. Ginny Garcia's EpiPen was enough to keep it from killing me, but not enough to totally get rid of all the effects. That's why the EMTs gave me a second dose. It's also why I slept so hard. This must have been such a concentrated and large dose. It hit me all at once and there was no symptom I could recognize in time."

"And you were going to tell me, or anyone else, about this little lethal issue when? What other secrets are you hiding that could end up killing you?" commanded Earl, raising his voice.

"Earl, you are still missing the point. The key is how I got this allergy. And who could find out about it and use it against me?"

"Obviously, it is not in your medical records," responded Earl.

"No. In fact, it is in only one record. And that record is beyond top secret, compartmented, and accessible to only a select few. People with the highest security clearances. Clearances that do not include the Vice President and President, for instance."

"Jesus, Nick, what are you talking about? What the hell happened?" he stared, concerned, and intrigued.

"Earl, much of my military record is redacted. Lots of activities in concert with CIA ops while I was in the various war zones, especially in the Navy, but also some while I flew. I can't tell you much. In this case, I ended up behind enemy lines in a country with little hope of rescue. I had to subsist on almost nothing but foul water and pistachios growing in the wilderness. This over reliance on this sole food, for several weeks, caused my body to develop a severe immunity to it. Hence the reaction. This information is only available in a report accessible by almost no one. Maybe the CIA director, but even that is unlikely. This tidbit is in one of those files they mark to open in a hundred years. How somebody got access to these concerns me. What else do they know?"

"What else is in there for them to find?" asked Earl. The look he got back sent a chill down his spine. For the first time, he saw there might be much more to his friend than he realized.

Nick smiled, reducing the tension. "Nothing, except some potentially embarrassing decisions made by various administrations. Their concern with me was much more around my knowledge as an observer, and what I knew, than my actions. My conscience is clear. But someone was able to tease out this little tidbit and obviously someone at Dolly's party knew enough about it to use it against me."

"Any way to find out, who or how?" asked Earl.

"I don't know Earl. Certainly not legally. I'll ask Jeremy if he has ideas. I remember little about the party."

"There were four hundred guests, staff, and security. Regardless, you are traveling with guards everywhere now. And food tasters."

"Doesn't sound negotiable."

"It isn't. Just be glad it is not the Administrations goons. I mean Secret Service." Nick and Earl smiled. Neither thought it was funny.

Chapter 41

Lauren sat in her condo in Buckhead. She was once again working in ANC headquarters in Atlanta. Her bosses announced they would not keep following Turner on the campaign trail. He was too insignificant.

Instead, they wanted Lauren to float between covering big rallies by Blackbird and the Vice President as they entered the home stretch of the campaign. Lauren disagreed, but Jeff, her producer, just shrugged.

"Not my call," was his constant response.

"Really?" looking at him as he turned away from her gaze.

"Let me get this straight. A candidate drawing twenty thousand to a rally at a state fair who has an assassination attempt on his life is now irrelevant. Then he goes down a week later at the party of the season? I suppose you think those are all coincidences for anyone, let alone a presidential candidate," she fumed.

"Lauren, the twenty-five thousand are there to see the bands. As for the party, he said it himself. It was just bad food. The doctors backed it up when they released his records. You're being melodramatic. Turner's peaked. He killed any chance at relevancy with his stupid stance, saying that Marine is innocent," finished Jeff.

"He did not say he was innocent. Just that he deserves a fair trial," corrected Lauren. Jeff gave her a questioning look.

"Does it matter? Fair trial or not, nothing changes six dead bodies at his feet. It was an amateur mistake by Turner. The kind you would expect from someone who has never run for office before. Shows we were wasting *our* time, money and *your* time following him around."

"I disagree. Have you read any of my articles?" she asked.

"Of course."

"About the response of the groups he talks to? Their reactions to his message? The size of his crowds in all these towns he rolls into unannounced. The grassroots orgs he leaves behind to continue his message. This is not someone who is irrelevant. This is a mistake to not have us following him and reporting on this. We are a news organization after all," finished Lauren stubbornly.

Jeff stared at her, surprised at her passion. He figured she would jump at the chance to be on one of the major candidates.

"Lauren, we are also a channel struggling with ratings, bleeding cash, and looking for relevance. We will not get this by talking about lunatic fringe candidates. Look at his polling. If everything you say is true, how is it after 6 months of continuous campaigning he has moved from three percent to six or seven at his high point?" stated Jeff.

Lauren smiled, showing her single dimple.

"You just answered my earlier question. Jeff, I have written multiple times and reported on camera about Nick telling his followers to lie to pollsters. This explains why he is low in the polls. If this is why we are not following him, it is a mistake."

Jeff looked at her again. "Nick?"

Lauren laughed. "I have been following him around for months now. Again, if you read anything I wrote, you would know his catch phrase with everyone he meets is 'call me Nick'. He hates being called Senator, even by his enemies in the press," noted Lauren, hoping she had covered her gaffe.

"Lauren, no politician tells their followers to lie to a pollster about their support. Even if they say it, they are doing it tongue in cheek. Without showing progress in the polls, how do they expect to get donations and endorsements? Oh, wait, Turner doesn't have either. Could it be because he is so low in the polls? I think this is good for you to get away from his campaign and back on a real one. Like I said, it is a moot point," he finished, walking away.

Lauren thought about this later, picking at the salad she grabbed on her way home from work, reflecting on her life. She had none. She worked and then came home to her condo, the company's condo in DC, or a hotel room for room service or takeout dinner. She was a beautiful and successful thirty-six-year-old career woman with her whole life ahead of her. And absolutely miserable.

#

Lexi stared at Roland sitting on a couch in her campaign headquarters. He stared back.

"Do you want to explain?" she asked.

"I have nothing to explain."

"I don't believe in coincidences."

"That makes two of us then," replied Roland.

"I am supposed to just believe you show up, with special skills at a critical time in both my campaign and the fate of the world."

"I do not understand what you are implying." He replied, still staring at her, standing in front of him in a green silk blouse, black skirt, and high heels. She looked the part of the corporate marketing executive.

Except for the obvious anger visible on her face. "What I'm implying is I'm in charge. Do you understand this?"

"Of course. What exactly am I being accused of doing? Taking care of the situation with a rogue presidential chief of staff preparing to spill all the secrets of how collectively you have been propping up a doddering old fool in the role of President? How he has been pumped full of experimental and certainly unapproved drugs? Or that you have been making the decisions and signing documents for which you were not elected? If this is what you are referring to, then yes, I plead guilty to saving *your* exquisite ass and that of *your* administration."

Lexi, fuming, headed toward the bar. She did not offer Roland a drink, knowing he would not partake. Making her scotch, she turned to him. "I guess I owe you thanks for that, though I have no idea what you are referring to regarding those baseless accusations."

Roland smiled, easing the tension.

"It is just us. Did you try to take out Turner?"

"Ah direct. I like it. I told you I did not. I am not a skilled enough sniper to attempt such a shot," confessed Roland.

Lexi took a sip of her scotch. Contemplating his answer.

"I meant the party. You asked me to take you to the party. I obliged you. Was Turner's 'incident' you?"

Roland paused.

"I too like direct," countered Lexi with a withering look.

"Poison is not my weapon of choice, as I am sure you are aware by now. To whom should I be listening? I believe there is a term in America. Plausible deniability. Up to now, you have not told me to do anything directly. It was my understanding this was the arrangement. If you prefer to give me the directives, merely inform me."

Lexi stared at him. "I must trust those around me. I cannot be unsure you or anyone else would be operating without my consent."

Roland gave a little bow. "You have provided my answer. From now on, I am your servant. I assume you will inform your chief of staff?"

Lexi ignored his statement. "If you didn't do this, then what the hell happened to him? A reaction to the food?. All of us ate the same food and no one else got sick. The prick even released all of his records."

Roland remained silent.

"Well?" she looked at him, frustrated.

"You may not like it, but perhaps it is coincidence? Perhaps he ate something before the party. Maybe someone else tried to kill him. He is making a lot of enemies."

Lexi paced, fuming. Then she stopped and turned to him.

"If he doesn't know what caused it either, then maybe we can use that against him in the future. He'll have to be even more careful. Not knowing what could cause a replay. Maybe I can use that in one of my speeches. An undisclosed illness or unknown malady that could pop up again at any time? Even the hint of this could be useful," mused Lexi, thinking aloud. She turned to Roland, who was smiling.

"Excellent idea."

She returned his smile and took another sip of scotch.

Chapter 42

'*This is the strangest bullet I have ever seen,*' read aloud Karen Coleman, acting director of the FBI, from the pages she was flipping through. "This is actually written in the ballistics report?" she asked, looking up at the two men in the room.

"It is Karen," replied a stocky man who looked like the former football lineman he been at Notre Dame decades before. "Our ballistics have concluded it was also somewhat directional. Do you see these tiny grooves?" He handed her the bullet, which was not deformed in the slightest. He also handed her a compact magnifying glass.

"What am I looking at, Caleb?"

"Frankly, we have no idea," replied Caleb Parker, the Director of the Secret Service. "We have heard of experimentation with ammunition, but nothing like this. It is also made of primarily tungsten carbide, with traces of molybdenum, cobalt, and iridium. That is one expensive bullet in your hands. Not something you pick up at your local Cabela's."

"Rhett? You're awfully quiet," said Karen, turning to the third person in the room. "Does the CIA perhaps know more than we do about this kind of ammo?"

Rhett held out his hand, taking the bullet and the magnifying glass from Karen. He looked at the bullet. It did indeed have three very slight grooves along the back half of the bullet.

He turned to Caleb. "What makes them think it was directional?

"Under a microscope they could tell there was some type of 'fin' or other faint residue of something in those grooves."

"Wouldn't anything outside the casing of the bullet be removed while traveling down the barrel?" asked Karen.

"On a normal rifle, yes. Like I said, this is speculation. Either it came from a special type of rifle, or it is possible the 'fins' may have projected at a certain velocity on the journey to correct the trajectory or aim. There is no other reason anyone can figure out why those grooves exist," concluded Caleb.

Rhett raised his hand to his face, pacing.

"You have something?" asked Karen.

"Not really. I know DARPA was working on directional ammo years, hell decades ago. There have also been others who sell bullets with microprocessors in them and rifles to fire them for $20,000 a pop. None of them turned out to be useful. Also, attempts to use GPS to 'guide' a sniper bullet along its path. I am unaware of any company or any country, including our own, perfecting this technology enough to use it. Maybe we are reading more into this than we should?"

"Tungsten carbide, iridium? You would need some pretty specialized equipment to create a bullet out of those materials. It is very expensive to get and to shape. This would have cost a small fortune in diamonds," noted Caleb.

"Diamonds?" asked Karen.

"Diamonds are one of the few substances harder than tungsten carbide. You would need a diamond lathe to grind down the metal. To do it precisely enough for a smooth bullet would take a lot of them. And you didn't just make one. Grinding it would wear down even diamonds. You are looking for a very well-funded sniper," replied Rhett.

"I'm confused. Why go to all this trouble to build a super bullet? If you wanted to kill him, why not use a standard .338?" asked Karen.

They stared at her until Karen answered her own question.

"Jesus. Are you saying he really did this to himself?"

"I'm not saying that," retorted Caleb. "Even a hit from this bullet could easily be fatal."

"But it wasn't," mused Rhett. "I bet your ballistics showed this bullet went in and passed through in a straight line. No fragmentation, obviously no tumbling. In and out like a surgical needle."

"Like a .338 needle. I read the report from the doc. Still left a hole an inch in diameter on the way out," added Caleb.

"True, but it lends credence to the idea the shooter might not have been trying to kill him," noted Karen.

"What do we do with this info? It is all conjecture and speculation. There is no smoking gun, and we have no clues to track down a shooter," noted Caleb.

"I'm not domestic, so this is not my problem. I will, however, offer this advice and you can do what you like. If you tell them, the Vice President or more likely Mel, they will leak it like a cracked egg. You are the acting director. If the FBI is seen disclosing information accusing a candidate of staging his own assassination based on a tungsten carbide bullet. You're going to be in a shitstorm every bit as nasty as some of your predecessors who couldn't help but meddle in elections, too."

Karen turned to Caleb.

"Don't look at me. No one knows my name. I intend to keep it that way. This is your show, Karen. I'm just giving you the info."

"That is my cue to leave. I don't want to know, and I want a clear conscience when I am called to testify. I do not recall any decision to disclose or not disclose any information, Senator or Congressman," smiled Rhett. "Sorry Karen. Welcome to the big leagues."

"Thanks for nothing," she replied through gritted teeth.

#

"There was nothing conclusive in the ballistics report. It appears the bullet did not fragment, showing it was likely at the end of its velocity. It hit Senator Turner at a subsonic speed," reported Karen Coleman.

"What does that mean?" asked Lexi as Mel also looked on.

"The shooter was a long way away. The bullet was traveling much slower than if it were a closer shot. When it hit Turner, it did not have as much of a punch. It did less damage than a typical sniper round at closer range. It would certainly still have killed him if it were a head shot or hit him in the center of his chest or lower in his abdomen. He got lucky."

"Any credence to the idea he did this?" asked Mel hopefully.

"None that our ballistics report shows. You would have to be suicidal to stand and willingly let someone take a shot at you from any distance. I have been shot in the line of duty and I can tell you it is not fun," replied Karen with a wince, remembering.

"Thank you, Karen. Do we need to release any of this?"

"Not with any formal process. We can release we recovered a single round and our analysis shows it was a .338 caliber rifle bullet at the end of its range when it hit Senator Turner. We can also reiterate he's a lucky man to have survived. No need to call a press conference."

"Good. The less press, the better. Thank you for your report, Karen. Caleb told Russ they don't have any suspects," added Lexi, referring to her Secret Service detail lead Russ Kramer.

"Correct. We have nothing either. An old, weathered playing card, a king of diamonds, was found on the roof. It could have blown there for all we know. There are no other clues and certainly no group claiming success. It will stay open, but with no leads…" she shrugged.

"I appreciate the quick work. Let's give it as little attention as possible," agreed Lexi.

Karen nodded as she left the office, feeling like she'd made the right choice for her career.

#

Denise walked into Nick's office smiling. In her hand, she held up a hardcover copy of a book. Across the front it said in bold printing *The Turner Doctrine* with a picture of Nick standing in the well of the Senate, giving his speech against removing the filibuster.

"I still think the title is presumptuous." Nick shook his head.

"It has to be catchy to get attention. Besides, you'll be happy. We have three hundred thousand pre-orders. Even the *Times* and the *Post* won't be able to deny you #1 bestseller status with those numbers."

"Poor bastards. They don't know what they're in for. It's not a Vince Flynn book," whined Nick.

"You never know Nick. Maybe you are getting through to folks. The people ordering this book are *not* the group listening to your speeches on social media. Where it is really selling is your audio version. You also have as many waiting on that as well."

"I sure hope they don't listen to it when they're driving. I don't want to be blamed for accidents from people falling asleep in the middle of my chapter on economics."

"Obviously, you didn't listen to your own recording. You actually make it come to life. The passion you bring to the recording can't be faked. I am so glad we had you do it instead of hiring a celebrity or professional. It's authentic."

"I'll take your word for it. I agree with the actors who refuse to go back and watch their early films. This is my first book, and likely my last."

"There is one other nice little tidbit," smiled Denise.

"What?"

"You may not know this, but because we self-published instead of going through the regular publishing process, we are cutting out the middleman. We also hired our own printer. They are churning these out as fast as they can. Do you even remember saying folks should buy it from the website instead of the usual online sites?"

"Vaguely," responded Nick.

"Well, Mr. #1 bestseller. You are about to bring in a ton of money to your campaign coffers. By having the campaign publish the book, all the profits go to the campaign. Nick, you are going to add $5 million to the campaign from book sales alone. Probably as much or more from audio too," said Denise.

"I had no idea. I directed all of this to the campaign, huh? Hmm, maybe I should rethink that. I can retire..."

"Hilarious. If we had published with the publisher, we would be lucky to see a million total from all these sales. That publisher made a huge mistake by pulling out of the deal. You can use that as another example of cancel culture coming back to bite them in the ass. I love it," finished Denise with a satisfied grunt.

"Thanks for making it happen, Denise. I probably wouldn't have finished it if you hadn't stayed on me about it."

She nodded in reply. "We've been printing up the actual Turner Doctrine, your twenty principles, as a one pager. The grass-roots groups have been handing them out for over a month. It really resonates."

"Yes, that one I *did* read. Good job," replied Nick.

"Now try not to screw the pooch with the 2J's. You sure you want to do that live?" asked Denise, hoping Nick would change his mind.

"JD been calling you?"

"Me? Hardly. The only thing he'd get from me is a free castration," she laughed. "He's been working Margie. Then she tells me. Just be careful. No more curveballs costing us supporters, please."

Nick ignored her not-so-subtle dig.

"It will be fine. What could go wrong? I have nothing to hide."

"Nick, everyone has something to hide. I would not want two AI holograms hooked up to supercomputers poring through every electronic record ever made of anything I did or said. Plus, if Jeremy and his team programmed them, no telling what security measures they have been able to penetrate. Legally, of course. No, thank you. Good luck."

Nick sat contemplating Denise's words as she left the office. Maybe this wasn't such a great idea. He had no idea how effective JD and Jeremy's computers were at digging stuff up. Or finding stuff best left buried.

Chapter 43

Nick was looking at a blank green screen waiting for the interview at 2JNews to begin. JD walked up to him. His forehead had a sheen of sweat. It wasn't warm in the studio.

"Nick, I appreciate your being willing to be our guinea pig for this. Honestly, I don't know how the programs will react. During the announcement, they seemed to hold their own with the reporters. We'll see what they come up with in this one. I have to be honest with you, I'm not comfortable doing this live. I would prefer to tape it. If it is terrible, we can always edit it," replied JD hopefully.

"Nope, I want it to go as is. People need to see what happens and I want you to show everyone this is live and unedited."

"This is an unnecessary risk. Denise has to be coming unglued."

"She is. I am close to driving her to drink again. She gave up coloring her hair and is simply letting it go gray."

JD did not laugh. "If this goes badly and tanks your campaign, you may bring down my network before we even get started. I'm taking an enormous risk letting you do this."

"It is your choice, not mine."

"Right," laughed JD. "If I stop it now, I lose. If you crash and burn, I lose. If my anchors screw up, I lose. I don't enjoy being out of control of my fate. More than that, I hate to lose."

Nick laughed too, turning in his chair to face the screen. "Me too. Let's do this. I'll be able to see them, right?"

"Yes. They'll be on the screen. Walter and Barbara have been told to limit the conversation to the book and the ideas in the books. So, we won't be going off topic to discuss any other activities, like the fact you should be the Opposition nominee or your crazy antics for that Marine," stated JD, showing his opinion of both actions.

"Oh geez, not you too. I was not in the Opposition primary, and I am not an Opposition member. That's why I didn't take Carson's call."

"She called you? You really could have had it?" asked JD, shaking his head at the confirmation.

"Woops. Keep that to yourself, please. No scoops. I didn't take the call, so I have no idea why she was calling. Maybe she wanted my seven-layer dip recipe? We'll never know."

"I think that was a mistake."

"Just make sure it doesn't come up in the interview or Walter and Barbara could get the Paxton and Bergamo treatment," said Nick, with a threatening hand chop.

"I wonder how they would respond?" asked JD, smiling.

"Let's not find out. We sort of already did at the announcement, but hey, your anchors don't lie, so we should be good there, right?"

"I hope so. They *shouldn't* lie, but I am still not sure they pick up on sarcasm. They haven't interacted with humans much yet. We do sessions with staff to help them better understand nuance, humor, sarcasm, and anger. Studying facial expressions and body language."

"I have to be honest, JD. This is kind of creepy. I'm giving a live interview in a political campaign where I'm the last hope our Constitution has, and I am relying on two AI holograms to give me the opportunity to explain my stances?" ended Nick with a nervous laugh.

"You can't stop progress. You can only make it useful and try to diminish the negatives. That's what I am trying to do. We don't need personality and opinion coloring our *news*. That is what opinion shows are for. You can turn them off. The news needs to be facts and let viewers form their own opinions."

"That is certainly not how American *Pravda* sees it," laughed Nick. "Their ratings appear to be dropping, so maybe folks are catching on."

"Let's hope we're doing our part. You ready?"

"Lead the lamb to slaughter," said Nick with a grin.

"Remember, they don't have a sense of humor," warned JD, truly sounding worried for the first time.

#

"Senator Turner, welcome to our first ever live interview on *What Really Happened Today*. Barbara and I have both read your book, *The Turner Doctrine*. We would like to ask you some questions and hear your responses for our audience," started Walter in a calm voice.

"Thank you, Barbara and Walter. I look forward to this groundbreaking interview. Let's have some fun," said Nick, smiling in reply.

They both smiled back but did not respond to his joke.

Nick continued quickly. "Thank you for reading the entire book. Most people who host book interviews do not read the book."

"As you know, Senator, we are not like most people," said Barbara, without a trace of humor. "We can read your entire book and research all of your statements and comments and come up with questions we feel help clarify the statements you made. We have reviewed over 10,000 prior biographies, including books by politicians who have published books during an election year."

"Your book lacks the extensive biographical information found in these other books, nor does it have the on average 81.4% statements about yourself and what you have done and how you have overcome adversity to achieve your position. Our question is, why did you not follow the standard format for these types of books?"

"81.4%, that's pretty accurate," said Nick lightly, again unaccustomed to his audience not responding to his humor.

Walter interrupted. "We could take it out to 4 decimal points, but we find that is unnecessary to make our point. In fact, your biography accounts for exactly 6% of your book."

"Walter, that is a good thing. My book is not about me, it is about my ideas and my thoughts on the key issues being faced by every American today. It educates and highlights what and how we got to the place we are in each of these cases. Then it describes plans for how we mitigate the problems we are facing, working together," responded Nick.

"Senator, it is our understanding in our review of books of these types, audiences prefer to learn more about the writer and their struggles than how they intend to fix the reader's problems," replied Barbara.

"Barbara, does your research also show you how many of the books were purchased versus given away and how many were bulk purchased by foundations with ties to the candidates?"

"One moment, Senator, we are researching."

"While you are at it, Barbara, you might also try to figure how many of the people who purchased these books actually read them."

"Sorry Senator, there are no credible statistics on the number of people who read the books purchased. It appears a majority of the books by candidates are indeed purchased by foundations and corporations in block buys, especially those published by Party candidates," he said.

"Walter, what that tells me is it is irrelevant what they write in their books. Few actual people are buying their books to read. I focused mine on issues, facts, and recommendations. Not on how I will fix them, but how collectively we all need to work to fix them. Not wasting words on my bio means my book *is* relevant. I'm hopeful regular people will buy it, read it, and act on its recommendations," explained Nick.

"Thank you for answering the question, Senator. Our next question concerns your position where you claim the country has strayed from the Constitution. You cite things like the removal of the filibuster as an example. Is the Constitution not a living document as witnessed by the twenty-seven amendments?" asked Barbara.

"Barbara, the first ten were passed when it was ratified in 1788. They ensured we had individual freedoms the government could not limit, such as freedom of speech, expression, and our right to bear arms."

Barbara broke in, not realizing Nick was pausing for effect.

"Senator, you say the government should be local, not federal. Is there not already local government?"

Nick laughed. "I can see I need to change the way I answer questions, Barbara. I had not finished answering the prior question. Pausing for effect is clearly not something you have experienced yet. I must remember you do not have a sense of humor, nor do you need to think about what I say, to digest it if you will, before I continue. I will help you learn more about interacting with humans today. Our brains are not computers. We need time to process what we hear, to think about it, and to understand all the implications or the words spoken."

"Senator, our apologies. We did not intend to cut you off. Please continue," responded Walter in a normal and emotionless tone.

"I like you guys because, even though you have access to endless information, you lack context. In many ways, you are like regular people who have so many things to do, but not enough time to research every decision. Let me try to explain how government that should be local is increasingly being ceded to federal governance."

"I can tie this into finishing the answer to the first question as well. The 27th amendment was one of the original 12 proposed," said Nick as Barbara interrupted.

"Yes, Senator, that would be the amendment preventing Congress from giving themselves pay raises. First proposed in 1788 but rejected and not ratified until 1992, by the states, not Congress."

"Barbara, can you look up Hermione Granger? A quote in the third book of the Harry Potter series, where Professor Snape makes a comment about her interrupting his lesson to answer a question, when she was not called upon?"

"Of course, Senator. May I ask why?"

"I am curious to understand if *you* can understand context."

"You believe I am 'an insufferable know it all'?" asked Barbara, again with no emotion on her pretty, but not beautiful, face.

Nick laughed again. "I may have met my match. Another time perhaps we can have a session on how to interact with humans in an interview. Let's press on. How about if I hold up my hand when you are interrupting and you let me finish my point before you jump in?"

"Of course, Senator. But we must point out, we have studied millions of hours of interviews, and it is our experience that interruptions between speakers are common."

Nick answered questions about how there have only been seventeen true amendments since eleven of the original twelve were proposed as the Bill of Rights at the original adoption. Most of those additions dealt with voting rights or repealed prior amendments. Not bad for a document almost two-hundred and fifty years old. His point was this was anything but an example of a living constitution.

He reiterated the stances he had explained on Tommy at the beginning of his campaign how the sixteenth and seventeenth amendments, namely the establishment of the income tax and making senator's elected by the people versus their state legislatures, were examples of how the Constitution was compromised. Intentionally.

Walter and Barbara were perfect foils for Nick, as he could have them cite facts from their enormous databases to back up his arguments of overreach and unintended consequences. This way it was not his opinion, but obvious examples of how neither of these amendments accomplished what they intended. How their proposers, the original progressives, knew this would happen. They were couched as changes to help the people and instead were two of the most egregious examples of the government turning these changes into weapons to control the masses, not punish the rich or powerful as they claimed they would.

Nick held his own as he was quizzed on his stances in the book, briefly touching on some of his more radical proposals like term limits, eliminating the federal bureaucracy, replacing the income tax with a consumption tax, funding police to re-establish deterrence and closing the border with an illegal immigrant assimilation plan implemented over decades versus the blanket and immediate amnesty the Vice President was proposing.

Nearing the end of the interview, Nick paused.

"Barbara, Walter, this is the most exhausted I have been in a long time. I feel like I'm on an eight-hour mission in my A-10," laughed Nick.

"Of course, Senator. You spent more time on missions in the war zone than any other pilot. We have only been talking for 87 minutes, not eight hours, so I am not sure how you can compare the two?" Barbara asked in a questioning tone.

Nick laughed. "Thank you for making my point for the audience. Now they know exactly what I mean.

"Senator, thank you for your answers and thank you for your time and explanations," said Walter in closing.

"Cut," shouted a producer.

"That was interesting," expressed Nick.

"Not bad," confirmed a relieved JD, coming up to Nick.

"It was hard to have a conversation with anchors who have no reaction to your answers. They just took my answer and moved on. It was so surreal. We'll see how others react," offered Nick.

JD smiled. "Indeed, we will Nick. I'll tell you what, though. There is no way someone like Lexi or Blackbird would sit for this. These guys will find any lies they write or imply and put them on the spot. They did it with you a few times, but you got them turned around. If you had lied to them, they would have done to you what you did to Diane and Bergamo. I know there were some who hoped that would happen tonight. It didn't, and that is a testament to your integrity and your positions."

"It's actually because I believe in my answers, so I can defend them naturally, without bluster or rhetoric."

"I'm just glad it is over," remarked JD. Nick smiled in reply.

Chapter 44

"Looks different doesn't it" said retired Super Bowl winning NFL Coach Alfred Sampson waving an arm at the now clear path down Venice Beach. The tent city was much smaller. The few still there weren't on the beach. Families pushing strollers. Fit and tanned young people once again strolled and skated up and down the path. Greg was walking in front of them, filming their conversation.

"It's fantastic, Alfie. You didn't waste any time," replied Nick.

"This is all because of you, Nick. You got people into motion. The inspiration was all you. This idea gave these people hope and purpose," replied Alfie.

"I started the ball rolling, but it took someone like you to organize and motivate people into action."

"Thanks. I have to say, I'm enjoying this as much, or maybe even more, than winning a Super Bowl. It is more satisfying, and it lasts. I don't have to repeat the next season and deal with failing," noted Alfie.

"What about the tents still here?" asked Nick, as Greg panned to show the dozen tents still on the beach, but in an out of the way corner.

"We can't save them all, Nick. Most of the ones left are mentally ill and refuse to seek treatment, which we offer, or they are new to the beach. We'll approach the new ones with offers to help, most of them accept after a few days of realizing this is no easy life. The tourists and locals are back, so the homeless feel more threatened now by the cops who patrol again now that we cleaned it all up," he explained.

"Did they provide any help?" asked Nick.

Alfie laughed. "Guess you didn't hear? I have already been arrested three times by the local cops on order from the Governor. Harassment mostly. It seems talking to a homeless person receiving government help and free needle exchange is considered harassment."

"You're kidding?" Nick had a suitably confused look on his face. Greg smiled behind the camera, knowing his boss's tactics.

"Talking to them to offer them non-governmental assistance is viewed as an infringement of their rights and if the conversation is not solicited by them, it is grounds for a harassment claim. We have had homeless advocates out preaching to them. It is their right to stay on the beach and live anywhere they like." Coach paused, shaking his head.

"They're pretty harmless. Their Antifa and ARL buddies are a different sort. They showed up to protest one day. About twenty of these thugs in the black hoodies and masks, knocking down tents and harassing our people, getting in their faces with the cameras rolling. You know, typical progressive tactics, trying to get a response so they can put it on the local news saying we are the problem. Trapper really came through." laughed Alfie.

"How so?"

"Smart guy, that one. And he knows tactics. He sent a group around the outside of the encampment to circle back around. Once they were in place, he approached the ARL leader with five of the biggest dudes from the encampment. He told him to leave and that he and his anarchists were not welcome in this or any community." Alfie was smiling big now, his white teeth contrasting against his dark face.

"One of them wound up with some sort of projectile to throw it into the group. Just as he was about to let it go, one of Trapper's guys hit him from behind with a water balloon full of urine. It splashed all over the leader and the guy with the projectile. What was even better was the thrower dropped his on the two guys standing next to him. Covered them in the white paint and whatever shit they had in it. Must not have been nice from their reaction." Nick started laughing.

"They started dancing around patting the stuff off their clothes. Trapper gave the word, and the group started getting pelted with water balloons full of piss from all directions. Once they were all covered, they ran off the beach like the little bullies they all are."

"Seems like justice was served," nodded Nick.

"We sent the footage to the local TV station about the homeless standing up to progressive intimidation tactics, but they declined to show 'our violence against fellow citizens' simply exercising their right to protest," shrugged Alfie. "That little stunt got us about half to join our effort. Let's take a trip. Let me show you how much the Pasadena Redemption village has changed."

#

They drove from the beach inland until they reached the original Redemption village, where Nick had made the announcement of the Blue Morpho Redemption Project in May. They parked their car in front of the welcome center.

Nick looked around. "You guys move fast."

"This is nothing. LA county is much more restrictive. They made us jump through all kinds of hoops to get permits to expand. We also have a couple of hotels in the area which were donated by our benefactors. We use them as initial housing until we figure out where folks want to go and the work they want to do. We have seventeen of these Redemption villages in various stages of construction. Five more in California, two in Chicago, one in Baltimore, outside Portland, Houston, two in Detroit, one in Pittsburgh, Austin, and Denver, and two in Seattle. I think that is all of them."

"Alfie, this is way beyond what I could even envision when we started this. Thank you for making this work. To be honest, I have intentionally not checked on the status to make sure no one says I am trying to use this for my own personal gain."

"Nick, I don't understand how getting tens of thousands of homeless off the street and into housing. How getting a majority of them jobs and treatment can be construed as anything but the Godsend it is," groused Alfie as Greg filmed their conversation.

Nick laughed. "Have you watched American *Pravda* lately? I heard they had a professor of humanities on one channel the other day, arguing that giving the homeless alternatives was akin to transporting innocent tribesmen from the wilds of Africa to the slavery of the American colonies. And the commentator agreed!"

"Senator, this country needs you to do what we have started here with the rest of our upside-down government. Common sense is not only uncommon, it appears to have been eradicated." Nick nodded as they walked down a lane. Greg would occasionally pan to the left or right, showing the neat rows of small modular houses and buildings.

"We're building as fast as we can here and in all the others. Blue Morpho has a total of 11,000 hotel rooms available in donated properties around the country. Your vision is working. We have tons of job openings from companies, and we are moving people from place to place to follow the work. So far, I would say we have about 5000 families in our villages and probably as many in our hotels either waiting for Pods to be built or waiting to transition to a new place for a promised job. You don't get into a Pod until we match them with a job. They are expected to pay minimal rent for the Pod and take part in the community with some type of service," said Alfie.

"Pod?" asked Nick as they walked up a well kept dirt street between the modular homes.

"Sorry, we call the modular homes Pods. They aren't much, but they have indoor plumbing, heat, air conditioning, kitchens and two bedrooms. We also have internet and cable connections, but they have to pay for these. Each village has a local school for home schooling support and a medical clinic, plus a general store stocked from donations. Nick, I gotta tell you, this is like the army. We have logistics and supply officers. We have strategy meetings and plan out everything. Each city has a 'general' and an operations manager."

"They are the genuine stars of the show. We even have our own internal security forces to keep the peace. There are local AA and other support groups, usually started by the locals who live here. It is drug free and everyone is tested before they get their jobs and during their time here. Most are cool with that. We have had a few back slide, but the community rallies around them and supports their efforts to get clean. It works well. Best of all, we keep the government away."

"Amen to that. I am sure that isn't sitting well with the Governor. What's he spending all those billions in aid on if there's no one to aid? His NGO buddies aren't making their payroll," offered Nick sarcastically.

"We've had a few social workers come by intending to shut us down for violating this or that statute, but they end up leaving disappointed. Nick, we also have lawyers in each village. They monitor everything. We have to be so careful to not give the local government any excuse to block us. Instead of helping us and celebrating our success, all they do is try everything they can to stop our efforts. Most of our lawyers are volunteers. Hell, a couple have actually been patrons as well as we found out," smiled Alfie.

"I can't say I am surprised. That they would try to stop you or that you have professionals who are homeless. Bad luck hits everyone."

"Nick, it isn't perfect, but it is much better than living on the streets and it is making a difference," said Alfie, shaking his hand and pulling Nick into one of his patented bear hugs.

"Thanks Alfie, it is a team effort," replied Nick, as Greg stopped filming. He noticed a woman walking her young daughter down the street. She saw Coach, waved, and smiled. As Nick and the Coach approached, he introduced them. "Nick, this is Cora and her daughter Amy. Senator Nick Turner."

The woman blushed as she realized who Nick was. She bent down. "Amy, shake the Senator's hand. He is the reason we have this house, and he got Daddy his job," said Cora as Amy came forward and gave Nick a hug around his legs.

"Whoa, that is way better than a handshake," laughed Nick, holding out a hand to Cora as Amy still hugged him. "Nice to meet you, Cora," said Nick, disengaging from her daughter. "You can call me Nick. It looked like you guys were on your way somewhere?"

"We were on our way to the schoolhouse for playtime. All the kids who are homeschooled get together a couple hours a day to do group activities," said Cora.

"You were on the beach?" asked Nick.

"Actually no. We were living with my parents," replied Amy. Seeing Nick's confusion, she continued as Alfie smiled, knowing what was coming. Greg had already started filming again.

"We were some of the first to arrive here at the village. My husband helped organize the city and has been helping build each of the homes since we started. You met him in March. Ryan?" noted Cora.

"Trapper? He was the inspiration for all of this. He was very persuasive," said Nick.

"Funny, he says the same thing about you. I need to get Amy to the schoolhouse. We try to instill in everybody the need to be on time. Ryan is on the edge of 4th street working on a new house. Senator, I can't thank you enough for what you've done for us and everyone else here. You gave us hope," she said, tearing up a bit.

"Mommy, are you OK?" asked Amy, her five-year-old voice showing concern.

"Yes, honey, just happy. Let's go, we can't be late," said Cora as she turned and walked quickly down the road to a house on the opposite side of the street.

"We're on First, so we need to go over four blocks and down to the end," said Coach, once again walking. "I would have taken a golf cart if I'd known we were going for a stroll," suggested Alfie.

"I need the exercise. All I do is talk all day Coach, or sit in cars or planes, traveling to the next talk. How many Pods are here?" asked Nick as they passed street after street of Pods in neat rows.

"120 so far, but we have permits to build out to 250. That took some doing, but like I said, our lawyers are both good and motivated by the good they do. The bureaucrats in the city halls try, but they are no match when our teams use their own regulations against them. They don't know what to do when we know the codes better than they do."

Nick laughed a hearty laugh. "I love it. Serves them right."

"250 would be what, 700 to 1000 people?"

"Sounds about right," said Coach,

They continued walking up Fourth street as they talked. The sound of hammering and pneumatic nailers increased as they came to a site where several Pods were being constructed. As they approached, a man straightened up at the sight of Coach. He took off his hard hat and walked over.

"Hey Coach, slumming?" asked Ryan. "Senator." He nodded once he realized Nick was behind Alfie.

"Trapper, you know it's Nick," he responded, shaking the outstretched hand. Trapper shook Greg's hand as well. "Where's Earl? No offence, but after Minneapolis you shouldn't be walking around without bodyguards. Especially in California."

"Same thing he said. We're working on it. Secret Service says I am too insignificant." Trapper and Coach laughed at Nick's delivery. "Earl's prepping a site for another meeting I have later. I'll tell him we saw you. He will be sad he missed seeing you and all the progress.

Ryan smiled back. "Been a while since anyone called me Trapper."

"Looks like you found a purpose," said Nick, laughing and looking around the construction sites.

"Indeed. I am the construction foreman. I'm in charge of all the building construction," said Ryan.

Alfie laughed. "Foreman? Nick, don't let ole Ryan shit you. He is also the 'General' of this village. His plans and processes are what we replicate in every village. He is the heart and soul of why this works."

Ryan's face reddened under his suntan. "Coach is fond of giving all the credit to his players. It is a team effort for sure."

"Looks like you have been busy. Regardless of who gets the credit, what you are doing is making a difference. It's exceeded my wildest expectations when we came up with this idea. Has it really only been five months?" asked Nick.

"I know. Hard to believe. It has been fulfilling. I've been able to watch many people come here, get their lives in order and move out to real housing. It's amazing," said Ryan, turning to look back at Nick.

"How many do you think you've helped?" asked Nick.

Coach looked at Ryan. "In all total, I'd say we probably have 20,000 we've moved through the program and onto jobs. Folks in the office can give you a more exact number. We keep track, of course," answered Alfie.

"Sounds about right. We've had a few issues, like everywhere. There are lots of folks who need help. Your donors came through again on that, Nick. They are funding additional beds at several local hospitals specifically for those in need of mental health services. Coach is probably right. Twenty, maybe as high as twenty-five thousand. We probably have capacity for that many in the program at any time. We need to move them through and into jobs. Getting their lives back on track so we can help others. It's still a drop in the bucket, sadly."

"We do what we can," said Coach.

"This is all you," said Ryan, looking at Nick as Coach nodded.

Nick shook his head. "Actually, when you showed me around Venice Beach and told me all these people had skills, they only needed a matchmaker. That sparked this idea," said Nick, waving an arm around. "This was your idea. I just pulled some folks together to make it a reality. You guys did the rest with your skills."

"The only problem we have now is getting people to leave," laughed Ryan. "People get here, like it, then get good jobs forcing them to move. It's tough. Just like getting new orders in the military."

"That's a good thing. Building friendships and comradery is irreplaceable. I know I can call any of my buddies from the service, and they will be wherever I am in a heartbeat. You can't fake that kind of bond. What you are building here is based on shared sacrifice. You've all hit the bottom and worked back for another shot. Everyone is so much stronger for having been through what you have done. It is an inspiration to all who struggle. You give them hope and you show them a path to purpose," said Nick, looking around again at all the workers.

"Our government misses the point entirely. Giving people money or food or housing or free education or anything else does not help. It does not encourage. It created dependency and dependency rots you from the inside out. What we are doing here is giving people purpose. Self-confidence, self-reliance, and the ability to own their own decisions. Both actions and consequences, but made by them. That's why this is working. Because the human spirit is *independent*, not dependent," finished Nick.

When Nick stopped, he looked up into the smiling faces of Greg, Alfie, and Ryan. They started clapping as Greg kept filming. "Nice speech Senator," smiled Ryan. Nick flipped them all off.

"Don't worry, we'll edit that part out," said Greg, laughing.

"When will you move on?" asked Nick, ignoring Greg.

"If Cora and Amy had a choice, never, they would stay here, but I know we can't. Most likely, I would move on to another Redemption village to plan and build it. Coach and I are trying to figure out what the next steps are. Until then, I will keep building these here. There are more homeless in California than anywhere. There are thousands of homeless in the LA area and we need to help all we can."

"Ryan, unfortunately, we need to go. We have one more stop before the Senator has to head out," said Coach.

Ryan held out his hand. "Nick, I can't thank you enough."

He gave him a hug, getting catcalls from the other workers who were watching. Ryan promptly flipped them off and yelled at them to stop loafing, and get back to work, but with a smile.

Chapter 45

As they walked back to their car, Coach was telling Nick how the traditional shelters, the city, the county, and the state were all working to stop their effort. "Thank goodness for our deep pockets and our lawyers. You would think getting homeless people off the street would be celebrated," said Coach with a shrug.

"Coach, the government is all about an old term from Europe. It is called *patronage*. You make someone a squire, or a count, and they owe you when you come calling. Nobility did this for centuries. Our nobility is congress and our government agencies, handing out patronage as government contracts to corporations and grants to NGOs."

"None of this is *solely* done out of the goodness of their hearts. With every dollar they spend, they are collecting leverage. They use this leverage to get something they want. Usually, it's a vote. Sometimes support for a re-election campaign. You're messing with their patronage system by taking away people who they are counting on to leverage at a later date. These organizations have invested a lot of time and your money to make these people beholden and dependent on them. They don't want to see all that go to waste. That's why lobbyists exist. To make sure the money and grants keep flowing," explained Nick.

"You're telling me, by *us* actually doing what they say they are trying to, we are being vilified so they can keep their clients from actually achieving what they say they want them to do?" asked Coach, confused. Nick smiled as Greg laughed behind his phone camera.

"You got it. Sort of like when a team owner says he is doing everything he can to put the best team on the field and then trades the team's best player to cut costs," explained Nick.

"Now *that* I can relate to. I think we call that talking out of one's ass," laughed Coach as they drove back into LA, then down into Orange County. They parked outside the local Turner for President office.

\#

"We volunteering to work the phones?" asked Nick, smiling.

"Hardly. You may not know this, but all your office workers are paid, and well above minimum wage from the start," said Coach.

"How do you know that?" asked Nick with a raised eyebrow.

"You'll see," said Coach as they walked in.

The office manager recognized Alfie immediately, and the folks in the office cheered and clapped. "Hey coach," she said as Nick walked in behind him and her eyes widened. "Holy crap. Senator, nobody told us you were coming," she said as the rest of the office stopped clapping and stood up to get a look at Nick.

Nick smiled and walked forward to shake her hand. "Laura Wood, Senator, I run the Turner for President office for Orange County."

"Nice to meet you in person, Laura. I've seen you on some of the ZOOM calls. How many folks work in this office? And call me Nick."

She smiled. Laura was a short blonde, who looked to be in her late thirties. "Right now? Probably 20 in the office. Alot of our team is out handing out the new *Turner Doctrine* pamphlet. Going door to door."

Nick looked at Coach. "How many of you are in or graduates of Blue Morpho?" asked Alfie in a loud voice. About two-thirds of the hands went up, including Laura.

"Really? This is great," said Nick. "Everyone is being paid right, not just volunteering?"

"We don't allow anyone in Blue Morpho to volunteer because of your involvement. Everyone is a paid worker," confirmed Laura.

"You were in the program, too?"

"Yes, I was on the beach when you came through with Trapper. I went through an ugly divorce, became an alcoholic, lost my job, and ended up on the street. I eventually made it to Venice and camped there. Trapper and then Cora, when she arrived at the village, took me under their wing, keeping me sober. I helped Trapper taking care of people. I had some nursing school training. But my profession was advertising.

"When we started Hope One, I was there with Trapper to get things established at the beginning."

"Hope One?" asked Nick.

Laura smiled. "Pasadena Blue Morpho Redemption village was too big a mouthful. We started calling it Hope One. Now each village is a Hope plus a number village. Technically, it is Hope One, California."

"Nice. I like it."

"I helped by doing outreach and building the database of companies willing to take a chance on our residents. Then, when we got someone placed, I used my marketing talents to create and market success stories. We had a few people with social media skills and the rest is history. Our success at showing the results of our efforts on various social apps and recruiting sites and we suddenly had companies calling us. It didn't hurt that it made them look good, giving back to the community. The HR departments love us."

"I knew there was talent there among everyone, just as Ryan said. I guess I never thought about the variety," admitted Nick.

"Nick, you have no idea. We have folks who have come through the program with PhDs and former pro athletes. We even had a JPL scientist who worked on spy satellites. You name it, we have it in our jobs database," replied Coach with pride at their accomplishments.

"It proves bad things can happen to anyone," remarked Nick.

"To finish my story, Denise was filling roles in the Orange County offices for your campaign. I interviewed, got the job, and we've been going gangbusters ever since. All your campaign offices have Blue Morpho folks. We want to pay it forward. There are many nights when I have to force BM people to go home. Best workers we have."

"You still live in Hope One?" asked Nick.

"Nope," said Laura with a smile. "Got an apartment nearby two months ago. Bought my first piece of furniture and a used car. You need to win so I can keep my job," threatened Laura with a smile.

"And if I lose, then what?" asked Nick carefully.

"Don't worry Nick. I'm confident in my abilities now. I could find another job. You and BM gave me back my self-respect and my confidence," said Laura with a smile. "But you're not going to lose. In fact, she said with a wink, I predict you win California."

Nick laughed. "I appreciate your confidence, but that would be an upset of colossal proportions. Please don't bet any money on that one. I wonder what odds the Vegas book makers would give that." They all laughed. He turned to Coach, "I thought you said you drug tested folks? Laura is obviously on hallucinogens. Maybe some of those legalized mushrooms," said Nick with a laugh and a wink at her.

"Totally clear-headed Senator. Would you like me to explain?"

"Clearly, you're serious. I apologize for joking. Please do,"

They sat around a small table while Laura laid out her theory.

"First, California is in terrible shape. We've had a huge outflow of money and talent, especially in the bay area. The net outflow of wealth has been even greater, as most who leave are the highest earners. Many are also some of the top donors who are disillusioned. They moved their residences and, therefore, their taxes elsewhere. California is suffering both a tax base *and* Party donation deficit."

Nick looked at Laura as she laid out her points, interrupting.

"The reason Blue Morpho exists is because many of those donors funded *it* rather than the Party this go round. If I'm not mistaken, the last election had the Party winning by over 6 million here?" said Nick.

"Actually 7.3 million after they counted all the votes, legit or otherwise," said Laura with a delightful laugh.

"See, it is even worse. They don't need fraudulent votes here."

"Nick, you don't live here. This place was once Shangri La. It was the place to be. Fabulous weather, great scenery, the ocean and fun all day long. Sixty years of progressive politics, poor leadership and unchecked immigration have turned us into a shell of what we once were. At one point, California was the fifth largest economy in the world *on its own*. Those days are long gone. Real Estate is unaffordable. The schools are now graduating illiterates. Don't get me started on the math scores. Our pensions are broken. The teachers are woke, *and* the highest paid in the country. The social services are crap. Our emergency rooms are full of people who do not pay any taxes. People, especially those not living in exclusive enclaves, are fed up." Laura delivered her news with passion.

"The brain drain to Texas, Florida, and Arizona has accelerated. Major companies have moved many of their workers to more business-friendly states. AI is also taking its toll on the low-skilled worker. With an influx of illegals who'll do menial work for a pittance under the table. You have a recipe for economic disaster in this state."

"It has gotten so bad, just like New York, we are now trying to penalize folks who leave the state with exit taxes. Thankfully, the Supreme Court overturned those stupid laws. Who knows what happens if Lexi wins? There is a storm brewing. This is why I think you have a chance. We talk to a lot of traditional Party members. Even people on welfare and Medicaid, who you would think would embrace the VP's policies, aren't. In fact, illegals who have been here for 10 or 20 years are the most resentful of the new opened flood gates. They're worried about losing their jobs to these new ones willing to undercut their wage."

Nick smiled as Laura continued her explanation. Nothing pleased him more than to hear others echoing his own words.

"Imagine the irony of that statement. The thing *most* shifting opinion is simple. Crime. It is a war zone after dark. Not just the cities, but in the suburbs and rural towns. When the sun goes down, the predators come out. Every central valley town now has gangs. We're just another Mexican state the cartels fight over," ended Laura.

"I've heard that," confirmed Nick, thinking of Duke's tales.

"Gun sales are through the roof and most of them are Party voters. It is ironic the very thing the VP wants to stop is being sped up by the administration's policies."

"Anybody using them?" asked Nick.

Coach jumped in on this one. "Surprisingly yes. These Party voters are very concerned when they are arrested and charged by the same DA's they voted into office. DA's who let the criminals who tried to rob them go free. Not prosecuting them for theft, robbery, grand theft, and aggravated assault. It comes full circle."

"When you finally stand up to them, if you don't kill the intruder, you are screwed big time for daring to confront an attacker. If they are an illegal, it is even worse. There is a whole cottage industry of ambulance chasing lawyers and government NGOs taking their cases, claiming they don't understand enough English to know what 'stop', 'leave' and 'hold up your hands' means. They are the innocent victims of the so-called trigger-happy gun nuts," said Coach in a disgusted tone.

"Not always Coach," laughed Laura. "It is only these new liberal gun owners who pay the price. The rest are smart enough to know it is kill or be killed. They have figured it out. When you go to gun training, the instructor makes it real clear the justice system is always against you as the gun owner. They tell you to make sure you shoot to kill. Dead intruders tell no tales. Crime is the big issue now. How the suburban moms go, so goes the state. You throw in your brilliant abortion compromise and that is how you win California," said Laura with a triumphant smile.

Nick smiled back. "An interesting theory, for sure. But you are in Orange County, the lone Opposition outpost in Southern California. I'm not nearly progressive enough in my views to captivate a majority of the California Party residents."

"I talk to my counterparts everywhere. Blackbird is flailing and you are getting all his support. You are easily going to beat him in the state. I know that is not saying much," admitted Laura. "Now it comes down to you and the VP. We are doing our part. I am now an optimist."

"Good. I won't tell Denise or Chuck. They will start putting California on our win board," smiled Nick. "You let me know personally if there is anything you need. More funding or people, OK?"

"I will, Nick," said Laura. Greg took pictures and filmed, before Coach took them to meet Earl. Nick stood, shaking Coach's hand. "Keep up the good work. You have done amazing things in such a short time."

"Nick, you need to win. If you don't, I worry the long arm of the law is going to come after us like a ton of bricks. They hate our success because it shows all the ways their own social justice and social welfare programs have only enriched those running them. Especially while all the 'clients' stay just as disadvantaged."

"For you to clean up Venice Beach, something the entire corrupt California Party government could not do is beating the hornet's nest with the stick. They'll come after you and God forbid you lose. Their vindictiveness will know no boundary," Coach was now pleading with Nick to acknowledge the danger as he finished.

"Believe me, I have seen it. There is no more motivated player than the one who comes to town on another team. He wants to prove to the world your team made a mistake letting him go. The Party will want to make an example of you. Showing the world no one dares to challenge their ownership of solving the problems of poverty and racism. Trust me," predicted Coach.

"I'll keep it in mind. You keep doing good," responded Nick.

"We will," finished Alfie as Nick headed into his hotel.

Greg followed silently. As Nick's shadow, he knew all too well exactly what Coach was saying. He worried Nick was not taking the threat seriously enough. There would be no place he could hide once Lexi came looking after the election. He was not sure what Nick's followers would do when this happened. Greg was afraid to contemplate that future.

Chapter 46

Nick was standing in the wings of the concert stage at the Tennessee state fair. Earl pulled him aside to an area where they could speak without yelling, as the band on stage finished their encore songs.

"I know a Secret Service agent who has shared stuff with me."

"Can you trust him?" asked Nick.

"Her. Yes, I think so. She doesn't agree with the stance of you not getting protection. She told me the ballistics on your shooting came back. They found the bullet lodged in the back wall of the stage. It was the weirdest bullet any of them had ever seen. She said it looked like attempts were made to make it directional. There was also no deformation at all. It didn't fragment, mushroom, or flatten upon hitting you. It was also most likely subsonic. At the end of both its range and velocity," Nick listened as Earl continued.

"What are you saying?"

"They are reviewing sniper records and assassinations to see if they have any record of this type of ammo being used previously. All very strange. Ammunition like this had to be custom crafted. It is also the opposite of what you want in a rifle bullet," shared Earl. "One other thing I got from her. They found a playing card on the roof of a building over a mile away. The king of diamonds. It was old and weathered, so they're not sure how long it was there. Could be coincidence."

"The plot thickens. Do you know any snipers who are good enough to hit a target a mile or more away and make sure to not kill them? I don't. And definitely not one I would trust to shoot at me."

"A special bullet designed to not inflict damage. This lends credence to the theory you did this to yourself. I saw no one in Special Forces I would trust to pull off that shot and not kill you."

"Maybe Bob does," said Nick, leaning his head toward a tall man standing off stage they had invited to join them this evening.

"I guess we could ask," said Earl, entirely serious.

They both walked over to him. He had a full beard and the universal look of Special Forces warriors.

Bob turned as Nick and Earl walked toward him.

"Do you know anyone who could have made that shot? Intentionally and be sure not to kill me?" asked Nick, without preamble.

Bob laughed at first. Then, seeing they were serious, shook his head. "Maybe a few who could try it. But none who could guarantee to not kill you. Not at a distance beyond a mile. I'm not sure I could even tell you anyone who would even try it. I wouldn't. Especially not with a presidential candidate. Odds are against anyone surviving."

"Aware of any directional ammunition?" asked Nick

Bob tensed up for a second. "Directional ammo?"

"Like a sniper bullet that could be directed to a target, like a heat-seeking missile or laser-guided bomb?" suggested Nick.

Bob paused for a second, looking at each. "I have heard of prototypes of both tracking ammo for snipers and attempts to guide bullets with lasers or GPS. At a very long distance, I might add. Are you saying that happened to you? Even if it was true, they are not designing these things to shoot from farther away to *not* kill their target. Kinda misses the whole point," suggested Bob.

"Don't know. The bullet certainly didn't do the damage one would expect from a normal sniper bullet. I should have a hole in my back the size of a grapefruit or a peach, at least," said Nick without flinching.

"I've heard stories. To my knowledge, none of this is a reality. Either the tech or the shooters to use it," replied Bob, thinking.

"Know anyone who used a king of diamonds as a calling card? You know, like Hathcock and his white feather?" asked Earl.

Before Bob could answer, the prior band was introducing Nick. He walked on stage, digesting Bob's statements and the info from Earl.

The last night of the Tennessee state fair had grown in significance year after year. Showcasing the most popular country acts in line with Nashville's increasing prominence. They'd even moved the fair to a larger site in Lebanon, Tennessee. Twenty-five miles outside Nashville, to accommodate the larger crowds.

This concert was now recorded and televised as an annual event. Nick was booked to speak for about 30 minutes between the last two acts. Both had won Grammy's and CMA awards earlier in the year. He knew the network would cut out his part of the evening.

Nick walked onto the stage at the intro from the prior band's lead singer to huge cheers. Arguably as loud as the prior act. Nick held up his hand. He was wearing jeans and an untucked dress shirt.

"How about that band? Weren't they fabulous?" asked Nick as the crowd shouted their agreement and began yelling 'Turner' over and over. Nick smiled and held up his right hand with the microphone. "I promise to be brief, or at least briefer than I normally am. As you can see, I am alive. I am not one of the 2J's holograms. See, I can turn sideways, and you can see me," said Nick, turning, as the crowd laughed.

Offstage, Earl and Denise shook their heads and laughed. Nick always knew how to poke fun at himself.

"Anyway, I guess there is a nasty rumor running around that somehow, I had myself shot. To raise my popularity." The crowd booed as Nick shook his head. "I know, I know, but let me explain a few things. First," Nick held up a finger. "The nearest place a sniper could have shot at me was over a mile away. That's not in this arena, it's not across the parking lot, it is across I-65 that way," he pointed.

"Now think about that some more. It was a little windy, so just imagine how much wind can affect a little bullet, about an inch long, traveling over a mile. Wind can make it move up and down or left and right. Then there is distance. As an object flies, it loses power, just like a paper airplane, baseball, or a can of beer you're throwing to your buddy."

"Eventually it starts to fall. But how fast, well that depends on a lot and over the course of a mile, that is *really* hard to judge. I'm not an expert in this, so you know what? I brought an expert along." Nick turned as Bob walked out on stage.

"This is 'Bob'," said Nick as the man came to stand next to him, wearing a ball cap and sunglasses. He shook Nick's hand. "Now Bob is not his real name, but take my word for it. He is a badass," the crowd laughed. "Bob here was a sniper in the Canadian army."

"Spec Ops, Senator, JTF2," corrected Bob in a lecturing tone.

"Hey, just trying to keep you anonymous," laughed Nick. "Anyway, Bob and I were both in Iraq and Afghanistan around the same time.

His job was a lot harder being on the ground while I rode an intel desk or flew above later in my A-10." Bob gave Nick a long look. This time, he laughed.

"Friends, don't believe that. The good senator here was involved in his share of danger if the stories could be told. Trust me," said Bob as they cheered.

"As I was saying, you have probably figured out by now, Bob is here because he was a sniper. He holds the record for one of the longest recorded sniper shots."

"Not one of, but the longest, Senator," corrected Bob again.

"You're making this really hard to keep you anonymous," responded Nick. More laughter. "Bob's shot was over 3000 meters. Math is not my thing. I believe that's 9000 feet. That's almost 2 miles.

"Senator, If you're going to tell the story, get your facts right, geez," said Bob in mock anger. "3,871 yards, which is 11,910 feet. Over 2 miles. Almost two and a quarter."

Nick raised his hands. "Everyone's a critic. Next stop ANC," said Nick, the crowd laughing. They were like an Abbott and Costello routine.

"In all seriousness, I brought Bob here for a reason. I want to put to bed any thought anyone would willingly stand to be a target of a sniper from over a mile and a quarter away. Take it away Bob."

"Thanks Senator. First, let me congratulate you on surviving being shot by a sniper. You know it is not the bullet that kills, it is the shock wave from the force of the bullet hitting the body. Think of a watermelon exploding. The bullet goes right through. The shock wave makes the watermelon disintegrate. That ripple spreads and kills you from the force of the ripple destroying your organs. Not only that, when a bullet hits an obstruction, it does not go in a straight line. It starts to turn and fragment, causing more damage as well to add to the shock wave." The crowd was paying attention to every word of Bob's description.

"As a sniper, your goal is not to hit the heart or any spot on a long-range shot. Your goal is to hit anywhere on the torso. For a long shot over a mile, don't believe any of the crap you see on TV. Trying to make a head shot from that distance risks missing completely and not bringing down your target." Bob shook his head at the TV portrayals, making it look so easy.

"You go for center mass in the chest. If you hit, the target goes down and stays down. Trust me, any hit anywhere with a high-velocity bullet is going to kill. The fact our good friend is standing here is nothing short of miraculous. No one, and I repeat, no one, would willingly put their life on the line and allow a sniper to shoot them. Anyone who says differently is not only wrong, but frankly incredibly stupid," finished 'Bob,' giving the mic back to Nick, shaking his hand as the crowd cheered.

"Please salute Bob, who risked his life many times in combat to enable us to sit here drinking our Coors Light and not worrying about ISIS. Thank you, Bob," said Nick, clapping as 'Bob,' waved.

"Ok, now we can get down to the business of saving the country. Does everyone here now understand I did not have myself shot?" The 'yes' was thunderous in reply. "I hope someone at ANC and 'Far Left Cable News', sorry FLCN, learned something they could have found on the web in 30 seconds. So much for fact checking," said Nick, shrugging.

"Let's get on with it so you can watch the final act, right?" prompted Nick as the crowd cheered and a chant of Turner, Turner, Turner started. "You were all given a pamphlet when you came in. It shows you what I think we need to do and what it means to all of us. If you want a deeper dive on any of the points, you can find it in my book, which is finally publishing after my original publisher chickened out." Boos from the crowd rained down at this revelation.

"You can buy it in various places, but if you buy it off my website, the money comes to the campaign. This helps us keep spreading the word versus going to corporate conglomerates. Companies, I might add who are actively trying to keep me from being heard. Unlike my fellow candidates, my book and pamphlet are not about me. I'm boring. It is about you and our problems. How we got to where we are through years of poor decisions by both political parties. How our collective inability to address our issues has led us here. *The Turner Doctrine* is about my positions and thoughts on how we fix it together."

Nick quickly highlighted many of the problems he had been campaigning against and repeating to these state fairs. These were his lone opportunities to talk to sizeable crowds live. As he wrapped it up, he finished with one last exhortation regarding the pamphlets they were now distributing across the country.

"I beg you, please look at the bill of rights. Look at what you are giving up. Especially amendment 1, 2, 4, 6, 8 and most importantly 10. The tenth amendment is the one that says powers not specifically enumerated to the United States federal government shall live in the states. States where you elect your friends and neighbors to deal with the local issues. Not the unseen bureaucrats in Washington telling you what to do in your small town." Nick stalked the stage as usual.

"Our Constitution is only 20 pages long. It is a simple and powerful document. When those oppressed by their regimes stand up against them, they wave the US flag. Not because we are the racists, the Progressives and American *Pravda* want you to believe you are. It is because *they* have read our Constitution and *they* realize the freedoms it provides for the individual. Freedom they do not have. Freedom they would like to have. Freedom we are squandering if we let the Progressives complete their takeover of our country. Wake up, think for yourself, read your Constitution and vote in person. Thank you very much, Tennessee, and enjoy the show." finished Nick walking off the stage.

The crowd continued to chant Turner, Turner, Turner as the band tuned up. They kept the chanting up. Nick smiled as he met the famous singer of the last act off stage and apologized to her for their continued chanting. Susie smiled, shaking her blonde hair. "Maybe you should do an encore, Senator," as she handed him the mic.

Nick walked back out to cheers from the crowd. "Ok you guys, you didn't pay to see me, you paid to see her," said Nick, pointing off stage as the famous country singer walked on stage. She gave Nick a hug and a kiss on his cheek, taking the microphone. "Ladies and Gentleman, Nick Turner," she said, holding the mic and clapping, before adding, "The next President of the United States." Nick stopped and turned to look at her. The bands had been careful to support Nick, but none had offered an endorsement. He bowed back to her. Finally, as Nick walked off, they started shouting her name as she started in on one of her famous hits.

Nick walked back to Earl and Denise, as people off stage shook his hand, got autographs, and took selfies.

"I'm guessing we put that one to bed?" stated Nick.

"Unbelievably well. Nick, Lexi has to come after you with both guns now. She can't ignore the reactions. That endorsement will set off a firestorm for her and her fans," mused Denise, nodding at the singer.

"It was going to happen, eventually. I hoped it would still be later," said Nick, pausing. "The attacks, I mean. Not the endorsement. I hope it doesn't hurt her."

"Based on the reaction, I think she'll be fine. Most of the country music scene is conservative or at least moderate, right where you are. Now if she were a pop singer catering to the teenagers and twenty-somethings, it might be a different story. There's only 6 weeks to go until the election, Lexi can't wait much longer. Something is coming. You can count on it," revealed Denise.

"Bob already gone?" asked Nick, looking around.

"Yep, we had a plane waiting to send him back to his undisclosed location," replied Earl with a smile. He left you a note. Nick took the folded paper and put it in his pocket.

"That worked well. You guys were great. Bob oozed credibility. It was a brilliant idea," admitted Denise.

"So how is she going to hit us?" asked Nick.

"Honestly, I don't know. You hardly have any record to attack. Your military records are not easily accessible and besides, that probably wouldn't work given the sacrifices you have made. I think the attacks are more on your policies rather than an October surprise."

"Blackbird is not making any progress, maybe a point or two, but you seem to be the one picking up the points he drops. You are inching up, but still too low to enter a debate. There are only two more. We'll see. Maybe we get lucky and get you in the last one," said Denise.

"We'll fly to DC in the morning for *The Sunday Hour* tomorrow night. You're still set on doing this live?" probed Denise.

"I am. Even more after the success with the 2J's. It is the only way to ensure they don't twist my words."

"OK," said Denise, shaking her head. Once again, Nick defied the norms of every candidate she had ever handled. She had to admit, his instincts were usually right.

Chapter 47

Nelson Lopez stood as Nick entered the sound stage for *The Sunday Hour,* the top-rated prime-time network news program. Nick walked over and shook the extended hand.

"Nick Turner."

"Nelson Lopez, Senator, but most folks call me Nelly."

Nick smiled. "You can call me Nick, but I suspect you're not going to, tonight?"

Nelson smiled and shook his head. "Not likely. Shall we sit and get ready? Do you need a water or a coffee?"

Nick shook his head and raised his hand, showing his stainless steel water bottle with its black top. They sat in chairs facing each other with a table for their drinks, hidden from the camera.

"Senator, since you insisted we do this live, I would only request you refrain from violating any FCC rules regarding banned words. There is no seven second delay. Your rules, your problems, OK?"

"Of course. I take full responsibility for my actions. Always have."

"Save it for the cameras, hotshot," said Nelly with a sneer.

Nick looked at the older man. He was about forty pounds overweight, with a thinning head of mostly gray hair. His round face and nose displayed the puffiness, one associated with too much alcohol. They had banished him from any regular programs on the network years ago. His only occasional appearances were now to report on immigration and crime issues, his specialties during his heyday.

He'd made his bones reporting from various war-torn hell holes in South and Central America and then in the Middle East. He was one of the last of a dying breed. Journalists who dug for stories, got dirty, hung out in shitty alleys and hotels in third world countries, traipsing through the jungle to interview the rebel leader. Nelly was a man time had passed by.

"We only have forty-four minutes with the commercials. Try to keep your answers to the point," said Nelly in an impatient tone.

"Been a while since you've done a live shot? Nervous?"

Nelly snorted, "Nervous? Son, I was doing live shots and being shot at long before you left kindergarten."

"Why did you get this gig?"

"Guess you're about to find out."

The producer started counting down and finally yelled for quiet.

"Welcome to this special edition of *The Sunday Hour*. I'm Nelson Lopez. Tonight, Senator Nick Turner, who has finally consented to an interview, joins us."

Nick laughed and shook his head. "Nelly, you can believe what you want. Any time. Any place, just make the call and I will answer…," Nelly cut Nick off.

"Senator, now that you *are* here," he drew the words out again to highlight Nick's lack of TV exposure.

"I'd like to discuss some of the more provocative accusations you have made against the United States. Let's start with your claim the administration has opened the borders, allowing unchecked immigration, so the Party can grant them amnesty and create a permanent voting majority. A statement, I might add, that not only impugns the value of these immigrant's lives but is both wild conjecture and downright dangerous. Inciting common citizens to view all immigrants as enemies of the state," finished Nelly.

Nick sat there, shaking his head, a smile on his face.

"What a mouthful of accusations. That's a lot of hateful rhetoric to unpack, but let me try."

"Your words, not mine. Do you deny making these statements?" asked Nelly, calmly.

"I'm sorry. Did you site a specific quote of mine?"

"No. I combined your statements from your rallies and…"

"Actually, you didn't. You paraphrased a serious situation and once again tried to turn words into the typical statements of hate our media is so proud to promote."

"Wait a minute Senator, you cannot…" he tried to cut him off.

"I can't what? Put words in your mouth. Doesn't taste so good, your own medicine does it." Nick held up his hand. "*You* asked me a question. Please do me the courtesy of giving me a chance to answer. The reality is we do not have a border."

"So, you claim," cut in Nelly.

Nick, ignoring Nelly, continued. "We are certainly not enforcing our border laws during this administration. Our CBP comprises fine patriotic Americans who are now babysitters, travel agents and court clerk schedulers. No attempt is being made to stop *anyone* from entering our country. Then we are putting them on buses and planes and sending them wherever they want to go. Hell, we routinely fly over 300,000 a year directly from *their* countries into heartland cities *in* the US. Just so we don't have to process them at the border. That is the worst rationalization I have ever heard of helping relieve the invasion at the border."

"Senator, you know that's not true. We deport at least 60,000 yearly. How can you say the border is open?" claimed Nelly, exasperated.

"Ah, a fact!" said Nick, throwing up a hand. "Good one Nelly. Yes, we send 60,000 back. That is less than 3% of the total who come across. The other 97% are allowed by this administration to stay until they have a court date. A court date 97.5% of them never show up for and which are now three years out. Nelly, do you know what cartel debt is?"

"Of course, I do, Senator, but that is not…" said Nelly, leaning back to respond as Nick cut him off.

"What is it, Nelly?" Nelson stared daggers at Nick.

"No answer?" Nick leaned forward. "Let me answer for you. Cartel debt is what you have if you cross the border as an illegal when you did not have the money to pay your way. You earn cartel debt. It is a marker the cartels call due once you're in America. It could be to transport drugs, sell drugs, steal, agitate, or do many things. It can take years to pay off. If you refuse, the Cartel kills your family in your home country in retaliation.

"Senator, that is melodramatic," said Nelly, trying to regain control of the interview.

"Is it? Let's see, and I quote directly this time, said Nick, raising his hands in the universal quote position. *'Onetime illegal immigrant Marcella Suiza, who lost her grandmother, grandfather, sister, and three cousins in Jalisco, Mexico because she refused to sell drugs for the Despardos gang in south central LA. She has overcome these tragedies to run for the LA city council on a platform of purging our inner cities of drugs and this insidious cartel debt.'* Do you know who said that in 2010?"

"I did," said Nelson reluctantly.

"True, and you won a Murrow award for the piece, I believe. Excellent work. I think we can move on to the next question."

"Senator, excellent redirection, avoiding the more serious question I asked. You claim the current administration is doing this to ensure a permanent majority of Party voters. Where is your proof?"

"As you know, Nelly, there is no proof, yet" replied Nick, taking a breath to continue when Nelly interrupted.

"So, you admit this is pure conjecture and right-wing conspiracy talking points?"

"Let me ask you a question…"

"Just answer my question. You admit this is rhetoric your buddy Tommy's been pushing and you're on 'The Great Replacement train'."

"How many illegals are in the US?"

Nelly shrugged. "Fifteen million is the last census count."

"Bad at math, are we?" asked Nick.

"Excuse me?"

"For 30 years it was 11 million. Then it was upped to 15 million after decades of over one, and sometimes two million documented illegals entering annually. Just in the last seven years of *this* administration, there are around fourteen million. At least who we admit knowing have been released into and actually delivered by this administration to all the lower 48 states. This discounts the ones who got away each year, a total estimated to be at least another five to six million."

"Even if you took eleven or fifteen and added ten to it, you would be at a *minimum* of twenty-five million. The number certainly does not go down. They aren't going home, that's for sure. Nelly, did you read the latest infrastructure bill that failed in the Senate?" probed Nick.

"Not entirely. It was 1200 pages long, Senator. I remember, though, that it was your vote that prevented these funds desperately needed for our crumbling infrastructure to be appropriated."

"I agree. Our roads and bridges need this funding desperately."

"Then why in the hell did you vote against it? And the funds for homeless shelters and other desperately needed services for the poor, including increased funding for your beloved CBP agents?" asked Nelly, leaning forward with a reddening face.

"Nelson, the bill was 1416 pages long. 6% of the funding was directly allocated to infrastructure. The rest was pure corruption. Almost a trillion dollars of it. Your and my tax dollars allocated for pet projects and frankly paybacks by Congress to supporters. Nothing new, wait please," said Nick, holding up a hand as Nelly looked to interrupt.

"I know pork is politics. But to tie this back to your 'Great Replacement' statement. Buried amongst the 1400 actual pages, which unfortunately for my Party colleagues in Congress I *did* read, were a couple of 'provisions' which caused me to vote against things I agreed with."

"These provisions provided Amnesty for every illegal above the age of 18 who arrived longer than twenty years ago–72% of whom are *still* receiving government help. It also provided a blanket amnesty for those arriving over ten years ago to be naturalized citizens in five years–88% of them are on state welfare too. These are the 15 million you claim."

Nelly shrugged while glancing down at his note cards and not watching as Nick continued.

"I am not heartless. I would prefer, we help make them legal, paying taxes, and off government assistance. What really bothered me and why I voted against the bill was the fact we would, with the wave of a pen, add ten, twenty, or more million voters to our voting base. These people owe their allegiance not to our Constitution or to our fundamental values. They owe their allegiance and gratitude to our government. Specifically, to our Party. Who would've made them eligible to vote in that bill."

"You, sir, are no longer in *our* Party."

"Sadly, true. Now you know why. The Party are the ones who are fighting to keep as many as possible on some form of government assistance. They are also the ones fighting tooth and nail to ensure the illegals are counted in the census so places like California, New York and Illinois do not lose any electoral votes or congressional seats. Replacing high tax paying residents who fled to Texas, Florida, Tennessee, and Arizona with low earning illegals. Good for politics, bad for state budgets."

"The next natural step is to ensure these twenty million would continue to benefit from our welfare programs, even after they become legal. Now, imagine we make these folks voters. My Opposition colleagues are on record for not supporting this amnesty and certainly for not providing welfare to illegals. Paid for by all our tax dollars. Dollars we desperately need elsewhere." Nick looked Nelson in the eye.

"Nelson, would it not be a fair statement, to say, if you were a newly minted American Citizen courtesy of amnesty from that bill. An Opposition candidate was threatening to remove your eligibility to welfare benefits? If their Party opponent was promising to keep your checks coming, who would you logically be expected to vote for?"

"This is pure theory, Senator. You do not know this would be a reality. They would vote for the candidate who best aligned with their values. Please don't use this time to promote your anti-immigrant stances," said Nelly.

"I am hardly anti-immigrant, Nelly. I am a second-generation immigrant. Just like you. I am pro legal immigrant, anti-illegal immigrant amnesty, and anti-government assistance. At least without a plan to get the recipient off it as quickly as possible and into responsible work."

"I voted against the infrastructure bill because my Party colleagues tried to hide this illegal amnesty vote amongst the 1400 pages. I wish we could poll your audience to see how many even knew these provisions were in the bill? I lost twenty-five and more likely forty million illegal votes, but so did my other competitors, at least on the Party ticket."

"You don't deny your statements support right-wing anti-immigrant racist discrimination?" asked Nelson, ignoring Nick's statement.

"Nelson, I believe both your math and hearing should be checked. I have explained my reasoning. It is your choice to see reason or to choose to twist the facts to fit *your* narrative," said Nick with a shrug, refusing to play the game.

"Nice deflection, Senator. Let's move on."

Nick simply raised his hand and 'Flipped' it while smiling.

"Senator, what are you doing?"

"Oh nothing, my wrist was stiff. Listen Nelly, I'm not going to have this argument with you. I have seen it with my own eyes. So have many others in small town America. Where they have seen these busloads and plane loads of supposed asylum seekers dropped off, with no job, no money and no help from the very administration who invited them. They stress the local governments, schools, hospitals, and social services who are now tasked with trying to 'help' these people."

"This breeds resentment, as these people have few prospects to survive other than stealing and paying back their cartel debt by dealing and distributing drugs. Or committing violence or other crimes. Since this is a family program, I won't even discuss the human trafficking and sex trade these poor unfortunates must submit to as well."

"Senator, please keep your generalizations to a minimum. These are just your opinions designed to make people afraid of immigrants. You have done nothing to convince me or the viewers that you feel any compassion for the plight of these immigrants. Let's get in another question before our first break, since we are doing this live at your request."

"Now, what are you doing? Do you need to stop?" asked Nelly as Nick held his hand up in front of his body, palm out.

"Me? No nothing, sorry, please carry on. What is your next accusation?"

"My next *question* is you seem to have a theme of supporting the expansion of police brutality through unchecked funding and stopping efforts to defund police departments with a history of violence against minorities. What do you have against the poor and minorities who are victims of this police brutality?"

Nick once again flipped his hand while answering. "Mr. Lopez, there are close to 650,000 full-time law enforcement officers in the United States. This number is plummeting because of the success of defunding efforts. Driven and supported by the Party and its activist wings."

"So, you *are* in favor of continued police brutality?" confirmed Nelly, shaking his head, prepared to move on.

Nick quickly answered before Nelson could go to break. "Nelly, of course I am not. Even you, someone who has covered crime for decades, have to admit the reduction in police presence has a direct correlation to increases in violent crime? Primarily in poor and minority neighborhoods."

"Sorry Senator, I do not agree. Maybe the reduction in the number of unarmed blacks murdered by racist police. Crime is crime in these neighborhoods, whether or not the cops are there. I grew up in one of those neighborhoods," said Nelson.

"Police killed how many unarmed black men last year?"

"Excuse me?" Nelson just stared, not rising to the bait.

"Thirteen," continued Nick. "All but one of them were resisting arrest. Only one of them was a true murder. That officer, who was black by the way, is now awaiting sentencing, our criminal justice system having worked correctly."

"The true crime is you and your American *Pravda* cohorts constantly harping about police brutality. Implying every black man walking on the street is just waiting to be shot by a corrupt cop. One out of 650,000 is six zeros before you get to a number in percent. One six-hundred and fifty thousandth percent. You almost have a better chance of winning the lottery than being shot by a cop," said Nick in an incredulous voice.

"Senator, I can throw out numbers as well to our viewers. It is disproportionate numbers of blacks being arrested and jailed. The police routinely profile and target minorities," said Nelson, still leaning forward.

Nick had held up his hand, palm down, and flipped it up again after Nelly's statement, before answering.

"The more blacks in prison statement, while true once, is no longer. Go look at our own government statistics and you will find there is now no difference between white and black incarceration rates."

"American *Pravda* and their allies, spreading this hate and outright lies, are the true criminals. Sadly, this is not limited to just the media, but some in the administration and Congress who continue to spew the true hateful rhetoric. They make our streets and our citizens less safe by breeding mistrust of our police and promoting the defunding of these departments. We have scared an entire generation of children and young people by this disinformation. Congratulations, journalists everywhere should be proud of their accomplishments," said Nick, with no sarcasm.

"Senator, crime in the inner city is not the fault of defunding police, and black incarceration rates are no myth," pronounce Nelly in response. "We need to break for commercial."

As the camera turned off, Nick sat back as Nelly looked down at his cards.

"What's with the gestures? You have epilepsy?" asked Nelly.

"You did little research. They just hand you the questions?"

Nelly kept staring at his cards as he prepared for the next segment. Nick took a sip from his water bottle and placed it back on his side table. The producer called them back to live cameras.

"Welcome back. Senator Turner let's switch gears. You are on record saying you would abolish the IRS. How would the government raise money without taxes? Please spare me the history lesson. I know when and how the IRS was created," said Nelly in a disdainful tone.

"Nelly, do you like paying taxes?"

"What?"

"Do you?"

"Please stick to the question," said Nelly, refusing to answer.

"Well, I don't. You know why?" When Nelly did not answer, Nick continued. "Because I don't believe those in charge of spending my taxes know what they're doing. Far too few of our population actually pay any federal income tax. Less than 10% paid 80% of the total taxes. The top 1% pay 40% of that total…"

Nelly interrupted. "Come on Senator, that is because they make so much money. It is hard to feel sorry for people who are millionaires and billionaires having to pay taxes on money in a year most others will never see in their entire lifetime of earning."

"Nelson, over 50% pay no income tax. These are your so called oppressed. And no, none of these are rich billionaires. Too many people have no skin in the game because it is not their money being spent on a host of bureaucratic boondoggles. So yes, I want to abolish the IRS. I would replace it with a tax system based on consumption. This ensures everyone pays taxes for what they consume.

"Criminals cannot hide. Billionaires cannot find loopholes in tax codes. This will ensure all the underground money; the money criminals and the underground economy spends, which is never taxed as income, would instead be taxed. When they buy their yachts and private jets and mansions with these ill-gotten gains, they would pay back into the system. And it will raise way more revenue than any proposed tax increases."

"The new tax rate for this new consumption tax would be what, 25%?" asked Nelson, astonished. "Every poor person now has to pay 25% more for everything? Exactly how does someone afford to pay 25% more for everything, if as you say, they currently pay no taxes? How does that not hurt the poor and help the rich?"

"Only if we continue to spend like we do. My proposals would reduce the need to raise as much for federal spending. Every citizen would be rebated back the taxes for the basic needs. Equally. The poor would not be burdened with this new system. It would instead raise most of its funds from those with higher incomes spending that money. In addition, with only tax on consumption, many of the embedded taxes in our labor, manufacturing, distribution, and other aspects of the supply chain would be reduced, if not eliminated, as well."

"How would you propose to fund the government? This consumption tax rate would have to be very high."

"You missed the rest of the statement. I would not only end the IRS, but I would also end most of the other bloated government agencies, taking them down to a minimal size to do true constitutionally federal efforts, such as protecting our country and enforcing our border. Many other federal bureaucracies are actually redundant, with efforts already completed at the state level. Safety, inspection, and compliance with regulations, for instance. Most of this governing would move to local cities, counties, and states, where it used to be and where it belongs. Nelly, do you know how many federal employees there are?"

"I know we spend way too much on defense," he answered.

"With Russia and China menacing our friends and allies, North Korea firing missiles over Japan and Iran funding terror groups all over the Middle East to attack Israel, I disagree, but let's not digress," said Nick before continuing.

"There are over 4 and a half million. Even taking out the million in the armed forces, we have well over 3 million federal employees. By reducing the bureaucratic state and moving many of these services local, we would remove a huge amount of the federal budget. These employees do not build goods for sale. Most of their 'services' are in support of regulations they passed. As one former Speaker of the House once said, 'We have to pass the bill to find out what is in the bill'. It is this bloated bureaucracy that finishes writing the bill, decides the regulations and then puts itself in charge of making everyone else comply. This is the good or service they provide us? This is a giant scam, on the rest of us."

"Wow Senator, are you insane? I thought some of your prior statements were ridiculous, but this one is out there. Good luck winning the vote of any of those 3 million federal workers you intend to fire if you win. Getting rid of the IRS and the FDA and USDA. I, for one, like knowing my drugs are safe and they inspected my meat."

"Me too, but that should be a state issue. In fact, it *is* a state issue. Why do we need the Feds doing it too? Totally wasteful," countered Nick.

"We ran long in the first segment. We need another break."

As they broke for commercial, Nelson stared at Nick in disbelief. "You have no idea how to win elections, do you?"

"I'm just trying to inform an uninformed electorate."

Nelson went back to studying his note cards and Nick took a sip of his water. Arranging his water bottle again, out of sight of the cameras.

"Guys, coming out of commercial," said the producer.

"Welcome back to the second half of *The Sunday Hour*. Tonight's guest is Senator Nick Turner. Senator, let's continue. It is clear you have some pretty radical ideas, which could be why you are so low in the polls."

"Am I?"

"Well, you love to cite facts. Every major poll has you between 5 and 8%. Why do you persist?"

"Nelson, first, I put absolutely zero trust in polls. They are used to facilitate voter suppression."

"Really?" asked Nelson, startled. "How so?"

"If I am low in the polls, why would my supporters come out to vote? Nelson, surely you have noticed. Look at the last election. The Opposition candidate was down 12 to 15% even 20% behind in some polls, the entire month of September and October before the election. To a President who even back then could not form a coherent statement and who managed, thanks to a second COVID pandemic and a host of executive orders restricting business and movement, to never campaign or debate at all during the campaign. Two days before the election, after 50% or more of the votes had already been mailed in, well after the only debate between the vice-presidential candidates, the final poll showed the Opposition candidate behind by 2%? How is this not voter suppression?"

Nelly shrugged. "People polled at the end changed their mind?"

"More likely, the polling companies wanted to be right for their final poll, the only one anyone remembers. By then, anyone who had chosen not to bother voting for a candidate 20% behind in a poll no longer had time to mail in a vote. It forced them to vote in person. There were fewer in-person voting sites in most states because of fear of the latest COVID variant. This wasn't considered voter suppression by the courts because of the prevalence of mail in voting options."

"To vote in person was taking one's life in one's hand and in some states practically not even allowed. Those that wanted to now vote could expect to stand in long lines for hours. I will hand it to my Party. It worked brilliantly. It is a common fact that Opposition voters have historically had better turnout at the polls and the Party voters favor mailing in ballots. So perhaps the polls are a sham designed to suppress voter turnout for certain candidates? Therefore, I put little stock in them."

"Interesting theory, Senator. I don't think anyone is intentionally suppressing your votes by keeping you low in the polls. I think your irrelevance is showing. Your radical policies don't seem to be gaining many followers," noted Nelson.

"We'll see Nelly. Only time will tell," said Nick with a big smile.

Nelson reordered his note cards. "Senator, you have been pretty hard on the media in your speeches, even alluding to the idea all media outlets are no better than Soviet propaganda outlets. Seems to me a candidate needs to have a tougher skin. Care to comment?"

"It has little to do with having a tough skin. I don't watch American *Pravda*, so I have no issues with what anyone is saying. Sticks and stones and all that. However, I do feel sorry for my fellow citizens. If you ever attended my rallies, there is one consistent theme. It is 'think for yourself'. This includes not believing everything you hear in the media or find in a search on the web. Certainly nothing on social media feeds."

"None of it is fact based as it claims to be. It is simply cherry-picked tidbits of information presented to make it appear as if facts support it. The last few presidential elections have born this out. Even the internet search giants have had to admit and pay fines for artificially manipulating search listings in favor of the Party."

"Senator, that is not what they were fined for doing and it was not widespread. You make it sound as if every search is illegitimate," said Nelly.

"Only on the political topics that determine who people vote for Nelly. Which is *exactly* what they were fined for. Just don't expect to have those *results*, or them admitting it, and paying the fines, show up in a search. Cat videos and celebrity gossip will be accurate," said Nick with a laugh. "You asked what I was doing earlier. If you had done any research, you would know I was using a technique called the Flip."

"Ok, I'll bite Senator. What is the Flip." Off camera, Nick could see a producer frantically waving his arms and slicing his arm across his throat in the classic 'cut' motion. Nelly apparently could not see this.

Nick held out his hand, palm down. "Nelly, I tell everyone to whom I speak to ignore anything they read, or are told by the media."

Nelson laughed. "That's one way to create ignorant believers."

"Instead, I tell them to use the Flip." Nick flipped his palm up. "You Flip whatever they are saying 180 degrees. If they say the science is settled on *anything*, I use the Flip, and now I know whatever you just told me is not only wrong, but the opposite is true. It makes me think about what the opposite of what you just said would logically be. The science can never be settled. Now I know the actual truth, thanks to the Flip."

"If you tell me all these illegals are coming because they need asylum, I use the Flip because I know that is a lie. They are coming to flee the corruption and economic disasters of their own country. Who wouldn't if given the chance? Because our administration has made it clear, we will let them stay and take care of them with your and my tax dollars and money printed or borrowed."

"If you tell me the polls are accurate, I use the Flip. You see Nelly, no one tells the facts anymore and my technique at least encourages the viewer to question info, do their own research, and form their own opinion. I tell them to use common sense and trust their gut feeling."

"It turns out, *not* believing you and all the networks blindly is *healthy*. Mentally and physically. Everything is manipulated and delivered in a way to ensure *your* viewer can only come away with a single viewpoint. Yours. That Nelly is why I am tough on the media. They, more than anyone, even more than this administration, are responsible for the decline of our country."

"Senator, I beg to differ with your opinion. The proliferation of 24/7 cable news now offers consumers even more facts from which to form their own opinions," countered Nelly.

Nick smiled in response, holding out his hand and flipping it.

"Nelly, you are entitled to your opinion. It is called the First Amendment. Something most others may no longer take advantage of if their opinion is counter to you and your media's accepted narrative. Cancel culture has its roots in the media and you are the stormtroopers of the Progressive movement. Quick to ruin folks for daring to have a different opinion. Is that not the entire purpose of finally allowing me to appear? To cancel me?"

"Believe what you want, Senator," replied Nelly, shrugging again, and looking down at his notes.

"Used to be we celebrated debate," continued Nick as Nelly studied his cards. "We delighted in the back and forth and the effort to sway an audience to one side or the other with eloquent argument."

"You are old enough to remember *The Firing Line* with William F. Buckley. His show would have lasted one episode in this current cancel culture driven media environment. His debate style would have offended everyone in some fashion. Discussing the truth is offensive to everyone these days. Tell me that is not true."

Nelson shrugged. "Whose truth Senator? We need to take one last break and return for our final thoughts," announced Nelson.

Nick took another sip and Nelson sat silently reviewing his cards, refusing to look at Nick or engage in any conversation.

"Welcome back to our last segment this evening," greeted Nelly.

Nick simply smiled, leaned back, and opened his hands as if motioning Nelly to bring it on.

"Senator, our closing question is philosophical. Why do you have such vehement disdain for the efforts to combat climate change and lessen the impact fossil fuels are having on our planet? Finally, please explain why you have such dislike of this administration's fact and science based pandemic responses?"

Nick smiled. "Here, I thought your earlier questions were full of rhetoric and broad generalizations and opinion."

"Your views, not mine. I am just paraphrasing your own statements," answered Nelly with a straight face.

"Again, you claim to use my own words, but you are too cowardly to actually choose a specific quote where I say as you say I do." Nelson sat up, prepared to counter the use of 'cowardly,' as Nick uttered a single "No." He did this in such a commanding tone, Nelson sat back, cowed.

"I am happy to offer facts in response to your attempts to paint me as something I am not. In short, you simply accuse me of disagreeing with the Progressive platform. To that, I am guilty as charged. I disagree with the Progressive agenda, certainly all the methods and most of the proposed outcomes. The climate is changing, as science clearly shows."

"As it has every day since it formed. The science of climate change can therefore never be settled. What is not clear is IF we are indeed having a measurable impact on it. I agree with trying to do what we can to reduce our carbon emissions. In a sane and sustainable manner. Without destroying our economy and with a clear understanding of what the full consequences of going electric are for our environment and the measurable benefits, if any."

"If you bother to check the facts and stop cherry picking only the ones supporting your narrative, you will find out electric cars actually cost as much or more to own and to run, especially as electric costs continue to rise. The entire supply chain for EV's use more water in their complete lifetime and creates long term hazardous waste problems we have not begun to know how to deal with. The same with discarded solar panels and wind turbine blades. Finally, power generation cannot keep up with the increasing demands because, frankly, the sun does not shine, and the wind does not blow consistently in places where people live. There are pros and cons to every solution. We never hear the complete picture."

"We make promises, impose mandates, and destroy people's livelihoods chasing utopian schemes that do not help the climate. Instead, we are making a majority of the population suffer while the donors of the Party and the elites who own the cobalt and lithium mines get richer."

"The current and former politicians and businessmen who take your money in return for carbon offsets that don't actually do anything to offset your carbon emissions. Just allow you to feel good about being able to afford to buy off your guilt at using fossil fuels. They gain the most from implementing these so-called solutions."

"Thank you, Senator, for confirming you are a climate denier."

Nick laughed while flipping his hand.

"Why Senator?" said Nelly, finding his voice, and upset at Nick's gesture, now realizing the purpose of his hand movement. "The Progressive agenda is all about helping the weak and minorities. About ensuring we have a plan from now on to combat climate change and reduce our dependency on the fossil fuels destroying our livelihood. Progressives are all about helping those who have suffered at the hands of our patriarchal, white male dominated society. Who achieved success using the poor and disadvantaged at the expense of all but themselves."

"Amazing," said Nick clapping. "Congratulations on your Public Service Announcement. If I could, were you quoting *Das Kapital, Mein Kampf, Rules for Radicals*, or perhaps Mao's *Little Red Book*? It seemed you worked them all into your statement of purpose. What I believe you are really saying is, once again, the Progressives, as so many previous utopian schemes, like you just referenced, promise you everything with only minor change. You just have to give up one teeny, tiny thing," said Nick, holding up his fingers barely apart. "Your freedom."

"Senator, you're missing the point and trivializing the problem."

"Am I? Nelly, I have studied history, specifically the history of how totalitarian regimes come to be. We are on the verge. All we need to do is give up on the Constitution. The document which guarantees our freedoms. Our freedoms to think for ourselves. To disagree, and work to change things we disagree with, not with violence or coercion but with debate and compromise. Something the Progressives are not inclined to allow. Their argument is not all that attractive to those giving up the freedom to choose. This is why we have cancel culture. They can't risk people discovering the truth about the policies. And worse, convincing others they are being scammed."

"Senator, I hardly think anyone is hiding the benefits of progressive policies. They are there for all to see," said Nelly.

"Then why do we have cancel culture?"

"To protect us from ignorance, racism, bigotry and misinformation."

"According to whom? American *Pravda* and this administration? The same entities who issues the proclamations and stifle the open debate?"

"Senator, there are many people who are misleading the public for their own benefit. We need a strong government to protect us from these lies and dangerous ideas. Much like many you have spoken of tonight."

"Nelson, I disagree. We need debate. We need open conversation and transparency on all aspects of our society and all policies that seek to change the way all of us lead our lives. Not amnesty buried in 1400 page bills. This is what the first amendment is all about. Make the argument. Convince others to agree with your points. Once a majority are convinced, this should then and only then become the rule of the land. That is democracy. Anything less, like what we have today, with cancel culture, is authoritarianism sliding toward totalitarianism."

"Nice speech Senator, but using your own words, you are polling at 6%. Clearly your ideas and your dissent aren't achieving support."

"Perhaps Nelson, but I am also not giving up. I am running for President because I refused to join the Progressive religion. That is what it really is, a belief in progressive dogma and a willingness to discount any who dissent or point out falsehoods in the reasoning. I am unwilling to give up and trade my freedoms for a life of servitude and obedience to the state in return for my food, shelter, and a job. As we've seen tonight, not joining the cult makes one an enemy of the state. Like every other totalitarian society, I noticed what happened to dissenters."

"Well Senator, if what you say is true, why are you here?"

Nick laughed. "Nelson, someone made a mistake. I guarantee you this will *never* happen again. I say to all of you watching, I am always willing to come on any TV talk show or news program. If you do not see me again, do not believe it is because I said no."

"Senator, I don't believe anyone is afraid of your words."

"We'll see Nelson." Nick turned to the camera. "If you approve of cancel culture, please do not vote for me. If you don't, then listen to what I have to say and make a choice yourself. Whether you like making choices or if you want others to make them for you. That is the choice."

"Senator, I am afraid that is all the time we have for this interview. We appreciate you coming to our program. I wish you luck on your effort to become relevant, and I am glad we have given more people a chance to make their own impression of some of your nontraditional positions," finished Nelly as the producer counted down.

Nick sat back in his chair. "What happened to you? You used to be legitimate. What did they do to you?"

Nelly looked up at Nick as he pulled off his microphone.

"Senator, I think you will find out what happened to me if you persist in your efforts. I admire your commitment, but I must tell you from experience, you will not beat them."

"So, you gave up?"

"Senator, you are so naïve. You think you can win with words?" Nelson said this in such a tone it surprised even Nick at their venom, and it seemed, regret. "They own the words. The narrative is in their hands. They control what people hear, see, believe and they never stop. *They never admit they were wrong, and they never give in.* **Ever.** Good luck," he said, leaving the stage.

Chapter 48

Lexi and Mel looked at the big screen in the campaign headquarters conference room late on Sunday night. Nelson was interrogating Nick at the beginning of the program.

"So far, so good," said Mel.

"This is a bad idea. Why'd they agree to do it live?" she asked.

"They really had no choice," answered Mel carefully, preparing to duck if Lexi launched her drink glass his way.

"I know. It's my fault. It was a rhetorical question," she said, giving him an icy stare. "They didn't have to agree. Claim live TV was too risky, especially with an out-of-control candidate like Turner or something like that," Lexi fumed. Mel stayed silent.

They continued to watch as Nick held his own and made cogent points to counter the questions from Nelly.

"Shit, he is eating him alive," complained Lexi. "I told you we needed to get someone who could hold their own against Turner."

"Lexi, he's doing OK. He's getting Turner's stances out there. Turner is wasting time defending instead of short ones denying."

"I hope you're right, Mel."

"The ratings have been falling for the show. The viewers for this network average seventy-five years old. Most of them are already set in their ways, already our voters mostly. They aren't going to be swayed by Turner," said Mel in an assuring tone he did not feel inside.

As the show continued, they watched as Nick started doing his Flip and Mirror motions.

"Stop him, you idiot," yelled Lexi at the screen, turning toward Mel. "Does he really not know what Turner is doing with his hand motions?" Mel shrugged in reply.

"Fuck," said Lexi, leaping to her feet. "No, no, no," she turned to Mel as Nelly walked into Turner's trap and let him explain the Flip.

Mel held up a hand, dialing his phone. He stood up, watching and talking into the phone. As they came back out of commercial to the last segment, they watched as Nelly asked his last questions and just as he confirmed Nick was a climate denier, the screen cut to commercial.

Lexi fumed, cursing, and stalking around the room as Mel continued to talk on the phone. After an exceptionally long break, an LN1 newscaster broke in to announce a missile attack in Gaza. After this special announcement, they finally returned to regular programming.

The screen returned in time to see Nelly thanking Senator Turner for appearing. Mel reached for the remote and turned off the TV.

Lexi's face was flushed with anger. She said nothing, knowing this was an unforced error on her part. Mel waited patiently for the inevitable explosion. When she spoke, it was surprisingly calm.

"Make sure they don't post it anywhere. He got his wish. Now he can't complain about not being asked to appear on a network show."

"Got it."

"I never want to see Nelly's face on my TV. Ever again."

Mel nodded and left the room. Behind him, he could hear breaking glass. He made a mental note to get IT to replace the big screen in the conference room. Thankfully, this late, on a Sunday night, the office was empty of staffers. He dialed a number on his phone.

#

Nick left the Washington studio of LN1 after his appearance on *The Sunday Hour*. He'd borrowed Chuck's car to drive to the studio. As he walked out into the parking lot, he could see Nelson Lopez sitting in a Mercedes sedan, drinking from a liquor bottle. Seeing Nick, he put the bottle down out of sight as Nick approached the driver's window.

He lowered the window.

"Why did they pick you?" asked Nick.

Nelly laughed. Nick could smell the booze.

"Senator, they thought I could handle you. Frankly, I think they thought the current crop of 'journalists'," said Nelly, holding up his hands, "would've been eaten alive." He laughed again. "They were right."

"You still didn't answer the question?"

Nelly sighed, looking at his bottle before answering.

"Senator, I had a reputation as a no-nonsense investigative journalist whose time was past and who had issues with the bottle. If I triumphed, it would have been because I was old school and you were inexperienced and emotional. If I failed, which I clearly did, it will be because I was old school and a washed up alcoholic. They still have me under contract, so I really had no choice."

"I see," said Nick.

"Actually, you don't. Because you have not sold your soul to get a network anchor desk or a prime-time show. Had to fight to get air time against a bunch of empty-headed J-school dolts who think they know everything. You have not had to play the game and smile while they stab you in the back. Forcing you to compromise your integrity because they know your secrets and have no qualms about sacrificing you on the altar of ratings. Which makes them and me dislike you even more," laughed Nelly.

Nick nodded and turned to go. Nelly called out as he turned.

"Senator, while I may dislike you and envy your easy path to success, I am not stupid. I *did* my research, contrary to your claim. While in my network-imposed exile, I have indeed done a lot of research on you. I know all about your Flip and your Mirror. They are both simple and effective and easy for the masses to understand. Bravo. I also understand your concerns. Yes, they gave me the questions to ask. But they did not tell me how to ask them. That was all me," said Nelly with a smile.

Nick smiled back. "You set them up?"

"Oh yes, I did Senator. I intentionally asked my questions to make sure we forced you to get your points across and not theirs. This is my revenge. For which I will no doubt pay. This is my contribution to your crusade. Not because I like you, but because I *loathe* them. I loathe what I have become because of swimming in their cesspool. You should know, they cut out the entire last segment. From right after I asked my last question. You were also on a 15 second delay, so many of your answers were truncated or simply not shown."

"So much for honesty in broadcasting," retorted Nick.

Nelly laughed. "You don't sound so surprised, Senator."

"Oh, I am not. That is why I recorded the entire episode." This time, it was Nick who laughed.

Nelly looked confused. "Not possible. They swept you when you came in. Any recording device would have interfered with our broadcast equipment. You had to leave your phone. How?"

Nick held up his water bottle and flipped up the lid. In the seam at the bottom was a tiny camera lens.

"I know some really smart tech guys. With the lid down, it was off and when I flipped it up, it recorded the entire show, both audio and video. Loaded it all directly to the cloud. We have everything and I would be surprised if it is not all up on multiple sites already."

"Senator, you are not very trusting, are you?"

"Nelly, you have been embedded with troops in combat. You know the paranoid survive."

"Nick," said Nelly, using his name for the first time. "They can't let you get traction. I know what you are doing and why, but you are almost forcing them to eliminate you, so you don't. This is bigger than the Vice President and this election. You know that."

Nick shrugged. "Maybe, maybe not. I am like chemo for the American soul. I have to take us to the brink. To get people to realize it really is 'a save themselves by saving our country or die' moment. It is a dangerous treatment for sure. We may not survive. I may not survive, but we have to throw everything at it, or their progressive cancer will end us."

"Maybe I do like you," said Nelly, holding his hand out.

"Better late than never," replied Nick, shaking his hand.

#

Nick walked into his Washington, DC, campaign office. Chuck and Denise were on their phones, and Greg was looking at his laptop.

"The conquering hero returns to thunderous applause and adulation," he said aloud. Chuck and Denise ignored him as they talked. Greg at least looked up with a smile on his face.

"Tough crowd," said Nick, sitting down. He threw Chuck's keys toward him. He caught them, sticking them in his pocket as he talked.

"Greg, give me some good news," ordered Nick.

"Well Boss, the snap attendance rating for the show was twenty-two million. That makes it the first or second highest ever for the show. About twice as many as they have been averaging. They were delaying the answers or cutting them short. And they simply cut away for the entire last question," said Greg.

Nick nodded, not saying what he'd heard from Nelson.

"Once they cut to the breaking news, and it became apparent this was a ploy to keep them from showing your last answer, some bloggers on the web started raising the alarm. No other stations were cutting into their broadcasts about a missile attack in Gaza. With us streaming the whole interview to Hibi, it got their attention, and they started embedding the link. We have fifty million views of the whole interview. This is backfiring on them. LN1 is going to have some explaining to do."

"Thank Jeremy for that. It was his idea to put the camera in the water bottle lid," responded Nick.

"Thank goodness for that," agreed Denise, joining the conversation. "That was LN1's chief legal counsel, threatening to sue us for breach of terms by recording the episode."

"I assume you pleaded innocent?" remarked Nick with a smile.

"Why, Nick Turner, are you telling me to lie? This is a first," said Denise in a feigned surprised tone.

"Not exactly a lie. And they started it. I spoke to Nelly after, he said there was a fifteen second delay. They broke the terms first, so I say offsetting penalties. No foul, replay the down," said Nick.

Denise smiled. "That explains it. We noticed there were a couple of answers missing from the broadcast that showed up on our recording. I made that point to them. I don't expect this to come to anything." They both looked up as Chuck came to them, smiling.

"Good news?" asked Nick.

"2J's finished analyzing the show and they are tearing LN1 a new one in terms of fabrication of facts and misquoting your statements. They're also now pointing out the obvious attempts to deceive the public by comparing our copy to what they broadcast. They have had a couple million tune in, on the web and on the providers broadcasting their station. Nelly is not coming across too well," said Chuck.

"It is too bad. He was the last of the true crusading journalists. They threw him away and brought him out to be the sacrificial lamb," lamented Denise, shaking her head. "I bet they thought he could handle you, Nick. They certainly didn't have anyone else. Of the current crop, only Adam Mullen at EXN could probably hold his own with you in a debate or interview. Thankfully, as far as I can tell, he's on our side."

"You made the most of it. We won't get on again. Of that you can be sure," said Chuck, smiling.

"The offer still stands. Happy to debate. Maybe this time they'll actually do it live," answered Nick.

Chapter 49

Jedidiah Forrest looked at the small, balding man in an ill-fitting suit seated across from him. His black-framed glasses perched on his nose. He looked up at the burly Jed, wearing overalls and a plaid shirt underneath.

"We are agreed?" asked the small man in accented English.

"Sounds good to me. How do we get to the cash?" asked Jed.

"Here are the account numbers and a debit card you can use at any ATM or bank. No withdrawals over $5000. We do not want to attract the attention of your FBI. And never from the same bank. You must stay on the move. That is critical."

"Fine with me. We have chapters all over the place now. Their campaign posts where all the rallies are in advance. What if we get arrested? Who do we call?"

"Turner. He has funds for this. You are a sanctioned Turner group, correct?"

"Yes, we are chartered in Idaho, but that doesn't mean anything. Lots of his supporters travel to out-of-state rallies," replied Jed.

"Good. He can help you then."

"From what I can tell, he'll tell us to stop."

"Even better. If he does not, we can broadcast his double standard as well. There is a cell phone number on there. Once they stop, we will get anyone out of jail. Do not worry. Make sure it is all on film. He invites the local TV stations to every rally. They should be more than happy to oblige us," smiled the small man.

Jed smiled back. "My pleasure. I just have to make sure none of the guys goes too far. They really don't like these ARL and Antifa punks."

The small man shrugged. Jed looked up at the man standing behind him. He stood silently throughout the entire conversation. His eyes bored into Jed's anytime he stared. Jed couldn't wait to leave.

"Are we done?" he asked.

The small man pushed an envelope across the table to him. He opened it and looked.

"It is all there, trust me. $50,000 and the same in your personal account. You succeed and you'll get even more."

Jed smiled. "A pleasure doing business with ya." He got up, with a look at the standing man, suppressing a shiver, he exited the room.

The small man sighed as he left. "I hate to put any faith in fools like that. Undisciplined and weak."

"Only for a time. They will serve their purpose and then they'll disappear," said the tall man. "We must go. There is a flight for you to catch and I have work to do."

The small man nodded, getting up.

#

Nick sat in his Washington office in the Hart Senate Office Building. His trips to his Senate office were now fewer and fewer. Almost exclusively to cast votes. He sat contemplating a stack of unread legislative bills. Carla knocked at Nick's open door.

"Senator, we forgot to tell you about this. It came a couple of weeks ago when you were out on the road." He took the plain padded envelope from Carla. Nick felt the edges. It seemed to have a stack of papers in it.

Everything sent or delivered to a senator's office was scanned for substances, bomb residues, or any metallic contents. Nick felt confident it was probably only documents. He looked at the address label. It was hand printed in block letters. Glancing at the return address, he paused.

It was a simple street address. 2013 Ayn Issa Rd Ft. Meade, MD. To anyone looking at this, it was simply an address. Nick doubted it existed in Ft. Meade, or the entire US. He quickly confirmed this by searching for the address on the web. Nothing.

He knew another Ayn Issa. It was a small town in Syria. A site of brutal fighting after the Arab Spring. During the uprising by the Syrian rebels against Assad. It had changed hands many times during the civil war. At one point, after the US intervention in 2014, the US coalition had freed it from ISIS.

Nick opened the envelope. There were thirty pages of what appeared to be photocopied pictures of documents. Looking closer, he could see these were coded files of after-action reports. Many of the pictures were blurry. Looking at a few, he quickly realized he was the subject of all of them.

Leaning back, he wondered where these reports came from. He'd seen none of them. They were obviously CIA reports about activities Nick had been involved in while on joint duty assignments.

Most of this was during his time with Naval Intelligence. He also noticed a few were during his stint in the Air National Guard. Nick had been involved in covert missions during that time as well. Flying missions over Syria before, during and after the official involvement of the US in the coalition of nations supporting rebel factions.

One mission was over Ayn Issa. This was why he recognized the address. His engagement was technically an act of war against a sovereign nation. One with whom the US was not at war. He noticed the documents were stamped with various designations. Secure Compartmented Information (SCI), Secure Access Program (SAP), and another stamp he had not encountered previously. Congressional National Intelligence, Q clearance level 5.

Q clearance was a mythical clearance in Intelligence circles. It was a cold war designation for materials dealing specifically with nuclear arsenals and information about nuclear programs themselves. Nick had actually been cleared for Q clearance level 4 for some information dealing with Iran, North Korea, and Pakistan's nuclear programs. He'd never heard or seen mention of a level 5.

Nick flipped through the pages, reading about assessments of actions he had witnessed or the aftermaths of which he had been involved in reviewing. He found it ironic how the facts, even in these reports, were whitewashed from what he'd seen himself. The last three were typed and printed, not copies. They had been typed on a typewriter, not a computer. As he read the words, he realized they must be encoded. Just a series of random letters and words. An unbreakable code without the proper key.

Nick stood, walked to his open door, shutting and locking it. Something he rarely did. He headed into the kitchen area in his senate office/apartment. His large fireproof safe was built into a wall in the kitchen. After entering multiple codes, he pulled out a large carved wooden trunk, about two-foot square.

Putting it on the kitchen counter, he opened the top. It was lined with felt, with several drop-in trays holding his various medals, citations, and military ribbons for his uniforms in neat stacks. Lifting out the trays, he fished around beneath these until he found a small notebook.

Nick turned the pages of his notebook until he found information about the raid at Ayn Issa. He found the code key for those orders. Applying the info he found to the pages of gibberish. He could now translate the first few words on the page. It took several minutes. '*Nick, you are in danger*', was the opening sentence.

He sighed. It would take hours to manually translate the words on the three pages using the key. He rolled up his sleeves and got to work.

#

Nick was about halfway through translating the pages when he heard another knock. He raised his head and looked over the pages spread across his desk. Walking to the locked office door, he opened it halfway. A startled Carla stood, not used to him opening the door.

He smiled. "What's up?"

"Sorry, you startled me. Not used to your door being locked. I found another stack of notes for you. I guess we probably need a better system of what to forward and what we should deal with." She handed him an inch deep stack of return call message forms.

He looked down as Carla continued.

"Chuck handles most of this and opens the mail he thinks is official or from cranks or constituents. We only leave the others that are personal for you. If you want, I can work with Margie to see about having these sent to the Denver office every few days?" suggested Carla.

"Thanks Carla. We're doing fine. If they were important, I think they would have tried to track me down again."

"I hope so Senator. Let us know if we missed something important and we'll make sure it doesn't happen again," she smiled, turning to go, as Nick shut the door.

Nick glanced through the stack, walking back to the table. He stopped. It was becoming clearer. Pulling out his phone and dialing the number on the message.

"Hello, who is this?" asked a firm male voice, clearly not the voice of the original caller.

Nick had a bad feeling and ended the call. His phone was not identified with caller ID, nor trackable, as a safety precaution for all members of Congress.

Sitting at his desk, typing in 'Daniel Jacobs', a recent obituary came up. Nick reviewed the story and closed the browser. His browsing was also anonymous courtesy of a Tor browser and various VPN and privacy services Jeremy had provided for his office and campaign computers. Emails were collected and archived as required by congressional acts, but not his browsing history.

Nick leaned back. He now knew who sent the package. And most likely why. He remembered Jacobs from a few interactions during the war. Nick dialed another number.

Chapter 50

"What can we do?" asked Harriet as she reviewed commercials various PACs and SuperPACs were producing on behalf of their candidate. "These are not helping."

Mel sat across from her as they both looked at a reel of commercials their team had recorded.

"Harriet, you know we coordinate with the key ones, even though we are technically not supposed to. They aren't the ones running these. Honestly, I don't even know who some of them are."

"What do we do? I mean the last one, just about accuses Turner of murdering those poor deputies himself, just because he came out to support a fair trial. They imply the administration is ensuring the Marine gets exactly what he has coming to him? How the hell do they think this is helping us? Who the hell are the 'Social Justice Officers Association'?"

"No idea."

"I tried to look them up. It's a SuperPAC front. We have no idea where the dark money funding is coming from," fumed Harriet.

Mel smiled. "You sound like the Opposition, when they start complaining about the money Pavlovich's WHS orgs spend on elections."

"It's fine when it is in my favor. Mel, I don't want to waste the time and money to counter program. If these idiots spend enough money on this kind of stuff, I have to almost defend Turner to make sure the public knows this is not from us."

"It'll die down. These guys all want to make their point. They run a few ads and the public forgets about them. The folks running it then pocket the rest of the donations as salaries or administrative fees."

"I hope so. Some of these are being played broadly in lots of markets. It has to be costing a pretty penny. We have this one about the Marine. There is another one saying he's taking away people's right to welfare. Not bad for us, but if you listen to the rest of the ad, it goes off the rails," vented Harriet.

"How so?" said Mel, looking at Harriet as she paced the office.

"It plays like it is a person's right to choose not to work and to choose to be paid by the government instead. There is another about homelessness being better handled by the government compassionately rather than removing them and making them work to get their life back on track." Harriet shook her head.

"On the surface, the message is one we support, but the subtlety of the message is what Turner supports. Means tested welfare and plans to get folks *less* dependent on government. The folks who are on welfare are not seeing these ads. Nor the homeless. The people whose tax dollars are supporting them are. And they probably agree with Turner."

"Harriet, let's be honest. How many people are watching political ads? It's why the remote has a mute button. You worry too much."

"It's my job Mel. I'm telling you, the folks who do watch these are our voters who are home during the day. Who have time to think about this stuff. I don't want them thinking about things we don't want them thinking about. Not in ads from folks who're supposedly helping us."

Mel nodded. "They are also the people getting those welfare checks from our administration. It will wake them up to vote to keep us in office. I'll do what I can. If we can't even identify who the SuperPACs are, it will be tough to stop. They all have their own agendas. Are we getting anywhere with any of our other efforts?" asked Mel, shifting gears.

Her face showed a look of skepticism. "We finished the interviews. It's pretty thin. Not sure it would hold up to any scrutiny."

"Doesn't have to. Just need the perception, even if it falls apart."

"Tell that to the people we ask to go public. You know what will happen to them if it doesn't hold up. EXN and his supporters will claim this is all a setup for bad publicity."

"Which is exactly what we'll get. His supporters can complain all they want. We want to plant seeds of doubt in the moderates he is courting. Anything to tarnish Saint Turner."

Harriet shook her head. She hated hanging women out to dry, even for political benefit. "He already started with the Marine. Why are we wasting time on Turner? Blackbird is who we should be worried about."

Mel smiled a knowing smile. Harriet stared for a second, opened her mouth to ask, and then shut it. It was better not to know.

#

As the calendar moved to late-September, the candidates and their vice presidential running mates were making multiple stops a day. Lexi was traveling through the upper Midwest, focusing on Minnesota, Wisconsin, Illinois, Michigan, and Pennsylvania. She would not make the same mistakes her predecessors did. Assuming these blue collar and urban Party stalwarts were firmly in her corner.

While her VP running mate Jimmy 'JJ' Jefferson hit the urban inner cities of the Rust Belt, Lexi focused on the suburbs. She made speeches in city after city. From high school gyms to Planned Parenthood clinics, to union halls, and rallies for all of her one issue voting blocs.

In each, she doubled down on the partnership between government and citizen. How together they could overcome the bigotry and hatred embodied in the Opposition. Now equally represented by the hateful and divisive rhetoric of Nick Turner. This was red meat for her followers. They were all bought into the need for the government to mandate and enforce these changes for all.

She aimed most of her invective at Blackbird, but she made it clear Turner was just as bad. His insistence on strict adherence to a Constitution that allowed slavery for a hundred years, and still continued to enshrine discrimination, was unforgivable. Progress demanded change and forward-looking actions. Not backwards and a return to rules that enabled all these issues in the past.

Her crowds were large, diverse, enthusiastic, and loud. Lexi fed off their response. She reveled in the love and her confidence grew daily. The entourage of attendant media dutifully reported on her adoring fans. Her polls continued to forecast a landslide.

Blackbird was having more trouble resonating. He, too, was barnstorming the country. At each stop, he attempted to paint Lexi's policies as too extreme for the majority. He was clearly courting the moderates. He rarely cited specific policies he would implement to rescind the administration's destruction of the constitutional checks and balances.

His crowds were smaller, older, and less enthusiastic. No matter what he tried to say or do, he always had protestors at his rallies. Not liberal protestors, but conservative Opposition ones. All claiming he was not doing enough to protect their family and fiscal values. He was not promising to start drilling again. Only discussing increasing oil production while also staying focused on alternate choices as well. Blackbird would not say definitively he would close the border, nor offer any concrete ideas on what to do with the millions of illegals already in the country.

He was also thin-skinned. On multiple occasions, he demanded to know why opposition voters were complaining to him about these things when Lexi was the real problem. Why were they wasting their time criticizing him instead of helping him beat her? He felt he was having to defend himself against the rest of his party instead of focusing on her.

Because of this, more and more of his speeches were aimed at Turner rather than Lexi. He explained how the radical nature of Turner's constitutional stances was the wrong message at the wrong time when the country was so divided. They needed to unite first and beat Lexi. Then they could discuss how best to repair the damage the administration had inflicted on the country these last seven years.

His vice presidential running mate was not having much success. Governor Kacey Carson's crowds were even smaller. She tried to focus on more conservative stances. Promising true abortion restrictions and trying to talk tough on the border and taxes.

It was clear she was not up to the task and could not inspire folks by herself. She was physically small in stature and could not project the power and command one expected from a national leader. Where she excelled was the heartfelt TV interview, but these were few with the media firmly in Lexi's court and EXN's opinion shows, preferring Turner's message to Blackbirds.

Turner, still in mid to high single digits, was suddenly being attacked by both major candidates. Pundits were pointing this out, suggesting their candidates get back to focusing on issues and their opponents. Even with all this 'free' commentary, they noted collectively, it was having little effect on his polling. Even as his crowds grew in size.

Nick continued to focus his energies in the small cities and towns throughout the country. When he stopped in the dense urban areas, it was typically in small venues filled with folks traveling in from the surrounding suburbs. He could talk to any group, finding the correct balance of moderation on social issues and conservative stances on fiscal prudence.

UAW hall, pro-life and pro-choice locals, teachers, school boards and concerned parent's groups. Fiscal think tanks, LGBTQ rallies, trial lawyers and VFWs. Nick's audience was every bit as diverse as Lexi's. The message was the polar opposite; personal responsibility and freedom to choose. This versus the cradle to grave care of the Party administrations.

He was resonating with both traditional Party and Opposition moderate voting blocks. He gave his message to all of them and listened to their concerns. In return, he told them his stances and always left them contemplating *their* futures and how each of them was responsible for their own, not him, or at least not him alone.

The pundits on both sides of the aisle were quick to point out Nick did not promise voters anything. Not more money in their pockets from lower taxes or more money spent to reduce their student loan and inflation burdens. Nothing to actually help any of them specifically.

With nothing to be gained personally from voting for Turner, both sets were mystified why he even continued. Clearly he did not know you could not win voters without offering them something in return for their vote.

As always, the challenge was how to get him in front of as many potential voters as possible. He was running out of state fairs. Without endorsements, he also lost the opportunity to both mobilize these groups in his favor, and the chance to talk to their gatherings.

Still relying primarily on word of mouth and his growing grassroots organizations. Guerilla social media was helping but was hard to quantify and missed entire segments of voters. The message was getting out, but his unwillingness to have his supporters respond to polls honestly also meant *he* had no good way to gauge his own support either.

Denise was a broken record, begging Nick to tell his supporters to start being honest with pollsters. Nick was adamant the time was not yet right. She countered with the fact that mail in ballots would shortly go out in certain states and if he was deemed irrelevant, potential supporters wouldn't be inclined to throw away their vote on an also ran.

There were several bright spots. In a parking lot of one of Martha Summer's largest stores, Nick gathered 11,000 people for a speech. A Guinness book of records adjudicator was present and certified this as the largest gathering in a retail parking lot for a political campaign speech.

Several noted Party and Opposition women, famous for screaming at each other about abortion rights, came together to discuss how they felt. They both agreed Nick's stance had a chance to work.

They also admitted what Nick proposed as a compromise solution, gave them both reasons to see the other's viewpoint. For the first time. Symbolically, they had a hatchet on a table between them. They put it in a clear plexiglass box on stage and each used a shovel throwing dirt in the box until the hatchet was buried. They then embraced, crying. The video had over fifty million views.

Naturally, the media pundits of American *Pravda* excommunicated the liberal feminist, claiming she was betraying both her party and her gender. The right celebrated her breaking free from group think.

With this tackled, they found they agreed on almost every other topic, as Nick had predicted in his speeches. Education, crime, immigration, funding police, social justice, and the pocketbook issues of inflation, taxes, and the economy. They even started a successful podcast together, '*Women agreeing, (mostly)*'. This emboldened others to speak up.

Even a majority of the ladies on *Women's Viewpoint* grudgingly admitted in one segment that Turner's message resonated, even if they were not willing to fully support any restriction on abortion. With several of them, they used it to fire a warning shot at Party voters to mobilize or face the consequences of ignoring the threat of Turner.

Finally, as the trial for Dusty Ingram approached, several heavy hitters, including Brad Hudson, with fifteen million radio listeners a day, came around to Nick's view of letting the trial expose the facts before jumping to conclusions.

Hudson originally criticized Nick for even involving himself in the controversy. Not because he disagreed, he told his viewers. Rather, he was rightly concerned Nick's stance would alienate potential supporters. He had invited Nick to come on the show to explain.

In a short phone call broadcast on one show, Nick responded he would be happy to, but he would not discuss the trial. If he wanted to talk about campaign issues, he'd be happy to join, or they could wait until after the trial began. Brad thanked him for being honest and said he would invite the Senator on once the trial began.

Denise and Margie were furious with Nick for not taking advantage of the initial invitation. Nick stuck to his principles and said he would not contribute to the media frenzy. Many of the subsequent callers into the show, as well as several guests, all expressed their admiration for Nick's principled stance, if not the stance itself. Many praised this as the attitude and integrity missing from the standard presidential candidates and the recent Presidents themselves.

As in every election cycle, millions of dollars were now being spent at all levels of the political races. From city councilman to mayor and state races, congressman, and President. The various political operatives reaped the benefit of the perpetual and seemingly endless campaign season American politics had become.

Each election was now breathlessly declared by the media as the most consequential election in American history. The election was six weeks away. This time, they would be correct.

Chapter 51

"Right this way, sir," said a youngish man wearing a T-shirt advertising some punk rock band Mel had never heard of. He looked at the man as they walked down the hallway in the warehouse. He had long hair, tattoos on his visible arms, his chest and neck above the T-shirt collar, with various piercings in his ear, nose, and lip.

All Mel could think was how much it would have hurt to do all that mutilation. And for what? To show you were a rebel? He continued following until they came to the main room of the warehouse. Inside it was organized chaos. There was station after station of tables. Some with computers, others with printers, and still others with people seated comparing printed lists with those on computer screens. As Mel entered, another man noticed, and came over, holding his hand out to Mel.

"Josh Stone," he said, shaking Mel's hand.

"Quite the operation you have going here."

"Actually, it is. Let me walk you around and explain things."

"Lots of people involved. Can you trust all of them?" asked Mel, looking around at what had to be close to a hundred workers.

Josh laughed. "Take a look. Do any of them look like Opposition to you? Most of them are members of Antifa or ARL chapters, or worse. All of them are dedicated to overthrowing the US government."

Mel stopped and looked at Josh before they got within earshot of the workers. "Last time I checked, the idea was to get the Party elected. Not to overthrow the Government," said Mel in a low voice.

"They don't know that. All they care about is sticking it to the man. We've done such a good job brainwashing these kids, or else frying their brains with legalized pot and worse, all they know is the Opposition is evil. None of them can explain why. We aren't here to debate ideas, just to mark the right circles. They can handle that much, as long as we let them vape while they work," laughed Josh.

As Mel looked, clouds of white 'vapor' rose around the heads of workers at the tables. "We're counting on you and your 'team' of misfits to get this done. They aren't too high to mark the correct 'circle'?"

"We got this, trust me. We've learned a few things during the last couple of elections. We're much smarter and way more capable. Every vote is now a legal vote. No more dead people voting," noted Josh.

"How are you doing that?" pushed Mel.

"Let me show you." They walked to a table where a young black woman sat comparing the list on a sheet of paper with rows of numbers on the screen. She, like the first young man, was covered in tattoos and the requisite body piercings. The markings of the tribes of anarchy.

"Maya is our floor manager. Maya, can you please explain what you are doing for our guest?" suggested Josh.

"Sure thing, Mr. J," said Maya, turning to look at Mel and Josh. "I'm working on Maricopa County, Arizona. We have a complete list of the registered voters for the county. I have a program that analyzes the voting patterns for the last 5 presidential elections. Using Machine Learning algorithms, we can figure out which registered voters have voted the least in the last 20 years or even not at all. We extrapolate the data to build a list of these voters most likely not to vote in this election and we use that as our baseline. Then we print official mail in ballots for each of these voters," she said, turning to wave at a table with printers.

"Next, we print the same ballots, with all the correct down ballot candidates and envelopes as the Secretary of States in all our targeted counties. We use the same printers they do. That one is printing Arizona," she said, pointing to a printer, spitting out ballots and envelopes labeled and addressed to these voters.

"Next, they are handed off to the painters." She pointed to a group marking ballots, picking them one at a time from the stacks.

"They are marking all of them for the Vice President with an occasional Opposition or Independent in the down ballot elections. The last person in the line is the forger. He or she looks at the signature on file, usually a driver's license, and signs the envelope."

Maya pointed to the end of a line of tables where stacks of boxes labeled 'Official Property of Maricopa County Elections' were stacked.

"Then it goes in the box to be delivered to the county for counting on election night. Those are the same boxes the ballots are put in from every collection box." Maya smiled in triumph at the operation. As she said that, the 'forger' at the table yelled out "lefty". Another person showed up at the table, looked at the signature, and signed it left-handed.

Mel watched in awe at the seamless nature of the effort underway. "It's brilliant. Quite the operation. Do we have enough of these to guarantee the outcome?" asked Mel, turning to Josh.

"Thank you, Maya," smiled Josh, turning and leading Mel away.

"No problem, Mr. J."

As Josh led Mel away, he explained. "Over there is Michigan. We have expanded this year to include counties all the way out to Ann Arbor and up to Flint and Saginaw. The current Governor of Michigan is such an idiot we're worried she's inspired lots of Opposition members to vote. Even some moderate Party members to switch allegiance."

"To make up for potential shortfalls, we are doing more counties. Of course, the risk we run is more Opposition who has never voted before, suddenly shows up. We are combing *all* the rolls, registered voter and just eligible. We are using anyone who hasn't voted recently *and* never voted," revealed Josh, turning to look at Mel.

"Here is the beautiful part. If the Opposition shows up and votes and they find a duplicate ballot from us, it will cancel both of them. No harm to us either way. Even if some of them are smart enough to go online and see their vote has been canceled and ask to cure the vote, it is going to have a negligible difference," explained Josh in triumph.

"It's perfect," agreed Mel.

"Most of our states have day of registration, so all these votes from non-registered voters won't be an issue. Michigan, and thanks to last-minute legislation, now Wisconsin and Pennsylvania too. Arizona and

Georgia are still holding out, so we are limited to only registered voters in both. It will make the turnout of registered voters suspiciously high."

Mel started to understand the diabolical nature of the process.

"Now we could take some of the historical Opposition voters and intentionally cast more duplicate ballots, but that could lead to more questions if there are suddenly a large number of duplicate mail in ballots. If these people are willing to sign legal affidavits, or they voted for Blackbird and not the Party and they find a friendly court, we could be looking at more scrutiny. I'd say we avoid that at all costs. To answer your question, in Arizona especially, if we don't have enough with all the extra voters, you have to rely on your voting machine algorithms," said Josh.

"What are those?" ask a somewhat bewildered Mel.

Josh gave him a strange look. "I'm the ballot whisperer. I don't do computers. Maya may not look it, but she has advanced programming degrees and came up with the algorithms we are using to isolate the non-voters who we are 'voting' for," explained Josh.

"I'm assuming the rumors of you having the software changed on the voting machines are true and you can turn on county by county to change votes or parts of votes for Lexi versus for Blackbird? That takes a different level of programming skill. You can do this, right?" asked Josh.

"I have been told so. Obviously, I can't explain it," replied Mel.

"If you're worried, we don't have enough ballots this way, then you need to talk to your computer geeks working the machines. I would be very careful using that method. Too many folks are watching for computer espionage. Too many smart hackers now. My way is old-fashioned and pretty foolproof. If some of these counties are forced to open up their machines for audits, you may have issues covering your tracks. If they find cheating on the machines, holy hell will break loose. They'll spend the time and money to look at the paper ballots as well."

"Not if we win," smiled Mel. Josh shook his head.

"I hope you're correct. Our scheme with the ballots is much more difficult to undo. After all, every one of these is a registered or eligible voter. It is a legal vote. The only way they undo this is if they were to take every vote and ask every voter if they voted and who they voted for. It would take way too long and cost way too much money to do a full audit. It's pretty full proof. The only red flag is going to be turnout. We got away with that in the past. Contentious elections bring out the voters because they are concerned about the outcome. Surely you have enough highly paid talking heads to make that case?" pointed out Josh.

"We do indeed. What about illegals voting?"

"Again, not my charter," answered Josh. "I'm assuming they'll send in their mail in ballots if they're sent them. Some will get canceled, but many will be counted. That is more likely to help you in Texas, California, and Arizona. I'm not sure how many mail in ballots will be sent to all the new illegals being seeded across all the red states. May take another election cycle or two before they have driver's licenses and stuff to be sent ballots. We should be OK this time. After this, maybe we don't need to have these contingencies anymore," shrugged Josh.

"How do you get the ballots to the counties?"

"Last time, the truckers tipped off the authorities. We almost lost Philly. This time, we're going to be smarter about it. We're moving them in produce trucks delivering groceries to warehouses. We have folks prepared to separate them out at each location and then deliver them by 'official' county vehicles to the county offices as if they were normal pickups from remote ballot boxes. Much less chance of anything out of the ordinary. We certainly won't be pulling bins from under tables this time," said Josh with a satisfied smile. "We got this. All it takes is money."

Mel smiled in reply. "Tell me again which counties we're doing?"

Josh turned in a semi-circle. "Our research shows the VP is in good shape in all the solid blue states. She only needs to win some of the swing states, but we aren't taking any chances. Over there we have Michigan. Five counties around Detroit to Ann Arbor. Wayne, Washtenaw, Oakland, Macomb, and Ingham. We added Genesee and Saginaw for Flint and Saginaw. Both are already blue, they'll be deep blue when we are done. High Party turnout in these is usual and if it goes to ninety percent or higher, we can get away with it."

Mel looked around at the effort going on around him. He silently thanked the technology advancements. There was no way they could have done all of this the old-fashioned way. Delivering harvested ballots stuffed in boxes in batches of fifty. Mel listened as Josh continued.

"In Wisconsin, we're concentrating on three counties around Milwaukee. Milwaukee, Dane, and Waukesha counties. We got away with 100% turnout the last time, hell some of those dopes brought in more ballots than there were actual voters. Luckily, the idiots in the press stopped reporting on it and your judges kept anyone from investigating." Josh was shaking his head in disbelief at the incompetence.

"It amazes me the people will put up with all this. Just shows you how docile and quelled they are. With the threat of being canceled, they won't even make a peep. So, Michigan and Wisconsin are fine. We left Minnesota alone this time. The entire state government is socialist."

Josh turned and pointed to a different area of the warehouse.

"Next is Pennsylvania. We are doing six counties around Philly this time. Philadelphia, Montgomery, Bucks, Lancaster, Delaware, and Chester. There was talk of trying to do something in Pittsburgh, but they threw out their District Attorney in a special election. Got some city-wide transparency laws and voter ID checks for every ballot, including mail in there, so we are leaving it alone. Six counties in Philly should be enough."

"We have issues in Nevada as well. As you know, there really are only two population centers to focus on; Reno and Vegas. We're hitting Clark county hard. The shenanigans last time cost us the Party Secretary of State and Attorney General, both of whom were replaced during the mid-term elections because of the last presidential election. They know there was cheating. They couldn't prove it because all the machines were wiped illegally, but they were wiped just the same."

Mel nodded, remembering the clandestine break in they'd arranged. They broke into the warehouse where the machines were stored and executed manual resets to wipe away all evidence of fraud. It had been a close shave.

Josh continued. "We are working the old-fashioned way, using the SEIU to drive more turnout. Clark is the key. I'm telling you, if there is a challenge, it is most likely coming from Nevada."

Mel nodded in understanding.

"They are on to us there and making it hard to use this process. Obviously, machines are out too unless you have something better than the last time. Georgia and Arizona are so obvious. You sure we want those this year again?" Josh asked, hoping Mel would say no.

"Yes. There is no way around it," affirmed Mel.

"As you can imagine, the Opposition was furious. They know we did something, and they would be right," said Josh, with a serious look on his face. "The laws passed, requiring IDs and transparency on the machines will make it hard. Mail in is still going to be a majority of the votes and there is no ID verification there yet."

"We are preparing ten counties in Georgia this time, including some of the smaller metro areas rather than just Fulton, Dekalb, and Cobb like last time. We are adding more of the metro Atlanta counties. Clayton, Forsyth, Hall, Cherokee, Gwinnett, plus Savannah and Macon, which are Chatham and Bibb counties. We'll have 100% ready, but I suggest we try to limit it to 80%. We'll have the other 20% for the 8 metro Atlanta counties nearby in 'official' vans, but only use them as a last resort."

Mel nodded in understanding.

"If you use them, they will definitely audit. A percentage of them will be invalidated from duplicate votes. Especially in Cobb and Cherokee and the Buckhead parts of Fulton County. It may call the entire state into question. Make sure it is worth it before you make the call," warned Josh.

"Ok, got it. Arizona?" inquired Mel.

"Arizona is even worse. It doesn't have very many counties. It is only Tucson, Phoenix, and Yuma. Six counties total we are working. Maricopa for Phoenix, Pima for Tucson, Pinal, Yavapai, Yuma, and Mohave. Again, keep it at 80% total turnout. They are really pissed after the last one because they know enough people did not support the President and yet it went for him."

"Yes, I remember, I was there," grimaced Mel.

"Right. They did some audits and thankfully they kept recounting until no one cared anymore. Once Pennsylvania was certified, it became moot, and you finally got a federal judge to stop it all as irrelevant, regardless of the outcome. The incorrect election night count showing the President winning by 5500 votes stood."

"Of course, enough people leaked it to confirm what they thought. Thankfully, that one state would not have been enough to change the outcomes, so it was irrelevant. That is the only reason we are having this conversation. If it had mattered, we'd have a different president. We would be back to voter IDs everywhere. No more mail in, and rightfully so," added Josh.

"You don't approve of our efforts?" asked Mel, concerned.

"Oh no, I approve. If they let us get away with it, shame on them. Hell, everyone knows Nixon won in 1960 and JFK's daddy used his mob ties to make sure he won. Ever since *Gore v Bush*, the Party has made an art of cheating. If the Opposition is too spineless to stop us, or too inept to do their own, then they get what they deserve." Josh explained.

"Deterrence works and without deterrence, you get exactly what you have. As long as we have elections, the Party is going to tip the scales. What bothers me, frankly, is we can't seem to win a big enough majority to support our ideas and make cheating unnecessary. We have done a terrible job of convincing folks our policies are the answer. Oh well, that is your issue, not mine," finished Josh.

"You have everything you need? Funding, People?" asked Mel.

"We're fine. Now that all the state ballots are finalized, we can print the official ones and the envelopes just like the states. We have enough people. Our networks of drivers, interceptors, and local distribution are all set. Remember, we will have Georgia and Arizona on ready 5, but we should not use them unless we have to. My polling tells me we won't need it, but it is only late-September," revealed Josh.

"We don't want to just win, we need to win big," said Mel. "Any chance you guys can do anything in states where we need to win the contested Senate seats. Ohio, Kentucky, Texas, Iowa, and Nebraska?"

"Too risky. All those states have voter ID laws and notary or ID requirements for mail in. The Red states are trying to stop us. We can't risk our operations by trying to work there," explained Josh.

"Too bad. I am more worried about keeping the Senate. Guess we'll have to resort to the old-fashioned ways there. Union turnout and intimidation. Are you involved in our harvesting efforts?"

"Nope. Since it is legal, the local party offices are in charge of efforts in California, Oregon, Virginia, Pennsylvania, Minnesota, Wisconsin, Nevada, Florida, and Washington. They are corralling the volunteers to go to the nursing homes, homeless encampments, and VA hospitals. I think the going rate for the homeless is a pack of cigs or 20 bucks. They are getting the voters who never vote the old-fashioned way, door to door. We didn't set up operations for those, since harvesting is legal and those are blue or purple, except for Florida. Surely you aren't worried?" insisted Josh.

"Presidential, no. I sure want those southern California congressional seats back. Thankfully, we have a tremendous advantage in Party registration and harvesting operations," grinned Mel.

"It's a well-oiled machine for sure," agreed Josh.

"Indeed, it is. Thanks for the tour," ended Mel.

Maya watched as Mel walked out with Josh. She turned back to her list with a smile.

Chapter 52

Nelson Lopez pushed the button on his garage door opener. It took three times before he got it right and it opened. Slowly driving his Mercedes sedan into the garage bay, he pulled in too far, compressing a plastic container against the far wall while his car sensors screamed. Nelson struggled to get the gearshift into reverse, finally backing away enough, stopping the alarm. It had been a rough couple of days since his interview with Nick. He'd been thrown under the bus by every liberal pundit.

Reaching over to the passenger seat, He grabbed the neck of the half empty bottle of scotch and slowly turned to exit the car. The garage was dark except for the interior light from the car. Nelson was not handy and had never replaced the burned-out bulb in his overhead garage opener. He stood up, wobbling, hanging on to the door frame with his free hand, wheezing. He had no chance to even fight back as the arm reached around, grabbing him in a chokehold.

Reaching up reflexively, he batted at the figure behind him. His other hand released its hold on the bottle, which tumbled back into the car. It did not take long for Nelly to lose consciousness. As he slumped, the assailant pinned his body against the car, maintaining the chokehold until it was clear he would not wake up soon.

Once finished, he let the unconscious body slide down the side of the car, arranging it back in the driver's seat.

The figure took Nelson's left hand and reached up the index finger to close the garage door. The now mostly empty bottle of scotch was on the floorboard between the pedals. Pushing the starter while simultaneously depressing the brake with one of Nelly's feet. The car started while he slowly leaned Nelson's head against the steering wheel. For completeness, picking up the liquor, unscrewing the cap, he simulated dropping the bottle from Nelly's limp hand. It landed on the floorboard, slowly gurgling out its contents.

Thankfully, Nelly's Mercedes was vintage enough and not diesel. It still spewed enough carbon monoxide to finish the job. To the police, it would appear he drove into his garage and passed out before he could get out of the car or turn it off. The figure exited through the door to the backyard he'd entered. Locking it behind him. It was already getting hard to breathe in the garage. It would not take long.

#

Mel sat in Air Force Two, going over the day's agenda with Lexi.

"The Marine's trial starts today?" commented Lexi.

"Yes. Too bad really. We have tagged Turner pretty hard with our relentless coverage of his support for a cop killer."

"True. It was still coverage," replied Lexi, looking at her tablet.

"For this, Lexi, I didn't mind. It hurt him with the conservatives. They revere the cops. This was a betrayal of their principles."

"We'll see. She scrolled through her news feeds as Mel returned to his daily agenda logistics."

"Son of a bitch," said Lexi, looking at Mel as he looked up. "Did you see this?" She turned the tablet to Mel. A headline read 'distinguished journalist Nelson Lopez was found dead in his house. Apparently, he passed out in his garage with his car running. No foul play is suspected.'

Mel looked up at Lexi. She was smiling. Mel did not smile back. He suspected Nelly did not die of his own choice, but he dared not ask.

#

Mel listened to the metallic Voice on his secure phone.

"You're getting sloppy. You cannot just kill anyone who is inconvenient to your campaign. Vincent and now Lopez? Taking out a drunk journalist because he embarrassed the candidate? Stop this."

"I had nothing to do with it," said Mel in complete sincerity.

"Of course not, but you give the orders. Don't get sloppy." It was clear the Voice wasn't happy at the scrutiny these deaths could bring.

"I had nothing to do with Lopez. Perhaps you should ask your man," repeated Mel with a slight annoyance.

"He does not act on his own. Who gave him the order?"

"Maybe Lopez really passed out. He was drunk, and the cops said they found a mostly empty bottle on the floorboard. Maybe you are jumping to conclusions?" suggested Mel.

"It is too convenient. Coming so soon after Turner's performance on *The Sunday Hour*. I know of your bosses' reaction."

"True, but I assure you it was not done on my order."

"He was sent to help you. You need to make sure she understands this as well. Settling petty scores helps no one."

"Understood."

Chapter 53

"Let's go to Lauren Bergamo, who is at the trial of Dusty Ingram. Lauren, what has happened so far?" asked Marty Nash from the ANC studio.

"Thanks Marty. The judge is not allowing the cameras into the courtroom yet. Today, the jury was seated and sworn in. The defense and prosecution lawyers both made their opening statements," stated Lauren.

"Both lawyers laid out their case. The prosecution claiming that Dusty Ingram ignored the obvious shouting of the deputies and the clear signs on their clothing stating they were law enforcement. He fired first and clearly intended to kill all of them, even after he realized they were not 'intruders'. He also explained how all the slain deputies and the father and baby killed by the sheriff's deputies directly resulted from Dusty's wanton disregard for the law and their orders to stand down."

"Lauren, that sounds pretty straightforward. Seems like this should be a quick trial," suggested Marty in a forceful tone.

"Marty, the defense made a compelling counter argument. The defense lawyer started to lay out the facts…"

"Lauren, sorry to interrupt, but we need to get to the White House briefing. Nothing the defense lawyer stated could contradict the fact he pulled the trigger on six sheriff's deputies, and they are now dead. We look forward to further updates once the witnesses are finished and we get to the jury's verdict," finished Marty.

Lauren handed her microphone to her cameraman, Paul, and looked down at her notes. No one wanted to hear the truth. It was pretty clear ANC had already decided on the verdict. They wouldn't play any part in getting out the truth or helping people form their own opinions.

She looked at her notes and thought through what she'd heard this morning from Duane Cooper, Dusty's defense attorney. He'd laid out a litany of procedural errors. None of which had received any coverage by the media. From the initial complaint, which was clearly a case of swatting and not a true Red Flag situation. To the unforgivable sin of listing Dusty's address rather than the address of the intended suspect. This, more than any, made Lauren rethink her position.

Duane then painted the picture of Dusty's mental state. His lingering PTSD, the fact he was mostly deaf, the lack of light, the shitty neighborhood, and the no-knock warrant giving the police the legal right to break down his door. Duane pointed out anyone who was concerned with their safety would've done what Dusty did.

Throughout the rest of the day, various medical experts were called by both sides and cross-examined to determine the hearing loss, PTSD and even to analyze the ability of Dusty to see and read the Sheriff's department on the deputy's clothing. The lasers flying back and forth would have contributed to Dusty not being able to focus on the lettering. Any flash of a laser in his eyes would have impacted his vision.

What Lauren found somewhat surprising was that none of the family members of any of the victims were in the courtroom. It would have been difficult, but many of them had appeared on various cable and network morning shows. Relentlessly attacking Dusty and then Nick for his support for a fair trial for Dusty. She also found it interesting that in the last few weeks running up to the trial, none of the family members were appearing on TV any longer.

She'd asked an ANC producer, and she told her it was not for lack of trying. Even with offers of free travel and appearance fees, all of them had politely declined to give any more interviews before the trial.

This made Lauren's investigative journalist senses very suspicious. To have all of them suddenly clam up in this day and age of constant media exposure was unusual. These appearances were the ticket to cashing in on book, appearance, and potential TV movies. It was not normal behavior.

Chapter 54

Kyle Combs, the evening news anchor for the *New World News* network, sat on a stool facing the bearded father of Eva Herrera. Behind Jack Herrera were fourteen other chairs. All but one filled with the parents or wives of the slain deputies and the widow of the man and baby killed through the walls of Dusty's apartment.

Kyle had a suitably somber look on his face as he began his interview. There was an audience of around 100 people in the studio as well who waited for the comments of the families on the first day of the trial, now completed. They were running this as a special live session of his normal evening news slot.

"First, I realize how difficult this must be for all of you. I have to ask, why are you here in New York rather than at the trial in Denver?"

"Kyle, as you know, I've been picked by all the parents and Jackie," he said, nodding at the widow. "Our shared loss has brought us all together. We felt it would be better to be here, together, away from the chaos of the trial."

He looked surprised at the choice of words. "He murdered your loved ones. I would think you would want closure. To be there when the man who took them away is convicted for his crime."

Kyle surveyed the assembled families, who sat stone faced, only the occasional frown meeting his gaze at his statement.

"This is exactly why we are here. Statements like that."

"If I can remind you, Jack. You came on this very program," he said, turning to look at the other family members. "In fact, many of you did. You all said how upset you were and how you couldn't wait for the Marine to pay for his crimes. Stealing your loved ones. Ruining lives and preventing them from having their own. These were your own words," finished Kyle righteously. There were murmurs in the crowd. They were unsure what was happening. They'd expected to see grieving and upset families screaming for justice. To attack the lies of the defense at the trial. Kyle was clearly perplexed and disappointed he was not seeing this.

Jack shook his head. "It's true, Kyle. We all came on this program and many others. Where we vented our anger. Demanding revenge. We wanted him to pay for our loss."

"Of course you do. So how do you feel after the first day of the trial? The defense attorney claiming your son's and daughter were in the wrong. Implying they were at fault for getting shot! How can that be when they were shouting at him to drop his gun and hold up his hands and he instead fired back, ignoring their commands," Kyle explained in a dramatic tone.

Jack stayed calm as Kyle tried to bait him into a passionate response. "Kyle, did you hear the testimony of the doctor about Dusty's inability to hear? How his hearing was damaged in Afghanistan and then further ruined by the treatment he received from the VA?"

"He had a hearing aid. Of course, they are going to claim he was not wearing it. I didn't believe the testimony. Even if he is mostly deaf, of course he is going to claim he did not have his hearing aid in when the sheriff's entered."

Jack turned to the other families, talking to one older father. "Jerry, you have hearing aids. Do you sleep with them in your ears?"

"Jack, I do not. It is very uncomfortable."

"That changes nothing," ignored Kyle. "He could see fine, no glasses needed. They all had 'Sheriff's department' clear as day on their vests."

Jack looked at Kyle, who was clearly getting upset at their lack of hatred in response to the day's revelations.

"Kyle, have you ever been in combat?"

"Of course not."

"I thought not," replied Jack.

"Now wait a minute…" Kyle fired back at Jack's dismissive tone.

"No, you need to listen. It was five in the morning. Pitch black. Dusty had no reason to believe his door was going to be broken down.

He had no record. Only PTSD and near complete deafness courtesy of Uncle Sam. I have served. In that situation, your door exploding in splinters, body armor clad people waving laser sights around your darkened room and shouting things you cannot hear. You don't think. You don't stop and listen. You don't pause to try to read words on their bullet-proof vests in the dark. And if you are a trained Marine, with combat experience in the hellholes we sent them to, you react as this country taught you to. You protect your life."

"But it is murder. He killed all of them. If he wasn't the target, he should have been. Someone like that shouldn't even have had a gun. Clearly, he was a menace! Look what he did!" shouted Kyle in response.

This time, some of the family members gasped at Kyle's statements. The audience appeared to be split as some cheered agreement at Kyle's statement. As one of the family members made to stand up, Jack held up his hand.

"This is exactly why we are here and not in Denver. Kyle, we have one more person we would like to bring out if it is ok with you?"

Kyle, fuming, nodded.

Nick walked in from the side of the stage and took the lone empty seat amongst the families. Several of them smiled and said hello to Nick. Kyle's eyes were as big as saucers as several in the audience booed.

"Well Senator, I must say you have a lot of nerve showing your face with these grieving families. I would ask that you please leave. Do you not understand the pain you have already caused all of them?" Kyle looked from Jack to the families. "Should I call security?"

"Kyle, the Senator is not a problem. We asked him to join us here," explained Jack calmly.

"Why on earth would you do that?"

"Like I said, we were all angry at our losses. At least we knew our loved ones were in dangerous jobs. Poor Jackie here had even less reason to ever worry. You were right, we were pissed. Even more so when Senator Turner posted his plea to ask for Dusty to get a fair trial. To let the facts speak for themselves. To let the justice system work as it is designed to. Innocent until proven guilty." Jack paused, taking a deep breath.

"I was almost homicidal. My wife Eileen had to practically tie me up to keep me from going after the Senator for what he said."

"See, Senator, I think you should leave," said Kyle, completely missing Jack's tone.

Nick stared at Kyle, not responding.

"Kyle, you don't get it," sighed Jack.

"Excuse me," replied Kyle defensively.

"Do you know the courage it took for the Senator to make that statement? He had no reason to do it. Nothing to gain. He didn't know Dusty. Coming out in support was sure to cost him votes. I know it totally flipped my opinion of him. Theirs too," said Jack, nodding at the families. "We hated Nick Turner as much as we hated Dusty Ingram,"

"Then why are you letting him sit there with a smug look on his face? Mocking your grief?" spewed Kyle.

"Because he did something else. Kyle, he knew how much his statement had to have hurt all of us. He also knew what he said, what he did, and why, was never going to be accurately reported by you or any of your cohorts in the media. You'll also notice that he never said Dusty was innocent. He just said to let the process play out. But none of us heard that. All we saw were story after story from *you* about how Senator Turner said Dusty was innocent of killing our kids."

Jack turned and looked at Nick, who sat impassively amongst the other families. The audience in the studio didn't know how to react.

"You can imagine my surprise when I open my door and find Senator Turner standing there a few weeks ago. No entourage, just him and a buddy of mine, a police chief from a nearby town."

"You have some nerve, Senator. Do you not have any compassion for their feelings? For their loss?" Kyle turned back to Jack. "I assume you told him to go to Hell?"

Jack smiled. "Kyle, for once you are right. I told him to go to Hell and get off my property before I threw him off, or worse," Kyle smiled in triumph. Jack smiled too. "You want to know what he said?"

Kyle nodded, assuming he was about to get his red meat moment.

"He said, 'tell me about Eva'," Jack choked up as he said it. Eileen, who was sitting next to Nick, reached out and grabbed his hand while she teared up. "He said tell me why Eva became a cop."

Before Kyle could break in, Jack continued. He looked up at Kyle with a fire in his eye. "I told the Senator about Eva and he listened. Not the way a politician listens and then moves on. No, he sat there and listened to me talk about all the things Eileen and I could remember. He sat there and listened and cried with us when we remembered all the little things that made her special. Then he talked, and *we* listened."

Jack continued as Kyle and the audience waited.

"When he was done. I arranged it so he could do the same with all the families and Jackie. He did the same thing with each of them. Listened, and then he explained himself. Why he did what he did. He never defended Dusty. He never tried to tell us what to think. He never told us we shouldn't be angry. Or that our grief was not authentic. He told us the facts. He also told us it was up to each of us to come to our own conclusions. *That* is why we are here. On your show instead of at the trial."

"Our eyes have been opened to the mistakes that were made. How these mistakes put our loved ones in the line of fire unnecessarily. Mistakes that caused an honorable warrior of our country to be put into an impossible situation through no fault of his own. How his reaction is the same that *any* of us would have done in his shoes. We no longer blame Dusty. We blame you, Kyle. We blame unseen bureaucrats and folks passing laws without understanding their consequences to real people. Our sons and daughters. Sacrificed needlessly by incompetence and wishful thinking."

Kyle's face was beet red. He didn't know what to do. The cameras kept rolling. To the producers, eyeballs were eyeballs, and NWN needed all they could get on this special edition of his show.

"I will finish with one more fact," continued Jack. "While all of you want us on here for clicks and ratings. Senator Turner asked us not to do this interview until after the jury was selected and the trial was underway. He did not want any of this to affect the trial. To prejudice any potential jurors. The exact opposite of what all of you have been doing since the day it happened. Using a good man, sacrificing him on the altar of sensationalism and ratings. We thank you for listening to us. Both before and now that we understand what really happened."

Jack and Eileen stood, as did the other family members. The audience began clapping and then stood as everyone filed out. Nick sat alone on his stool.

Kyle looked at him, anger and resentment on his face.

"I hope you feel good about using their guilt to help your campaign, Senator," accused Kyle as a few in the audience booed.

Nick stood and shook his head. "You have learned nothing." He walked off the stage as the crowd clapped.

The next morning, Jack and Eileen appeared on ANC. The mid-morning show host, Constance Tipton, who had interviewed them previously, was now grilling them on their change of heart on NWN.

"Help me understand why you've changed your mind regarding your daughter's murder?" asked Connie, her unlined face pinched up in an unattractive scowl. Before Jack could answer, she continued. "I mean, you were here only three weeks ago railing against the Senator and his inhumanity in supporting the murderer. Did he pay you to change your story?" she accused.

"What?" said Jack. "You mean like when ANC offered last week and we refused to appear for money?"

"We do not pay guests, Mr. Herrera, but it seems Senator Turner might have, by your reaction."

Jack laughed as Eileen fumed next to him. "Connie, you obviously did not listen to a word we said yesterday, did you?"

"I heard enough to know you have changed your story one-hundred and eighty degrees, from the grieving family to one where you support finding the murderer of your child not guilty," she accused.

Jack's face darkened as Eileen grabbed his arm. "You've got some nerve. We come on here as a guest of your program and you insult the memory of our child. Implying we changed our opinion about the guilt or innocence of Dusty for *money*? What kind of human being are you? We did not need to be paid by Senator Turner or anyone else. All we needed were the facts, which we finally got from Senator Turner. Not from any of you so-called news organizations. Nick is right to call you American *Pravda*," finished Jack, his voice quivering.

"Congratulations. The person who murdered your daughter may go free because of your actions. How does that honor her? How can you live with yourself knowing this?" asked Connie, not giving in as Eileen rose as well.

"The only person preying on people is you," replied Eileen as she hit Connie in the nose with a left cross. Connie was not expecting violence from anyone, let alone a fellow woman. She was surprised and tumbled off her stool, landing with a thump, her designer glasses askew.

Eileen stood over her. "I'll see you in court, you miserable piece of shit." They walked out as others came on set to help Connie back up. She was too stunned to reply. The cameras kept rolling through the whole segment.

Chapter 55

The six black-clad men stopped at the chain-link fence surrounding the compound. Two groups of three. Using bolt cutters, they quickly cut holes in the six-foot-tall perimeter fencing.

Streaming through, each carried a backpack over a shoulder. The leader nodded and made a hand gesture as they spread out. They moved forward toward a group of buildings under construction.

The leader reached into his backpack and carefully removed four glass jars. Quickly removing their tops, replacing them with perforated tops with rags sticking out of them. Giving the rag a second to soak up some of the liquid in the glass jar, he set them on the ground.

Removing a lighter, he quickly lit the four rags. Screaming voices were yelling 'fire'. Smiling, he picked up his projectiles and quickly threw them at four of the buildings under construction. The glass bottles shattered, spreading their fuel on walls and floors immediately igniting the wood frames.

Picking up his bag, he turned and began trotting back to their entry point. After a few steps, perimeter lighting flashed on, illuminating the entire compound. He hadn't counted on this and broke into a sprint.

Spying the hole in the fence, making for it as fast as his adrenaline assisted legs would now carry him. Just as he thought he was in the clear, two large men moved in front of the exit. Both were wearing sweatshirts, shorts, and carrying aluminum softball bats.

He looked to his right as several more of his companions arrived. By this time, six more men had arrived, boxing four of the hoodie clad arsonists in from behind. One of them shouted.

"Ryan, the fire brigade is on the way. Seventh street is a disaster, all the buildings under construction are on fire. Sixth is about half.

Thankfully, the ones these assholes threw at on Fourth didn't do well with the fireproof siding on the house. We got the folks out. Don't think anyone is hurt. We got two of them. Jacob is holding them for the cops."

"Thanks, Spence," replied Trapper, looking with menace at the four anarchists in front of him. By now there were three more angry men standing next to Trapper. "Well gents, looks like your little party got interrupted. We can do this the easy way or the hard way. Your choice."

The leader looked to his right and nodded. One guy pulled out a Molotov cocktail and lit it, holding it in his hand and waving it around. The leader laughed. "I think maybe you should move before we barbecue you." A second thug had also pulled out another cocktail, lighting it. Trapper looked at the leader, shaking his head.

"Who paid you to do this?"

"Pay? Hell, we did it for free. Homeless shelter? Some shelter you are running here," he said, looking around. "More like a prison. Fences, lights, guards. I am just trying to help free people from your jail. Now," yelled the man as he made a break for the fence.

One of them pulled back an arm to throw and was hit in the back with a stone, causing him to drop it, immediately setting himself and one other ablaze. Both started screaming and rolling around on the ground.

The other got his off. As it headed toward Trapper, the guy next to him stuck out a bat to knock it away. It deflected, broke, and landed, setting the nearby grass on fire and that person's pant covered leg. He calmly rolled to the ground and doused the flames.

The leader and one of the others were tackled by Trapper and his other buddies. As he squirmed, the leader pulled out his knife. In desperation, he began wildly slashing at anything he could reach. He was met with grunts and howls of pain as one set of hands let go of him.

Trying to squirm away and run to freedom, he made one more motion with the knife stabbing and lost his grip. An arm went around his throat and pressed until he saw stars and then darkness.

"Ryan, stop, you're gonna kill him," yelled Spencer, helping put out the flames on the other two arsonists as more people arrived with water and fire extinguishers to stop the grass fire.

Trapper had the leader in a chokehold and was not paying attention to the shouts of his guys. Finally, Spencer disengaged and pulled him off the man. As Trapper let go of him, he flopped to the ground.

"Shit, he's not breathing. Go get help," Spencer said to another man who ran back down the street between the buildings toward the now arriving fire rescue and EMTs. Trapper stood, taking deep breaths, oblivious to the knife sticking out of the fat part of his thigh.

He kneeled next to the guy. "Move over. We've got to start compressions." He pulled the knife out of his thigh and used it to cut the hoodie the man was wearing. He looked up at his face in the hood. He was a young black man, probably not even thirty yet.

Trapper began chest compressions. In his head. He played the song *Staying Alive* by the Bee Gees. It was a trick used to teach people how fast to go on CPR compressions. Trapper had done this many times as a medic in the army. Now he needed to do it to save his own soul. He'd just violated his oath to do no harm.

As he kept up the compressions, the other thug they'd wrestled to the ground was now shouting about how Trapper had killed his buddy. He was going on about getting on TV and suing and making sure he fried his ass. Two EMTs ran up to them as Trapper continued.

One of them took over as Trapper leaned back.

The other was setting up a defibrillator. "How long?"

Trapper thought for a second. "Compressions for probably three minutes. The EMT nodded. He had the paddles ready.

"Clear" he shouted as the other EMT moved back. He shocked the man on the ground and his body twitched. The first one checked and shook his head, continuing compression as the unit recharged. He backed away, and they shocked him again.

"I have a pulse," said the one EMT.

Trapper leaned back with a sigh of relief.

"Good job. You saved his life," said the one with the paddles as he looked at Trapper.

"My fault. I choked him out too long after he stabbed me," said Trapper, looking down. The EMT followed his glance.

"Jose, we got a bleeder here," he said as Trapper slumped over, *his* adrenaline now subsiding while his thigh continued pulsing out blood.

#

"Coach, what the hell happened?" asked Nick on the phone.

"Some Antifa thugs tried to burn down Hope One in Pasadena."

"No! How bad?"

"We lost 15 houses and two streets of half-finished houses. Thankfully, we evacuated the families in the fifteen houses without an injury, but they lost the few possessions they had."

"Thank God for that. Everyone else alright?"

"That's the main reason I am calling. Trapper and the guys caught all six of them. Two of them got burned when they dropped a Molotov cocktail and it lit them up. Mostly first and a few second-degree burns."

"Serves them right," stated Nick.

"Unfortunately, Trapper got stabbed and two other guys have some minor knife slash wounds."

"Is he OK?"

"Should be. The leader of the thugs stabbed him in the thigh and it nicked his artery, but the EMTs got to him in time. He should be fine. There is a problem, though."

"What?"

"Nick, they arrested Trapper and are charging him with attempted murder. When the leader tried to escape, they tried to make a break for it through the guys. That's when the other one dropped their Molotov cocktail. A second one was thrown at Trapper and the guys. They deflected it and only one guy had some minor burns. The others, including Trapper, tackled the two thugs and wrestled them to the ground. The leader had a knife and started slashing and stabbing anything he could find. He's the one who left the knife in Trapper's thigh."

"I see. Shouldn't the charges be the other way around? That sounds like an obvious attempt to inflict harm on multiple people and a stab wound is at a minimum assault with a deadly weapon," replied Nick.

"You'd think. Trapper immobilized the guy. Put him in a chokehold until the guy went limp. Then he stopped breathing."

"Shit."

"I know. Just like that guy on the NY subway years ago. Anyway, Trapper was a medic in the army."

"Right, I remember."

"He started doing CPR until the EMTs showed up with a defibrillator. They got the guy breathing again. Of course, his thug pal witnessed the whole thing and immediately went to the DA and told a story about how Trapper had intentionally tried to kill his buddy. Even to the point of one of Trapper's friends telling him to stop the choking. All of that is unfortunately true. Trapper's buddy yelled at him to stop."

"Crap. Does he have a lawyer yet? We can help."

Coach laughed. "Don't worry. We have plenty of lawyers courtesy of Howard and Everett. When they heard what was happening, they immediately went into crisis mode. Hell, we had an army of contractors show up the next day to start removing debris as soon as the arson inspectors gathered their evidence. They are fixing the partially burned houses and ready to rebuild the ones that were under construction."

"I knew I liked those guys. What's the next step?"

"I wanted to let you know we are going to do a PR campaign to support Trapper. Get folks on the TV stations and make it clear it was self-defense and if the guy got choked out, it was his own fault. We also have the doctor's saying Trapper could easily have died from the exertion of doing CPR, causing more blood loss from the stab wound."

"Good, let's fight their misinformation with the truth."

"That's the plan. Of course, all the thugs have been released without bail. Except the one who attacked Trapper. He is still in the hospital claiming he has brain damage from his attack. I wanted to let you know we aren't going down quietly and some of this may spill over to you for supporting this effort and Trapper."

"Thanks Coach. This is exactly what we set the TRDF up for. Any idea who funded this?"

"Nope, and since the no bail laws here prevent them from being questioned, my guess is no one will face charges other than the one who fought back. With sympathetic TV coverage, I doubt he gets charged either. What is wrong with our justice system?"

"I know Coach. How's Trapper taking all this?

"He's upset. He feels like he let us and you down."

"You tell him I'd have done exactly the same thing."

"Roger that. Thanks Nick," finished Coach, ending the call.

Nick leaned back in his chair. His fists were clenched. This kind of injustice just boiled his blood. First Dusty, now Trapper. Folks who already have it tough enough being shit on by people not being held accountable for their own actions.

He closed his eyes and began his mantra. His meditation seemed less and less effective as the campaign wore on. Trying to banish his desire to mete out justice himself was becoming impossible. He rarely slept, as his mind worked through innumerable issues. From scenarios to reach more people in the waning weeks before the election, to how to protect his supporters from the increasing flurry of attacks.

Occasionally, his mind was also filled with fantasies of running away from all of this. The only problem was, even his dreams couldn't decide which of the women in his life to take with him.

Chapter 56

"What do we do?" asked Margie.

Denise looked at her. They were in the DC headquarters.

"Frankly, I am not sure. I've never been involved in a campaign with this level of protesting at events. Or this level of uncontrolled grassroots folks. Nick's support is so widespread. It has a mind of its own."

"It doesn't help that we post every event on the web. Makes it easy for the protesters to organize too," offered Margie.

"True, but with the cameras and the invites to the groups, we are covering our ass too. At least we have all these protests on camera."

"Looks like that's working both ways. Who are these 'Gabriel's Angels' groups? They seem to be the ones who are involved in most of the fights at the protests. Responding and retaliating to the words and taunting from the protestors," asked Denise, looking at Steve Gaines.

"Denise, they're a group we sanctioned out of Idaho. It's pretty popular and has recruited folks to support Nick in most states. They have claimed their charter is to protect Nick's supporters from the violent ARL, LGBTQ, and Antifa protesters. Their website is also pretty preachy, 'All smite the wicked' and stuff like that," explained Steve.

"Sounds more like a white supremacist militia," frowned Denise.

"I agree. It's not a good look. The footage all showed our supporters throwing the first punches. Of course, those on our side were all arrested. We used the TRDF to post bail and defend them. All of them said they were part of local Gabriel's Angels' groups," he confirmed.

"Steve, can we issue a directive?" suggested Chuck.

"We can, but you have been to some of these rallies. It is all emotion. When the bad guys are insulting your mothers, wives, daughters, calling you Nazis, it makes their blood boil," shrugged Steve.

"I know, it's difficult," sighed Chuck.

"The other problem is it always couched as race and hate related. It doesn't help these Gabriel's Angels' are predominantly white. They're pretty redneck as well. Sorry, but I'm just saying what the liberal media says about these attacks," pointed out Margie in an apologetic tone.

"No harm in pointing out the obvious. Nick needs to do something," agreed Denise. "Let's get him."

#

"What do you need me to do?" asked Nick, joining the team.

"We were saying you need to give some orders to your white supremacist militia followers to tone down the attacks," ordered Denise.

"Good morning to you as well. Things getting out of hand at some rallies? We're still filming everything, correct?"

"Yes. We get the folks out of jail on bail and provide defense attorneys and use the footage," replied Steve.

"Good. What's the problem?"

"Some of the violence is instigated from our side. We throw the first punches," answered Earl, earning a look from Denise.

"Our folks are getting pissed off being yelled at by Antifa, ARL, and climate change activists? The ones gluing themselves to roads preventing pregnant women from getting to hospitals? Groups burning down Redemption villages? Shooting and running over cops at traffic stops. Breaking into stores in packs. These are who we punch?" asked Nick.

"All good professor, but you don't watch ANC or FLCN or get your news from social media. Everyone else does. It looks like you are condoning your lunatic fringe to commit hate crimes every time they react to words with violence," argued Denise, her voice rising.

"What do you want me to do? I'm already proposing a non-violent solution. If we revoke the charter of these Angels, does it stop?"

Steve shook his head no.

"Bob?" asked Nick, looking at the Colonel.

The gray-haired, still crew cut ex-Colonel looked at Nick for a second. "You know what this is, right?"

"Of course. But it changes nothing. If not this way, it would happen some other way."

"Ok, what the hell are you two talking about?" asked a pissed off Denise, not understanding their conversation.

Nick nodded at Bob.

"It's called counter-insurgency. Someone is paying folks to disrupt our protests from within our own grass-roots organizations. Force us to react to lots of little fires. Distract us from the primary goal. They are using the most stereotypical anti-government, anti-liberal looking demographic they can find to publicly do exactly what they say the right-wing has been doing for generations. Except now it is us," recited Bob.

"Exactly," responded Nick. He looked at Steve.

"How many additional charters have been requested for these Gabriel's Angels? The last couple of weeks? Ten, twenty?" asked Nick.

"Thirty in the last two weeks. In thirty different states."

"When did the violence from these guys start?" asked Bob.

"Last two weeks, we have seen a spike. First time we have been the instigator," replied Margie, looking at notes.

"Always against ARL too, I bet. White on Black," noted Nick.

"And gay," added Margie, nodding.

"Any charges elevated to hate crime status yet?"

"Not yet, but the press sure makes a point that our followers are getting pissed you are still so low in the polls and are taking it out on the LGBTQ and ARL protestors. Even Blackbird is saying you are attracting the far-right wing lunatics from his party. He says good riddance to them. Lucky for us, he includes everyday religious conservatives in that group too, not just the supremacists," added Margie.

Chuck spoke up as Denise was getting ready. "Doesn't matter. Nick, this is giving them fodder. Every news item about you is negative now. The Marine, these fights at the events. Right or wrong, white against black. Your statements on *The Sunday Hour* about amnesty of some type. They conveniently forget you said 'over decades'. Trapper almost killing the arsonist. You throw in Lexi and Blackbird, and their surrogates appearing on endless news shows trashing you without you going on any except *Tommy* to rebut. Your silence is seen as fear. They figure you aren't out denying them, so it must be true," ended Chuck.

Nick looked around the room and could tell they all agreed.

"Don't I get any credit for persuading the parents of the slain deputies to at least wait on the results of the justice system before speaking further?" responded Nick.

"You know you don't. Everyone assumes you bought them off. NWN never even posted the footage. Did you see any articles after? Were there any appearances after Eileen cold cocked Connie?" challenged Denise, her tone rising.

"There weren't and we are spending TRDF money to defend her from the lawsuits there, as frivolous as they may be. There were a few articles about that. 'Rabid Turner supporter assaults news anchor', that got the most views out of all of that. They barely even mentioned she was the mother of Eva," Denise was clearly frustrated.

"What do you want me to do?" repeated Nick angrily.

Those in the room tensed, having never seen this tone from Nick.

Denise was not intimidated in the slightest. She was well schooled at delivering bad news to candidates in prior campaigns. She'd been yelled at, cursed out, had things thrown at her, and even fired on the spot for delivering bad news or challenging her candidate.

"She held up a hand. First, post something and tell your supporters no more violence. Second, tell these Gabriel's Angels to fuck off. Threaten to stop defending them if they get arrested. We are the sane ones. We don't need to stoop to these tactics. Third, ask for some donations. It is going to be a near thing to make it through at the pace we're going. The slightest hiccup, again, slowing down funding and we are laying folks off the last week in October. Fourth, tell people to start telling the truth to pollsters." Denise paused, thinking of more asks.

"Is that all?" asked Nick, leaning back, his anger under control.

"Don't push it. I could go on all night. No more controversial stances. We are less than five weeks from the election. You need to be on message. And you need to be everywhere. We need everyone who is a Nick Turner supporter driving folks to the polls. Helping harvest ballots where it is legal. The grass roots folks have to hit the pavement. Your only hope is turnout. It has to be through the roof. Everyone who hasn't voted in twenty years has to cast a vote for Nick Turner."

"Now how hard was that?" smiled Nick.

"So, you'll do all that?" asked Denise, warily.

"Except the polling. Two more weeks. It is still too soon."

Denise refused to give in. "Nick, the ballots are already in the mail in some states, shortly in all the others. If our numbers don't rise, making people think they aren't wasting their vote on you, we risk losing a bunch of the early, older voters to Blackbird. No one donates to a losing cause."

"Denise, we got this far. You have to trust me. It is October in a few days. We all know what that means. I don't want to open the spigot until we can turn it into a waterfall," replied Nick cryptically.

"What do you know?" she asked suspiciously.

"Nothing concrete. I have a gut feeling. You know Lexi. She will not trust fate and her polling lead. Everyone, be on your toes and on the lookout for attacks on all flanks. I promise you Denise, I will release the polling restrictions soon. Promise."

Denise stared, as did everyone else in the room, at the 'parents arguing'. Eventually, Chuck broke the silence.

"Let's go film a short of Nick begging for money, before he breaks his promise," getting up as Nick scowled at him.

Chapter 57

Luc sat in a small hotel in the outskirts of Geneva, Switzerland. For the last two weeks, he'd been staking out the multi-story building nearby. This was the destination of the autistic 'students' Lauzon had been graduating to the Doctor's care these last few years.

This was where the suicide bomber who had killed Jean Paul Gaspard had been trained. Something was happening. Large panel vans had been arriving and departing for the last week. He figured this might have something to do with the events outside Lyon. Eventually, even de Monfort would figure out none of the bodies were Luc.

After fleeing in Lauzon's Maserati, he drove south to Marseille, a town he knew well. Ditching the car in a parking garage, disabling the battery, GPS, and removing the license plates. Then he holed up in a cheap hotel, far from the tourists and prying eyes.

Opening Lauzon's box, inside was €100,000, along with passports and several large file folders full of notes and records. With the additional cash, he could now hide easily. He spent a few days in Marseille, moving from hotel to hotel each day while he reviewed the documents.

The notes showed Lauzon was approached and offered a preposterous amount of money to locate specific autistic patients exhibiting particular traits. As he read, it became clear these records were what the rolling pin wielding thug was trying to destroy.

Lauzon had scoured the hospitals in France, offering to take over the care of these autistic patients, paying the hospitals to transfer them to his private facility. His staff were trained to care for the patients in ways to determine their suitability for 'graduation' to a facility in Switzerland.

It was all cold-blooded and precise. The fact these were human beings seemed of little relevance to Lauzon or this 'Doctor'. He'd sent over fifteen prospective 'students' to Switzerland over the last few years. Luc eventually pieced together information leading to the exact location of the facility in Switzerland.

Boarding a train, he headed to Geneva, continuing to use cash. Entering the country using one of Lauzon's fake passports. He would leave no trail for de Monfort or Chaumont to follow.

Luc dyed his brown hair blonde and grew out his beard to further disguise his appearance. Having worked undercover many times in his service at Interpol, he knew how to watch without being seen. To move without being noticed, and to vary his appearance, clothing, and mannerisms. To not attract attention. He had the time and the target. He would watch and learn.

#

Luc saw an older gentleman going in and out, always with two bodyguards in proximity. After a week of vans arriving and going, there were none in the last twenty-four hours. The older gentlemen lived nearby and walked home, shadowed by his escorts every evening.

There was a security system, but not any that looked too sophisticated. No cameras appeared to be focused on the building during his casual observations, circling the building several times.

Sensing his prey was closing up shop, Luc knew he needed to hurry. Approaching a dark corner of the building at 3am and throwing his rappel over the edge of the fire escape ladder. Climbing to the second story ladder and to the roof of the three-story building.

There was a lone door hatch on the roof. Using his lock pick tools to open the padlock. Raising the hatch slowly, listening intently for the telltale sign of alarms or a distant siren announcing a silent alarm to law enforcement.

Waiting, he counted to thirty, then sixty, and finally ninety. When there was neither, he climbed down the ladder into a utility closet on the upper floor of the building.

Slowly opening the door from the roof access closet to a hallway, glancing each way in the darkness before going right. Making notes of the layout of the building as he progressed, the light from his small flashlight illuminating the corridor. The hallway intersected with a larger one going the length of the building.

A sign on the left read dormitories. He pushed through this door. A hallway showed a series of doors with glass windows and locks. Flipping the switch in one of these, not sure what he would see. Looking through, he saw what looked like a prison cell but with a carpeted floor, a cot and a sink, toilet and what looked like a TV monitor mounted on the wall. The room was empty. There was no sign of recent human habitation.

Luc continued down the hallway. Each was the same, though some showed more recent habitation with books and other personal items in several of the rooms. Most were simple books one would give to a 10-year-old. He checked his watch.

Eleven minutes so far. Continuing to wander, he located a stairwell. Down on the second floor were more rooms, similar to hotel rooms. These rooms were larger and without locked doors. Perhaps these were the quarters of the staff? No one was home. It was clear they had only recently vacated the premises. They were indeed shutting down.

Luc, mindful of the time, began to quickly search the rest of the facility. Locating another stairwell, and headed to the ground floor. There he found a kitchen, which still had some provisions in the refrigerators and freezers. There was also a cafeteria, capable of holding thirty. Finally, he came to a wing that looked more medical.

There were examination rooms, and a full operating room, that thankfully did not look to have been used recently. Luc had half expected to find a fully outfitted dungeon torture chamber. Arriving at the last corner of the building were several offices. The last one was the one he was looking for.

This appeared to be the office of the older gentleman. He was in a couple of pictures on the wall, receiving some sort of award. The men with him in several of the pictures caused Luc to open his eyes in surprise. He took out his phone and took a few pictures. Looking around the room, there were several file cabinets and a desk.

Luc sat down at the desk, opening the drawers. One was locked. Going to the file cabinets, which were also locked. His lock picks would not work on these. Contemplating his situation, his intent was to go in and out undetected.

Since it was clear, they were closing up shop. Luc found a screwdriver in his backpack and went to work on the file cabinets. There was no hiding this kind of abuse. As he opened the cabinets, they were full of named file folders. Hundreds of them. Others with code names. He took several with his gloved hands and put them in his backpack.

Luc turned to the desk, using his screwdriver on the desk drawer. After much abuse, he popped the lock and pulled the door open. There were other files in here, some showing their age with yellow edges and faded writing, again mostly code names. One he recognized. It made his blood run cold.

Taking the entire contents of the desk drawer, he placed them in his backpack as well. Looking at the computer, he shook his head. There was no way he could carry all the files and the computer. Without Annie, he did not know what he would have done with it anyway. Glancing at his watch, turning to go, Luc intentionally dropped an empty file folder on the top of the desk. He had been here too long already.

Retracing his path, he made his way back to the roof access. Turning off all the lights as he did, not that it would matter once the owner of the office arrived. Back to the roof and slipping back down the side of the building, Luc flipped his rappel line loose. Walking calmly back down the road, he had no idea the impact the information he had in his backpack would have on history.

Chapter 58

The Doctor sat in his office sweating as he waited for the call to complete. He never initiated contact. It was always the other way around. Eventually, he heard the familiar pops and clicks of the security his benefactor always employed when they talked.

"Yes," answered the metallic voice of Pavlovich.

"There has been a break in."

There was a pause on the other side as the Doctor waited.

"You were shut down, correct? The subjects already dealt with?"

"Yes."

""What information could they have taken? Did they try to take your computer and did the protective measures fail to engage?"

"They only took paper. No one touched the computer. The explosives did not go off."

"Why did they not attempt to take the computer and its data? Strange. What was on paper? You know you were told to confine your records to the computer for expressly this reason. There was to be no trail of your efforts, or of our plans."

"There is nothing. Only patient records, fake names, and medical histories. Nothing of note," lied the Doctor, convincingly he hoped.

"And yet I detect fear in your voice. You would not have reached out to me without sufficient reason or concern."

"He broke into my desk and took *my* files. Old files. These do not pertain to the current plans, but there is some information in there that may be of note. To certain people."

"He?"

"The thief was Luc Gauthier."

"How do you know?"

The Doctor could hear the concern and anger even with the masking technology.

"We kept the facility free of security cameras for the same reasons we wired your computer with motion sensors to explode if anyone removed it from the floor. How do you know it is him?" demanded the voice.

"He left an empty file folder on the top of my desk. Only he would know to do that."

Again, the pause on the phone was long.

"You will leave today and return to your laboratory. The building will be destroyed immediately. Do you understand?"

"Yes. What can Gauthier do?"

"Nothing. He just signed his death warrant," said the disembodied voice, sounding menacing.

"I will return to my lab and supervise our projects there."

"Doctor, this was a mistake. I am not usually lenient in my punishment for mistakes. Do not assume your unique position and my needs afford you protection from my displeasure. I have the formulas to all of your elixirs. It is only the hope of breakthroughs soon that keeps you breathing. Understood?"

The Doctor was glad he was not on video, his shiver undetected.

"Understood. I shall not disappoint." The call ended. The Doctor leaned back in his seat, looking at the empty desk drawer. His memory was not what it used to be. He brought his files so he could refer to them. Only the more recent projects were limited to the computer. He closed his eyes, remembering what was in the drawer. Most of it would mean nothing to Gauthier.

He merely recognized the code name from his prior investigations that had cost him his family. The actual contents of the file were meaningless. But if he looked hard enough, there were hints and fragments someone could put together of other activities, which could have repercussions.

He could only hope *that* person, who could put it all together, never saw the information. The Doctor leaned forward now, looking at the computer tower. All he had to do was attempt to lift it and it would all be over. He could join *his* wife and children, dead now for decades.

He could end his servitude. Guilt for their death was long since purged. But remorse and revenge? He took a deep breath and summoned his remaining staff. It was time to remove any remaining evidence and vacate the location. Operation *Esprit Simple*, was now ended.

#

Roland was in his office in Lexi's campaign headquarters when his secure satellite phone rang.

"One moment," he answered as he shut his door. "Yes."

"Gauthier found the Doctor," said Pavlovich.

Roland closed his eyes, his body tensing. "Is he dead?"

"No, but apparently our absent-minded Doctor brought some of his paper files with him to this assignment and Gauthier now has them. I do not know what was in them, but he was scared enough to admit to this lapse of judgement."

"This is my fault. I was overconfident that my plan was foolproof. I will clean this up. I assume you want Gauthier neutralized once and for all? What about the Doctor?" asked Roland.

"We have too many missions underway to which the Doctor and his 'skills' are critical. I delivered a warning. It should suffice. As for Gauthier, yes, he must be neutralized in case there is anything in the material he pilfered. Find him, end him, and recover the files. I too want to know what information our Doctor has been documenting."

"Understood."

Chapter 59

The sprawling Morstead resort in the Shenandoah valley west of Washington, DC, had hosted this meeting in years past. The entire private and exclusive resort was reserved for the meeting. The perimeter was secured by private security, augmented by many of the attendees' own security teams. This weekend's gathering was further enhanced by the United States Secret Service.

The Konigschloss Group was a who's who of world elites who met once a year to discuss the globalization of the world. Similar in style to Bilderberg, this meeting was truly exclusive and entirely focused on conserving the planet through a united governance approach. There were no reporters or celebrities. Only a select few knew this forum existed.

Lexi was in attendance again this year. She worked the room during the cocktail reception. She'd received an exclusive invitation to join the group a decade prior when it became clear her political rise would put her in a position to make American policy happen. The fact she was also the granddaughter of a prior member helped with her selection.

No wives, husbands, girlfriends, or mistresses. Just the rich, powerful, and global elite. All sworn to secrecy. There were no notes, no recordings, and no devices allowed in the meetings. Most had arrived by private jets at obscure airports spread around the countryside. Lexi was one of the few women in attendance this year among the 100 in the room.

She was the queen bee, surrounded by her drones. Amongst the sea of men in black tuxedos, Lexi stood out in a blue Chanel chiffon and silk off the shoulder dress, with a deep V displaying ample cleavage. The floor length dress, slit to mid thigh on one side, showed off her legs.

She paired this with open-toed sandals sporting a 3-inch stacked heel, opting for comfort over additional height. As she mingled around the room, she drew the admiring stares of all in attendance.

"Ah Alexis, stunning as always," delivered in a French accent from a distinguished-looking gentleman with gray hair, mustache, and goatee. He oozed sophistication as he took her hand and raised it to his lips.

"Count, nice to see you, as always. How is Switzerland these days?" asked Lexi with a sweet smile. The Count was an actual Count many times removed from any court. In charge of one of the largest consortiums in the world. He controlled massive telecommunications, shipping, airline, and satellite technologies, among many other industries.

"Boring as ever, so perfect," laughed the Count in a deep voice.

"And the Countess?" asked Lexi with a mischievous smile.

"She is, of course, paying me back for leaving her this weekend by buying out Milan," said the Count with a frown.

"This is the price to pay for marrying such a young beauty," said Lexi as she walked away, leaving the Count smiling and remembering their own trysts so many years ago. The price of these had been exerting significant influence in her first senate campaign. Alexis Smythe-Thomas gave nothing away for free.

Lexi was trying to make her way across the room but was frequently stopped, often by well-wishers and those seeking to be seen talking to her. Even in this elite group, perception was still of value in negotiation. Looking to be friendly with the soon to be most powerful woman in the world would be useful.

She said hello to Sir Percival Lowry, the Australian Mining magnate who asked about her health and that of the President. She next had to say hello to one of the few women present, Lady Elaine Robinson DeWynter. Recently widowed and finding herself the chairwoman of a European manufacturing empire at the tender age of 83.

She was kind, but her gaze was sharp and her reputation nearly as fierce. Rumor had it one of her late husband's paramours had required a dozen plastic surgeries to repair the damage Lady DeWynter had inflicted on her face with a horsewhip during a hunt.

As Lexi continued to work her way across the room towards her target, she exchanged hellos with Carlton Alexander, the legendary chairman of a powerful international energy syndicate with both Astor and Rothschild pedigree in his lineage. Carlton was a large, dark money contributor to the Party coffers in exchange for continued restrictions on American energy development and exploration.

Just as she was getting close, a short, young, and eager Indian blocked her path. Sanjay Chakrabarti was the leader of one of the wunderkind companies of India, making billions on security and surveillance technologies. He was a self-made man, a profligate spender, playboy, and absolutely insufferable.

It was also his first time at a KSG event. Sanjay was working the room like a hooker at a Congressional retreat. He was donating obscene amounts of money to the Party coffers through his PAC. While also sourcing the surveillance products the Chinese were busily installing in their insatiable appetite for surveilling all aspects of their citizens' lives.

"Sanjay, nice to see you," said Lexi, holding out a hand.

"Lexi, may I say you look good enough to devour tonight," leered Sanjay in his singsong accent, having never studied proper English.

Lexi gave him a look. Sanjay either ignored it or did not understand the inappropriateness of his comment and her reaction.

"Are you enjoying the party" asked Lexi, hoping to disengage.

"It is quite the who's who. A little light on female representation," Sanjay replied, surveying the crowd of old men in tuxedos.

"I agree. Perhaps you can turn over your companies to a female CEO? It would be quite the statement and help advance the cause of female leadership in your country. You could be an inspiration to a generation of entrepreneurial Indian women," suggested Lexi sweetly.

He laughed nervously. "One day perhaps. A pleasure to see you, Madame Vice President," replied Sanjay, disentangling himself from the feminist discussion Lexi intended to have with him.

Lexi smirked. "Men," she said under her breath. Finally, she approached two men wearing perfectly tailored tuxedos in one corner of the room. They couldn't have been more different. The tall one was six foot six at least, muscular, and handsome, with a head of light brown hair and deep blue eyes twinkling as Lexi approached.

The second was a wizened old man standing maybe five foot six, hunched over with sparse hair on his head. His amber eyes were so intense with fire, no one could hold their gaze for long. He spoke first.

"Alexis, you are a sight for all to see. A splash of color in this dull room full of dull people who believe the world revolves around them," greeted Maksim Pavlovich. "Your gown is spectacular."

Lexi did a mini twirl. "Max, how kind," she said, leaning in to brush her lips against each cheek. They felt like wrinkled parchment.

"Do you know Archer?" asked Max, looking up at the tall handsome man in his mid-fifties.

"I don't believe I have had the pleasure. Archer Collins," he answered in a deep voice, taking her hand and brushing it to his lips.

"The pleasure is all mine," said Lexi devilishly.

"Don't get any ideas, Lexi. Archer is queer as a three-dollar bill," said Max with a laugh.

"Sadly, he is correct. You are not my type," conceded Archer, with no hint of anger at how Max referred to him.

"I like challenges Archer. Perhaps you have never met the right woman?" purred Lexi seductively. "How is it we have not met before? I am sure I would remember *you*." This last bit drawn out for effect.

"Archer has been out in the field, literally," laughed Max. "He is the scion of the Collins-Davis-Gordon agri-business conglomerate."

"Ah, CDG. I didn't know it was a family company. Your land and farm holdings around the world are enormous," observed Lexi.

"CDG feeds the world," commented Archer with a grin.

"You clean up nice." Lexi responded, not giving up.

"I have unfortunately been pulled from the manure laden fields to the boardroom by my father. He retired, and the board voted me chairman. Over my strenuous objections, I might add."

"Prefer to keep your hands dirty Archer?" asked Lexi, lightheartedly, her icy blue eyes dancing.

"Call me Archie. Yes, I do," responded Archie, holding her gaze.

"My dear, how is the old boy?" inquired Max, changing direction.

"He's fine. He sends his regards, of course," sighed Lexi.

"I bet he does," doubted Max in a tone, clearly implying he did not send his best wishes. "How's the campaign? We get little info here."

Lexi laughed a hearty laugh as Max and Archie both smiled.

"Really Max? None of your twenty-seven NGOs, all of which are based or spend a majority of their money in the US, send you updates? Your hedge funds are US based and you probably have a direct feed into every major newsroom on the planet. To imply you don't know exactly what is going on is disingenuous. In fact, I am assuming your sure hand is on the tiller of many of your NGO's spending supporting my campaign," said Lexi knowingly.

"I would not want to get in trouble with any of your many regulatory agencies. Being accused of collaborating with a candidate on how my non-profits direct their contributions and spending for candidates," smiled Max in a crooked, yellow-toothed grin.

"But of course," smiled Lexi in return.

"As always, you see right through me," said Max, holding up his arms. His tux jacket, though perfectly tailored, still seemed to hang on him.

"I think that is my cue to mingle. I need to network as my father would expect of the new Chairman of CDG. Madame Vice President, it has been a pleasure," concluded Archie.

"Please call me Alexis, or even Lexi."

"Alexis, it shall be then. It is more suitable for such a beautiful and capable woman," said Archie, bowing to Lexi with a twinkle in his own eye this time at their game.

"Are you sure you're not interested? I would make it worth your while," goaded Lexi as Max looked on with a smile.

"Ah, the temptation, but I fear your efforts would be wasted."

"Maybe for you, but I would risk it," laughed Lexi. "I'm sure I'll see you around this weekend."

"Indeed. Max, good evening," nodded Archie.

Max lifted his glass in response.

"He is luscious. What a waste," commented Lexi, watching as he walked away. She turned back to Max. "Are you positive?"

"I am. His father was furious. He was expected to father the next generation of Collins and now he will be the last. His father even suggested he marry to have a child and continue to dally on the side, ala the old Hollywood arranged marriages. He refused. That's why he was surprised when he was made chairman. His father wanted a Collins in charge rather than let either Davis or Gordon put their lines on the throne," explained Max.

"I see," said Lexi, turning back to Max. "Shall we sit?"

"I am not as frail as I appear, but yes, we can sit. You are in the heels after all," noted Max.

"These are like sneakers compared to what I normally wear," laughed Lexi, sitting and arranging her dress so she showed her leg to the rest of the room.

"Lexi, how have you managed to not get murdered by some jealous wife after all these years?" wondered Max aloud with a guffaw.

"Because their wives don't want to lose the Botox and plastic surgery, their husbands pay for. I never choose a man whose wife has the money," said Lexi nonchalantly. She waved over a waiter. "Macallen 30, two ice cubes. Max?" asked Lexi.

"Pellegrino, with ice, please."

"Always the teetotaler. Max, you are such a bore," noted Lexi dangling a sandal.

"What is up with this Turner fellow?" asked Max, turning serious.

"He is a little snot, that's all," fired back Lexi quickly with a scowl.

Max laughed a deep, knowing laugh, earning a stern look from Lexi whose own eyes could be almost as piercing as his.

"He turned you down, didn't he? Is he gay too?"

"No, he is not gay, at least as far as I know. Yes, he appeared to be immune to my charms and any offers of power. He is a fucking boy scout," growled Lexi as the waiter appeared with their drinks.

Max thanked him and Lexi simply slugged down half her drink.

"Do we need to be worried? We have a lot riding on you winning. I've spent 100s of millions supporting your American Progressives. My return on those investments has been well below expectations. Now I have spent even more putting progressive radicals in every elected statewide office I can buy. Attorney generals, prosecutors, district attorneys, secretaries of state, election officials and even police chiefs and sheriffs now. There is little more I can do. You had better win or we," he rolled his eyes to include the room, "will find another way to accomplish our goal," pointed out Max.

"Is that a threat?" snapped Lexi, preparing to respond with anger.

Max fixed her with that stare without saying a word. She looked away and took another sip of her ultra smooth and ultra expensive scotch.

"I do not threaten. I act. You are in this group for a reason. You know our goals. Our plans. So did your boss. He failed us. America is the last firewall. It must be removed. You can be a true influencer in our group. To help us achieve our goals. Just get the job done. What else do you need? I have arranged for as much money to flow your way as possible. I used my influence to ensure all the good Opposition candidates stayed out of the race. Blackbird is weak. You have his secret. Use it," ordered Max. "Where is the spanner in the works this time?"

"Excuse me" asked Lexi confused.

"Sorry, you Americans call them wrenches. Where is the wrench in the works to mess things up? Is it Turner? Is it someone or something else? Any of your skeletons getting out? Apparently, it's harder and harder to assassinate anyone anymore with all the cameras, cellphones and now it seems accurate shots," opined Max in a tone suggesting Lexi had tried to kill Turner.

"It wasn't me. I figured it was you or one of our friends here being impatient," observed Lexi.

"Hardly. Trying to kill him only made him stronger. I assure you when I order extermination, they do not get up," extolled Maksim in such a sinister tone, Lexi had to suppress a shiver. She had no doubt he'd ordered many. She knew this could be her fate if she lost this election.

"We have it under control. Turner is a distraction. He is getting a following, but his polling is still in the low single digits."

"Is it?"

"What does that mean?" asked Lexi suspiciously.

"The Party does not have a good track record of accurate polling."

"Our polling is great. They report exactly what we want them to hear," retorted Lexi with a snort.

"Precisely my point. You are so used to instructing the pollsters to give the results you want. They don't know how to do their job any longer. Look what happened before. Your polling was all wrong, and we suffered an enormous setback. We spent all this money on judges and DAs and secretaries of state, to cover our asses when we have to be more obvious. We need to make this one stick and slink back to the shadows to reap the benefit of your progressive platform. There cannot be a one world viewpoint if the United States continues to espouse personal freedom. Especially when that freedom comes at the expense of order and our planet. It must be stopped before we destroy our habitat completely. Don't fail us, Madame Vice President," finished Max, getting up and nodding to Lexi.

She sat for another minute and finished her drink. Pasting her smile back on, she continued her rounds amongst the most powerful elites in the world. Throughout the course of the weekend, these people would discuss the globalist goal of uniting beyond sovereign borders and creating global governance of all aspects of society with unified economies to maintain order and prosperity for the civilized world. The fruition of over a century of planning and manipulation was now upon the world.

The weekend culminated in a speech from Lexi where she assured attendees America was on a path to committing to these global priorities. Working in concert with the leaders of the world to suppress individual priorities in exchange for becoming world citizens. Complying with what was best for the world rather than what was best for the individual.

America had become a behemoth on the backs of the world, and now it was her turn to give back. Once the election was over, Lexi promised the first 100 days of her administration would be paradigm changing. Starting America on an irreversible course toward joining the global community once and for all.

Only as part of this community could America apply her resources to solving the problems of the globe. Climate Change, overpopulation, water scarcity, and systemic racism. This would also enable the eradication of those who stood in the way of progress. The anarchists and religious terrorists causing so much mayhem and destruction. The world would rejoice at the calm they would bring. Lexi finished her speech to a standing ovation from the crowd of globalists. Archie stood and clapped, as did Max and, among others, Senator Baxter Banks, the only other elected US official in the room.

Chapter 60

Judge Harris sat behind her dais. Dusty and Duane were on one side of the courtroom. The district attorney and her aides sat at another table. The bailiff entered the courtroom, holding the door as the jury filed back into the courtroom taking their seats.

"Has the jury reached a verdict?" asked Judge Harris.

The jury foreman, a middle-aged Hispanic man, stood and faced the judge. "We have, your honor."

The cameras, allowed into the courtroom for the verdict, arranged themselves to catch the response of as much of the crowd as possible and the defendant. The assembled crowd in the room, consisting mainly of members of the press and most of the families of the victims, all held their breath, waiting for the result to be read.

"Very well, if the defendant would please rise to hear the verdict."

Dusty dutifully rose, standing ramrod straight as he had on so many occasions as a Marine. The jury foreman unfolded his piece of paper and put on his reading glasses.

"On the two counts of voluntary manslaughter, the jury finds the defendant not guilty." The members of the gathered press let out collective comments of astonishment. The widow who had lost her husband and child from the gunfire penetrating the walls of Dusty's apartment sobbed and put her head on the shoulder of Eileen Herrara. The judge banged her gavel. "Order please. Continue."

The foreman nodded. "On the six charges of murder in the first-degree, the jury finds the defendant not guilty of all charges." This time, the gasps were accompanied by shouts of outrage. 'What. How. No way,' came cries of disbelief from the audience. The families of the lost loved ones hugged each other, crying as the results were announced. The judge banged her gavel.

"Order in the court, please!"

The bailiff took the piece of paper and handed it to the judge.

"I thank the jury for their service. This case is closed, and court is adjourned. Mr. Ingram, you are free to go." She banged the gavel as the crowd murmured loudly.

Dusty remained standing at attention and simply said, "No," in a loud and firm tone.

The crowd stopped talking. The judge turned to him.

"Excuse me? I said you are free, Mr. Ingram. The trial is over."

"This is not right. I don't accept this." He turned to the jury, then to the families in the first few rows of the courtroom. "I have to pay. I killed your sons and daughter. Your husband and child died because I fought back. This can't be right. It is not right," Dusty was quivering as he made his statement. Duane stood up next to him, putting his hand on Dusty's shoulder.

"It wasn't your fault. It was an awful accident. All of those decisions, with their flaws and mistakes, made this happen. You did not murder anyone," he said calmly, worried Dusty was going to breakdown in the courtroom.

He stood there, shaking his head. As some in the crowd murmured louder again, and before Dusty could say anything, Eileen stepped forward. She walked to him. He once again stood ramrod straight, prepared for whatever she would do in retaliation. The judge glanced at the bailiff, who took a couple of steps closer to them.

"Dusty. We know the facts now. All of us. We know you only did what you were trained to do. You defended yourself. Our Eva was also doing what she thought was her duty too. It was an accident. A horrible accident. You are not to blame. They put you in an impossible situation," she said, waving her arm toward the DA.

"Any of us would have done the same in your shoes. I forgive you. We all forgive you," again she waved her arm, this time to encompass the other families. She wrapped her arms around him as he sobbed.

The families in the audience came forward in a show of support. Some in the crowd started yelling. "See, he even admits he is a murderer." Saying he just got away with killing eight people with no consequence. Dusty shook loose and turned to the judge before she could leave.

"Your honor, please. Don't do this. This is not justice," he pleaded.

She looked confused. "I don't understand. You are not guilty of the crimes charged. A jury of your peers has listened to the evidence and come to this conclusion. Justice *is* served. There is nothing else I can do."

"I accept your forgiveness," he turned to look at the surrounding families. "Even though I don't believe I deserve it. It doesn't change the fact they are dead because of me. I need to pay. Where do I go? What do I do? I have no job or a home to return to." He pointed out the door. "They have ruined any chance at a life I might have. I am not innocent in their eyes. They clearly don't agree with the verdict."

The judge took her glasses off and looked at Dusty. "I am sorry. I realize your life is forever changed." She looked with disdain at the now open courtroom doors, the reporters being held back by police. The media held dozens of cameras, all pointed into the courtroom to capture these moments. "I am afraid I have no other advice. Except to live your life. I wish you luck," she said as she exited the court to her chambers.

Dusty, Duane, and the families left the court to a bank of reporters shouting questions at him, asking if he really disagreed with the verdict. Dusty did not respond. Duane turned to the assembled reporters.

"The facts were allowed to be heard. The mistakes that caused these events to occur were exposed. My client is not guilty of murder in the first degree. He fully acknowledges he killed the children of all these parents assembled behind me. They have forgiven him. The reality is this will happen again if egregious mistakes made are not corrected. My ask, our ask," he nodded at the parents assemble behind him and Dusty. "Is that you use your incredible influence to right these wrongs," said Duane, relishing this moment where he finally could speak about those who really made this tragedy possible.

"Use it to pressure the prosecutors to examine the Red Flag laws. Question the judge and system that allows approval of no-knock warrants without proper due diligence. Examine and demand changes to the processes, allowing the incorrect address of the perpetrator to be used on six sets of documents with no oversight or double checking. Finally, this was all set off by a swatting incident. Where is the punishment for this? Where are the charges? Do this and I will be impressed."

They started yelling at the parents if they agreed with the verdict. Eileen Herrara stepped forward and grabbed Dusty's hand. "Shame on all of you. We have told you we do. We have seen in our hearts to forgive Dusty. He was defending himself after he was put in an impossible position. We agree with Mr. Cooper. Pursue those who made this happen. They are the guilty ones. Ask the Colorado Governor who continues to push these laws. Leave Dusty alone," she said with the fierce tone of a mama protecting her child.

Dusty broke down and Eileen hugged him. As the reporters continued to shout questions, the other parents formed a circle around Dusty, leading him through the crowd of reporters into the courthouse and away from the public areas.

Chapter 61

"I'll be damned," said Mel, watching the verdicts announced live on ANC. "Unfrickinbelievable." He shook his head, holding his phone for the inevitable text or call from his irate boss.

#

"Are you kidding me?" asked Chuck, turning on the TV in his office in DC. "Sure, I am watching it right now. He said what?" Chuck listened as Margie explained what Dusty had said in the courtroom.

#

Nick sat in his office in Denver, going through documents about grass roots efforts. Again, impressed with the organizational skills and clarity Steve Gaines had brought to managing the efforts of his various volunteer groups. He was reviewing their finances, get out the vote, and registration efforts. How many people they had directly interacted with, including probable conversion rates. It was all very professional.

"Come in," he yelled at the knock on his door. Margie, Jenny, Earl, Greg, Jer, and Denise all filed in with giant smiles on their faces.

"What?"

"Duane did it," said Jenny, beaming.

"Not guilty?" asked Nick, sitting up.

"On all counts. The families stood up after and told Dusty they forgave him. It was wonderful for all. A complete sense of closure," said Jenny. "Thank you, Nick. He could not have done it without you."

Nick nodded his head. "Good. A win for the rule of law in a time when so much of it is weaponized. It is nice to see it work."

"Unfortunately, this man's life is ruined," interjected Denise.

Nick looked at her.

"She's right Nick. The cable news and networks are running non-stop smear campaigns calling for retrials, disbarment, and flat out saying the jury got it wrong. 'How could they possibly find a person not guilty of killing the six dead bodies at his feet?', is one of the more tame statements being spewed," noted Margie with disgust. "Social Media is even worse. Full of hateful suggestions."

Nick shook his head, looking at Earl. "He has a chance. What he does with it is his choice alone. Jenny, reach out to Duane and let him know we're here to help Dusty. A job if he needs it, funds from TRDF to help him get back on his feet. I'm sure he has nothing."

"Already have Nick. I will pass on the offer for a job as well. Duane is making sure he has a hotel and some spending money until he decides what he wants to do next," replied Jenny.

"Good. We may also want to find Duane something to do. I am sure there are going to be more court cases. We can team him up with Penrose. Now that is a formidable pair," laughed Nick.

As everyone filed out, Denise and Earl stayed behind.

"Nick, I owe you a huge apology. You were right. I was wrong. I didn't trust your judgment. I certainly didn't trust our justice system to be impartial. You saved that Marine's life. All I could think about was the hit we were going to take," admitted Denise.

"Apology accepted. I assume there are some pundits on our side, pointing out how first-degree murder was an obvious case of overcharging? How the facts are what they are and trying to minimize the mistakes in the processes looked like a coverup?"

"A few, but they have been saying it all along. I think now that the trial is over, it might be good for you to do an interview with Tommy or, even better, Brad Hudson. Maybe a post explaining why you did what you did. There is no tainting the jury pool now that the trial is over."

"We'll see. I am not taking a victory lap for our system working the way it is supposed to."

Denise sighed as she got up to leave.

Earl stared at Nick. "Thank you."

"I know Earl, but what does he have to look forward to? Think about the poor kid from Illinois. And the other cops who were in the right but excoriated by the press for defending themselves and following the law. There is no one to protect them from the violence of digital ink. Our town square and American *Pravda* are going to cancel poor Dusty. Just as they have so many others. Help Jenny with anything Duane might need. The kid needs to know he has people who do care about him."

"Will do. Just so you know, Eileen stood up in court and told Dusty she and all the families forgave him. He wanted the judge to change the sentence. His sense of honor mattered more than the verdict. Even with the families there, saying they forgave him, the guilt is crushing him."

"Duane didn't tell him about the family's change of heart. Or there going on TV to say so?"

"He did not. He was afraid the verdict would be guilty. He wanted to save that revelation for an appeal or to help Dusty deal with it if he was found guilty. Dusty was truly surprised when Eileen approached. I watched the footage. Everyone expected her to slap him."

Nick interrupted. "That shows they have successfully suppressed the footage of the families from the other night. The jury, I expect not to know since they were sequestered, but others should have known."

"I know," agreed Earl. "Instead, she forgave him and hugged him. He lost it. Hibi has the footage. It probably won't be shown on any of the cable channels. Is there anything we can do to shut them up?"

Nick shook his head. "Earl, I assume that was rhetorical? You know, when they don't accept the verdicts they dislike, they turn to digital lynching as the remedy. They are the ultimate judge and jury. They choose who is innocent or guilty. No facts or laws get in their way."

"Maybe you can change that when you become president."

"Not unless I become Emperor Turner the first. We have to take the good with the bad."

"I like the emperor approach better," said Earl as Nick laughed.

#

Dusty sat in his pickup, in the parking lot at the top of the promontory on the Boulder Turnpike. It was a magnificent view of the snow covered back ranges of the Rockies. Boulder, with the red-tiled roofs of the University of Colorado shining in the setting sun, sat nestled against the foothills. Now blazing with the yellow aspen leaves of fall. It was one of the best views in America.

He looked at the fast-food wrappers on the seat of his old pickup. It still hurt when he ate from his poorly healed jaw. He was on his way to a hotel Duane had arranged. With a thousand dollars and a debit card he could use until he decided what he wanted to do and where. Duane told him Senator Turner was offering work on his campaign. He told him to tell the senator he appreciated all he had done. Especially his time spent explaining the facts to the families. To help them heal.

As he looked over the horizon at the setting sun, he reflected on his life. He had been through so much in the war and after and now here he sat. Dusty had never expected to be a free man again. He assumed he would spend his days in prison, paying penance for his deeds.

He no longer woke up every night with Billy Ray dying in his arms. This nightmare was now replaced with the deep brown eyes and the wide pupils of Eva Herrera, staring at him in terror, as he shot her between those eyes.

He picked up the well-worn service pistol they'd returned to him, put it in his mouth, and pulled the trigger.

Part Three

Battle Stations

"Running for President is physically, emotionally, mentally and spiritually the most demanding single undertaking I can envisage, unless it's World War III."

Walter F. Mondale

Chapter 62

"It appears the guilt of his deed was too much for Dusty Ingram to live with. He took his own life yesterday outside Boulder, Colorado. As our viewers know, in a surprise verdict, he had been found not guilty of the charges of murder and manslaughter for the six sheriff's deputies he killed and the husband and baby who died in the crossfire." This was reported in a righteous tone by Diane Paxton, formerly of EXN. Now an anchor for FLCN's midday news program.

"We have Dennis Sims, a former DC police chief, now the head of the Order of the Thin Blue Line police union. Welcome Chief," replied Stuart Adams, Diane's partner on the midday news.

"Thanks for having me on the program," replied Dennis, an overweight white man with graying hair and big glasses.

"Sir, you've been on the program previously to discuss the trial. It's been an eventful couple of days. Your thoughts?" she asked.

"Diane, first, it seems there is cosmic justice, after all. That young man was clearly guilty of killing those deputies. As I said, during the trial, there can be no doubt he killed them. Any excuse for not following their commands to surrender and then to cease firing is unacceptable. That his slick lawyer could convince a jury he should get a pass for murder was the first mistake. The DA botched the prosecution," he said, raising his voice and gesturing with his hands.

"Thankfully, even he understood this and did all the grieving families the courtesy of ending his miserable life." The police chief ended his statement forcefully, as if pronouncing judgement.

Both Diane and Stu were taken aback at his statement.

"Sir, is that the position of your union or your own opinion?"

"I can't speak for all of them Stu, but all those I have spoken to were appalled at the verdict. It was a travesty and shows the decline of our criminal justice system. Turner keeps claiming he wants to return to the rule of law. This was an example of the miscarriage of that very justice."

"Chief, he was tried by a jury of his peers. The evidence showed many mistakes were made, mainly because he was not the target of the raid," replied Diane reluctantly. "Seems to me a charge of involuntary manslaughter might have been more appropriate."

"It doesn't excuse him from taking their lives. There is no fact that changes he shot them. Anything else is irrelevant. I say good riddance, and I genuinely hope the families sleep better, knowing justice has been served."

Stu, a handsome black man in his thirties, tried to change the tone of the conversation.

"Chief, your union has yet to endorse a candidate for president. Can you tell us how you and the union are leaning? Will you be breaking with tradition and endorse the Vice President this go round?"

"Stu, that is for the leaders to decide tomorrow. Two months ago, I would have told you many were leaning toward Turner and his clear support for law enforcement. What I *can* tell you is since his betrayal and support for the Marine, that sentiment shifted dramatically. Even more, once the not guilty verdict came down. Many blame Turner for the verdict."

"It seems the Vice President has an insurmountable lead over Governor Blackbird. It would seem prudent for your union to back the winner," replied Diane, her true feelings more clearly evident now that she was on a left leaning media outlet.

"We'll see Ms. Paxton. It wouldn't surprise me if we endorsed no candidate. Everyone, it seems, is against the cops."

#

"Shit." This from the normally mild-mannered Greg as he watched the TV in the conference room.

Denise shook her head. "The chief is going to have to issue an apology for that statement. It's one thing to disagree with a verdict, but insulting the jury, the judge, the entire criminal justice system, denying mistakes were made that should have prevented the incident and *then* celebrating suicide. Yikes. He must really be pissed."

"Denise, they all are," responded Earl, shaking his head. "I can't tell you the number of my sheriff buddies who have called. None can see beyond the dead deputies."

"At least the jury did," interjected Jenny in a small voice. "Did we do wrong, trying to defend him? He'd still be alive if he was found guilty."

Earl shook his head. "Jenny, don't think that for a second. He wouldn't have lasted long in prison. Inmates love the cop killers, but the guards hate them. Eventually, he would get sideways with the gangs. He wouldn't have gotten any help from the guards and one of the gangs would've killed him. Though I hate to say it, his life was ruined either way. In prison or out."

"What is wrong with our country?" asked Greg in a pissed off tone. "This is just wrong. We have *police chiefs* on TV celebrating an innocent man's suicide, telling us his union agrees with his position. I have been reviewing social media. It is all filth, just like this. #DeathtoDusty had millions of thumbs up before he killed himself. There is no remorse. Did any of these people look at the facts?"

Many around the table looked down. No one answered Greg's rhetorical question.

"It's called lack of moral courage," said Nick, speaking for the first time from his seat at the table. "You're right, Greg. There is something wrong with our society. I am not sure we can fix it, but we can't sit around and complain about it."

"How're you doing, boss?" asked Margie, cautiously.

"Margie, I'm pissed. That man's life was wasted. It reminds me of the gladiators of Rome. Fighting and dying for the pleasure of the rabble in the stands. Our youth is increasingly this rabble. Salivating and spewing hatred to goad others into killing each other for their pleasure. If any of *them* ended up in the pit, they'd pee their pants and die of fright."

"Nick," warned Denise.

"Denise, I want to record a spot for Hibi."

"You shouldn't do things when you're angry," countered Denise.

"She's right," agreed Earl, as the others nodded.

"Nick, Jack Herrera's on EXN right now," blurted Greg, looking at his phone.

They changed the channel to EXN, where Jack was on a feed from his California home talking to Billy McCall.

"Billy, I would offer condolences to Dusty's family, but he had none. Instead, I will give you *my* thoughts. One last time and then I'm done with our American media circus. Understand I'm no longer speaking for all the families, but I think they feel as I do. Thank you for putting me on, but as soon as I saw the crap the former police chief was spewing, I had to respond. Also, if I know Nick Turner, he is about to go online and speak out and I want to stop him. He has already done enough for all of us. It is our turn to help him."

"Ok Jack. Obviously, you saw what chief Sims said. You disagree, I assume, by your tone?"

Jack took a deep breath before speaking. "Billy, I think many know I served in the army. When I did, I swore an oath to protect our country. To abide by the Constitution. To the rule of laws as laid out in that document. We may not always like our criminal justice system and it makes mistakes. It did not in this case. You can be bitter, you can disagree, but the facts spoke for themselves. The chief obviously has forgotten the oath he swore. To protect and to serve. *Us.* He worked for us. He agreed to abide by and enforce these rules. For our benefit. To protect us from evil."

Jack paused, but Billy didn't interrupt.

"He has fixated on the dead deputies, including my daughter, and not the entire facts the trial exposed. We were guilty of the same. After all, we lost our sons and daughter. If anyone had a *right* to ignore the facts, it is us. Once the facts were known, we were forced to understand our anger was misplaced. The system, and a breakdown in processes and sheer incompetence by many, caused the death of our children by putting them in a no-win scenario." Jack paused again, trying to settle down.

"Dusty Ingram, through no fault of his own, was put in the same position. I forgave him and so did my wife, and Jackie and the other families. We are the injured parties. The chief is not. I do not need him standing there spouting hateful rhetoric designed to further weaken our already tenuous commitment to law and order and the justice system. I would ask him to apologize for his hateful commentary." He raised his hands, using them to make his point.

"Most of all, I would like him to apologize for maligning the reputation of an upstanding citizen. A decorated Marine who put himself in the line of fire for eight years to enable our misguided youth to sit around in the safety of their parent's basements or dorm rooms texting out support for #DeathtoDusty. I frankly am ashamed of a large swath of my fellow Americans today. Thank you for your time."

"There you have it. Thanks for your response, Jack. Unfortunately, you're probably right. We are hearing and seeing many of the liberal media channels amplifying the statements of chief Sims."

"Then only God can help our Republic and preserve our future," replied Jack as they went to commercial.

"I guess that takes care of that. We need to send Jack a case of his favorite whiskey," said Earl, exhaling while looking at Nick.

Nick sat staring at the monitor, now a muted commercial.

"Call Duke," ordered Nick.

Earl looked at him, confused, and then started shaking his head.

"NO. Abs-a-fucking-lutely not," replied Earl vehemently. "Nick, Jack just saved your ass. And likely another drop in your polling. I'm stepping into Denise's territory here now. You cannot go out and do this."

"Earl, call him. I want to talk."

"What are you talking about?" asked Denise, pissed and confused again at not knowing what they were discussing.

"Nick wants me to call Duke Wayne. The police chief buddy of mine, who is also co-chairman of the convention of the TBL union. They're meeting tomorrow to decide if they offer an endorsement to the VP. The same union chief Sims is the head of."

"Still don't get it. What are you suggesting?" she asked.

"He wants to talk to them," revealed Earl.

Everyone in the room immediately burst out in agreement that it was not a good idea.

"Nick, you're gonna get killed, maybe literally. You can't convince them. There is nothing you can say. If they are like the chief, it will be downright dangerous," pleaded Earl.

Nick stood up. "Fine, I'll make the call. You can come or not, your choice," replied Nick, looking at Earl as he left the room.

"What the fuck does that mean?" blurted Denise at Nick's back as she turned to look at the pissed off face of Earl.

"It means he is going to go whether or not we like it."

"Is it televised?" asked Margie, fearfully.

"Thankfully no, but word will get out and people with phones will film whatever happens. Geez." Earl shook his head.

"Earl, you've to get him under control. His fuse is burned to the end. We can't suggest anything to him any more without him blowing up," noted Denise, looking at him.

"Denise, I try. He's closing down. Dusty killing himself is the last straw. Now, seeing this pile on in the media, I'm afraid he's just going to lose it completely."

"Earl, if he goes on a rant or does something stupid, we are toast. Talk to him. Where is the speech?" asked Denise.

"Dallas."

"Good, you'll have a couple of hours on the jet. Then he goes to Austin to speak at the Creating Change gathering. That is another tinder box. If he lays into them, the same thing. Talk some sense into him. He needs to be careful, calculated, and in control. He needs to act Presidential. Not emotionally. Only four more weeks..."

Earl stared at Denise in disbelief, shaking his head.

"I have to go arrange for some security in Dallas tomorrow." He stood and left the room.

Denise looked at Greg, Margie, and Jenny. All of them had scared looks on their faces.

"Any updates?"

"I actually had some good news," commented Greg.

"Good, we could use some," nodded Denise.

"We put Nick's spot up asking for money, nothing greater than $100. Then we had the Dusty verdict and all the drama. We've raised $75 million in five days. Denise, we've had donations from 1.5 million people. That's huge. It's still coming in. If for no other reason, we need to make sure he doesn't piss these folks off who are coming back to our side."

"That *is* good news. I guess we'll get paid this month."

Chapter 63

Nick walked onto the stage at the convention center in Dallas where the Thin Blue Line police union was having their gathering. He was immediately met by a chorus of boos and various curse words thrown his way. He grabbed a microphone and stood at the foot of the stage.

There were a thousand police chiefs and various union representatives. They'd spent the last two days ratifying a slate of proposals they would send to Washington. Proposals to improve overall law enforcement capabilities, including better training, diversity, and safety measures for both officers and citizens. They also highlighted how more funding was necessary to restore order in the mostly Party ruled urban cities where crime was out of control.

Nick looked out over the crowd of angry faces.

"First, I read the proposals you've adopted. I agree with every single one of them. All of them. I would do everything I could to make them a reality. How many of you agree with chief Sims? A show of hands please," asked Nick in a controlled tone.

About half the hands in the audience went up.

Nick looked out over the crowd.

"Really. Wow. I would ask how many of you actually bothered to look at the evidence. Or watch the trial. Does it not matter the families spoke about forgiving him once *they* knew the facts?"

"Fuck you!"

This from a policeman standing, yelling, and pointing at Nick.

"He shouldn't have had a fucking gun. God Damn crazy vet. He's why we have these laws. He should've been the target of the raid, even if he wasn't. Look what he did." Some officers near him tried to get him to sit down.

"I will not sit down. You stand up there all righteous and proud of getting a cop killer off. I don't know what you did to those poor family members, but whatever it was, it doesn't change anything. He killed them and now he is dead. Nothing you say changes any of that." He stood glaring at Nick.

Nick stood there thinking for a second, trying to remain calm.

"Half of you think a vet who kills himself after he is *illegally* assaulted is a fitting end? What the fuck is wrong with all of *you*?" vented Nick in frustration.

There were murmurs at his statement. The other cop sat down.

"From the beginning of my run, hell, since I joined Congress, I have been unwavering in my support of all of you. More funding, more training, better equipment, and laws stressing safety for all of *you*. No more crazy Red Flag raids. Putting you in danger to fulfill the state's desire to seize firearms by any means. Mental illness causes most mass shootings, not guns. We need more hospital beds, not laws allowing people to send officers into the houses of unsuspecting and law-abiding gun owners based on *their* opinions," Nick was shouting, his voice reverberating throughout the auditorium.

"If half of you no longer care about facts, or the rule of law, or letting the criminal justice system work. If you don't believe in innocent until proven guilty, then screw you."

"You swore an oath to uphold the law. To have that law applied equally to all. No favorites. It is a code of conduct. It has to be upheld. The evidence collected. The trial tried. We have to agree to abide by the verdict regardless of how we feel. That is the oath. If we selectively apply it, then what?" Nick stopped looking to see if anyone disagreed. The crowd was now quiet.

"Eva's parents and the others all forgave Dusty. I did not convince them. The facts did. They arrived at their own conclusions. Dusty knew this and still he committed suicide. Because of the reaction we just saw. If you in law enforcement can't objectively admit mistake after mistake by the authorities, put him in a no-win situation. What hope did he have with the uninformed masses? Those same uninformed masses who think all of *you* go around shooting unarmed black men *every* day? For fun! I know you know how that feels. Now you know how Dusty felt."

"Yes, he had PTSD. And yes, he had his gun, and he knew how to use it. Despite what you may have read or what you want to believe about soldiers with PTSD, he didn't go crazy. Instinct kicked in and he did what we trained him to do. Unfortunately, he was put into that position. Red Flag laws mean well. I believe in the outcome they hope to achieve. Yet they never work. They never stop random mass shootings. Nor do gun grabs. All they do is disarm the law abiding. Not the mentally ill or the criminal. The best answer for this is an armed and aware population." Nick stalked the stage.

"Ask any burglar. They are way more afraid of an armed homeowner than they are of you. Because if they run into him, he has every right to shoot the burglar for being in his house. Sound familiar?" Nick fixed the cop who had attacked him earlier with a stare. He would not make eye contact.

"Now we can add Dusty to the body count. American *Pravda* has contributed to this without even getting their hands dirty. Now it seems I can add half of you too." Nick shook his head sadly. "But hey, now he's dead. All is right in the world. The parents of the slain deputies can now mourn his death, too. The police chiefs, anchors on cable news, and those who thumbed up #DeathforDusty on social media can take a victory lap in their parent's basement. Hooray for you!"

"With their relentless megaphone and no one to hold them accountable, he knew it would *never* stop. The same megaphone used to smear all of you, by the way. You should be the most sympathetic group of people to his treatment. You live it too." Nick paused to let this statement resonate.

"While all of this is horrible, and horribly predictable, it is not what disappoints me most. Frankly, it is the rest of you. Those who know the facts, who watched the trial. Who understand the errors. None of you are screaming to fix these obvious mistakes. No, you are shouting at *me* for demanding accountability for all of this. You are complaining about *me* for daring to demand we let our criminal justice system do its job.

You are yelling at *me*, because you lost six of your comrades. Now he's dead. Do you feel better? Are you going to yell at me now for telling you what I think of your protests and your insults?"

"It could have been any of you. It will be many of you if things are not changed. You are going to continue to be sent out to enforce these rules. I suggest you ask everyone to verify the addresses twice. I would make the judge who issues the no-knock warrant, the governor, DA and AG, stand behind you when you break down the door of the next Red Flag target. Because after this, fewer people are going to just open their doors and let you ransack their premises looking for weapons based on the word of anonymous sources."

Nick was marching up and down the stage, punching the air to make his points. His face was red as he shouted at his audience, his anger palpable. No one could fake these emotions.

"Last, I want you to understand. If you pull the trigger to defend yourself against someone trying to take your life. I will do *exactly* the same thing I did for Dusty. I will, and perhaps I alone, will stand there advocating on your behalf to let the evidence speak. If it does and it acquits you, I will also be here. To defend you from American *Pravda* and, apparently, your union. Who demand that justice was not served and that you should be taken out back and shot. Or who will be happy to give you a gun you can stick in your mouth."

Nick stopped in the center of the stage, staring over the now fidgeting police officers.

"My hope is, when faced with the same situation, you will not end up taking your own life. Not because persecution in the public square after American justice, the most free and fair system on the fucking planet, has done its job. Shame on all of you."

Nick stood for a second and walked off the stage while the assembled police officers in the room didn't say a word. Many of the female officers were crying and others were hanging their head in embarrassment. It was definitely not their finest hour.

As Nick left the stage, Earl met him. Nick did not stop and kept walking to the green room of the conference hall. He glanced up, seeing it was just the two of them. Looking at a wooden table in the room, Nick hit it with the side of his hand, letting out a shout of pent-up anger. The table split in two as cleanly as if hit with an axe.

Earl stood there. "Feel better now? Your hand, ok?"

"It's a start. Let's get out of here." As they turned to go, Duke came into the room, glanced at the broken table and then Nick.

"Nick, can I convince you to come back with me? For just a minute. It's important."

"It's too late, Duke. Words and deeds have been said and done that can't be forgiven with an apology. From them, and I am certainly not sorry about what I've said. I don't care how badly Denise says I need your endorsement."

"Fair enough. I get it. I think you embarrassed them. We'll see what they do."

"Duke, if this is what we are up against, we are way farther gone than I thought."

"Nick, you have to remember, the police have been persecuted for decades. They are not feeling a lot of love."

"No excuse, Duke," said Nick, shaking his head. "I'll support them even if they don't support me or don't like it. Earl, let's go. I'm sure I'm in for the same at the Creating Change rally. People don't like to hear the truth. To fucking inconvenient." Nick headed out of the room while Earl shook Duke's hand and shrugged.

"Earl, the cop in the front. His brother was killed by an Iraq vet. High on drugs," said Duke in a small voice.

Earl nodded and put his hand on Duke's shoulder before he followed Nick.

They got out to the car without a fight or a potshot from an angry cop. Even if there was no endorsement, one out of two was fine in Earl's book. He just hoped they could do the same at the next one.

#

Two hours later, a video of the beginning of Nick's speech and the cop yelling at Nick for supporting a cop killer was being posted and shared from the #DeathforDusty chat group. It did not include any of

Nick's rebuttal, only Nick telling the police they sucked. By the time Nick landed in Austin, the post had been shared a million times on the rest of the social platforms. No Ministry of Truth demands to take that one down.

On Hibi, the entire speech was posted, but it only had 25,000 views. Supporters were starting to counter program, by tagging it into the feeds on all the other social platforms. Of course, these platforms were blocking the reposts from Hibi. Claiming Nick's full response was hate speech and misinformation. That he was making incorrect claims about the facts of Dusty's trial. The 2J's made a headline of fact checking the statements by the censoring channels, but again, their rebuttals were being taken down as fast as they were reposted.

Chapter 64

Nick raised an arm to block a wild swing, bouncing off his forearm harmlessly. He countered with a leg sweep and a quick shove as they collapsed in a heap at his feet, dazed but unhurt. On either side of him were his Green Beret bodyguards, all trained and instructed in non-lethal methods of disarming and dealing with inexperienced attackers. Earl had his back to Nick, covering the final flank.

Unlike the TBL union talk, a late addition to Nick's appearances, the Creating Change conference was both planned and posted on Nick's website. They had security, cameras posted, and followers in attendance who supported Nick. This was good and bad. It meant they had a record of activities. It also meant they had folks who could be baited by inappropriate behavior to respond.

As Nick continued to punch, kick, and block his way out of the center of the melee, he could see out of the corner of his eye other supporters responding more violently. Black clad protesters going down in heaps, being punched and kicked by some of his followers, whipped into a frenzy. He started barking orders, telling them to stand down. To stop fighting.

The police and security stood on the perimeter on one side, hesitating to get involved. The scrum was losing momentum as Nick's people prevailed. It seemed the protesters were retreating or stopping, but a segment of his followers were still pressing the fight. Now attacking rather than just defending.

As this became more apparent, the cops finally got involved, often using their clubs on Nick's followers. Again, he was alternatively shouting for them to stand down and for the cops to stop using force.

Eventually, Nick, Earl and his two bodyguards stood alone in a square, back to back, as a dozen protesters writhed on the grass in various states of pain and moaning. None had broken bones or any damage beyond a few bruises.

A couple of cops approached Nick and his team with guns raised, demanding they surrender. Nick and his team made no moves. An officer arrived, saw it was Nick, and told his men to stand down.

"Well Senator, congratulations, you've started another riot. I'm sure Homeland will enjoy prosecuting this one. I don't think your followers killed anyone, so you won't have to defend a killer again."

Nick's bodyguards made a move, but Nick held out a hand.

"That's exactly what he wants. He's probably being paid to instigate a violent response. Know your enemy, right!" said Nick to the officer. He looked pissed for a second, then turned, not taking the bait.

Nick and his team marched out of the grassy area of Austin's Zilker Park, where the gathering was staged. They were being endlessly heckled by LGBTQ supporters holding banners espousing gender transitions, gay rights, and various other slogans telling the state to leave them alone to live their life as they chose.

As they reached their vehicles, some of the other local teams showed up as well. Bringing the cameras and footage. Many had bloody noses, black eyes, cuts, and bruises.

Nick frowned as he was approached by his local Turner Rabble leader for this Austin group. She was a lesbian herself and had a rapidly blackening eye and a split lower lip.

"Jill, are you OK?" he asked, turning to Earl. "Find some ice."

She smiled. "I'm ok Nick. You should see the other guy. At least I think she used to be a guy," laughed Jill, showing a sense of humor despite the chaos.

"How bad?" asked Nick

"It'll look bad on the film, because of all the punches, but anyone who pays attention to what you actually said, how the fighting got started, who threw the punches, and how it escalated, will realize it was all a setup."

"Is it that clear?" asked Nick, handing Jill an ice pack.

"Yep. You did nothing but preach tolerance. You were even making a few folks see your approach made sense. You support adults making their own choices, no special treatment, but also no restrictions. Your only request is to leave the kids alone. To get it out of the schools. Let the parents be involved in the choices their children make. Most of us agree with you. Once they saw you were getting some cheers, they started throwing the frozen water bottles."

"We have it on camera?"

"Oh yeah. The usual suspects. Black clad with hoodies. This time, though, some of those idiot redneck Gabriel's Angels started fighting back. It looked staged," said Jill, shaking her head.

"How so?"

"They had three groups. ARL on the sides with mostly blacks and a few Hispanics. Some may have even been gay. The ones in the middle were definitely Antifa. All white, young, and not even LGBTQ. Once they attacked, there was a convenient smaller group of these Gabriel's followers. One near each of them. Pre-positioned. Of course, both groups are wearing the normal uniforms. Black hoodies for the bad guys and ball caps for the Angels."

"Would probably stand out amongst all the other hair colors," smiled Earl ruefully, holding an ice pack on his forehead as well.

"Makes it easy to find them on the footage. Like I said, it looked almost choreographed, not organic. The ones who charged you were not the organized ones. They were back in the crowd. As soon as it started, the Angel's got to work. You know how this works. The Antifa and ARL crew are not fighters. They are bomb throwers. I wish I could say the same for 'your' side. The Angels were out for blood. They spilled a bunch. All those ambulances you see over there are for the ones our team hurt. Lots of broken limbs and concussions.

"Shit. I have already disavowed these guys. I didn't pay for the bail or the defense of those at the last rally when they got arrested. Who is paying for them?"

"Somebody is. These guys don't seem to be too worried about being arrested or who they hurt."

"Nick, Denise is going to come unglued," noted Earl.

"I know. We need to get out of here. Jill, you and your team OK?" asked Nick as he noticed more news vans arriving.

"Sure. I'll let you know if they come after any of us. We followed your approach. Stayed out of most of the fighting. But the nightly news is going to be all about your violent militia followers."

"We will counter with our own footage. It was worth a shot."

"Some will hear. A few have open minds. All we can do is keep trying. The footage should be uploaded to the Hibi cloud. Available for Steve and Greg to cut and get on the websites. Good luck Nick."

"Thanks Jill."

#

Jed smiled a bloody smile. He had lost a tooth in the fight, but he was sure his benefactors would be more than happy to pay the dental bill. It had gone even better than planned. He sat in a jail cell at the county lockup. Twelve others from his group were also arrested.

They'd done their job. He knew he had broken at least half a dozen arms and legs of a bunch of the queers and sissies at the rally. He just wished he could have done more.

After listening to Turner carry on about tolerance and respecting their choices and their rights to do whatever perversion they wanted as adults. At least he told the perverts to leave the kids alone.

Jed agreed with Turner on closing the border, but obviously not on assimilating the illegal aliens. They were all drug dealers, murderers, and freeloaders. Coming to America to take the jobs from Americans and leech off the welfare system. The gays, trans and whatever's were ruining the schools, high school athletics and messing with the heads of the kids. If he had his way, he would send them all to Canada or Denmark, if not straight to hell. Or better yet, to any Middle Eastern country where they'd all be stoned in the square. Jed rarely sided with the ragheads, but on this, he was in violent agreement.

As he gleefully replayed the day's events, a sheriff's deputy arrived. He knew what was coming. Travis County had recently followed in the footsteps of LA, San Francisco, Houston, Seattle, Portland and other Party run urban cities and instituted no bail laws. Since no one died, he knew they would all be out soon.

The deputy opened the door, and Jed tried not to smile. He knew his release was not because of Senator Turner's TRDF staff. The first few times they had been bailed out by Turner's people. No longer. Just as his benefactor had claimed, when Turner disowned them, they started bailing them out or providing lawyers to do the paperwork.

Leaving the county lockup, he looked up his secret bank account from his phone and smiled. He saw another $10,000 deposit. He'd have to check Turner's website and see where to go next.

#

Cheryl Thompson, assistant director of Homeland Security, stood at a podium. "I stand here today to announce we are opening up an investigation into various events occurring at Senator Turner's rallies and other gatherings. We can no longer ignore the violent tendencies of his followers, as we saw in Austin," she paused.

"Nineteen people are hospitalized, some in serious condition from broken bones and internal injuries sustained while defending themselves against the attacks of Turner's followers."

"We must warn you; the following images are graphic. As you can see from our footage, you can see many of his followers clearly utter hate speech and use racial and gender preference slurs as they attacked the peaceful protesters and conference attendees."

"While Senator Turner has paid lip service admonishing these more militant groups supporting him, ultimately, we still believe they are triggered by his message of bigotry and sedition. We hold him accountable for instigating violence against the LGBTQ community."

The press started shouting questions as Mel muted the TV.

Lexi sat and rubbed her hands together. "What is with this guy? First the cops and now the gays? He is a glutton for punishment. Does he honestly think lecturing these people is a good way to get their support?

What a moron. And these redneck followers. Wherever did you find them? How much is this costing us?"

Mel looked at her worriedly. "Lexi, I assure you we are not paying them."

Lexi looked back in disbelief. "Really. Hmm. Not sure if that is good or bad. If we aren't controlling them, how do we keep them from hurting us? You'd better figure out who is controlling them. You know how this has a habit of going too far. So far, it's working brilliantly. But for how long? If this is being funded by one of those Super PACs we can't control, if they are exposed, we don't need that. Thankfully, by the time the stupidity of her bought and paid for dossier was revealed, it had little impact. She still lost. Find out who is funding this."

"Got it." It worried Mel as well. Yet again, Turner had footage and he and his team were using it and the triangulation of Hibi and the 2J's discrediting everything the liberal outlets were doing to promote the propaganda angles. His message was getting to more people. It was also becoming clear the over-the-top sensationalism of all the liberal media channels was approaching critical mass. Making even the ignorant question their message. Mel worried they were pushing it too far. The election couldn't get here fast enough.

As Mel walked from his office, he made one more call. When he got an answer, he described what he needed next. He'd been holding this card and decided now was the time to call in the favor.

Chapter 65

Nick and Earl sat in the conference room in Denver with Denise, Margie, and Greg.

"Nick, I told you."

"I know Denise, but I had to try. The cops needed to get the message. We were never going to get their endorsement, anyway. Same with LGBTQ. If I can even get a small percentage to think for themselves, it was worth it."

"Nick, they are going non-stop trashing you. How is that good for us?" accused Denise.

"Margie, how are their ratings?"

"Good on EXN, still going down on all the other stations. They've been steadily dropping for the last two months. A slow decline in total viewers, especially the hard news programs."

"And Hibi and the 2J's?"

"The opposite, growing and the curves look like hockey sticks," smiled Margie.

"Before you start patting yourself on the back, remember the law of small numbers. Even with the growth, it is a fraction of all of them. Nick, I get it. But our coverage is all negative. We get to counter it with the actual footage and debunk the fact checkers. It only gets to those who choose to follow us. Those not listening already aren't getting the chance to be convinced to join our side," explained Denise.

Nick stared at her. "What now? The news is not sunshine and roses. I can't tell them it is or will be if I'm elected."

"Why not Nick? Look, I get it, but this is not a debate. They want to hear hopeful things. They want to know you are going to make their life better. How you are going to give them a chance to improve their life.

Reduce their bills, improve their kid's schooling, make it safer to shop or walk in their neighborhoods. Something uplifting. Instead, you keep kicking them in the nuts." She glared at Nick.

"Denise, those cops were not looking for sunshine and promises. They wanted to kick me in the nuts. The LGBTQ folks wanted me to give them unfair advantages and accommodate their views on gender transitions and women in sports. The climate activists want me to ban all gas cars in less than ten years. How can it be hopeful when I am against all these things they want?"

"Nick, it is not winning us enough votes. We are now at the point where folks are getting their mail in ballots. When they do, all it takes is one negative press item, at the right time, to sway a voter who does not see our posts, see you on EXN, or watch the 2J's. Their only view of you is coming from American *Pravda*."

"Denise, in case you didn't notice, hopeful got Dusty killed. Me cursed out by cops who should embrace me. Attacked at a conference where I was telling them I agree with almost everything they want. I almost got killed at a state fair being hopeful, poisoned at a Gala and finally mobbed in the parking lot by right-wing religious fanatics. Oh and I forgot, I now have right-wing militia followers breaking legs and arms in my name, ignoring my commands to stop. Hopeful is working really fucking well," finished Nick, getting up.

"What is the fucking point? If people are too stupid to see their decisions and lack of curiosity are leading them into a totalitarian regime? Maybe I should let them," he'd raged, leaving the room.

"That went well," said Earl. They could all see Nick had reached his boiling point.

"Don't blame me," blurted Denise. "Somebody had to tell him. He is talking us right out of followers."

"What can we do?" asked Greg in a meek voice.

"Beats the fuck out of me." Denise threw her hands up.

The intercom on the conference table buzzed. Margie pressed the button. "Yeah."

"We have Jeremy Kwan on line two."

"Thanks Carla."

"Jeremy, you've got Margie, Earl, Denise, and Greg. Nick stepped out. Anything we can help you with? Should we go get him?"

"Probably just as well Nick is not here," said Jeremy, concern coming through in his voice.

"Uh oh, what happened?" asked Margie.

"TruthinNews, the fact checking org that rates sites based on their so called 'truth'. As we all know, it is founded and run by Party operatives. They just published a review of our programming on the 2J's since we launched. Of course, it was all negative, claiming it has one of the lowest scores ever in terms of truth and in spreading misinformation disguised as free speech."

Jeremy paused on the conference line.

"2J's lost all our cable and satellite channels. FCC told them we were promoting sedition and hate speech with our programming and fact checking, showing support for misinformation under the guise of truth. That means we are streaming only now. We are filing appeals. I'm not hopeful. Our only chance is to get to the Supreme Court. I'm not sure we can get back on satellite and cable before the election. None of them could risk defying the FCC or they would lose their entire broadcast license."

"Shit, what else can they do?" asked Margie shaking her head, staring at the conference phone, head in hands.

"They can't stop us from streaming, at least in the US," added Jeremy. "The EU, that is a different animal. They are proposing to ban Hibi from being seen inside the EU. Canada is looking at the same as well. Citing the same provisions. KooKoo gets defended for killing kids and sharing personal info with the Chinese communists and they are talking about banning us for sharing truth? Go figure. They say we aren't doing enough to take down hateful content. We're promoting violence, bigotry and now riots. Allowing folks to post positions reflecting negatively on some aspects of transgenderism, homosexuality, climate change, bigotry, and racial terrorism."

"Geez, what did they leave out? Picking on the Atlanta Braves name change?" asked Denise rhetorically. Those in the conference room at least cracked a slight smile. Jeremy did not laugh.

"If we get shut down around the world, I am not sure how that doesn't set a precedent for Homeland to use the same approach stateside," finished Jeremy.

Denise ran her hands through her hair, stopping to cup her face. She looked up after a few seconds of thought.

"We can't lose Hibi. Jeremy, can you prevent some of the more provocative posts? Would that work?" asked Denise.

"Denise, honestly, I've thought about it. That's why I'm glad Nick is not there. We all know what he would say. I doubt it would make a difference at this point. If they decide to use this, they could take anything out of context and at least tie us up in court."

"The hits keep coming," commented Earl.

"Sorry, but I wanted you to know. I'll let you know if any of these threats become real. Homeland is pressuring the FCC, so let Nick know we may need some heavy hitters and some EXN appearances. It will be the only outlet left."

"Thanks Jeremy."

Margie ended the call, looking at Denise.

"After that last conversation, if we tell him, he is going to explode," offered Margie.

Denise looked at Earl. "Any ideas?"

Earl shrugged. "It's a Hail Mary, but I think we are at that point in the game."

"Call the play," said Denise.

Chapter 66

The next day, Nick sat in the passenger seat, reviewing seemingly endless emails and texts on his phone as Earl drove. Nick looked up as they turned off C-470 and up interstate 70, leaving Denver climbing steeply west into the mountains.

"It's too early to ski. Where we headed?"

"Someone wants to see you. We're headed to Lookout Mountain," replied Earl, taking the first exit, heading up to the promontory overlooking Denver to the east.

"Buffalo Bill's grave? I hope it is not symbolic."

Earl laughed. "Hardly. They wanted to see it while they were in town."

"What's with all the spy stuff? This isn't a Ludlum book. An overnight bag, no computer or notebook, only this leash," said Nick, holding up his phone.

"You'll see," replied Earl cryptically.

Earl pulled into the parking lot next to an SUV parked in a far corner. As he parked, a woman with coppery red hair, wearing a flannel shirt, jeans and hiking boots, got out. Nick smiled, looking from Earl to the woman.

"Ma'am, are you lost?" asked Nick as he hugged Natalie.

"Nope. Right where I need to be," she quipped right back, staring into Nick's eyes as if Earl wasn't even there.

Earl cleared his throat as both looked down with a laugh.

"Much as I appreciate the visit. Why *are* you here? Why am I packing an overnight bag? Where we headed?"

"Your team has decided you need a break. I volunteered to chaperone and keep you out of trouble," grinned Natalie.

"Ya, right? Whose idea was this?"

"Grab your bag and let's go. Thanks Earl. Pass caught," commented Natalie, ignoring Nick.

Earl laughed as Nick grabbed his bag, threw it in back and headed for the passenger seat.

"No way, mister. You're driving. I have no idea where I'm going. The address is programmed into the GPS. I'm a flatlander, not a mountain girl," she explained as they switched places.

"Have fun kids," waved Earl as he returned to his car.

"Thanks Dad," smirked Nick as Earl flipped him off.

Nick drove them back to I-70, following the GPS system.

"Where too?" asked Nick, glancing at his passenger.

She turned, smiling. "No idea. A cabin outside Breckintop."

"Breckinridge."

"Whatever. That's what the GPS is for."

"Ok, spill. What's up? I thought we were waiting until I lost."

"Pretty presumptuous, Senator. Can't two adults of the opposite sex just have a leisurely visit?"

"Guess I'm about to find out," replied Nick in an ironic tone.

Natalie kept smiling in reply. They drove up I-70, through the Eisenhower tunnel under the continental divide. Exiting the interstate toward Breckinridge. Nat filled him in on Grace and all the activities of her Turner Rabble group in the heartland. She purposely steered away from any of the recent campaign news.

Nick said little, staying focused on driving. He continued to follow the prompts from the GPS. They went through Breckinridge proper and out into the countryside, winding up a mountain road until they were told to turn off on a dirt driveway.

They found the cabin, which was more like a small house in a picturesque location with glorious vistas. The sun was dipping.

"Nick, it is absolutely beautiful out here. Look at all the colors," marveled Natalie, throwing her arms wide.

"You picked a good year. The fall colors were especially vibrant this year and are lasting longer than usual at this elevation."

"Grab the bags. Let's see inside," she said in an excited voice.

"I hope they left some food," quipped Nick.

"I asked them to have it stocked, so we should be good."

Nick looked at her suspiciously.

"What?"

"How many folks were involved in this?"

"Your team is worried about you. I drew the short straw, the Dr. is in," she said with a smile as they both headed into the house carrying their small overnight bags.

They explored the cabin and Natalie confirmed the food was indeed in the fridge, so they wouldn't starve.

Nick looked at the coffee machine. "A little too early to eat. Up for a coffee and a sunset?"

"Sounds good."

Nick brewed two coffees and they headed out onto the porch. Conveniently aimed at the sunset over a high mountain meadow and lake with soaring peaks in the background.

Nick lit the fire pit as they sat on a loveseat and covered their legs with a convenient quilt.

Sipping their coffee, they watched the sun dip below a peak.

"A little different from watching the sunset in Omaha," said Natalie, awestruck.

"First time in the Rockies?"

"It is. I am a Texas and plains girl. I could get used to this."

"Really? I have a cabin just like this. Better views though, not too far from here as the crow flies. As the car drives, though, it is a couple of hours."

"Get up there much?"

"Actually, no. Not in years. I often rent or loan it out to friends. I always figured I'd end up there when I give all this up."

"It's good to have plans and choices," she agreed.

"So, Miss Williams, exactly why have you abducted me and dragged me to your secret lair? You aren't going to go all Scarlett Johansson on me, are you?"

He loved her laugh. "You wish. Sorry, I left my Black Widow costume at home. Just my flannel and hiking boots."

"Seriously. I know my team by now. Sending me away anywhere that is not election related, less than a month before it is not insignificant. What did I do?"

"Nick, they're worried about you. First the pastor, then the cops, and at the gay conference. The constant attacks at the grass roots rallies and in the media. Now Homeland and the FCC. They know how much you don't want to lead anyone else into trouble. We all know how badly Dusty's suicide hurt you. Especially after all you did and risked giving him a chance."

Nick tensed up at the mention of Dusty.

"I have dealt with loss, Nick. You can't bottle it up. It eats you from the inside out. Trust me, I know."

"Natalie, people deal with grief and stress in different ways. I find sharing does not help me with mine."

"I'm going to tell you something I've never shared with anyone. When they told me Patrick was dead, I was crushed, but part of me had prepared for this outcome. It was the rest I couldn't handle. They shared they'd found his severed hand. He'd been tortured. The four fingers left were all broken, with their fingernails removed before they cut the hand off." Natalie shivered as Nick reached out.

"They told you that? Why on Earth?" responded Nick, getting angry.

"Nick, I forced it out of his best friend. I wouldn't let it go. I had to know." Tears were streaming down her face as she turned to him. "How did he do it? How does someone withstand this abuse?" Nick put his arm around her as she buried her head in his shoulder, sobbing.

Nick pushed her up so he could look into her eyes.

"Natalie, I spoke to Henry Burket about Patrick when I saw him in El Paso. He told me what happened. About the rescue mission. You know what Patrick did, fighting back to protect his partner?"

Natalie nodded.

"Only someone with something to lose can go through that kind of torture and not break. The fact they kept going meant he didn't give them what they wanted. He did this, knowing if he gave in, they would just kill him. The amount of money they asked for was never going to be paid. He knew this, yet he endured whatever they did to him so he could get back to you."

She gave him a fierce look. "How do you know?"

"He had a reason to live. You and Grace. Trust me."

"Show me," she demanded.

"Show you what," responded Nick, confused.

"The scars on your back."

"How do you know about those?"

"Your doctor, after you got shot. He told Earl what you told him. It didn't match the lie you told Earl about how you got them. The Doctor said you were lying too. Earl told Jamie, and she told me."

"I see. Why does this matter?"

"Because I want to know. I need to know what that kind of resolve looks like. I need to understand. How were you able to withstand it?"

"I told them the truth. I got it through an accident."

"Nick, you're a horrible liar. You can't hide forever. I called Dr. Guraji when I knew you were coming. Earl gave me his contact info. The doctor told me his story about Afghanistan and the tribal leader who was found hanged. That was you, wasn't it?"

"I see no secret is safe in my campaign," frowned Nick.

"Nick, they care. *I* care.

"I'm fine. Running for president isn't supposed to be easy."

"Show me."

"It's freezing," lied Nick as it was indeed dark, but the firepit was throwing off plenty of heat. Her green eyes flashed in response.

Nick took off his shirt, presenting his back to Natalie. She gently ran her fingers up and down the ten to twelve vertical scars. Each was raised slightly. As she traced them, Nick shivered. She reached her arms around, laying her head on his shoulder from behind.

"How do you survive this? How did you not give up? How did Patrick not give up?"

Nick turned around and faced her, looking deeply into those emerald eyes.

"You don't have a choice. You fight. With each blow, you bury the pain and plot your revenge. You dig deep inside and find the ability to block out the pain. You focus on the hate. You think about how important it is to survive. To have a reason to survive."

As he talked, Nick's eyes lost their focus, as he remembered.

"Then you plan. You plan for how you're going to make your captors pay. If only you get the chance. You focus on everything around you. Like a trapped animal. Looking for a way to escape. Knowing if you can, if only they make a mistake, how they will pay."

As he said this, it was Natalie's turn to shiver as Nick made his statement with such passion and determination. She kept eye contact, hearing Nick's conviction, describing his motivation for retribution.

"Is that what you did?"

Nick turned. "This is hardly how I expected this visit to go."

Natalie laughed. "What did you expect? A booty call?"

Nick smiled back. "Hope springs eternal. I should have known it was an intervention," he ended, shaking his head as he leaned back.

Natalie looked at him. Her green eyes now softer, her youthful face wearing a worried look. She smiled her crooked smile.

"Nick, they're right. What you did with Dusty was noble. You did all you could. Sometimes you can't save people from themselves."

"The system killed him. Plain and simple. Gross incompetence with no consequence. Social media mobs and American *Pravda*. Lynched in the public square," commented Nick, his determined tone returning as he put his shirt back on.

Natalie paused for a second. "Yes, they did. What can you do about it?" She paused as he looked at her. "Get your M-16 and shoot as many as you can before they take you down? Fly your A-10 and bomb ANC headquarters?

Nick didn't comment, so she continued.

"No, what you're going to do about it is fight. Just like Patrick did. Just like you've been ever since you came to Washington. You're going to fight to preserve the right. Your right. My right. Our right to control our own destiny. To not let these elites and pieces of media shit ruin lives and kill more innocents with their lies."

Nick was surprised at the passion of Natalie's reply.

"You sure you can't join my campaign team?"

"I do my part, buster. Stay focused and see this through."

"When you put it that way…"

"Quit stalling." She fixed him with her stare. "Now answer my question. How did you survive? Have you ever told your story to anyone? Nick, you can't keep it inside. It's eating you alive. Earl and Denise, Chuck and Margie, they all saw it during the time with Dusty. Now with the attack at the rally and what you said to Denise and Earl. Earl called Jamie, and she suggested I might help you. You have to come to grips with it. Earl said you talked to chief Wayne about getting treatment for PTSD. You lied when you told him you talked to someone, didn't you?"

Nick looked her in the eyes. This time, she turned away.

"Who would have thought my chief of security is my mole? No more trips to Nebraska for Earl. You are a very perceptive and dangerous woman, Natalie Williams."

"Nick…"

"Natalie, I have seen things I care not to remember. Most, I'm not able to talk about without putting you at risk. And violating all kinds of national security rules. I've made my peace with my demons."

Natalie's green eyes narrowed in anger.

"I don't care about rules. I care about you. About you surviving to the end of this journey. They've already tried to kill you twice and probably would have beaten you to a pulp in Dallas and Austin if given the chance. If you won't share with me, share with someone. The pressure relief valve has to pop Nick. It eventually did with me. I could pick myself up from the fetal position on the floor and make a life for my daughter. We all need you to survive. You are the only one who can save us from ourselves. I, we, all of us, know this to be true," finished Natalie breathlessly.

Nick stared back for a few seconds.

"I was in a helicopter in Afghanistan on the border with Pakistan. We were doing a SEAL team insertion into a remote village. They were there to infiltrate Pakistan and assassinate a Taliban leader. I planned the mission and tagged along to monitor. It was night. Someone got lucky or, more likely, we had a leak in headquarters. It didn't matter. We were flying low. There was nothing the pilot could do. The RPG hit us before he could even try to maneuver."

"It took out a turbine and two rotor blades on the Blackhawk. The Army pilot barely had time to try to auto rotate us to the ground. When we hit, I was thrown clear at first contact. The helo rolled and then burst into flames. No one else made it."

"When I woke up, I was in a building across the border in Pakistan. I won't bore you with the details. The very Taliban leader we were trying to locate was standing in front of me. He was a butcher. Known for killing his own supporters at the slightest provocation. They had no idea who I was, just that I was an American soldier."

"They spent the days torturing me as only terrorists can. It was not pleasant, but I didn't give them any satisfaction. I was pretty beat up by then and weak. They tied me up, naked between two poles in a building, and left me hanging there by my arms. I figured castration was probably next on the menu."

Nick took a breath before continuing as Natalie shivered, wrapping the quilt around her shoulders.

"He walked in. A big burly pig of a man. He started spouting off the unpleasant things he was going to do to me in Pashto, not knowing I could understand him. Then he shifted to English and repeated his plans as best he could. Some things I wouldn't wish on my worst enemy. Then he showed me the whip." Natalie was wide eyed listening to Nick's story.

"He told me how it had been used by the puppet ruler of Afghanistan the British had installed in the mid-1800s in their failed attempts to control the area. How that ruler used to flay traitors alive with it while his British allies would sit nearby drinking their tea. He was working himself into a frenzy." Nick's tone changed subtly as he continued. As if he were still there, living it.

"By this time, I figured maybe this was my fate rather than castration. He started whipping me. With each stroke, my resolve grew greater, along with my hatred. Each time he hit me, my body would be thrown forward, pulling at the ropes. It was ripping the skin from my wrists and hands where they were tied by the ropes." Nick looked down at his hands as he continued his story. Ignoring the tears streaming down Natalie's face.

"There were only two other rebels. They'd laid down their weapons and were sitting at a nearby table. I knew exactly where everything in the room was. I plotted my vengeance. Hit after hit. I no longer felt them. I only burned with the desire to return the favor. All I had to do was wait and survive long enough."

Natalie interrupted. "Survive long enough for what?"

She shivered again as Nick smiled. "On the tenth or eleventh swing he hit me so hard my right hand, slick with blood now, pulled free from the rope. As I had expected, the force of the blow swung me around toward the table where his two cohorts sat, no longer paying much attention."

"I swung toward them, the table, and the knife they'd conveniently stabbed in the table's top when speaking about my imminent neutering. I grabbed the knife, slicing one guard's throat before he could even react. The second guard was bringing up his AK when I shoved the knife through his left eye socket."

"I turned back toward the Chief. He swung the whip at me. I let it wrap around my still trapped left arm. Reaching up with the knife, cut the rope, and that was that."

"What did you do to him?"

Nick returned her gaze with one of no remorse. "Dr. Guraji didn't fill you in?

Natalie shook her head no.

"That is between me and God. I was not very Christian in my treatment. I chose the Hammurabi code for that one."

"Oh Nick, I am so sorry," said Natalie, tears streaming.

"Don't be. It was my fault for going along on a mission. I had no right being on it. I was cocky and thought I was invincible. It was how I operated. I knew the risks. It all worked out in the end. There is a saying, 'what doesn't kill me only makes me stronger', or something like that. It was true."

He looked at her, tears on her cheeks, wrapped in the quilt, the light from the fire pit bathing both of them in rippling shadows.

"It also taught me about limits. He showed me how to suppress pain and feelings. This has come in handy a few times since. You asked how Patrick survived? He did it the same way I did. I have no doubt, if the building hadn't blown up, he too would have found a way back to you. I can guarantee you, he never stopped trying."

Natalie turned to Nick and hugged him, sobbing full body sobs now. Wishing she had never asked and never heard what Nick had been through to earn those scars.

"I'm supposed to be here to help you," she said against his chest as he held her close.

Eventually, he pushed her away. "Careful what you ask. You may not like the answer. Now, I'm hungry. Surely this intervention isn't designed to starve me into submission, is it?"

She smiled through her tears. "I can probably make you a peanut butter sandwich." Nick frowned as Natalie rose.

"I'll see if I can do better. Open the wine. Least I can do after forcing you to relive that."

Nick turned serious for a minute. He took Natalie's hands, and her smile faded.

"Natalie, you can never tell anyone this story. This is so buried in CIA archives, if you even breathed a word of it, they'll have you in rendition to find out what else you know. Even though you don't, they won't care. Promise me. Swear on Grace."

Natalie had never seen fear in Nick's eyes or in his voice before. She had no idea what 'rendition' was and didn't want to know.

"I swear."

"Some questions are best left unanswered. Not a soul Natalie, not even Jamie." She nodded as they walked into the kitchen.

#

"Much better than PB&J," said Nick as he pushed away his plate. Only a few bones of the rainbow trout were left.

"Had to make do with what they had available in town."

"You're kidding right? Rainbow trout is a delicacy up in these parts. Though, I still remember that halibut you served. Best ever."

"Flattery will get you everywhere. Return to the fire pit?"

"A wonderful idea," agreed Nick.

"Here, take the wine and re-start the fire. I'll clean up and be there in a minute."

Nick dutifully headed outside and re-started the fire pit, pouring two more glasses of red. It was considerably colder, so he turned up the fire pit until it was putting off a good glow of heat. Kicking off his shoes, he sat on the love seat and covered his legs with the quilt. He turned and yelled. "Hey, the last one out gets less wine."

"Easy boy."

Nick turned his head. Natalie came through the door, wearing only her flannel shirt. Realizing how cold it was, she scurried under the quilt. Nick handed her his glass and grabbed the other one.

She snuggled in under his arm as they soaked up the warmth from the fire. They clinked glasses.

"Natalie. I appreciate what you're doing. And everyone else. I got to sit here for a minute and look at the stars. I know all of you think this is getting to me. It is. And it isn't. I think I was made for this. Almost forged. My experiences are very different from most. Certainly different than most who run for President. These combined have prepared me to shoulder this burden. I don't say that out of some misguided pride or martyrdom. Frankly, it scares me sometimes. Then I think, if not me, who? Again, not out of ego, but necessity. I literally have nothing to lose. Who truly runs for office with this mindset?"

Natalie sipped her wine, thinking through Nick's statement.

"Well, say something."

"How do you know you have nothing to lose? We all have something to lose. You." She turned to face Nick and found his lips. He leaned over and set down his wine and then hers, while still keeping the kiss going. He laid her down beneath him on the loveseat. As he fumbled, trying to flip the quilt to cover them, she laughed.

"You think you can do better?"

She kissed him in reply.

Their hands roamed as they kissed. Nick undid the buttons on her shirt, cupping her small, firm breasts as she moaned. She reached down, pulling his shirt up. He leaned up and took his shirt off, looking down at her smiling face. Kissing again, his hands rubbed down her body, across her flat and toned middle, finding her panties. Using his hand, he pushed them off her hips. She moaned and turned her head away, breaking their kiss while reaching a hand down.

"Nick, we can't do this. A promise is a promise," she panted, trying to catch her breath. Nick propped his weight on his elbows, resting his chin between her bare breasts, looking up at her. He smiled.

"Really?"

"I'm sorry, I'm sorry," she said as the tears came.

"Whoa, Nat. It's fine. You're right. We made a pact. It seems like we're cheating, doesn't it?"

"Exactly," she agreed with a sniffle. "I want it to be perfect. While this would be wonderful, it wouldn't be the same. Can you wait a little longer?"

Nick leaned over and kissed each of her pert nipples. "That will have to tide us over," he said, as Natalie shivered. He covered her and pulled the covers back over them while he returned to kissing her. After another minute, she pushed him away.

"Not fair. You're breaking my resolve."

Nick smiled wickedly. "Sorry, I'm taking what I can get. To get me through the waiting." He heaved himself off her, standing and pulling her up to a sitting position.

"Geez, lady, button up your shirt. I mean, really. What kind of man do you think I am?"

"One that's good at camping. Looks like you already have a tent pole," she fired back, buttoning her shirt, as Nick looked down at his still obvious erection pushing out against his pants.

"What a waste," he said, shaking his head with a smile as he turned off the fire pit.

They carried the wine inside and closed up the house.

As they headed to the bedroom, Nick was going to grab a pillow and sleep on the couch in the living room.

Natalie shook her head.

"If you can keep your hands to yourself, you're welcome to join me," she smiled at him.

"It's not my hands that have a mind of their own," he quipped back. "*They'll* be the perfect gentleman. The rest? We'll see."

"I'll have to risk it. I hate sleeping alone. Especially now that the world is going to hell in a handbasket."

They snuggled in the queen-sized bed, Natalie with her head on Nick's chest. She quickly fell asleep while Nick lay there thinking about the women in his life. It couldn't be any more fucked up.

Now that the moment was passed, he realized Natalie was right to wait. He was thankful one of them had willpower. Rolling over, he spooned around her body, throwing a protective arm over her.

#

In the morning, they packed up and Nick drove Natalie back down the mountain to Denver International. During the drive, they discussed the remaining election efforts. What the final push would look like. Nick told her he knew it would only keep getting worse. The attacks had to keep coming because Lexi couldn't afford to lose.

He thanked her for all her help and for the intervention. Mostly. They didn't mention anything he'd shared.

"Be strong Nick Turner. We are all counting on you to see this through. We have your back. Just keep moving forward. Until the next time," she promised, her hand on his face after he kissed her goodbye.

Nick watched as she entered the terminal. Dropping off the car, he took the A-train from the airport into the center of Denver, then walked the couple of blocks from Union Station to the office.

Entering, he was greeted by a smiling Earl, Denise, and Margie. He stopped, shook his head, and headed to his office without a comment. They looked at each other, surprised he didn't have something snarky to say.

They followed him into the office.

"What's on deck today?" said Nick, booting up his laptop and opening his purple notebook he'd left in his desk.

With that, they started discussing the things they needed to do. They quickly realized he was not going to comment on his day in the mountains. They would have to wait for a report from Natalie about whether the Hail Mary worked. If the pressure was released.

#

Nick looked up at Margie and Denise standing in his doorway. "Now what?"

"Do you know a Tiffany Myers or Sharice Jones?" asked Margie tentatively.

Nick shook his head. "Don't ring any bells. Should I?"

"They both were just on ANC accusing you of sexual harassment. As well as making racist and homophobic statements when they were students of yours during you time as a history professor at Colorado State. The university president is already opening up an investigation. As is the state AG who announced their investigation into the allegations," finished Margie in a meek tone.

"This is how it always goes, Nick. Think really hard. Can you think of anything you said or did that could be misconstrued? Did you ever meet with students in private in your office? What could you have done that made them think you were harassing them?" prompted Denise, as the three sat at his conference table.

Nick had a pensive look as he tried to recall any incidents.

"Guys, I was always friendly and accessible to the kids at school. I never shut my office door for the reasons you state, Denise. You can't be too careful these days. My teaching methods were a bit more lively than most history courses. We did some role playing. Where I would have random students from the class come up front playing historical parts and giving historical lines and stuff."

"Sounds pretty harmless," said Margie.

"They liked it. It was always the highlight of the comments at the end of the semesters. They said they learned more by seeing things acted out than by droning lectures," responded Nick.

Denise stared at Nick. "That wouldn't perhaps have included them talking about things like slavery, emancipation, woman's suffrage, the Klan and things like that, would it?" asked Denise disingenuously.

Nick smiled in reply. "Well Denise, unlike my former Party, American *Pravda*, and Howard Zinn, I did not rewrite the inconvenient parts of our history. If we don't study it, we are doomed to repeat it.

Denise shook her head. "You are both the most naïve and stubborn man I have ever met."

Nick leaned back and opened his hands. He got up and headed to his kitchen while his advisors looked at each other. He came back with his wooden trunk and set it on his 'kitchen' counter. He lifted out two trays and set them aside as he dug around looking for a book.

Denise and Margie got up and wandered over as Nick pulled a notebook from the box and started replacing the trays. Denise noticed all the medals and ribbons.

"What the fuck are those?" she accused, pointing as Nick closed the box.

"Nothing."

"Nothing, my ass. Those look like a pile of medals. Jesus Nick. If you have a bunch of medals, why in the hell are we not talking about them? God damn it. We need all the help we can get, and you are hiding this shit?" Denise was as mad as Margie had ever seen her.

Nick carried the box back to his kitchen, replacing it in his safe. When he returned, he looked at Denise. "Drop it."

She was about to explode. "I mean it Denise. Not another word on this. Now let's figure out how to counter this latest shit."

"What's in the notebook, Nick?" asked Margie, trying desperately to change the subject.

"There are a few folks I want you to start contacting and see if they will issue statements or get on camera," instructed Nick.

Margie and Denise both started making notes as Nick rattled off names, email addresses, and phone numbers. After giving them extensive lists, he leaned back.

"Sadly, in this day or age, even trying to have a discussion about our founding fathers, the difference between the prevailing attitudes of each era, and the actions in the context of the time, is impossible. I can assure you; I did nothing inappropriate with any student during my time. In fact, you may also want to call the university president and have her dig up a file on these two professors." Nick showed them an entry in his notebook.

"For?" asked Denise.

"Just do it. Then we can ask a question if there is ever a press conference where she appears. I legally can't comment on it *directly*, but that doesn't mean I can't direct you to ask," answered Nick, smiling.

"Why are you smiling? This is serious, Nick," growled Denise.

"Denise, they are grasping at straws. I feel bad for the young women they obviously duped into giving these statements. Did they provide any specific dates, times, things I supposedly did or said?

Margie shook her head no. "The AG said they would provide more details soon.

"So just good old-fashioned character assassination. The usual Party tactic; the politics of personal destruction. Even now, they're still running her playbook." Nick sat and shook his head.

"Nick, they still run it because it is highly effective. Even if it isn't true, the words are out there. A certain group of low information voters now assume you're a creep," ended Denise, her frustration with the situation clear.

"What else is new? Those people already think I'm a creep for any number of other reasons. What do we need to say to the press? I can also do a quick one with Tommy."

"Great," sighed Denise. "Nick, I have to say, this is much worse than the last time I did this. Social media was just getting started. People were more willing to listen. Now it is nuclear Armageddon with every bombshell. Frankly, I don't see how this ever changes, regardless of who wins."

"Have faith Denise. There are a lot of people who feel like you do. Disgusted and silent. Who are afraid to complain for just that reason. We can change it if we stick together and don't give up. Let's get that press release out."

Chapter 67

Luc had crossed back over into France and was holed up in a house on the outskirts of the town of Dijon. Here he studied the files he'd stolen from the office of the Doctor.

At noon on the day after his break-in, an explosion blew in the windows of his hotel and all the nearby buildings. Exiting to see what happened, he noticed the building he had staked out was now a mass of rubble, with small fires burning. It had been destroyed by the explosion. The smell of natural gas was still in the air. Luc knew he was the reason this had happened. Because of the file, he'd left. They would know it was him. Just as he'd planned.

He had little to lose. Only a few friends, and his only living sibling, was the first lady of France. She was about as safe as possible. Annie was the only person he really cared about. But it seemed the people he interacted with were in danger merely by associating with him. Caroline, the engineer, Lauzon, and now perhaps Annie and even Gabi. Like it started the last time. This time would be different.

His gaze returned to the stack of papers. Many of them were of little use to him. The new ones just detailing the repetitive nature of the training to 'teach' the autistic students the responses and actions they would need to perform as suicide bombers. Month after month, with mixed results. He found the idea both intriguing and repulsive. Both the lack of empathy for their lives or the consequences of their efforts. They were a means to an end.

The older files from the drawer were the most interesting. They detailed experiments with drugs and projects from what seemed like decades ago. It was clear the doctor specialized in some type of bioengineering and molecular biology from what Luc could glean.

The photo he'd snapped of the framed pictures on the wall had yielded a name. Mehdi Khan. He was listed as a onetime professor at the Swiss Federal Institute of Technology with PhDs in Molecular and Cellular Biology and a second PhD in Nanoscience, Nanomedicine and Bioengineering. In the frame on the wall, he was pictured as a member of the staff standing behind two scientists accepting a Nobel prize.

In several others, he was pictured with famous American technology entrepreneurs and former leaders of a couple of European countries. Mehdi, 'the Doctor', had since disappeared from academia. He was no longer listed on any university faculty, nor had he published anything for the last two decades.

The notes Luc reviewed implied he continued his research in a private laboratory in either Moldova or in or around Odessa in the Ukraine. Luc had trouble following all the technical references and jargon. What was clear was his work was focused on nanotechnology and viral biology. There were complex formulas on cellular manipulation at the molecular and atomic levels. None of it made sense to Luc.

Other files talked about experiments trying to regrow limbs or regenerate organs in both labs and in subject patients. None appeared to be successful, their failures described in gruesome details. All were clinical. Luc's head was pounding as he continued to push through the files. He sat back and took a drink of his scotch, stretching and rubbing his neck as he grabbed the next file.

This one was not as old as some others. It detailed an interrogation of a prisoner. It stood out from the rest. The notes described a particular brutal torture session. While reading the details of the methodical torture, Luc was reminded of what the Paris doctor had told him of Caroline's injuries.

Mehdi was advising the interrogator he would kill the prisoner if he continued with his particular methods. Luc sat up abruptly, reading the handwritten notes.

I told Daboia I would not be responsible if I could not resuscitate the subject again if he continued. He laughed and told me it was up to 'Cap' as he called the man. He also pointed out this was not this man's first episode of torture. I noticed he had healed scars on his back. Clearly from a whip. They appeared to have been inflicted quite a few years previously.'

Luc reread the passage. *Daboia.* The torture continued until this 'Cap' passed out again, slumping to the ground. Mehdi checked him and screamed at *Daboia. 'See I told you, his heart has stopped. Daboia shrugged. 'Bring him back,' he commanded me, as if it was as easy as turning a switch. This would be the second time. I had no choice but to inject him with another sample. It had worked the first time. I had no idea if it would work a second time or the results if it did. It was untested. Its effects unknown. I did it, injecting an entire syringe this time. He did indeed revive, writhing around in pain on the floor.*

Perhaps mindful of my admonishment, Daboia instructed his two men to pick him up and take him back to his 'cell'. It was at this point I witnessed the result of my efforts.

As the two men picked him up, apparently feigning weakness, he hit the first in the throat with a sideways chop of his hand. The man fell gasping for a breath he would never get again through his crushed trachea. Grabbing the neck of the liquor bottle on the table, 'Cap' struck the base of the bottle into the nose of the second with such force it drove his nasal bones into his brain, shattering the bottle and killing the man instantly. Before I could even fear for my life, he turned to face Daboia, who had turned at the sound.

With a feral growl, he slashed Daboia across the face with the fragment of the bottle in his hand and grabbed him. As Daboia reacted to the gash in his face, lowering his head in pain, 'Cap' wrapped his arms around Daboia's neck in a wrestler's chokehold and squeezed. Daboia did all he could to dislodge the man. Pummeling his midsection with iron fists. I could hear the ribs cracking from the blows, but Cap did not relent. He just grunted. Desperate, Daboia tried to lift the bigger man and slam him against anything. All it did was hasten his demise. With a slight crack, Daboia fell to the ground, his balaclava clad face bleeding from the gash through his face covering. I knew not if he was dead or unconscious.

I had stood silent, terrified during the entire incident, still holding the syringe. In less time than it has taken me to write these notes, it was over. He turned. I assumed I would join my departed wife and daughter. I felt no fear, instead a little exhilaration at the prospect of this final release from my servitude.

Cap reached me, a wild look in his eyes. He grabbed my throat in his large hand. In English, he asked. (we had been speaking Arabic during the interrogation).

'What is it?' glancing at the empty syringe, I dropped it from my hand.

'An experimental drug I have been working on to regenerate tissue and organs. Molecular assemblers, nanoparticles, and nanorobots. Mitochondrial with modified ATP and DNA, stem cells, HGH and adrenaline, among other components. You were dead three minutes ago.'

He looked at me, confused at my answer, squeezing slightly. 'Why?'

I looked at him, perplexed.

'Why are you doing this research?'

'My benefactor employs me to develop this, hoping to extend his life.'

'How long will it last?'

'I do not know.' He squeezed again, looking at me, lifting me to the tips of my toes. His dark eyes blazed with vengeance.

'What will it do to me?'

'I do not know. It is experimental. I have never injected it into a human before. I have not been able to study the results. I was desperate. It contains adrenaline. It was all I had here to use to bring you back. You were dead, and you were not telling them anything useful about US troop strengths, plans, or movements in Syria or Iraq. He just kept torturing you. I told him his torture would kill you. And it did. Twice.'

'Who are you?'

'They call me the Doctor.'

He asked me for my benefactor and my name, and I told him. Then he squeezed until I blacked out.

"NO!" shouted Luc aloud, leaping to his feet. "Who is *Daboia*? Who is your benefactor? You cannot *not* tell me. Who is he?"

Luc raged silently, pacing the room. So close and yet no closer to finding out who employed this Medhi Khan and presumably *Daboia*. He stopped. If this Cap killed him, then who was his *Daboia*?

He refilled his scotch and sat, his glass against his forehead. He returned to the handwritten notes, curiously all in English.

No one was more surprised than me when I awoke. I could not have been unconscious for long. I scanned the room with my eyes without moving in case he was still there. Once I knew he was gone, I slowly got to my feet and surveyed the carnage. I did not know the inventory of the room, but it appeared he had left with minimal items as nothing appeared out of place. The two helpers were both obviously dead. Daboia was still lying on the floor, but I could see he was breathing. I moved toward him and checked the back of his neck where there was a lump.

His eyes opened, and he moved.

'Stop. You may have cracked vertebrae. Can you move your fingers and toes?' I asked as he stared at me, fear replacing the anger.

'Yes.' His eyes reviewed the room, seeing the dead rebels and no prisoner. 'Where is he?'

'I do not know. He knocked me out, too. I woke just before you,' I lied to him. I did not want him to know of our conversation.

'We must recapture him. He can't have gotten far. We broke all his fingers and toes and most of his ribs.' I remember his smile of delight as he said this.

Daboia tried to move. I put a hand on his shoulder.

'You have a lump at the back of your neck. If you continue to move, you may die immediately or become paralyzed. You need to remain still until we can arrange a helicopter transport.'

He paused. I could see the calculation in his head. He told me to send for one of the men. Daboia explained to them to send a tracking party to find the prisoner and allowed me to use the satellite phone to contact our benefactor.

He told me what to gather to take with us on the helicopter. There could be no evidence to be found, nor any clue of our participation. This included taking the cracked helmet of the prisoner. Apparently, he was a US fighter pilot. The back of his helmet read Lt. Colonel Nick 'Cap' Turner.

Luc leaned back and closed his eyes. The current Senator from Colorado and independent candidate for President. The only person who knew the name of Khan's benefactor. Clearly, there was more to this story, as none of this had been made public. A presidential candidate enduring torture and escaping would certainly have used this in his campaign to prove his toughness.

Pacing the room, trying to decide what to do next, Luc contemplated what he had learned. First the Doctor, and presumably *Daboia*, were behind the assassination of Gaspard. The empty folder he had left on the desk in Geneva was the code name of the Interpol case he was working on when his wife and child were murdered.

It was a human trafficking ring, responsible for the disappearance of thousands of European migrants, primarily refugees from North Africa, but many also from the war-torn Middle East. He'd been on the verge of tying all of this back to a syndicate of rich European elites. He had convinced one to turn on the others.

On the same day his wife and daughter were gunned down in broad daylight, in protective custody, in the middle of Paris, his informer was also found hanging in his safe house, his tongue cut out while still alive. His three guards murdered as well. From the information he found in that folder, it was clear this doctor was using some of these 'disappeared' refugees as the test subjects to give his benefactor everlasting life.

In addition, Luc seemed to remember talk of a lab in Ukraine possibly having something to do with the origins of the COVID virus or being involved somehow in the manipulation of the virus. Having seen viral biology, plus molecular and atomic cellular manipulation mentioned in several of the folders of notes, it was possible Khan had been involved in other activities or his lab was part of this.

Now he also knew there was a connection to Nick Turner. In his gut, Luc suspected *Daboia* was tied up in the death of his family. He would not stop until he knew the complete truth and *Daboia* was dead. He had to talk to Turner, and he needed to use Annie's skills to find out more about all of them.

#

"Any idea where Luc is?" asked Chaumont.

"None. After we confirmed he was not one of the bodies in the burned house of Byron Lauzon, he already had days to disappear," replied Leon Thibault, Chaumont's Minister of Justice.

"Maximilian knows this?"

Leon laughed. "He does. Now he has two bodyguards with him everywhere he goes. Gauthier on the loose has him paranoid."

Chaumont nodded, but did not respond.

"We located Lauzon's Maserati abandoned in a parking garage in Marseille. Luc must have left his car with our tracker and drove Lauzon's to Marseille. Nobody realized the car was unaccounted for until days after the fire."

"What is he doing?" mused Alain aloud.

"His job. Or rather, his old job, I would suspect. You know how Luc is. He's the best. Sniffing out clues no one else can find. Relentlessly tracking down every lead. Would he not contact you?"

Alain shook his head.

"Leon, you know our relationship is not the best since I sided with Maximilian against Luc regarding responsibility for his family's death. He only tolerates me because of his sister."

"Yet you involved him in our investigations?"

"For the reasons you stated. He is the best. I did not want to end up like Jean Paul," explained Alain.

"I see," replied Leon, adding casually, "the man is dead."

Alain flinched, feigning ignorance. "Man?"

"The man Luc interrogated. After his fingers were repaired in the hospital and his face stitched up, we had no choice but to release him. He did not wish to press charges."

"When?"

"Two days after. Floating in the Seine. His throat was cut. It did not appear to be a robbery."

Alain leaned back again. "My friend, what is happening?"

Leon stared back, wanting to ask questions he would not get honest answers to. Instead, his face impassive, he replied with the Gallic shrug made famous by the French, complete with raised hands.

Chapter 68

Harriet ran into Lexi's office in their HQ. She was on the phone.

"Excuse me," she said in an annoyed voice as Harriet turned on ANC. '*Supreme Court Justice Marvin Moore died this afternoon while traveling back to Washington after giving a speech,*' said the talking head.

"Let me call you back," said Lexi, hanging up the phone. "What the hell happened?"

"He had a heart attack on the plane, and they were unable to resuscitate him. He had a history of heart disease and two prior heart attacks, so not entirely surprising. By the time they landed, there was nothing anyone could do," Harriet answered breathlessly. Trotting down hallways was more cardio than she'd had in years.

Lexi picked up her phone when the second line lit up. She punched it. "Hello" she said, listening. "Yes, I just heard as well."

Lexi looked at Harriet and motioned her to leave the office. Harriet gave her an annoyed look, but walked out and closed the door. Lexi flipped the switch under her desk, engaging the SCIF mode to secure her communications. She put the phone on speaker.

"… the fuck do we do?" came through the concerned voice of Sal Fontana, the Majority Leader of the Senate.

"Nothing. We can't risk wasting a good nominee and have Turner and Crawford block them from being approved. We do what the Opposition did. Wait until after the election," ordered Lexi.

"Too bad it wasn't one of the younger ones. Moore was probably going to retire, anyway. He is the only black. I guess we can at least replace him with a nice progressive black judge," laughed Sal.

"And female. Sounds good to me," suggested Lexi. "You'll make the announcement?"

"Yes. The official statement is to wait until after the election and let the new president choose their candidate," laughed Sal.

"It will look magnanimous," agreed Lexi.

"Ok, later," he said, hanging up.

Lexi turned off SCIF mode and dialed Harriet's phone.

"All good."

Harriet came back into the office. "What's the plan? Wait?"

"We don't have a choice. Without a majority in the Senate, we'd need to convert someone, and it's not worth the risk. Especially this close to the election," explained Lexi.

"Timing sucks. Now Blackbird can use this as a point to drive conservatives to the polls in the hope they can pick the nominee to replace their black conservative justice," groaned Harriet.

"Blackbird and Turner both. It is unfortunate. They are already claiming we are going to pack the courts, so I doubt this makes their argument that much stronger," commented Lexi.

"Let's hope so. We'll just highlight your stance the next president should be the one to pick the justice.

#

"Shit," snarled Denise, watching the TV with Chuck.

"It really hurts if there are any election shenanigans. The conservatives are now four versus three, with the 'conservative' Chief as the decider. We know he hates controversy. We can expect him to side with the Party. No better than a tie in every case. He's never going to be the deciding vote in any landmark decision," explained Chuck.

"I hadn't thought about that," admitted Denise. "There are sure to be lawsuits. We're screwed. You know the state courts are going to side with the Party every time."

Nick sat silently through their conversation, his face showing on a ZOOM screen on the main TV in the office.

"All we can do is keep doing what we're doing. Denise, please find out about the services so we can arrange my schedule. I want to attend if I can. I only met him a few times, but I read his biography. He was a perfect example of everything America offers to those willing to work hard," said Nick.

"Got it."

"Can you get me on *Tommy* tonight to comment?"

"I'll have Margie give her friend there a call. He likes her," said Denise, smiling.

"Don't tell Jer," snickered Chuck.

#

"To comment on the tragic loss of a scion of the Supreme Court, we welcome presidential candidate Senator Nick Turner," introduced Tommy.

"Thanks Tommy," said Nick, once again broadcasting through a webcam on his laptop in yet another hotel from the road. "It is truly a sad day for America. Justice Moore was a perfect example of the American dream. His nomination hearing was the stuff of legends. Born into poverty, raised by his grandparents, earning his way through school and attending Harvard on his own merits."

"He succeeded despite the perception that affirmative action led to his higher education opportunities. He constantly fought the damage affirmative action did to those minorities who *earned* their accolades. He told me his proudest moment was when he got to see this declared unconstitutional," informed Nick.

"I agree. It was a milestone for the court. For now, anyway. I hear the Vice President is looking for a way to reinstate affirmative action in some form. Lots of pressure from the Ivy League alumni donors," countered Tommy.

Nick's head in his window nodded. "It will be our job to keep it merit based. Not sure why they are complaining. The Supreme Court did not put an end to legacy based admission. Your name can still get you into the Ivy League regardless of your grades or effort," smiled Nick on his camera.

"Ouch," grinned Tommy in reply.

"We will miss his common sense jurisprudence and his stalwart defense of the Constitution. Most of all, we will miss his ability to listen.

When he spoke, it was with profound retrospection, jurisprudence, and wisdom. His legacy and shoes will be hard to fill," finished Nick in a solemn tone, showing his concern for the replacement measuring up.

"Did you know the Justice?"

"I met him a few times and enjoyed the conversations. He was also a history buff, so we connected on that level. What the administration is doing is the right thing. Still, I am worried. We are going into a contentious election cycle, with our populace having less and less faith in our election systems. While the Supreme Court has tried to not be part of picking winners and losers, they have also shirked their duty to rule on the unlawful changes of state election rules by various governors."

"Senator, the elections are run by the states, not the federal government. The cases have to be brought to the court for them to decide," pointed out Tommy.

"True Tommy. But many of these changes contradict state constitutions. These rules clearly state these kinds of changes can only be enacted by state legislatures. The Supreme Court can certainly rule on the overreach of governors, ignoring their own legislative rules. Without a majority on the Court, there will be gridlock on rulings we may need to have in this election cycle," explained Nick.

"You bring up good points, Senator. Especially when the Supreme Court clearly could have ruled on these egregious and unlawful changes late in the last several election cycles. Not to mention their decision to not even hear your arguments about why you should be allowed on the ballots in Pennsylvania, Michigan, and Wisconsin. By not taking the case, the states did not even have to defend what is clearly a decision designed to favor the major party candidates. Allowing this overreach to stay in place was a travesty of justice."

Nick shook his head on the screen, interrupting. "We did what we could. In all fairness, the Opposition gave up pretty easily and didn't even all agree this should be pursued in the *last* elections."

"It's still a wanton disregard for the stated duties of the Supreme Court," Tommy finished, his concern clear.

"Tommy, our Supreme Court has become political and is more concerned with public opinion and offending American *Pravda* than in reviewing the Constitutionality of laws. I don't know if some of them are afraid they won't get invited to the best cocktail parties or if they're afraid to make consequential and potentially unpopular decisions."

"Senator, I know why. They are afraid their houses will be picketed by protestors and activists. What I find worse," continued Tommy ominously, "is many of these activists are encouraged by people like the current and former Senate Majority Leaders who use inflammatory language to goad these protesters on. As someone who has frequently had this treatment. I would not wish it on my worst enemy. If you have a wife and family, it is very effective. Especially given the state of our police, who are not inclined to enforce the law."

"I understand Tommy. I do. However, they have lifetime appointments for this reason. They do not have to face an angry mob of voters in order to be reelected. There are laws against protesting a Supreme Court Justice's house. As you mentioned, our own elected leaders in our Party encouraged this violence. Clearly, this has a chilling effect on justices. Worried about the consequences of following the letter of the law and ruling on the constitutionality of the laws and cases they review, may now have personal consequences."

Nick paused and took a sip of coffee. Tommy did not interrupt. He always felt the words coming from Nick carried much more authority than him saying the same things.

"We need to fix this by holding anyone accountable who implies or issues a threat to a jury or judge, claiming they will be punished if they rule one way. Too often in the last few decades, our court has been weak and bowed to public opinion rather than the strict canon of the law. Lady Justice is wearing a blindfold. We need to add noise-canceling headphones to drown out the partisans on all sides."

Tommy laughed loudly. "Nice. Great analogy."

"The other thing, Tommy, is the role of the court. Too often lately we saw judgement after judgement dealing with the merit of the law or case in question. The merit of a case is not for a Supreme Court judge to determine. They are strictly limited in their review. That is the whole principle of *judicial review*. They don't get to decide if it is a good law or a bad law and they certainly don't get to 'make' law. We have two branches of congress and fifty state legislatures held accountable for their good and bad laws. By voters."

"As Judge Moore showed time and time again in both his majority rulings and his minority dissents, he constantly reminded his fellow Justices that theirs was not to question good or bad, just whether it violated the Constitution. Simple and straightforward."

"As always, Senator, you back up your opinions with strong facts and defend your position well," noted Tommy. "Justice Moore was not afraid and was one of the strongest advocates for strict interpretation of the Constitution. It is unlikely we will see his sort again on the Court," Tommy said with a visible sigh.

"That is true Tommy. Certainly, if the Vice President is elected, there is no hope. I can tell you. I'd only nominate strict Constitutional Justices. You can count on that," stated Nick.

"Thank you, Senator. Unfortunately, I must also ask about the latest accusations against you."

Nick sighed in his little window on Tommy's broadcast.

"Tommy, have you ever noticed how the bombshell headline makes the front page of the papers of record, but when they admit they lied, the story and admission are buried on page fourteen?"

"It always seems that way," agreed Tommy.

"Yet it still enables them to say they retracted their accusation or admit their fault, even if no one reads it or knows it happened. The damage is done. They win either way. Public opinion has been swayed, and their mission accomplished for their masters."

"A sad truth, Senator."

"Tommy, not only did I not do any of the things these students have claimed, they never actually cited anything I said or did. Or a time and place. Funny. Last time I checked, even in America, it took evidence to accuse someone of a crime."

Tommy was laughing on his side of the screen.

"What I have done is provide over one hundred witnesses, debunking the charges. Students, faculty, and administrators. Many are concerned at the implied stain on my reputation and the university's reputation, too. Allowing such a weak accusation with no specifics. It makes it look more and more political, given the timing."

"Ya think?" quipped Tommy. "How could anyone misconstrue this attack as anything but an attempt to smear your reputation?"

"Exactly. Which is why I have contacted these colleagues as character witnesses. They are available to be interviewed, interrogated, and put through the wringer to confirm both my character and teaching style as both entertaining, honest, and highly effective."

Tommy laughed again at Nick's expectation his witnesses would be tortured by the press.

"If discussing topics such as the slave trade, slavery itself, Jim Crow, reconstruction, Wilson and FDR, women's suffrage, Vietnam, prohibition, Kerouac, and the sexual revolution, makes me a racist or sexist, well too bad," Nick was getting worked up, raising his voice.

"Tommy, shit happened in our history. We need to discuss it with an open mind and understand the root causes and where we failed. And where we succeeded. If these kids make it through high school or college without facing hard truths, that's too bad. They weren't going to get through my class without an understanding of our history. No revisionist history in my class. I was equally critical of all parties and their boneheaded decisions on these topics. Including the fact slavery was not abolished in the Constitution initially. And why."

"Senator, I wish I had a history professor like you."

"Tommy, they had to expand the size of my classrooms almost every year. I must have been doing something right."

"Did I hear you were voted professor of the year your first year?" asked Tommy.

"Yes, I was. I also won it a second time."

"Now I understand your statement about the retraction on page fourteen. I guess that answers my question of why it is buried."

"Let's just say I welcome the time when they can quote time and place and the exact transgressions. I'm happy to defend my actions as a professor. Or anything else. I take responsibility for my actions."

Tommy nodded. "Apparently, many others feel the same way. I believe we are now up to over eight thousand of your former students who have posted videos and testimonials on social media. How they learned so much in your class and how you treated everyone as equals. And how only snowflakes, using their terms, not mine, were offended by having to learn the inconvenient truth of some of our history and how it came about."

"Tommy, it was an epiphany for many, debunking much of what they had been indoctrinated with in high school and earlier. Especially learning we would not have had an America if slavery were not still allowed when the Constitution was first ratified."

"I bet that was a shocker, learning that," laughed Tommy.

"Today it looks unconscionable. Back then, it was impossible to remove. A non-starter to any compromise and adoption by both Northern and Southern states. Much like it is impossible today to talk about reforming Social Security, Medicare and other entitlements. Governing is compromise and that one inclusion, while heinous, is also what enabled us to fight a Civil War eighty years later to right that wrong. There was no way to accomplish it in 1786."

Tommy shook his head in agreement, not interrupting Nick.

"No one considers the alternative of not ratifying the Constitution with slavery. They assume things would have turned out fine. There wouldn't have been an America. And we would not be having this conversation about 250 years of American success. It's easy for pundits today to talk about that decision as if it was just one among many, but they have not studied the Convention, nor the debates and the tiny margins with which it was adopted," finished Nick.

"Always teaching Professor. Thanks for the lesson. I hope folks are as curious as they have been in your prior lectures on this show. To look up some real facts on this. Thank you for your time, Senator."

"You're welcome."

#

Roland listened to the metallic voice emanating from the metal brick on his desk.

"Excellent work. It appears no one is any the wiser. Their court will not meddle now."

"He was in poor health. It took little effort," he responded.

"No one is going to suspect I trust?"

"People should be more careful with mail order prescriptions. The right dosage, especially for someone with serious heart conditions. It is too important to trust to some faceless machine or pill packer in Thailand, not to mention the delivery services. Anything could have been swapped in the warehouses," replied Roland in mock seriousness.

"Excellent," replied the metallic voice. "Where are we with Gauthier? Have you found him yet?"

"I have spies everywhere in Europe. We have a lead. I will take care of him. He does not possess limitless resources as we do. He will surface. When he does, I will strike."

"And the photographer?"

"Eliminated. He swore he gave nothing away. But it was too convenient that we lost track of Gauthier during his captivity. The man had broken fingers and a cut cheek. Our friend is showing a more ruthless demeanor now that he is free from the restraints of the law."

"Geneva?"

"Complete. All evidence was destroyed, and the authorities wrote it off as a large gas leak."

"There are too many loose ends and mistakes. *Daboia*, you are getting sloppy. We cannot afford mistakes. We are so close. Finish this."

He fingered the faint scar on his cheek as he replied.

"Understood. I am tying them all off. There will be no one left to betray our efforts by mistake or through coercion," replied Roland, knowing Pavlovich was right. There were so many operations in flight at once. With him being tied to Washington, many of the ops he would have completed himself were now being farmed out to others he did not fully trust. Any of them being exposed could bring the others down. Like pebbles starting an avalanche.

"Israel still going according to plan?"

"It is, just as we laid out. Tell me when you would like our 'friends' to be betrayed."

"Begin." The metallic brick went silent with a few clicks.

Chapter 69

Mel knocked at the door to the suite in the Waldorf Astoria in DC, near the Capitol building. After twenty seconds, he was getting ready to knock again, when the door was opened by a large, rotund man, wearing a robe, with a glass of some liquor in his hand and a big smile.

"Ah, Professor, please come in," said the man, returning to a table with a spread of expensive hors d'oeuvres.

"Caviar, scotch, champagne?"

"No, thank you. A bit too ostentatious for my tastes," replied Mel, noticing the door to the bedroom side of the suite was closed. Judging by his attire, he figured there was someone in the bedroom.

He was looking at one of the world's most notorious hackers. Sebastian Kolsten was the mastermind behind several very destructive and lucrative ransomware gangs. He'd made millions from extorting corporations and sovereign nations for decryption keys to unlock data.

The FBI cybercrimes division eventually tracked him down, extraditing him from Croatia. He was hiding in a manure truck, trying to cross into Bosnia. A country without US extradition for cybercrimes.

Once the FBI got him, they charged him with several counts of murder for a particular attack which had shut down life support systems and stopped robotic surgeries at a hospital in Maryland.

The resulting chaos killed several patients before backup generators could come online. The inability to access patient records data, key MRIs, CAT, and x-ray scans, and drug dosages resulted in additional harm and eventual loss of life from delayed treatment.

In a secret plea deal, he'd agreed to become a white hat hacker for the government. Helping harden cyber defenses for key military systems and infrastructure. For this, many of his frozen assets were returned to him as well as deferred sentencing on the various murder convictions as long as he played ball.

Many in the FBI objected to this arrangement but were countered with the realization they and Homeland were hopelessly outmatched. There were no resources to keep up with the teams of state sponsored hackers trying to breach their systems. Sebastian was a necessary alternative to continued national security risk.

He was also well compensated by several private sector companies who contracted with him to help harden their systems against increasingly sophisticated attacks. Primarily those companies with various government contracts. TrustedVoter was a client and one of three voting machine contractors.

Seb shrugged at Mel's statement. "What's the point of having the money if you don't enjoy it? He glanced at the bedroom door. To what do I owe this visit? You summoned me to Washington."

Mel saw the glance toward the door. He set his phone down on the table. It emitted a white noise hum, with occasional harmonics, almost like monks chanting.

"I would hardly call it a summons. You are being well compensated, sometimes from both sides," added Mel in a careful aside. At this Seb paused, cracker and caviar poised in front of his mouth. He finished the motion after a slight hesitation.

"I don't know what you mean," he said, crunching the cracker.

Mel shook his head.

"Sebastian. May I call you Sebastian?"

"Seb."

"Ok, Seb. You forget how we caught you. And your deal. Which you are clearly not adhering to completely. We are well aware of your aliases on the dark web and how you are still dabbling in, shall we say, less than honest and illegal hacking activities. Remember, the charges are only deferred, not dropped. With your background and what you know. There are many who would be concerned. Accidents can happen. Ask Epstein. Oh, that's right, you can't."

Seb sat down in a chair, the robe parting, mercifully revealing he was at least wearing boxers underneath, if not entirely covering his bloated belly. His face was slightly pale at Mel's revelations. Like most who caused mayhem behind computer screens, Seb was a coward.

"That is not why I'm here," pointed out Mel.

Seb shook his head, still processing how they could have discovered his new extracurricular activities.

"Now you know we know. Is someone in the bedroom?"

Seb nodded yes.

Mel picked up his phone. He added a jazz music track to mask their voices from the other room. His prior efforts were to thwart any listening devices. Miles Davis played loud, as he pulled his chair closer.

"Hey, no worries, she's in the shower," he laughed nervously.

"Just in case," answered Mel in a low voice, leaning in. "Now talk to me about the voting machines. Are they ready?"

Seb, glad to change the subject, brightened.

He explained the complex code he had inserted into the executables and binaries of each of the system's boot up processes. Mel finally held up a hand.

"Enough. I don't care how. I care about results. And I care about this not being discovered. Explain in English, please."

"Sorry. Each machine will have these subroutines imbedded in the final upload of software before the election. They will not be detected because they are set up as monitoring programs. As each machine is booted on election day, the subroutines are coded to execute based on the activation of the Election Day ballot code. In the machines and states you have chosen, it will present to the voter exactly what they vote. In the database it will tally a vote for the Vice President at 1.33 and a vote for Governor Blackbird at .66. Every three votes, a vote is added to the Vice President and subtracted from the Governor. With me so far?" asked Seb in a whisper, as Mel nodded.

"The tricky part is the paper ticket. As the votes are tallied in the database, my code clones it and journals the changes," Mel's face showed he was frustrated at the technobabble again.

"Hang on, I want you to understand this part. It is how we show them their vote, put it on the paper ticket and still have it recorded the way we want. The machine's code is working, collecting the votes and storing them in the database correctly. I make a copy of the database in DRAM. Think of it as a scratch pad. In my copy, the votes are adjusted as I described. The voter hits submit. His vote is committed to the database, and the outcome sent to the print routine of the paper output." Seb paused as he leaned forward, excited to be explaining his expertise. "Got it?"

"I think so. At this point, everything is as it should be, right?"

"Right. Now for the tricky part. My database is sitting there as well, with the altered counts. What my code does is spoof the tally system into accessing my copy of the database when it requests the information for the tally of the votes in the system. My altered counts are all that are used to pull from and compile this data from each of the machines." Seb leaned back and took an opened bottle of champagne from an ice bucket and poured himself a glass.

Mel was still trying to follow the logic. He had an MBA from Harvard and a PhD in international relations from Georgetown. His last statistics course was many years in the past. His only computer course came when floppy disks still reigned.

"If your copy is still there, won't they find it? Even if there isn't a formal audit, won't TrustedVoter technicians eventually find this if it is going to be on all the machines?"

"Good question Professor. If they knew what to look for, sure. Even a dumb technician could eventually find it if they looked. But it won't be there the day after the election," smiled Seb.

"How are you going to ensure that? There must be thousands of machines being used. Remember, it can't be obvious," prodded Mel speaking louder in a worried voice. He did not trust machines and AI was worrying him even more.

"No worries. DRAM is purged when a machine is power cycled. My cloned copy disappears when they power off the machine. Leaving only the database copy with the actual data. My program has an erasure code in it. At noon the day after the election, if the machine is on, my program erases itself if they have not turned the machine off. The shadow copy of the database and any record of the code ever being in the machine. It also does a hard reset of all the event logs. This happens in every machine." Seb loaded another cracker with caviar, crumbs spilling out as he smiled in triumph.

Mel was thinking through audit scenarios he'd heard of.

"What about an audit? What if the machine is off? And turned on and done by someone in an audit. Can they get around your self destruct mechanism?"

"To the head of the class, professor. Excellent question. The machines can be booted in audit mode. This prevents many other programs in the boot sequence from executing, including those having to do with the election and the databases."

"Shit," muttered Mel, shaking his head in disappointment at the risk. They'd been through this before and had to physically alter machines en masse in a warehouse to prevent audits from discovering some of their antics with voting machines in the prior presidential election. He did not think they could do it again.

"Easy. You did not pay me all that money to leave you exposed. Remember, if the machine is off, my cloned copy is gone. However, if they try to do a recount, they will use the original database with the original tallies. Those *not* sent up to be counted. I added a second program, again, simply disguised as a sniffer program, not an executable. If they boot in audit mode, it detects this and then *it* issues the self-destruct code to the other code to execute the wipe, *after* the boot sequence. This time it is a full wipe. Everything. Logs, databases, everything. It also overwrites all the used sectors on the solid-state disks with random generated characters. TrustedVoter will take the heat for the reset."

"Why does this matter?"

"When you hit delete on your computer, you think you have deleted your file and your information. All it has done is delete the pointer in your little folder to where that file existed on the disk. In the computer on the memory, the solid state disk or the physical disk, the blocks where your data is actually stored in the computer are all still there. It is pretty easy for any tech to access this data. Unless you go in and physically erase and copy over those sectors on the storage, your data is not truly gone. I started my hacker days by accessing celebrities' phones and selling nudes they thought they'd deleted." He smiled in delight at the embarrassment and money he'd made from those threats.

"The technical term is called data shredding. Like you shred a piece of paper through a paper shredder, we do the same for digital data. Scramble it and make it impossible to reassemble. It's a brave new world professor."

Mel's head was pounding. He was tempted to take Seb up on the offer of a drink.

"What else do I need to know?"

"As you know, TrustedVoter owns the contracts for Alaska, Arizona, Nevada, California, Oregon, Washington, Montana, Colorado, Idaho, Wyoming, Utah, New Mexico, and Hawaii. We have only scheduled Nevada and Arizona, per your request.

"Yes, too bad you don't have Georgia, Florida or Texas."

Seb shrugged. He didn't understand the politics of government contracts and kickbacks. He had no idea how the states chose what voting machine vendor they used.

"Maybe next time," replied Seb with a smile.

"Hopefully, we won't have to resort to this anymore. After the election, you will see the last half of your payment."

"Pleasure doing business with you, professor," finished Seb.

#

As he closed the door, Seb let out a gigantic sigh. He hurried to the closed door to the bedroom of the spacious suite. Opening it, he made to say something when a black gloved hand grabbed his throat, holding a finger up to signal silence.

Seb was practically peeing his pants as he watched the man, with a barely visible scar on his cheek, pull a device from his pocket. As he turned it on, he released Seb's throat.

"Jesus man, that hurt. What the fuck. I did what you asked."

"So, it is all ready? Everything is loaded into the machines and all your code will activate as you explained."

Seb was still rubbing his throat, pissed at his treatment.

"Ya, it's all done. It will all auto execute. Watch and wait."

"Can you still add this to the machines in the other states?"

"No, it is too late. They have already gone out for delivery and the patches are scheduled to download and install on each machine. The code is already locked down. I can't get to it anymore. You should have said something sooner." He paused, looking at the man.

He stared back, dark eyes boring into his own.

"After the patches are installed, the machine goes into read-only mode. This means no more changes from the outside are accepted by the machine. They can monitor and extract the results, but nothing will be allowed in to alter the code after that. It was one of the concessions after that election when the data was flowing out to servers overseas and then being written back into the machines to be tallied. Of course, *nothing* was being done to alter the data then, right?" smiled Seb.

"I see," the man responded.

"Besides, none of those other states have voted Opposition in decades. They don't need to cheat," shrugged Seb, rubbing his throat.

"A pity. You might have enjoyed your money a bit longer," the man said in a satisfied and slightly sinister tone.

Seb, startled, looked up in time to see the small caliber pistol with a sound suppression muzzle aimed at his forehead flash. The man stood over the corpulent corpse, looking down to make sure his two shots were sufficient.

He was tempted to spit on the man, but that would mean DNA. It was one thing to look into the face of your target, another to sit behind a computer screen and anonymously cause mayhem. It was no different from bureaucrats and politicians watching video game monitors of the results of their drones, missiles and bombs destroying people's lives and livelihood. With no risk came no remorse. He was determined to provide remorse to people for actions and their unseen consequences. It also helped that he enjoyed delivering his 'messages'.

Walking carefully from the room and out the door. Neither his shoes nor his fingers would leave any marks behind for any forensic tracing. He walked to the stairwell, keeping his head low, with the brim of a hat pulled low to prevent any surveillance from picking up a clear picture. One more loose end dealt with. There would be no leak or public testimony from the hacker.

#

"Son of a bitch," thought Ken Holcomb as he listened. He continued to listen to the conversation, making occasional notes. He had headphones covering one ear while he fiddled with the equipment, trying to get as clear a recording as possible. The walls in the old hotel prevented some of their technology from transmitting as clearly as they would have liked. They got about every third word. Bits and pieces of sentences. It had been a rush job to get the bugs in at all.

He was startled as his partner, Carlos Garrett, tapped him.

"Geez," shouted Ken, removing his headphones while looking at his tall and skinny black partner.

"Sorry man, foods here. Club sandwich on rye. What's up?"

"I'm not sure, but our busy little hacker is explaining how to hack a voting machine. At least, I think he is. I am not getting all of it. But someone else is in the room asking a few questions. I don't think he is a hacker. There is a lot of jazz music in the background and a nasty reverb from something. Any way you look at it, old tubby is definitely violating the terms of his agreement. We should have fried his ass the first time," commented Ken in a righteous tone.

"Way beyond my pay grade. He sure is living high on the hog. This prick gets a suite at the Waldorf and we're in a closet. I figured we'd be in for another orgy. The only way he gets any is paying for it."

"I think I heard a door close. Nothing. Maybe he is calling the girls now. Hey, leave my club alone. Eat your own damn sandwich," said Ken as he grabbed his club and fries from the room service cart.

Carlos looked up between bites.

"This what you signed up for when you joined the FBI?"

Ken snorted. "I wanted to be Clint Eastwood from *In the Line of Fire*. Couldn't get in the Secret Service, so here I am. Eavesdropping on fat pig hacker informants in $1000 a night suites at the Waldorf courtesy of Uncle Sam. Buddy, there's something rotten with this."

Carlos nodded as he ate. He'd get the recordings transferred and shipped over to the techs to see if they could clean it up a little more. Maybe they could actually put the words together into better sentences. They'd been tipped off that Sebastian was coming to town and only had a few hours to set up their surveillance. It was not ideal, but it would give them ammo to maybe put his ass in jail for violating his deal with the Feds. Carlos smiled as he ate his hamburger. Seb would not do well in prison. Maybe there would be justice after all.

Chapter 70

"Today, we welcome a true American icon to *Face the Press*. Thomas Culhaven, Secretary of State for three presidents, Ambassador to the UN, Great Britain, the Soviet Union, Japan and China. You have been involved in nearly every major event in our country's history since World War II," finished David Johanson.

Culhaven smiled, showing his fake teeth in his famous grin.

"Thank you, David," he replied in a slow, yet firm, voice. "What you did not tell everyone is I am also a six-time failed primary candidate for president. Or that I accomplished all those other tasks simply by being one hundred years old."

"Mr. Secretary, that does not diminish your obvious love for our country and dedication to serve," replied David in a solemn voice.

"You are too kind. My genuine passion these last thirty years have been my books on the state of the world," admitted Thomas.

"You have recently published your latest commentary. '*1914 Again? Is History About to Repeat Itself.* In it, you state the world is retreating to nationalism, similar to Europe in 1914?"

"That is correct. It is becoming clear. The rhetoric, the saber rattling, the locking down of resources and access to key materials. It mirrors both the land and resource grabs of the new world resources by the European powers during the era of exploration."

"In the past, it was gold and silver, then spices and silks, finally oil and iron ore. Now it is rare earth minerals, lithium, and cobalt and to a certain extent still oil." Thomas delivered his summary in a lecturing tone, as he had for decades as a professor at Georgetown.

"Sir, I would be remiss if I did not ask your opinion of the current situations and who's best equipped to steer the United States through these perilous times," asked David in his serious anchor tone.

"David, I am not sure it is worthy of such dramatics, but I will offer my opinion. It is true I have seen and been involved in many consequential decisions for our country. What I can say is experience trumps instinct. Now is not the time to trust instinct. We face dangerous times, both here and abroad."

Johanson broke in as the Secretary paused.

"So, you believe the Vice President is the wisest choice?

"Without a doubt. She has spent years in the Senate in leadership positions and now almost two full terms as Vice President. Rarely have we had a more qualified candidate for president. It is critical we have someone with proven leadership as the world faces these precarious times," he finished in slow and thoughtful sentences.

"Clearly her opponent does not have anywhere near her resume, with only Congress and a few years as a governor of a small state. Very little international political experience as well," said David.

"Yes, her opponents are fractured and adrift. They cannot even come together around a single candidate. Our country is at risk as long as we remain apart. We need to unify around common goals and objectives. I believe the Vice President has articulated these well. Her opponents not so much," explained Secretary Culhaven.

"Opponents? Do you even consider Turner a viable candidate? He is polling less than ten percent with some dubious positions and his support for the cop killer Marine. He hasn't even stood for an election before and he aspires to the Presidency?"

"David, I've seen much. Nothing surprises me any longer. As you noted in the title of my book, we are indeed returning to the imperial days of old. Nationalism is the order of the day. This drives pride in the superior nature of one's own country and people. A desire to drive out diversity. To shut down the doors to the assimilation of new ideas and people. An appeal to restricting social freedoms for perceived unity instead. Turner is appealing to the lower classes. Speaking to their baser needs and stoking these fears."

"There is no doubt he is espousing violent rhetoric, as we are seeing in his followers attacking minority protesters," agreed David.

"I spent my career fighting against fascism and communism spreading around the world. What I see in Turner is the same tactics and message that led to the rise of both ideologies around the world. It is easy to rouse those who have nothing. By branding everyone who has what you want, who looks and leads their life differently from you, as their enemy. You can blame them for your lot in life and how they are stealing your opportunity. It is a dangerous path. We have consistently fought to preserve the path of freedom for over 200 years. Turner claims to want to return to first principles, to the rule of the Constitution. Perhaps he should read it and understand the true meaning of what it means to be free."

"Mr. Secretary, those are some powerful words. I hope we can get them spread far and wide. To make sure those in our electorate understand what they are giving up by being duped by Turner. We thank you for your time and wish you well with your book and continued health," finished David as they broke for a commercial.

Secretary Culhaven's aide and bodyguard quickly pulled him in his wheelchair from the dais and off the sound stage so the next guest, Senator Freddie Garcia, could take the chair.

"Ah Senator Garcia, a pleasure," he said, holding out an emaciated hand.

"Mr. Secretary," replied Freddie, looking down at the wizened old man. He didn't have the heart to tell him that yet again, his insight was wrong. He'd been a failure in every position he held. Often with significant loss of life as a result of poor counsel and bad decisions.

Yet, as a prominent member of the Party, they and the media had shielded his reputation from any harm. It was how Washington worked. And Turner was the threat? Only to men like him in a Party where continual incompetence was rewarded with lifetimes of praise.

"Good luck up there Freddie," the Secretary smiled, knowing his words about Turner would be the ones broadcast by the media. He'd done what he could to help his party, ever loyal to the end.

#

"Senator, former Secretary of State Culhaven, had some pretty harsh words for you this morning," noted Tommy Charles.

"Thanks for having me on, Tommy. I think Senator Garcia, who appeared right after him, did a pretty good job countering his arguments. However, seeing as he accused me of trying to be the next fascist dictator, perhaps a little history lesson is in order," answered Nick, staring into his phone from the passenger seat as Earl drove them from a rally in North Carolina back to DC. Tommy smiled in reply.

"Secretary Culhaven has two things in common with our current president. They have both been in DC for sixty years or more. The second thing is they have both been wrong about every major policy decision since the sixties. From escalations in Vietnam, to a host of diplomatic blunders during the cold war, the Iran hostage crisis and then, in Culhaven's case, his antics prior to the first Gulf War proposing to allow Saddam Hussein to keep Kuwait as a path to peace. Finally, both of their anti-Israel stances have been harmful to American-Israeli relations in every Party regime since they arrived in town," explained Nick in an impassioned voice.

"Senator, that is a lot to unpack. I think you offered an excellent summation of your own on the futility of the Secretary's efforts. Is there anything else?"

"There is Tommy. Specifically, his claim that I am like so many dictators before. I can only assume he meant the standard defense of the Party against anyone who criticizes their stances. Those who stand up against them are eventually labeled as the next Hitler or Lenin. Those despots did indeed speak both a populist and nationalistic message. Rousing their poor and disenfranchised to rise against the ruling elites." Nick paused in his window from his phone.

"What he neglected to note is that in each of these cases they were speaking to homogeneous peoples. What I mean by that is Germans,

Russians, North Koreans, or Chinese. America could not be farther from this appearance. An American is a true melting pot of different cultures, ethnicities, races, and orientations. We don't have hundreds or thousands of years of animosity against those who are different. This is still a problem in most of the world, but not here."

"You are right Senator. We are all made up of unique pieces of our immigrant family's experiences," agreed Tommy.

"Shaped by the freedom in America to be and do what you want. Free from coercion. Here is the crux of the argument. It is easy to twist words into the shape you want, but it is the actions that truly show what your intentions are. Go listen to any speech by any of these totalitarian dictators. They all tell you who the problem is. Who you should hate and blame for your lot in life. They use this hate to mobilize their followers into fanatics and channel this hate into violence against the enemies of the elected leaders until they can get absolute power. Who pays the price? It is always these poor, disadvantaged followers. They simply trade one yoke for another, but in the end, they are still serfs or slaves to a ruler, with no way to fight back." Nick paused.

"Here is my point. Ask yourself. Who among the candidates is telling you what to do? Who is telling you who to hate? The candidates telling you what they are going to do for you are the ones making promises they won't be able to keep. Only one candidate is truly talking about you keeping and exercising your freedom."

"Only one candidate is not espousing censorship or vowing to shut down media outlets daring to offer different opinions. Those who know their ideas are not supported by a majority shout the loudest that the other guy is the problem and must be silenced. Keep this in mind. If you don't think for yourself and let them do it for you, don't be surprised when they turn on you after they no longer need you, or your vote. This is exactly why I created and explained the Mirror concept. They are the ones who are *doing* exactly what they claim we are. Taking away people's freedom and the right to choose. Just hold up your mirror and you can see who the real fascists and future dictators are."

"Thank you, Senator. Anyone who actually pays attention to your words can see exactly what you are saying. They only have to open their eyes and ears. And use the Mirror."

Nick nodded in his window as the live shot ended.

He glanced to his left at Earl driving and behind at Greg.

"Good job, boss. We'll get it up on the website and posted on Hibi as soon as we can," said Greg.

Earl looked at Nick, concerned. "Feeling better?"

"Earl, when dickheads like Culhaven pop up, I feel so helpless. He has single-handedly screwed up so much. He was one of 'the best and the brightest' the Kennedy admin pulled out of the Ivy League to join his cadre of experts. We've been saddled with their ineptitude for more than half a century. The saddest part is they are responsible for training and leaving behind an entire army of acolytes in all branches of the bureaucratic state. They are the real problem in our country. Smarter than me or you and always right. And accountable to no one. The voters don't even understand how this shadow government works. They are the true enemy of the people."

"Nick, we solve the problems we can solve. Then we move to the next one. You've said this before. Let's win this one before we worry about the next one."

"More Sun Tzu?" asked Greg with a grin.

"It's just common sense. If he created common sense than I guess he can take credit." Earl grinned back at him.

Nick smiled. "Not Sun Tzu, but valid none the less."

Chapter 71

"We unequivocally condemn the attack by Hummus on our ally Israel. We stand behind Israel and support their right to defend their territory and their people," slurred the President of the United States in a shaky voice, standing at a podium.

There was no press in the room.

"Cut," yelled a producer, looking at Amy, the President's press secretary. Lexi, who was standing behind the President, came up.

"That was very good, Mr. President. Let's try it one more time. It is 'Ha-mas'." She sounded out the name of the terrorists for him.

They moved back to their stations and rerecorded the speech. There'd been another terrorist strike into the heart of Israel by Hamas terrorists an hour previously. A car bomb detonated in the parking lot of a sporting event, killing seventy-five attendees. They'd also attacked a kibbutz only recently rebuilt from the prior war.

Killing a dozen and making away with four hostages, two women, and two children. The President was appointing Lexi to be his point person to work with Israel on response and aid.

As they finished a suitable recording, the President was led off by Amy and his secret service team back to the residence.

"Thank God it wasn't Hezbollah, or we would be here all day to get him to say that. Just what I need three weeks before the election. A high-profile task to divert my attention," fumed Lexi to Mel as she walked down the hall in the West Wing.

Mel shrugged. "Not much for you to do at this point. We are done with the major campaigning. A few high profile stops to large crowds. Might actually look good for you to take time from campaigning to help our strongest ally in the Middle East. Very presidential. Also shows how confident you are."

Lexi gave him a look as they entered her office. The footage announcing her role would play shortly, stage managed as a live event.

\#

"We cannot continue like this," accused Willa Kreutz, the Secretary of Commerce. They were at an emergency cabinet meeting.

"We have to invoke the 25th amendment. The president hasn't been in a cabinet meeting in six months. He hasn't been in public beyond a few waves walking to Air Force One. You have illegally been functioning as the President for almost a year. This charade must end."

"Thank you for your support," replied Lexi sarcastically. "Once again, let's consider this rationally. The 25th amendment would put me in charge, correct." This was met with a majority of nodding heads around the table. "What exactly are we going to gain by formally going through the motions?" asked Lexi, holding up her hand at Willa.

"Let's consider what would happen. It is mid-October, we have an election in less than a month. To invoke the 25th would cause chaos and no doubt spur lawsuits about what and when the President became incapacitated and demands for proof of his incompetence. This could delay the transition of power or the acknowledgement I truly am the rightful president. Would this not embolden our very enemies you keep telling me to worry about, Admiral?" asked Lexi, looking at Admiral Jason Kensington, the head of the Joint Chiefs. He'd been invited to this cabinet meeting by Lexi for this very reason.

"Indeed, it would Madame Vice President. This is exactly the confusion our enemies look for. To take advantage of knowing our attention is focused inward versus toward external threats. If there were any question regarding who was in charge, they would use this to execute some of their plans. Taking advantage of our inability to react quickly. Even without the Israeli issue, I would recommend against any attempt to invoke the 25th amendment. Even discussion of it is dangerous for us and our allies and already emboldens our enemies. The speculation in the press because of the lack of visibility of the President has increased chatter in the terrorist circles we are monitoring. It is why Hamas has attacked so close to the election."

"Homeland, Defense, do you agree?" asked Lexi.

"Yes, Madame Vice President, I do" agreed Roger Brody. Issac Roth, the SecDef, merely nodded his head in concurrence.

"What other issues would the 25th cause?"

"Lexi, we would probably see the stock market crash 40%. The market hates uncertainty. Especially with an election so close. It might even be worse," offered Rosemary Hurst, former CEO of a Wall Street bank and now Secretary of the Treasury.

"We can't have that now, can we?" replied Lexi with a snort.

"True, it would not be a good time for a market crash. We are just starting to really recover from the two pandemics and all our Fed interest rate increases. We'd risk sliding back down," conceded Willa.

"If I may, I would like to add my thoughts," interjected the First Lady. "My husband is no longer capable. It is true. I know he wouldn't want to cause any damage to our country. He'd want us to continue on, to transfer power in the same manner we have throughout our history. There is precedent for the continuation of a President while incapacitated in office. If you recall, during the last year or so of Woodrow Wilson's second term, a stroke had a debilitating effect on him. His wife continued to provide the support and direction necessary while the cabinet carried on as the President continued to live but not be an active participant in governing. The election occurred and the peaceful transfer of power was completed. The population was none the wiser about how disaster, mayhem, and confusion were averted. This is our job, to ensure this disaster and confusion is not willfully cast upon our people, *by us*," she finished.

The cabinet sat in silence. They contemplated the words she'd spoken; the situation described and the potential disaster they might usher in by removing the man who was president but no longer knew his name. Many were surprised at the support of the First Lady.

Lexi responded. "You are *his* hand-picked leaders of our executive departments. Our departments. Either way, I'm the leader of this country, whether or not officially. I'm willing to stay in the shadows for the good of the people. We know I'm in an excellent position to become the next president. If I win, we can ensure the public never knows the extent of the president's ailment and his legacy will be safe."

"If we invoke the 25th amendment, I'll become president for the next three and a half months and maybe this will prevent me from becoming president. It will certainly be hung around the neck of each of you as the group that forced out a sitting president. You will always be branded as the traitors who put me into the presidency before an election. Is that how any of you want to be remembered?"

"Will anything change if I am president versus the Vice President acting as the head of his cabinet? Ask yourself, is it worth it? What do we have to gain? We know we have a lot to lose. As long as the health of the President is not terminal, I believe we continue on, maintain his low profile and continue to do the jobs all of us have been assigned by him. Do we need to discuss this further?" asked Lexi, looking up and down the table from her seat at the center.

"Javier, are there any legal issues with us *not* invoking the 25th amendment?" asked Lexi of the Attorney General.

"Madame Vice President, the 25th amendment is a tool. It allows the cabinet and the Vice President to agree to remove the President if *all* agree he or she is incapable of executing the duties of the office of the Presidency. Nowhere does it state the cabinet *has* to implement the 25th amendment if the President is ill. It is defensible if we choose not to."

"Then it is my recommendation. We continue as we are, get through the election and have our usual transfer of power. Any further comment?" finished Lexi in a presidential tone. There was none.

"Then this meeting is adjourned. See you all next week, unless the Middle East escalates."

Everyone left the room, acknowledging the Vice President and First Lady as they exited. Finally, it was the two of them. They sat eyeing each other.

"Thank you for your support," commented Lexi, graciously.

"You insincere bitch, fuck you," spewed the First Lady, rising to leave, her eyes ablaze. She was so angry she was shaking.

Lexi calmly replied, "You may want to compose yourself before you leave. Wouldn't want anyone thinking you've lost control, or that there is any issue with your husband."

"You are an evil woman. I told him not to nominate you. The Party gave him no choice," admitted the First Lady, sitting back down.

"Your husband has never had an original thought in his entire life. He has been a parasite living off the body of the government. A fat bloated tick. You have done well living off him. As have your children and now grandchildren," replied Lexi in a calm tone with a slight smile as she leaned back in the President's chair at the table.

"I can take you down. I can expose what a vindictive and power-hungry whore you are. How you've sold your soul and spread your legs to gain the power to rule," spat the First Lady.

"Please do. We can also discuss your husband's concessions to China, Russia and Ukraine, and the blackmail that made these conflicts possible. The kickbacks, the deals he's made during his 60 years in public service. While we are at it, perhaps we can discuss the affairs both of you have had. Or the troubles of your daughters and sons. There are how many grandchildren no one knows about? Your legacy would be ruined. Or perhaps the DNA results of who the father of your third child really is?" The First Lady's eyes widened a bit at this revelation.

"I suspect jail time would be in order, as no jury in the world can overlook some deals you've been part of. Many have died because of some of them, correct? And for what? I am still going to win the election. I can admit to trying to hold it all together as your husband declined into his current state. Of sparing this country and its people from suffering because of his poor leadership. I may even be seen as selfless, putting the needs of the country ahead of ambition or the chaos of invoking the 25th. Is this what you want?"

The First Lady had her manicured nails buried in the arms of a leather chair across from Lexi, glowering at her.

"I thought not. My advice is for you to pull yourself together. Put a smile on your plastic face and walk out of here with me arm and arm for your husband, for your family, for yourself and your future, free from him when he finally passes. Who knows, you are young enough, you may even ensnare another unsuspecting man in your web. Believe me, you do not want me as an enemy and worse, if I somehow fail to win this election, your fall will be fast, hard, and spectacular. Trust me. Now let's go," commanded Lexi.

The First Lady squeezed the chair for a few more seconds and finally released her grip. There were now eight slits cut into the arm of the chair from the force of her nails.

"Now look what you did. More taxpayer money spent on your behalf," lamented Lexi. The First Lady glanced down at the arms.

"Coming?" asked Lexi sweetly, standing at the door. As the First Lady hesitated, Lexi held out her hand.

"I am only going to ask once. Come now or pay the price."

"The First Lady hesitated, then took the arm of the Vice President as they left the cabinet room arm in arm, laughing and smiling as the photographer in the atrium office took the requisite pictures.

Chapter 72

Greg led Dan Baker through the office toward Nick's office. As they passed by Steve Gaine's office, he glanced up. Immediately recognizing Dan. He had been listed as an FBI person of interest and was under mild surveillance at all times because of his exposure of various governmental shenanigans.

Steve knew there were teams assigned by Karen to continuously monitor his internet and phone activities. He was also smart enough to know a guy like Dan, about his own age, had come of age in the digital era. He was smart enough to use publicly available tools to mask most of his online activity from the FBI.

Sadly, the FBI rarely had the best and the brightest, especially given the tarnished nature of their agency's reputation these last two decades. They could no longer recruit the top talent based on a patriotic desire to protect their country from the enemy. In fact, were he being honest, he wasn't sure he didn't agree that many of his agency's tactics and efforts were worse than those they claimed were so dangerous to democracy.

As Greg walked by with Dan, he could see they were talking and smiling with a familiarity only a long friendship could instill. This was no random visit from Dan to the office. He made a note to do some digging. Dan Baker was a Pulitzer prize-winning pain in the ass investigative reporter. One of the last. The FBI had been unable to intimidate him with either cancel culture or Patriot Act threats. The fact he was here was both curious and worrisome.

Nick looked up at the knock, smiling as Greg led Dan in.

"Nice to meet you, Dan. I'm a big fan."

"Thank you, Senator. I am a fan of yours as well," he replied, shaking Nick's hand.

"Call him Nick," said Greg, as Nick smiled in reply. Greg shut the door, and they sat around the small table in Nick's office.

"Get you anything to drink before we get going?"

"Sure, a coffee would be great."

Nick headed over to the machine and waved at Greg to sit. Greg looked at Dan and smiled.

As Nick worked the machine, he complimented Dan on a story he'd done, exposing the infiltration of the FBI into several local organizations and then their obvious manipulation to coerce and convince them to commit a criminal act.

They had instead pulled a sting on the FBI, allowing them to infiltrate the group. Meticulously documenting all of their activities. Proving without a doubt, the FBI did indeed act as agent provocateurs. Entrapping everyday citizens simply expressing displeasure at the government. Encouraging, steering, and then clearing obstructions out of their way to help them commit crimes. Sometimes, even arranging access to weapons they would not have been able to acquire otherwise.

This had given the FBI a huge black eye and should have earned him a second Pulitzer. Instead, it had led to relentless attacks by the liberal media against *his* integrity for giving oxygen to right wing conspiracy theories. An audit from the IRS and being 'mistakenly' added to the terror watchlist preventing him from flying overseas to receive a key journalism award were other rewards for his effort exposing their malfeasance. He was quietly removed from the watchlist with little fanfare shortly after missing the award show and publicity. They cited an honest clerical error as the reason.

Nick returned with their coffee and sat.

"Greg tells me you've once again been busy uncovering uncomfortable facts," started Nick.

Dan nodded, sipping the coffee. Adding sugar as he talked.

"Nick, I was contacted by Sam Vincent..."

"The dead chief of staff?" interrupted Nick. "When?"

"Two days before he died on the street in New York. Nick, he was on his way to meet me. His last text was to a burner phone number I gave him," replied Dan, looking Nick in the eyes.

"Wow," he answered, leaning back, his hands behind his head.

He looked at Dan. He was sandy-haired with soft features and no facial hair. His blue eyes burned with intensity.

"That's not all," Dan continued. "His last text was telling me he got my text and was on his way to a new Starbucks location. I sent him no such text. I replied with two question marks and waited."

"Hmm." Nick still had his hands behind his head. He raised his head to look at the ceiling. "Someone sent a text to his phone and diverted him. But they had to know he was meeting someone."

"My thought exactly. After thirty minutes, I looked at my regular phone and saw the headline he'd been hit by a bus a few blocks away. I knew then, someone else knew Vincent was trying to tell his story. I did the only thing I could think of," laughed Dan nervously. "Just like the movies, I removed the battery and threw the burner in the trash. I'd paid cash, so there should be no trail."

Nick lowered his hands and looked at Dan. His assumption would be true if he were dealing with anyone but the world's most powerful surveillance organization. He didn't have the heart to tell him the FBI had tracked the phone number and location from Vincent's phone and would access many surveillance data sources. If not in the store, then on the street. They knew who Vincent was heading to see.

"Did Vincent tell you what he wanted to talk about?"

"Only that he was working on an autobiography and he wanted to also do an 'exposé' with me. About the VP and Mel Arenson."

"Pretty heady targets. Did you get any info?" probed Nick.

"Not directly."

"It's an interesting story. I'm not sure how it affects me or why you are telling me. It seems Vincent's death was convenient, but absent proof it's still an accident."

Dan smiled. "Give me a little credit. I wouldn't be wasting your time if I didn't have more."

Nick returned the smile, opening his hands on the table as Greg smiled brightly as well. "Dazzle me."

"After I took the long way home assuming I was about to be run over or shiv'd on the street by an operative, I calmed down enough to think things through. Here is my theory."

Dan took a sip of coffee. He told Nick how he figured Vincent was being pushed out of his position of power by the VP because of the President's obvious decline. In fact, he figured the VP was really acting as the President and it was only becoming clearer as the President was seen less and less since the State of the Union. Today's brief comments on the Israel Hamas situation and appointment of the VP to handle it just proved his point.

Vincent had no money. Dan had discovered he had a big mortgage on a house in Georgetown. His wife was younger, and they'd only been married for a short time. The new wife had left a lucrative corporate job to come to DC to be with Vincent in his chief of staff role for the second term of the administration.

He was living on credit. Champagne tastes on Bud Light wages. Counting on cashing in after the Presidency with a lobbying or cable gig. Neither of which would be forthcoming if he was being frozen out of key decisions by Lexi. He did the next best thing. Write a tell all and cash in on the sensationalism. Dan finished his summation.

"He called me. He wanted me to legitimize his tell all."

"Instead, presumably Lexi or the FBI or someone was watching, and he was foolish. He probably didn't hide his outreach to publishers and they blabbed to the VP," speculated Nick.

"Most likely."

"You still have nothing but theories. No offence, Dan, but I'm three weeks from an election, and my campaign manager is probably pacing a hole outside the office."

Dan laughed. "Right, sorry. I tracked down the widow. Told her I was helping Sam with the book and was wondering if I could look around the house. She was pissed because the house was the only thing Sam had left. That and a pretty impressive wine collection."

"She also told me the FBI had taken everything, including the computers and all his notebooks. She didn't even know the passwords to access the bank accounts. Bottom line, the FBI ransacked the house looking for his notes and manuscript."

"Think they found it?"

"Honestly, I am not sure. She told me he was extremely paranoid. As you can imagine, if you are planning to write a book exposing the most powerful woman in the world," offered Dan.

This time, Nick laughed. "You have no idea. He was right to be paranoid, trust me." Dan raised an eyebrow at this statement.

"We really need to finish," added Greg, looking at Dan. "I'm the one Denise will draw and quarter if we don't wrap this up."

Nick had been in intelligence for most of his adult life. He could spot all kinds of 'tells' and non-verbal communications. One thing he prided himself on was an indifference to the preferences of his staff. He could tell Dan and Greg had been more than friends. He suspected as they walked in, a bit too comfortable with each other than two business acquaintances.

"I snooped around and found something in his wine cellar. I found this." Reaching into his bag and pulling out a wine opener with a logo of a famous Napa winery. He handed it to Nick, who looked at it and smiled as he turned the USB drive out of the handle.

"The FBI missed it?"

Dan nodded.

"His manuscript is on it?" He nodded again.

"What are you going to do with it?"

Dan held Nick's gaze. "Nothing."

This was not the answer he expected from a journalist famous for exposing corruption in politics.

"Why?"

"I can't corroborate any of it with the key witness dead."

"They think theirs is the only copy? If he was as paranoid as you say, it is unlikely he made a copy to the cloud," mused Nick.

"His wife confirmed he did not have a remote account for storage. I confirmed as best I could without giving myself away. I think that is the only copy outside of what was on the laptop."

Nick made to hand it back to him. Dan held up his hand.

"Nope. I don't want it. I can't do anything with it. The temptation to try is too great, and I know what would happen. You, on the other hand…"

Nick stared down at the corkscrew tchotchke USB drive.

"I don't have a copy. My techie friend who broke the password also promised me he did not make a copy either. I told him it was a matter of life or death. I believe him. He has worked with me before and he understands this isn't a game you want to play with government agencies. No one wants to end up like Seth Rich. Or Jeffrey Epstein."

Nick nodded. "What's on it?"

"The short answer is the President's a puppet, pumped full of drugs to fight various cognitive issues associated with his age. The VP is running the country, and the cabinet is going along."

"Dan, none of this is a surprise to anyone with eyes and an ounce of curiosity in America. It is hardly worth Vincent's life."

This time, Dan nodded. "There are dates and times and specific actions he has documented. The reason I am giving it to you is because of what they did to win their two elections. Nick, how I wish I could publish that book with ironclad proof and a witness to testify in front of the people. He tells how they did it. Everything we suspected and then some. How they have been using government funded 'get out the vote' grants and non-profits to focus on helping poor and disadvantage people vote only for the Party. From absentee and mail in votes, to dead people voting, organized ballot harvesting and ballot box stuffing, to bought and paid for judges and finally the machines."

Nick sat back and took a sip of his lukewarm coffee.

"Dan, I can't do anything with it either, without proof."

"I'm not giving it to you to expose the past. I am giving it to you so you can try to keep them from running it again in three weeks."

"Not exactly a lot of runway," Nick added in an ironic tone.

"I know. It took longer than I thought for my guy to crack his password. It was ten digits long. It took him five months."

Nick smiled. "He paid attention to the security classes they make us take. Mine is over twenty. Supposed to take seven quadrillion years to brute force through it. Jeremy Kwan said he could do it in a year or two," finished Nick, looking down at the device in his hand.

"Dan, I thank you for this. You are right, it wouldn't have made a difference. This DOJ is clearly not going to take any of these accusations seriously. They were certainly complicit in many of the past election 'actions', if only from inattention or unwillingness to investigate legitimate concerns. Or force transparency at a minimum."

"I knew Greg worked on your staff. I figured if I couldn't expose it, I might help the next target of their actions."

"Blackbird is more of a target than I am," countered Nick.

"No offence, Senator. *If* the Vice President is smart, and unfortunately, I believe she is, she and her staff should be smart enough to know you are the real threat. The country is a powder keg. Half the citizens are not happy with their choices. You offer the potential for something different. I wish you luck. My only ask is if you ever uncover a way to corroborate any of this info, I get the chance to break the story. Deal?" offered Dan, holding out his hand.

Nick stood as well. "Deal. Thanks Dan. Thanks Greg for arranging this. Oh, what is the password?"

"Was wondering if you would ask. Ellsberg&?, with a capital E and the L's are number 1's."

"Pentagon Papers, nice," responded Nick, smiling.

"You should change it immediately, too."

"Will do." Nick looked at Greg. "If Denise gives you a hard time, tell her I said it was worth every minute."

A smiling Greg led Dan from the office.

#

Steve was waiting for them to leave Nick's office. As they got near, he conveniently exited, bumping into Dan.

"Oh sorry, didn't see you. Looking at the stupid phone," he stated, holding up his phone. They all laughed and smiled.

Steve widened his eyes. "Hey, aren't you the guy who quit that New York magazine and won a Pulitzer?"

Dan smiled as Greg introduced him.

"Nice to meet you," replied Steve, heading down the aisle toward Margie's office. He smiled once they couldn't see him. Looking down at his phone, he could see Dan walking away. The malware he had airdropped to Dan's phone was working.

He had tried to do the same to the other staff member's phones, but they were all too secure. Jeremy Kwan was smarter than the FBI's smart guys. He'd made a note of this in his last update to Karen. Having Dan Baker make a visit was probably worth another undercover meeting with her.

Chapter 73

"Nick, where are you guys? I need you to turn around and head back to DC pronto. Tell me where to send the jet," announced Denise from the speakerphone.

"We're in Tennessee driving between Knoxville and Nashville, I think. What happened?" asked Nick.

"Senator Fitzpatrick is asking for a Censure vote against you for your speeches and all the violence of the past few weeks. He claims you've delivered inflammatory rhetoric, are recommending seditious behavior, and are inciting citizens to open rebellion against the government," read Denise.

"He cites the specific speeches at the Police Convention, the Creating Change gathering, your university speech and he also refers to the violence you've been involved in with Pastor Mill's bodyguards and at the LGBTQ conference. He is asking for an immediate vote."

"Shit. We finished our voting already. There was no pending legislation for this reason. That's why we left. Now he expects all the Senators who left to turn around and come back for this? Is Fontana giving him his wish with a quorum call?" asked Nick.

"It appears so. You know the Opposition has more contested seats this year, even though the Party has nineteen up vs. their fourteen. This could be designed to hurt those candidates, and it takes you off the road for a few more days, too."

"Crap. There is no way they vote for this. There is also no way he gets folks, his and the Opposition Senators to turn around and immediately head back. This is lunacy. I find it hard to believe Fontana is going through with this."

"Boss, it's about 7 or 8 hours from where we are to DC. No need to send the jet. Let's drive it," added Greg from the back seat, where he was studying the GPS. "Straight shot, interstate the entire way."

"Hang on, Earl," said Nick as Earl got off at the next exit to turn back east. "Pull over up there at that store," said Nick, pointing. "Denise, let me call Chuck and see if he can find out when and if this is going to happen."

"Sorry Nick. I know you wanted to talk to more folks this week," sighed Denise, hanging up.

#

"What the hell is going on?" he asked Chuck.

"Beats the hell out of me. You have no idea the number of calls I am getting from senators from both parties. Everyone is pissed at us instead of at Fitzpatrick. I am telling them you could give a shit, and this is all silliness. There is no way this is going to pass."

"I agree, but it sure gets us off the road. And thirty-three senators in the middle of re-election campaigns. Any idea when he is going to schedule the vote? No way he can pull this off this week, right? Folks have made plans already," stated Nick.

"I have a call in to the Leader's office. As soon as I know, I'll let you know. Where are you guys?"

"Just outside Knoxville. I believe we are headed to one of Martha's stores in Cookeville."

"Go. I will let you know as soon as I know something. Worst-case scenario, we'll send the jet to Nashville to pick you up. I'll let you know what I find out."

"With the Israeli's threatening to invade Gaza again in retribution for the attacks, the death of a Supreme Court justice, and an election in three weeks, we have better things to do than listen to one hundred Senator's bloviate about election campaign speeches. Not our finest hour for sure. I have half a mind to not even bother showing up. So what if they censure me? I'm out in less than three months anyway," speculated Nick.

"Not a good look. They'll make it look like you are afraid to defend your words. You have to go," confirmed Chuck.

"I know. I was just daydreaming out loud. Punch it, Earl. Let's get to Cookeville and keep going until we hear otherwise."

#

Sal Fontana held the phone away from his ear as he listened to the screeching voice of the Vice President. He set the phone down and punched the speaker, leaning back in his chair.

"…fucking control our own caucus. What does that prick Fitzpatrick think he is doing? The last thing I need is a bunch of televised speeches defending Turner's right to say whatever he wants. We are already crucifying the guy in the press for inciting all this violence. No one is hearing his rebuttals. Look at Secretary Culhaven. He did *his* duty and tagged Turner good. And he is one hundred fucking years old. Still doing what he can to help us. I want you to stop this," bellowed Lexi, stopping to take a breath.

"Lexi, I can't. The rules of the Senate allow anyone to call for a censure vote," responded Sal, sipping his bourbon.

"The fuck you can't. When I was Leader, I would've told Fitzpatrick I'd put his balls in a jar on my shelf if he didn't get things back in line with what the Party needs. Make it happen and cancel the vote and the speeches, Sal. Before I do. Or better yet, postpone them to after the election. We can send Turner out with one last black eye."

"Lexi, the rules changed since you left. I tried to talk to Colin and convince him now was not the time. We have nineteen of the thirty-three seats up this go round. Pulling them back after we just sent them home looks bad. He wouldn't go for it. I also told him you didn't appreciate the distraction. He laughed and said it will help you. I'm thinking sometime next week is the best we can do. I need to get it done as fast as I can, or Fitz will make a stink. That we definitely don't need." Sal could imagine Lexi on the other side of the phone. He was glad they were not in the same room.

"Start grooming a replacement. No money for him in two years when he is up for reelection," growled Lexi.

"Lexi, that seat's been in the Fitzpatrick family for generations. He doesn't need our money to run again. He is popular in Massachusetts," he replied, trying to calm her.

"Sal, I never forget betrayal. I won't tolerate it. Find a woman and start the process to get her ready. I will campaign every day of primary season if that's what it takes for her to win. Got it?" ordered Lexi in a tone offering no rebuttal.

"Got it."

"Make this go away, Sal. Limit the speeches as much as possible. Too bad we can't ban cameras. I swear, if he gets a bump out of this, Fitzpatrick may have to resign before the next election. Or he can transition to FitzPatricia, and we add another woman senator after I cut off his balls."

"Whoa Lexi. We need his vote for your agenda. Let's not be too hasty. You can get your revenge *after* we expand the court and add more states."

"Sal, I don't need this shit right now. Keep your house in order. Everyone is replaceable." Sal looked at his phone as Lexi ended the call. He slugged the rest of his drink.

Chapter 74

'Professor Bishop' was getting a cup of coffee from the carafe on the credenza in the conference room outside the FBI director's office. He stood sipping the very hot coffee and leaned against a windowsill, looking around the table and chairs.

John North, aka Steve Gaines, often wondered what his career at the FBI would have been like if he hadn't shown so much potential as an undercover agent. He pictured himself like so many of his FBI agent brethren. Career climbers scurrying from meeting room to meeting room just like any other corporate drones. Showing PowerPoint presentations and pontificating on strategies to increase profit margins, or in their case, higher arrest rates, all to rise in the ranks.

He knew he would have either quit, shot himself, or someone else out of frustration. He was definitely not cut out for office work in a bureaucratic government agency. The field was where he felt alive. When he infiltrated Turner's campaign, it was just another assignment.

He'd attended a few of his smaller rallies at VFWs and American Legion halls in the early days of his grassroots efforts. What he saw was a mostly older group of fed up blue collar and middle-class parents nodding at the bravery of someone standing and saying exactly what they all felt. Articulating their worries and concerns.

What he found most surprising was what he did not hear. It intrigued him that Turner could say these things, rile up these crowds, motivate them to do things they would not have done themselves, and then not tell them to do anything to help *him*.

This mesmerized John. He'd *never* encountered any leader building movements or protesting government, not ask his followers for money, or recruit them to do some deed to show their loyalty, or at least vent their anger for his cause.

He looked up as Karen Coleman walked into the room, shutting the door behind her.

"Ah 'Professor', nice to see you again," she smiled.

"Director."

"Sit. How is it going? Is Turner beginning to crumble? He has to be getting desperate with all these attacks," continued Karen gleefully as they sat.

"It is chaotic. How much of this mayhem is us?" asked John.

"I wouldn't know what you mean?" replied Karen, smiling. "Seriously, not as much as you would think. This guy pisses off people left and right. They don't even need any prompting. The ARL and Antifa crowds are funded by the usual dark money SuperPACs and Pavlovich's NGOs."

"And Gabriel's Angels? Do we have anyone in those orgs? They are pretty violent. If they don't tone it down, you guys are going to have to step in and stop them."

Karen looked at her top undercover operative. John had accomplished so much. Helping the FBI unmask unhinged groups, planning dangerous activities within the US. He looked nothing like his actual appearance with his wig and prosthetics.

"To my knowledge, we have not infiltrated this org," she lied convincingly. "They seem to be ultra-violent. Who do you think is funding them?"

John laughed. "Funding is not their issue, trust me. You know, from all my other work. Money is rarely the issue with any of these white supremacist outfits. My concern is more with the outcome."

"How so?"

"Karen, they're going too far. It ends up helping Turner, for all the wrong reasons. He has disavowed them. Yet they still claim to support him. Every time they show up, he has footage of them doing all this mayhem. Not heeding his directions. Hurting people. Going to jail and either getting out because of liberal no bail laws or getting bailed out by someone."

"So? How is this helping him? Seems to me as long as they keep claiming to be his supporters, it will hang around his neck."

John shook his head. "Not this time. You have to understand. He is always thinking two or three steps ahead of everyone. He sees the opportunity, and he milks it until that last possible ounce of value, and then he stops. He never pushes it. Every risk is calculated, but he knows the odds of success." John was leaning forward, speaking quickly as he described Nick's masterful grasp of tactics. It was quite an energetic performance from what looked like a sixty-year-old philosophy professor.

"He took their support until it was no longer useful. He bailed them out until they started going from self-defense to offense. Now he pivots. With his cameras, and his use of the footage and carefully timed statements, he tags whoever is funding them with the obvious shades of conspiracies against him by most likely us and some other nefarious Party operative or NGO. It is brilliant, and it's working. Everybody who thinks, now assumes this as another plot by the state to discredit and meddle in a campaign. Most probably assume it is the FBI."

Karen laughed. "Working? 'Steve', I think it might be time for you to have a sick relative and leave this campaign. You're blinded by his rhetoric."

She stood to get a cup of coffee.

"Turner's tactics are *not* working. He is getting attacked from all sides. Now he even has to go defend his dangerous speeches in front of his Senate colleagues. He has students claiming harassment and racism. He's riled up the LGBTQ community against him as well as pissing off both the pro-life and pro-choice crowds. He even turned one of his staunchest support groups against him, the cops." Karen returned to her seat.

"He lucked out on the Marine, but even that backfired when public opinion, the very thing you say is on his side, clearly thought he was guilty and should have been put in prison. If he hadn't committed suicide, they would have continued to write stories about how it was all Turner's fault he was free. Even then, the cops were still going on TV hating on him."

John sat and listened. For the first time in his career, he questioned his loyalty to his agency. Karen was the obvious choice for the directorship. She no longer remembered what it was like in the field. She couldn't read the signs. Maybe he *was* too close.

"What's next? I assume you came with something?" asked Karen tersely, not getting the reaction she expected from John to her comments. She would have to pull him out and reassign him soon.

"You are right. It is chaos. The staff are feeling the stress more than Turner. He rolls with it mostly. I see occasional outbursts or body language suggesting he is internalizing a lot of anger. Especially as you said regarding the Marine. The fact he's being physically attacked, with the cops doing nothing, weighs on him."

"Good. One of these times he is going to go too far and then we have him," she nodded righteously.

"Don't hold your breath. He knows this and he will let them kill him before he hits back," answered John.

Karen shrugged. "That works too."

John hid his surprise at her response.

"How's his money? You said last time he was running out?"

"The book helped a lot. They published it themselves, so all the profit came to the campaign. Despite your opinion on Dusty, when he was found not guilty, and the families forgave him, that brought in a ton of additional money. All small dollars from millions of donors."

Karen leaned back. "Hmm, that's somewhat concerning. Can you get the donor lists? It will come in handy after the election to know exactly who supports his message. We can track them down if they don't behave after he loses. Do you think the Homeland investigations is going to affect his ability to get the message out?"

"Some. The biggest challenge I see between now and the election is his ability to speak to sizeable crowds. He only has a couple of state fairs left. Though, this Censure thing could be a boon to him. It will be televised and give him a chance to once again speak to millions who'll turn in to see what this is all about. I think they'll be surprised. Everyone else will pile on and Nick will hit them between the eyes with common sense. Karen, this was a mistake."

"I was surprised as well. Especially after Congress adjourned for the break. It's pissing off the Party as well," agreed Karen.

"I don't know if the Vice President sanctioned this or not, but watch out. The only way he gets any traction is with mistakes that put him in front of lots of people who have not heard him. *The Sunday Hour* was a perfect example. They were ecstatic, especially with the fact the network tried to censor him and he had the proof. He went in knowing this would happen, prepared for it, and caught them with their hand in the cookie jar. This stuff plays right into his 'us against the world' narrative."

"We are just observers, John," noted Karen carefully.

This time it was John who smiled.

"Still, if you are ever asked. My advice is to dial back on the scandals if they can. Each one he just turns in his favor. Look at the one with the students. Whoever came up with that one should be prosecuted. They threw those girls in front of the train trying to slow it down. Now they are getting creamed on social media, by feminists and activists, for making shit up and setting back the cause for true victims of abuse."

"I suspect that was not the campaign. And he got tagged pretty bad with front-page headlines. For lots of folks, that is all they will remember, the accusations. With all the dark money and the importance of this election. We have to let it all play out from our perch. Unless it crosses the line."

"Understood. I have one more bit of interesting info."

Karen sensed from his tone this one might be important.

"Dan Baker came by the office yesterday. That's really why I asked for this meeting."

"Baker? What the hell is he doing visiting Turner?"

"My thought exactly. I wasn't at the meeting. Only Dan, Greg Simmons and Nick. I did some checking. Greg and Dan were classmates in college at Columbia."

"Interesting. What do you think?"

"No idea. I planted our tracing software on his phone. I bumped into him on the way out. As you know, I can't get it on any of Turner's staff," commented John.

"That damn Kwan. We're going to have to deal with him."

John nodded. He handed a note to Karen.

"That's the id of the tracker I put on his phone. With that, you should be able to access his phone and his whereabouts. Maybe that will help you figure out why he visited."

"Thanks John, good job. See if you can find anything else out."

John nodded.

"How are we doing on outside interference? The usual suspects up to their dirty tricks?" asked John, fishing.

"You know how it is. The usual state actors. We have a lot of efforts on ensuring the integrity of the drop boxes. Making sure no one has access to the voting machines, that kind of stuff. You stick to your assignment. Just a few weeks to go and then we'll see. Depending on how bad he loses, we may move you over to the Opposition side to make sure we have a seamless transfer of power. You stay focused until the election. We can't meet again. If something comes up, switch to the drop off method for any other data we need to know."

John stood as Karen did. The meeting was clearly over.

#

"What is this?" asked Irving Paradowski.

"It's a code to a tracker on Dan Baker's phone," answered Karen.

"No shit? How did you get it?"

"No questions. Just use it and see what you can find out. Maybe this can help explain why Baker visited Vincent's widow. Any luck finding Vincent's phone?"

"No. We even looked in the storm drains on the street side. Nothing. Probably dropped it and someone pocketed it and sold it after wiping it clean," answered Irv.

"Apparently Baker stopped by Turner's office. Any chance this is related?"

"How did we find that out? You have someone on the inside?"

"Need to know. Irv, you were the lead investigator on this. Did we find anything connecting Turner and Vincent on his laptop?"

"Nothing. We couldn't find the phone at the scene. You got the tip about him meeting with a publisher in the city. We put the screws to them and seized the computers. We had to return them pretty quick once their lawyers got involved, but reviewing the emails, it was all just meetings and a promise of a juicy tell all."

Karen nodded. "The notes and outline on the laptop, were it?"

"It was all we could find. He didn't even have a first draft. Just a bunch of random events. Dates, times, participants. All pretty damning stuff if he had published it. We had surveillance of Vincent's widow. That's when Baker entered the picture."

"You talked to her after. What did he say to her?"

"Vincent had contacted him about helping with a biography of his time in the White House. She hadn't heard of him. She said he looked around, mostly to see all the damage we left behind. By then, she was very pissed off at the FBI and threatened to call her lawyers. We backed off. We'd already been through the house with a fine-toothed comb. There was nothing for Baker to find."

"You sure?"

"Karen, it's been four months. If he had found anything, shared it with anyone, or was planning on publishing, he would certainly have done it by now. We kept him under surveillance for two months and he did nothing suspicious."

"I don't like it. His ties to Vincent. What we know he had and was going to do. Now Baker shows up at Turner's? See if you can come up with anything and let me know. Thanks."

"Since I am here."

Karen looked up from her desk. "What?"

"We had a surveillance team following Sebastian Kolsten, as always. He checked into a suite at the Waldorf two days ago. Our teams said he met with someone, but their audio is garbled and incomplete. We only got bits and pieces of dialogue. The techs are trying to piece things together. It sounded like they were talking about hacking and something to do with the election. No specifics, though."

"If he violates his terms, we'll fry his ass. He shouldn't even be out of prison. Claude spearheaded that one. I have no idea why."

"No worry about that now," said Irv in a deadpan tone.

"Why?"

"The do not disturb sign was up, so the hotel staff left him alone. It was a $1000 a night suite. Our teams heard nothing the next day and thought nothing of it, since they didn't get any devices into the bedroom. He is known for dropping big bucks on hookers."

"Get to the point Irv,"

"The cleaning crew found him dead this morning. Double-tap to the head. Very professional. Coroner says it happened about thirty-six hours ago. Right after the meeting, our guys recorded."

"Karma is a bitch. Let me know if you get anywhere with the recording."

Irv hesitated for a second. "Karen, he's one of the world's most notorious hackers. We heard the words hacking, voting and election. Shouldn't we dig deeper three weeks from an election?"

She looked up again, already late for her next call.

"Irv, we get five hundred of these a day, even more now that we are three weeks away, as you just said. He's dead. Whatever he was planning was obviously stopped. I'm late for another call," she finished, picking up the phone.

Irv nodded and left the room, closing the door. Too many coincidences. Baker showing up. A notorious hacker dying after having a conversation about elections. Vincent's missing phone. All FBI agents hated loose ends. He headed to the FBI labs to see if they'd made any progress on the recordings.

#

"Karen, to what do I owe this visit?" asked Mel as he welcomed Karen into his office in the west wing.

"Mel, I didn't want to waste Lexi's time with rumors and pieces of intel, but I need you to know some of what we are finding."

Mel motioned to a small table in his office where they sat.

"Like what?"

"You know who Sebastian Kolsten is?"

Mel's stomach knotted up as he kept his demeanor calm.

"Sure, the super hacker."

"Right. And you remember we did a deal with him to have him play ball on our side or go to jail for his murder convictions?"

"If I recall, that part was kept pretty quiet," replied Mel.

"Indeed. He was found dead this morning in a suite at the Waldorf. He'd been there for a couple of days. Anyway, we always have him under surveillance. We had some agents monitoring his conversations," explained Karen.

Mel was trying to maintain his outward calm as he tried to remember the conversation he'd had. How much had he implicated himself. He didn't recall admitting to Kolsten they were the ones paying him to alter the voting machines.

Karen continued droning on, not recognizing the outward signs of Mel's rising discomfort.

"Anyway, our recording wasn't any good. We only got a few snippets regarding the election and hacking. Nothing concrete or specific. In short, nothing we can use. But with Kolsten dead, I thought you'd want to know. You can decide if you want to tell Lexi."

Mel's blood pressure dropped back into the semi-normal range at the revelation they had nothing. Now his worry was in the other room, and why was Kolsten dead? Who else may have seen him or heard his conversation?

"Thanks Karen. I doubt I'll bother Lexi with this, since she has a few other things on her mind. Hamas and Israel about to re-kindle World War III."

"I get it. That's why I didn't ask for her time. One last tidbit. Dan Baker visited Turner's campaign. We don't know why. But as you remember, we were able to tie Baker to talking with Vincent about his potential tell all from Vincent's widow. We don't think Vincent shared anything with either the publisher or Baker."

"Yet, he is meeting with Turner, and you are here telling me about it. Why?" asked Mel pointedly.

"Call it a gut feeling. Or a dislike of coincidences. Again, passing it on to you rather than her. Just be aware. It is October and surprises appear. I wouldn't want Turner springing one on you guys with no warning."

"Thanks Karen," said Mel, thinking, if she only knew what the next three days would bring.

Chapter 75

"Should we panic now" asked Harriet, walking into Mel's office at Lexi's campaign HQ and shutting the door.

Mel sighed. It had already been a day of revelations, with more to come.

"Why?" asked Mel, looking up from his desk.

"Have you seen the latest polls. *Our* latest polls?"

"No, which ones?"

"All of them. Turner is approaching double digits with Blackbird in the high thirties and Lexi falling to the low fifties. She's lost about six points in the last few weeks. Turner is up about three, even after all the shit we have thrown at him," warned Harriet.

"I wouldn't worry. This is typical. Lexi had a rough go in the last debate. She is trying to save the free world. She'll do much better in the last one in a couple weeks. JJ will slaughter Carson this week in the VP debate, and that will bring us back up."

"What about Turner? If he keeps climbing, we won't be able to keep him out of the last debate," said Harriet.

"He's not there yet. Even if he makes it, so what? By then, the mail in ballots are coming in. Anything he says is going to fall on deaf ears, plus I'm not convinced he is going to stay that high. We still have what, two more polls before they choose who gets in the last one."

"What do you know you aren't telling me?" asked Harriet, surprised at Mel's nonchalant attitude over a six point drop in Lexi's polling.

"Who, me?" said Mel, leaning back in his chair. "What is today?"

"October 16th, but you know that as well as I do."

"Give it a couple of days and then we can see if Lexi is still as low," said Mel prophetically.

"What is about to happen? You have a trick up your sleeve? Care to share so I can be prepared?" asked Harriet, a smile beginning.

"I know nothing, but it is October. We've had a few surprises in this month, especially during presidential elections."

"I see, Nostradamus. What kind of scale? Firecrackers, bottle rockets, roman candle?" questioned Harriet.

"4th of July," replied Mel with a smile and hand gesture.

"Holy Shit, really?"

"Let's just say there will be rats jumping from the sinking ship on this one."

"Won't most of them go to Turner?" the smile fading from Harriet's face, suddenly worried, doing the math.

"Turner will have his own worries. Trust me."

"Glorious. This is why you're known for being such a bastard."

"Why thank you. I take that as a compliment."

"You know it was meant as one," smiled Harriet.

#

"How are the House and Senate races looking?" asked Lexi, walking around her desk to sit down.

Mel stood up, walking to the front of her desk, and looking at a tablet in his hands.

"We're looking good. Ballot harvesting is in full swing in Southern California, so we should get the seven seats back. We are also going to take full advantage of some of the new harvesting laws in Michigan, New York, Virginia, and Pennsylvania, so we should pick up some seats there, too. I would guess we will be plus 20 in the house."

"The Senate will be close, but we will get Colorado back solid and probably pick up a seat in Ohio and another in Pennsylvania. Texas is a possibility but remote. We keep running Bozo the Clown, hoping one day he'll get lucky," said Mel, referring to a certain high profile Party candidate who always won primaries and lost elections in Texas.

"I would say 52 solid and maybe 53. It will be enough. With the filibuster gone, you'll be able to have the most impactful first 100 days in the country's history. We'll have all the bills ready to go, since they are essentially the same ones which were just voted down."

"Nice," said Lexi. "Any luck with Georgia and Arizona."

"Unfortunately, no. Both the Governors tried to implement looser rules for harvesting, but the Supreme Court of both states ruled their executive orders were unconstitutional. We have other measures in place to ensure we have enough votes to win."

Roland made a rude noise from his place on the couch in Lexi's office.

Mel turned to look at him. He merely smiled. Lexi tried to hide a smile of her own as the two alpha males squared off.

"You disagree. With your copious amounts of experience winning elections, you have perhaps a better way?" sneered Mel.

As Roland opened his mouth to reply, Mel interrupted.

"One that does not simply involve killing all our enemies?"

Roland leaned back and smiled, declining to trade insults with Lexi's chief of staff. "There is a time and a place for all tactics. The key is knowing when."

Mel, sensing an opening, continued. "In America, unlike other parts of the world, it is not acceptable to use assassination as a political tool. I would ask that you contain your efforts to keeping our campaign secure and stop bumping off Supreme Court justices, presidential candidates, chiefs of staff, or super hackers."

"Boys, behave," purred Lexi with a smile.

Roland stood. "I am not sure what you are referring to Mel. Justice Moore died of a heart attack. I have already admitted I do not possess the skills to shoot Turner and *keep* him alive. As for Vincent, accidents happen, and I have no idea what you are referring to regarding any hacker's death."

Mel stared at him. If he had killed Kolsten, he was indeed a cool character. Mel had thrown that in to see if he reacted. He knew he was lying about Vincent and probably Turner. He suspected he had something to do with Justice Moore, because Lexi didn't react, either. He knew he was losing some of his grip on power. Now he knew how Vincent felt when Lexi froze him out. He didn't like it.

"Anything else Mel?"

"Karen said Dan Baker came by Turner's office. She has nothing beyond that. If Baker had anything from Vincent, we would know by now. He isn't the type to sit on a story. She said she's going to keep digging. I wanted you to know." Mel was baiting the trap.

"Shit. I thought that one was behind us. You sure he doesn't have anything? Why visit Turner?"

"No idea. If there is something, we'll ferret it out."

"I need to discuss the security for the next few weeks with Roland," she announced casually.

Mel knew he was being dismissed. As he left, Roland smiled while meeting his gaze.

#

"You know you don't have to rub his nose in it. He is good at what he does. I wouldn't be where I am without him. Just as you are good at what you do," responded Lexi provocatively as she walked to the bar, hips swaying.

"You realize he is hiding things from you?"

"Of course. Just as we are hiding things from him right now."

"Yes, but he feels threatened. I do not," he counseled, staring at her as she turned, drink in hand. She was pure energy. Roland had never encountered a woman like her in his life. It took all his willpower to remember his mission and not be consumed.

"I need you to play nice. I cannot afford to have Mel working against you *or* me. Make it work. What is so important that you need me to banish him?" asked Lexi, posing suggestively.

"I know where the hostages are being held in Gaza."

"What! How?" burst Lexi, all thought of play vanishing.

Roland shrugged. "Neither are important. What is important is for you to look Presidential providing this information to the Israelis so they can go rescue the hostages."

"How will I explain the intel? They aren't going to tell their IDF and Kidon teams to head into Gaza tunnels based on my word."

"Yes, they will. Here is how and why."

\#

"I know Mr. Prime Minister. It is very detailed and exact. As I have told you, we too have our intelligence sources. Just as you do in our country. In the interests of not repeating the horrors of the prior Israeli-Hamas wars, I suggest you take my word this is good intel," stated Lexi in a commanding tone.

The Prime Minister of Israel, somewhat shocked at the tone from Lexi, hemmed and hawed about having to verify the information with his own intelligence teams.

"Look, Elad, I know we have not yet met face to face. This is a trial by fire. You must decide to trust us. We are your biggest ally in the world. This intel is good. If you don't act quickly, we both know they will move the hostages and we will continue to escalate a conflict neither of us wants. Including the new Palestinian President who is still claiming to have no knowledge of this heinous attack."

Lexi could see the giant projected face of the Israeli Prime Minister on the screen in the situation room. He was only recently elected in yet another of Israel's complicated and multi-party compromise governments. He was clearly struggling with taking orders from the American Vice President.

"Is the President aware of this?" he asked, stalling for time.

Lexi didn't even hesitate. "He is and has publicly put me in charge of assisting you to rescue your people. I have an election in three weeks. If we cannot capitalize on this information and rescue these hostages, I may have no choice but to leak our efforts to help and your delay in using this info. I have to look Presidential. It would not look good for you to ignore our help or arrive too late."

"Is that a threat?"

"More like a lifeline. Both of us know if something happens to those hostages, or the conflict escalates, the public opinion in America will quickly turn against Israel if you start bombing Gaza just as the Palestinians are rebuilding from the devastation of the last conflicts."

"A moment Madame Vice President."

His head disappeared from the screen as they muted.

Admiral Jason Kensington and her Secretary of Defense, Issac Roth, both looked at Lexi during the pause.

"Are we sure on our side? If we send them into an ambush, it could be just as detrimental to our relationship. I would feel better if our own intel agencies could review your material. It is awfully detailed. It seems like a trap," said Roth, a veteran of both the military and the intelligence agencies.

"I agree. It seems a bit too perfect," chimed in Kensington.

"Gentlemen, I have more to lose than anyone. I assure you I have vetted the source and I trust them."

Before she could continue, the giant head of Elad returned to the large overhead screen.

"We thank you Madame Vice President. We are dispatching our forces to execute the raid. We humbly thank you for this information and let us both pray for a successful outcome."

"Amen, Elad. Let us know if we can assist. Shalom."

Chapter 76

Beverly Johnson sat at her desk, finishing the copy for her explosive story. Ever since the packet arrived a month prior, she'd spent most of her time researching and verifying the facts and allegations described.

She believed she'd corroborated all of them. People were on camera confirming the accusations. There were copies of official documents. All legally obtained and certified by various state entities.

Beverly had reviewed it with her producer Wil a thousand times. An accusation like this required rock-solid background and confirmation from multiple sources to withstand the scrutiny and pressure it was sure to bring on her and her network.

To drop this kind of bombshell three weeks before the election would rock the campaign and potentially change the course of history. She did not take this task lightly. Nor did she deny the pleasure she felt, exposing the level of hypocrisy this story would reveal.

It would also not be bad for her career. For now, she did not contemplate any potential accolades. Instead, she reviewed the material a last time. Beverly would break the story on the NWN *Nightly News*.

\#

"You are absolutely positive about your sources? There can be no chance any of this is wrong," claimed Kyle Combs nervously. He was the anchor of the NWN *Nightly News* show and had already been embarrassed by the families of the slain deputies on his program. He did not wish to repeat that episode.

"We are Kyle. Every source has checked out and verified the information we intend to share," assured Beverly.

"This one is ironclad," agreed Wil.

Kyle's producer, Joseph, sat in the corner, his hands in a steeple in front of him.

"How did you get this?"

"It was delivered by messenger about a month ago," replied Wil sheepishly.

"Geez," wailed Kyle, throwing his hands up.

"It's anonymous? You could not track down the source?" asked Joseph, ignoring Kyle's histrionics.

"We could not, but we were able to verify everything in the dossier. There are court records, we have interviews and affidavits," Wil padded the stack of notes. "It is all there. Doesn't matter how we got it. We did the legwork and confirmed it all. The info is truthful."

"Did it come from the Vice President's campaign?" asked Joseph, continuing to push.

"We don't know," admitted Beverly.

"Oh God. It's the dossier all over again. Come on guys, they are setting you up," whined Kyle.

Joseph was looking through the various notes and statements.

"That will be everyone's first question. If we say we don't know, the assumption's going to be the VP sent it to us. Did you ask?"

"We did. They said they had no idea what we were talking about," shared Beverly.

"Of course, they didn't. They claim they have no knowledge and let us take the risk and do their dirty work. I don't like it. It's not good for the network, and it is frankly not good for the country. I would say we push back and tell them to do their own mudslinging," suggested Joseph, as Kyle nodded in agreement.

"Does Harry know?" asked Kyle.

"I have told him. He is aware of what we have and how we got it," confirmed Wil.

"If the President of the network knows about it and hasn't stopped this," probed Kyle, trailing off while looking at Joseph.

"Hang on, I'll call him," said Joseph, pulling out a cell phone.

"Hi Liz, Joe, does Harry have a sec to discuss a hot one for tonight's show? Sure, I'll hold," he said, standing in the corner.

"Thanks Liz. Harry, you aware what Wil and Bev brought to us?" asked Joe, listening. "Sure. Alright," replied Joe in the one-sided conversation. "You'll take the call and issue the statement? Thanks."

"Ok, we go with it," he said as Beverly and Wil smiled and Kyle looked relieved. "Harry understands the risk. He knows the sources are verified, and he is alright with the anonymous nature of the information delivered to us. He already has a statement ready for the inevitable calls he'll get after. Congrats guys, you are about to put Lexi Smythe-Thomas into the White House."

#

"Welcome. Tonight on NWN *Nightly News*, we have some breaking news. This may disturb some of you, but we feel it is our duty to the citizens of America to share the information we have obtained. This information came to us anonymously, but we have spent the last month diligently tracking down and verifying both the sources referenced and the people involved in the allegations. The timing of this announcement results from us completing this comprehensive confirmation of the facts. To tell you more, here is Beverly Johnson," uttered Kyle Combs, doing his best Brokaw.

"Thank you, Kyle," she responded.

"Beverly, before we get to the allegations, can you explain how you got this information and what you did to confirm its veracity?"

"Absolutely Kyle. The original package was delivered by registered mail about five weeks ago. It contained information and photocopies of relevant documents and a timeline detailing the specifics of the allegation." Beverly made a conscious effort to slow down, articulating her message.

"We were able to verify the copies of documents by visiting courthouses and viewing the originals archived there. The still living who were identified and involved were interviewed and we have received signed and notarized affidavits. We were also able to get court orders to unseal juvenile court records because of the potential impact on the election. In short, we have validated and confirmed the allegations in the packet of information. This is neither opinion nor conjecture," she paused for emphasis.

"Thank you, Beverly. I want to assure our viewers this information is not a rumor. It is not an allegation. It is simply the facts as verified by Beverly and her team. The media have learned our lesson, blindly believing in information provided by third parties during elections. This time, we've done the work ahead of disclosure. Please continue," announced Kyle, his ass now covered.

"When current Opposition presidential candidate George Blackbird was eighteen, he fathered a child with one Louise Elaine Konrad. She was fourteen at the time. This occurred in Minnesota, where both lived and attended high school together."

"According to court records, Miss Konrad's parents filed statutory rape charges against George Blackbird. It appears Mr. Blackbird was dared into convincing Miss Konrad to have sex during homecoming that year. This resulted in Miss Konrad becoming pregnant with Mr. Blackbird's child."

"Mr. Blackbird denied the child was his. He admitted he had sex with Miss Konrad once the teammates on his football team were deposed and admitted to daring him to have sex with her." Beverly was referring to her notes as she continued.

"This was sufficient for the judge to continue to charge Mr. Blackbird with statutory rape. In a plea agreement, Mr. Blackbird agreed to marry Miss Konrad to make the child legitimate in the eyes of the court and society. Once the child, Lois Georgina Blackbird, was born, it was confirmed by blood test. He was the father."

"Mr. Blackbird was granted a divorce on the agreement he would pay support for both Lois and Louise and provide for Lois' college education. In return, the statutory rape charge was dropped. While the charges were expunged from the record, the notes of the attorney and the court reporter up to that point were preserved in the county archives and we could get official copies to validate all these statements," said Beverly holding up a stack of papers.

"Beverly, this is quite a revelation. How is it this has not been discovered previously?" Kyle asking what many were now speculating, given the number of elections Blackbird had completed.

"Sadly, there is more to the story, Kyle," shared Beverly.

"Mr. Blackbird and his family provided child support and spousal support for both Lois and Louise. He lived up to his part of the agreement with the DA. However, Louise never recovered from the shame of the event. She dropped out of school and joined a convent. Her parents raised Lois as their own."

"Sister Maria, as Louise became known, choosing her name after St. Maria. The patron saint of forgiveness. She spent 20 years in the convent. While there, she succumbed to long undetected thyroid cancer at the age of only thirty-five."

"According to the sisters, she suffered from acute depression receiving large doses of lithium for years, including two overdoses. It is possible this may have led to her thyroid cancer. She led a solitary life, contributing to no one noticing her thyroid issues."

She never saw her daughter again after she joined the convent. It is pretty safe to say, and this is my opinion now. Her life was altered by those events with Mr. Blackbird.

"Lois' grandparents legally adopted her, giving her their last name, Konrad. She went through high school in Minneapolis, far removed from the childhood home of Mr. Blackbird and her mother Louise in Brainard, Minnesota. Her grandparents died when she was 23 and a recent graduate of the University of Minnesota." Kyle continued to nod as Beverly detailed revelation after revelation.

"In the review of her 'parents' papers, she found out who she really was. Someone had been paying child support and her college tuition through her parents. She now also knew her parents were actually her grandparents. She found information her mother had joined a convent and legally given her up to her grandparents to raise.

"There was nothing in her parents' papers about Mr. Blackbird. The support payments all came from a trust fund set up in her name by a shell corporation. By this time, Mr. Blackbird was already a successful businessman, married with his own family, and had just become a first-term congressman from South Dakota."

"Lois built a life working in advertising and marketing. She married and divorced twice with no children. In her early forties, a decade ago, she was diagnosed with thyroid cancer herself. As part of her research to treat the cancer, she wanted to know more about her family lineage."

"She researched her family, her grandparents, her mother, and, hopefully, her father. Because of this effort, she discovered she was the daughter of then Congressman and soon to be Governor Blackbird. At first, she was surprised. She assumed he did not know her and there was no reason to get involved in his life."

"Doctors treated her thyroid cancer successfully. She carried on with her career. Three years ago she had a nasty car accident, became addicted to painkillers, lost her job, her house, and ended up in a shelter in Minneapolis."

"She approached now Governor Blackbird with a request for help. At first the Governor ignored her, but much like us, she showed him the research to prove she was indeed Lois Blackbird and produced the birth certificate as well."

"Not wanting any publicity, he agreed to set Lois up in a small apartment, providing her with a monthly allowance. Everything became better until the Governor ran for president."

"Before announcing, he gave Lois a one-million-dollar trust for her silence. She also signed a non-disclosure agreement to not tell anyone she is his daughter," said Beverly.

"Quite the cover up," noted Kyle, shaking his head.

"I'm still not done, Kyle. There is more."

"We interviewed Lois and have a sworn statement from her. Once we showed her the complete story, including all the details of how she was conceived, she became understandably upset. Both for the deed itself, and the coverup. She learned of the destruction of her mother's ability to lead a normal life. Her decision to give Lois to her grandparents and enter the convent. Louise's depression, premature death, and finally the continued efforts of the Governor to clear his conscience with money. Those last are her words," said Beverly.

"When we showed all this to her, she confirmed to us, both in sworn statement and in a video deposition, that she is indeed Governor Blackbird's daughter. She is also more than willing to confirm this via a DNA test. The payoffs from Governor Blackbird to her and the trail leading back to him from her grandparents leave little doubt. Lois Konrad, formerly Lois Blackbird, is in an undisclosed location for obvious reasons now that we have publicly aired her story," finished Beverly with a big sigh.

Kyle shook his head. "Governor Blackbird has gone to extraordinary lengths to conceal and silence his daughter from this event. Clearly, he understood the concerns people would have with his deeds and the subsequent actions to cover up the story. This is explosive. Do we have any official comment from the Blackbird campaign?" queried Kyle.

"No, we sought comment prior to going on the air, but we did not receive any reply from the Blackbird camp."

"Well, there you have it. Excellent work Beverly. We await an official response from the Blackbird campaign," concluded Kyle.

"Thank you, Kyle," said Beverly.

#

"Wow, what a prick," remarked Lexi. "I knew I didn't like the schmuck, but this is even worse than I imagined."

"It makes him look like a grade A asshole," agreed Mel.

"What happens now?"

"All the major news networks will run wall to wall stories, hell even EXN can't resist this one. My guess is he'll try to point out how he took responsibility and paid for all the kid's education as some sort of good guy move. This will backfire. All the women will hate this entire episode, from the date rape to the quickie divorce to the 'ain't I responsible, I paid for everything'. He is finished with the opposition women," suggested Mel.

"What about the woman?" asked Lexi.

"You heard NWN. She is in an undisclosed location," smiled Mel. "NWN has video recordings of her deposition. She is very sincere in her belief Blackbird ruined her mother's life. It comes through she is more concerned with him paying a price than getting more money."

"Can we keep her off the air so she won't undermine her sympathetic appearance?" asked Lexi.

"That is the plan."

"How bad is the hit? Will it stick?" she asked, watching the muted television showing coverage of the 'bombshell Blackbird Rape case', according to the crawler and pictures of Beverly talking.

"Yes, I think it will. The women cannot stomach this. He'll probably lose 60-80% of them. The men, maybe 25% will bail."

"That's a lot of fallout," mused Lexi, thinking aloud.

"Tonight's VP Debate now requires Carson to defend him. It will put her in a horrible position. It starts in less than an hour. She can either throw him under the bus and save her own reputation, costing them even more votes with men, or she can defend him, tarnish her image, defending a child rapist, and risk losing even more of the Opposition women. I do not envy her handlers right now trying to change her prep."

"JJ will hit her hard, but not too hard. We prepped him. Her response to the Blackbird allegations will be the only thing that matters and the only thing people will remember," expressed Mel gleefully.

"Trial by fire," mused Lexi with little sympathy. "So how do we keep them all from going to Turner?"

Mel replied with a smile.

"Good, no need for me to know details, just like this," smiled Lexi herself in reply.

#

"Ouch, that is going to leave a mark" grimaced Denise, watching the Beverly interview from the conference room in Denver.

"Holy shit, that's one hell of an October surprise," noted Chuck. "How the hell did he get through elections with this baggage?"

"Investigative journalism is dead," said Denise. "Too much work. Hell, this was handed to her on a silver platter. She even admitted it.

They probably already had a judge and a subpoena for records release teed up and ready. They did everything but lead her to the courthouse. This has Lexi and, more likely, Mel Arenson written all over it. She always lets others do her slimiest work. Classic dirty tricks. They love to use sex because it sells," concluded Denise.

"How bad does this hit Blackbird?" probed Nick, having just arrived from the airport at their Denver HQ once it was clear he did not need to head to DC for the Censure vote until next week.

"He was already fading. This is probably the last straw. The question is, can we convince a majority of his voters to come to you rather than stay home?" stressed Denise.

"How do we do that? Is there anything we can do we aren't doing already?" Nick glanced around to see who had suggestions.

"We have the southern swing of state fairs next week, South and North Carolina, probably not the place to be overly aggressive since Carson is their darling, though I feel sorry for her tonight. This is really unfair. She is going to get pilloried for something her boss did and through no fault of her own, her biggest night is going to be overshadowed by this," lamented Denise.

"Sucks for sure," said Nick. "What's after the Carolinas?"

"Georgia, Alabama and Arkansas," revealed Chuck.

"Georgia and Alabama are the perfect place to make a direct appeal to Blackbird's voter base. Maybe we can talk about integrity or something like that," mused Nick.

"No matter how tempted you are, Nick, you never claim to be more virtuous. It always comes back to bite you in the ass. No one is entirely clear. Remember, you have tons of staff now and they have pasts too. Look around our office, half of us are has-bins. Be careful about claiming to have more integrity or better morals or better ethics. It is an avoidable pothole. Trust me," cautioned Denise.

"She's right Nick. Keep it issue based. If they are already disgusted, you just need to give them a lifeboat," nodded Chuck.

"Nice analogy. I may use that," agreed Nick. "You should write speeches."

"If only you would actually give them," retorted Chuck.

Denise had been flipping through news channels looking at the coverage. "Blackbird is so screwed," she said, shaking her head as Nick and Chuck turned back.

"Lexi really called in the markers on this one. Every station is wall to wall with victims of rape. Experts in law critiquing his plea deal. Others wondering why no one who knew about this from back then didn't come forward sooner. Questions about who else he may have paid off to keep this so hidden."

"Have they issued a statement yet?" asked Nick.

"They called a press conference for tomorrow morning. If it were me, I would have at least put out a statement these news orgs would have to read to at least give an alternate view," replied Denise, her tone showing what she thought of Blackbird's PR team.

"I guess we'll find out tomorrow how many folks will leave his campaign," stated Chuck.

"If Blackbird becomes less of a threat, Lexi isn't stupid. She has to know a certain number of these are going to come to me. I can only assume she is going to turn both barrels on us now, right?" said Nick, looking at his chief lieutenants.

"Even more than she already has. It looks like you deflected the student accusations with your list of references. The Censure thing is definitely not Lexi. There is going to be more. If things go the way we think, you are going to qualify for the last debate. Unless they change the rules again. Lexi, or rather Mel, will try something. Guaranteed," warned Denise.

"Any clue from your sources or networks?" asked Chuck, looking at Denise.

"A friend in the Pentagon said there were requests to view redacted military records, but even if there were anything there and Nick assures us there is not, they would get in big trouble disclosing classified material publicly," commented Denise.

"If they aren't going after Nick?" said Chuck questioningly.

"I'm already ruined. My secrets are well known. Can't exactly call me a home wrecking, washed-up alcoholic again, that's no secret," laughed Denise.

"We've done basic background on everyone, but not real deep. What about Neill?" Chuck looked at Denise.

"Frankly, he is the same as me. He comes with a lot of baggage, but it is known baggage. He ran for president in the primaries once too. I doubt they would expect that to get much traction. It has to be something else. Can you think of anything they might dig up in your past?" asked Denise, staring intently at Nick.

"I honestly can't. My military intelligence work is classified. The rest is pretty straightforward. Some of the 'who's' were interesting but nothing likely to sabotage my campaign," lied Nick. "There is some stuff from my time leading the air wings, but nothing that embarrasses me, only the various administration's ineptitude," replied Nick in a nonchalant tone.

"That where you got all those medals?" asked Denise.

Nick gave her a glare.

"Medals? Am I missing something?" asked Chuck.

"No," said Nick as Denise sat silent.

"Something is coming, and we need to be ready. We need to start thinking about debate prep too. Especially since you have never been in one," muttered Chuck.

"If something happens, we need to react fast. Let's keep the core team together for the rest of the campaign," suggested Nick. "Be good to pull Neill and Ellie in as well. Where are they?"

"Good idea. They are in the northwest and heading down through California and into the southwest. I can pull them in if you think it would be better," offered Denise.

Nick thought for a second. "Let's see what happens, but let them know we may need them to come in if it does."

"Got it."

Chapter 77

"The Opposition is already exploring if they can replace the candidate this late in an election," said Margie, reading headlines from her phone.

"Fat chance of that. The ballots are already printed. The primaries are over. They are stuck with him," responded Greg.

"He had a closed door with the national committee, and they didn't like his answers. Somebody leaked the reaction," guessed Chuck.

"Here it comes," waved Denise. "Anyone bring the popcorn?"

They watched as Governor Blackbird approached the podium. He did not look good with bags under his eyes.

"Ladies and gentlemen, first let me say, the facts of the reporting by NWN last night are indeed mostly correct. I got a young woman pregnant. The sex was consensual. It was not rape. The rape charge was a threat by the parents to force me to do the right thing. Marry their daughter. Which I did. I gave the child a legitimate name. I also ensured both the mother and the child would be financially supported, including a college fund to enable the child to attend college, which she did. I did not know what happened to either the mother or the daughter. What I agreed to do, I did. The story the NWN reporter told about the life of the mother and of the child was news to me. I was approached by Lois Konrad, who claimed to be my daughter." He read from the teleprompter, his tone never varying.

"As a continued act of benevolence, I agreed to help her out, as she was in desperate times. I paid for an apartment and an allowance to give her a chance to get back on her feet. When I decided to run for president, I did approach Lois Konrad with an arrangement to provide a large sum of money in exchange for stopping the payments on the apartment and the allowance." Blackbird took a sip of water.

"She took the money and signed an agreement saying she would not discuss or go public with her relationship to me. She violated the terms of her agreement by talking to the NWN news reporter, but I have no desire to seek any charges for this breach. So yes, I made a mistake years ago, and I have lived up to my responsibility and supported the mother and child well beyond what was required by law," finished Governor Blackbird.

#

Denise practically leaped out of her chair. "You sanctimonious SOB. How can you sit there and read that speech without an ounce of empathy? You might as well be talking about suicide bombers in Tel Aviv or a garbage strike in Chicago. This guy has no feelings. He deserves every piece of hate he gets." Denise turned to Nick.

"Take a good look. This is a Master Class in how not to handle a crisis. His handlers must know this is going to go over like a ton of bricks. Who let him read this shit? Look, he is getting slaughtered by the questions," Denise turned the TV back up.

#

"…but Governor, you were 18, an adult. You slept with a 14-year-old on a dare. You took advantage of a child who was probably infatuated with you. Captain of the football team and homecoming king. This was just wrong," accused Lauren Bergamo.

"As I have said, the sex was consensual. There was no rape," replied the Governor, showing no empathy as Denise noted and totally misreading the point that Lauren was making.

"Sir, now that you know what happened to the mother, do you not feel some sense of remorse for the way her life turned out? Abandoning her child, joining a convent, essentially dying from depression. Do you not think you bear some responsibility for this tragedy?" asked another female reporter.

"I do not. As I have said, we were young and immature. I did the right thing. I gave her daughter a name and financial stability to both. Then we went our separate ways to build separate lives. What choices she made after that were strictly her own. I cannot be held accountable for every decision someone I never saw again made. That's an unreasonable standard to be held too," said Blackbird, as if he had just answered in the only logical and acceptable manner.

#

"Oh my god, he thinks he's right. He honestly thinks his answers are good ones," blurted Denise, looking at Nick. A wild-eyed look on her face. "It's not his handlers. This guy is soulless." She was almost shaking. She got up and walked out of the room. Nick followed her with his eyes, wondering why she was so upset.

"She's right. It's almost as if a lawyer advised him how to answer. Technically, all of his answers are correct, if he were arguing facts in a courtroom. Except this is the court of public opinion, and he is coming off as an uncaring ass. Nick, this is what I was talking about. It's digging a hole and jumping in. If he keeps this up, he's going to start filling the hole in on top of himself," said Chuck.

#

Blackbird continued to get questions from the predominantly female press corp. Finally, yet another female reporter asked him a question about the hush money. "Governor, would you characterize your money paid to Lois as hush money? Especially the last payment in excess of a reportedly one million dollars?"

"No, I would not call it hush money. I would call it a final restitution. An act of kindness and generosity. Look, I have done more than most. Perhaps more than any, in a situation where they find themselves supporting a mother and child who led a separate life. I took care of them. I saw they did not want for food or shelter. I made sure she got an education which she used to build a life."

"When she came to me, destitute, the victim of our medical and insurance professions, I once again stepped up and took care of her, providing shelter and food again. Finally, as I ran for president, I did not want this to become a story my enemies would attempt to use against me. To ruin her life through sensationalizing it. I paid her enough money to allow her to do whatever she would like, in return for severing our ties. She was pleased with this and agreed, signing the agreement to receive the payment. It is not hush money, it is compassion," finished Blackbird righteously, almost expecting cheers.

He failed to read the room. Every woman in the room was disgusted. Several appeared on the verge of physical sickness. Lauren Bergamo couldn't let it go.

"Governor, I'm sorry, but one does not sign a non-disclosure agreement out of compassion. They sign a non-disclosure agreement when one side is threatening the other, worried someone else will find out what that person is hiding. I may not speak for everyone here, but I suspect most of us find your answers repugnant. You claim to be a knight in shining armor when you are really just an entitled predator. We can understand why *your* daughter is upset and bitter about the way you treated her mother and the way her life was wasted because of your dare in high school." Lauren's voice went up an octave and anger flashed in her eyes.

"Now hold on a minute, you are putting words in my mouth. I love my daughter, I supported my daughter, I helped her mother. I am not ashamed of her. I made a mistake, I owned up to it and I did the right thing, over and over," said the Governor, still defending.

This was the last straw for Lauren, who stood defiantly. "Love? Governor, everything you have described can be called many things, but none of them were done out of love. They were done to cover your ass," snarled Lauren. With that, she turned to exit the press conference. Stopping, she turned. "Oh, and by the way, she has a name. It is Lois, and it was given to her by her mother, Louise. Because the father took no responsibility other than providing some sperm and a bank account number," Lauren was quivering in anger as she turned, not waiting for the Governor to answer, exiting the room.

As if on cue, all the other female reporters also got up and left the press conference. The scene was one of the Governor standing at a podium while the stream of female reporters turned their backs on him and walked out, leaving a handful of male reporters in a sea of empty chairs. This image would be how the Governor's presidential campaign was remembered. Forever.

\#

Nick couldn't help but feel admiration for Lauren and how she handled Blackbird's answers. Responding to his hypocrisy by clearly making the points all women in the country were sure to remember. He almost felt sorry for Blackbird. He was over-matched and should never have aspired to the presidency with this in his background. A secret like that was bound to come out, in this, the nastiest of nasty businesses, running for president.

\#

"Oh my god, He was even worse than I thought," said Lexi, giddy as a schoolgirl. She uncharacteristically broke her icy persona, high fiving Mel, who was equally surprised as they watched the press conference in her campaign office.

"This is unbelievably bad, even for his campaign. Whoever prepped him with those answers should be taken out back and shot. The women of America now have a new favorite person to hate," agreed Mel.

"You got that right. I want to kick him in the balls right now. Bergamo sure ripped him a new one. I like her. She is a real bitch," laughed Lexi. "We should look at adding her to the administration. She is wasting her talent at ANC."

"She sure added the exclamation point to the conversation," declared Mel. "That is all anyone is going to remember, her leading every female reporter out of the press conference."

"What's next?

"Working on it. Your friend Bergamo may come in handy once more," offered Mel cryptically.

Chapter 78

Khalid Yousef Hassan sprinted down the tunnel. Behind him were flashes and loud echoes of automatic weapons and small explosives. Somehow, the Israelis had found their hideout. They had breached the front entrances to their tunnels, five stories beneath a rebuilt hospital in Gaza City.

During the reconstruction of the destroyed hospital, they'd built a new set of tunnels below the ones the Israelis had destroyed and sealed. Going even deeper this time, with more exit and entry points. He'd been confident they wouldn't be found this time. Too confident.

Approaching the interior chamber where the four hostages were being kept, he burst through the doorway. Gun ready to kill them in a hail of automatic weapon fire. Already thinking how to set up the booby-traps to cover his exit after he killed them.

As he entered the room, he was met with multiple shots to his torso. Sending him against the wall with their force. He slid to the ground, dropping his unfired AK-47. He was staring at an elite Israeli Kidon team. They'd breached the compound from the rear as well. The hostages were already gone.

As a man approached, Khalid knew he'd been betrayed. There was only one person who could have done this. He breathed a name and a prayer as the light left his eyes.

Kidon team leader Haim Edelman kneeled down in front of the dying terrorist. He'd uttered the name *Daboia*, followed by a partially completed Allahu Akbar.

Haim was astounded at the level of intelligence he'd been given for this mission. The complexity of the tunnel systems, the multiple exits and entries, all in private homes, had each been mapped out. The exact chamber where the hostages were held and the number and locations of the entire terrorist cell.

It was as if one member reconsidered and provided everything. He didn't care. All he cared about was they had rescued all four hostages and killed all the terrorists without losing a single member of his team. He could not agree more with the terrorist. God was indeed great, and on their side this day.

#

"I cannot thank the United States and specifically the Vice President enough. Without her specific help and information provided to us by her directly, we would not have been able to execute this rescue mission. The nation of Israel is in your debt forever, Madame Vice President," said Elad Goldman, the Prime Minister of Israel.

"Prime Minister, thank you," beamed Lexi, standing at a podium with a projection of the Prime Minister in Israel behind her. Our entire nation is glad you were able to successfully rescue your citizens and dispose of this terrorist cell. Further, it seems this was indeed a splinter cell. Not one sanctioned by Hamas. This is good news. We can continue to work toward lasting peace in the region.

Denise pointed the remote at the TV to mute the rest of the press conference.

"The pundits are going crazy lauding her leadership during the crisis and how well she has managed this compared to her boss's ineptitude these last few years," offered Margie in a disgusted tone.

Nick sat contemplating the events of the last few days. First Blackbird, then a miraculous turn of events in Israel, apparently from intel directly from Lexi. He did not believe in coincidences.

"What are you thinking, boss?" asked Greg, as the rest of the team turned to look at Nick.

"I'm thinking Lexi has read her Sun Tzu. She is playing to her strengths. Manipulating public opinion to destroy Blackbird while showing the world how prepared she is to handle an international crisis at the same time. She is everything the President has not been for almost his entire two terms. This is way too choreographed to be real."

"You're saying she had Hamas kill folks at the concert and then take hostages so she could look presidential? That's quite a stretch, even for Lexi," suggested Denise.

"Not directly, for sure. But you have to admit, the timing is certainly suspect."

"Whatever it is, it is working. Folks are rejoicing at the success of the raid. She gets her victory lap. Carson got slaughtered at the VP debate, and Blackbird shot his campaign in the head at his press conference. The next polls are going to be brutal," stated Chuck.

"Nick, hit it out of the park tomorrow at the Georgia state fair. You've got to give Blackbird's followers a lifeline. They can't stay home. Tell them why and give them something to care about."

Nick nodded, not saying what he was thinking.

#

Earl knocked on Nick's office door. Nick looked up.

"We've got to leave for the airport soon. You've got a visitor. Says you two have met. An Israeli named Ammi Chaffetz?"

Nick stood smiling and waved his hand.

"Bring him in."

Ammi soon entered Nick's office, shaking his hand. Earl tapped his watch as he closed the door.

"Ammi, good to see you. Congrats on the wonderful news of the rescue of your citizens," smiled Nick as they sat.

"Nick, Earl told me you only have a few minutes, so I'll get to the point. This was all staged."

"How can you be sure?" asked Nick, not surprised in the least.

It was Ammi's turn to smile.

"You don't seem surprised."

"Ammi, you know my background. From the way it was described. Even with the little information shared and the way they were implying, it came directly from Lexi. This had to be planned. The Vice President was obviously fed the intel from someone."

"Nick, I spoke to the Kidon team leader. He explained to me what they were given. Maps, plans, exact layouts and locations of terrorists, booby traps and the hostages. It was 100% accurate."

"Somebody have a change of heart from the inside?"

"Not that we can figure out. This was also not regular Hamas. That much was true. It was a well-funded splinter group. Even this tunnel system was unknown to the Palestinians and Hamas, as far as we can tell. That means it had to be funded by someone. Starting a year ago when the hospital was being rebuilt. It means the construction also had to occur with no leaks. The intricacy of the system was brilliant."

"A pretty expensive sacrificial lamb," agreed Nick.

"To spend the money to do this and then to expose it to make the Vice President look good? Nick, we are talking millions of dollars. Probably tens of millions. Who spends that and then will throw it all away and burn it?" finished Ammi with a giant question.

"Ammi, someone with deep pockets who has a lot to lose if the Vice President doesn't win," replied Nick.

"Do you recall our conversation in Ms. Monroe's library?"

"You mean the one where you told me Maksim Pavlovich was trying to rule the world?" smiled Nick in reply.

"Yes, where you lied and tried to convince me you know little about him. He has the money. You saw his interview on GBTV?"

Nick simply nodded, ignoring Ammi's accusation.

"You heard it straight from him. He's not even trying to hide it any longer. Lexi and the US are the last domino to fall for his one world globalism. Looks to me like he is protecting his investment and putting his foot on the scales to ensure the outcome."

"It seems that way, given the choreographed nature of the attack on her prime opponent," agreed Nick.

"Nick, our new Prime Minister is weak. He was a compromise leader to form the government. The hard-liners were sacked because they wanted to eradicate Hamas completely. Public opinion and primarily the US administration of the President, and now presumably Lexi, made it clear they would not tolerate our efforts to extinguish the threat if it meant leveling all of Gaza and potentially Lebanon."

"And your point is?"

"We are weak when we need to be strong. I have it from someone on the call that Lexi strong armed our PM into launching the raid based on her info."

"Well, it did work and freed the hostages," noted Nick.

Ammi smiled. "Yes, but at what cost in terms of our sovereignty? Lexi now knows we will fold like a chair to her threats. This is a dangerous precedent. We know Hamas is reconstructing as we speak. History will repeat itself. Both in Israel and elsewhere."

"Thanks for the info, Ammi. Let me know if I can help."

He hesitated.

"Ammi, I'm sorry, but I have to go. I have a speech to give," said Nick, walking him to the door.

Ammi stopped him at the door.

"Nick, the Kidon leader, told me something. When he shot the leader coming to the hostage room. No doubt to execute the hostages and flee through a rear exit. After he shot him and he was dying, his last word was *Daboia*." Ammi looked at Nick to see if he responded. He did not.

"Yes? It's a snake, right? What is the significance?"

Ammi smiled, opening the door. "I know you are late, a story for another time."

"Until then. Thank you again, Ammi."

"Good luck Senator."

Chapter 79

Lauren sat in her cubicle working on the final touches of her story, excoriating Blackbird and his tone deaf and righteous response. She had interviewed a few of his supporters for the story.

A majority, maybe seventy percent, were no longer planning on voting for Blackbird. Almost all the women she'd talked to were repelled by his cavalier attitude toward the mayhem he caused

A few felt it was a hit job by the media, typical of the Party's October surprises every election year. Some tried to defend Blackbird and the anonymous nature of the revelations and the delivery. To them, it was clear this was a ploy by the Vice President, akin to the usual dirty tricks the Party was so famous for manufacturing.

She pointed out Blackbird admitted the truth of the accusations. People just shouted back at her. It didn't matter because it was an attack by the Party. She intended to highlight this to show both signs of the argument. She'd already flown up to New York in the wee hours and back to Atlanta on this busy morning.

Jeff stuck his head around the corner and caught her attention, admiring her legs in their heels, dark hose, black leather skirt and blue silk blouse.

"I'm almost done," she said, taking out her earbuds.

"Good," said Jeff. "That's not why I'm here. Great segment on *Women's Viewpoint* this morning. You're getting to be a regular."

"Hey, maybe I should ask if they have an opening," suggested Lauren with a smile, as Jeff frowned.

"The boss wants to see you upstairs."

Lauren assumed Jeff meant Susan, the managing editor, who probably wanted to chastise her for interjecting her own opinion into the questioning at the press conference. And her doubling down on them on *Viewpoint*. Lauren was prepared to defend herself. Various pundits said her comments were the reason the Opposition women in America broke from Blackbird.

"I'll walk with you to the elevator," said Jeff as Lauren got up. As they walked, Jeff commented. "How's the feedback on your comments at the press conference?"

"Mostly positive. Some sites are saying it crossed the line, but it was heartfelt and true. I suppose that's why Susan wants to see me. To extract an apology?"

"Susan?" said Jeff, laughing. "No, Susan was all girl power. She loved it." He kept walking past the elevator bank to the corner of the floor where the private elevator door stood.

Now Lauren understood. Hallberg wanted to see her. Her stomach did flip-flops as she waited for the ding of the arrival.

"Mr. Hallberg wants to congratulate you himself," smiled Jeff. "Enjoy the moment. You earned it," he finished as the elevator door opened and Lauren entered for the trip to the top floor of the building.

She exited the elevator, greeted by Sherman's matronly assistant, Bess. After the last network president's office shenanigans with staff, Sherman was sending an obvious message of his intentions.

"Ah Lauren dear, you look lovely. Mr. Hallberg is on the phone. Let me set you up in his conference room. Coffee?" she asked.

"Yes, please," said Lauren, setting her purse down. Bess brought back the coffee and handed Lauren the cream and sugar. There is a bathroom over there if you need to freshen up, said Bess, pointing to a door in the corner. "He should be right in."

Lauren dosed her coffee with sugar and some cream and took a sip. The conference room was very luxurious, with old wood paneling and plush chairs around a small table. Ducking her head into the bathroom, noticing the luxury extended there as well. Taking a seat at the small table, waiting nervously for the network president.

Glancing at her phone as she waited, she saw a text from Nick after her *Viewpoint* segment. It was simply a thumbs up. She smiled.

Her stomach was finally recovering from the nausea she'd suffered almost daily since the procedure and the attempts on Nick's life. Her emotions were on edge. She often still woke at night crying. His simple responses to her texts made her sad, but she understood. They'd made their choices. Lauren looked up as Sherman entered from the door to his private office. He waved at her as she started to get up. He was carrying his own cup of tea as he sat down with a sigh.

Lauren often wondered how he bore the weight of a network in terminal decline. The ratings had been gradually falling for years and nothing he tried was making any difference. Lauren and her reporting, with the clashes and antagonism against Turner, were one of the few ratings draws they had.

"First, let me congratulate you on a delightful press conference. While you couldn't upstage the top act, you gave yourself second billing. You even came out of it with kudos from EXN. That's saying something. Nice job this morning on *Women's Viewpoint* as well."

"Thanks for flying me up and back this morning on the jet. It was very nice. I just spoke from the heart. Any woman with any compassion for their fellow human beings would've reacted like I did."

"Yet a room full of your female peers failed to express their opinion. You did. For that, we thank you," replied Sherman, smiling.

"Thank you," accepted Lauren like a paralyzed mongoose awaiting the cobra strike. She knew this was just the prelude. She wondered what else he could need from her.

He handed a stack of photos to Lauren. "You've been a busy beaver." Sherman smirked at his clever choice of words.

Lauren looked through the pictures. Many were her surveillance photos of Nick. Meeting with Lexi, going in and out of Senator Banks' house. There were photos of Nick and Earl walking with Reverend Ray in Chicago and them leaving the house with Kayla. Then she gasped. She was looking at pictures from San Francisco. She and Nick were on the scooter. Another on top of Coit Tower, holding on to each other in the wind. She was stunned, speechless.

"Where did you get these? Did you access my phone?" accused Lauren, with a combination of anger and concern.

"I own your phone plan. Therefore, I own the content and can access it. That is the contract you signed," explained Sherman.

Sherman pulled another envelope from his sport coat pocket and pulled a letter out of it. He unfolded it carefully and laid it down in front of Lauren. "Is it true?" he asked.

She took one look at the paper, leaped to her feet, and rushed to the bathroom. Sherman smiled and sipped his tea. He could hear the toilet flush. Lauren came out of the bathroom, dabbing her mouth.

"I assume the answer is yes. You never cease to amaze me. On the surface and in public you put up a front of being this hard edged pain in the ass. Yet somehow you found time to get pregnant by a presidential candidate the world thinks you hate and who everyone thinks despises you?" chortled Sherman, shaking his head in admiration. "You may win an Emmy for your reporting today, but you should really be up for an Oscar."

Lauren finished wiping her mouth and returned to her seat, with what little dignity she had remaining. Taking a sip of her coffee, hoping to calm her tummy, she looked down at the admission form to her clinic. Where she had marked out 'unknown' and written Nick Turner in the 'father' space.

"Where did you get it? There are laws against this," she croaked, ignoring his question.

"Indeed, there are. Should we call a press conference to announce this violation of HIPAA? Seems the admitting nurse recognized you and the name you added to the form. Being a clever girl, and in student loan debt, we were able to come to a suitable arrangement for the acquisition of the original of this form. Feel free to sue. Hell, you can even write the article about the lawsuit," he said with a small laugh.

Lauren stared at the form on the table in front of her.

"Turner knocked you up, and you had an abortion. How poetic. Are you two still seeing each other?"

"It was a one-night stand. In San Francisco. I was trying to sweet talk information out of him, and things suddenly turned romantic. If you are curious, it was mutual. I did not Mata Hari him," said Lauren in a cynical tone. "What do you want?" she asked, trying to sound brave.

"Does he know?"

"Know what?"

"Don't play coy with me. You are way out of your league, little missy. Did he know you were pregnant? Does he know you got an abortion?" asked Sherman, in a ruthless tone.

"No, on both."

"You are either incredibly stupid or in love with him?" questioned Sherman. "I see," he continued as she did not answer, but looked away, her cheeks reddening.

"So again, what do you want to know? If you release this, it isn't going to hurt his campaign. He has already made his abortion stance clear. It was my decision, and he would have supported it."

"You sure about that? Does he feel the same about you?"

"Of course not. It was a one-night stand and my birth control failed. Bad luck for both of us, but more for me," sniffled Lauren.

"I think it is good luck."

"Why?"

"Because it gives me more leverage," sneered Sherman.

"I already told you it won't hurt him," she answered.

"Not over him, over you."

"You already made your leverage pretty clear at the beginning of the year. What did you want, my first born too? Guess you missed out on that one, sorry," she said in a cynical tone.

"Where is your story on the drug deal you witnessed in April in Chicago?" asked Sherman.

"I don't have a story on any drug deal in Chicago," deflected Lauren carefully.

"Why not? I am told you have some excellent footage complete with visible participants, flying bullets, and screeching tires," accused Sherman.

"I still don't know what you're talking about. I haven't discussed putting a story like that together." Lauren tried appearing confused, sensing danger.

"Your photographer, Paul, asked Jeff about the status one day. He described it as kick ass and how you guys 'almost got our asses shot off in a drug deal gone south'. I used my access to all corporate accounts, and what did I find? These photos I just showed you, and some very interesting video footage you took of a drug deal going down. With one Senator Nick Turner wearing a hoodie, but clearly seen holding what looks like heroin in his hand. Other drug dealers with guns and cash standing by. The footage then shows shots being fired and everyone ducking for cover as the car drove away." The blood rushed from Lauren's face.

"Now exactly why didn't you run with such an exposé as this? When I got this little gem," he held up the abortion check-in sheet and dropped it back in front of her. "I understood why. In fact, your coverage of young Mr. Turner seems to have been decidedly more civil these last few months. I bet you were relieved he didn't die from the assassination attempt?" revealed Sherman.

"Like most people were. I do not want to see anyone killed over politics. I have a conscience," replied Lauren, indignant.

"What are these?" asked Sherman, pointing to the stills from her surveillance of Nick. She had followed him a couple of times to Bank's house.

"Nothing. Senator Turner has been to Senator Bank's occasionally this year. He usually stays for an hour and then leaves," said Lauren.

"I see," said Sherman. He pulled the photos of the two of them embracing in the wind on Coit tower. "You two make a cute couple. Too bad." He showed the pictures Lauren had taken of Nick kissing Dolly outside Bank's house. "I bet these didn't make you very happy," smirked Hallberg.

Lauren sat glaring back, waiting for the inevitable.

"You are going to prepare a story, describing what you saw, how you tracked the Senator. How did you track the Senator by the way? In any case, I want a story talking about what you saw, the drug deal, the conversation with the dealer, the actions leading up to the shooting. Feel free to embellish. The others are no doubt dead by now and unable to sue you for slander or libel," laughed Sherman.

"I'll do the story. I won't present it," croaked Lauren defiantly.

"Is that so? You'll do it, or Mr. Turner will find a copy of this in his mail. He may respect your decision, but he'll hate you for murdering his child, especially without his knowledge," ordered Sherman in an icy voice.

"I want the story ready for prime time on Marty's show tomorrow night. I expect to see the Lauren Bergamo who enjoyed skewering him, not the one who enjoyed screwing him," laughed Sherman at his own pun. "You can keep that copy. I have the original in a vault." He stood and exited to his inner office.

Lauren sat and held her now throbbing head in her hands.

Chapter 80

"Ms. Monroe?"

Dolly looked up from the desk in her study to see her assistant Nina standing in the doorway with an express envelope in her hand.

"Ah, Nina. What is that?"

"This arrived via messenger. It is international from France. The return address is Ms. Marie Durand and an address in Paris," read Nina from the envelope.

Dolly had stiffened at the name.

Nina noticed this. "Are you OK?"

"Yes," smiled Dolly, trying to appear casual. She held out her hand for the envelope. "Thank you, Nina. That will be all for now."

Nina gave a slight bow and retreated from the room.

Dolly held the envelope in her hand, trying to calm her racing heart. Marie Durand had died almost three years ago, gunned down in broad daylight in Paris with her 11-year-old daughter, Celeste.

They met at the Sorbonne and became best friends. She was from Provence and had taken Dolly under her wing and showed her the differences between life in France and her English boarding school. They carried on during university, two independent women, looking to change the world. Then Luc Gauthier entered their lives.

Dolly sat back, remembering how both she and Marie had vied for his attention. Luc was the classic bad boy. Dark and daring, devil may care and reckless. Recently graduated and working for Interpol as a junior detective.

He'd initially been smitten with Dolly, but over time had instead warmed to the charms of Marie. Dolly had graciously stepped aside, as she knew her destiny would not be to marry a penniless French detective. Her parents had made that clear.

She was happy for Marie, as it soon became clear she and Luc were a perfect pair. She curbed his wildness with common sense. He brought her out of her shell, teaching her to enjoy the moment and not sweat every detail. Dolly had been Marie's maid of honor.

When Dolly moved back to the states, they had slowly lost touch. Luc moved up the ranks in Interpol, earning accolades and some fame in Europe. Marie continued her schooling, eventually opening a private psychiatry practice. Then Celeste had been born. Dolly's own inability to have a family further caused them to drift apart. She was happy for Marie, of course. Whenever she got the odd Christmas postcard showing Marie's family, she was envious. It showed Marie having everything she could not.

Then William died, and she spiraled into depression. By the time she finally found her footing, she had alienated many of her closest friends. Especially those who had tried to help in her initial grief. She had rebuffed all attempts by Marie in this period.

After, she was too embarrassed to patch things up. Then Marie and Celeste had been killed. All she could do was send a brief note of condolence to Luc. It was never answered.

Dolly contemplated all of this as she sat, turning the large envelope. Opening it with her letter opener, a smaller envelope fell out. This envelope was addressed to 'Just Dolly'.

She smiled, a single tear falling from one eye as she choked up. Luc had insisted she tell him what her real first name was. He was certain Dolly was a nickname or shortened from something like Dorothy. He had kept teasing, insisting she was not being honest, until she stood up and yelled at him it was 'Just Dolly'. He'd made it up to her shortly after. From that point on, he called her 'Just Dolly'.

Wiping a hand on her face, the opener slashed the end of the envelope. She pulled out a single sheet of paper.

Dolly, I know this is all very strange. I cannot risk committing much to paper. I saw in the tabloids you are close to, or at least know, Nick

Turner. It is imperative that I speak with him as soon as possible. It could be a matter of life or death for many. You know I am not prone to melodramatics. Bon Ami.

   Picard

Despite the ominous nature of the note, Dolly felt a pang of regret in her stomach at their young love. She had called him Jean-Luc, to counter his calling her Just Dolly. He told her his mother named him Luc after Jean Luc Godard, the famous French New Wave director. So, he had become Jean Luc to her. She joked it was really because his mother had the hots for Patrick Stewart, who'd played Jean Luc Picard in a *Star Trek* series popular when he was born.

What could he need to talk to Nick about? She noticed Luc included an international phone number at the bottom of the note. At this point in the campaign, she knew it would be next to impossible to get Nick's time.

Pulling out her phone, intending to text Chuck to see if Nick had a couple of minutes. Dolly felt bad for even bothering them. It was clear Nick was having a terrible couple of weeks. She'd seen the news coverage of his last few rallies with the violence and then the riots breaking out at his grassroots events. Even having to defend himself from physical violence. Relentlessly attacked from all angles. She didn't know how he could withstand all the pressure. It made her queasy thinking about how he must feel.

Still, she was also feeling the sting of his rejection. Dolly did not offer her favors to just anyone. She'd done everything but tie herself to the bed naked to get his attention. And he claimed he was doing this to spare *her* feelings. Men! Nick reminded her of Luc, clueless at love, dashing, and resourceful at everything else.

Sighing, she pressed send on her text to Chuck. The last thing she needed was another round of heartache from Nick Turner. Luc wouldn't have contacted her if it were not urgent. Prudence trumped hurt feelings in this case.

Chapter 81

"My friends, as you know, I am not shy about sharing my opinion," said the emcee at the Georgia state fair's final night festivities. He was a well-known, semi-retired comic, with successful sitcom TV shows, who'd made his career skewering mostly Party supporters.

"So why change now?" he said as the crowd cheered. "As you are no doubt aware, it turns out our Opposition candidate is guilty of being a schmuck and an ass," he paused for a second. "Just like most Party leaders." He finished with a sour look on his face as the crowd laughed and cheered in agreement.

"So much for your choices, huh?" Loud jeers this time. "He got caught doing bad things and covering them up. Sound familiar? Then trying to make us feel like he did the right thing," he shook his head as the crowd booed loudly again in agreement.

"Honestly, I was never very impressed with him, anyway. I'll tell you who I *am* impressed with," he paused. "And it ain't the Vice President." Louder cheers this time.

"It's our national hero. Once in the Party, like a lot of us, he came to his senses and left. He continues to protect us from their flawed policies as a US Senator. Just like he protected us from terrorists in New York City and, before that, in the Navy and the Air Force." The crowd hooted and cheered at Nick's service and heroics.

"Unlike our Opposition candidate, Nick is stepping up again. This time to stop the unrelenting creep of the freedom stealing Party and their future Empress. Please welcome Nick Turner, our last hope," he finished, shaking Nick's hand and handing him the microphone.

"Can't ask for a better welcome than that. And before I get tons of hate mail from my comrades, it was Navy and Air *National Guard*, not the regular Air Force." The crowd laughed accordingly as the comedian bowed off stage.

Nick's face turned serious, looking out over the crowd.

"Georgia is ground central. You and Arizona seem to be the new key states in our Union. That puts the pressure on you. It is a tremendous responsibility. Think about it. All of *you*," he said, pointing sharply at the audience. "Will make this monumental decision. You think you don't matter? There are 20,000 of you in this audience. The presidential election in this state was decided by a margin of less than 5000 of you last time. Of all the hundreds of millions of citizens in this country, look to your left and right. Count three people. One out of every four of you will decide the future for all 350 million of us."

Nick paused as the raucous crowd calmed, looking around at each other. Realizing how few people could alter their way of life.

"Only a few of you will cast those deciding votes to determine if we have nine or fifteen Supreme Court justices next year. You'll decide if you are still allowed to buy a handgun or a rifle. Or a gas powered car, gas stove, or now air conditioning. Whether you can keep the guns you have, including your rifles. If we add more states with guaranteed Party senators like Puerto Rico and DC, or how quickly we expand our eligible voter pool to include recent illegal arrivals. People who can't speak our language, read our Constitution, and who certainly cannot pledge allegiance to our flag. They will suddenly get an equal voice in our elections," Nick paused again, walking the stage as the crowd booed loudly at his last revelations.

"It won't be California, Texas, Florida, or even Pennsylvania. It will be Georgia and Arizona. You few, you band of brothers and sisters, will decide if we ever have a fair election again. This gives you more power than you ever thought. I bet you didn't realize that, did you?" The crowd announced they now knew.

"That's good. You realize how important you are. I have spoken to a lot of you at state fairs like this. The response is almost always the same. So why are we so f'd up?" Nick walked back and forth as the crowd laughed.

"I'm serious. If you are right and you agree we are in danger, why are we losing? I see young people out there in the crowd. You can't all be brainwashed, right? For those of you who are too young, I want to say, don't worry. The planet will not die in the next eight years. By my count, we are in the fourth iteration of the twelve-year pronouncements of our impending climate doom. Almost forty years of the sky is falling. Chicken Little was clearly a member of the Party." A few older folks in the audience laughed, knowing the comic strip.

Nick marched the stage, working the crowd up. Preaching his message of common sense and self-reliance. Denise fidgeted off stage. He still hadn't addressed the need to win over Blackbird's followers.

"You know what worries me?" asked Nick in a serious tone. "Apathy. Apathy is when we are assaulted day after day by lies and propaganda to where we no longer have any faith that justice or right will prevail. There is a psychological term for it. But I don't know it," laughed Nick.

"If a majority of us feel this way, why do we let it keep happening? Apathy. That's why. We have lost faith in our systems. In our justice systems. We lost faith in ourselves and each other. That we can change this. By voting for officials who will do the right thing. Pass and enforce laws to hold criminals accountable for their crime. Today, this is not the reality. The only way it stops is for us to break free from our apathy."

"We now live in a fearful society where anyone can be attacked with impunity. What kind of society allows this to happen and stands by and does nothing? This is happening to our country and we are standing by and watching as thugs beat people at my rallies because we are exposing their lies. When I become president, THIS STOPS NOW," articulated Nick, speaking each of the words forcefully. The accompanying cheers were loud and strong.

"No more black shirts, brown shirts, Antifa, ARL, or Gabriel's Angels. They go by many names. It is up to us to make sure the CIA, FBI, IRS and NSA are not added to that list. It is time to hold them all accountable to *the law*. We are the people. And this is a democracy. We all have an equal say in how we live."

"We need to put people in elected office who will stop this abuse of power. Honest people, serving us, not themselves or the elitists who control the money. Honest people who will hold our agencies and our leaders to the high standards our founders expected our citizen politicians to deliver."

"Instead, we have corrupt career politicians who go from the public sector or military to the private sector and then on to lobbying the same government they worked for, raking in millions, and serving their corporate masters. This is just wrong. This too will stop when I'm president. I'll break the merry-go-round and stop this revolving door of corruption. We're infected. We need a serious dose of antibiotics."

"It is supposed to be about what is right and what is good. If you have to explain your actions to tell how it is right or good, hey newsflash, it isn't either. Look at the Opposition candidate. How did that go over?" The crowd booed loudly, being reminded of Blackbird's lack of remorse for his deeds.

"Good and right are easy to spot. They don't need rationalization. Government and government service are now about money and control. Of you. You have a choice. We have already seen how money, power and control have corrupted the current administration. We have seen what lack of empathy, and any idea what it is like to be in your shoes, has done to the Opposition candidate. I am afraid you have a choice to make." Nick stopped pacing and stood in the middle of the stage. The crowd quieted down as he stood looking out of them.

"I can promise you one thing and if you know anything about me by now, it is I don't make promises to you. But I will make this one. I will do good and I will do right. I will fight evil and corruption and every other effort to move us farther from the Constitution." The crowd cheered at this.

"I will fight the slide we have been on. Stop the shredding of our Bill of Rights by the Progressive agenda. They are lying to you. Telling you they care. That they will take care of you. As soon as they no longer need your vote, they will revert to form and treat you like a slave on their plantation. You have choice, but worse, you have to rely on increasingly flawed systems to ensure you vote is counted and not invalidated by their increasing efforts to diminish legitimate votes." The arena, filled with over 20,000 fans waiting to see a band, was as quiet as a church.

"If you want freedom. If you want a choice. You must make your stand. You must take the risk, stand up and be heard. Be seen. Inspire your neighbors. You must vote against Progressivism and choose to stand. They have a 125-year head start on us, but we have to start pushing them back. It starts in less than three weeks. One way or another. It is your choice."

"Ok, enough doom and gloom, bring on the main event. Thanks folks and for your own sake, Wake Up, Stand Up, Think for Yourself, and vote in person," said Nick, walking off the stage as the crowd finally let loose with full throated cheers.

#

Nick started shaking his head as soon as he got offstage to the team. "That sucked. I'm sorry Denise. I couldn't do it. I couldn't go out there and tell them to not vote for Blackbird," apologized Nick.

Denise gave him the 'are you crazy' look.

"What are you talking about? Do you hear them? They are still cheering and yelling your name, even if you think you sucked," laughed Greg. "You'd better make another appearance, or the band will be mad when they won't stop."

Nick stuck his head back out on the stage and waved for thirty seconds before giving them a thumbs up and heading back off stage.

"Nick, have you thought what you will do or where you will go when this is over?" asked Denise, a truly scared look on her face as they left the stage, heading to the parking lot. One of Nick's bodyguards was in front and one in back of the group, scanning ahead and behind. Earl and Nick were also on alert, as always.

"What the hell kind of question is that?" growled Earl, looking at Denise.

"Nick, you are getting pretty close to preaching open rebellion. If you lose, you are not going to go down quietly. You are going to have millions behind you who feel the same way. A general with an army in occupied territory. Lexi is not going to tolerate you running around preaching against every move she makes."

"Welcome to America. They run around, attacking us daily. Turnabout is fair play," replied Nick off-handedly.

Denise sighed. "Listen to what you said today. Really listen and pretend you are Lexi, leading that progressive army. What you hear is a challenge. A challenge that says even if we don't win, we will keep fighting. Unlike in the past, when the Opposition slinks away, fragmented, like a whipped dog. You are making sure she, or more likely the intelligence agencies you so subtly called out tonight, has to deal with you either way. Be careful. She doesn't have to shoot you. She can arrest you, perhaps even the day after the election. You may want to dial down the rhetoric a bit," suggested Denise.

"She's right," added Chuck.

"Bullshit, if we lose, it may come down to sedition," said Earl, jumping into the conversation, countering Chuck and Denise's cautious approaches.

"Look at that crowd. How they reacted to what Nick said. They're not going to go down quietly either. So are a lot of other folks Nick has connected with. None of them are going to go down without a fight. If she tries to take their guns or the ability to assemble and have different opinions, then the result is on her, not Nick."

"Earl, that is fine, but she has the power and the armed forces, Navy SEALs, Deltas, FBI QRT. She can snatch Nick and we won't even have time to blink. Just remember that," pointed out Denise.

"Nick, Denise is right. We need to up the security. I have some more ex-special forces guys who I'll have following us all 24x7 for the rest of the campaign. Now that fundraising is on the uptick again, we can afford it," commented Earl.

"I think it's a good idea," agreed Nick. "I realize what I am preaching is not pretty. It is also the same things Sam Adams and Dr. Warren and others preached at Sons of Liberty meetings. It is the same thing being talked about in every Turner Rabble gathering. Every Woman for Turner rally and every Vets for Turner meeting. At every other one of our grass-roots groups. They'd have to arrest them all," promised Nick.

Denise shook her head.

"No, they don't Nick. You've heard the analogy, 'cut off the head and the snake dies'? You are that head," responded Denise.

"Maybe, but this movement is less about me and more about not losing their freedom. If I am not here, someone else will step up."

"Are you fucking kidding?" asked Chuck, incredulously. "They've had years to rise. You are the reason this is happening. You and you alone are the catalyst. What if you did not stand up and stop that terrorist attack? Guess what? No one else did. If you hadn't stood up against the filibuster, we wouldn't have Crawford and we would instead have fifteen Supremes and two additional states already. Or forty-five million new voters. Just like no one else is going to do what you are doing. You need to face this and you need to make sure you survive and don't get disappeared," rattled off Chuck, holding up two fingers to make his point. "You said it yourself. In a totalitarian regime, they can do what they want, and no one can stop them."

"Chuck's right, Nick," said Earl. "Without you, we are just a bunch of people complaining while we watch our rights disappear. Same as before you showed up. We wanted to do something, but we didn't know what. Until you started leading us on that path."

"Nick, you are the movement," said Greg, who had been listening to the entire exchange. "They bring you down and we all crumble with you. Crawl back under our rocks and hunker down," Greg stopped abruptly. "Look," he said, pointing.

Nick's bodyguards went into a crouch around him.

Greg laughed. "Sorry." He pointed to the row of cars in the well-lit parking lot. They all showed either an 'I am Nick Turner', 'Who is Nick Turner?', or a 'Think for Yourself' bumper sticker. One even had a WST4Y acronym sticker of Nick's trademark phrase.

"Where did these come from?" asked Nick, confused.

"No idea. Some enterprising entrepreneur?" lied Greg. "Or maybe from our website? You should look at it sometime. T-shirts too. Wake up, Stand up, Think for Yourself. WST4Y gear is also a big seller."

"Somewhere John Galt is smiling," laughed Nick.

"And Ayn Rand. I think she'd have approved of your campaign," mused Denise.

They piled into the Suburban along with the bodyguards.

"I hope you guys are wrong. If I cannot convince people each of them together is more powerful than each alone, we will lose this fight. It cannot be about me or Lexi alone. If it fails because I fall, then I have not achieved my goal. You're also right that we cannot devolve into an armed insurrection. It is exactly what she wants. A fight with guns and violence is the surest way to totalitarianism."

His staff understood what he was saying, but they all knew people were afraid of the alternative and without Nick to lead them, they would not risk standing up. Alone or together. The cost of standing up was just too high. Nick was the key. The problem was the enemy knew this, too.

Chapter 82

Mid-morning the day following the Georgia state fair, Nick, Denise, and Chuck were in the conference room in their Denver office. The jet had flown them during the wee hours to get them back to their office. The sun was shining brightly, with a bright blue sky only Colorado showed in the middle of October.

"The next two and a half weeks look like this," said Chuck, standing at the whiteboard. "Next week you are at the Arkansas state fair and then at the end of the week we have the Arizona one. Those are the last chance for the sizeable crowds," Chuck wrote as he talked.

"In between, we'll have you stopping at local rallies in Martha's store parking lots. Maybe a stop in New Mexico as well," rattled off Denise, as Chuck was writing various cities in the south they planned on routing Nick through between the state fairs.

Nick looked on, now used to not having much of a say on where and when he went anywhere. "What about the Midwest and the write-in states? Shouldn't I be trying to capitalize on the people being pissed? Especially in Pennsylvania?"

Chuck stopped writing and glanced at Denise. She spoke up. "Nick, it will take between three and four million votes to win Pennsylvania. Maybe a few less with three viable candidates. The idea we can rouse anywhere near this number of folks to write in your vote…" trailed off Denise, with a sad look on her face.

Nick nodded. "If you can, send me anyway. Maybe a quick swing. You can ignore Philly. But get me into coal and steel country. Scranton, Harrisburg, Allentown, and Pittsburgh. Even if it is only a rally in Martha's parking lots. I'm sure those towns have her stores."

"Nick, it is a waste of your time. We need you where we can actually influence voters in states we might have a chance in. Georgia, Arizona, Nevada, maybe even Virginia or Colorado," replied Chuck in a conciliatory tone. With Blackbird dragging down Carson with him, we'd be better off sending you to the Carolinas. At least they already hate Lexi. Maybe they hate Blackbird enough too. The Blue wall of the rust belt is too entrenched with the Party to make this effort pay off.

Nick stood up and went to the map tacked up on the wall. Many of the states were crisscrossed with green lines showing where Nick and now Neill had been. Wisconsin, Michigan, Pennsylvania, Minnesota, and Illinois had very few spots of green.

"We can't win if I never even give it a try. Can we see if I can squeeze in a visit?" continued Nick. Denise and Chuck looked at each other in concern.

"Here's an idea. How about we send Neill and Ellie?" offered Denise. "There just isn't enough time. You'll spend most of your time on the plane. Arkansas to the Midwest, then to Arizona, back to the Midwest and finally back for the debate in Virginia. If we send them, they can spend the week on a bus. Maybe start in Pennsylvania and head across. They can even dip into West Virginia too. Ellie was born there."

Nick turned and looked at them. "You're right. I hate leaving stones unturned. I didn't make it to Hawaii or Alaska either."

They smiled as the door burst open. Margie quickly entered.

"You'd better look at this." She grabbed the remote and turned it onto *Liberty News One* for breaking coverage.

"That's correct Dan," said a young reporter to Dan Rodriguez, anchor for LN1's *Morning News*.

"Senator Turner was one founder of the Blue Morpho Redemption Project, a 501(c)3 non-profit whose charter is to offer homeless people a better alternative than relying on state and federal help," the young man was speaking quickly, obviously excited.

"The Senator has been receiving a lot of favorable press for cleaning up tent cities in Seattle, California, Austin and other urban areas, getting homeless folks off the street. Turns out it may not be as wonderful as it seems," he announced.

"How is that Mason," asked Dan patiently, with a tilt of his perfectly coiffed hair and an interested look on his face.

"We got a tip to investigate Senator Turner taking advantage of these vulnerable homeless people, making them work on his campaign in return for food and shelter while being paid a pittance."

"That is certainly not how Turner's campaign explains it," countered Dan. Mason nodded on camera as he continued.

"Every Turner office in state after state has these homeless workers from his Blue Morpho org. They are in paid jobs, doing menial jobs like stuffing envelopes, making get out the vote phone calls, and even going door to door dropping off pamphlets in crappy neighborhoods where they are at risk of being abused and attacked."

"You said they are being paid, correct, Mason?" asked Dan.

"They are, but it is a subsistence wage. Those we talked to admitted they are paid, and they are grateful to be off the street and to have shelter. However, they complain about the stipulations they have to agree to in order to live in one of these 'Redemption Villages'," commented Mason.

On the screen, a video showed snippets of typical homeless looking people bad-mouthing the Blue Morpho program. One of them complained because he was constantly being drug tested and was kicked out of one village for testing positive twice. Another complained because he was turned in for stealing from a car on the street. Even though no charges were filed, he was kicked back out on the street by the program.

"It seems his program comes with some pretty strict restrictions to qualify," commented Dan after the montage.

"There are lots of rules and regulations," agreed Mason.

"This is the same type of village, with the high fences, where one of the guys running them attacked the protestor and nearly choked him to death a few weeks back, correct?" pointed out Dan.

"Yes, it is, Dan. Ryan Erikson is the man's name. He is being charged with attempted murder. This confirms some of what we heard from folks who have been in the program. They talked about having to agree to mandatory drug testing, forced labor, and to live in the shelters built by the organization until Blue Morpho says they could leave," stated Mason, looking down at his notes as he spoke.

"Blue Morpho appears to want to keep tabs on their enrollees besides the forced drug tests as a requirement to stay employed at Turner offices and other places they are placed, like Martha Summer's discount stores. They have to sign contracts and agree to a host of other restrictions, including mandatory wage garnishment to pay for their housing and food."

"There are also questions about state or federal funds being diverted or collected and not used or given to those in the program. We are told the local DAs and several federal agencies are looking into this issue with an indictment looming."

"Those are pretty serious allegations, Mason? Abusing and redirecting federal funds. Do we have any official statements from the DA's office?"

"Not yet. We asked. They only confirmed they were investigating. Some of those we interviewed confirmed they were cooperating with the authorities and providing testimony."

"Mason, do we have any comment from Blue Morpho?"

"Not yet Dan, we tried contacting them, but we have not yet heard from them for comment."

"And the Turner campaign?"

"We are following up with them as you speak for comment."

"There is another angle as well Dan, we believe some of the major donors who are donating land and abandoned property like hotels and office buildings are taking massive tax loss write downs to shelter and launder more income. There could be implications and charges of tax fraud as well. We have turned over all our findings, including some documents we got from a whistleblower inside the Blue Morpho LA office. They show massive transfers of wealth from donors like Carson Williamson, Martha Summers, Everett Spalding, Howard Patterson, and others to the Blue Morpho coffers."

"On the screen next was a blurred video of a whistleblower offering claims of knowing these big donors were donating millions of dollars in cash, property, and services without supposedly asking for anything in return or taking the charitable donation tax breaks. He'd heard from others the main reason they were doing it was so they could launder a lot of their offshore profits and fully depreciated assets without being taxed for reshoring the money to the US."

"Mason, that list is a who's who of some of the richest people in America," noted Dan in a surprised voice.

"Dan, the whistleblower has also provided a list of the assets and their values to the US attorneys so they can follow up on the allegations of dodging taxes on these items. There appear to be billions of dollars of assets transferred to the Blue Morpho org. If these allegations are true, you are talking very large penalties at a minimum, if not jail time," finished Mason.

"It's no secret Turner assembled a lot of well-heeled donors to fund this project. He's been busy spreading his claims of fixing homelessness and taking credit for accomplishing things the state and federal government is not," remarked Dan in a not friendly tone.

"My thoughts too, Dan. We'll continue to dig and interview more of the victims of the Blue Morpho programs."

"Thank you. That was Mason Sexton, investigative reporter for LN1 news" finished Dan as he segued to a story about Lexi visiting a low-income health clinic pledging to improve funding for this and all local community clinics serving the poor.

"Here we go again," said Chuck after watching the interview.

"Margie, did we receive any inquiry from LN1 regarding the story?" asked Nick.

"Nope,"

"So that is the first lie," stated Nick. "Who is this guy? I've never heard of him."

"Mason is one of the network's new J-school reporters. The new breed of investigative reporter. Short on field experience, long on a desire to build a brand and cash in on sensationalism. He's building a following on social media," snorted Margie.

"Journalism is really just a branch of Hollywood now. These guys want to get on camera, look tough, and get a book deal. They increasingly want to be the story. Gone are the days of real investigative reporters who met their sources in back alleys, who travel to drug dens reporting firsthand on life on the seedy side of town. Nelly was one of the last. These guys wouldn't know what to do if they were confronted with a pusher or drug deal gone bad," groused Denise. "They'd crap their pants and call 911, begging for help from the same cops they shit on in every story."

Nick snuck a quick look at Earl, who smiled at the change in Denise these past months.

"What do we do?" asked Greg.

"Get out a statement right away denying the allegations," suggested Margie.

"Hang on," said Nick, taking out his phone to answer a call.

Nick walked to a corner of the conference room, listening. He laughed twice before hanging up the phone.

"Who was that?" asked Denise.

"In a minute," replied Nick. "First, let's call Coach and setup calls with Trapper and several others who can go on camera and refute everything they are claiming about Blue Morpho goals and results. Let's talk to our Orange County chair, Laura Wood."

Margie nodded, dialing. "Six months ago, she was homeless. Now she is running our office. She can refute the statements and show how all of her people are being paid, well, in contrast to the millions of hours of free time Lexi is getting from her volunteers. We can also see if she knows anything about a whistleblower or what data on assets is lying around the LA office. That sounds fishy." Margie walked away from the crowd as she talked to Laura on the phone.

"Nick, we probably shouldn't involve Trapper. He *is* still facing attempted murder charges. To come out on camera might be used against him. Maybe check with Penrose?" suggested Jenny from a corner of the table.

"Ah, good point Jenny. Maybe talk to Duane Cooper too?" Jenny smiled, nodding in reply as she started dialing.

"They must be desperate, because this is not well thought out," said Nick. "She is really the one using slave labor and benefiting from cheap student volunteers. That charge should be easy to refute. Next, I think we need to be prepared to open the books and show how all of our work is paying off. Coach can arrange that."

"Was that who was on the phone?" asked Denise impatiently.

"The call was from one very pissed off Everett Spalding. They should think twice before they start throwing out accusations of tax fraud and other stuff. He is going to come down on them like a ton of bricks. He wants to know if we need his help. I asked if he could call Martha, Carson, and Howard. Maybe they could go on the networks to show how their contributions to Blue Morpho instead of the Party were finally paying off. Maybe even work in a 'revenge' angle to redirect their donations. Lexi will love that," laughed Nick.

"Doesn't seem like Lexi. Too much speculation. When she is involved, I expect a complete package. Like the Blackbird takedown. She doesn't make mistakes like this," commented Denise.

"Maybe Kaufmann, the president of LN1?" said Chuck. "We know he is a big supporter of Lexi, and he loathes the Constitution. Maybe he figured he could take you down or keep you from attracting the Blackbird refugees?"

"Maybe, but it is a tactical error. Getting really rich people mad is not a good recipe for success. They have both the means and the will to fight back that your average citizen slandered in the news does not. Is Kaufmann an ex-journalist?" asked Nick.

"No, he is a businessman. Why?" asked Chuck.

Nick smiled. "A veteran journalist would never have allowed that story with so many assumptions. That's why Everett is so pissed. He knows it is going to be easy to refute the charges, but he also knows the charge makes page one and the retraction page sixteen. He's not going to let this go quietly with a simple apology. This is a swipe at us, to turn public opinion against us with salacious accusations. It is effective at getting us chasing our tail at a time we should be wooing Blackbird voters," lamented Nick,

"It doesn't have to be true if we have to spend time fighting it. Look at the time it took us to refute the harassment charges from the two students," said Denise.

"If this is the best they can do?" asked Chuck, trailing off.

Nick looked pensive.

"What?" asked Denise, seeing Nick's look.

"This is a diversion. Like Denise said, this gets us to marshall our forces in one direction while they attack another flank. Let Everett, Coach and others handle this. Hold back our full response. I don't think this is the best they can do."

"Ah, Nick," said Greg, looking first at Earl and then at Nick. Greg flipped the channel to EXN.

The President's press secretary was standing to the side of the podium as Roger Brody, the Secretary of Homeland Security, stood.

Nick's phone started vibrating in his pocket. He got up again, retreating to a corner as Denise gave him an irritated look.

"Today, I am here to announce we are opening an investigation into the response by a private company to an apparent cyber-attack on their company computer systems. It seems in their efforts to combat an aggressive cyber-attack, the Hibiscus companies retaliated against the hackers in such a forceful manner it has brought down part of the power grid in a major Serbian city. Their ambassador has lodged a formal complaint with the US ambassador, and we are opening our own investigation."

"Apparently, this has caused a widespread blackout and damaged both their power grid infrastructure and the ability for the region's major hospital to continue operating. They are transferring critical cases to other area hospitals as we speak. These are serious allegations. If they are true, we will have to bring Hibiscus up on charges of espionage against a sovereign nation. I would warn every private entity that while we understand the concerns regarding cyber terrorism, you cannot take matters into your own hands. All attacks need to be reported to Homeland Security so we can organize any responses and lodge complaints using proper channels."

"I will add, this is not the wild west. Where anyone with a revolver can challenge someone to a duel and randomly respond with attacks. There are rules and the stakes are bigger than a company's computer systems and data. Let this be a warning to any other companies who are or plan to take retaliation into their own hands. We will not be sanctioning or shutting down Hibiscus until we complete our investigation and confirm the veracity of the accusations of the Serbian government. Questions?" asked Roger.

Denise muted the commentary as Nick came back to the table.

"Jeremy?" asked Chuck.

Nick nodded.

"How bad?" asked Margie, her concern clear at the potential of losing this last method of getting their message to the masses.

"Bad. They haven't shut them down, but they now can if they choose to. National Security is one of the few triggers they could use to justify going after them alone and restricting their access to the world," explained Nick.

"What's Jeremy going to do?" asked Denise.

Nick laughed. "He has balls. I'll give him credit. He is putting together a documentary of exactly what happened. What the hackers tried to do and how they stopped them. He is also gathering the information to prove the collapse of the Serbian electric grid is actually self-inflicted. It was an attack by a rival Serbian crime organization trying to take out a competing syndicate by destroying their equipment with a power surge. It got out of hand and took out several power stations."

"He knows this? How?" asked Greg.

"He started to explain it to me, and I told him I already had a headache," smiled Nick as everyone laughed. "The bigger worry is Homeland is smart enough to know this, too. If they are not, we're all in big trouble. Either way, this shows we are getting to them. They fear

Jeremy and Hibi. They set this up to use it to shut him down anytime he gets too bothersome. He is going to hit back with the documentary and expose the duplicity of Homeland. Try to get public opinion on his side before they taint the listeners."

"Crap, Nick. This is not a good time to pick a fight. If he goes down, we go down with him," pleaded Denise. "Can you tell him to wait until after the election, at least?"

"Denise, it is his livelihood. I can't tell him to cower down in fear and play nice with the sword of Damocles hanging over his head. Frankly, I think his move is the right one. They expect defense, so we hit them with offense."

"I know, but if he loses, and he will eventually, trust me, then we lose access. We'll literally be the Sons of Liberty, passing notes from horseback rider to rider," finished Denise.

"I can't stop him. All we can do is support him."

"Shit, that's two, and it's only noon," broke in Chuck, trying to change the subject.

Nick smiled, appreciating Chuck's efforts.

"True. Still early. In the meantime, I want a video of before and after on Venice beach and I want interviews on the boardwalk from tourists and residents about the change. Then I want to hit California's Party government hard. Statistics about homelessness, money spent, that was for nothing, and how Blue Morpho turned all this around. Let's hit them so hard they will think twice about doing this again. Can we do all of this in a couple of days?" asked Nick, acting like the commanding officer he had once been.

"Yes, we can," said Margie now charged up. "We can absolutely go on offense. With Coach's help and the mega donors going on other networks, we should be able to not only stop this but turn it around. Blame LN1. Imply they were working at Lexi's behest and turn it into a positive highlighting how shitty California has been. How well you and Blue Morpho did for the homeless."

"Great." said Nick, "Let's go, but keep an eye open. They are not done. Where else are we weak? Stay alert."

"You know, Nick, they may rue this day. They are hitting you too soft and at the wrong time. They are ensuring you get coverage by forcing all the networks to cover this, when all of them previously wouldn't touch you with a ten-foot pole," pondered Chuck, laughing.

"My thought exactly, they're committing a strategic error, telling me their plans. Giving me time to use it to my advantage."

"Oh God, not more Sun Tzu. Please don't encourage him," said Denise, listening on the phone for an answer on one of her calls. She turned away as the voice on the other end started talking.

Margie finished her call. "We're all set. EXN is going to go out and do some interviews on the beach about before and after. We're lining up Penrose to appear on EXN with Coach to answer any legal issues regarding the whistleblower. Laura in Orange County set all this up. She knew as soon as the story dropped, you'd need all this. She's good, Nick. We'll call the other office managers to be transparent about their hiring and staffing. It was a brilliant move to make sure we paid them all well over minimum wage. All our volunteers in state offices are in Turner Rabble groups. Everyone from a Blue Morpho is on the payroll. None of the other campaigns can make that claim."

Nick nodded.

"One more thing. Find out who they interviewed, and if they really worked for us or not. If yes, when and if they were paid and why they left. Also, let's make it clear what our programs look like and make sure every interview stresses it is all voluntary and they can opt out of the drug testing and leave the Redemption Villages any time they want, no questions asked. Coach can explain this."

"Got it boss," said Margie. "We'll get the info."

#

A couple of hours later, Nick had his feet up on the corner of the desk. He had his hands behind his head, staring at the non-descript ceiling in his office. He'd spent the last two hours talking to Jeremy, Everett, Martha, Howard, Coach and even Trapper. Everyone was clear on the next steps. They would make the enemy rue the day they attacked without doing their due diligence.

As Nick reflected on this, having explained it for the sixth time, it became clear, none of these attacks were supposed to land a knockout punch. As someone had said, they were merely a distraction. To keep them chasing their tail. Keep him off the campaign trail, doing what he did best. Chatting up the common citizen and turning them into an apostle, spreading the gospel of Nick.

The Censure vote was another of these, he was sure. Designed to pull him back to DC at a critical time. But it also pulled everyone else back, too. There were a handful of critical senate races on both sides. This one did not seem like it was part of Lexi's grand plan.

As he tried to get into their heads and anticipate their next attack, there was a knock at the door.

"Enter."

Chuck, Denise and their campaign finance manager, Theodore Perkins, can in quickly. Denise was as white as a ghost. Theodore, who refused to go by Ted, was even paler.

"What happened?" asked Nick, standing, pointing folks to the small table in his office.

"Nick, they're debanking us," said Denise in a panicked voice.

"Settle down. What does that mean?" he asked, looking from Denise to Theodore.

"Sir, it means we no longer have accounts at the banks where we keep our campaign funds. Without accounts, we can't pay bills or issue payroll checks. We can't do business," explained Theodore.

"How did we find out?"

"The three major banks we use, the top three in the country I might add, all sent me notices our accounts were closed immediately and where would we like the money transferred?"

"Did they give a reason?"

"They cited the homeland investigations into the speeches and violence and finally the upcoming Censure vote. According to them, the accusations are sufficient to allow them to cite breach of contract and end our accounts," answered Denise.

"Can we appeal?" asked Nick, looking at Theodore.

"No. It is arbitrary and completely at their discretion. Frankly they don't need a reason or even have to give us an explanation."

Nick stood and paced the room.

"Nick, what do we do? If we don't make payroll, or any number of other payments to advertisers, we are screwed," blurted Denise in a panic.

Nick turned to Theodore. "What's our burn rate?"

Surprised to be asked a finance question in the proper lingo, Theodore hesitated.

"How much a day?" pushed Nick.

"Now, in October?"

"Today and tomorrow specifically. Come on Ted, give me a number," prompted Nick, getting impatient.

"Payroll is the big payout, and it's a week out. Probably one to two million, maybe as high as three. Each day," he replied, flustered, not even correcting Nick for calling him Ted.

"Chuck, can you get Jenny in here, please?" Chuck nodded and left the office.

"Theodore, what are the rules of paying for bills out of my personal bank account?"

"Ah, let me think. Like a loan? We don't need the money, we need an account and a bank to transact with."

"Right, so I want to use the money in my account to pay our bills. They haven't tried to debank me, right? My accounts are USAA. It runs differently from these others not having any shareholders and not being a corporation. I have all of my own accounts there."

"Nick, I think we would be ok. The FEC rules say you, as the candidate, can contribute unlimited funds to your campaign. I'm reading between the lines to mean there is no rule against you doing transactions from your account for the campaign," explained Theodore, looking up from reviewing the FEC website.

"Good, that'll buy us a day or so," disclosed Nick. Chuck re-entered the office with Jenny in tow.

"Denise, you and Margie, and anyone else need to call all our creditors or anyone who is expecting payment. Defer what you can. Find out what we absolutely have to pay. Make it clear we're not out of money, just experiencing challenges for processing." Denise nodded.

Nick turned to Chuck and Jenny. "Jenny, I need a quick contract between the campaign and me personally. I am about to spend my life's savings paying the campaigns bills until we find a bank to take us. I want to reimburse myself for the payments. If I can't, that's ok too. I don't want my paying the bills to be a contribution, but a loan *transacted* from my account. Make sense?"

"Yep, got it. Can I take Theodore with me? We'll have to comb through the FEC rules to make sure you can get paid back from the campaign for the loan of the account. Nick, if your bank figures this out, they are going to shut this down fast, too," remarked Jenny.

"I know. I like USAA, so I don't want to put them in that position. This has the heavy hand of the Treasury and DOJ all over it. That's why I want to find an alternative fast." Jenny and Theodore left the room with Denise as well.

"What are you thinking?" asked Chuck.

"Switzerland, possibly Australia or China, as a last resort. Any of them look terrible, doing my banking outside the US because my country thinks I am the equivalent of Iran."

"Sucks to be us right now. All this money and unable to use it. How about crypto? You know, like Bitcoin?"

"I don't understand it, so I also don't trust it. It can't be a currency the masses will accept if they can't understand the concepts of block chains. I'm not converting my good old cash to tulip bulbs either. A stable currency doesn't fluctuate like a tech stock."

"I'll see if anyone has any other ideas."

"Good. One thing is for sure. This one is *not* a sideshow. The recon is done. Here come the tanks."

#

"Oh, bravo Mel. This is fantastic," declared Lexi with a beaming smile and a little clap. They'd been watching the wrap up of the market day on a business channel, when they had breaking news that Nick Turner's campaign accounts were being debanked by the three largest financial institutions of the United States.

The commentators explained what this would mean for the Senator and his ability to transact business in the United States. Without access to clearinghouses and various other financial services provided by SWIFT and other financial processing entities, much like Iran and North Korea, Turner would be cut off from his funds. No way to pay bills meant he'd be unable to arrange for advertising or even make payroll for his employees.

"Let's see how Saint Turner squirms out of this," gloated Lexi.

"Lexi, this approach is not without risk. Both to Turner and public opinion. We need to hide our glee. Of course, we had nothing to do with any of these investigations, allegations, or their recommendations of these banks or agencies," cautioned Mel.

"Of course, Mel. It's not my first campaign, you know. I've seen every dirty trick in the book. How are we doing?" she asked.

"The co-ed accusations are done. The papers already printed their retractions. The girls are being excoriated, just as Harriet thought they would. We made our point. A certain group of people assume he got away with harassment as a professor. That's all we could ask or hope for from that one. It was a longshot."

Lexi nodded, not concerned at the collateral damage of the two co-eds and their lives being trashed on social media *forever*.

"The Blue Morpho story aired on LN1. It wasn't done very well. They got lazy. Lots of accusations and innuendo. They had the story and could have done the legwork like Beverly did on the Blackbird material. I don't think Kaufmann took our info seriously."

Lexi made a rude noise.

"We're shielded. My sources are telling me Spalding is going to come after them with both barrels because of the slanderous statements. He's got the deep pockets to do it too. We'll see how the public responds. The good thing is we got the man on the street footage out there, shitting allover Blue Morpho and making it look more like a concentration camp than the utopia they make it out to be. Lots of additional coverage on other stations, assuming the donors are at a minimum, dodging taxes if not collecting taxpayer funding for the shelters as well. Lots of confusion and no time to unravel it."

"Good. They can spend some of the money they didn't give me, defending their asses instead," seethed Lexi.

Mel continued. "Homeland is doing their thing on the violence. It won't result in any charges before the election, but it contributed to the debanking. Even if nothing comes of it, it gave the banks air cover and it is no doubt causing mayhem for Turner."

"We only need to get through the election anyway, then I have plenty of ways to deal with Turner."

Mel kept going. "You saw the announcement regarding Hibi and the investigation there. I can't believe we lucked out on that one with the Serb's complaining. I hope the CIA had time to confirm the accusations before Roger went public. These cabinet secretaries are not the bravest or smartest bunch. If it is true, it gives us the leverage we need to deal with Kwan."

"Shit, Mel, I don't care if it is true or not. We decide what is the truth. Especially for the cyber stuff. Must have been bad if the Serbs tried to blame us."

"Agree. I think that brings you up to speed on the big ones." Mel wisely did not bring up the Censure vote, which was now being scheduled for next week. Pulling the Senator's back two weeks before an election did not bode well for the future of Senator Fitzpatrick.

"We on track on everything else?"

"Oh yeah. Showtime tomorrow."

Lexi rubbed her hands together and smiled.

Chapter 83

Nick's HQ was like a beehive at harvest time. Everyone was in motion, countering some aspect of the various attacks. The conference room was set up as a war room. On various whiteboards and flip charts, each incident was listed, the response plans, and where they were in the response, all diagrammed out.

Nick huddled with Margie. "How'd it go?" asked Nick.

"So far, so good. I was on the EXN morning show. Coach did the morning show at LN1 and knocked it out of the park. Everett, Martha and Carson are going on together tonight on NWN. They will do fine. It is terrible optics when Party mega donors get on and trash Party policies. They are going to let LN1 have it as well and announce a defamation lawsuit, while releasing all their relevant donation and tax records. They poked the wrong hornet's nest on this one," laughed Margie. "I wouldn't want any of them as my enemy. Lexi has pissed all of them off."

"Good. Let's get Laura on somewhere and get that video of the man on the street footage," suggested Nick.

"Working on it. Should be on EXN sometime today. The other networks are already backing down a bit from coverage. I'm sure Everett's lawyers worked the phones last night. The *Times* and the *Post* both published front page hit pieces as news and, of course, scathing rebukes and calls for special prosecutors on their opinion pages. Plus, the usual kick you out of the Senate rhetoric, and to add these charges to the Censure motion."

"Ah, nothing like being pilloried in the public square without facts or the chance to defend yourself," commented Nick dryly.

"They're all ready for the presser outside."

"Let's do this. And let's limit questions to a few. I don't have time for an hour-long one today. Any national guys?"

"Not sure. No Bergamo. I think you have pretty good coverage. You're the hot topic now and everyone wants to pile on."

\#

Nick walked outside his office to the podium. There were about thirty reporters and the requisite number of news cameras.

"Good morning. Actually, it's a splendid morning for the thousands of homeless in the Blue Morpho Redemption Villages across the country. Those who are now helping themselves leave homelessness behind and working to improve *their* lives and return to society with the support of Blue Morpho."

"You have seen some interviews already this morning from participants in the programs. About how they have succeeded because Blue Morpho gave them a chance to help themselves. You will also hear tonight from the major donors behind the organization. They do not need my help to counter the baseless and frankly slanderous charges leveled against the organization and each of them personally."

"The facts speak for themselves. It took their willingness to do what our state and federal governments could not accomplish. A reduction in homelessness and an increase in hope. And they did it with their own money." Nick was speaking faster, his voice louder.

"They do this because they are problem solvers. Because they are patriotic Americans. Americans who have lived the American dream and want to ensure others also have that chance. Perhaps it is time this administration and our government approached their job in this way. Blue Morpho was founded to give hope to those who have given up on hope," finished Nick.

"As for some of my own issues. Where do we start? You know, I was told to expect all manner of dirty tricks when I decided to run for president. I figured the person who had the best ideas would win. The one who did the best job articulating these to the most people. Convincing them they meant what they said? How naïve. Clearly, I am mistaken. I promise nothing to anyone. I am not sure why my opponents find this so threatening? Apparently, they do, or they would not be relentlessly attacking me."

Nick held up his hand. "I would appreciate all of you spending as much time apologizing to me as you did accusing me of sexual harassment, sexism, and racism. As much time as you spent praising the two students who made those baseless accusations."

"They were sought out and convinced to make these accusations by faceless, nameless, and coldhearted Party operatives. People who do not give a shit about what has happened to them. They are the real predators. Find and expose them, and I will praise you." Nick's anger was coming through in his delivery.

"These poor young women's lives are being trashed on social media. Because all of you used them. Oh well, they were adults, right? And none of *you* have to pay any price for your part contributing to their misery. Congratulations." Nick held up the palm of his hand.

"Take a good look in my Mirror and congratulate yourself. These could have been your sisters or daughters. You are not blameless in their suffering." He stopped to calm down. The reporters threw out questions about the investigations and the debanking. Nick fixed them with a hard stare, not answering until they stopped. Then he shook his head.

"We welcome the various investigations of violence and so-called rhetoric at my speeches. If one were to look at *all* the footage at my rallies. Both the ones I'm at and ones I'm not. You would see all the so-called violence is self-defense. 'The peaceful' protesters are the ones with hoodies, face masks, frozen water bottles, rocks, and Molotov cocktails. The ones hurling the racial and ethnic slurs."

"All caught on the recordings, including the audio. Footage we make available to anyone. Yet every story I see accompanying these accusations against our campaign does not show any of this. Instead, it shows an organization for which I have no affiliation and to whom I have disavowed all relationship. I am perfectly happy for Homeland or local police to track down and charge *all* of those who are instigating violence at rallies, be they ARL, Antifa, Gabriel's Angels, or any other organization, including my own. I am not afraid. I have faith I can still get an impartial judge and jury. Bring it on." Nick stared defiantly into the camera. His message delivered in firm and clear tones. No bluster, no rhetoric. Just facts and confidence.

"Third, Censure. Really? Again, go to my website. I have a host of videos of my senate colleagues calling on their supporters to do violence against Supreme Court nominees. To stalk and disrupt Opposition congress members and their families anywhere they encounter them. At restaurants and on the street. Others are on record supporting terrorists and claiming Israel has no right to exist. Give me a break. I don't see anyone bringing up Censure against them. Senator Fitzpatrick, I am happy to debate and expose the hypocrisy of the 'world's greatest deliberative body'." Nick smiled for a second, causing the reporters to wonder what he was smiling about.

"I may not have been able to stop nefarious deeds from removing the Legislative filibuster, but the individual right of any senator to filibuster is still sacrosanct. A word of warning. I am in excellent health. I figure I can probably stand at that podium for two or three days. My memory is also very strong. I am sure I can quote chapter and verse every hateful statement my colleagues would prefer were not brought back to the surface. Especially for some of them up for re-election. Who knows, a couple of senators may even be willing to join me. We could be like the Party in 1964 when they filibustered against the passage of the Civil Rights Bill. We could keep this up through the election. We all have better things than to show to our citizens how we are *not focused* on things important to them."

The reporters in the audience started yelling questions at Nick. Asking if he was threatening his colleagues? He ignored them.

"Finally, debanking. How many of you understand what this is and what it means?" There were a few nodding heads, and even some smiles. Nick was not talking to them, but looking squarely into the cameras.

"Now imagine, you get a call from your bank. I bet you didn't know they can decide to stop doing business with you for no reason. Anytime they want. No questions asked. No appeal. And no explanation given to you. Even if you ask. Did you know that? Your bank issued credit cards stop working. You can't write a check. You can't withdraw cash from an ATM. Can't get a loan, can't pay your mortgage without access to the banking system. Your life is effectively over. Does this seem reasonable in any way?"

"This happened a few years ago to a high-profile politician in Great Britain. It was clearly politically motivated. Payback for his stances and actions. Nothing illegal. They wanted to make him pay. Or maybe not be able to pay." Several in the audience couldn't resist smiling and laughed at Nick's pun. Many were amazed he could still laugh, knowing he had no way to use his campaign funds.

"Typically, your bank is nice enough to tell you to F-yourself, but with some notice. Well, I got zero notice for my campaign. And from the three largest banks in this country, simultaneously. Hmm. There couldn't be any coordination there now, could there?" Again, Nick paused to let this sink in.

"Now it is not because I can't pay my bills, trust me. We have hundreds of millions of dollars in our accounts. The banks are making tons of money in transaction fees from our using them. No, this is much more sinister than that. This is banking being used as a weapon. A weapon to stifle free speech. A political weapon. If they can use it against me, perhaps they will find a reason to use it against you."

"We have a fourth and sixth amendment for a reason. We are protected against illegal search, seizure or warrantless activity, such as denying access to millions of campaign dollars. To hear our so-called crimes and to have a jury of our peers to judge our guilt or innocence. Especially when charged with something serious enough to warrant them trying to cut us off from all banking services. We reserve this for terrorist states like Iran, North Korea and Syria. Do I look like a terrorist state? I am a lowly politician who is still barely at double digits. Why am I being treated like a rogue nation state? Is this the future for anyone who dares challenge the incumbent Party nominee?"

"This will not stop us. Even now we are arranging other ways to pay our suppliers and our employees. It is simply an inconvenience. But I ask all of you who are watching this. Do you trust companies that would treat me this way, for simply voicing an opinion? Is my opinion really that radical? Is it that different from your own? Do you want your livelihood tied up in an institution like this who can pull the plug on your ability to lead a financial life? I ask you to think about this. Decide and express for yourself how you feel about this action."

"I think that hits the major topics. Fire away."

"Senator, what about the allegations you are preying on the homeless and forcing them to work in your offices in return for Blue Morpho services?" asked Meg from RBS, the third major network.

"Meg, have you contacted any of my offices?" asked Nick, looking at Meg who didn't respond yes or no. "I thought not. You can go to any of my campaign offices, and they will be happy to show you the books. You can talk to anyone in our office. They will be happy to talk to you about how they are paid, if they are part of Blue Morpho, and if there is any restriction on their employment."

Nick paused, gripping the raised sides of the podium harder.

"My state offices are staffed with *only* paid staffers. All of whom are making more than the minimum wage in the state. I can guarantee you if you were to go to *any* of Lexi's offices, you will find young people who are volunteering their time and providing free services to Lexi's campaign."

"Why are you not examining this as an in-kind donation? Why are you not doing a story on the thousands of unpaid workers in Lexi's offices and the thousands and thousands of hours of free labor she receives, for which these students get no pay, no social security wage deposited, and no income tax for state and federal coffers?"

Meg did not respond to Nick's question, though her cheeks reddened a bit.

"All aspects of the Blue Morpho program are voluntary. You take a job voluntarily. You live in a Redemption Village voluntarily. You voluntarily agree to take a drug test as a condition of employment, like you do in many other businesses and the military. And if you don't want to do any of this, you are free to go without penalty. Period," finished Nick, his frustration apparent in his tone.

"Senator, does it not concern you these donors are getting massive tax breaks by donating all these goods and services to the Blue Morpho organization? It seems dishonest to pay less tax by transferring so much wealth to this effort?" asked Ned from EXN

"Ned, philanthropy is a fundamental part of our society. As a whole, we give more to support charities as a country than the rest of the world combined. We are a giving society. I will let them speak for themselves tonight, as I am sure each of these generous donors will be asked to defend why they are willing to invest billions of their own money, not your tax dollars, to help people less fortunate than they are. Why would anyone not want to get the homeless off the streets? Our government sure doesn't want to solve the problem, unless it is for a few days to impress the Chinese premier in San Francisco," Nick's voice dripped sarcasm. Denise was off camera, cringing at Nick's tone.

"Again, I cite the hypocrisy of the statement and the questions. Are you investigating the offshoring of so much wealth in the Caribbean islands? Are you investigating the donations to the Anti-Racist League chapters and how these funds have been used to buy multi-million dollar houses for the leader of those non-profits? Did anyone ever track down the millions raised for Haiti by ex-presidents and movie stars and demand an account of how much of that donated money made it to the starving citizens?" Nick continued to challenge the press gathered in front of him. They continued to not hear a word he said. Circling like a pack of cowardly hyenas, waiting for their opening to lunge in for their bite.

"I challenge every other company or person who has donated to social justice causes and NGOs to be as transparent and forego their tax benefits as the Blue Morpho donors have. I know this will never happen, but at least one side will bet their money against the American *Pravda* hypocrisy," ended Nick.

He looked over the crowd and reluctantly picked out Al from FLCN. "Senator, do you care to comment on the allegations regarding your staffer? I believe his name is Greg Simmons, having inappropriate relations with a junior staffer in your office."

Nick stood at the podium for a second, processing the statement. Margie bent to his ear. "This is airing on FLCN right now," she whispered, her eyes wide.

"Al, I am just being made aware of this allegation. I cannot comment on this until I better understand the facts," deflected Nick.

"Ok, that will do it," said Margie as she and Nick walked back inside the office as reporters shouted more questions at his back.

As they entered the office, the beehive was now chaotic and confused. The phones were ringing off the hook. Chuck saw Nick and waved him over.

"He's in the conference room. Nick, he's a wreck. I'm worried about him. They're going after staff now. You better get ready to get it from all sides. Good job out there today. Too bad they have moved on to this one," finished Chuck with a sigh.

"Thanks Chuck. Let me go in alone."

Nick walked into the conference room and closed the door behind him. Greg immediately jumped to his feet.

"Nick, you gotta believe me. It's all a lie."

"Greg, relax," answered Nick, waving him back into his seat and taking one next to him. "Of course, I believe you. But this is not about whether I believe you, it is about what they are saying and how we handle it. Tell me everything."

Greg looked down. "I know you never asked, and I appreciate that, but I'm gay. I've known since high school. Even though things are better to be publicly gay, politics is a dirty business and for that reason, I have been very careful to not do anything which could impact you or your campaign. Ever since I came to work for you, I made a pact to never be the story. I have had no dates or relations with anyone of any sex in the last 18 months. I would be happy to take a lie detector test or anything else you need to confirm this," offered Greg.

"What's the story then?" asked Nick.

"Kevin was on FLCN and he says not only did I have relations with him, but it was non-consensual," admitted Greg, who put his hands in his head as he finished.

"I assume, from your statement, this is not true?"

Greg raised his head and laughed. "He is not my type. I was counseling him. There are some in the office who can confirm we were together. We could be seen leaving the office together. I am sure there are others who have guessed, if not figured out, that both of us are gay. We'd always go down the street to Starbucks for a coffee and chat, but those could be construed as having a relationship. They also had the barista confirm we were there together frequently."

"What were you counseling him about?" asked Nick quietly.

"Kevin wants to come out, but he is afraid of the response. From his family, from all of us, and most importantly from you," revealed Greg.

"He ought to know me well enough to know I wouldn't care."

"Nick, you really are obtuse sometimes. You think you are just this 'normal' guy walking around solving the world's problems. To these kids, you are like Ironman and Captain America, all rolled into one. You are larger than life to them. They idolize you. The last thing in the world any of them want to do is disappoint you," finished Greg, looking at the bewildered look on Nick's face. "Man, you really don't get it, do you?"

"I *am* just a regular guy," said Nick, sheepishly.

"OK, let's table that one for now," laughed Greg. Nick hid his grin. He was trying to get Greg to relax and focus.

"Anyway, what I was doing was telling him most people suspected or knew I was gay, but I didn't have to announce it and I just lived my life. Things like explaining to him the added burden a gay man has in the political world. I also explained to him I don't date and why. While being gay is no longer an issue, there is still a stigma in part of the country. Nick, I told him I don't want to risk becoming the story if an indiscretion or relationship were to be used against you."

"That's ironic. It's almost as if you gave him the playbook on how to hurt you and us," noted Nick.

"I know, I know. I've been asking myself that as well. It also makes little sense why he would do this. He loves the job and is really a good kid. His home life is a wreck. Abusive father he hasn't seen in ten years and a mother in and out of rehab. He's stable, if that is what you are thinking. Others in the office like him. I don't know what he has to gain by doing this. I was honestly trying to help. I swear, I made no suggestive moves at all. He is way too young. God Nick, what am I going to do?" He put his head in his hands.

Nick put a hand on his shoulder.

"Greg, the first thing you are going to do is tell the senior staff what you told me. Then you are going to tell the office the same thing. I don't want anyone in here to think there is an ounce of truth in these allegations. Then we are going to fight it tooth and nail. Just as we are all the other dirty tricks. Maybe we will televise a lie detector test. This is more Lexi bullshit designed to fragment us and keep us from focusing on getting out the vote," confided Nick.

"Nick, I am so sorry."

"Greg, this is a shitty business. They can make up crap about anyone without repercussions. I intend to make sure those people face some level of retribution for their reprehensible actions." Greg nodded and Nick left to get the senior staff.

#

Later, Nick sat in his office making calls, checking in with all the Blue Morpho donors, making sure they were all set for their interviews tonight when he heard a tap at his door.

"Enter."

This time it was Chuck, Denise, Greg, and Margie. He could tell by their face it was more bad news.

"Geez, what a day. Now what?"

"Boss, there is a story on RBS and now the cable networks have picked it up. During a traffic stop in Detroit earlier today, the cops pulled over a delivery van. In the back, they found twelve bins full of mail in ballots. All of them filled out with your name on the write in line of the ballot. About 80,000. For Wayne County, Michigan," explained Chuck.

"Really?" Nick shook his head.

"Lexi has already made an appearance claiming you are trying to cheat at the ballot box since you couldn't cheat and get on the ballot in Michigan. The driver is claiming he picked them up in a warehouse outside Ann Arbor with instructions to drive them to another warehouse near the Wayne County Convention Center. This is a staging area where the ballots will be collected and transferred to the Convention Center on election night for counting," continued Chuck.

"A warehouse. Is it an official warehouse?"

"Actually, it is. They collect the ballots from the ballot boxes and store them in this warehouse. They don't open the ballot and separate the ballot from the envelope with the signature. That will all happen on election night. They were all in official election cardboard boxes, sealed with official tape," noted Denise.

"These are the boxes where they would be put after the signatures were verified on the envelopes and then the actual ballot is stacked in these to be fed into the tallying machines. Lexi is calling for you to admit this fraud and drop out of the race," fumed Chuck.

Margie looked up from her phone.

"Nick, Blackbird is saying basically the same thing. 'There is no place in the election or the country for any attempt to thwart the will of the people'."

"We need to issue a statement. We unequivocally deny any attempt to influence the outcome of the election. This is obviously an attempt to frame me because I have been rising in popularity and it scares the establishment. We will vigorously defend our reputation and immediately ask for a special nonpartisan review of the information and the evidence. We will be happy to comply with any requests for disclosure or interview with non-partisan authorities. Last, I ask every thinking American to look into their conscience and ask themselves who they believe. Me or American *Pravda*, the Vice President, and the current administration with their track record," quoted Nick. "Can you get that out word for word?"

"You got it, boss. The gloves are off," said Margie, heading out to put the statement out on the wire.

"Shit," said Denise. "They're pulling out all the stops. It's getting to where even the average American is going to ask themselves if it is just a little too convenient that all these allegations are coming out so close to the election. And only against Blackbird and you."

"I sure hope so, Denise. At least these are getting broad distribution. They want as many as possible to see and hear these."

"Nick, this is a real hard one to refute. Unless we can come up with an eyewitness willing to say they were coerced into doing this, it is going to be their word, with the evidence against ours that we have nothing to do with this," warned Denise.

"I know. Can you ask Earl to join us, Chuck.?"

"We need to get our hand on some of those to see if there is anything we can trace back to a source," revealed Denise.

"Fat chance of that," scoffed Nick, as Chuck and Earl came in.

"Earl, can you track down some crack investigators? I need them to find out where this came from and get evidence of who perpetrated it. Fast. Can you do it?"

"I already have a good idea of who I need. We'll figure it out, Nick. Keep the faith," urged Earl.

"I'm trying," agreed Nick with a smile. "I just spoke to the Blue Morpho guys. They're ready for tonight, assuming the network hasn't moved on to these other stories."

"Nick, you know they're going to cancel. That story is already three bombshells ago. Like you said, they stir the pot, detonate the IED, and walk away. That is what they are doing, leaving us to pick ourselves out of the debris field," grumbled Chuck.

"Chuck's right. I'd say it is 50/50. If NWN cancels, we can at least get EXN to take them and get a recording we can use on the website," suggested Denise, as Nick nodded.

"I guess we'll see. They are scheduled for what, 6pm mountain?" asked Nick.

"Yes," said Greg. Margie came back into the room.

"Dare I ask, how is social media?"

Margie looked at Greg first. "Pretty negative on the Greg stuff. You know young people are pro-gay, but the way this is being presented is predatory. They don't like that, and it is a big negative. The only way to change this is if we find out what is being used to pressure Kevin and get him to recant. Sorry Greg," said Margie with a weak smile. Greg nodded, "Thanks."

"On the ballot stuff it is a little early, but the trends are actually in your favor as many are claiming this is more Party dirty tricks. No doubt the trolls will flood the media channels with disinformation, but for now, we are holding our own."

"Alright team, hang in there. Our first goal is to figure out how to exonerate Greg. Guys, we have to get to Kevin. Anyone know where his mother is?"

"Rehab again in Malibu, California, I think. It's been weighing on him pretty heavily. And I think it's expensive," shared Greg.

"Earl."

"Got it. I'll see what I can do with some local help. If we can dig something up."

"See if you can get anything from her. Visits, money, threats, promises, there has to be something. I feel like this is the weak link," commented Nick.

"OK, I'm on it. Anything else? If not, I'm going to start making calls," added Earl, getting up and heading for the door.

"Let's roll folks, we all have day jobs. Keep the pedal down. Don't let this distract us from our efforts to keep getting the word out," declared Nick as optimistically as possible. Everyone but Denise left the room.

"Nick, there is a chance this hits your poll numbers, and you get left out of the last debate next week. We expected to pick up enough of Blackbirds to get to the threshold. Can you record a PSA telling your voters to answer truthfully now to any polls? What can Lexi do now that she is not already doing?" asked Denise.

"I'll consider it," offered Nick. "Let's see how the polls do in the next two days."

Chapter 84

Nick picked at his Caesar salad in the conference room with the entire senior staff. They were watching NWN ask questions of Martha Summers, Howard Patterson, and Carson Williamson in the New York studio and Everett Spalding was on a big screen behind them on video conference.

Martha was explaining why they helped fund Blue Morpho. They saw the possibility of what Nick had described and saw it as an alternative to the failed policies and actions of the local, state, and federal efforts. Maybe something from the private sector would have a better effect.

They made sure it was clear that it was Nick's plan and his strategy to accomplish the goals through individual work ethic, hope and faith in humanity's desire to control their own fate. To break the cycle of poverty not through handouts, but accomplishment. As Everett was starting to layout the financial arrangements and position his lawsuit, Margie's phone buzzed. Then Denise's and Chuck's.

"Somebody nuke Israel?" asked Nick questioningly.

"Boss, we're recording NWN. We need to switch to ANC," declared Margie as she changed the channel.

#

"That's right Marty, I have video taken in April of this year of Senator Nick Turner involved in a drug deal in North Lawndale, Chicago," reported Lauren Bergamo.

"Let's play the footage," ordered Marty.

The group in the conference room watched as the video shot from the interior of a car showed it pulling up to the stoop of a house. On the steps were several black men of various ages, most wearing hoodies or dark t-shirts. There is one white guy standing in the background, his hood pulled up. Earl can be seen staring down from the steps, looking into the car. Denise recognized him and turned to stare at Earl in the room.

"What the *fuck*!" she almost screamed.

"Shush," ordered Nick, as they continued to watch. In the footage, the white guy was holding a packet of heroin as the person in the driver's side of the car talked to the dealer leaning in and the passenger, apparently Lauren, filmed from her seat as the conversation happened.

In the distance, a car could be heard approaching as the dealer leaning into the car stood up. Nick turned to look, the camera catching his face clear as day, holding the drugs in his hands. Right then the squeal of tires, the sound of gunfire, the shattering of Lauren's window and glass shards falling into the frame of the camera as it headed down in her hand. The image shifted to a rear camera, which showed everyone running and ducking, including Nick and Earl covering a woman on the ground, as Lauren and her photographer drove away.

"That is amazing footage, Lauren. Were you injured when the bullets were flying?" asked Marty.

"No, Marty, luckily both Paul, my photographer and I were unhurt as we drove away. I'm not sure what the Senator was doing there. We tracked him that day when he went to a shelter and visited another house for a couple of hours in a dangerous neighborhood. We saw him go up to that stoop with another young black woman and his head of security, Earl Greene. That is when we did the drive by and got the pictures for the story," explained Lauren.

"Lauren, if this happened in April, why wait until now?"

"Until now, it really wasn't relevant. Given the other various issues with the Senator's campaign and the dishonesty being shown, ANC's management decided this footage must also be disclosed to the voting public so they are aware of all the activities of the presidential candidates," deflected Lauren.

"We have reached out to the Senator's staff, but we have no response to the footage or the accusations," stated Lauren.

"Thank you. Lauren Bergamo with breaking news and footage of Senator Turner in an apparent drug deal in Chicago earlier this year. The day keeps getting worse for the Senator," ended Marty.

They went to a commercial. Lauren jumped off the stage, her mic ripping loose from her blouse. Marty looked over at her.

"Lauren, are you OK?"

Lauren looked up, tears streaming down her face, and shook her head, fleeing the studio. Sherman stood off camera, smiling.

#

Everyone turned and looked at Nick and Earl questioningly.

"So that was her? Son of a bitch," said Earl. "How the hell did she track us that day? We were walking around the whole time."

"I don't know, but it is not the first time she has just showed up. Earl, you say you swept my phone and there is no tracking device. We had better check my clothes and shoes, watch. For the life of me, I can't figure out what she could be using," speculated Nick.

"Screw that, Nick. This footage is the most damning in a long day of damns," said Denise, her voice breaking under all the tension.

"I know. We'll figure it out. The video is out of context and I think we can prove it." Nick looked at Earl.

"Kayla?" asked Earl

"And Ray," added Nick as Earl nodded.

"Care to explain? It might be important, you know?" growled Denise.

"Let us make some calls and then we'll fill you in," replied Earl.

"And in the meantime? Jeez Nick, the cops are going to bust in here and arrest Greg for rape and you for drug dealing. Now is not the time to hold back," exploded Denise angrily.

"Ah Denise," broke in Margie. "And you for election fraud. Apparently, the driver told the cops you were the one coordinating the pickup and delivery of the ballots."

"What!" wailed Denise in despair.

"Ok guys, keep it together. No one is going to be arrested. ANC is not outside the door to film it, so I know the FBI is not on the way," joked Nick.

"I don't know how you can be so calm about all this," blurted Denise, almost hysterical.

"They are all just attacks, Denise. We'll deal with them. Shore up our defenses and counterattack. Earl, I want another sweep of the offices and use a different firm this time in case the other one has been bought by Lexi."

"First thing in the morning, Nick."

"Flip back to NWN please," directed Nick.

NWN now had a series of talking heads on, not talking about the interview with Blue Morpho donors but showing the drug deal footage and talking about the need to bring Nick up on charges immediately and move to have him resign from the Senate. And to, of course, end his presidential campaign.

Margie flipped to LN1, then RBS, and finally back to cable and FLCN. All were talking about the footage, and all were asking for the same resignation. Margie turned to EXN, where Tommy was now on.

"Has anyone asked themselves how all of this is coming out in one day? What we lack is context and evidence. Evidence other than hearsay about Turner staffers and context on the ballots and the footage ANC showed. Conveniently held for six months. It is not as difficult as you think to print up fake ballots. It would be easy to do this to just gin up talking points against the Senator."

"The same with the drug deal. I know Nick Turner and I can tell you, in fact I will bet my show, that he is no drug user or dealer. I'm looking forward to hearing from the Senator so he can expose the truth of what was happening in Chicago."

"We already know the Blue Morpho stuff was pure BS and LN1 should be ashamed of their reporting. Ed Murrow and Walter Cronkite are rolling in their graves at the tabloid exploits of these networks. Time will tell, keep the faith, and continue to stand against the creeping socialism and cancel culture of the administration and their stormtroopers in American *Pravda*. Senator, we are with you and do not let them beat you down," said Tommy, signing off his show.

"Where's Greg?" asked Margie, looking down the table to Greg's empty chair.

"Shit," said Nick, leaping up from his chair. "Earl, call security. Find him."

Nick ran out of the conference room, looking through the mostly empty office. He asked a staffer if they had seen Greg, but they could only say they saw him heading out.

Chuck was standing next to Nick. Earl stuck his head out. "Nick, he's on the roof."

"No!" Nick sprinted to the elevator.

Earl and Chuck made it to the elevator just as it was closing with Nick in it. They reached the top floor and carefully opened the roof access door. Greg was nowhere in sight. As they moved forward, Nick could see him standing on the West side, in the light of the full moon, looking at the mountains. Nick motioned Earl to go around the flank as he and Chuck moved toward Greg.

"Greg," said Nick in an even tone.

"Nick, please stay back," responded Greg in a surprisingly calm voice.

"Greg, this won't solve anything," reasoned Nick. Greg was still facing west and had not turned to face Nick. Out of the corner of his eye, he could see Earl creeping up low and slow from the right. Nick turned and walked to the left, hoping to get Greg to turn away from Earl.

"Nick, this is the only way I can help you. It is my word against Kevin's. He already has sympathy on his side. You heard Margie," explained Greg, turning slightly to face Nick.

"That's far enough. I've already decided. I put a video recording on my phone. Get Tommy to play it if no one else will. It may help resolve this."

"Come back from the edge. Let's use the info and get to the truth. You know I believe you. You know I will stand by you no matter what," pleaded Nick. Earl was about ten feet away, almost close enough to grab him.

Greg smiled. "I know Nick. Everyone who knows you does. Dusty knew, yet it wasn't enough to save him. You would stand by me even if it cost you the election. You would stand by any of us. It's why people who know you love you. But I cannot allow you to sacrifice the greater good protecting me. I'm sorry I failed, Nick. I am so sorry," ended Greg.

"Now," yelled Nick.

Earl lunged, and Nick ran forward as Greg hurled himself over the sill of the building. Earl grabbed a pant leg, turning Greg briefly as he went over. Earl lost his grip, reestablished it on Greg's foot as he went over. Earl looked at Nick as he got to the edge. He had only a shoe in his hand. Greg made no sound as he fell the twenty stories to the ground below.

Chuck was on his knees behind them, not just crying, but sobbing. Nick and Earl had both lost comrades in battle. They stood looking out, their grief and guilt internalized. Nick glanced at Earl with a nod. Earl set Greg's shoe on the ledge. He half carried Chuck as he tried to comfort him. The door to the roof closed silently behind them.

Nick looked down at the ledge, first at the shoe, and then picked up Greg's phone. He listened to the video. After, he was so pissed he almost threw the phone off the building. He stood there looking at the Rocky Mountains as the beams of moonlight bathed the snow-covered peaks in the distance. The sound and wail of approaching police and ambulances arriving below carried to the roof.

Turning away, his eyes now hardened with hatred, his mind was full of vengeance and his body a coiled up spring, ready to release violently. He would find who started this and he would make them suffer, as Greg had suffered. As Nick was suffering, as countless others had suffered, under this regime's dirty tricks. They didn't know it yet, but the whirlwind was upon them, and its name was Nick Turner.

The End

The Cost of Standing Up

Connect with the Author

- Author website: www.ejriceauthor.com
- Facebook author site: https://www.facebook.com/ejriceauthor
- Substack Blog site: https://ejriceauthor.substack.com/
- Twitter account: https://twitter.com/EJRiceauthor
- Instagram: https://www.instagram.com/ericriceauthor.
- TikTok: https://www.tiktok.com/eric.rice.author